TRINE RISING

THE KINDERRA SAGA:
BOOK 1

By C.K. Donnelly

This is a work of fiction. Names, characters, places, and incidents either are the product of the author's imagination or are used fictitiously. Any resemblance to actual persons, living or dead, events, or locales is entirely coincidental.
Copyright © 2020 by C.K. Donnelly

AI DISCLAIMER:

First hardcover edition 2020

PHOTO CREDIT: *Mike Harvey/Peak Image Photo*
MAP CREDIT: *Emily Rakić/Emily's World of Design*
COVER CREDIT: *Jennifer Givner/Acapella Book Cover Design*

ISBN 978-1-7350518-0-2 (Hardcover)
ISBN 978-1-7350518-3-3 (Softcover)
ISBN 978-1-7350518-2-6 (Ebook)

Published in the United States by Kibbe Creative Media, LLC

www.ckdonnelly.com

CHAPTER 1

"Great need and greater love can beget miracles."
—The Codex of Jasal the Great

"If I don't understand my ciphers, I won't get to be a seer. They'll never let me choose an amulet," Taddie whimpered. His breaths turned to little puffs of steam in the chill air of the stable.

Mirana Pinal bit her bottom lip and furrowed her brows in amused concern at the little boy's predicament. "You were born a seer. Nothing and no one can take away the gift the Aspects Above gave you."

She knew that all too well.

She scooted across the stable's hay-strewn floor to sit closer to him and wiped the tears from his cheeks. "It's not the end of the world. It's just a cipher problem."

"If I can't understand my numbers," he sniffed back more tears, "how will I understand my seer's visions when I'm older?"

Mirana waved her hand, sending a small current of intent to the lamps with the gesture. They flared to life, dispelling some shadows and creating others as evening descended outside of the stable.

"Taddie, you're only six summers old. I think you have some time to learn your numbers. You saw Falantir in shambles just like me. Just like the rest of the seers."

Taddie wiped his nose with a sleeve. "*Ai*, but you were the only one who saw it was the Ken'nar."

He was right. Her interpretation of that vision had led to the order extending her father's tour of duty. And may have sent him to his death.

She tensed, her own throat tight with emotion she could not let come. No. She would know if he died.

The boy blinked, his tears momentarily forgotten. "Did I say something wrong?"

Ai. "No, of course not. I just—never mind."

He lowered his watery sapphire-blue gaze. "I'm stupid."

"You are not stupid. Just because you don't understand something, doesn't make you stupid. If anyone is failing here, it's me. I'm not doing a good job explaining things to you."

Taddie played with a piece of straw. "You never fail at anything."

He could not be more wrong.

Mirana laughed anyway. Maybe he would think she thought his comment humorous.

"My *maithe* has us older *scholaire'e* teaching you younger ones to help us both learn our lessons. So, like it or not, we're in this together. Let's try something different."

She searched the monstrous stable for something that would help the little boy learn the simple sum. The horse paddocks made up one quarter-mile-long arm of the massive, multistoried square of the learning hall, all guarded by the imposing watchtower, Jasal's Keep. The three aisles of paddocks housed hundreds of warhorses for Kin-Deren province's army. Despite the wet snow falling outside, the bodies and breath of the horses made the stable nearly comfortable. And Taddie loved horses.

Horses. Horses running. Fast. Fleeing.

"*Scholaira* Miri?"

Mirana pushed back the particular nudge the Seeing Aspect made when it wished to antagonize her. She rubbed her eyes. Horses charged all the time. It was nothing.

She rose to her feet, brushing at the straw clinging to her heavy cotton leggings. "Come with me." The boy followed her to the first paddock of one of the long stable aisles. "All right. Let's try it again, except we're going to use the horse stalls this time. Four plus six."

Ten. It was important. The most important number there could be.

The probing sense of an impending vision prodded her brain. Ten? What the heck was ten? And why was it so important?

Taddie cocked his head and scowled. "Are you all right?"

She took a quick breath, pushing back her irritation. She didn't want to see a vision. They were seldom good ones. "I'm fine."

He nodded, dragging the heel of a hand over his nose and continuing through the riot of pale-yellow curls on his head.

Mirana frowned. "Ugh. And when we're done, it's off to the bathhouse with you."

He shrugged.

She strode down the row of stalls, stopping at the fourth one. "I want you to tell me how many horses I need to pass to reach the answer." She began to walk backward.

"Keep going." He waved her on.

Horses whuffled and neighed as she passed. A gray palfrey stuck its nose out over the paddock gate and blew out a greeting.

"Not now, Bankin." Mirana stroked the filly's velvet muzzle. "We're busy."

Taddie laughed. "Go farther." She continued past a few more stalls. "Stop. There."

The paddock was empty. The crib belonged to Ashtar, her father's warhorse. Her *paithe* hadn't been home for most of the last Reckoning. Fourthmonth in the new Reckoning was only a sevenday away. He and his strike force had been sent to reconnoiter just what had befallen Falantir so far to the north. Because of the interpretation of her prescience. Her *paithe* was all right. Of course he was. He was the most skilled defender in Kinderra. Nothing could take him down.

Right?

"That's ten," the little seer boy piped.

Father. Her *paithe*.

Ten. Ten beasts. All claws and fangs.

She shook her head to dispel the image. Had Taddie called it somehow? "Well done."

"I wanna do another one."

"All right."

The stable boy fidgeted up and down on his toes, his face expectant.

"If this stall is 'ten,' show me the horse in the stall of ten minus seven. Only this time, don't speak the name or point. I want you to call to my mind an image of the horse."

Taddie thrust out his lip, this time in a thoughtful expression. The lip pulled back in when his mouth turned in a smile. He held her gaze intently with his own. An image of a magnificent stallion with a mahogany coat so dark it was nearly black popped up before her mind's eye.

"Excellent! See? You're ciphering—and calling—just like a real seer."

The young seer boy squealed with joy and ran over to her, throwing his arms around her waist. She brushed a blond curl from his eyes. "I knew you could do it."

He grinned, turning his bright little face absolutely cherubic. "*Gratas Oë*, Mirana."

She returned his smile. "Don't thank me. You're the one who did all the work."

She walked over to the stallion. The steed tossed its head and sputtered. "Always a testy one, aren't you, Traga?"

The massive stable door groaned on its hinges, all but drowning out the groan of the one who opened it. They both lifted their heads to greet the visitor. Mirana's smile grew. So did the sudden warmth that spread through her.

"*Ben dia*, or should I say '*Ben nöc*.' That sleet out there is making this one miserable evening." He shook the icy rain from his hair, the moisture making it look a darker shade of brown than it was.

"Oh, I don't think it's so bad." She rushed over to him and took his hands, warming them in hers. "Teague, I'm so glad you're home." She pushed the hair out of his eyes, her smile not fading an inch. His grin matched hers, several freckles disappearing into the dimples of his smile. A giggle behind them reminded her they were not alone. People, presences, just about everything tended to fade into the background when she was with Teague. "Taddie, go help Herbsman Beltran with his

horses." She gave the stable boy a gentle push toward the mounts.

"Is that because you two want to go all mushy?" he asked as he took the horses' reins.

"*Ai*," Mirana replied, nodding. "Now, scoot."

"Ew. I'm never having a girlfriend. Ever." The little boy clicked his tongue and led the horses farther into the stable's interior.

"I'm not an herbsman just yet," Teague said, watching Taddie disappear among the seemingly endless rows of paddocks, "but we did manage to collect a good supply of willow bark and even some callas leaves that had sprung up early."

She stepped closer to Teague. "I can't believe you and your father stayed out an entire sevenday. What healing plants could you possibly find in this weather?"

"We would have stayed out longer." He pulled his forest-green gaze away from her to stare at his boots. "My father's Healing Aspect warned him we'll be seeing a rise in grippe cases after this storm."

Why was Teague sad? He'd done a good thing. Callas leaves were tiny and difficult to find. "But I'm certain it was your brilliant intellect that remembered callas plants grow at the base of willow trees."

He laughed, however, he was anything but happy. "Brilliant intellect? I saved us with my brilliance from an epidemic of toothaches. Thank the Aspects Above."

She lowered her head to meet his even lower gaze. "Have you ever suffered a toothache? I think finding the callas leaves is worthy of an herbsman." When he lifted his head, she put a hand on his arm. "At least to me."

She and Teague Beltran had been born within months of each other. And she cherished every single day of those nearly sixteen summers spent together.

He took her hand from his arm and held it. "How can I hate that pale color of snow on the ground so much when your silver eyes chase away any chill?"

Mirana raised an eyebrow. "Is that supposed to be romantic?"

He smiled. "*Ai.*"

"Try again."

"It's better than 'your black hair makes even coal beautiful.'"

She squeezed her eyes shut in a wince. "Not only is that perfectly dreadful, it doesn't even make sense."

He leaned closer. "Maybe you'd prefer I did something else with my lips instead of using them to speak dreadful flattery, hmm?" He pulled her to him and covered her mouth with his.

"That's much better," she said through his kiss.

She reached up to cup his face. He said her eyes chased away his chill. Chill? What chill? She never felt cold in his arms.

Without lifting his lips from hers, he rushed her backward and into Ashtar's empty stall—and tripped over the feed pail. They tumbled into the straw together, laughing.

"Somehow, I always imagined we'd be someplace more dung-free when you ravished me for the first time." She hitched a thumb to the corner. Taddie had missed a spot.

His hazel eyes twinkled. "Ravish you? I've been nothing but a gentleman."

She giggled. "*Ai.*" She kissed the faded freckles on his nose. "That's been your problem all along." She brushed his lips with hers.

"If this is the greeting I get from being gone just one sevenday, what would you do if I were gone ten?" He pulled her over to a cleaner corner of straw.

Ten.

The Seeing Aspect. Ten beasts. Grynwen. Twice the size of wolves. Black as midnight. Eyes as red as fresh blood. Long, pointed muzzles with uncounted long, pointed fangs. Carnivores charge out of the forest and leap upon a band of riders.

She stiffened. This time, there was no ignoring the vision as it forced itself before her mind's eye.

"Mirana?"

Fangs shred flesh. Agony shreds nerves. The Healing Aspect. Bleeding, bleeding, away, away. Snow-white uniforms stained red with blood. Shrieks of pain, man, woman, beast.

"Miri, are you all right?"

Chill sleet falls, the same sleet, the same storm that's outside now. Ice sizzles on the smoldering carcasses. The Defending Aspect. A burning in her chest, burning, burning. She must release it through an amulet. Amulets fire. Defenders. A man with silver-frosted black hair and silver eyes turns. Screams. Falls. The forest stills. Ice and wet snowflakes fall. Like here.

Like now.

"Father!"

Mirana sat up out of Teague's arms, sucking in rapid gasps.

"Mirana! What happened? Did I do—? I would never make you—Miri?"

"What? No—he's dying!" she said, breathless.

Teague shook his head in confusion. "Who?"

"My father. I have to reach him." She sprang to her feet.

He sat back on his heels, looking up at her. "Isn't he still in Kana-Akün? That's more than a hundred leagues from here. I know your mind-calling ability is better than most, but that's too far to reach anyone."

The Trine Prophecy

"'And it shall come to pass that Kinderra will cry out in such agony as to deafen even her birth. The chosen shall be like a ship without a keel. Aspect will appear where there was none. Light will be dark; dark will be light. One will come forth, thrice-cursed, to destroy. One will come forth, thrice-blessed, to rebuild. End and beginning in one, in both. Only hope shall remain.'"

—The Book of Kinderra

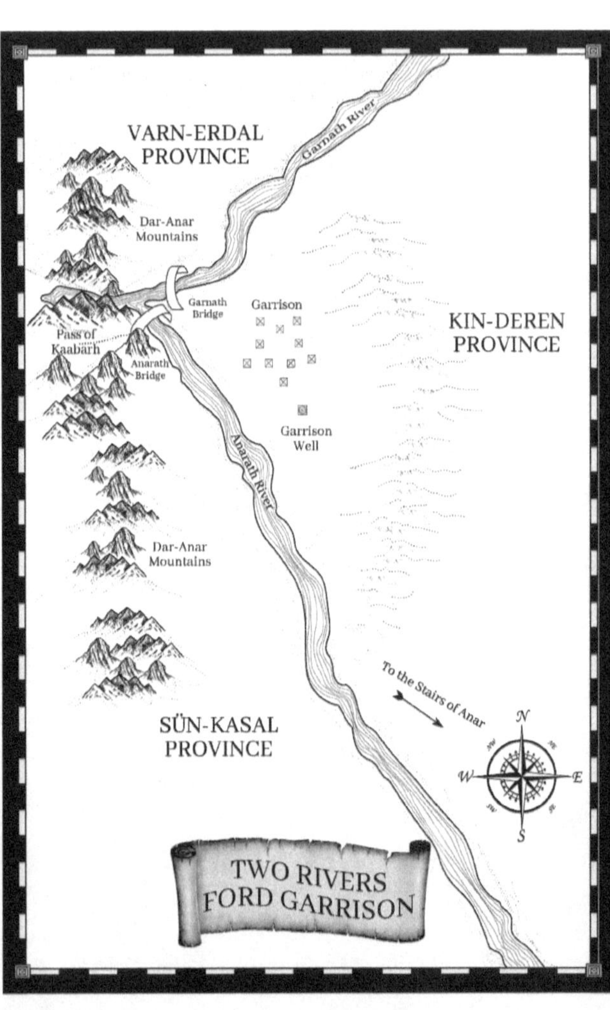

VARN-ERDAL PROVINCE
Garnath River
Dar-Anar Mountains
Garnath Bridge
Garrison
KIN-DEREN PROVINCE
Pass of Kaabärh
Anarath Bridge
Anarath River
Garrison Well
Dar-Anar Mountains
To the Stairs of Anar
N
W
E
S
SÜN-KASAL PROVINCE
TWO RIVERS FORD GARRISON

Pass of Kaabarh
Stairs of Anar
Silveren Lake
Salmasalar
CITADEL OF DEREN
Jasal's Keep
ANARATH RIVER
Passem's Rise
KIN-DEREN
DAR AL-JAD MOUNTAINS
Unadar
JAD-ANUNA JUNGLE
Kasan
SÜN-KASAL LOWLANDS
DAR-TAL SI MOUNTAINS
Vale i Dùadar
Pass of Dùadar
Sündalan
DAR-TAL NA MOUNTAINS
Parsalon
RÜN-TARAN PENINSULA
Rhadaz
TASH-HAMAR DESERT
MER-LIMA SEA
Qadar
Nuralima
Shoals of Taran
N
S
E
W
NE
SE
SW
NW
LEGEND
Learning Hall
1,000 miles East to West
2,000 miles North to South
1/2" = 1 day's ride
(10 mi/hr for 10 hrs.)
or approx. 100 miles
KINDERRA

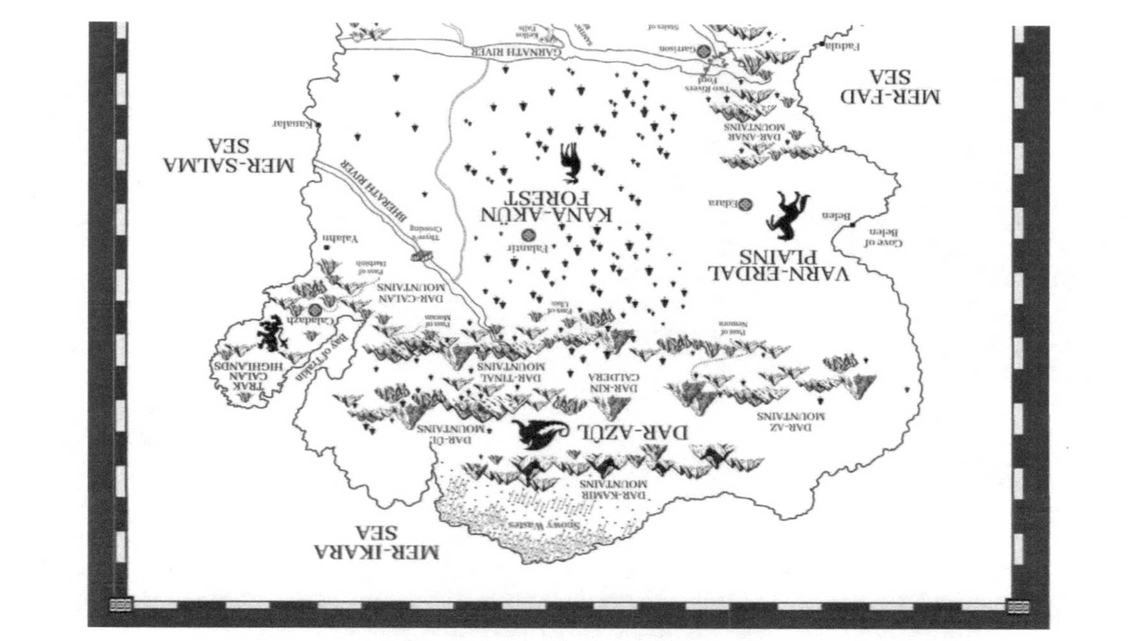

MER-IKARA SEA
MER-SALMA SEA
MER-FAD SEA
TRAK CALAN HIGHLANDS
Bay of Tralin
Calaelgh
DAR-CALAN MOUNTAINS
Pass of Naubenh
Yalahtu
Kanalar
BHERATH RIVER
Thane's Crossing
DAR-OI MOUNTAINS
DAR-TINAL MOUNTAINS
Pass of Mastan
DAR-AZÛL
DAR-KIN CALDERA
Spiney Wastes
DAR-KAMIR MOUNTAINS
DAR-AZ MOUNTAINS
Pass of Nenmira
Tower of Ular
Palamir
KANA-AKÛN FOREST
GARNATH RIVER
Kellos Falls
SANTO...
VARN-ERDAL PLAINS
Edara
Belen
Cove of Belen
DAR-ANAR MOUNTAINS
Two Rivers Ford
Garrison
Stairs of
Faduhi
MER-FAD SEA

Luke 1:46-48, 49

"My soul proclaims the greatness of the Lord; my spirit rejoices in God my savior. For he has looked upon his handmaid's lowliness, behold... The Mighty One has done great things for me, and holy is his name."

ACKNOWLEDGMENTS

It is said that writing a novel is a solitary profession. For me, nothing could be further from the truth. So many people have helped me for years—and in some cases, decades—to create the book you now hold. I want to thank my editors, Ann Videan, Elizabeth Evans, Susan Barnes, and Melissa Frain for taking a chance on this little book that just wouldn't die, and helping to make it the best it could be; my Beta Reader Tribe, especially Carrie, Jonah, Tim, Angela, Darlene, Heather, Lisa, and Anat; my incredible designers, Jennifer Givner and Emily Rakić, who made Mirana and Teague, and their world of Kinderra come alive; my representative, Sherry, as well as Claire and her team, for letting the world this novel exists; my photographer, Mike Harvey, for his magical camera and even more magical talent; my lawyers, Wendy Anderson and Leia Dingott, for making sure this world I've created is truly my world; and a special thanks to my husband, Wayne, whose tireless support helped me endure so many times when I wanted to quit. *Gratas Oë!*

"I know, but I've got to try."

Teague stood. "We need to go to your mother with this."

She shook her head. "There's no time." She curled her hands into fists and closed her eyes.

"Mirana." He put a hand on her shoulder. "Your mother is prime of this province. You have to tell her."

"Later. Right now, I have to warn my father or he's going to die."

She closed her eyes and reached out with her mind. Too many horses, too close. She growled in frustration. Mirana tore from the stable and into wet snow falling in the gray twilight of the learning hall's courtyard, Teague rushing behind her.

The learning hall complex housed hundreds of steeds and people, but in the courtyard at least, they weren't right on top of her. And there simply wasn't time to run out of Deren and leave the city behind for better isolation.

She sank to her knees on the icy cobblestones and centered herself again. She pushed her senses beyond the murmur of minds the way one would listen for a single voice in a crowd.

… Father … Where are you? … Answer me …

She searched for his presence, his essence, a life force singing all he was within the grace of the Aspects Above. His life, his power, sang in her veins, as he and her mother gave her life. And if she didn't find him in time, the echo of him that resided within her would be all that was left. She would never let that happen.

… Father … Please … Answer me …

The jumble of innumerable minds and presences swirled around her as she searched for one and only one. So very impossible. She needed more focus, more power.

An amulet.

The thought bloomed in her mind, and she shrank from it. A bond with an amulet would be demanded of her when she saw eighteen summers, the duty expected of all those who possessed the gifts of the Aspects. The pure gemstone of an amulet would confer upon its bearer the ability to focus the Aspects so tightly, he or she could accomplish actions far beyond the limited control of innate power. As for her, she would accomplish amazing things. Terrible things.

Mirana let her Seeing Aspect spread through her. Fragments of visions, premonitions, prescience drifted as they would through her consciousness. She could only pray something of her father would rise above the tantalizing yet useless information her Seeing Aspect now showed her. Without an amulet, she was at the mercy of her powers, unable to control what—and who—she wanted to see. With an amulet, however, Kinderra would be at *her* mercy. She squeezed her eyes shut tighter. Not that. Anything but that. Unless there was no other way to save his life, she would not even touch an amulet. She still had time, two summers, before she faced such a decision. Her father still had time. Just.

Would he be in the forests of Kana-Akün searching for the Ken'nar, or on the plains of that province's southern border, on his way home?

Neither her mother nor the other seers had made any mention of the information he and his strike force had discovered regarding Falantir, so he was not yet far enough away from the Ken'nar to safely contact them. He must still be in the forest.

Mirana couldn't create any serious manifestation of her powers without an amulet, but she didn't have to "see" with just one power. The Aspects Above never bestowed more than one gift, never gave more than just the Defending, Seeing, or Healing

Aspect alone to an individual. She gritted her teeth. Unless they gave all three.

Gifts. What gifts? Having all three powers of the Aspects made her a Trine, one of the few ever to be born. But gifts? No. Her powers were a curse, or at least they might be someday. She had seen what would happen when she took up an amulet, the horror of destruction at her hands etched permanently in her mind. So she never told a soul what those so-called "gifts" made her, except for Teague. Sometimes, she regretted telling him. She wished she didn't know herself.

Images, hazy with uncertainty, flitted past her mind's eye. She pushed away Teague's warm energies and the cold of icy pellets of sleet hitting her skin, and awakened her Defending and Healing Aspects, letting them listen for her father with her Seeing Aspect.

The preternatural wariness of the Defending Aspect gave rise to an awareness of where life hummed. Tall, thick conifers rose from the ground hardened by winter. Icy, wet snow fell in spattering taps on tree trunks and coated naked black branches. Mice scurried down holes under barren shrubs. A rabbit paused its browsing through the prickly pine needles of the forest floor. A deer, no, a buck picked its way through the darkening woods. It stood motionless except for its ears. They swiveled, listening.

Mirana did not *see* the stag as much as she fathomed its essence. Unable to draw more of its presence to her without an amulet, she forced herself to remain patient and let the animal's being fill her. It was hungry, starving from the cruel northern winter. Her Healing Aspect told her of its want. A want desperate enough for two animals. Two *exact* animals.

Her hope swelled with the odd sensation. Perfection did not exist in nature. Two completely identical presences simply could not be. Every creation had flaws except for the Aspects Above themselves. She could attest to that.

Mirana's heart hammered in her chest as she thrust the thought away. The life of the buck mirrored itself, as did some rabbits, mice, a weasel. Duplicates of animal essences, exact in every way except reality, shimmered within the Aspects. They were too far, too faint for her to detect any more than a mere whisper. But they were there. Only a person with the powers of the Aspects could manifest such a duplication, a duplication with one purpose—to hide one's life energies—and none were better at performing the technique than those possessing the Defending Aspect. Defenders like her father.

She opened her mind further. If her father had cloaked his presence, she would never be able to call specifically to his mind. She could call to anyone in the vicinity of the false animals, but any Aspected mind would hear her telepathic communication.

She froze. What if the false presences weren't her father and his patrol group? What if they were Ken'nar cloaking themselves? And if she called out? Their enemies—the latest generation to engage the Fal'kin in three thousand summers of bloodshed—would know he was near.

The Healing Aspect within her sought to bolster her failing strength. Sweat turned to cloying ice on her skin in the bitter air of the courtyard. She opened herself deeper to the strange sensations of life in the distant forest. Hunger and wariness. And pain. Exhaustion. These people had fought, had been injured. So had the Ken'nar in sacking Falantir, but they now had a garrison, a place to rest, to eat, to heal. No, these Aspected who masked themselves had not paused to recover. That meant urgency. An urgency born of necessity. They had to flee Kana-Akün to warn Kin-Deren province, her home, that the Ken'nar were on the doorstep.

A sudden, bloodthirsty counterpoint slashed the soft harmony of animal presences within the Healing Aspect.

Grynwen.

Some said grynwen hunted with some primitive form of the Aspects. Even if the rumor were true, if her father and his strike force had cloaked themselves, the predators would sense mice, not people. They couldn't divine the duplications of essences, much less search for them, could they?

Before her mind's eye, the grynwen pack loped on long legs with primal confidence toward her father and his men and women, the drumming of their paws echoing through her Defending Aspect. Why? Their bellies were full. They had no young to defend, no blooded prey to bring down. These were not normal beasts. They hunted, she sensed, but not for food.

They wanted to kill. Because they *liked* it.

If the beasts hadn't tracked her father with ordinary senses, hadn't hunted him for food, they couldn't possibly know his location. Unless they were sent. Unless they had been given her father's position and sent to kill him.

To warn her father, she'd have to call wide, as if she were shouting across a crowded room. Any Aspected mind—Fal'kin or Ken'nar—in the local area would hear. The risk was worth her *paithe*'s life.

The Seeing Aspect now joined with her Healing Aspect and Defending Aspect, merging of its own accord within her. It spoke of no future skein of time, no distant, uncertain knowing. It demanded her attention, present, real. Now.

… Father! … Grynwen! … Ride! …

She poured as much of herself as she could into her mind's voice, into those words. The Defending Aspect burned within her chest at the resounding need trapped within the prison of her body.

The illusion of the second stag shattered. Shock and disbelief exploded in her mind. A presence surrounded her consciousness, full of awe, of love. A moment later, the presence disappeared as if it had never existed, replaced once more by a buck.

But it was enough.

The raw need to send a warning slipped away. Her chest tightened, her lungs could not draw air. The presences, even the Aspects, faded. Something hard, rough, and cold pressed against her cheek and temple.

"Mirana!" a voice cried.

Hands, strong yet gentle, lifted her and placed her right palm flat against a solid, warm surface. A thud, pulsing with life. A heartbeat. Teague's heartbeat. His life sang out to her Healing Aspect, reviving her.

"Mirana, wake up!" His confident fingers pressed her neck, her heartbeat throbbing against his touch. She looked up at him as she lay in his arms on the courtyard's frozen cobblestones, her breath now wreathing his face in the cold air.

He blew out a loud exhale. "Thank the Aspects Above." He stroked her cheek and blinked back the sleet. "Miri, you dropped like a stone. You didn't move. I couldn't wake you. What happened?"

The clatter of small boots on cobblestones interrupted her reply.

"What's wrong? What happened? I heard you both!" Taddie said as he approached.

Teague frowned. "I didn't even yell."

The stable boy shook his head. "No. Your minds."

Teague's frown deepened.

"I'm fine," Mirana said as Teague helped her to sit. "I just slipped on some ice, that's all." She caught her herbsman's eye.

Calling to him would do no good. He couldn't hear her, and Taddie most certainly would. He made a slight movement with his head. Few would notice the simple gesture, but such responses had become a language all their own. She hated making Teague a party to her lie, but she couldn't very well have Taddie run to the hall seers, who would, in turn, run to her mother with the truth of what she had just done. Far too many questions would need to be answered if that happened.

"Now, get back inside before you catch a cold," Teague ordered. "You don't want me to use the nasal pot on you again to clear your stuffy nose, do you?"

Taddie's eyes grew as round as trenchers at the suggestion of such a horror. "Aspects, no!" He turned and pelted back inside the stable.

Once the boy was gone, Teague asked again, "What happened?"

Mirana looked up into his forest-colored eyes. "I found him."

The watchtower of Jasal's Keep loomed behind her beloved, dark and foreboding, its crenulated pinnacle crown lost to the icy precipitation and the gathering night.

Her father was safe. But for how long?

CHAPTER 2

*"A warning often comes, not with the clang of swords,
but with the softest of whispers."*

—The Book of Kinderra

Kaarl Pinal tightened his grip around the bloodred garnet amulet hanging at his chest. At his touch, the Defending Aspect rose sharply within him. He opened himself to the union his soul made with the amulet, a connected sense of rightness he would find with no other crystal.

He focused deep within himself, reaching for the power that lay there, a twinning of the harmonics of his life with that of the gemstone. His Aspect and his amulet became one—separate yet insoluble—as he willed his power out through the pure red crystal. A tongue of vermilion lightning engulfed the last of the ferocious grynwen as it moved toward him for the kill. The deadly light reduced four hundred pounds of muscle and sinew to a pile of blackened bones and ash, leaving the cold rain to hiss on the burning remains.

"How could they have found us? We were hidden," Seer Binthe Lima shouted to him from farther in the forest clearing, her breath rising like smoke in the frigid forest. "Unless my Aspect is as frozen as I am, I never saw them." She grimaced with disgust as she yanked her long knife free from the throat of one of the carnivores.

He shook his head. Cold air stabbed his lungs as he breathed deeply from the exertion of the vicious but brief scuffle. "The Ken'nar. It seems they're training mongrels to do their dirty work now." He had no proof, of course, just an intuition honed from summers of warfare.

"Then they did see us from Falantir's ramparts," Morgan Jord said, clawing the ice from the beard outlining his face with one hand, the other still gripping his amulet.

Seers in Kin-Deren province suspected the Ken'nar had sacked the city, their visions filled with dark armor and violence. Kaarl and his troops had proved their suspicions were correct.

Binthe's shoulders fell. "I made sure we left no trail." She clutched the emerald amulet that hung about her neck. "The vision of the forest battle I saw was the Ken'nar assault on Falantir. I did not see the grynwen. I should have."

The defender second stepped closer to the seer woman, his blue eyes hard with guilt. "Binthe, I know this wasn't your fault. I would never blame you."

Kaarl held up his hand, silencing his lieutenant. They had more pressing problems, and he wasn't about to waste the advantage the warning call had given them.

"These beasts had nothing to do with you, Binthe."

No one should have been able to find him to call a warning, for his presence was hidden. No one. He had wanted to reply, desperately, but he dared not. He could not risk the discovery of his men and women. Nor the one who called him.

He turned to the rest of his unit. "Everyone, back to your horses."

He scanned the forest as he perched a boot in the stirrup of his warhorse. A mount remained without a rider.

"Gannah!"

He ran over to a fallen defender woman slumped against a fire-blackened conifer and knelt next to her. Clumps of singed fur, bone, and ash smoldered at her feet. She clutched a deep wound in her side.

"Commander, tell Jord to move his arse next time when I tell him to get down." She tried to laugh, but her labored breathing turned it into a wheeze.

Kaarl pressed his hand over hers. Fresh, hot blood oozed over her ebony skin, saturating his glove and steaming in the cold air. Her armor and chain mail had been torn away from her flank. He clenched his jaw. More grynwen and Aspects Above only knew what else would be drawn by the scent of blood. "Damned beast thought he could nip you, did he?"

"I'll be fine. I just need a moment." Her eyelids fluttered.

Binthe and Morgan crouched down. The seer placed her arm around the defender woman, supporting her. "Gannah? *Siba?*" Her sea-green eyes held his, intense with concern when the woman didn't reply.

Morgan's gaze darted around the thick woods. "Do we have time to cauterize the wound?"

The woman was hardly more than a girl but was already one of the best defenders her far-flung southern province of

Jad-Anüna had ever sent to his strike team. She had her whole life ahead of her. Kaarl nodded. "*Ai.*"

"No," Gannah breathed. Her hand fell away, revealing torn flesh and ribs, shockingly white in the twilight gloom. "Go. I'll cover your backs. You have to get word to Deren that Falantir has fallen."

"Gannah—"

Binthe sucked in a breath and closed her eyes. Her hand flew to her amulet, verdant light spilling from between her fingers. … *Riders* … The seer called an image to his mind's eye.

He fought a gasp of his own. "There must be several dozen."

… *Fifty* … she called again, her lids remaining shut. He knew better than to ask her to speak when his battle seer was working a vision.

"Can you tell who they are?" Morgan asked. "Maybe some of the Fal'kin survived."

The seer shook her head. … *They have black armor* …

Kaarl nodded, tensing his shoulders to hide the rising dread. Black armor. Ken'nar. The incessant war against their enemies had long ago erased panic but never the sinking dismay that came before a bloody fight. Panic would do nothing to protect Mirana and Desde, nor the Unaspected, those without powers whom he was sworn to guard.

"I thought I heard something earlier, just before the grynwen attacked. Do you think one of the Ken'nar scouts found us?" his lieutenant asked.

"No," Binthe replied. She took a deep breath and pushed a lock of mist-darkened auburn hair away from her face. "I heard it, too. It seemed desperate."

Kaarl stripped off his cloak and bunched it against Gannah's side. "It was Mirana."

Morgan's eyes widened. "Your daughter? But how—?"

The injured woman lay slack in Binthe's arms, her breathing jagged. Kaarl tugged his sword belt free and lashed it around her, holding the makeshift compress in place. "Her warning will be for naught if these riders find us."

The Ken'nar were the ones who had laid the grynwen ambush, he was certain of it. The attack was never meant to wipe them out, only to slow them so their sentries could finish them off.

The enemies of the Fal'kin for thousands of summers, the Ken'nar consumed everything in their path. They and their ruthless leader, the Dark Trine, sought to subjugate Kinderra with the Power from Without, a manipulation of their innate powers to steal life to fuel their Aspects through an amulet. Fal'kin, like himself, devoted themselves to protecting all of Kinderra through the Light from Within, directing only the powers the divine Aspects Above granted them at birth in communion with a crystal amulet.

His daughter had known about the ambush. She must have seen it. She found his mind when it should have been impossible to do so and called to warn him.

Kaarl cinched his belt tight around the dying defender, swallowing against rising bile in his throat from the fresh rush of blood over his hand. He and his fighters were only a handful of leagues from Falantir. Could those black-hearted bastards have heard something of his daughter's warning call as Binthe and Morgan had? Could the Dark Trine?

He clamped down on the thought with the same strength the grynwen had on Gannah. Right now, he needed to get Gannah and the other eighteen men and women around him— and the information they carried—home.

… Binthe, take your unit and move left into the brush … he called to the seer. … *Morgan, take your group and my horse, Ashtar, and go right … If the Ken'nar think a pack of mangy curs can finish us, they're about to learn differently … Let's see how they like to be ambushed … The rest of you … Hide yourselves and your presences … Do not fire your amulets until I give the call …*

Kaarl scooped up Gannah in his arms and hurried into a copse of thick brambles. He looked down at the unconscious woman in his arms. She exhaled a wet, slow leak of breath.

… *Stay with me, Gannah … Please …* The woman's eyelids fluttered but did not open. … *Your man waits for you … You don't want to keep him waiting, do you? …*

He strengthened his focus within himself and amplified outward more of the life energies of forest creatures thrumming around him. U'Nehíl, the "not nothing." The technique had saved his life as often as his sword and his amulet. He tensed, bowstring-taut, ready to launch himself at this new threat, amulet in one hand, sword in the other.

Dozens of uniformed riders charged out of the frozen fog into the clearing. A tall, helmeted warrior on a black stallion emerged as fighters bearing the black-and-silver livery of Dar-Azûl province fanned out behind him.

Kaarl shot to his feet. "Tetric! Thank the Aspects! Hurry. We have wounded." He waved the tall rider closer. He carried Gannah from the brambles as the Fal'kin reappeared from deeper in the woods.

Tetric Garis removed his helmet and quickly dismounted. "We followed the grynwen, thinking they might be tracking survivors who had fled Falantir." He knelt beside the fallen young woman and grimaced as he peeled away the makeshift bandage.

"Defender, can you hear me?" He closed his eyes and gripped his dark, silvery hematite amulet with one hand while placing the other over the gaping wound in the woman's side. A glow emanated from the crystal. "Listen to my voice."

The defender woman's eyes flew open, and she flailed her arms against the man's ministrations as though fighting against some unseen foe. Kaarl struggled with her. "Gannah, stop. It will be all right. Lord Garis is here to help you." He released her and stepped back, giving the tall rider room to work.

"Do not fight me. You will no longer be in pain." Tetric gripped her wrists, immobilizing her.

Kaarl studied the man as he used the Healing Aspect on the injured woman. Fal'kin seers like Binthe Lima could peer into the skeins of time and anticipate an enemy's sword strike. Others healed those broken and diseased of body far quicker than nature. Fal'kin defenders like he and the riders around him had the unique ability to release amulet fire. Nothing—not wood, not metal, not stone—could withstand the intense light of amulet fire. He frowned at the absolute futility of the Aspect at this moment.

Tetric, however, was something yet again. He held all three powers, an exceedingly rare Aspected known as a Trine—one of the few individuals in recorded history to be thrice blessed by the Aspects Above. More than once, Tetric's presence alone had turned the tide of battle against the Ken'nar, sending them into retreat as he rode through the fray. Kaarl himself was known for his stature, but the Trine stood a few inches taller still. That only added to his formidable reputation.

At this moment, however, Kaarl cared nothing for the other man's knowledge from the skeins of time, his amulet's fire, or his imposing appearance. It was his Healing Aspect he so desperately needed now.

Morgan drew closer, followed by Binthe. "I had her under my cover," the young defender said. "The grynwen—"

"—were everywhere," Tetric finished, opening his eyes. He sat back on his heels. The wound in the defender woman's flank had faded into pale scars across her dark skin, but she remained in the muddy, bloody, icy pine needles, her eyes open, fixed on nothing. He rubbed his face and gave a long exhale.

Kaarl cursed. This should not have happened. His troops were the best on the continent, with all the powers of the Aspects at their command. He had been warned they would be ambushed. Yet somehow one of his defenders lay dead in the melting snow.

Fal'kin were created by the Aspects Above to protect all of creation and the Unaspected peoples. Or at least that's what the ancient sages, who wrote the holy books, had said for three thousand summers. After decades at the battlefront, he wasn't certain any longer if the Fal'kin, who had the blessings of the Aspects, could even protect themselves, let alone protect the Unaspected, who did not.

The forest stilled once more, save for the gentle pattering of rain on armor. Blood from the dead Fal'kin woman and the carnivores stained red the remaining shreds of crusty white snow. Kaarl wiped the sweat and blood from his eyes. He kept them closed for a moment, the emotion taking a few heartbeats longer to recede.

He rose wearily to his feet and opened his eyes. He reached to grasp the chain of Gannah's amulet when the Trine stayed his hand.

"Leave it."

The fallen woman's amulet glowed, golden light from the yellow sapphire emanating between the man's fingers. Was she still alive? No. He was being a fool. Tetric's touch ignited it, not

Gannah's. A Trine could connect with any amulet, chosen or free, not just the one oh-so-ineffectual crystal that hung heavily from his own neck. "Her man will want it."

"I will not remove it from her as if she were a criminal," Tetric replied. "Her man. He will understand."

Binthe stepped closer to Kaarl. The fair skin of her face grew paler against her cold-reddened cheeks. "Gannah and I came to the il'Kin together. Both of us were so far from home. I will bring the news of her death to her family."

"I will send word to her family and her man in Jad-Anüna. That is my responsibility. Not yours."

The heavy rain began to turn into ice once more, so many needles stinging his face. "We can do nothing more for her," he said to the rest of his troops. "The scent of blood will draw more grynwen. We had best leave now."

As he walked back to his mount, he said to Tetric, "How long have the Ken'nar been in Falantir?"

The Trine pursed his lips. "I would guess they've been there for some time. I sense no urgency among their minds."

"Meaning they've settled in and aren't expecting a counter-attack." Kaarl sighed and lifted his head toward the waning daylight. He let his chin fall back down in a nod. "Where are the rest of your men and women?"

"Some are in the woods. Others in the thickets just outside. Where are the rest of yours?"

Kaarl said nothing, letting a glare answer for him.

The Trine shook his head slowly. "Do you still feel it is better not to unite our forces? How many more do you have to lose?"

Again, he let the question hang and climbed into Ashtar's saddle, gritting his teeth against the cold stiffness in his body.

"We will ride with you to Deren," the Trine said as he retrieved his helmet from the frozen ground. "There is much I would discuss with you and your prime." He swung his long leg over the back of his mount. ... *I heard her call as well* ...

Kaarl cursed, the steam of his breath adding substance to the invective. The man would only follow up with inevitable questions. And that horrible little thought that her call had gone far beyond the immediate area pierced his brain like the tip of a stiletto. He snapped that sharp thought off before it could grow further.

Tetric trotted his horse next to Kaarl's and gripped his arm, initiating a private connection to his mind. ... *We were all under U'Nehíl* ...

He jerked his arm away. ... *Such communication is not possible* ... He clicked his tongue, guiding his horse forward through the trees.

... *It is possible* ... *For one who is more than a seer* ...

He looked over his shoulder. "I know what you are insinuating."

Tetric had not moved. "I am the only one in Kinderra who can be certain of it. You must let me test her."

Kaarl reined his mount around to face the other man. "My daughter is a seer, Lord Trine. You know we misinterpreted her Seeing Aspect to be the Defending Aspect when she was a young child. It is not unheard of, especially for a child born so early before her time. And she certainly does not heal. *Ai*, she is uncommonly skilled, but she is nothing more than a seer."

... *Kaarl—* ...

He drilled his silver gaze into Tetric. ... *If the Dark Trine believed for one moment she was anything else, he would send every last one of his Ken'nar to kill her* ... *Her life would be in as much danger as your own* ... *I will never let that happen* ... *Never* ...

He kicked his horse's sides, leaving the Trine's reply and the dead to the sleet.

CHAPTER 3

'What is power? Is it might of the sword? Wealth?
Followers? Strength of the Aspects? No, it is the ability
to decide when to use none of these.''

—The Codex of Jasal the Great

The Ain Magne led his horse away from the others as they made camp for the night. Irritation needled him like the dampness that leached through his cloak and under his armor. He must keep moving forward with his plans. Especially now, after the girl's call. Which made this delay unnecessary.

He took a breath to calm himself. A pause in their ride might have been unnecessary for him but not for the others. Those with whom he traveled needed their rest more than he, as did his horse.

"My lord," one of the defenders said as he jogged closer, "do you wish a guard to accompany you while you rest?"

He removed his helmet and tucked it under his arm. "That won't be necessary. I'm easing my horse from the ride. I'll be back soon." The young man nodded and returned to the camp.

He hung the helmet from straps on his horse's saddlebag while the animal pawed at the crusty snow in search of grass. He pulled his cloak tighter against the incessant rain. The stallion did not prefer the company of others. He understood. He, too, often needed solitude.

My Lord. Ain Magne. The Great One.

He pressed his lips tightly against his teeth in frustration. The men and women he led conferred these monikers upon him. The Fal'kin and the Unaspected whispered another name—the Dark Trine. *Ai*, he was a Trine, but he was not dark. Those who refused to augment their innate Light from Within with life forces pulled in by the Power from Without, those who preferred war to peace—they were the dark ones. Not he.

Titles were desired by those who needed to know where they stood in the hierarchy of order. He, however, stood at the head of the Ken'nar, and soon at the head of the Fal'kin as well. All of Kinderra. No one sat above him, except for the Aspects Above. He was not a deity, of course. He was not one of their godhead trinity. He was a man, yet he was no more like the men and women who surrounded him now than his stallion resembled a draft horse. They did not know him. In truth, no one did. One day, however, they would know and understand and accept.

The Ain Magne removed his horse's saddle. He wiped some of the water from the stallion's neck as a vague sense of discomfort from the animal returned to his mind, mediated by his Healing Aspect. The beast was not a companion and certainly not a pet, but a tool, even a weapon, one of the most valuable he had. Because of that, he lavished attention on his mount. He removed a waterskin from a saddlebag and took a drink. He would eat later, after he had attended to his horse.

Securing Falantir, the capital of Kana-Akün province, had been a costly affair. Costly in terms of lives. Costly in terms of something almost more precious: time. He pursed his lips tighter and, again, an ember of frustration burned in him. He had no one to blame but himself. The Kana-Aküni forces had put up more resistance than anticipated. In his hubris, he had not followed his Sight far enough, a mistake he'd thought he was long past making. Like hubris. He was not above learning from his mistakes, however. It would not happen again.

The Ain Magne led his horse away farther still, shouldering the heavy saddle. He glanced back at the camp. There would be no fires tonight with the sleet. No fires also meant he could melt into the gloomy darkness, wrapped in dark leather and armor and U'Nehíl.

He set the saddle down on the ground and reached out to search the Aspects for the mind of his seer second. The young man was leagues away in Falantir with the remainder of his forces. Although he knew the seer's mind as well as his own, the distance still made such contact difficult. Difficult, *ai*, but hardly impossible.

Like his horse, his servant was an exceedingly important tool. The young seer's sensitivity toward divining visions, and his interpretations of them, were extraordinarily accurate. His servant was also another source of his frustration. A most infuriating one at that.

… Eö hac, my lord … I am here … his lieutenant's mind-voice returned.

… Your grynwen attack—one I did not order—was not successful … the Ain Magne called.

… Pinal and his lackeys reached the bulwarks of Falantir and our garrison here … I saw an opportunity … I was merely acting on your desires …

The Ain Magne ground his teeth. *… You have no idea what my desires are …*

… Forgive me, Lord Trine … I exist but for your will … I had no right— …

He sent a searing reprimand into his second's mind, his Healing Aspect feeding on his lieutenant's very life force, pulling at it, drawing it from the seer to inflame the young man's nerves. *… How dare you even presume to make such a move without my orders? … Did it not occur to you that I might have wanted the il'Kin to glimpse our presence there? … Knowing something of my might would more likely draw the Fal'kin out in our next engagement …*

… Forgive me! … Please! … I beg of you! …

Ai, sometimes his seer second and others under his command needed to be taught a harsh lesson, but inflicting pain for its own sake repulsed him. He seldom abused the Healing Aspect in such a fashion.

The Ain Magne loosened his hold on his second and blew out his breath. He had spent more than fifty summers learning forbearance. His second, having seen but twenty-two summers, still had lessons to learn.

His stallion nickered at his loud exhale. He drew his hand down his horse's fetlock, as much to calm himself as his mount. He lifted the hoof to examine it.

His seer's mind, soft with repentance, nudged his own. *… Shall I eliminate the il'Kin who survived? … Say the word, and even their amulets will not be found …*

… No … I will deal with Kaarl Pinal and the il'Kin soon enough …

Kaarl Pinal. He threw down his horse's hoof. The name filled him with as much vexation as respect. When his mount tossed its head in annoyance, he stroked the animal's flank.

For summers, the Ain Magne had fought against Pinal and studied him on the battlefield. Not just his skills and tactics but *him*. He knew the man's many strengths as well as his weaknesses. The defender showed far fewer of those, but they were much more important. Like the use of a man's own life to fuel the Power from Without, a man's weaknesses were weapons to be used against him. He now knew which particular weakness would be the man's undoing.

… We have lost too much time in capturing Falantir … he called to his servant.

… Allowing the il'Kin to remain is not a wise move, my Trine …

The Ain Magne smiled without humor at his second's impudence. Perhaps his servant's usefulness was growing less useful. He cocked his head to one side, stretching the muscles in his neck to relieve the returning tension. For now, he required the young seer's Aspect as well as his brutally efficient talents with a blade.

He trailed a gloved palm along his horse's flank as he walked to its hindquarters. *… Let me ask you this: how do the provinces view Pinal and his il'Kin defenders? …* He sensed his servant's wary confusion.

… They are considered heroes …

The Ain Magne bent down and raised the hind hoof of his horse. He frowned. A small, sharp stone had embedded itself against the sole in frozen mud. *… And if they were all killed? …* When his seer second made no answer, the Trine continued. *… Martyrs … The brave il'Kin and their noble Defender Commander Kaarl Pinal cut down in the defense of Kinderra—they would be hailed as martyrs … But alive, with just a handful limping home, they are* *failures … Whom do you think the provinces would be more likely to place their faith in, a martyr or a failure? …* He paused again, allowing his words to take effect. … *Oë comprende? … Do you understand now? …*

… Ai, my lord … Ëo comprende …

… I hope you do … You are not above being made an example of what happens to those who counter me … Which you have done … Twice … That is twice more than any other living man or woman …

… I am your servant, my Trine … You have more than my fealty … You have my life … his lieutenant returned, his mind's voice full of contrition.

The Ain Magne ignored his humility. Let the boy worry for a while. He preferred the loyalty of the Ken'narren to come from respect, but fear was sometimes a very appropriate—and effective—motivator.

He unsheathed a small knife from his belt and began to pick away at the mud under his horse's hoof. … *What of Kana-Akün's healer prime? …*

… She cannot keep up the pace of harvesting you have demanded … Her body fails, and we must wait until she revives …

… She will soon have assistance …

The Ain Magne heard raised voices coming from the camp and turned to face the noise. The shouts degraded into raucous laughter. A call from one of the defenders came to his mind, inviting him back to the camp. He gently repelled the contact, hoping the defender would honor his need for privacy.

… Stay present a moment … he called to his servant. … *I may have more need of you …*

He continued to pick away at the packed dirt under his horse's hoof, but the stone refused to dislodge. He would have to use much stronger means to remove this frustration. As he would with building his forces.

Some Aspected, like his seer second, freely chose the Ken'nar way and fully embraced the Power from Without, but there were never enough of these for his needs. He added to his armies through a skill most in Kinderra believed was a terrifying rumor: the Soul Harvest.

Oh, it was no rumor. It was very real.

The Soul Harvest was a dramatic description, perhaps, but an apt one, for those harvested were left bereft of anything that once made them individuals. It could be accomplished only through the Healing Aspect. With that most precious of Aspects, he winnowed away self-awareness like needless chaff.

The ancient sages were right to forbid the Soul Harvest's use, and Kinderrans were right to fear it. In a way, he agreed with both conclusions. The arcane skill was a despicable act, but it was necessary for peace. He would do anything necessary to accomplish that goal. Even kill. Even perform the Soul Harvest.

Although gaining control of Kana-Akün province and Falantir, its capital, had been an unexpected struggle, it did result in a very important victory. Healer Belessa Tir, prime of the woodland province, now harvested others by his command. It freed him to enact the rest of his plans to conquer Kinderra from anywhere he chose while she harvested warriors for him.

The Ain Magne shoved his belt knife back into its sheath. He cupped his amulet with one hand and held the horse's hoof with the other. Reaching deep within himself, he harnessed the innate power of his Defending Aspect through the Light from Within and enjoined the crystal in his amulet to condense it. He let it build a moment, then sent a thin beam of light toward the frozen mud holding the stone. A tiny cloud of steam lifted in the damp night air as the muddy ice melted. The stone fell away. He let his Defending Aspect recede and called to his Healing

Aspect, mending the knife prick in the flesh of his mount's sole. He stood and again stroked the horse's black coat.

The Light from Within. The Power from Without. Using one's Aspect alone. Supplementing it by bringing in more life forces from outside of oneself. It was the same damn power, the same Aspect. Only the road to touch it was different. That was all. Just a difference of connection. Why would Kinderra not accept this? It was so bloody obvious, and yet the Fal'kin preferred war to understanding, embraced killing over enlightenment.

His stallion stomped and neighed again in irritation. He received the distinct impression of hunger. The Ain Magne reached into his saddlebag for a small sack of oats and set it down. The horse paused, waiting for a command from its master despite the gnawing in its stomach. He obliged the steed, and the animal buried its nose in the feed.

Now that he had Falantir and a secure location from which to stage his armies, he needed only two more conquests to make Kinderra his: Two Rivers Ford and Deren. Securing the ford bridge complex stretching over the Garnath and Anarath Rivers was just a means to an end, though. Deren, the citadel and capital of Kin-Deren province, *ai*, that was the key to everything. The other eight provinces might be Kinderra's limbs, but Kin-Deren province was her heart, and Deren, her soul.

The Ain Magne wiped the chill rain from his face and frowned. Kaarl Pinal's daughter Mirana and her warning call were now additional frustrations in gaining Deren—and perhaps his greatest ones. Petite, raven-haired, with the penetrating silver eyes of her father, the girl held the Seeing Aspect and was considered quite gifted in that expression. Speculation about the girl had swirled across Kinderra for summers since she was a small child. What was first believed as her defender's acute reflexes was later explained away as manifestations of her Sight showing her when and how to move.

It wasn't the fact that Mirana was able to call to Pinal, even at a great distance, that concerned him. A caller needed only to sense the presence of another with the powers of the Aspects. Distance, and the noise of all the minds in between, did, however, make calling more difficult by diluting that connection. It was the circumstances in which she accomplished the feat that he found deeply troubling.

To find minds at a distance? And call to them? While those minds were hidden? That skill was difficult even for him—with an amulet. She was hardly more than a child, certainly not old enough to have chosen an amulet yet. Had she taken one in secret? It was possible. He had bonded with the crystal for his amulet when he was but ten summers old, unwilling to wait until he was eighteen as customary.

Interpretation of a vision, however, rested solely on the brilliance and insightfulness of the seer, something completely separate from amulet use. In that, he truly had no equal. Perhaps still. Perhaps not. Her abilities were more than impressive, they were daunting in their implications.

The Ain Magne glanced again at the camp. It was quiet now. He retrieved the now half-empty oat sack from his horse and stowed it back in the saddlebag. When he was certain he would no longer be disturbed, he reached out to his seer second's mind again.

… We may have a complication … Pinal's daughter … She warned the il'Kin your beasts would attack … I'd like to know how she knew …

… I sent the grynwen in utmost secrecy, I assure you … his lieutenant returned. *… How is this possible? …*

… How indeed … The Ain Magne noted his second had changed the subject most skillfully, deflecting his scrutiny back to the girl.

What if Mirana Pinal's Defending Aspect had *not* been misidentified? A child's Aspect was known at birth, often before. Misidentifying an infant's Aspect rarely happened and certainly not after the child had seen one summer. Then again, his own Aspects' alignments would be sensed as blurred by others, superimposing themselves over each other, unless he chose to use one alone.

… Do you think she is another Trine? … his servant called. *… There has never been any mention of the girl possessing the Healing Aspect …*

… No mention? … Or outright lying? … While Kinderra's Aspected had never been numerous—perhaps one babe in a thousand was born with gifts—centuries would pass without a Trine coming into the world. *… Pinal could be hiding his daughter's true identity …*

… He would not dare …

… Oh, would he not? …

Pinal—and maybe his wife, too—risked removal of his amulet and expulsion from his home province of Kin-Deren if he deliberately withheld Mirana's Aspects from service to Kinderra.

He yanked at the strap, closing the saddlebag. There could be only one reason Pinal would hide his daughter's Trine gifts with such a sentence hanging over his head—he feared for her life because of the Trine Prophecy.

Ai, the Ain Magne knew of Kaarl Pinal's weaknesses, and Mirana was his greatest.

His seer pushed at his mind in alarm. *… If she is a Trine, do you think she is one of those predicted in the Trine Prophecy? … It says— …*

… Aren't you a little old for minstrels' tales? … he snapped back.

He was far too pragmatic to believe in the dire words written by a forgotten soothsayer thousands of summers ago. What exactly did the prophecy say, anyway? Chronicled in the Book of Kinderra, a thrice-cursed and a thrice-blessed, a Dark Trine and a Light Trine, were cast as mortal enemies. It portended in dramatic fashion great upheaval in Kinderra as one of the Trines would come to destroy, the other to rebuild. He remembered well those who cared for him as a boy had remained vigilant for signs that the Trine Prophecy was being fulfilled, lest his own young life be in danger.

Regardless of Kinderra's belief—and his disbelief—in the prophecy, Mirana Pinal was a concern, Trine or no. If the girl found her father's hidden presence and had correctly interpreted his seer second's grynwen attack without possessing an amulet, what else could she deduce? The idea chilled him more than the sleet. He would have to alter his tactics for his strike on Two Rivers Ford. Immediately.

… I have a new strategy for the ford …

The Ain Magne wove an image of the bridge complex into a precise tapestry of time and space—the ford as the warp, the Ken'nar as the thread of the weft—and called it to his second's mind.

… Are you certain this is the right course of action? … We will be left vulnerable … his young seer called.

… Then you understand precisely the false advantage I will present the Fal'kin … They will be even more likely to take this bait …

… Ëo comprende, Great One …

He sensed his servant's mind lingering in his own. *… What is it? …*

… Mirana Pinal … If she is a Trine, your life could be in danger, my lord … The Trine Prophecy says— …

… I know what it says … he replied, his mind-words clipped. *… And it is as vague as it is sensational …*

… If there is even a chance the prophecy is true, she must be killed … I will not let Pinal's brat destroy all we have built together … Nor destroy you …

The Ain Magne considered the option as he hefted his horse's saddle. His second's concern regarding the prophecy, to say nothing of his life, was unfounded. The girl, however, did appear to possess formidable talents, ones that could become troublesome. He did not take the decision to kill lightly and would not do so until he had more information.

Embracing his Seeing Aspect, indistinct images began to fill his mind, then slowly resolved themselves with greater clarity.

The walled city of Deren, the capital of the Kin-Deren province. A vast expanse of bodies heaves in the torment of war. The watchtower of Jasal's Keep juts two hundred feet into the sky. Mirana's face pales in agony. Her silver eyes hold desperation. The watchtower explodes in white light.

He gasped and dropped the saddle, startled by the vision. The explosion of white light from Jasal's Keep. The Book of Kinderra said the deserter's keep saved Deren from certain destruction by the Ken'nar. Somehow. It was never explained. This legend lent strength to the myth that Deren would never fall, a myth he was looking forward to proving quite wrong. Was Jasal's Keep a weapon? It must be. Yet, the vision of the keep appeared along with Mirana. The keep and the girl must be connected. His Aspects were telling him as much.

The shock from his seer second's mind speared through his own. *… My lord! … The keep … In Deren … The light … Such power … And Mirana Pinal is— …*

… You are not to concern yourself with her … Make certain Falantir remains secure … Prepare for the ford, and be ready to ride on my order …

… Ai, Great One … It shall be done …

The Ain Magne let the connection to his seer second slip from his mind. He ground his teeth together. He hadn't expected to see Jasal's Keep, let alone allow his seer to witness it. The boy was talented and ruthless. And ambitious. He had trained his second himself. Perhaps too well.

The keep could be a weapon of such stunning proportions, whoever possessed it would control all of Kinderra. With his Ken'nar and the keep, he would be invincible. The Fal'kin would be forced to accept him as their sole leader.

He ran his hand along the stallion's back. It shivered under his touch. His steed would feed freely from farm fields of fresh, sweet grass instead of browsing for bloody stubble from battlefields.

Once the unconquerable city and its mysterious keep came under his amulet, the other provinces would know resistance was pointless. One by one, they would fall under his amulet. Kinderra would be his, and the needless waste of death that had run unchecked for three thousand summers would finally come to an end.

All logic told him to kill the girl. She endangered everything he had spent his life building. She and the watchtower were somehow connected, though. If he wanted to gain control of Jasal's Keep and end the war, she must remain alive.

The Ain Magne lifted the saddle across his mount's back once more and returned to the camp. He nodded a greeting to the defenders keeping watch.

One of them rose and came over to him. She reached inside an oilcloth bag and held out two leathery strips of meat to him. "Some dried beef, Lord Trine? It's not roast pheasant, but it will keep you from starving."

"*Gratas Oë.*" He took the pieces and tore off a bite with his teeth. It was tough and tasteless. He gave her a tight smile in gratitude.

"Please take your fill, my lord. You fight three times as hard as any of us."

He shook his head. "I have three times as many Aspects to help me endure, too. I shall be fine. Make sure the others have enough."

She dipped her head in a polite bow, but the emotions that flowed from her mind to his held wonder, even astonishment. Why were people so surprised when he cared about their welfare? As a Trine, was not the welfare of the entire continent his ultimate responsibility?

The Ain Magne continued through the camp and chose a spot close enough to the others to be seen, yet still far enough away where his meditations would not be disturbed. He made a crude lean-to from his bedroll, draping one end over his mount's back and the other across the hilt of his blade plunged in the hard earth. He crawled under the thick cloth and out of the elements.

He let the vision of Jasal's Keep fill his mind once more. He would make certain Mirana Pinal lived. For now.

CHAPTER 4

"Etís nunqa onoír cinen u'verdas. Verdas revelaré en
tempre, birente tuda pián thet ísié maent ísi runhé."
("There can never be honor within a falsehood.
Truth shall be revealed in time, bringing all the
suffering that was meant to be hidden.")
—Ora Fal'kinnen 89:75–76

Mirana looked at the spoon in her hand, but she saw
clouds. Rain was coming. Rain always came in Fourthmonth, as
spring defeated winter at last. True sunny warmth would not
come until Sixthmonth, with the summer season. The thunder
rumbled throughout the learning hall, muted by thick stone
walls. It had rained, too, when her father had been attacked by
the pack of grynwen. She pushed the thought away and

concentrated on filling a medicine jar with sticky, pain-relieving numbweed salve.

Numbweed was made from delicate peda blossoms. The tiny, yellow blooms flourished in Sixthmonth. *Paithe* would be long home by then, and the grynwen and her warning would fade under the summer sun like winter frost. The incident would be forgotten and not mentioned again.

The Choosing Ceremony, when the province's Aspected *scholaire'e* chose their amulets to be elevated to Fal'kin status, was held on the first day of Sixthmonth as well. The same day as her birthday. She frowned as she scooped salve into a small clay medicine jar. She'd turn sixteen.

Birthdays were considered almost sacred by the Fal'kin because so many saw so few with the constant state of war. When she was younger, her parents had given her a doll for her birthday. At fourteen, now old enough to attend the Quorumtide pavanes, she received a beautiful dress. Her birthday this time only brought her another summer closer to the Choosing Ceremony. When she turned eighteen, she would trade a dress for armor and a doll for an amulet.

And a dream for a nightmare.

She closed her eyes and took a long, slow inhale. Patients in the healing hostel were in pain. They needed numbweed, and the sooner she filled the jars, the sooner people would stop hurting.

The healing hostel, housed within the learning hall, was large enough to convalesce one hundred patients. The hall itself, however, was an enormous compound that could hold with ease twenty times as many Fal'kin. At the moment, she didn't care if it could hold a thousand times as many people. She wanted it to hold only one right now. Father. *Paithe.*

Mirana picked up a cork stopper. The alarm from his mind at her call was the only thing she had sensed from him since the warning. It had been sevendays. Was he now simply better hidden, his presence better diluted by those of forest creatures? Of course he would be hidden. He must be. What if he wasn't, though?

The memory of the gnashing fangs of the grynwen that had ambushed her father and his Fal'kin gnawed at her. Ambush. Her stomach constricted. He had not stumbled upon some hunting pack of wild beasts in the forests of Kana-Akün province. That, she knew for certain. The vicious carnivores had made straight for them. The attack must have been premeditated. His strike force, the fabled il'Kin, was meant to be eliminated. Murdered.

She shoved the cork into the jar and let out an explosive exhale. She glanced behind her. No one in the apothecary had heard her. She reached for another empty jar.

Some evil warlord—whom everyone called the Dark Trine—controlled the Ken'nar. Was it he who had sent the grynwen after her father?

The Trine Prophecy spoke of a thrice-cursed, who would destroy, and a thrice-blessed, who would rebuild. Would this "thrice-blessed" only be considered, well, *blessed* because he—or she—destroyed the Ken'nar's Dark Trine? She swallowed and stared at the jar in her hand. Not all gifts were blessings.

Mirana took another deep, slow breath. She'd never get all these jars filled with those kinds of thoughts. People would need this medicine. People like her father.

Paithe.

She wasn't supposed to act alone on visions she saw because she hadn't chosen a crystal amulet yet. Studying images in detail without one was all but impossible. There had been no time, however, to have the vision of the attack on her father examined, questioned, and debated by others.

She gestured to the large pot of numbweed salve, wrapping it with an Aspected intent of movement. It drifted across the workbench, closer to her.

Calling to someone's mind through the powers of the Aspects was one thing. Anyone gifted with the powers of the Aspects could do that, even without an amulet. Just like moving a pot. Her father's presence existed as a metaphysical embrace of love, devotion, and protection strong enough to be an Aspect of its own. The Aspects Above created him, as the indivisible deity had created her, her mother, all life. They blessed him with a breath of their power through his Defending Aspect.

Her call this time, however, had been wholly different. Of course it was. She was a Trine. She beat the spoon against the jar rim with quick, violent blows to deliver more clinging salve into the container.

Why would the Aspects Above give her abilities such as this only to have her destroy Deren someday, summers from now? By the Light! It just made no sense.

She had known by her father's surprise once he had dropped U'Nehíl that he had heard her. Then, he'd disappeared and never contacted her again.

What if *she* was the reason he never contacted her again?

She gripped the spoon tighter.

Had her journey toward darkness and destruction already begun? She set the spoon in the serving pot and gripped the workbench, calming herself.

Should she search for her father once more? What if this time she searched, and she truly found nothing? Had she distracted him with that call at a critical moment? She paused in her ladling, holding the handle so tightly, its edges pressed into her palm. What if he, Morgan Jord, Binthe Lima, and the other il'Kin had died, and only she knew what had happened to them?

She threw the spoon down on the table and rubbed her face. No. She squeezed her eyes shut behind her hands. No, her father was not dead. She would know if he was. She would know it in her heart, in her Aspects.

She laid her hands on the workbench, calming herself.

No. No, she didn't have an amulet. She couldn't be that powerful without one, could she? Just because she had all three Aspects didn't mean she had to use them, right? She could remain the seer everyone thought she was. *Ai*, she was a seer, maybe a powerful one, but a seer. *Ai*, that Aspect and only that Aspect would be the one she claimed. Aspects Above knew she'd never admit aloud to being a Trine.

Mirana retrieved the spoon, then scooped more into several waiting containers. How come she didn't feel unburdened by her decision? She did save her father by seeing a vision. She saved her father.

The spoon hovered over a jar.

What would her mother do if she had been successful and saved their lives?

What if her father returned home, whole and safe, because she accomplished something almost no other Aspected individual in Kinderra could do? Her mother was Seer Prime Desde Kellis Pinal, leader of all of Kin-Deren province's Fal'kin. She might ask her to choose an amulet early, that's what she might do.

Mirana bit her bottom lip as she stoppered the jar and selected another empty one.

She slapped heaping dollops of numbweed into the container, spilling some on the workbench. Could she honestly ignore her Healing Aspect? She would always try to save her father's life. Anyone's life. To willingly let someone die when such a thing could be prevented was unthinkable. More than just her duty, she wanted to use her gifts for the good of Kinderra. Desperately.

Should she have told her mother what had happened? Should she tell her now, after so many days? What would her mother do if her father had been injured—or worse—because of her call? Or—or what if her call itself had killed him, ripping his mind to cut through his cover?

What if instead of saving him and the others from death, she had caused it?

The medicine jar fell from her hands, smashing on the stone floor and spilling salve around her feet. "Oh!"

"Mirana, dear, perhaps a little more attention on your jar and a little less on daydreaming," Gemma cautioned, coming out of the storage room in the back of the apothecary.

"I'm sorry. It slipped. My fingers are numb."

The herbswoman handed her a rag and a scullery pan. "That's why it's called numbweed. Don't get any more on you, or your whole arm will fall asleep."

The woman pushed a graying black curl back up into her haircloth and gathered from the table several of the small jars Mirana had already filled with the viscous analgesic ointment.

A particularly loud thunderclap boomed through the hallway outside the hostel. Gemma's dark-skinned face creased in a wince at the noise. "Not exactly the spring weather for daydreams. Then again, unlike mine, your dreams actually come true."

Mirana hesitated in mopping up the spent salve and pottery shards. Dear Aspects Above, she didn't want any of her dreams to come true. Ever.

"What did you study today with your mother?" Gemma asked.

"We analyzed the Battle of the Vale i'Dúadar." She groaned in not-quite-feigned disgust. "For the life of me, I don't know why we call it a victory. It was a bloodbath." She brushed the pieces of pottery from the pan into a copper waste bin, where they fell with a declamatory crash.

The herbswoman wore a grim expression of her own. "*Ai*, it was. But it was a victory, too. Thousands of Fal'kin forces from three provinces had hidden in the mountains surrounding the valley to turn back an incursion of Ken'nar. The ambush they set up sent the black-armored bastards packing. It was more than ten summers before those *vermihn* mounted anything close to a serious attack after that." She carried the filled jars to the storeroom.

Ambush. Mirana hated that word. She flexed her hands, her fingers tingling from where she had touched some of the numbing salve. Recalling the grisly images her mother had projected through her amulet during their lesson earlier that day, she realized the Fal'kin façade worked brilliantly. The Ken'nar, however, did not give up easily. Thousands on both sides were killed before the dark-armored warriors were finally forced into a bloody rout.

"You were there?" she asked as she wiped up the spilled salve on the workbench.

"*Ai*," Gemma said from the storeroom. "It's been thirty summers now. I was twenty-five before I tended patients on the battlefield for the first time. My parents were killed by the Ken'nar when I was a few summers younger than you. Traders from Kana-Akün found me." She returned with a clean rag. "Healer Prime Belessa Tir herself finished my herbswoman's training. It was a long journey from growing up in Jad-Anüna to practicing here in Kin-Deren. I'd like to think my parents would be proud."

Mirana looked at the woman with even more admiration than she had already held for her. Teague's parents, Fal'kin Healers Tennen and Niah Beltran, might be the *priore'e* of the infirmary, but the herbswoman had no shortage of lives she, too, had pulled back from the brink of death. If Gemma Piaar had survived that battle, she could survive just about anything. No wonder she had been named senior herbswoman of Kin-Deren's healing hostel.

"I only sew up wounds with linen, so watching the Beltrans and their Healing Aspect was a sight to behold," the graying herbswoman continued, her gaze resting on a pile of clean bandages at the corner of the workbench. "Niah and Tennen were so young then, just a few summers older than you, but the number of lives they saved that day was nothing short of miraculous."

After a moment, she gave her shoulders a little shake and straightened them. "I don't understand how you seers can ever tell much from a vision."

If the swift topic change wasn't clear enough, the distinct impression Mirana received not to ask further questions about the vale certainly was. Fine by her. Studying every gory nuance for hours on end with her *maithe* and her fellow seer *scholaire'e* was more than enough.

"You can tell plenty," she replied. "The angle of the sun or the position of the stars tell you when an event occurs, sometimes even a precise date. Landmarks like mountains or rivers can give you a location. You can even compare a vision of one army against a mind's eye impression of an army of known size and get an estimate of troop counts." She looked down at the rag in her hand. "That is, if you have an amulet. *Maithe* and the senior seers sometimes call a memory or a vision directly to our minds, but more times than not, they just send it out through their amulets and the images hang there in the air." Like ghosts.

Gemma wrapped an arm around her and hugged her. "Don't worry, sweetling. You will have an amulet of your own soon. Just two more summers, isn't it? I can't believe it—you've grown up so quickly."

Cold fear stabbed through Mirana. She must not choose an amulet. Not unless she found a way to become who she wanted to be, rather than what the skeins of the future portended she could be.

She frowned, hoping the older woman hadn't noticed her reaction. "Grown older, *ai*, but not exactly 'up.'"

The herbswoman laughed. "I guess you've caught up now as much as you're ever going to. I'm afraid you'll have to settle for a bit less than your *maithe's* stature. You were so small when you were born, I could almost fit you in my palm. You might have come to us early, but you certainly did not come willingly. Your *maithe* labored a full night and day. Stubborn little kit you were, even then." Gemma gave her another squeeze and released her.

Why did they always bring up the circumstances of her birth, as if she should be proud of the agony she'd caused her mother? She didn't ask to be born, certainly not born with the Aspects. Sometimes, she wished she hadn't been born at all.

Another presence drew near. A flight of sunlarks took to wing in her stomach as she recognized the young man before the sound of his footsteps reached her ears.

Teague sped into the apothecary. Seeing the other woman, he slowed to a more sensible pace. He shook the rain-soaked hair out of his eyes. "*Ben dië*, Senior Herbswoman. Mirana."

She smiled broadly. "Teague." She caught Gemma's raised eyebrow and eased her mouth into a more sensible grin.

The herbswoman's expression, however, remained. "Miri, I thought your *maithe* had you helping out in the kitchens after your lessons today."

Teague began to place lids on some of the jars she had filled. How could hands be so gentle yet so strong at the same time? And warm. And tender. When they touched her arm, her face. What would his caress feel like when he, at last, touched her—

"Mirana?" Gemma nudged her elbow.

She shook herself. "What? Sorry. I already did. I think I peeled every potato in the province. My fingers are permanently curled from holding a paring knife. After studying a battle all day, I didn't even want to look at another knife. So, when I finished in the kitchens, I came here."

"*Ai*, of course. Completely understandable, as there are no sharp instruments here." The herbswoman gestured to a set of gleaming scalpels on a tray on the workbench. "Young Master Beltran, help our potato peeler fill her jars, would you?" She left through the apothecary door to see to her patients in the adjacent convalescence room, chuckling as she passed them.

"Have you heard from your father yet?" Teague asked once Gemma was out of earshot.

The question was simple. The answer, however, was far from it. She shook her head.

"Are you worried? I mean, really worried?"

"No. Maybe." She sighed. "I don't know. If only he had called—" She stiffened and cocked her head for a moment, sensing something.

Pain. Nausea. Fear. Anger. Bleeding. Bleeding. Bleeding.

He moved closer. "What is it?"

She quickly looked over her shoulder. They were still alone. "There's a patient. He's hurting. It's a deep cut of some kind."

"Teague? Would you come here a moment?" Niah Beltran summoned her son from the convalescence room.

He nodded, handing Mirana a lid. She covered a jar and followed him out of the apothecary.

"What is it?" he said, entering the patient wardroom. Gemma and the learning hall's quartermaster held worried expressions as they stood next to Teague's mother.

On a cot lay a boy Mirana and Teague's age. The youth was pale and sweaty. His left forearm was wrapped in a cloth soaked with blood.

"This is a good one for you to attend to, Teague," Niah said. "The laceration on his arm is deep. It will be good suture practice for you. Just use plenty of numbweed for your deeper sutures."

Teague's parents were Mirana's own parents' closest friends, nearly family in their own right. She shared *Matrua* Niah's jet-black hair and admired its thick waves much more than her own poker-straight tresses. What she appreciated the most, however, was the healer woman's honest and reassuring smile. Teague had *Patrua* Tennen's lighter coloring, not his mother's rich, caramel skin from the southern province of Tash-Hamar. He and his father both had hazel eyes—even a dusting of freckles across the nose when they saw too much sun—but his warm expression was a perfect reflection of his mother's. It was one of the qualities she adored most about him.

At the moment, the wounded boy looked like he needed smiles from both the mother and the son.

Niah pulled back her hair, tightening it into a coil at the nape of her neck, and rolled up her sleeves. "What happened to him?" she asked the quartermaster.

"I found him lying in the street by the markets," Haarlen Lasen replied. "He didn't want to come." His frown sank into cheeks turned apple-red from summers manning the learning hall's kitchen hearths.

Teague's mother sighed. "It is a sentiment that grows regardless of who wins battles."

Gemma's eyes widened as she pointed to the large man's shirt. "I'll bet you did more than just find him in the street." A long tear rent the fabric. One that might have been made protecting oneself—or someone else—from a large knife. "You're a good man, Haarlen."

He shrugged his massive shoulders. "Let me know how he does."

The healer woman nodded. "I will."

The quartermaster grinned down at the boy, the expression nearly buried within his bushy brown beard, and left the wardroom.

Mirana blinked as a memory flashed from the boy's mind to hers. He had tried to steal some bread from a vendor in Deren's markets. The baker was not about to have his wares pilfered by a street orphan. The dough knife he'd used on the boy was meant to take off his hand.

The herbswoman was right. Quartermaster Haarlen was a good man. How many others would have left the young thief in the street as just another petty criminal?

As *Matrua* Niah carefully unwrapped the cloth from the youth's forearm, the rose quartz amulet around her neck began to glow a soft pinkish hue.

The boy snatched his arm back from her. "Let go of me." His breath came in short bursts through clenched teeth.

Mirana grimaced and caught Teague's gaze. Obviously, the young thief was terrified and in a good deal of pain, but underneath those emotions, she sensed anger. More like fury.

The healer sat back and put her hands on her lap where the boy could see them. "You can relax now. You are safe here. You've got yourself a nasty cut. I want to help you."

The injured youth recoiled in fear and hissed in pain. "You're one of them."

Mirana winced, this time from the thief's comment. Unaspected, like the boy, didn't have powers to protect themselves. They could not see the skeins of time to know when an attack would occur, they could not heal injuries hundreds of times faster than letting nature do the work, and they could not defend themselves with amulet fire.

The Ken'nar ransacked the homes and farms of the Unaspected for food, horses, livestock, supplies, and anything that could be melted down in a smithy fire to create weapons. If the Unaspected resisted, they were killed. Sometimes, they were killed anyway. Killed by their own life forces, fueling the very amulets that struck them down.

After three thousand summers, could no one find a way to end the war between the Ken'nar and Fal'kin? The people the Fal'kin were sworn to protect often suffered the most.

"*Ai.* I am a Fal'kin healer," Niah replied. "This is my *biraen*, Teague. I would like him to care for you if that's all right."

The boy eyed Teague fearfully. "Your son? Where's his amulet?"

The healer woman looked down at her hands resting in her lap. "My son heals in a different way."

"Mother, please." Teague turned to the youth. "I don't have an amulet. I'm not old enough but that doesn't matter. I'm not 'one of them.' I'm like you. I don't have the Aspects. I heal, well, the regular way."

"He will have you as good as new in no time." *Matrua* Niah moved over to make room for her son. "Mirana, dear, you might want to leave."

More impressions pushed at her Aspects. The boy's mental state was as concerning as his physical injury. "I'd like to stay and help if I could." She glanced at Teague. "It's good for everyone to learn some healing skills, even, um, seers, isn't it?"

... The boy is frightened enough of us Aspected ... I don't want you to upset him even more ... Teague's mother called to her mind.

... I have no amulet, either ... Maybe he won't be so frightened of me ... she returned. *... I just want to help ...*

Niah regarded her for a moment. "You may spend as much time here as your parents will allow." Her dark brown eyes glinted with humor. "Provided you learn."

Mirana turned her face away from the healer to pick at a hangnail on her thumb. "I do learn so much here."

"All right. You may stay and help. Get a basin of clean water and some fresh bandages. Teague, what else do we need?"

He rattled off a list of other supplies.

"Did you get that, Mirana?"

"*Ai.*" She hurried and gathered the supplies from the apothecary. When she returned, she set down an additional jar. "I brought some allium tincture as well. The cut is so deep, there will be a risk of infection. Teague says it works better than strained honey alone," she added with a smile.

A dark eyebrow rose on Niah's face. Teague grinned and nodded. "I think I got this."

Now, a corner of his mother's mouth lifted like her eyebrow. *... He needs to practice his stitches ...* "You come get me if he runs into any trouble."

Oh. No.

Did his mother suspect she had the Healing Aspect? Or did she think she was just here to dally with her son? Was it too late to run from the infirmary? Probably. She couldn't move anyway because panic bound every limb. She swallowed and forced a smile.

"*Ai,* Healer Niah, of course." She nodded vigorously. Maybe too vigorously.

"Gemma, let's get more of those bundles of thyme and mint ready," the healer woman said. "With this damp weather, it's a wonder the entire hall hasn't come down with croup." She rose to leave and squeezed Mirana's shoulder. … *I am here for you, too, if you need me … Always …*

She did not return the healer's call but focused instead on the boy's wound. His forearm had been sliced open down to the muscle. Thankfully, no bones were exposed. She had taught herself to control others' pain without an amulet over the past few summers. It was difficult, at the limits of her abilities, but possible. Holding the youth's pain at bay from such a deep wound would require considerably more effort than she was used to, however. This was by far the most serious injury she and Teague had worked on together. *Matrua* Niah was one of Kinderra's few Fal'kin healers. Could she do it without Teague's mother or anyone else noticing? She bit her lip.

She glanced around the spacious convalescence room. A few patients lay in cots and appeared to be asleep. Three other herbsfolk tended them while an apprentice made up a cot with fresh linens. They were all busy enough not to notice her. Good. She took a breath. They were safe.

As Teague cleaned the boy's forearm, she sat in the chair by the cot. She reached out to grasp his good arm in greeting. "*Ben dië.* My name is Mirana. What is your name?"

The wounded thief batted her hand away and locked a moan of pain behind gritted teeth. "You're a Pinal. All of you in the Pinal family have those eyes. The silver eyes that will take away my soul."

She folded her hands in her lap. "Don't be silly. The Aspected don't take away souls."

"Your family is cursed." The boy curled the hand of his uninjured arm into a fist.

After more than twelve hundred summers, Fal'kin and Unaspected alike still looked at her family with a certain amount of mistrust. By the Light, she did not want to continue Jasal Pinal's sins. Then again, some Unaspected were beginning to look at anyone with powers with mistrust.

"I only want to help you." She tried to send soothing thoughts into him, but that was harder to do if he wouldn't let her touch him.

"Help?" The youth swung his feet off the cot. "What do you know of help? Help might have saved my mother and father when the Ken'nar overran our farm. Where were the Fal'kin and their saving amulets then? If there were no racking Fal'kin, there would be no racking Ken'nar to fight them, there would be no racking war, and my parents would still be alive!"

She started to speak but, instead, blew out her words through pursed lips. He was wrong. Very. Her father hadn't been home since before the Reckoning had turned, putting his own life in danger to prevent tragedies exactly like this. Then again, would she feel any different if a Ken'nar amulet had reduced him to ash? Or if a grynwen had torn out his throat? She willed the thought away.

"I shouldn't have come here." The young thief rose from the cot. He groaned in pain and swayed when his legs wouldn't hold him.

Teague caught him before he could fall to the floor. Mirana helped ease the injured boy back down to sit on the cot and sent a calming intent to his mind. The boy's breathing now came in pants. Maybe she should call *Matrua* Niah after all.

"If you leave now, that wound could fester," Teague said. "You could lose your arm."

"I will leave if you want me to," Mirana added, "but at least let Teague put a clean bandage on you."

The thief's gaze flicked between the two of them as he sat hunched over, guarding the wounded limb.

Teague sat back in his chair. "Look, I trust her with my life." His gaze now drifted to her. "I would do anything for her. As I know she would for me."

Her cheeks flushed. That was indeed true, but so much more existed behind his words that the youth could not perceive. Only she could.

The boy hesitated a moment more, then nodded and fell back on the cot.

"Give me the numbweed, Mirana." She passed the jar to Teague, and he slathered some on his patient's forearm with a thin, metal spatula. The youth flinched as the salve touched his wound.

"Give it a moment. It will help lessen your pain," she said. She threaded a thin filament of catgut through a fine needle and some silk through another slightly larger one, and handed both to Teague. Reaching for the jar of numbweed, she pretended to scoop out a dab of the salve. She moved to sit behind the boy's head and placed her fingers on his temples. He winced.

"I promise I won't hurt you." Her Healing Aspect rose in earnest in response to the boy's wound. She brought him into a deep sleep. When he awoke, he would believe his slumber was due to the anesthetic effects of the numbweed. Or, rather, she hoped he would. Everyone else whose pain she dampened had come to that conclusion. What if he knew it was her, though? She bit her lip again.

Was this all really worth the risk? To the boy *and* of perhaps letting her secret out? She glanced up at the rafters. They were up there, the Aspects Above, somewhere far beyond the ceiling, the clouds, and the sun. Maybe if she kept doing good things like helping to heal people, the divine entity would lift her curse from her.

Ai, it was worth the risk.

The boy tensed as she massaged his temples, but at least he didn't pull away this time.

And she could always tell Niah and her own mother she didn't heal anything, merely controlled some pain, and used her Sight to predict an immediate-future prognosis. *Ai*, that would work if it came to that.

Wouldn't it?

Teague washed the blood away from the wound and treated it with the honey and allium. He thought her name, ready for her help. She closed her eyes, centered herself, and pushed away any distractions.

Wrongness. Muscles laid bare. Bleeding. Blood vessels cut. Bleeding. Raw flesh bleeds.

The shrill notes of the boy's laceration scraped at her mind as she struggled to diminish his pain with her Healing Aspect. She clamped her jaw as the boy's deep ache pulsated through her before fading. His breathing calmed as his body relaxed under her fingers. She opened herself more fully to her Healing power and sent the youth into a deeper state of unconsciousness.

"Is everything all right over there?" Niah called from the apothecary.

Mirana froze at the sound of the healer's voice. Teague replied to his mother with a confident answer, but the alarmed emotion she caught from him matched her own. To lose concentration now would put the boy in even greater pain. The pungent, camphor-like scent of the numbweed burned her nose as Teague applied more salve into his patient's wound. A moment later, his thoughts bade her to continue. She pulled from within herself and coaxed the boy's nerves to remain quiet, fighting against the strain.

A new note, a dissonant chord separate from the street boy's painful music, rang out. Soft at first, the shrill sense grew sharply louder. A burning sensation centered itself in her chest. Images of the youth's injuries began to shift. What was happening? A vision from her Seeing Aspect superimposed itself over her Healing Aspect and into her awareness.

"Miri," Teague whispered, "could you try to—"

Water rushes over rock. Two stone bridges span river chasms. Lightning flashes. Thousands of riders, hazy with the insubstantiality of a time yet to come. They pound across a narrow bit of land and surge through an outpost of tents. The landscape plunges into darkness. The all-consuming bloodlust of the riders remains. Fighters rise to meet the riders. Amulets fire. Burning, burning. Death. Massive wolf-like creatures leap high, their fangs fastening on throats. Death. Power grows within her, burning, building, consuming. Her chest burns. Lightning flashes again. The rivers and the riders disappear. Jasal's Keep. Her chest burns. Burning, burning. The watchtower stands entombed in white light. Rage. Desolation. Agony. Death. Thousands. Light. Exploding.

"—because I'm awfully close to a nerve."

"I can't," she gasped, attempting to keep her shaking fingers locked on the boy's temples.

"It's all right. It's all right. I just need to close him up," he replied. "Keep him asleep a little bit longer." He reached for the numbweed jar again.

She nodded and closed her eyes once more as she fought to catch her breath. Beads of sweat rolled down her face.

Long moments later, he thought a clear notion of relief. "I'm done. You can let him go now."

Mirana slipped out of the youth's mind and removed her hands from his temples as Teague spread more of the analgesic salve on the wound. A row of tiny, meticulous stitches now closed the gash in the boy's forearm.

Moments later, the youth blinked and slowly sat up. He looked down at his arm. "What happened?"

"You fell asleep. Our numbweed is, um, very strong," Teague replied. "I just need to put this bandage on you. You should be good as new in a few sevendays." He took a clean strip of linen and wound it around the youth's limb.

When he had finished, the street boy touched the bandage, his brows drawn together. "I was talking, and then I just fell asleep." His words sounded more like a question. Mirana certainly had questions of her own at the moment.

She wiped her forehead with the back of her hand, still shaking. She peered behind her. The other herbsfolk had left. The apprentice herbsgirl, however, gave her a curious look, pausing in the middle of stuffing a pillow in a case. Mirana feigned a nauseated grimace and gestured to the wounded youth with a tilt of her head. The other girl smiled and nodded in understanding, and finished making the bed.

"That happens." Teague now stared at her with a questioning scowl.

The young thief looked back down at his arm. "I don't know what to say."

She took a slow breath. "You are starving. Find your way to the kitchens."

Teague nodded. "Tell them Healer Niah said you could have as much as you want. They might need some help, too. If your family had a farm, you probably know good produce when you see it. Maybe you can assist Quartermaster Lasen with choosing provisions?"

The youth rose from the bed and started to leave. When he reached the door, he paused. "My name is Maark. Maark Bedane. *Gratas Oë*." He nodded at Mirana. "Both of you."

She nodded absently and watched Maark leave the hostel.

Dear Light Above, what had she just seen?

Teague blew out an exhale. "That was a close one. What the bloody hell happened? I thought he was going to come back around before we were done."

She remained in the chair and didn't answer.

As happened for any seer, disturbing visions came unbidden on occasion. This one terrified her. A wave of thousands upon thousands of riders, more than she had ever seen, swelled across Two Rivers Ford. It had to be the ford. She had learned in her primary lessons that the stone bridge complex spanned the confluence of the Garnath and Anarath Rivers, joining three provinces. Were all those riders Ken'nar? It was impossible to tell. In the vision, it was nighttime, and she could only see between flashes of lightning. Was it truly a vision or was it a memory of the boy's? A nightmare of his? Of hers? It happened so fast. She rubbed her chest where the burning sensation still stung.

"Miri?" Teague nudged her with his elbow.

"What? *Ai*. I'm fine."

He rinsed the blood from his hands in the basin. The blood. The riders. Death. She gasped and squeezed her eyes shut.

"You don't look so good. Are you all right?"

To make light of her reaction, she waved him off and tried to laugh. It sounded fake even to her.

Glancing at the apothecary where his mother worked, he stepped close to her. "Did you see something?"

In a rush, she wrapped her arms around his waist, burying her face against his chest. He stroked her hair. "Maybe. I don't know—" She gasped and pulled back from him.

Matrua Niah walked into the convalescence room. "Done already?"

"*Ai*," he said, nodding as he rubbed his suddenly empty hands on his breeches. "It, ah, wasn't as bad as it looked after I cleaned him up. He finally told us his name was Maark Bedane."

"He left?"

"He was famished," Mirana said. "We sent him to the kitchens. I think if we waited any longer, he would have eaten the numbweed."

Teague avoided his mother's gaze, pointedly so, and busied himself with gathering the medical supplies. "He should be fine."

"I wanted to inspect your sutures. How am I supposed to tell how well you're doing if you don't show me?" the healer woman said, but she kept her eyes fixed on Mirana.

Mirana glanced over at Teague. He looked just as pale as she felt.

"Mother, I'll bring Maark back. You can inspect my sutures. If you think they're sloppy, it's because I don't have your, well, your skills."

Matrua Niah rounded her mouth into her reassuring smile. "You are very skilled, but I must check your progress."

He turned to face his mother. His shoulders and fists tensed, readied for the struggle he combated so often. Mirana fought the urge to hold him. "If I'm as skilled as you say, why do you need to check on my progress?"

"You are very talented, but you are still an apprentice—"

"You think Mirana distracts me, don't you? Don't take your disappointment in me out on her."

The healer woman stepped close and held her son's face, her own full of pride and pain. "I am not disappointed in you, *ama*. Ever." Her gaze moved to Mirana. "And I never said she was a distraction. I'm just not so sure she's letting you practice your herbsman's skills on your own."

Mirana lowered her gaze at Niah's comment. Did Teague's mother really think she would ever prevent him from caring for a patient? He was everything to her. He held her deepest confidences, her deepest fears. He held her heart. But hadn't she, in fact, interrupted his treatment at a critical moment? She'd nearly lost her hold on the boy's pain when that vision or whatever it was stormed its way into her mind. He had to calm her and treat Maark at the same time. Her shoulders sank. What if she hadn't been able to regain control? Maybe it was time to put an end to this ridiculous attempt to heal in secret.

She shook her head. "Please, don't, Teague. I never meant to be a distraction to you. I thought I was helping you. Your mother is right. I didn't realize my, well, using my Seeing Aspect in front of you was like flaunting it and making it more difficult for you to concentrate."

He held her, ignoring his mother. "You are not a distraction. Ever. I've never felt that you were using your Aspect to make me feel bad. You know that. I know that's not what you're doing."

Matrua Niah folded her arms. "That injury should have taken two jars of numbweed, yet neither of you returned for more. I know something is going on here."

He released Mirana. "Mother, I—"

The healer held up her hand, silencing him, and turned to Mirana. "Teague's father and I have noticed far less use of numbweed when you help. *Ai*, all Aspected have some ability to heal minor injuries and lessen pain, but that is only within themselves. Not others. How do you explain what's been happening?"

She looked away from Niah's penetrating deep-brown eyes. "I just wanted to help. That's all." That would be enough. That would be everything. "I should go. I've probably been here too long anyway." She turned to leave.

"Miri, wait," Teague pleaded.

Before the healer woman could search her thoughts further, another mind brushed her consciousness.

"Shouldn't you be helping your mother?"

Mirana whirled around. "*Paithe!* You're home!"

She flew into his arms. He was soaked to the skin from the rain. Mud and blood stained his white uniform. His chain mail bore great rents. Fatigue roiled off him like storm clouds. But he was alive!

He held her tightly, pressing his lips to the top of her head. *... Ai, biraena, I am ... Because of you ...*

CHAPTER 5

"I, at last, beheld my child."
—The Codex of Jasal the Great

Kaarl lay next to Desde, drowsing in the stillness of their chamber. Thick raindrops pattered against the window, punctuated by the occasional tap of sleet. Oh, to be out of the elements at last and in a warm bed next to his warm wife. For long moments, he simply breathed her in, clinging to her as she held on to him. He laid his cheek on her breast and listened to her heartbeat. He was so inexpressibly grateful to hear and to feel her living presence again after so much death. He could not remember anything as fragrant as his wife's skin. Nor anything as soft. Nor could he imagine anyone as beautiful as she. Hair like summer wheat shimmering in the sun, eyes like burnished wood. Her body gave life back to him after the Ken'nar had left only death in their wake.

His hand followed the sinuous curves of her body up from her hip to rest on her arm. … *Why do I ever leave you?* …

She brushed her lips on his head. … *Because you are a fool* … She entwined her long legs around his.

… *Ai, I am a fool* …

"The bravest, most brilliant fool the Aspects Above ever chose to defend us."

"In that, you are very much mistaken." He raised himself on one elbow and kissed her, again drinking in her love.

She pulled back from his mouth. … *What happened in Kana-Akün, Ëi ama?* …

He did not return her call this time. He slid his body over hers, pouring more passion into his kisses.

She gently pushed him back from her. "Kaarl. What happened?"

He rested his forehead against her collarbone and sighed. Kaarl rolled off her and sat up, the coverlet sliding down his bare chest to his waist. He studied his hands in his lap, the scars, old and new. If his body was still as lean and strong as it ever was, why did he feel so powerless? Her fingers brushed at his hair and traced down his neck to a healing wound on the back of his shoulder.

"Kaarl?" she asked again.

He shook his head, dismissing the question as he peeled off the blankets and rose from the bed. He slipped his arms through a tunic and went over to the fireplace. Kaarl stoked the embers back into a comfortable blaze to ward off the deep night's chill.

The Defending Aspect flowed through his veins. He'd once wondered if, when the Aspects Above created the Aspected, they made defenders first. So wedded to the ideal of protecting Kinderra and her people were defenders, maybe it made some sense to the deity to create fighters ahead of seers or even healers. Now, he wondered if making defenders at all had been a mistake.

He held his deep-red garnet. *Ai*, he was blessed with calling forth amulet fire. Yet, his blessing had failed one of his defenders entirely. He let his amulet fall back to his chest.

"They were," he paused, "they are all so young. Even Morgan has seen only thirty summers."

"They are also very skilled and highly trained, and they are led by the best defender Kinderra has."

He laughed in derision at her comment.

Just past fifty summers he had lived, and most of those had been spent in combat with the Ken'nar. Fifteen of those summers he had served as the commander of the il'Kin, and he had fought as a defender in its ranks longer still.

Long summers ago, the renowned strike force unit comprising the finest Fal'kin in the nine provinces of Kinderra numbered one hundred amulets. When the snows had melted last spring, he rode out with thirty defenders. It was spring again, and he had marched home with eighteen. Never had so many fallen under his command in so short a time as in these last months.

In other labors, a man could walk away when he became too old or too disheartened. Being a Fal'kin was not a choice; it was a birthright. How did one escape one's destiny?

"You cannot, but you can control how you face it," Desde said, answering his unspoken question. ... *What are you hiding from me?* ...

He was silent. What could he say? What was there to say?

He poured himself what was left of the wine from a carafe on a small side table near the bed. He held up his cup as a means of asking his wife if she wanted some. She shook her head.

She raised herself on her elbow and propped up her head with her hand. "I am a seer, and I was a student of my father. He was seer prime of this province for nearly fifty summers and twice as cagey as any defender. I think that entitles me to know brilliance when I see it."

Kaarl sat down next to her again. "That is very true." He leaned over to give her a tender kiss on her forehead. "I miss Toban. Very much."

Their room, one of the hundreds in Deren's learning hall, contained little more than a bed, a fireplace, some chairs, and a small table. It was Desde's right as prime now to take up residence in the largest suite in the hall. He was glad she had not moved them to the prime's chambers down the hallway. Too much of her beloved father Toban remained in it.

"Could the healers do nothing?"

His wife sighed. "Even Fal'kin do not live forever."

"I wish the Aspects Above would have made him an exception."

"You have no idea how hard I prayed for that as well. However, you sidestepped my question. What happened in the forest?"

He stared into his cup. "I already briefed you, my prime. What more do you need to know?"

She sat up and rested her lips on his shoulder. "I need nothing more. You need to rid yourself of the poison left behind."

He swallowed a large draft of wine. "I do not wish to discuss it."

… Dici Oëa cerebus a Ëa, Ëi ama … she called to him in Anqa Lingua, the old tongue of Kinderra.

… I do not wish to speak my mind to you … Not now … It is too soon … he returned.

"No. I fear it has already been too long."

He said nothing. In the firelight, the wine looked like blood.

"I have known you your whole life. Never have you allowed adversity to defeat you. You've lost good fighters before. Why does this one haunt you so?"

"It's not just this one. It's all of them. It's thirty summers of them. Of seeing them die." Kaarl regarded his cup once more, now disgusted by its contents. "I fight and I fight and I fight, but my sword and amulet never make one damn bit of difference. I have grown useless in this war. Why does this one haunt me so? I'll tell you why. One moment, we were riding through the woods. The next, one of my defenders was dead."

… By nothing more nefarious than a simple pack of beasts! … Beasts, Desde! … And I couldn't do anything to save Gannah … Not one … Damn! … THING! …

His Defending Aspect flared as the cup hurled across the room and shattered within the fireplace. The flames rose as they consumed the wine.

Desde tensed. *… Ama? …*

He never brought the war to their home. To their bed. To her. He buried his face in his hands.

"I remember all too well what it's like to lose people you care about, *Ëi ama*." Her voice dropped to a whisper. "Skilled battle seers died from a strike they had successfully blocked a hundred times before. And the most inept of fighters lived another day." She held one of his hands and pulled it down. "I also remember all the battle lust. The stench of blood. The noises the Ken'nar made as I slit their throats. I was drowning in guilt from the deaths I caused. Becoming pregnant with Mirana and remaining a hall seer in Deren was a blessing for me beyond just bearing a child." She brought his hand to her lips. "Now, I merely see deaths by the hundreds instead of causing them."

Kaarl studied Desde's hand in his. He also remembered holding his wife month after barren month, her guilt-ridden sobs blaming her empty womb on her sins. "Gannah Tesabe died."

"Oh, Kaarl."

He squeezed her hand and released it. His amulet glowed softly as his Aspect called to the deep red garnet with the memory. "She was just four summers older than Mirana. She had so much promise. Few older defenders could fight better than that girl."

Gannah Tesabe, born to the far-flung tropical province of Jad-Anüna, had woven her scimitar in combat like a master craftswoman weaving a tapestry. So much talent. So very much. He cursed under his breath, his body growing rigid in an effort to hold back his anger. "I couldn't even save her from those bloody grynwen. Do you call that brilliance?"

"Grynwen are not merely large wolves." She covered his amulet with her hand, her fingers cool and soothing against the skin of his chest. "Even a man such as Tetric Garis cannot save everyone." When he did not comment, she continued. "Gannah was not a child. She had seen battle. Many of them."

He deflated back into the bed. "I shouldn't have lost her."

"It is said grynwen hunt with the Aspects."

"So do we." He sighed in frustration. "I had hoped Tetric might have been able to do something, but…" He stared at the beamed ceiling high above him. The supports no doubt came from Kana-Akün centuries ago.

"He came?"

Kaarl frowned. "After we'd taken the loss. Again. This time, it was sheer luck. We didn't even know he was in the vicinity."

He closed his eyes and sighed. He was weary, and for this one moment, he let himself feel the full weight of his fatigue. "The war has changed, Desde. The Ken'nar. They have always been brutal, but now?" He slowly spun the thin gold band encircling his left wrist. His wife had given it to him the day they joined in union, forever committing herself to him. She wore one just like it, his eternal promise to her. Her love and their daughter's love were the only things he held closer to him than his Aspect. Sometimes, their love was all he cared about. "We fight them, but they do not stop. They are relentless."

His wife gently caressed his mind, trying to comfort him, but nothing could take away this hurt anymore. "Our corpses were not even recognizable as bodies," he continued, "That is, those the Ken'nar did not turn into ash with their amulets. For summers now, grynwen are at every engagement, not just large-scale assaults."

He sat up again and swung his legs off the edge of their bed, his back to Desde. He looked down at his hands once more, staring at them helplessly. "Last autumn, fighting out on the borderlands in between Varn-Erdal and Dar-Azûl, I rode past one felled Ken'nar. His leg had been cut from him, he was pocked with arrows, yet he still tried to stand and attack. He ripped out an arrow from his side and stabbed at the fetlocks of my horse. We are all but powerless against evil such as this." He let his breath out slowly in a staccato exhale. "Do you remember when Tarn Salka died?"

"*Ai*. It was at that skirmish at Thyre's Crossing. Two summers ago now."

The amulet pulled at the back of his neck, its burden hanging even more heavily on his soul. "We fought in the provincial forces together. We were both called up to the il'Kin together. I didn't think another loss could hurt more. I was wrong." He stopped fighting the weight of his garnet and let it sag his shoulders. "The Ken'nar do not stop. We must butcher them just to press any advantage at all. This is not war. This is savagery."

"I know you fought bravely."

"And yet one of my own was brought down by animals. Not even a blade."

Desde touched the shadow of another scar on his arm. "One could have been all twenty of you, regardless of whether Tetric arrived or not." … *And we would not be having this conversation* …

He shifted uncomfortably. "That has more to do with Mirana's warning than Tetric."

She dropped her hand. "Warning? What warning?"

"Mirana's call." He scowled as her shock leaked from her mind to his. He turned to face her. "Did she not tell you?"

"Tell. Me. What?" She cut off each word as if with a knife.

"She called to me. She should not have been able to."

"Granted, the distance—"

"We were hidden. We were under U'Nehîl."

Her hand went to her mouth.

The fact that Mirana had not told his wife of this warning meant their daughter knew precisely the magnitude of what she had done. She was certainly adept in her interpretation abilities, foretelling with accuracy many events, despite being given just fragments of unbidden visions. Their daughter, once so exuberant in expressing what the Aspects Above revealed to her through her Seeing Aspect, had grown more and more withdrawn in recent summers. Now, she barely discussed any vision beyond its facts. Even with her reticence, though, she had never been deceitful.

Maybe she was beginning to understand her sight meant so much more to Kinderra than merely receiving some skein of time before her mind's eye. Was the Dark Trine beginning to take notice of their daughter's talents as well?

A chill rippled through him having nothing to do with the night air.

He and Desde would do anything to keep their child safe. Anything. If deceit saved lives, was it still a sin? He did not know. He wasn't sure he cared anymore. If Mirana remained safe, that was all that mattered to him.

Kaarl reached out now for their daughter's presence in her small room across the corridor from theirs. She was awake. She had been as relieved to have him and the others home as he was to be home. He had held her and not wanted to let go, deciding to save the discussion about her warning for the morning.

She was still so petite despite seeing nearly sixteen summers. It was as though her small body never made up for the sevendays she missed coming nearly two months early when she was born. His tiny girl. Eyes like moonlight on water. Like his. Hair as black as midnight. Like his. Having to bear the weight of his ancestor Jasal Pinal's damned reputation for failure, cowardice, and betrayal. Having to do more, be more, just to counter it. Like him. Like all in the Pinal lineage.

"Does she actually think I would punish her for saving your life?" Desde crossed her arms, hugging herself. "She is not supposed to act alone on visions yet, but this was a matter of life or death. Why would she hide this from me?"

"If you were honest with yourself, you would know why."

She now rose from the bed and put on her robe, cinching it around her slender waist. She walked over to the window. Mirana's high, rose-petal cheeks on porcelain skin, her rosebud mouth—adorable when she pouted, glorious when she smiled—those were all Desde's. As were their daughter's shoulders when she tightened them in fear. As his wife was doing now. Desde closed her mind from him.

He frowned and went over to her.

She swallowed audibly. "Perhaps she sensed the grynwen hunting you and found you that way?"

Kaarl shook his head. "Binthe did not sense them."

"Maybe you weren't hidden as well as you thought. You and the others were exhausted from sevendays of fighting and riding."

He thought about this possibility for a moment, then rejected it. When the vicious carnivores had attacked, he could not sense Morgan Jord until his defender second dropped the cloak of U'Nehíl to fight, and he had been only a few yards away.

"She called me," he replied, his voice a whisper. "She found me."

His wife turned. "We cannot continue to do this. It is time. We must speak with Tetric."

"He already knows."

Her eyes widened. "Everything?"

"No, but he suspects it." ... *He heard her, too* ...

The sleet and fog he'd encountered in the Kana-Akün had followed him home. Icy pellets beat at the window the way unwanted conclusions beat at his mind. Rime ice coated the metal escutcheons of the window and the torchlight embrasures in the courtyard below. Beyond the learning hall sat the many homes and shops of Deren. Beyond that, the great walls, as thick as two men lying head to toe, encircled the city. Somewhere beyond the apple orchards and the fields flowed the Garnath River far to the north and the border with the Kana-Akün province. He was no seer, but his father's heart conjured up an image of the frost-paled fields blackened by dark-armored Ken'nar, all marching down from Falantir to take his daughter from him.

He turned to face his wife. "Do you think she knows?" As soon as the words left his lips, he wished he hadn't asked the question. He didn't want to know the answer.

Desde shrugged sadly and shook her head. "I would have thought she would have come to me if she had questions. She doesn't speak with me like she used to, but I thought that was because she's becoming a young woman. It's a natural part of growing up, I suppose. The Aspects Above know I didn't tell my father half of what I did when I was her age."

A small smile tugged at one corner of Kaarl's mouth. More often than not, he had been the reason Desde had not told Toban how she was spending her days. "But to not speak up about this?" she continued. "To willfully keep silent? I don't know whether to be furious or terrified."

"I have fears even darker than Mirana's silence on this."

His wife stiffened. "I know what you are alleging. Do not dare speak it. He would have had to know where to look, when to listen to have heard her. Kaarl, with this call of hers, we can't protect her anymore. It is time. We need to give her to Tetric."

"No." He again clenched his hands into fists. This time they were balled up not in anger, but in determination. "We are her parents. We know what's best for her, and we will protect her. As we've always done."

"Our lies can no longer keep her safe. She's nearly sixteen. She will choose an amulet in just two more summers. If she doesn't understand now, she certainly will by then. We must speak with her and tell her. Everything. She needs Tetric Garis now. Not us."

"We agreed to wait until she's ready to choose an amulet. When she can defend herself."

She held his arm tightly. "I don't think we can wait that long anymore. Not after this. Tetric Garis is the Light Trine of the prophecy. We all would have come to believe it through his success at turning back the Ken'nar time and again, even if the Aspects Above hadn't placed that destiny on his shoulders. He's the only one who can protect—"

He now gripped both of Desde's arms. "He's also a man, and he's not invincible. I've seen him bleed."

"*Ai*, exactly. It terrifies me to say it, but what if Mirana is the one to rebuild like the prophecy says—because Tetric will not survive?"

He dropped his hands. "Is that supposed to make me feel better? The Ken'nar are no longer loosely aligned bands of barbarians raiding unsuspecting farmers. They have become preternaturally skilled in attacking us. They must be led by the Dark Trine. No mere warlord ever won such victories against the Fal'kin. With Tetric Garis as the Light Trine, the Ken'nar bastard will want nothing more than to see him dead. If we give Mirana to Tetric, she could be killed in his wake. And if he dies? The Dark Trine's eye will be fixed on Mirana." His amulet gave off a ruddy glow in the firelight.

Desde cupped her topaz amulet in her hands, staring into its sulfurous facets. ... *If she understands why she could make such a call to you, why hasn't she come to us, ama?* ...

... *Ëo no compre* ... Kaarl pulled his wife into his arms. ... *The only thing I do know is that our lie is the only thing keeping her alive* ...

He hoped the conviction of his words would strengthen Desde's. And his own.

CHAPTER 6

*"Like a thief in the night, the Power from Without
steals. Remain watchful that even thy Aspects are not
taken from thee."*

—The Book of Kinderra

Mirana gave up on sleep, her thoughts advancing and
retreating like defenders in battle. Somewhere behind the
overcast skies, the midnight stars wheeled ever closer to dawn.

The army of riders. Thousands of them. At Two Rivers
Ford. Were they Fal'kin? Ken'nar? The images had appeared so
quickly in her mind, she never had time to look for uniforms,
standards, anything.

She rose from bed, slipped on leggings and a linen tunic,
and stomped into her boots. She reached for a woolen sweater.

Woven for a man more than twice her size, it hung nearly to her knees. She inhaled its scent as she pulled it over her head. *Paithe.* She would always keep something of his when he went away on a tour of duty in case it might be the only thing she'd have left of him.

She cinched the sweater with a belt around her waist and picked up her small belt knife. She paused, studying it. The blade was not much longer than her index finger, meant more for slicing apples than anything else.

She had never really used a weapon before, other than a few months of training summers ago with the defenders. She had certainly never seen combat before. Well, not with her mortal eyes. She had seen plenty of battles and studied them—in all their gruesome, if insubstantial, detail—through her Seeing Aspect with her mother and her fellow seer *scholaire'e*.

Someday, warfare would be all too real, no longer just moving pictures in her mind. She regarded the knife a moment longer, then tucked it into the sheath on her belt.

She flopped back down on the bed and listened to the sleet scratching at the window. Thoughts, elated and fearful, came at her again, vanguard legions of worry bent on breaking the line of her battalion mind's effort to repel them.

No doubt her father would tell her mother she had called to him when, in all likelihood, she should not have been able to. Sick little rushes dribbled through her belly.

She sniffed the sweater's fabric once more, another smell now tickling her nostrils. Ashtar.

Her father's enormous chestnut warhorse stood seventeen hands high if he was a finger. He was all muscle and hooves, nearly impervious to the charges from Ken'nar steeds. He used his great head as a battering ram to unseat any black-armored warrior who dared approach him. Her father once remarked

Ashtar seemed more like a war machine clad in a copper coat than a living, breathing destrier.

Her father was home in one piece as much from Ashtar's efforts as her warning call. The very least she could do was feed the horse a midnight snack.

Mirana stepped out of her room, crept down the hallway, and hurried into the night. Sleet prickled at her face as she darted across an exterior portico. She blinked back the icy droplets and ducked into another interior corridor.

The dozens of rooms on either side of the hallway were still empty. Lord Garis and the fifty troops from his Dar-Azûlan provincial forces that had ridden to Deren with her father from Kana-Akün must be embedded elsewhere in the hall. At one time, every single room in the learning hall had been occupied. The never-ending war was very good at creating vacancies. The Trine's men and women helped bring some life back into the compound, but the months of fighting had been as hard on them as on her father, the il'Kin, and Kin-Deren's provincial forces. Most of the Dar-Azûlans' minds were either closed or somber. A few suffered pain as they recovered from wounds, both physical and otherwise.

She could not keep up the charade of healing in secret with Teague much longer. She risked exposing her Trine powers whenever she did so, but how could she possibly leave someone in pain—or worse—when she could do something about it? At least she was trying to do something useful and not completely shirk her duty. Still, his mother, if not both his parents, already suspected she might have the Healing Aspect. How long would it be before they would tell her own parents? She gritted her teeth.

She trotted down a set of stairs and paused under a covered portico. Torchlight around the yard glowed in diffuse orange spheres in the cold fog. Mirana dashed across the learning hall's courtyard toward the stables, squinting against the stinging ice and frigid rain. Once inside, she shook the wet hair from her eyes and wiped away the rain from her face.

A presence rang through her Aspects. Taddie.

She frowned. Any other time, she would have welcomed spending time with the young stable boy. Tonight, however, she preferred the company of animals.

Taddie jumped up as she drew near. "Oh. *Scholaira* Mirana."

She smiled. "I didn't mean to startle you."

"You didn't startle me. My Seeing Aspect told me you were coming," the boy replied proudly, then his mouth stretched in an enormous yawn.

She raised an eyebrow. "Did it now?" She brushed a blond curl from his sleepy eyes. "Are you guarding the horses all by yourself tonight?"

The boy shook his head. "Defender Isel just stepped out for a late dinner after he gave me mine. It took us a long time to get the horses of Lord Garis's troops settled. I wanted to stable the Lord Trine's stallion, but *Patrua* Isel said he was too much for me. The beast didn't even like him, pulling against him and all."

"That is surprising. Defender Isel knows horses almost as well as the horses know themselves."

Taddie smiled brightly. "He says if I spend as much time learning about horses as I do my Seeing Aspect, someday I could be as good with them as he is."

She patted his shoulder. "I bet you will be."

"What are you doing down here? It's late." The little seer yawned again.

"No, it's very early. I couldn't sleep. I guess I'm too excited to have my father home. I'm going to see to Ashtar for a bit."

She began to scoop some oats from a large barrel into a nearby bucket, then jumped back with a yelp. Several mice scurried out. Taddie gestured to a broom against the wall, and it flew into his hand. He swept at the mice and sent them squeaking and running into the straw.

Mirana laughed. "Maybe you should be a battle seer instead of a horse breeder."

The little boy stuck out his chest. "I am going to be both."

"You certainly did very well learning your numbers and glyphs in our lessons earlier. At this rate, you'll be ready for your amulet before me."

He looked down at his boots for a moment. ... *When you get your amulet, will you help me see some past skeins of time? ... I miss my maithe and paithe ... Seeing them will almost be like having them here again ... Even if it is only a vision ...*

"Oh, Taddie." She gathered the boy in her arms. "I have a better idea. I'll show you how when you get your own amulet. That way you can see them whenever you want." He nodded. "Here. Help me get some more oats for Ashtar."

When she and the boy finished doling out the feed, she asked, "Do you have a curry brush and a sheepskin mitt handy?"

The young seer *scholaire* nodded again and gestured toward the items hanging among some stable tools pegged to the wall. They floated to his hand as he called to them.

She sent a notion of thanks when he gave them to her. *... Why don't you get some more sleep ... I don't think even horse thieves would be out on a night like this ... And I promise I won't tell Defender Isel ...*

He looked up at her with a bashful half-grin, dimples dotting his cheeks, and nodded. She squeezed his shoulder, picked up the feed bucket, and made her way down the line of paddocks.

Mirana peered up at the timber beams of the stable's ceiling as she walked, each one as thick as her body. They had to be strong to support four more stories of the learning hall rising above the stable. The immense aisles of paddocks always made her feel as though she stood in a roof-covered city, the stalls like homes to hundreds of horses instead of people. Legend said the stable was so large, it once housed every horse in Kinderra. It was a preposterous claim, of course, but it did take a small army of Fal'kin and Unaspected to maintain it.

An army. Thousands.

She shook her head to clear it. As she neared Ashtar's paddock, she looked over her shoulder. Taddie's mind had quieted in slumber. A deep-throated whuffling rumbled as she approached a stall on the left.

"Ashtar, you big brute."

She set down the brushes and the bucket, and threw her arms around the horse's great neck. She buried her face against his coat as he greedily ate the oats before she could pour them into his feeding trough. He smelled of leather and the sweet grassiness of fresh hay. She inhaled again and now detected a more pungent odor. She scowled. A poultice was wrapped midway down his left hind flank, secured with bandages.

"You were wounded?"

She rubbed the white blaze running down Ashtar's face, then swept a hand along his side as she walked to his hindquarters, stopping at the poultice. The horse snorted. His muscles shivered at her touch, and he stamped his white-socked hoof. She made a low, soothing noise.

Torn flesh. Four lacerations. Claws. Muscles intact. A painful redness spreads.

The wound wasn't deep, but infection had started. Thankfully, her father returned when he did and got the horse some attention. Untreated wounds easily festered in the wilds.

She returned to the horse's head and stroked his broad, velvety nose. "If I only had an amulet, Ashtar, I would fix this in a heartbeat." And yet.

Could she tell Teague's parents—her own parents—that she had been a healer all along and hadn't realized it? That her temporal visions had simply been lifted from other seers' minds because she was so acutely attuned to their bodies? Every time she had a vision, she'd just say it was some other seer's and she picked up on it as she healed the person. That way, she could keep using her Trine gifts in secret and honor her duty privately, and no one would be the wiser. *Ai,* that might actually work. She scowled and bit her lip.

Wouldn't it?

She picked up the brush and began to curry the horse's ruddy coat, staying well away from his left hind leg.

Ai, she would be able to heal wounds, even life-threatening ones, with an amulet. It would be such a greater use of her healing gift than merely blunting some pain as she did now. She wanted to heal. Oh, Aspects Above, how she wanted to. She wanted to embrace all her gifts, honor her duty, and serve as a Fal'kin, fully in communion with an amulet and her Trine Aspects. Someday, though, an amulet in her hands would not heal. It would threaten lives, not save them. She knew this. She had seen it. Almost every night for four summers.

Jasal's Keep. Rising two hundred feet in the air, wreathed in lightning. The sense of a desperate battle, thousands fighting, dying. A physical agony more than a mortal could bear. A rage so incendiary, it burned as bright as a thousand amulets. Grief, a desolation so deep, it bled the life from her. Betrayal so raw it shattered her soul into countless shards. And a white light. A light of awesome power. Of terrible power. Of magnificence. Of destruction. The explosion of light left her with a complete and utter "endness," at once glorious and final.

What exactly was the white light in Jasal's Keep? Some manifestation of her evil? The Aspects Above reaching down from the heavens to destroy her for her sins yet to be committed?

Something rubbed Mirana's leg. She cried out and dropped the curry brush.

"Cider, you scared me half to death." A large cream-and-orange-striped tomcat purred against her calf. She glanced down the dim row of stalls. Taddie was still asleep.

She picked up the cat and nuzzled the soft fur between his ears. "I think you came to the stables not so much to see me and Ashtar as to catch the mice eating his nighttime snack." She kissed the cat and set him down. He padded over to the corner of the paddock, curled into a knot, and closed his eyes to slits. "You can't fool me. You're no more asleep than I am."

She retrieved the curry brush and ran it along Ashtar's sinewy forequarters.

If her parents, if the other Fal'kin, found out she was a Trine, they would compel her to choose an amulet right away, regardless of the age custom. They would think her possession of the Trine powers was a blessing—her three Aspects were desperately needed to stop the Ken'nar. To create the enormous destruction she sensed in her keep vision of white light, however, would most certainly require an amulet. To leverage that kind of power without one would kill her. If she told them she could not take up an amulet because of the destruction she would bring at Jasal's Keep, they wouldn't believe her and would say it was impossible. They would say she misunderstood what she was seeing, that it was perhaps just a dream. But she knew it was no dream. Someday, some mistake, some choice, some path would lead her to perpetrate all the horror she saw at Jasal's Keep. She would destroy all she loved and bring to ruin all for which her people fought. She would rather disavow her duty, her birthright, than let that happen.

She'd rather die.

A soft note from her Healing Aspect whispered to her again. Her hand neared a scrape on Ashtar that had scabbed over.

She sighed and looked up at the rafters. "Why? Why give me these powers if I can't use them?"

In hindsight, she knew she had been born with the Healing Aspect, too, as well as her other powers. As a child, however, she had been too young to understand visions of a bleeding wound or a lung filling with fluid were any different than the visions of seers. It wasn't until she was older that she realized what she truly was.

She and Teague, both just past twelve summers, had climbed one of the apple trees in the orchards outside of Deren's walls. Teague, showing off for her, climbed too high on a branch too small. The tree limb snapped, and he fell. The stark picture of the two jagged white ends of the broken bones in his arm had speared into her mind. Bleeding, inflammation, and other symptoms of which she had no concept, pulled at her.

A power had welled up in her, an almost undeniable need to correct the cacophony of "wrongness" she sensed, but she didn't know how to direct it. In the end, she had done more harm than good. Tiny bits of bone, so small they could only be seen by a trained Fal'kin healer, fused in the wrong order. She had fainted from the ordeal, and Teague's parents had to re-break his arm to keep him from being maimed.

The vision of Jasal's Keep had come to her that night and forever changed her. When she awoke from unconsciousness, she finally understood what she was.

She was a Trine. And she would someday destroy Kinderra.

Mirana paused in currying Ashtar. "I don't want to hurt anyone. Why have the Aspects Above cursed me like this?"

The horse snorted and resumed munching on the oats.

"Some help you are."

She walked around to the other side, stroking his neck as she crossed in front of him. She set the curry brush down and picked up the sheepskin mitt. His copper coat gleamed under her long strokes, and she made sure to stay away from the scab.

People could call the one who led the Ken'nar whatever they wanted, but she knew better. She wasn't just a Trine. She was a Trine of the prophecy. She would become the Dark Trine. As evil as the Trine at the head of the Ken'nar was, she had yet to hear of him doing anything like she would do someday. *Ai*, he decimated armies and outposts—all horrific enough—but laying waste to the entire citadel of Deren? And the hundreds of thousands that lived there? No. That would be her.

Someday.

She stopped stroking Ashtar.

The damnable thing was that an amulet could help her control and understand her power, but she couldn't possibly choose an amulet and put Kinderra at risk for the destruction she saw.

How could she *not* choose an amulet and use her Aspects when they might actually do some good, at least in the immediate present? Was the only way to save Kinderra's future to refuse to choose an amulet and let horrible things happen now?

Choose an amulet and risk all she loved. Not choose an amulet and turn her back on all she loved. It was an impossible choice.

A cry of frustrated desperation escaped her throat, and she threw down the mitt. She wanted to cry, but weeping had long since ceased to comfort her. She rested her forehead against the horse's shoulder, feeling him breathe, hearing the beating of his heart, sensing the robust life within him.

"No matter what I choose, *Ëi cara*, Kinderra will suffer. There must be some way. Why would the Aspects Above make me their Trine if they didn't want me to use my powers? What would make me do all of what I see at Jasal's Keep? I love Kinderra." She lifted her head, searching once more for a godhead who created all but only gave her silence.

She retrieved the sheepskin mitt and wiped Ashtar's coat forcefully, scrubbing away the memory of the nightmare.

Ashtar whinnied and stomped his left leg. The muscles near his wound trembled under her mitted hand. "Ashtar. I'm sorry. I'm so sorry. I'm trying." She pulled the mitt off, letting it fall, and stared at her hands. So powerful. So powerless. "By the Light, I am trying. I'm trying to do good, to *be* good. I'm trying to do the right thing. I keep hoping that if I do enough good, it will change my destiny. But it doesn't. Nothing I ever do changes it."

Her hand drifted to her belt knife. There was always that. She let her hand fall away.

She dropped to sit in the hay next to the cat. The indecision paralyzed her. "You have no idea how lucky you are." She gave Cider a sad smile and stroked his fur. He stretched, kneaded her with his paws, then coiled back into a sleepy ball.

She picked up the brush and traced her finger along the stiff bristles. "Skeins of the future always change. Little things.

Big things. Only until the future becomes the present do we truly know what is to happen. Why doesn't my keep vision ever change, Cider?"

And if the destruction was so terrible, why was it that no other seer—even her mother, even her grandfather—ever mentioned it or accused her?

She tilted her head back, searching the unforgiving rafters for answers. "You've given this future vision to me and only me, haven't you? Why? Why are you torturing me? What have I ever done to deserve your punishment?"

She set the brush back down and dug the heels of her hands into her eyes until sparks danced against the insides of her eyelids. They looked all too much like flashes of amulet fire.

Even though his cowardice tainted her family's name to this day, maybe Jasal Pinal had been right to leave. Maybe his own Trine powers proved too overwhelming, too damning, so he left Deren. Maybe he believed abandoning his people to their fate at the hands of the Ken'nar was better than remaining and bringing about wholesale destruction at his own hands. If she, too, abandoned the Fal'kin, would she save them?

She could run away with Teague.

"I don't want to leave you, Ashtar, nor leave *Maithe* and *Paithe*, but maybe you'd all be safer." Her heart beat wildly in her chest at the sudden hope of an escape from her dilemma. "*Ai*, Teague and I could join in union and run away to the ocean. Oh, we could have a little cottage and even a garden. And…and chickens! Oh-oh and apple trees! I could grow medicinal plants for him. He could use his herbsman's skills to care for the people who homestead on the coastal plains." He could hide her. Hide her Aspects from Kinderra.

Ashtar snorted as he munched on oats. She frowned. "*Gratas fár Oëa comprendean*, you big brute."

Mirana sought Teague's mind from among the hundreds in the learning hall. He was awake and waiting for her, hoping she'd come and find him.

She rose and paused at the paddock's gate. A thought spiked, stealing her breath. Would he be caught up in her destiny of destruction? She gripped the gate with both hands. "No. Please. Anything but that."

She would not let that happen. If she had to put hundreds of miles between them to save Teague's life, she would.

Hundreds.

Lightning flares. Five hundred riders race over the hills outside Two Rivers Ford. Black armor encases them like charred skeletons. Ken'nar. Inhuman howls fill the air. Grynwen. Their blood-red eyes wink with an insatiable hunger in the lightning. Rain falls. Down, down, a deluge from the dark sky. Lightning flashes again. A massive force of fighters surges to meet the Ken'nar. Red eagles on a gold field. Fal'kin. From Kin-Deren province. Thousands. The Fal'kin engulf the scant hundreds of Ken'nar. A sea of amulets and swords. Kin-Deren fighters drive the black-armored warriors toward the ford's southern bridge over the Anarath River.

Power grows within her. Building, consuming. Her chest aches, burns. The power demands to be freed. She must release the power.

Shreds of clouds reveal the bloody dawn. Gabrial, the Guiding Star, slowly fades in the west over the Dar-Anar Mountains. Distant lightning flares again. Jasal's Keep. Rage. Desolation. Agony. She grips a sword, raising it against an unseen foe. Power grows within her. She must release it. She can no longer contain it. White light. Exploding.

Mirana screamed.

The stable snapped back before her eyes. Her fist clutched the knife from her belt.

*… Mirana? … *came Taddie's sleepy call. *… Are you all right? …*

She gasped, trying to recover her breath. It was the same attack on Two Rivers Ford, the same premonition she'd had in the healing hostel—except it all had changed. She thought she saw thousands of Ken'nar in the earlier iteration she had in the hostel, but it happened so quickly, she wasn't even sure it was a true vision. Now, the thousands she saw were not Ken'nar at all, but Fal'kin.

"How could I have been so wrong? I've never made a mistake like this before." She gripped her head. "What is happening to me?"

"Mirana?" Taddie jogged over to her.

She held both his arms. "Did you see something? Just now, or-or at all today? An unbidden vision?" The boy looked down at his boots and nodded. She gave him a gentle shake. "What? Tell me."

"I saw I would be thrown from that gray palfrey mare your *brepaithe* used to ride. Bankin. I was frightened, so I didn't exercise her as I should have." He kept his gaze lowered. "I'm sorry."

"Taddie." She held him. "Just walk her tomorrow morning. Ride her later when you feel more comfortable."

"You're upset." He lifted his face, bottom lip trembling. "With me?"

"No." She stared at the knife in her hand. "With me."

Mirana sheathed the small blade and ran from the stables. Once outside, she passed a man, his face battered by more than just the elements. His right leg, wooden from the knee down, told even more of his past.

"Mirana? What the blazes are you doing up at this hour, girl?" he shouted as she ran past.

"I can't talk now, Defender Isel. *Ben nöc!*" She did not stop.

"It's more like *'ben dia.'* If I find young Herbsman Teague loitering about again this late, it's not me you'll have to talk to," he called after her. "Your father's home, I hear."

Aspects Above! If only all she had to worry about was a late-night kiss from Teague.

And not an impending calamity.

CHAPTER 7

"Ama u'vide tuda. Ama tudsa vide tuda."
("Love blinds all. Love also sees all.")
—Ora Fal'kinnen 32:68–69

Teague shifted on the frozen flagstones just outside the corridor entrance leading to his family's rooms. He breathed on his even more frozen fingers. The springtime sleet had drifted off to the south, but the stars and the rest of the learning hall were still obscured by icy fog. The cold penetrated through the cloak he had thrown over his homespun shirt and breeches.

He heard footsteps race up a flight of stairs. On the opposite side of the landing spanning the courtyard, a torch sprang to ruddy life, its light softened by the mist.

Mirana emerged from the shadows. Her raven hair was plastered against her forehead and neck in a rain-soaked sheet and the old woolen sweater she wore hung down to her knees with the weight of the wetness. She rushed into his arms, and he wrapped his cloak around them both.

"I almost thought you weren't coming."

"How long would you have waited?"

He smiled down at her. "As long as it took." He held her tighter, a very good thing as he was freezing. She had a way of making him warm up inside and out. Her body was warm against his, but she was shaking. She wasn't cold.

Oh no. She was scared. So, she did see something in the infirmary earlier that afternoon.

"What is it, Miri?"

"I saw something I don't understand."

He hated it when he was right about Mirana's fear.

"Well, I mean I do," she continued, "but it doesn't make any sense. It's completely different." Her words came out in a rush.

He stroked her hair. "Does this have to do with what happened with that boy, Maark?" When she looked up at him, he smiled. "I knew something happened."

"A premonition came to me. At least I think it was a premonition. I wasn't sure at first. Then I had it again. The same one. Now? I'm so confused. It was—" she shook her head slowly, "only it was completely different."

"Different? How can that be?"

"I don't know," she cried into his chest. "I have to say something to my mother, but I don't know what to tell her."

"The truth?"

She stood back from him. He curled up one corner of his mouth. "I've never lied to her. Not in so many words. I've just decided to say nothing. About some things. For a while."

He continued to grin. "So, lies of omission are not really lies?"

"Teague." She glared at him.

"All right, all right. We'll save that debate for another day. C'mere." He pulled her back into his arms. "What did you see that has you so upset?"

She breathed into his chest in exasperation. "I saw two completely different versions of the same event. Or I think so, anyway. No one's called an alarm yet, which means no one else has seen this battle. So, I'm the first to see something. Again." She turned her face to rest her cheek against him. "Details change all the time as an occurrence gets closer to reality, but a completely different vision? That never happens. To me, anyway."

Teague rested his lips on the top of her head. Even wet, her hair smelled good. "So, tell your mother both versions."

She leaned back, frowning. "It's not as simple as that. To figure out what's going on, regardless of whether others have seen something or not, my mother and the seers would all work together to corroborate the vision. We all enter each other's minds and look at everybody's visions. That's how it works. That's how seers work together."

It was his turn to frown. "I know how it works. Just because I can't do it, doesn't mean I don't understand it."

She waved her hand, dismissing his comment. "You know I didn't mean it like that. We see everyone's visions. And the more similar they are, the more something is likely to happen that way, right?"

"Right." What was she getting at?

"And sometimes, we have to read deeply. Without an amulet, reading someone's visions from her mind and having mine read is the only way I have to study and learn a vision."

Her nightmare vision. The keep. Everything for the last few summers was about Jasal's Keep. "So you can't risk them discovering details they shouldn't."

The frustrated expression in her moonlight eyes became one of defeat. She turned into his chest once more. "They wouldn't believe me even if I told them about the keep. They'd say I got it wrong somehow."

"But they would see what you'd see," he whispered into her hair. "Wouldn't that help?"

She let out a growl of frustration. "No. Because they wouldn't *feel* what I'm feeling. Sense what I'm sensing. They're not…me. And, on top of it all, I'm going to have to speak up about the grynwen and my warning to my father. I'm sure he's told *Maithe* by now."

"Miri." He held her tighter and kissed her forehead. "Why didn't you tell her right away?"

"I intended to. I got scared when I didn't hear back from my father." She frowned. "I thought, well, I thought I might have killed him."

"I don't think your father is so easily killed, even if you startled him with your call."

He held her back from him to see her face in the diffuse torchlight. "Or maybe the real reason you haven't told your mother is that you're afraid you did the *right* thing? And she'd want to know more about how you did manage to call him. Which, if you told her the truth, you know full well how she'd react. She'd want you to choose an amulet. Two summers early."

She frowned at him and shook her head. "I can't let that happen. At least, not yet."

"Not until you find a way to change your keep vision. Or avoid it altogether." Teague exhaled, his breath turning to smoke in the damp, cold air.

It was a keep vision, all right. It kept hold of her and never let go. And not in a good way, like he would.

She nodded slowly and rubbed her eyes. "Besides, with *Brepaithe* Toban's death just a few months ago and her having to take over the province, she's got enough to worry about without me adding to the heap." She let her hands drop to her sides.

Jasal's Keep stood in the center of the learning hall's courtyard. Without the moon, it was an imposing black spire shrouded in the frigid gloom. Maybe she wasn't wrong to be frightened. If he saw that monstrous thing exploding on top of him night after night, he'd probably be a bit jumpy, too. But what he could never understand—refused to—was she somehow felt responsible for the white light she claimed was destructive.

Mirana scooped butterflies out of horse drinking troughs to save them. That hardly sounded like someone who would turn into a mass murderer someday.

Then again, he saw what the war did to good defenders as he served in his parents' healing hostel. The endless rampage of death turned decent people, well, *not* decent.

He'd never let that happen to Mirana. She might not like it, but he had never been so happy as when her parents decided she would become a hall seer instead of a battle seer serving on the front lines.

Teague rubbed her arms, brushing some of the frost from her sweater. "Maybe you'd be removing something from your mother's heap? I guess I can understand why you're not ready to tell her yet you're a Trine. But your mother's not stupid. She knows your Seeing Aspect is as strong as it comes. She could maybe use your help."

She blew out her breath, its mist slowly rising in the cold, damp air. "I should have told her right away about *Paithe*."

"Probably."

"Now that he's home, it's ridiculous to pretend anymore."

"Definitely."

She rolled her eyes and huffed an irritated but amused laugh. "You're no help."

He took a lock of damp, jet hair and twined it around his fingers. "No, I'm very good help. You're just a terrible listener."

She put her arms around his waist. "Probably."

He laughed. "Definitely."

Teague held her in his arms in silence for a few breaths. Instead of relaxing into his embrace like she usually did, she tensed. "Mirana?"

"Seriously, though. Does this make me a bad person?"

He screwed his mouth into a grimace. "You're not a bad person, but maybe keeping your warning a secret wasn't a good thing." He lightly kissed her forehead. "You can still come clean, you know."

"I know, I know. I will. Maybe she'll just take my word for it and not pick around in my brain for more."

"And if she does?"

She pushed him away. "Dammit, Teague." She turned and strode away a few steps, her hands clenched into fists.

Sometimes, there was no winning with her. "*Ama*, I didn't mean to upset you. But it just might be time to get some help with all of this. Your warning is going to come out. And so is whatever the hell you saw in the infirmary today. Your Aspects. The damn keep thing. This is bigger than you can handle alone." He moved closer to her. "I'd do anything to help you, you know that, but all of this might be bigger than the both of us. It's ripping you apart. And I can't stand to see that."

"You're right." She spun suddenly back into his arms. "Take me away. Now. Tonight. I'll tell Mother and Father about the grynwen and these two confusing forewarnings, and then we will run to the ocean and never come back." She pulled him by the wrist toward a stairway. "Please, let's just go. We'll leave everything behind. Please."

"Look, there are days when I hate it here at the learning hall. With all the Aspected—" He shook his head. Oh, how he'd love to leave some days. But it wasn't like there weren't Fal'kin—to say nothing of Ken'nar—everywhere. Deren was as much a hell as anyplace else.

He took her hand from his wrist and held it in both of his. "*Ai*, you should tell them. Everything. If they start to question you about things you don't want to answer, well, we'll figure that out. Maybe then you can give them a proper lie."

"That's not funny." She pulled out of his arms and walked over to lean on the landing railing.

He just couldn't say the right thing tonight. "This double premonition thing. Was it a battle?"

Once again, she tensed. "I can't keep asking you to put yourself in danger for me. You've already done so much. Keeping all my secrets."

Huh?

"What—?" The halted question died in a puff of frozen breath. "Danger? Because I haven't told a soul what you asked me to keep confidential? My parents aren't that cruel." He shrugged. "Then again, they could make me haul the healing hostel refuse to the midden pits. I do that already, though, so I guess I don't know what they would do."

He rested his forearms on the walkway railing and knocked his shoulder against hers. "I was trying to make you laugh."

She bit her bottom lip as her eyes began to shimmer. "It's better you don't know."

Oh, Lights. The lip. She was really upset. "You're keeping secrets from me now?"

She covered her eyes with her hands. "I have to tell my mother. I know this. Lives are at stake." She slapped her palms down on the railing. "If I do, though, all the rest could fall apart."

"So, you're afraid that if they read your mind deeply enough to understand the inconsistencies of whatever you saw, they will find out you're a Trine? And maybe even see your vision of Jasal's Keep?"

She nodded.

"You can't be the one who brings all that destruction. You just can't be."

"Then why doesn't the vision ever change? I've done all I can think of to change my future in some way, but it is always the same. Always."

"I don't know." He held her shoulders then slipped his hands up to hold her face. In the flickering torchlight, her eyes shone with unreleased tears like moonlight reflecting on ice. "But I do know you are not evil or another Dark Trine or anything like that, and you never will be. If you truly want to leave, I will take you anywhere you want to go. I'd do anything for you. You know that."

Mirana leaned into the warm safety of his arms. Teague touched his lips to her forehead, the bridge of her nose. She lifted her face to his. He bent his head down, resting his lips on hers, letting the heat of his body and his love fill her. He pressed the small of her back toward him and deepened their kiss. She opened her mouth to his, inviting him in, and he eagerly accepted. Teague had no Healing Aspect, but he could feel her heartbeat quicken against his chest, mirroring his own passion.

Mirana made a small gasp of surprise. "Your parents are coming."

Teague swore under his breath and stepped back from her.

His father walked through the corridor door onto the landing, Teague's mother just behind. Teague adored his father for so many reasons, not the least of which was the great lengths he went to heal his patients. But he hated—hated even more than Mirana's keep nightmare—the deep, barely discernible sadness behind his father's stoicism when Teague couldn't help patients himself.

If anything would boot him out the door, it was his father's pity.

Teague resembled his father closely—green and brown and gold eyes like a sun-dappled forest, gilded-brown hair—but he rarely wore his father's serious bearing. The very one his father wore right now.

"It is late, Mirana. Unless you have an emergency that requires healing, I'd suggest you go back to bed. Teague, go to your room."

Teague kept his arm around her. "Father, can't you see she's upset?"

The pale-purple sapphire in his father's amulet began to glow. The crystal's hue always reminded him of spring-blooming star lilacs. Except for now. "She appears to be many things but not upset. Mirana, your father is exhausted from a very long tour of duty. I would not want to have to wake him to collect you. Go to bed."

"I had a nightmare, *Patrua* Tennen. Teague comforted me."

He and his parents lived above the healing hostel. The location of their chambers was very convenient for patients and very inconvenient for Mirana and him when they wanted to be alone together.

Tennen frowned. "Apparently. Teague. Inside."

Teague stood his ground. "I am not a child."

His father's frown hardened into something more dour. The older man planted his feet and crossed his arms, not yielding, either. "Maybe not, but you are an herbsman's apprentice living under my roof."

Teague turned to his mother. "Is this about her working with me this afternoon? If Mirana is going to be a battle seer someday, doesn't it make sense she learns some aid? The battle seer unit is the first to be hit in any attack."

His mother could look remarkably stern when she wanted to. "Her parents decided against her becoming a battle seer summers ago."

Bloody hell. He was no better a liar than Mirana.

"Well, *ai*, but—"

His mother held up her hand, silencing him. "*Biraen*, I'll not have you become ill from lack of sleep and this chill air." His mother pointed to the door. "Go."

He stepped closer to his parents. "You cannot make me—"

Tennen made a slight movement with his hand. The corridor door nudged open wider. "Now."

"No, dammit. I'm sixteen. I might be an apprentice, but I'm not a child. I'll see Mirana when I want to. And I'll go to bed when I'm good and ready."

"Teague." Mirana laid a hand on his arm. He let out an explosive exhale. She turned to his parents. "I didn't mean to keep him out in this foul weather."

Niah drew closer to them. "You didn't have a nightmare, did you?"

Maybe if Miri said something to his mother and father this time, it would help her. Aspects knew he was at a loss for what to do.

Her gaze, however, dropped to her boots. "I am so sorry if I interfered with Teague's training in the healing hostel this afternoon. I like spending time there. It's better than seeing. Sometimes, anyway."

"Then why haven't you come to us before?" his mother asked. "We could have spoken to your mother. We've often thought a seer working with us would be of great benefit. It would help us to know when an onslaught of casualties was to come. Or an epidemic. Or looking into the future for a prognosis when one eludes us."

She had a point, a very good one. Teague reached for Mirana's hand. It was cold.

"My mother said she needs me to concentrate on long-range forecasts. Weather. Ken'nar troop movements. I really shouldn't spend time at the hostel at all. I didn't mean to be in Teague's way. I swear it." She let go of his hand and turned to leave.

"Mirana, wait." He started after her.

"Miri, Teague, please. Wait a moment," his father said, his voice becoming the compassionate tenor he used when Teague came to him for help. "I am not blind. I know you have feelings for each other. Don't you understand that this will harm you both?"

Harm them? Teague looked from his father to Mirana and back, and dug his fists into his hips. "How exactly, Father?"

"Son, she's destined to be a Fal'kin. And you're…not."

"I can't believe—" He shook his head, fury stealing the rest of his words. What was the point of finishing?

Tennen turned to Mirana. "Every day, he is surrounded by those who can touch the Aspects he cannot. It is like a spring of cool water just out of reach of a man dying of thirst." His gaze shifted back to Teague. "I feel your pain. And it breaks my heart that there's nothing I can do about it."

"You're right," Teague replied. "There is nothing you can do about it." He looked at his mother. "Either of you." Even Mirana. The Aspects Above made him a failure in the eyes of his parents. But not Mirana. He put his arm around her. "But whether I can touch the Aspects or not has nothing to do with her." He pulled her closer.

She peered up at him. "You don't feel that way about me…do you? That I make you feel somehow 'less than' when I use my—well, when I see something?"

"Of course not!" He then glared at his father.

Tennen turned his own hard expression on Mirana. "I also know you have indeed healed to some degree more than a few of those who have come to the hostel. Just exactly how, I do not know."

"I have not healed anyone—" She started to protest, but he held up his hand, silencing her. His hazel gaze bore down on her. "If you truly are a healer, if you truly have the Healing Aspect and are constantly showing our son that rare gift, one he desperately wants and can never have, it will shatter him—"

"Father!" Teague shouted.

"—I will not let that happen. If you care for him at all, you will let him go."

"I would never hurt him. Ever. We love each other. You must know that."

Teague threw his hands out wide. "How can you stand there, Father, and say these things?"

"Teague, I'm trying to save you both from making a mistake," his father replied. That shocked him. He fully expected a harsh reprimand. "I know you care for our son, Mirana, just as I know you'd never intentionally hurt him. But none of that matters. I am trying to spare you pain as well. It was difficult enough for his mother and me—" Tennen gestured to Niah, "—joining in union despite coming from different provinces. No province ever likes to give up even just one Fal'kin to another province under any circumstances. An Aspected espoused to an Unaspected is far more difficult. Far more."

"It's not too difficult," Teague replied. "Nothing I could do is too difficult for Mirana."

His father shook his head sadly. "Teague, you're not being logical."

"*Patrua*, I know it must have been difficult for you and *Matrua* Niah," Mirana nodded toward Teague's mother, "but you found a way. You travel back to Tash-Hamar province every few summers to heal her people, and in doing so, you received the blessing from not one but two provinces. If you found a way to have a future together, why can't we?"

"Such a union just cannot be, no matter how much you both want it," his father answered. "The chasm is just too wide. You both need to put this foolishness aside."

Teague stalked up to his father, his hands clenched into fists. "How dare you?"

"Teague, that's enough," Niah cautioned. Teague took a breath and stepped back. "Tennen, we came out here to speak with Mirana, not about their relationship. That's a discussion for another day. He's nearly old enough to begin a journeyman's sabbatical away from Deren anyway."

She reached for Mirana's hands. "Miri, *biraena*, seeing an injury from inside the body with the Healing Aspect can be frightening, but the Healing Aspect itself is nothing to be frightened of. If we have another healer in our midst, we would be blessed beyond all telling. The Aspects Above know there are enough injuries and disease in this land for a thousand Fal'kin healers."

Teague put his hand on Mirana's back to let her know—feel within him—his resolve to stand by her. No matter what happened. Even the keep. Maybe now she would say something.

But she didn't. She just bit her lip and stared at Jasal's Keep. Was she trying to prevent an intimate psychic connection with his mother? Seeing something about her nemesis? He couldn't tell. He never could tell.

Mirana let go of his hand and flexed her fingers. He hadn't realized he had crushed it in his grip.

"When you were born, Miri, your Aspect was so very strong but undefined," his mother continued. "Could there be a reason you're drawn to the hostel? A reason besides our son?"

Mirana tensed beside him. If he didn't know better, he'd swear she was about to bolt. He sure as hell wanted to. He'd never been so angry and so worried at the same time.

Tennen sighed. "I didn't mean to upset you, Miri. I, too, held you moments after you were born. I felt your gift then, but it was impossible to tell which Aspect was shining within you. We all thought it was because you came to us so early. Do you think your Aspected sight might be the Healing Aspect? Or even something else? You can trust us. Please. Tell us."

"Have you ever made a mistake with your Healing Aspect and killed a patient instead of saving him?" Her voice was quiet, distant. It would grow soft like that when she was frightened. Again, he put his arm around her, willing his love to her for her to sense.

His mother's dark brows drew together in confusion as she glanced at his father and back to Mirana. "Not everyone can be saved, *ai*, that's true. Wounds can be too grave, illness too advanced—"

"That's not what I mean," Mirana answered. "What if you wanted to use your Aspect to save lives, but you ended up harming people instead? What if you meant to do something, well, good, but ended up doing something horrible? How do you stop that from happening?"

Niah's eyes widened. "Wh-What? Mirana, what are you trying to tell us?"

Mirana stepped out of his arms.

"Miri?" Oh, this was so not good.

His father's face, however, lost all expression. "*Ëi biraena?* Have you—" He swallowed. "Have you hurt someone?"

"No! I would never want to hurt anyone."

He shook his head slowly. "I didn't ask if you wanted to. I asked you if you had."

"No! I—no." She did not meet his gaze.

He reached for her, but she moved farther away. "Mirana."

"I am so sorry. I never meant to stand in Teague's way. Ever. I need to go."

"Miri, we want to help you. If you have the Healing gift, please let us show you how to use your blessing," his mother tried once more.

"You don't understand," Mirana said, her voice dropping to a strangled whisper. "Sometimes the powers the Aspects Above give are not blessings. I won't trouble you in the healing hostel anymore."

She turned away from Teague, no longer meeting his eyes, and hurried down the stairs, snuffing out the torchlight as she disappeared into the night.

Teague fought the urge to run after her, but he'd only alienate his parents from them more if he did. He had to do something, that much was certain. If he didn't, he'd lose Mirana forever.

CHAPTER 8

"Confian ísi passenae tré qua seconda necesit íre."
("Trust is a passage through which two must journey.")
—Ora Fal'kinnen 74:4

Mirana hurried back through the corridors of the learning hall. She tripped on a broken slate tile, her feet numb from the cold, her heart numb with grief over her fading future with Teague.

Her mother had not sounded an alarm, nor had any of the other seers. No late-night—or early-morning, as it were—strategy session had been called. Had no one else seen any attack on Two Rivers Ford?

Regardless of whether other seers had a vision of what was to befall the ford garrison, she had to tell her mother. She would have to submit her mind to examination by the seers. They could see so much more than she wanted to reveal. What then? Elope with Teague? Leave alone?

Dread now dragged at her and chained her footfalls. Could she run away with Teague? She loved him with her whole heart, and he loved her just as much. Even if they had yet to make love, the stolen moments they had shared told her as much of his feelings for her as any Aspect. A fourth Aspect in its strength. She knew he held deep pain from his lack of powers, but he had never hidden it from her. Did her three add to his unfounded sense of inadequacy? Was he hiding that? What if his father were right, and her love would break her beloved? Would he grow to hate her?

She paused when she reached the door leading to the hallway where her family's rooms were located. The grynwen warning. The ford premonitions. Her Trine Aspects. The keep. Now Teague. It all suddenly became too complicated, and she wasn't sure she had the strength to bear it anymore.

Her mother's primeship office was also down this hallway. It used to be *Brepaithe* Toban's chambers. How many times had she run down the hall to *Brepaithe* with a difficult school lesson or trouble with a classmate or when *Maithe* scolded her?

Why couldn't he have taken her with him when he died?

Desperation billowed up from the marrow of her bones. A sudden compulsion gripped her to run up the spire of Jasal's Keep and beg the deadly white light she saw in her hellish vision to come down on top of her now and end any horror before it could begin.

She pressed her forehead against the entryway's wood. "I don't want this. Aspects Above, please take this from me. I beg of you." She wanted it to end. All of it. All of it, except for Teague.

She gave the iron pull a hard tug and entered. She had taken two paces into the still hallway when another door opened, forcing her to stumble to a halt.

"What are you doing up at this hour?"

She sucked in her breath and looked up. And up.

"L-Lord Garis. You startled me."

His black eyes glinted down at her like obsidian shards. A hematite amulet glowed in the center of his chest like a demon's eye. The argent griffin of Dar-Azûl province's heraldic on his black tunic appeared to glare back at her, too. Had she not met Trine Tetric Garis a few times during Quorumtide celebrations, she might have been frightened of him. Or maybe she was frightened anyway.

"You are far too talented to have anyone startle you."

His dark hair was streaked with silver, and a frown tugged at the close-cropped beard outlining the sharp angles of his face. Was everything about him all hard and black and silver?

"I apologize if I disturbed you, my lord. I couldn't sleep after all the excitement of having my father home. Why are you awake?" She winced. She didn't mean the comment to sound so forward. This was Lord Tetric Garis, for Aspects' sakes.

The tall Trine's scowl deepened. "I have had a vision. I was about to see your mother despite the inconvenient hour."

Oh, thank the Aspects Above. Someone else had seen the attack.

"I have heard you are quite adept with your Seeing Aspect. Perhaps we are well met after all." His expression softened into a smile. Well, not exactly a smile. She didn't think the serious man was capable of expressing anything more jovial than mild annoyance.

"My lord?" She blinked as his mind pressed in on hers. Maybe it was too soon to feel relieved.

"I think you couldn't sleep because you had a vision as well. I also think you are concerned, even frightened by what you saw. I am as well." Although his voice was soft, its deep register drummed in her ears.

"I might have seen something." She swallowed. "Well, that is, I think—"

"I'd like to know exactly what it is you saw." Lord Garis gestured for her to enter his room.

She quickly looked down the hallway to her parents' chambers. "I wasn't sure what it was. I was going to my mother with it right now."

"Before we concern her, shouldn't we try to understand what 'it' is, first?"

When he did not move, she sighed and stepped into his quarters. "*Ai*, sir."

He shut the door behind him. "I have seen a battle at Two Rivers Ford. I think you have as well." A chair scraped across the floor as if pulled by the unseen hand of his Aspects. "Sit."

She stood rigid. "I—"

He pointed to the seat. "Sit."

The Trine's longsword rested on its tip in the far corner of his room. It probably came up to her chin. She quickly sat on the edge of the chair.

His mind pressed heavily against hers again. "Now. What did you see?" He balled his hands into fists and rested them on his hips. Very. Large. Fists. Lord Garis took a step closer. He seemed as tall as Jasal's Keep, and just as ominous.

She eyed the door. She couldn't simply walk out on a living legend. "Maybe we should both just go to my mother?"

"And tell her what? I'm not exactly sure of what I saw, either. I don't want to tell the Seer Prime of Kin-Deren province that something might be true when it is, in fact, wrong. Everyone thinks because I have three Aspects, I'm somehow infallible." He examined a scar on the back of his hand. "I'm not. Believe me."

She was about to tell her mother and probably all the other seers in the hall. What was one more person? It was said he had spent many summers in a hermitage when he was younger before he came back to Fal'kin society. Maybe he knew of a nice but desolate place in which to live. She hung her head. Tetric Garis, *Trine* Tetric Garis, of all people, would understand just how frightening the power she held within her was.

She blinked. He just might understand. Truly.

"I think I saw a battle, but I'm not sure I picked up anything of consequence," she said at last.

He folded his long arms and continued to stare down at her. "Your fear moments ago cut through my mind. Like your warning call to your father."

She tried to speak several intelligent replies, but shock stomped them all flat. "Oh?"

He studied her a moment. With a sigh, he walked over to a small side table and leaned on it, his back to her. "I know you must be troubled by some of the things you see and what you can do. Seeing yourself do things in the future that you don't understand in the present." His voice was subdued, and his shoulders sank a bit. "Finding a hidden mind and calling to it. I've never known anyone else who could perform such an action, other than I."

His emotions leaked from his mind to hers. He was concerned. About the ford? About her? What was happening here? "It was my father, Lord Garis. I suppose I could find his presence anywhere."

"Even under U'Nehíl?" He turned to face her again. Then, he did smile. A real, genuine one. Unfortunately, it was because he knew he had her.

She couldn't quite match his expression with all the guilt she held. "I love my father. I love both my parents. I would do anything to save their lives."

"I know. That's why we need to understand what is to happen at Two Rivers Ford. I could use your help. I need corroboration for what I've seen. It's not exactly easy for me to go to your mother, the prime—or any prime, for that matter— and tell her she needs to commit men and women to an action that will likely get some killed. The blood of the fallen is on my hands as well as hers."

All her life, she had heard of Lord Tetric Garis, the Trine of Kinderra. He was larger than life, almost literally. He was like one of the heroes come to life out of the stories *Brepaithe* Toban would read to her at bedtime. Standing in front of her now, however, was not a demigod, but a war-weary man whose enormous burden weighed heavily on him. He reminded her more than a little of her father.

He returned to her and crouched in front of her, making his height less threatening. His gesture stunned her, so like her father would do when she was young and scared.

"You can do things other Aspected cannot. This makes you stand apart. I felt just as alone when I was your age."

Mirana blinked once more. He was a Trine. Did he know? About her? Could he sense her own Trine Aspects? "*Ai*, it can be frightening sometimes. Seeing. Things."

Lord Garis was perhaps the only person on the continent who could even begin to understand her deepest fears. Could he find a way around her destiny that she could not? Maybe that was too much to ask.

She sat up straighter in the chair. "I saw an attack on the Fal'kin garrison at Two Rivers Ford, only I saw two different versions of it. Or at least I think it's two different versions. I saw one this afternoon just before you and Father arrived home. I saw thousands upon thousands of riders. I had another premonition later tonight, but I only saw several hundred riders, not even a thousand."

He stood slowly and rubbed his beard. "That smaller force. That is what I saw tonight."

She ran her fingers through her wet hair, trying to recall what few details she could. "In the earlier version, I thought, well, maybe I had seen an army of Ken'nar. Larger than any army I've ever seen."

He dragged over another chair and sat across from her. "Start at the beginning. Tell me exactly what you saw."

She hesitated. What was the point of her silence now? She'd told him this much, she might as well tell him everything. Well, almost everything. "The attack comes at night. During a storm. A sea of riders. I saw fighters resist them, but they were outmanned many times over. By the time morning breaks, thousands lie dead. Between the darkness and the loose weaving of the time skein, it was hard to tell who was fighting whom."

He frowned and nodded. "From what direction did the riders come?"

She furrowed her brow in concentration. "I couldn't tell, at least not in the first premonition. The fighting was already engaged. In the second, the Ken'nar, if that's who they are, appear to come from the north. They cross the bridge over the Garnath River."

"You saw the Ken'nar as the smaller force?"

She nodded. "In the second vision, the images were much clearer, but—" She searched for a word to explain a sense that defied description. "But it felt different."

"Go on."

Wasn't that enough? She didn't want to tell him any more. She wanted to bolt from the room. His mind continued to touch hers. It supported her, however, encouraging her. "At dawn, the clouds had broken. A star—Gabrial, I think—was setting west of the Dar-Anar Mountains. It was cool but not cold. Springtime, maybe. This may occur in only a few sevendays."

"And the troop counts? Who is attacking whom?" the Trine asked.

She shook her head. "That's just it. I don't know for certain. Both visions lasted only a heartbeat or two. I could only see the armies between flashes of lightning, and then, not clearly. In my first premonition, I thought I saw more Ken'nar. A lot more. Maybe as many as five thousand, but that's just a guess. The Fal'kin armies we had in the Battle of the Vale were of similar size, and we've studied that attack in depth. I thought the larger force had black armor like the Ken'nar, but the vision was at night during a storm, so I couldn't be sure."

She lowered her eyes away from his probing gaze and picked at a hangnail. She winced when she jabbed the quick.

He covered her hand with his, stopping her. "It's all right."

She took her hand from his and rubbed her forehead. "In the second premonition, the one I had just a little while ago, I thought I sensed far fewer Ken'nar. Just a few hundred. I thought maybe I could be seeing a battle from the past and from the future, two different ones at the same location. The stars would be in different positions if that were the case, but with the storm, there was no way to get a timeframe. And I doubt two different battles would occur at the same location on the same date. So, if it is indeed the same battle, the skeins of time must be woven very loosely for such a drastic difference. Taken individually, though, they seem—" She paused as again a clear explanation eluded her. "Well, they seem certain. I've never had this happen before. Ever."

"Let's call to the Seeing Aspect and study this together." He took her hand once more, and this time, he placed it on his amulet.

"My lord, I don't think that's such a good idea." She tried to pull her hand back, but he held it firmly.

"Trust me."

Her parents had drummed into her that it was an extreme offense to touch another's amulet. It was a sacred relic, not a piece of jewelry. Since she was twelve, since she had learned her destiny, she avoided contact with another's amulet at all costs. A Trine could join in union with any amulet, not just one, like those bearing a single Aspect. Would Lord Garis be able to detect that she had all three Aspects? Maybe he'd be so focused on finding the right skein of time he wouldn't notice. Maybe this was all a really, really bad idea.

"Lord Trine, maybe we should just speak with my—"

He continued to hold her hand. "Please."

Mirana nodded slowly and closed her eyes as he reached out to her mind. His presence, heavy and unrelenting, pressed down upon hers. A tug pulled deep within her. It was not painful, just odd, like she slipped or faded further away from herself somehow. Her Seeing Aspect billowed inside her. Once again, flashes of lightning and amulet fire revealed armies locked in deadly combat on the stone bridges of Two Rivers Ford.

An aberrant vibration, a grating sort of discord, now quivered through her. Lord Garis's amulet. It called to her, needed her, reached for her.

His amulet. It was—she was connecting with it!

She tried to pull away as images flared before her mind's eye. The vision, almost identical to the first one she remembered, resolved with brutal clarity. Almost identical. Except now, it was obvious the thousands of fighters were not Ken'nar but were Fal'kin from Kin-Deren province, like in the vision she had in the stable.

The vibration from his amulet against her Aspects grew more insistent, begging her to match her harmonics with it. She fought against it, but his mind and his Aspects held her fast as he sought to understand the images playing before them.

Lightning slashed within the prescient pictures, and the scenes that held her captive changed yet again.

Jasal's Keep erupts with hellfire.

Mirana yanked her hand from his grip. No. Oh, Aspects Above, no. Did he see it?

The Trine sat back in the chair and blinked as the corner of his mouth curled up. "You did well. *Gratas Oë.*"

She lowered her face from his to study a crack in one of the stone pavers on the floor. The keep appeared for only the briefest of moments before she broke their connection. Maybe he hadn't seen it. If she concentrated on the crack, that would be the only thought he would read easily.

"I have to tell my parents," she said. "I should have told them as soon as I saw the ford the first time. It's just I've never misinterpreted a vision before. Never."

"Mirana, if what you're telling me is true about your first version—the darkness, the rain, the lack of clarity—it would have been nearly impossible to discern which army is which without an amulet. Those thousands you saw? They could have been Fal'kin. In fact, what we just saw together all but corroborates that. You saw thousands from Kin-Deren fighting in the second version, correct?"

She scowled. "*Ai*, but—"

"And the smaller force, a scant five hundred? The garrison at the ford typically doesn't have much more than that. The Ken'nar may believe they have an easy target, so they don't attack in large numbers."

The first version of the attack on the ford happened so quickly, and she had been in the midst of healing the youth, Maark. But the sense of it all? The bloodlust, the maniacal glee of meting out death, and a myriad of other things besides? That had to be the Ken'nar. Then again, her father never spoke of what he did as he fought. She had heard of Fal'kin going nearly mad on the battlefield, driven to extremes by the Defending Aspect. Was that what would happen to her someday?

She pounded her fist on the chair arm and groaned in frustration through clenched teeth. "How could I have been so wrong?"

"It is all but impossible without an amulet to get the precise information one needs from a vision. Even I would have had a hard time without an amulet. It came to you. You did not go to it. When you saw the vision of Two Rivers Ford again, you saw a further refinement, the Fal'kin defending the ford installation in larger numbers. The same one I had. More than likely, in both cases, you were doing something else at the time and not prepared to analyze what you saw. Aspects know I was startled."

She sought his eyes with her own. "You were?"

"Of course." He held his amulet, studying it. "It was a frightening vision. Armies coming starkly into view in the lightning, only to disappear then re-emerge, closer and more violent. Visions are always frightening when—" he paused, "when death occurs." He let his amulet fall to his chest. "I hated it when I was young. I still do."

She sank back farther into the chair and followed the crack on the floor with her eyes. "So, it doesn't get any easier?"

He leaned forward and rested his forearms on his thighs as he stared at the floor. Maybe even at the same crack she had been studying. He shook his head. "Seeing death. Feeling it, sensing it is coming. Knowing sometimes there's nothing I can do to stop it. No, it doesn't get any easier. It's been that way ever since—"

"Ever since always."

He raised his head and nodded.

Would he understand the agony of her dilemma? Could he find a way to save Kinderra when all she saw was death at her hands?

He rose from his chair and helped her up. "Come. Let us see your mother. Perhaps she can shed some light on this for both of us."

The Trine escorted her down the corridor. His hematite amulet winked in the soft light of the hallway's rush lamps. It was dusky yet held a metallic brilliance all its own, a piece of the winter midnight sky.

When she and Lord Garis called upon the Seeing Aspect together, had it reached out to her? Or had she reached out to it? She looked up at the tall man. If he had sensed her manipulating his amulet right from his chest, he said nothing about it.

Joining in union with an amulet was supposed to be an experience of ecstasy, a marriage of the sacred and the worldly. What she had experienced with his amulet, however, was frankly a bit disturbing, even physically unsettling. That couldn't be like what it was to choose an amulet, could it?

Maybe her avoidance of taking up an amulet reflected more than just her desire to deflect her destiny. Tetric Garis was the Light Trine.

And she was not.

Mirana came to an abrupt halt outside her parents' room. "Do you believe in the prophecy?" The words rushed out before she had a chance to consider them.

He turned around and scowled. "What?"

"The Trine Prophecy. From the Book of Kinderra. It predicts a great cataclysm of some sort between a Light Trine and a Dark Trine. Do you believe it?"

"Prophecies are written by seers to preserve their power long past their usefulness. They are meant to strike both awe and fear among Aspected and Unaspected alike. Each time a Trine comes into the world, that prophecy rears its head in the land. As a boy, I don't think I was allowed out of my learning hall until I was nearly twelve."

"Are you not the Light Trine, the thrice-blessed? Is not the one leading the Ken'nar called the Dark Trine? Is he not the thrice-cursed?" What did the prophecy then mean for her?

Lord Garis squared his shoulders. "I am the Trine of Kinderra. The Aspects Above created me for one purpose—to save Kinderra from the senseless bloodshed we've endured for millennia." He smiled down at her. "Maybe with a little help, I can accomplish that."

Her mouth hung open for a moment. The prophecy ended with the stanza, "Only Hope shall remain." Could he be that hope? Her hope?

He placed his palm on the door and closed his eyes. Moments later, Mirana's mother opened the door as she tightened her robe around her. "Prime Kellis Pinal, I apologize—"

She held up her hand. "I want Kaarl to sleep." She stepped into the hallway and shut the door behind her. "You've seen something. *Ai*, I have, too."

"We both have."

Mirana looked up at Lord Garis. He nodded.

"Mother, I have seen a vision."

CHAPTER 9

"Solis, Ëomus com siber, cin inimica rithente tré Ëome com gháinn'e i'gainem. Atuda, Ëomus defende as ain."
("Apart, we are like a sieve, with the enemy running through us like grains of sand. Together, we fight as one.")

—Ora Fal'kinnen 125:56–57

Kaarl awoke to sunlight streaming in through the window. He stretched and reached over to find the other side of the bed empty and cool. He frowned and sat up. Desde would be in her father's study, working. He corrected himself. Toban's study was now his wife's.

Toban Kellis had been prime of Kin-Deren province for as long as Kaarl could remember. Toban had returned to the Aspects Above in Twelfthmonth. Four months ago, the il'Kin had been tailing a detached unit of Ken'nar through the frozen borderlands between Varn-Erdal and Kana-Akün. He had no idea the man lay on his deathbed. He loved the old seer as much as he had his own father. He never got to tell either man goodbye.

He rose from the bed and splashed his face with cold water from a basin on the nightstand, washing away the last of his fatigue. Out of the lead-camed window, the sky was as blue as a sunlark's egg. The hoarfrost sparkled like tiny amulets. Sixthmonth was only a few sevendays away and would usher in the summer season. The cold that had followed him home from the forests was an ill omen.

He shook his head. When did he start believing in omens? He was a defender. He believed in his Aspect, his amulet and sword, and little else.

Long ago, men and women more learned than he had pegged the beginning of a new Reckoning to the dead of winter. Those ancient seers perceived with their Aspect daylight growing longer by minute increments after the solstice to mark the beginning of Firstmonth. Had it been him, he would have started the new calendar when days were at their longest and warmest, and the land had fully awakened to give life again. When the light of his life had been born. The weather, however, followed its own wisdom. His smile faded. The heavy frost out the window looked uncannily like the thin, crusty patches of snow upon which il'Kin Defender Gannah Tesabe had died in the Kana-Akün forests.

The sun was high. It was late. He had not meant to sleep so long.

Kaarl dressed quickly and left his and Desde's chambers. He paused by Mirana's door. She was not in her room, either.

He wanted to thank her once more. Or maybe to ask her to never again look for him when he was away from home.

He walked down the corridor to the primeship study and found the door ajar. He brushed Desde's mind with his as he entered. She smiled at him, but her eyes were red-rimmed. He walked over and sat on the corner of the desk, taking her hand in his. He wished he, too, could mourn. The Ken'nar had killed off that capacity in him long ago.

"The ice has lingered even though it's Fourthmonth. Do your seers know when the weather will break?" he asked.

"Soon. Then again, it is easier to march on frozen ground than mud." She sighed. "There's still so much of him here."

He nodded and picked up from the desk a small, green jadelite carving of a mountain tiger. Toban had gotten it after some conflict in the distant mountainous province of Trak-Calan. It was a seal stamp, and very old, but because of the stone's fragility, it now served as a piece of art.

"He is with your mother once more." His wife nodded and quickly wiped her eyes. He sat in one of the chairs fronting Toban's—Desde's desk. "You should have awakened me."

"You needed your rest." She reached for his hand again.

"That is especially true given your welcome home." He caressed her fingers with his thumb. They both smiled. He continued to hold her hand. "You left last night."

"*Ai*, however, it was more than just you that kept me awake."

"I didn't mean to upset you. I was concerned about Mirana. Have you seen her, by the way? She wasn't in her room."

"She's not a layabout like her father." Desde lifted one corner of her mouth. "She's studying with the other seers this morning. I've given her a noontime break before our lessons this afternoon. Unless she's decided to skip her meal again, in which case she's probably someplace with young Herbsman Beltran."

"Teague?"

"Oh, Kaarl. Surely, you can see what's going on? It's been summers."

"*Ai*, I know, but—" He looked out the door, imagining with difficulty the young woman who had replaced his little girl. "They're in love?"

She raised her hands in a helpless gesture.

"They've always been close, but this? And you approve? Teague's Unaspected."

She sat up straighter. "Teague is a wonderful boy. It makes no difference if he's Unaspected or not."

He shook his head. "Of course. I didn't mean it like that. It's just relationships like that are, well, complicated to say the least. You know I care for the boy. Deeply. He reminds me a bit of myself when I was his age."

As a young boy, he had suffered through many scuffles of his own with those who thought less of who he was, too. He would swear a curse on Jasal Pinal if he thought it would add to his ancestor's damnation.

"Aspects Above." He exhaled, suddenly weary again despite his slumber. "Have I been gone that long?"

"I see her every day, and I cannot believe she's ready to lose her heart."

By the Light, his little girl had grown up, and he had missed so much of it. She was nearly sixteen. She would choose an amulet in two summers. Two summers! In two summers, other mysteries would have to be explained, if not before.

"How serious are they?"

"The war will end it for them before they will, I fear." Desde sat back in the high-backed oak chair as her elegant, tapered fingers curled around the armrests. She looked remarkably like Toban at that moment.

Later. He would deal with all of these issues later.

"So, who have you chosen as your prime's second?"

His wife shook her head. "No one yet."

He raised an eyebrow. "Your father died four months ago. Succession should not be left open like this, especially given what's happened in the north."

"*Ëo comprende*," she replied. "And I need your advice."

He had hoped he would have missed all the cutthroat maneuvering and backroom deals that always accompanied the selection of who would be next in line for the primeship. At least when Desde did select someone, all the political wrangling and gilded backstabbing would be well out of the way to ensure there were no gaps in a province's leadership. That was the point. When a prime died or was incapacitated, the elevation from second to prime was immediate.

He stroked his beard for a moment. "Dav Koehl is the obvious choice."

"*Ai*," she replied, nodding, "but I need him focused on the war as my defender commander, not splitting his time in council meetings."

"What about Tennen Beltran?"

She tapped one of her fingers on the armrest and grew thoughtful. "That's an interesting choice."

"The man's a healer, so you have your compassionate viewpoint for the greater good. He also has defender's blood in him. I swear, he doesn't so much cure injury and illness but attack them with the Healing Aspect."

Desde folded her hands and bounced them against her chin, thinking. "I hadn't thought about that. He worked tirelessly to cure my father and gave him a peaceful death when he couldn't. And you know how insightful he is. He's also well respected by the Fal'kin." She inhaled and made a guilty grimace. "But he's not exactly charismatic. Which, unfortunately, must be near the top of a provincial leader's list of skills. I'll have to think about that one."

"Well, who do you want?" Kaarl asked.

She smiled and took his hand again. "The two people I want to offer my council as choices are the two people who they'd least likely approve."

He squeezed her hand and released it. "She's too young."

Her smile faded but did not disappear. "Your illustrious ancestor Jasal was sixteen when most of the province wished to elevate him to prime."

He shrugged in agreement. "He was not installed as prime until he was twenty-three. Because he was too young." He held out his hands, rendering her choice moot.

"And, unfortunately, you'll be otherwise occupied. I'm afraid my choice in second will have to wait a bit longer." She straightened in her chair. "I'm glad you came. There has been a development overnight."

If his wife's sudden change in demeanor hadn't raised a warning, the whisper his Defending Aspect gave him would have. "What is it?"

"I had a vision. Tetric and Mirana saw it, too."

"Two Rivers Ford will be attacked," came a deep voice behind him.

He turned to look over his shoulder.

Tetric Garis strode into Desde's study. "Seer Prime Kellis Pinal," he said as he inclined his head in a bow.

She waved him off. "Tetric, you've known me for thirty summers. It is hard enough to hear that title from others, even more so from you."

Kaarl turned back to face his wife, more than a little irritated that his wife and the Trine were wasting time on pleasantries. "What? Why didn't you wake me? The ford will be attacked?"

"You have been fighting since before the Reckoning turned, *Ëi ama*. I wanted to give you at least one night's rest. Besides, there is little you can do at the moment," she replied. "We saw what we think are several hundred Ken'nar make a play for our garrison at Two Rivers Ford. We saw a second, much larger force, presumably our own, engage them. We believe we will be successful in turning them back, but it appears many will still be killed. We are working to understand the plan of attack and divine a precise time frame."

Tetric nodded and sat in the chair next to Kaarl. "The vision was difficult to interpret for many reasons. There are still many questions to be answered."

Kaarl gripped the chair's armrests. "Those bridges are the gateway into southern Kinderra. If the Dark Trine controls the ford—"

"The Ken'nar will march across the rest of the continent, *ai*," the other man finished. "But, as Desde said, the attacking force does not appear to be large. Kin-Deren has more than enough Fal'kin to stop them. Your daughter had the same vision as we did."

"Meaning?"

"Meaning, the more seers that receive the same vision, the greater the likelihood the event will actually occur," the Trine replied, his words clipped with annoyance. "This one, however, still remains a bit unclear. Young Mirana was quite disconcerted by it when she told me."

Desde leaned forward. "One moment, Tetric. Are you telling me my daughter came to you first with this? Before you both came to me?"

He waved a hand to dismiss her concern. "Do not be upset with her. Apparently, she had been awakened by this vision, as you and I had been. I heard her in the hall. She was obviously distraught, so I comforted her, and together we walked through the vision. Then we came to see you."

She tugged at her bottom lip, then slapped her hands down flat on the desk. "Damn that girl. What is wrong with her? She should have come to me immediately."

"My prime, it was only a matter of moments between the time she came to me and when we both spoke with you," he said.

She gripped the armrests tighter. "You do not understand. She has been most disobedient of late. Criminally so."

The Trine pursed his lips. "You are more afraid than angry."

"Forgive me for troubling you with Kin-Deren's—and a mother's—concerns," she replied.

Kaarl regarded the tall man. "I would think you would be the last person she'd want to speak with. She hardly knows you."

Tetric held his gaze. "Sometimes a stranger is the best person with whom to speak."

Was that so? The memory of their conversation after the grynwen attack came back to him. The man had no interest in comforting their daughter. No, he wanted to pry into her mind. "What do you mean by that? We love our daughter."

"Exactly. How much did you tell your father—or Toban, for that matter—when things troubled you?" he replied. "I don't believe, however, I was first on her list either. I think her little midnight escapade might have involved a certain herbsboy. She was coming in from the outside."

Kaarl sat up sharply. "Escapade?" He turned to his wife. "Just exactly how close are Mirana and Teague?" He remembered more than a few midnight escapades of his own. With Desde. She frowned and shook her head, quelling the notions that had flown up in his mind.

"The real concern here is the ford, not your daughter's adolescent transgressions," the Trine continued as annoyance crept back into his voice.

"I appreciate your kindness to our daughter, but the next time Mirana is distraught from a vision, we will be the ones to comfort her. We will discuss with her what she may or may not have seen," he replied, not disguising his own irritation.

The Dar-Azûlan stroked his beard with his long fingers. "I don't think you can comfort her regarding some of the things she sees. They are enough to terrify a Trine."

Kaarl straightened in his chair. "What are you—"

"Gentlemen, please. I will deal with Mirana later," Desde said. "Tetric is right. We have other priorities at the moment."

He sat back. His wife was correct. "You said there would be several hundred Ken'nar. Do you have a better estimate?"

"Perhaps five hundred," she said.

For the first time in a long, long time, hope warmed him. "Kin-Deren province has nearly two thousand Fal'kin. If the dark bastard thinks he can have our ford, he's about to be proven wrong."

She nodded. "My thoughts exactly."

"We il'Kin are few now, but we will serve at your word. How soon are we talking?" he asked.

"That is the one great concern. Timing will be an issue," she replied. "We're trying to narrow it down, but we think it will be in a few sevendays."

"Within the month," Tetric replied.

"That soon?" A sudden thought occurred to him. He glanced at his wife with a confident sneer. "That might be a boon."

The tall Trine shifted in his seat. "How so?"

"The contingent from Varn-Erdal province is due at the garrison for their tour of duty about that time. We met up with some Varn-Erdalans late last autumn as we patrolled the border. They said Defender Prime Vallia Edaran has been so—what was the word that the defender used?—so 'displeased' with the incessant attacks in Varn-Erdal by the Ken'nar in the last few summers, she wished to inspect the readiness of the Two Rivers Ford garrison herself. She's even sending her daughter Defender Second Liaonne Edaran to be stationed there."

Desde grinned, her mahogany eyes as hard as burl wood. "With Vallia and Liaonne both at the ford, I almost feel sorry for the Ken'nar."

Kaarl chuckled evilly. "Almost."

Tetric settled deeper into his chair and folded his hands. "I seldom have come across defenders more vicious than you, Kaarl."

"I am not vicious. I am thorough," he said, "Vallia. Liaonne. They are vicious."

"Vallia's displeasure is not unfounded," the Trine said. "Varn-Erdal has suffered more than any other province of late save Kana-Akün. Now that not one, but two provinces stand broken, it is time to change how we look at this war. That is also why I am here." He turned to Kaarl. "We need to unite our forces. It is time."

"That is not your decision to make," Desde said. "It is the decision of the Steward of the Quorum of Light." She gestured to Kaarl with her chin.

"What?" He shook his head in disbelief. "Surely your father would have made you steward upon his death?"

"No, thankfully, he did not. Being a prime is burden enough to bear." She pushed a piece of parchment toward him. "He named you steward in the interim until the Quorum of Light convenes in the autumn. With you half a continent away and on the move for most of the Reckoning, I had no way to reach you with the news until now."

"Toban can't do that," Tetric said. "Kaarl's not even a prime."

He nodded. "I agree with you for once, *Ëi cara.*"

She tapped the document. "*Ai,* it flies in the face of a thousand summers of Kinderran tradition, but there is nothing in either the Book of Kinderra or the Ora Fal'kinnen that bars it. My father knew our laws better than those who wrote them."

"My place is on the back of a horse—an amulet in one hand, a sword in the other. Not hiding behind walls, sitting on a stone chair in the Quorum chambers."

She raised an eyebrow. "Is that what you think the Quorum steward does? Is that what you think I do?"

He exhaled, frustrated. "No, of course not. But I am a defender. My life exists to be in defense of Kinderra."

"And could still be," the Trine said. "Perhaps Toban's move isn't so ridiculous after all."

He scowled. "What do you mean?"

Tetric leaned toward him. "I want you and your il'Kin to fight with me. Only the steward can order when and where the il'Kin fight. With you as steward, there is one less impediment to their deployment."

Shock and anger fought for control of Kaarl's emotions. "I wouldn't be fighting *with* you. I would be fighting *for* you. I take orders from no one."

"You took orders from Toban," the Dar-Azûlan said evenly, "and, you took orders as a provincial Fal'kin once."

The naked ambition of Tetric's request was beyond belief. Kaarl rose from his seat. "You've spent summers trying to extinguish the il'Kin, believing it is a waste of effort when Kinderra has your Dar-Azûlan provincial troops as a strike force. Now, you are trying to do the next best thing by controlling it outright."

The tall man stood. "It *is* a waste of effort. My province, if you can call it that, has nothing for my men and women to protect. Barren steppe. Nomads who herd stinking deer. I willingly commit my troops to safeguard all of Kinderra's provinces. I am a Trine, and such is my duty. The il'Kin are bound to no specific province for much the same reason. We both exist to support provincial troops. We have exactly the same mission. The only reason the il'Kin exists at all is that, for most of Kinderra's history, no Trine lived to intercede for her on a continental basis. It makes no sense to have two units with the same goal—one answering to me and one answering to you."

Kaarl remained standing. "I see no problem with that. Neither did Toban. Neither did the Quorum itself. For summers. Kinderra is large, and neither of us can be everywhere at once. There are more than enough black-armored bastards for both of us to fight."

As he expected, the other man did not back down. "There is no greater sword and amulet in the land than yours. I would put you at the head of the entire combined force. You could do with them as you will. Have units embedded in every province, ready for your orders at a moment's notice."

"You don't think I've already petitioned for that?"

"You would be greater to me than my second."

"I am no one's second," he growled between locked teeth.

"Two Rivers Ford is about to be attacked. Despite the small force, the fighting will be brutal, from what I've seen. The Fal'kin will suffer losses. Ask your wife." The Trine gestured toward the door and the hall beyond. "Aspects Above, man, ask your daughter!"

Kaarl took a step toward the other man. He was well aware his silver gaze could be unsettling to others, even more so when he was furious. As he hoped it was now. "I will find a way."

Again, the tall Trine did not acquiesce. "You lost half of your forces within two seasons. How do you plan to protect the garrison there with the paltry nineteen of you?"

"Gentlemen!" Desde warned. "Tetric, obviously Kaarl's being facetious."

Kaarl ignored his wife and leaned in close. "You stood by and watched them be slaughtered," he said, bitter memories dropping his voice into a low snarl.

The other man moved closer still, standing toe to toe. "How many times must I tell you? I had to attack when the moment was right. The loss of your tens would have been hundreds. Sacrifices had to be made."

He squeezed his hands into fists. "Those sacrifices were not yours to make."

"I said, that is enough!" Desde jumped to her feet. "Sit down. Both of you. Now. That was two summers ago, Kaarl. It is over. Nothing can change the outcome now. *Leten pone morte cin morte.*"

Let the dead lie with the dead. Would she feel that way if it had been her men and women who had been cut down? He glared at Tetric a moment, then sank into his chair as the taller man took his seat. His wife was right again. They were dead, and nothing could bring them back.

"Lord Trine, you hold my awe with your Aspects," she said, "but what you are suggesting is no less than cutting out the heart of the steward's responsibility. How could Kaarl possibly serve you and the Quorum at the same time in a position like that?"

Tetric steepled his fingers and stared at him. "The only reason your husband would even consider honoring your father's directive is that he would still be in command of the il'Kin, is that not so?"

Kaarl's hands remained in fists. He said nothing. The answer was obvious.

"*Ëi cara*, I am not trying to take away your power." The Trine held out his hand, expecting him to take it. "I am giving you a way to accept the role and still hold your birthright."

"I cannot make a decision like this now. To join our forces and accept your offer would essentially dissolve the steward's position. That will be for the Quorum to decide. Not I. Furthermore, we have a battle to plan for."

"There is no time to wait," the Trine pressed. "The Quorum members will decide whatever you decide. Do you want to be a protector or a politician?"

Anger began to tug at Kaarl's Defending Aspect. His amulet warmed the skin of his chest. "We have disagreed on many things, Tetric, but I have never called into question your dedication to your duty."

"Kaarl, please," his wife said, holding up her hand to stop any more of his replies. She turned to Tetric. "My husband is right. Your proposal affects the whole of Kinderra. War is on our doorstep, and I am never one to believe any victory is easy. I need your help, both of you, to stop Ken'nar at the ford."

The Trine rose again from his chair and moved around it to place his hands on its back. "I hope you will reconsider my offer. Is not our ultimate goal to end this war? Combining our forces will go a long way to achieving the peace I thought we both want so desperately." He left, and the door swung shut, closed by an unseen hand.

Kaarl could not shake the unmistakable feeling of dread coiled like a viper in the pit of his stomach. He had learned to distinguish between his Defending Aspect and common intuition well before he chose his amulet. This time, he felt both.

"What do you intend to do?" Desde asked quietly.

"I don't know. I'm not a seer." He rose and picked up the jadelite carving. "If I become steward, I won't even be a defender anymore."

He crushed the stamp with his hand and his Aspect, leaving the pieces on the desk.

CHAPTER 10

"What an enigma the Aspects are. They reveal all but say nothing."
—The Codex of Jasal the Great

"I've taught you better than this. Or at least I thought I did. Perhaps this is as much my mistake as yours."

"No, Mother," Mirana said. "This has nothing to do with you. You're right. I should have come to you immediately and told you about the grynwen attack. I was terrified I might have distracted Father at precisely the wrong moment when I called to warn him." She glanced at her father. "When you didn't call later, I didn't know what to think. I was frightened, so I didn't say anything."

Her mother's hands were folded in front of her, a false semblance of calm. Her knuckles were clenched white. Her father leaned back against her mother's desk, his mind closed as tightly as his folded arms.

Her father shook his head slowly. "You've studied enough military tactics with your mother as a seer. Tell me why you think I did not return your call?"

She lowered her eyes to avoid the accusation and the disappointment in her father's silver gaze. She focused instead on the shards of jadelite scattered on her mother's desk. *Brepaithe* Toban's tiger stamp. It was broken. She used to play with it. She loved that stamp. She picked up a jadelite fragment.

"You had to remain under U'Nehíl so the Ken'nar in Falantir would not sense your location."

She could stare at the stone shards all she wanted to avoid her father's gaze, but her mother's mind was not to be ignored.

"Were you planning not to tell me about Two Rivers Ford, either?"

Mirana snapped her head up and closed her hand around the shard. "No. I swear it. I was confused. I needed some time to figure it out. I first thought our troops at the ford were the Ken'nar." Her shoulders slumped. "I made a mistake in interpretation. It's not often I don't understand what it is I am perceiving. I guess I was frightened about this, too."

"And Teague helped you get over your fears. Would that have been before or after you went to see Tetric Garis?" her mother said.

Mirana bit her lip.

"I am your prime, not Lord Garis. You should have come to me first with any inkling of any vision. Mirana il'Kellis il'Pinal, what is the matter with you?"

She closed her eyes and exhaled. It did nothing to rid her of her guilt. "I am so sorry."

Her mother sighed in bitter frustration as she sat back in her primeship's chair. "You are no longer a little girl, and I am no longer just your mother. I am the prime of Kin-Deren province now. Not speaking to me about the grynwen attack, and now your delay in coming to me about Two Rivers Ford? These are not things I can simply forget or pass off as childish foolishness. Your interpretation skills are worthy of a seer far beyond your summers. Consequently, when you are done with your lessons each day, you will now remain with me and my senior seers. If you have any more unbidden prescience, you need not be frightened because you will be surrounded by seers who can help you."

No. Oh, Aspects Above. What if the keep vision appeared to her while her mother and the other seers were in her mind?

Her father reached over and squeezed Mirana's shoulder. "Desde, she was frightened that she distracted me at the wrong moment when she called the warning. With Two Rivers Ford, you said yourself the vision was difficult to interpret. She did come to you only moments after speaking with Tetric. I think she knows now to never do this again."

"If she has been seeing more than her share of unbidden visions and can call to you across hundreds of leagues but also find you while you were hidden under U'Nehíl, she will need close supervision." Her mother spat out her words like bitter medicine.

She was angry, certainly, but she was also scared. Mirana scowled. Why was she frightened? What was going on here?

Her mother's expression softened. Finally.

"I am not doing this to be cruel, Lightness, but you need to remember why it is so vitally important we know any scrap of information. It can save lives." She now sent a caring notion to Mirana's mind. "You may go."

She nodded and walked to the door. Fear had kept her from doing her duty and coming to her mother—no, her prime—as was required by law. Fear of no longer trusting her instincts. Fear of no longer trusting herself. Fear this misstep would lead to another and another until she believed evil choices weren't evil anymore.

Her hand lingered on the door handle. Could she tell them? Tell them what she was? Tell them the awesome and atrocious things her destiny held for her? Would they believe her?

She turned around. "I really am sorry. For everything. Father, the grynwen weren't hunting you like a herd of deer. They were sent. I had to warn you. I had to. I also know the kind of call I made—" She swallowed. "The call I made is beyond what most Fal'kin can do. That frightened me as well. The thought I might have killed you in the end and not saved you, that is what terrified me." She crossed her arms tightly, holding herself. "With Two Rivers Ford, Mother, I could have given you incorrect information. If I came to you with bad information, it would have been worse. I didn't want to cause more people to die." She tried to keep the sob in her throat from escaping, but it slipped through her clenched teeth anyway. "I don't want people to die because of me."

Kaarl crossed over to her and held her face in his hands. "Gannah Tesabe did not die because of you."

Her mother rose and stroked Mirana's hair. "You must never be afraid of what you see, *ai*, even if the visions are terrifying."

The keep tower and its deadly light flared in her mind. She squeezed her eyes shut and shuddered, her folded arms unable to suppress the trembling.

"Miri, what is it?" Desde asked.

"You always told me you gave up being a battle seer to raise me. It was more than that, though, wasn't it?" Her voice dropped to a whisper. She wasn't sure she wanted to hear her own words. "It was all the death, too. The guilt of taking so many lives over the summers. It had left you empty inside. That's why you thought you could never have a child, isn't it? You thought the Aspects Above were punishing you?"

Her mother blinked, her hand now still. "What?"

Mirana inhaled. Would they understand? They had to. This burden was killing her, heartbeat by heartbeat. "Father, you fight evil every day until you know of nothing else. The bloodlust on the battlefield. It nearly overwhelms you sometimes, doesn't it? Sometimes your Defending Aspect controls you more than you control it."

She stepped out of her parents' embrace. "I know these things about you both. I've seen it, heard it from you, in bits and pieces of thoughts you don't even want to admit to yourselves. We all have horrors like that inside. All of us."

Her mother's eyes held concern, *ai*, but it was her fear that shot like an arrow through Mirana's heart. "What are you saying, Lightness?"

"Please don't call me that anymore." Her words tried to fight their way out just as strongly as she was trying to hold them back. "We call the one who leads the Ken'nar the Dark Trine. Was he born evil? Did he suddenly wake up one morning and decide to turn his back on the Fal'kin and forsake the Light from Within for the Ken'nar and the Power from Without? What choices did he make in his life that led him down the path to become evil? You both are the noblest Fal'kin I know. If *you* can't fight the darkness in your hearts, how can I?"

"Mirana," her father said, "you made some mistakes, and, *ai*, they were serious ones, but you are not evil. They were just mistakes."

Her mother looked once more at her father, then nudged Mirana's mind. "The Aspects Above gave us our gifts, and we are compelled to use them, but they also gave us a conscience. They gave us free will." She reached out to cup her cheek. "You are not evil. You could never be evil, *biraena*. Ever."

She pulled her face away from her mother's hand and stepped back farther. "How do you know?"

"I carried you beneath my heart for almost eight months. The Aspects Above wanted you so badly for Kinderra, they called you to be born that much sooner. Your gifts were once my gifts. I know you. I know you are not evil." Her mother tried to smile, but her worried brow defeated the expression.

Mirana slowly opened her hand to see the piece of the broken jadelite tiger still in her palm. "Do you think the Dark Trine's mother said the same things to him when he was young?"

Her mother reached for her father's hand. *... Mirana ... You know we love you ... Is there something else you haven't told us? ... Have you done something? ...*

"No." She shook her head quickly. "Why would anyone want to become the Dark Trine, the one to destroy Kinderra? I can't even imagine what his mother and father have gone through, seeing what he's become. If they're still alive. Maybe it's better if they weren't."

Her father held his hand out toward her. When she did not reach for it, pain shot behind his eyes, then disappeared behind the walls of his mind. "Power—seeking it above all else—turns good men into evil men. I've made my share of serious mistakes, but I like to believe that maybe I've done a little good, too. I took up an amulet summers too early so I could kill the Ken'nar who killed my parents. But I later learned it was far more satisfying to save the lives of my comrades and the Unaspected we are sworn to protect than it was to take the lives of the Ken'nar. I also want you to know this: whatever sins I have committed, I committed them to keep you safe."

Mirana placed the jadelite shard back on her mother's desk. *... Please know I would do the same ...*

CHAPTER 11

*"A bhéth en aonta cin anelies ísi a bhéth en aonta cin
Kin e U'Kin i'anelies aspecaem. Acceptem ísi tuda o
nehíl."*
("To join in union with another is to join in
union with another soul's Light and Dark.
Acceptance is total or not at all.")

—Ora Fal'kinnen 130:45–46

Teague ran up the last of the four hundred and thirty-eight
stairs leading to the parapet at the summit of Jasal's Keep. His
heart beat faster than even the exertion could make it.

He used to love this place. He and Mirana would steal away
when their lessons and chores were done for the day—and
sometimes before—to sneak up the tower and look out from its
heights. He hadn't been up here in four summers. Not since

Mirana had that terrifying vision the night he had broken his arm.

When he and Mirana were younger, they would race each other up the stairs to leap up and tag the divot gouged out of the door's lintel stone. He was taller, his legs were longer. She was Aspected and therefore faster. When they were younger, they were an even match. Now, they were no longer children. He was a man. He gritted his teeth, frowning, as he held onto the parapet door to catch his breath. Well, he was trying to be a man.

"I looked everywhere for you." He gulped a lungful of cold air as he walked over to Mirana.

She didn't turn to him but remained facing the landscape. "How did you find me?"

He wasn't all that surprised she hadn't been startled at his arrival. She probably heard him coming since his first step. She might have even sensed his presence from the moment he left the healing hostel. Aspects Above knew his thoughts were a loud, messy jumble at the moment. It was a wonder someone hadn't stopped him already.

He leaned on the capstone railing, smiling. Hills rolled away to the south, the dun-colored stubble of cornstalks and wheat chaff emerging from the thick frost as the afternoon sun warmed the land. Soon those hills would flush green with the first of the season's crops.

"The padlock on the door was open. I don't know why they even use one. It's not like it will keep any of you out."

"You shouldn't be here."

Her face held no emotion, and her voice was just as flat. Something was wrong. Mirana usually ran into his arms if no one was around.

"Neither should you."

"If your parents catch you here, you'll be in trouble."

"So will you."

"I've been granted a momentary reprieve from my sentence to eat. My mother and her seers are now to watch me like bloodhawks on a field mouse. After the grynwen and everything else, I don't blame her." She turned to him at last. "You really shouldn't be seen with me. Your mother and your father made it perfectly clear they didn't want you near me."

Maybe that was why she was troubled. She had gotten the same bloody talking-to he had. "No," Teague said as one side of his mouth arched upward into a scoundrel's grin, "they didn't want you near me. They never told me I couldn't be near you." She rolled her eyes in disgust. He nudged her with his elbow. "C'mon. That was supposed to make you laugh."

At last, she gave him a sliver of a smile. "I think your distance was implied."

That was better, but he wanted her happy. He had a lot of talking to do. "I've been granted a bit of a stay of sentence myself. I'm on my way to fetch some tallow from the kitchens for poultices."

A light breeze ruffled the waves of his hair. She reached up to smooth them back. That was much, much better. He loved it when she played with his hair. "Your mother and the other seers had a vision before dawn of a battle at Two Rivers Ford. They told my parents and the rest of the hall this morning. That's what you saw, isn't it? In the healing hostel yesterday, and last night? That's what you were upset about."

She nodded. "I told my mother what I saw, but I ran into Lord Garis first." She gave a small laugh. "Literally."

He leaned back from her in surprise. "And you told him?"

She frowned. "I didn't have much of a choice, but, *ai*, I told him what I saw."

He reached for her hand. Her fingers were cold against his palm. "Everything?"

"Of the ford, *ai*." She pulled her hand away and brushed the remaining frost from the stone. She then slammed her fist on the stone.

He started at her gesture. This wasn't like Mirana. This wasn't like Mirana at all. "What's going on? What else aren't you telling me?"

"Teague, I completely misinterpreted what is to happen at Two Rivers Ford." She lightly pounded the stone with both fists now. "That's never happened to me before." She leaned over the parapet wall and looked down. "Is this the start of it all? Is this where I begin to lose my ability to do good?"

"I don't think that's possible."

He followed her gaze but couldn't see anything interesting other than it was a long way down. A long way. A water bucket by the courtyard's well looked like a thimble. He turned back to her and noticed the pallor on her face. Dark circles under her eyes marred the diamond-bright beauty he so wanted to see right now.

He reached for her, but she leaned away from him. She had never before refused his embrace. The fluttering chill that suddenly decided to make a nest in his stomach had nothing to do with the cold air. Did she already know what he wanted to ask her? Had she already thought of an answer?

"What if I misunderstand something else, something important? Something where people could die?" She bit her lip. Oh, no. She only did that when she was upset. "Maybe you really should leave."

Surely, she knew how he felt about her. He would say it to her once again, so she could hear it with her ears as real words, not magically mediated perceptions. "I don't care what you see or don't see. I don't care what you think your destiny holds for you. I'm not going to stop being with you. Ever."

The wind blew a silken ebony lock of hair across her face. When she made no move to brush it away, he did. Her expression, though, remained strained, even frightened. That frightened him. "Miri?"

She let her breath out and watched it for a moment as it rose toward the keep's crowning pinnacle. "Why were you looking for me anyway?"

Oh, this was so not going the way he had planned, and certainly not the way he had hoped. If only he could get her to smile again. "You were pretty upset last night. I wanted to see how you were doing. And," he leaned in close, grinning, his body touching hers, "we were interrupted." Mirana blushed, chasing away a bit of the paleness. *Hope shall remain*, the good book said. "I wanted to find you to give you something." He dug into his belt pouch. "I made it for your birthday. I know it's still a few sevendays away." He shrugged. "I don't know. After everything, I thought now might be an even better time."

He placed a small pendant in her hand. Three tiny flowers, their yellow petals deepening to red in the center, were pressed between two thumbnail-sized plates of colorless mica. A crudely crafted thin frame of gold sealed the edges.

Mirana opened her mouth and, for a moment, he couldn't tell if she was happy or horrified. "Teague, I—*Gratas Oë.*"

He had known his entire life he wanted to spend each of Mirana's birthdays with her—and every other day in between.

"I made it myself. It's not very good. I know the gold leaf is uneven, but I hoped you'd like it anyway. It took me sevendays. I kept breaking the mica. I hoped to find a gold chain or at least a silk cord to string it on, but maybe this will do." He unlaced the leather cord from his tunic. He took the pendant from her and threaded the cord through, then placed it around her neck.

She touched it as it lay over her heart. "This is the most precious gift I've ever received."

The chill that sat in his stomach now flew up into his throat, thudding along with his heartbeat. "It's no amulet, I know. Or a gold band." He placed his hand over hers, feeling her heartbeat against his fingertips. He searched those silver eyes, the ones he knew so well. He wanted to lose himself in them forever. In truth, he already had.

"A gold band? You want to join in union? For forever? With me?"

He laughed. "You say it like I'm the one who's settling for something less. I'm the one who's Unaspected."

"That's never mattered to me. You know that. But I'm a Pinal." She traced the outlines of the pendant with a finger. "And a liar."

"And now, according to your mother, apparently a felon." He and Mirana both laughed. He pulled her close and rested his forehead against hers. "I know we're still too young, but it's my pledge to you for the future. Our future."

"I want to spend the rest of my life with you. More than anything." She rose on her toes and met her lips with his.

He made her happy, and that made him happy. No, it made him ecstatic. Mirana once told him that she could feel what he felt when they kissed—emotional and otherwise. He slid his hands up to hold her face and drank in her kiss, parting her lips with his. He didn't want this moment to end, but all too soon it would. That was the whole reason why he wanted to see her now. He might not get another chance. That fluttering bird of cold plummeted back down his throat, past his belly, and into his limbs.

She pulled back from him slightly. "What's wrong?"

He parted from her and turned to stare at the railing to avoid her gaze. It didn't work. From the corner of his eye, he saw her staring at him. Who knew those starlight eyes of hers could rest so heavily on him? "I just wanted to let you know all of this before I left."

She scowled. "Where are you going?"

He took a breath before answering. This was the other thing he needed to do to be a man. Whether he'd live long enough to become one was another matter entirely. "I am going with my parents to the ford."

"What?" She grabbed his arm.

"They expect a victory, but there will still be wounded. Gemma and a few of the others will remain here at the healing hostel. Most of the herbsfolk, however, are headed to the ford."

Mirana shook her head. "You can't go. You could be killed."

It was one thing if he thought it, quite another if she did. Mirana had the annoying tendency to always be right. "*Gratas.* Thanks for the encouragement, unskilled Unaspected wretch that I am."

"You know that's not what I meant." She held his other arm now, too. "You can't go. It's too dangerous."

He pulled himself away from her. "What's that supposed to mean? You don't think I can survive because I don't have the Aspects?"

"No." She shook her head. "I didn't mean that at all. Teague—"

"This is what I'm supposed to be doing as an herbsman. Someday, anyway."

Her eyes remained wide in shock. "I can't believe your parents are making you do this."

He started to say something but gave up in frustration and now looked out on the thawing fields himself. She had asked him last night to take her away, begged him. He wanted nothing more than to build her a little cottage somewhere, maybe on the bluffs of Parsalon overlooking the sea, where they could care for the countryfolk together. He would never be able to have her as his wife, to make a life for her, if he didn't learn how to take responsibility for his own life first.

He couldn't fight demons he couldn't see like Mirana could, he wasn't Aspected. He could only fight the ones he could see and, only then, if he knew what they were. She was a Trine, and someday when the Ken'nar found out about her, he would need something more than a poultice to protect her.

"They aren't making me. I volunteered to go," he said finally. "I demanded it, actually."

She leaned forward into his view. "Why would you do such a thing?"

"It makes sense if you think about it. If I am skilled enough to train someone else, it's high time I put my knowledge into practice. If I stop acting like a child, my parents will stop treating me like one. They're going to have to start respecting my choices."

He scooped up some of the remaining frost and compacted it between his palms into a tiny snowball. He threw it down toward the stone pavers below in the courtyard. She thrust out her hand. The snowball hung suspended in mid-air. He glared at her. She released it, letting it fall to the pavers below, where it spattered into icy dust.

"By choices, you mean me," she said. "Oh, Light Above, I would never want to come between you and your family. You have nothing to prove to me or anyone else by going to Two Rivers Ford. Teague, don't do this. Least of all for me."

"It's not just for you." He laughed sadly. "Well, *ai*, it is, mostly, but I'm doing this for me, too. I want to be strong for you."

She gripped his arms again, tighter this time. "You are strong for me."

"No, I'm not. Or I guess I don't know if I am or not." He raised his hands to hold her. "The only way you truly know a sword's mettle is to test it in combat."

"You are not a sword!" Her breath ascended into the cold air with the force of her words.

He gave her a strained smile. "Not yet." Her face remained pulled taut in disbelief. "You're not laughing at any of my jokes today."

"This is not funny. This is the least funny thing there could be." Her shoulders fell. "I don't need you to be a weapon for me. I don't need your protection. All I need is you." She drew a ragged breath.

Oh, Lights! Was she going to cry? Had he made her cry? "Maybe not today, but someday you're going to need help. Even a Trine is just one person."

Mirana held his pendant. "You shouldn't be going to the ford. I should be the one going. Maybe it's best if we're apart from each other for a while. My life has become such a nightmare. I don't want you to get hurt." Her hand dropped to her side.

Teague's heart fell along with it. "We shouldn't be gone that long, but that's not the point." He reached for her again. "You can't hurt me."

"I would never want to. Ever." She refused to let him pull her back into his embrace and turned from him. "Why can't I just disappear like your snowball?"

Rank dread now replaced the fluttering chill. It was hot, sitting there in his belly, and far worse. "What are you talking about?"

She was silent for a moment, her gaze fixed on the southern horizon. "Have you ever been to the ocean?"

He scowled as concern fought for his attention with his confusion. "What? *Ai*, a few times with my parents. We'd sail occasionally when they went on their sabbaticals to Tash-Hamar. The only way their provinces allowed them to join in union was if my mother came home to heal the sick there once in a while. But I don't see—"

"It's wide. Oblivious," she replied, not listening to him. "It doesn't know who I am or what I do, or even care."

He reached for her, but she stepped back from him and hugged herself. "Miri, you're not making any sense."

"Nothing's changed." Her voice had dropped so low, he could barely hear her. "Which means everything's changed. It has to. I have my own choices to make." She turned around to stare up at the keep's pinnacle. "Maybe we—" She swallowed loudly. "Maybe we aren't such a good idea after all."

The keep. Her damn keep vision! Because of that racking vision, she believed she would lay waste to Kinderra. It had to be wrong. She wasn't capable of that kind of evil. He knew her. She was the most loving person he knew. She fought herself every time she walked into the healing hostel to help him with patients, even though it terrified her to do so. Those weren't the actions of a demon bent on wielding death. They were the actions of someone trying to do the right thing, the good thing. The Light thing.

Worried, he moved closer. "Maybe it's time to tell your parents what you are. Maybe it's even time to let them know about the keep."

"How can you even suggest such a thing?" She groaned in frustration. She hid her face in her hands a moment, then threw them back down.

"I want to help you. I think you know that," he said. "Please listen to me. My parents know we've been doing some sort of healing together. How long do you think it's going to be before they tell your parents? We can't hide anymore."

She spun back to face him. "Hiding the fact that I'm a Trine is what's saving everyone from me right now."

"Tell your parents about your Aspects," he pleaded once again. "We'll find a way to deal with whatever happens. I won't let you go through this alone."

"Don't you understand? I *am* alone." She held her arms out in an appeal. "Don't you think I want to tell my parents? Don't you think I want help to stop all of this? For Aspects' sakes, Teague, I'm trying desperately to honor who I am called to be, yet avoid who I am to become!" Tears began to shimmer in her silver eyes. "I tried to tell your parents. But if they don't believe in us, believe that we can overcome any hardships, how will they believe that I'm going to cause all of *this*?" She slammed her hand down on a parapet capstone. "I even tried to tell my parents earlier. I want to tell them, but I can't. My father still calls me 'his tiny child.' By the Light, it's like he still sees me as that infant born two months early sometimes. They won't believe me. They would never believe me. Even you don't. How do you expect them to?"

"Mirana—"

"If I told them I was a Trine, they would demand I choose an amulet immediately, and choosing would lead to this damned watchtower exploding and death and nothingness!" She threw her hands out to her sides. "To prevent that from happening, I would have no other choice than to leave in exile. What then,

Teague? My Aspects will still speak to me. I can run away from every Fal'kin and Unaspected on the continent, but I can't outrun my Aspects. What if I see my father's life threatened again? Or someone innocent like Maark Bedane? Or-Or you? I'm living in the wilds of Kinderra somewhere. What then? Do I ignore what I see, what I sense? Do I ignore the fact that I could help? Do I let my father die this time? Do I let you—" She curled her fingers into fists. "No matter what I do, people will die. My Aspects have given me a birthright without honor. They have left me with a life I cannot live."

Teague rushed over and wrapped his arms around her, but she did not return his embrace. He held her closer still and whispered into her dark hair, "You think this is what will happen, but you don't know for sure. You've never truly told anyone the whole of it except me. Tell. Your parents."

"Teague—"

"Maybe they actually will believe you. If they don't, well, you're not much worse off than you are now. We'll leave. Together."

The tension melted from her body. That was good. Wait. Now, she felt completely limp. That was bad.

"Maybe you're right. Maybe they will believe me. They and all the Fal'kin will drag me out beyond the Great Gates. Their amulets will solve everything." She laughed, a cold sound he'd never heard her make before. She turned, peering out over the vista. "Everyone would be safe then. You'll be safe. Maybe that would be for the best. For everyone."

His brows drew together in confusion. "What do you mean?" When she didn't answer, he held her back from him. "You're joking. Right?" She was joking. She had to be. She better be.

"Of course, of course." She waved him off, however, she wouldn't meet his eyes. In fact, she wasn't looking at anything, just sort of gazing past his shoulder.

He pulled her close once more and held her fiercely. "I know you are not evil. I know you will never become evil. Mirana, you don't really know what your keep vision means. Talk to your parents. We'll see this through together."

She pushed him away, gently but resolutely. "Go tell your parents you spoke out of turn. Stay here and help Gemma prepare supplies. There is much to do before the Fal'kin leave."

"Mirana."

"Please leave me."

Tears began to scald his eyes. "I love you."

"Leave me."

When Teague reached the stairwell door, he paused and turned around. He watched her take off his pendant—along with the promise it held—and put it into her belt pouch.

She fought demons he could not see and never would. No matter how hard he tried.

CHAPTER 12

"In the stillness before the war horns sound is the true
moment of decision: Will you answer the Aspects' call
or the call of fear?"

—The Book of Kinderra

A raindrop splattered on the back of Mirana's hand. It blew
in from the small clerestory window high up in the seer's training
room. On sunny days, light would pour through the opening to
form a tightly focused shaft ending in a brilliant square in the
center of the floor. Today, however, it only focused the rain
from the spring storm.

The weather had finally changed, bringing warm wind and
downpours. It melted the ice. It saturated the roads. It drowned

the new crops. She brought her hand to her mouth and sucked off the drop. It was no better than winter.

The bare room featured no decorations or furniture, nothing to distract a seer from visions. Unfortunately, the sparseness of the room only left her with her thoughts to consume her.

She tried to pay attention to her mother's lesson, as the other twelve seer *scholaire'e* around her were, but her mind kept drifting. Uneasiness about the Two Rivers Ford visions continued to prickle her mind over the last sevendays like a splinter just below the skin—always nagging but impossible to remove.

Lord Garis had said she couldn't possibly have gotten accurate information from her first viewing of the ford vision, the one where she thought she had seen thousands of Ken'nar. Aspects Above knew she didn't see every vision the other seers did. She couldn't without an amulet, even if she wanted to. Her Seeing Aspect, however, had only been part of what had led her to believe a Ken'nar horde of that size would attack the garrison. Her other gifts added to her convictions—the sense of so very many bloodthirsty lives around her mediated by her Defending Aspect, the sudden stillness of life notes amplified by her Healing Aspect.

Not once, though, had she misinterpreted a vision she did see. Not once. Had she lost what little control she had of her Aspects? Whatever hope she had begun to feel from Lord Garis melted away like frost in a warm rain shower.

Her mother called images of Two Rivers Ford to Mirana's mind and the minds of the other young seers, as much to teach and test them as to perhaps have them reveal some unnoticed detail of information the Kin-Deren Fal'kin could use to their advantage against the Ken'nar.

The scenes her mother sent were the same ones Mirana had been seeing for sevendays. Nothing had changed. How could she be wrong when she had sensed so much with all three of her Aspects? Yet, she had not seen, had not sensed, anything like the thousands of Ken'nar again.

"As I view this scene, can anyone give me an estimate of how many Ken'nar he or she sees?" her mother asked. Her voice sounded soft, mesmerizing. Her yellow topaz glowed, spilling golden light around the room.

"Five hundred. Maybe five hundred and fifty," Pelen said. He had not stopped talking about all the frightening images he would conjure up with his amulet to terrify the Ken'nar on the battlefield when he chose next summer. Why couldn't she feel like that—excited and eager to choose an amulet and use it? "The number of Ken'nar troops at the ford appears to be similar to their forces at the Dawn Point Incursion of 3358."

Her mother nodded. "Excellent. That has been our estimate as well."

Pelen's observation was right. Only a few hundred Ken'nar appeared to ride on the ford now, as had been foreseen for sevendays. How could there possibly be two completely different versions of the attack on Two Rivers Ford and both still be correct?

One of the very few skills in which she once had placed her confidence was her ability to interpret what she saw. Now, she no longer trusted herself. How many more visions would she not understand correctly?

"Can anyone surmise from where the Ken'nar have come?" her mother questioned.

"From the north. The span of that bridge is narrower than the other one. It's the Garnath River bridge," Yenira said. "Also, we heard from the defenders Ken'nar entered the Kana-Akün interior during the winter. Perhaps they came from Falantir, its capital." The older girl was always so smug, but Mirana supposed she had every right to be. She, too, was seldom wrong in her predictions.

Desde nodded. "*Ai.* Good. We believe that as well. You are more than ready for your amulet, Yenira."

The girl sat back, smiling in satisfaction.

Teague would be going. Even five hundred Ken'nar would fight viciously. What if there were ten times as many, like at the Vale i'Dúadar? She ground her knuckles in the rough stone pavers, wanting the pain to blot out the thought.

"Landmarks like mountain ranges are also good reference points," her mother said. "Although it helps if there are recognizable peaks or a profile. Closer in, well, one rock ledge can look pretty much like another."

Mirana wiped her bloody knuckles on the sleeve of her father's woolen tunic that engulfed her over her clothes. The spring weather was too warm for such a heavy sweater, but she hadn't put it on for warmth. She put it on to be comforted. It wasn't working well for that either. Her father had been named interim Steward of the Quorum of Light. Would he stay in Deren or head to the ford with Kin-Deren's provincial troops and the il'Kin?

"Sometimes, such a vague reference point can be of benefit. It helped the Kin-Deren forces as they hid in the Dar-Tal Si Mountains at the Battle of the Vale i'Dúadar," her mother continued. "As you remember, our split forces were a complete surprise to the Ken'nar and led to their rout that day."

Mirana frowned. Who was she kidding? Her father was a defender. He lived for one thing: to defend. Her mother would be going, too. She was the prime of a province now. Any physical threat to the province demanded her presence.

"Good work today, all of you." Her mother rose to her feet. "Before I release you for the day, I wanted to say how very proud I am of each one of you. This will be my last lesson with you for a while. I will be riding out with our forces for the ford tomorrow. I have asked Seer Vesta to remain behind and continue your training. My only regret is I will not be able to officiate this summer's Choosing Ceremony. I cannot believe eighteen summers have passed for so many of you, and you will be choosing. I remember when you were all just babes. *Rememore Kin e Forte.* Remember the Light and the Keep, *Ëi cara'e.*"

If her mother held any fear of the upcoming battle, she certainly did not show it. Her voice was full of emotion, *ai*, but not fear.

Her mother and the seer *scholaire'e* filed out of the training room, leaving Mirana alone. Remember the Light and the Keep. She didn't want to remember it at all, she wanted to forget it ever existed.

Running away would have solved nothing. *Ai*, it would keep an amulet from hanging around her neck, but her Aspects would continue to constrict her like a hangman's noose. If she left, the knowledge that people would die who could have been saved would be just as damning as killing them through the fate awaiting her at Jasal's Keep. As always, telling everyone of the impending destruction at her hands would get her nowhere. They'd think the notion was ludicrous. She highly doubted the Fal'kin would see her as a threat serious enough to require immediate execution with their amulets—something that hadn't been done in centuries. At best, they'd write it off as a nightmare, at worst, she was imagining it. No, her revelation would be dismissed out of hand by everyone, even her parents. They loved her. Because they loved her, they would never understand. Or believe.

Mirana reached for her small belt knife.

She knew of one sure way, however, to stop her future. To stop it all. Forever.

She frowned. As she sheathed the blade, her fingers brushed her belt pouch and the cherished rectangular object within it. Teague's pendant.

She removed it and traced its delicate lines. The mica reflected the heat from her palm.

Teague. Her parents. Teague's parents. Binthe and Morgan, her father's il'Kin. So many others who were friends, mentors. They would all be at the ford. With only five hundred-odd Ken'nar, the Fal'kin from Kin-Deren would be victorious. How could they not? The Kin-Deren forces outnumbered the Ken'nar four to one. As her mother had said only a moment ago, it would be like the victory the Fal'kin claimed at the Battle of the Vale when they had split their forces. How could she have been so wrong about the ford?

Unless she was not.

She gasped. *Split forces. Victory.*

An avalanche of understanding careened through her mind. She *had* been right all along. The first viewing of the ford attack was not simply a preamble to the second. It was a separate and distinct prescience of its own. She had truly seen two different visions. Both versions of the attack on the ford installation were correct. The Ken'nar's Dark Trine would split his troops. Her first vision, the one with thousands of Ken'nar, came *after* the second one with Kin-Deren's more numerous forces. She'd first seen the attack's conclusion, the Ken'nar rear guard. When she saw the vision again with Lord Garis—that refined premonition, with just five hundred Ken'nar and thousands of Fal'kin from Kin-Deren province—that was the Dark Trine's opening ploy!

Five hundred Ken'nar would indeed attack from the north. The Ken'nar Dark Trine would hold back more than four thousand to attack later when the Fal'kin were fully engaged with the smaller force. The Fal'kin would be annihilated.

She brought her shaking hands to her mouth. "Oh, Aspects Above, no. What have I done?"

If she had only listened to herself—trusted herself as the person she was now and not some distant, horrific version of herself—her mother and her troops could have prepared for a larger force, even sought help from neighboring provinces. Instead, her self-denial and her silence had left Kin-Deren to march into a trap where they would be decimated. And it was all her fault.

Mirana jammed Teague's pendant back into her belt pouch and tore out of the training room.

CHAPTER 13

"Like leaves unfurling in the spring, so didst my dream unfold before my eyes. Whether for good or ill, I could not tell. Its conclusion still lay behind the curtain of understanding."

—The Codex of Jasal the Great

Mirana threw the door open to her mother's study with a swipe of her hand and her Aspects. "Your vision of the ford. It's a trap."

"Ah, there you are—" Her mother froze. "What?"

"The Ken'nar will split their forces. We're marching into a trap."

Her mother's council gathered in her prime's study—her senior seers, provincial defender commanders, Morgan Jord and

Binthe Lima from her father's il'Kin, Teague's parents. Her father. Lord Trine Tetric Garis.

"The Ken'nar Dark Trine will split his forces." She gulped a breath. "Five hundred will indeed attack, as we all have seen, but he will reserve the majority of his troops until we're occupied with his vanguard. The others will then charge in and surround us. By the thousands."

Her mother rose from her chair. "How do you know this?"

Mirana's heart banged in her chest, striking out at her ribs. "I saw it. I didn't understand at first. As we know, the vision was hard to understand because it mostly takes place at night. By the time I studied it again with Lord Garis, it had become what we see now. I had two separate visions of the ford attack."

"Mirana—" the Trine said.

Her mother held up her hand, stopping his comment. "You saw a different version of Two Rivers Ford? A vision before this one? One you did not tell me about?"

Mirana nodded slowly. Her breath turned into soft, jagged gasps. "I thought I was wrong, and that it was just a fuzzier and earlier version of the one we've been seeing for sevendays. I never saw it again. So, I didn't say anything. The one we've all been seeing will take place *before* what I saw the first time. My first vision was the conclusion of the attack, not the beginning. He will attack with five thousand, only he's split that single force into two—a smaller one and a larger one. I saw them both." She swallowed and tried to breathe at the same time. "I saw. Them. Both."

"Withholding a vision is a crime. A grave one. You know this," her mother said, her voice hushed with horror. "If you were a full Fal'kin with an amulet about her neck, I would have to consider expulsion from the province. What have you done, child?"

The minds of those gathered assaulted her. They leaped upon her like grynwen on prey. The senior seers stood around her, judgment and downright disgust emanating from their minds. Binthe, her sea-green eyes full of compassion, full of trepidation. Morgan, his handsome, bearded face wearing the hard, stoic expression of a man who knew he might not be alive in a matter of days. Niah Beltran turned away from Mirana, her mind closed. Tennen Beltran's, however, was not. His mind bored into hers with the precision of an amulet-driven scalpel. Tetric Garis, his face remained as inscrutable as his mind. Her father—

"*Paithe*, I thought what I saw was wrong. I swear it." Mirana's trembling blurred the sound of her words. Her cheeks flushed with heat. "Maybe the Ken'nar Dark Trine was going to attack with his full might, then changed his plans to what we see now. I don't know. I saw only once the single force of thousands. It never happened again. I thought I was wrong. I'm so sorry."

Her mother ran over and dragged her to the center of the room with an iron grip on her wrist. She slapped Mirana's hand over her topaz amulet. "Call to us what you first saw."

She tried to pull her hand back from her mother's unyielding grip. "I can't—"

"Call. Your. First vision. All of it," her mother repeated, snapping off each word like a dry twig.

Mirana's shoulders fell in bitter defeat. Her transgressions stood naked, her sins exposed, with nowhere to hide. Fear of her fate had driven her to turn her back on the shred of belief she had in herself. She had begged the Aspects Above for more time to find a different future for herself, one without corrupting her Aspects. Her actions to prevent her fate had only brought her closer to her downfall. Thousands would now pay for her fear, her hesitation, and her cowardice because there was no time to seek help from other provinces. Kin-Deren would be fighting on its own. Her people would pay for her sins just like they had centuries ago with her ancestor, Jasal Pinal. Time had run out. For the Fal'kin. For her.

She was the Dark Trine.

The amulet called to her, slowly drawing her Aspects from her. Her breath left her lungs in short, useless bursts. Her stomach clenched, and bile seared her throat. She swallowed and closed her eyes. A brilliant yellow light burst from her mother's topaz between their fingers as Desde projected Mirana's memory out through her amulet. Ethereal fighters floated like specters in front of the Fal'kin.

Rain falls, a cold, liquid curtain. Lightning flares from roiling clouds, illuminating the night, only to plunge it back into darkness a heartbeat later. Cries of blood-thirsty grynwen pierce the night. A wave of black riders pounds down a rise above Two Rivers Ford. Three thousand. Lightning flickers again. Four thousand. Riders flood across the Kin-Deren landmass and charge into the ford garrison, an endless wave of dark bodies. Five thousand. The landscape fades as night descends once more between the flashes of lightning. A smaller force of fighters fans out to meet the riders. The darkness and the storm and the uncertain skeins of the future hide the heraldics of the combatants' uniforms. Another lightning bolt explodes across the dark sky. Grynwen howl like demon hounds unleashed from the Underworld, ripping flesh from bone. Tents erupt in flames. Screams of the dying fill the air. The battlefield fades once more under the shroud of darkness.

The crystal of her mother's amulet began to take on a life of its own with its nearness, pulling at Mirana, drawing, bleeding the memory of the images out of her.

On and on they come, this terrifying mass of horses and grynwen and swords and amulets, visible one moment in the lightning, only to disappear in the next. Amulets burst in jets of their own colored lightning as the two forces hurl death at one another. Bodies fall and grynwen feed. The smaller force of fighters is pushed southward, toward the river chasm, unable to beat back the onslaught of the larger army. Corpses of the dead impede fighters, sending men and women from both forces off the ford bridges to their doom into the river ravine below.

Her heart constricted within the cage of her ribs with a sharp, visceral ache. Her legs grew weak, her bones dissolving along with her resolve. Her Defending Aspect rose, searing and urgent, in response to what she witnessed again in her memory. Her Healing Aspect begged to be released upon the mortal wounds that had yet to come. The demand from her mother's amulet was insistent, incessant, as it wrenched from her the memory of that first vision of slaughter awaiting Two Rivers Ford.

Gabrial, the Guiding Star, quivers over the backbone of the Dar-Anar Mountains in the west, a piercing silver eye in the red dawn. Bellicose chanting overtakes the refrains of fading life notes. The cries of grynwen sing a descant. Lightning flares again then dies.

Jasal's Keep.

The watchtower explodes in light, unleashing white fury.

Mirana tore her hand away from her mother and staggered back, gasping for breath. Her hair clung to her forehead with sweat.

"This is a completely different vision," Morgan said, his voice hushed. "It is—" The defender swallowed. "Deeply concerning."

"Call it to me again," her mother ordered, reaching for Mirana's hand again.

She backed away. "Mother, please don't make me—"

"Now."

She clenched Desde's hand and forced her memory of the vision once more from her mind.

"Wait. I will hold it here," her mother commanded.

An image of the battlefield, hazy with the loosely woven skeins of time, hung frozen in front of the Fal'kin from Desde's amulet. A massive army in black armor darkened the land, briefly illuminated by lightning. Individual fighters could not be made out clearly, but the dark armor they wore was apparent. The armor of the Ken'nar. The murmuring in the room ceased.

"There must be four, five thousand Ken'nar," her father whispered.

Binthe shook her head slowly, her gaze riveted on the image. "We have seen nothing of this."

Desde released Mirana's hand, and the ghostly image of fighters slowly disappeared. "Tetric, you both came to me and told me we would be attacked by five hundred Ken'nar. The very same vision I had. The same one I've had—we've all had—all along."

"*Ai*, I, too, saw some hazy thousands of fighters," the tall Trine said as he stood from his chair. "She told me she had been confused by what she saw, a greater force attacking a lesser force, but both armies were indistinct. When we reached for the Seeing Aspect together to understand just who those fighters were, it was as we see it now. The Fal'kin are the thousands, not the Ken'nar. The vision has remained so ever since."

The muscles in her mother's jaw tightened.

"Mother—"

"You blame my daughter for this?" Desde questioned Lord Garis.

"No, not at all. And neither should you. Nor should any of you." His dark gaze traveled around the room. "This is a memory of a vision, Desde, not an actual one. That's why I didn't have her call it to me." He gestured to the empty air in the middle of the room where the translucent images had been displayed. "As I said, by the time I called on my Seeing Aspect and we viewed the actual vision together, it appeared as it does now. There is no way the girl could have possibly understood at the time what she was seeing. Without an amulet, she would have had absolutely no way of controlling the vision to examine it."

"She understands it now," her mother hissed, "and it appears she may be correct."

"I can explain—" Mirana stepped closer to her.

"If you must assign blame, my prime, put it on my shoulders," Lord Garis said, stopping her reply. "None of us even considered looking into different skeins of time for something different. Did we not all believe we had seen enough? Only your daughter had the wisdom to think of other possibilities."

The Trine's mind pushed against hers, not to condemn her but something else. To comfort her? She didn't deserve his comfort and certainly not his defense.

"How do we know this memory of hers," her father gestured toward her, "is any more correct than the one you all have been seeing? You seers tell me visions change all the time. I agree with Tetric. Mirana doesn't have an amulet to bring in the precision required. I've been around enough seers to know it wouldn't be the first time emotions skewed an interpretation of a vision, and certainly the memory of one."

"My memory is not wrong, Father," she said. "My vision is correct."

He gave her a worried smile. "I know you believe it to be correct."

It was time to tell them before she put even more people in jeopardy. Everything. All of it. She had no choice. Maybe she never really did.

She stared into the faces around the chamber, giving in to their condemning expressions. "It is difficult to see the armies at Two Rivers Ford if one only looks at the vision with the Seeing Aspect. My awareness of the battle around me spoke to me of thousands more than you can see in the mind's eye. I felt them, their presences, their bloodlust. My chest ached with the need to release amulet fire. I sensed their heartbeats, too. Their wounds cried out to me. Their deaths. So much death. My first vision is right because I sensed it with my Aspects. All three of them." She took a breath, and, for a moment, it would not leave her body. "I am a Trine."

"Mirana," her mother cried.

… *Hush, now* … her father called to her, his strident mind-voice resounding within her. … *All will be well* …

She tried to block out the shock of the others from her mind, but it was impossible. It engulfed her like the wave of Ken'nar that would engulf the ford.

"This is all my fault. I am so sorry." The words sounded so pathetically inadequate. Nothing would make up for this. Nothing. The wall of deceit behind which she had hidden for summers crashed down around her.

She was the Dark Trine.

"I've hidden my Aspects from you because I was trying to stop a far more horrific nightmare than all of this. I am a Trine. I am the Dark Trine, and I will destroy Kinderra. Someday."

Desperation, mirroring her own, escaped from her father's mind to hers. "Mirana, quiet now. You are overwhelmed." He turned to the others. "She's obviously distraught. Our daughter is not a Trine. She certainly could not destroy anything. She's a seer."

Lord Garis folded his long arms. "Are you so certain?"

"I think I should know my own child's gift," Kaarl snapped.

"Tetric may be right," *Patrua* Tennen said. "She has been healing, or close to it, for a while now." His gaze, so like Teague's yet so unfamiliar in its raw disbelief, bored into her. "And she has not said a single word of it."

Her father gave a disgusted laugh. "How do you know it has been Mirana who has done these supposed healings?"

"We started to notice them several summers ago after Teague fractured his arm," *Matrua* Niah replied. "That injury itself made no sense. The break was fresh, yet there had been some partial remodeling. Performed incorrectly. The only way this could have occurred was by a healer. At first, we thought maybe Teague had finally— But then summers went by, and, well, we knew it wasn't Teague who had tried to heal." The healer woman's hands curled into fists for a moment, then relaxed. "These past few summers, our use of numbweed in the hostel has dropped by magnitudes. Maybe Mirana has yet to mend flesh and definitively set bone, but she has been suppressing the pain of our patients nearly as deeply as we could."

"There is nothing to debate—" Mirana started.

… Be still, girl … her father called sharply. "Niah, we all can shunt away pain. My Light, if I couldn't, I would have never made it past my first battle."

"That has more to do with endurance than the actual calming of nerves," she replied. "She's been suppressing pain with the Healing Aspect. On others. Which is the utmost any healer can do without an amulet, and even that is difficult."

Teague's father nodded in agreement with his wife. "Kaarl, even we remember how quickly she progressed in training as a battle seer. She nearly bested Dav and Niall both inside of six months. No seer child of ten summers could do that. Unless she is a defender, too. This is a blessing. One we desperately need, given what's about to take place."

"She does not defend, Tennen," her father snarled. "She's a seer. She saw their moves. That's all. Dav and Niall know her too well and didn't press her enough. That's why she appeared to excel so quickly with a sword. My daughter is no Trine."

"I do not think the leaders of Kin-Deren's provincial armies would willingly shirk their duty in training," the healer rejoined.

Healer Niah moved to stand beside her husband. "I was there when that girl was born. Her Aspect was so incredibly powerful but had no alignment. We thought perhaps it was because she had come two months early or even because of her difficult breech birth. Perhaps, though, it was due to all three Aspects superimposed over each other. Ask Tetric."

Her father flicked his eyes to Tetric Garis then back to Niah Beltran like a bullwhip. "Mirana is no Trine. Just you speaking such words could put her life in jeopardy."

"I love her as much as you do. I would never do anything to harm that child," *Matrua* Niah said, pointing to her.

"Except try to make it impossible for her to be near your son," her father seethed.

Her mother reached for her father's arm. "Kaarl, please."

Tennen took a step towards her father. "Are you alleging my wife would attempt to get your daughter killed to prevent her from joining in union with my son?"

Her father moved closer still. "A father will do anything to protect his child."

"Stop it, Father!" Mirana cried. "Listen to me! All of you. I have to stop pretending to be something I'm not. I'm not a seer. Or not *just* a seer. I'm a defender and a healer as well. I am a Trine."

Stark hopelessness etched itself on her father's face. "Mirana. Please. Don't."

Her mother uttered a sob. "*Biraena*, Lightness, please. Don't do this."

"I didn't know at first. My Seeing and my Defending Aspects were almost always joined." She wove her fingers together. "But healing?" She glanced at Tennen and Niah, then looked down at her boots. "I didn't understand until Teague broke his arm. Then it was no longer just sight. It was a power. An Aspect. I had to heal him. I had to."

"Why didn't you come to us then?" *Patrua* Tennen asked.

Binthe Lima clutched her emerald amulet. "Why would you keep this to yourself? You know we love you. I would lay down my life for you."

Mirana shook her head quickly. "Binthe, you don't understand—"

Lord Garis moved to stand close behind her as if he were guarding her against the others. "She said nothing because she is terrified. It is not easy knowing every single Ken'nar would kill you instantly if he or she could, especially when you have seen so few summers. It was the same for me when I was a child. Kaarl is not wrong. Her life will be in danger with this revelation."

"None of you will speak of this. It means her life," her father added, the warning unmistakable in his voice.

Mirana slipped a hand inside her belt pouch to hold Teague's pendant for comfort. All that did was remind her that he, too, could be caught up in this nightmare. She dropped her hand to her side. "I tried for summers to hide my Defending and Healing Aspects, and look what's happened. I can't hide this anymore. Too much is at stake. You call the one who leads the Ken'nar the Dark Trine. Are you so certain he is, in fact, a Trine? Have you ever seen him in the flesh? Have you ever fought against him, face-to-face?"

The Trine gifts. The three Aspects. That was more power than one mortal should hold. It was an abomination. She was an abomination. She was the Dark Trine.

"What are you saying?" Her mother's voice quaked in a way she had never heard before—a strangled, almost wheezing quality diluting her normally melodious alto.

Her parents. All of them. They didn't understand. "The Trine Prophecy speaks of the Light Trine and the Dark Trine. There is nothing written anywhere about three Trines. I know. I've looked. Lord Garis is our Light Trine. What role, then, does the prophecy leave for me?"

The minds of the other Fal'kin burst through her consciousness like exploding amulets. Voices shouted, but it was all just noise in her ears. Her heartbeat pulsed in her eardrums until it, too, faded into a ringing.

"Mirana." Her father ran to her and gripped her arms so hard it hurt.

"You are frightened, child," Lord Garis said, "but you are not the Dark Trine."

She pushed her father away and backed against the tall Trine. "Kinderra will be destroyed. Because of me. I've seen it." Her voice sounded strange to her, someone else's words echoing through her ears.

How many Ken'nar had Lord Garis put down with his amulet? If she asked him, would he do it? Was it not his destiny as the thrice-blessed to stop the thrice-cursed? Ice replaced the burning bile in her stomach, a smothering, chill blanket, oddly comforting. Maybe he would respect her for finding a shred of courage at the end. Maybe he would be quick.

Her mother rushed over, pulled her from the men, and held her. "You are not the Dark Trine. You cannot be." Her voice grew shrill. "I don't know what could have possibly made you think that. You are just frightened. *Ai*, it is your fear making you believe these things. Perhaps it is an actual nightmare. *Ai*, that is what it is. It is just a nightmare, *biraena*."

Ai, it was a nightmare. Of apocalyptic proportions.

Her father's silver eyes drilled into hers. "I don't know why you are saying all of this, but you are not the Dark Trine. You are not any Trine. You are a seer. Do you hear me? A seer. Just. A seer."

Desde's face turned into a pale mask of surrender. "Kaarl. Enough."

"You should have given her to me long ago." The tall Trine glared at her father. "Only I can protect her from those who would kill her at the ford."

Her father's hands curled into fists and turned to her mother. "She's not going to the ford."

"*Ai*, she is. She must."

"Surely you don't mean to bring her there. We can't."

"I have no choice," her mother continued. "If there is even a chance she is correct, I will need every Fal'kin in the province I can send. We will be outnumbered."

Morgan stepped forward. "I will leave tonight, my prime, and be in Kasan within a sevenday. We will get aid from Sün-Kasal. That province has one of the largest complements of Fal'kin in Kinderra."

"There is not enough time." Desde closed her eyes for a moment and swallowed audibly. "Even if you left this very moment, Sün-Kasal's defenders will never be able to reach the ford in time. Why do you think we leave at dawn? You've seen the position of Gabrial from our visions. That gives us less than two sevendays to reach the ford ourselves. I will have to order any *scholaire'e* of at least sixteen summers to choose their amulets now. Those of at least fifteen summers will choose and serve in support roles. We cannot spare experienced Fal'kin to provision weapons and tend horses during the battle."

Mirana's heart constricted. By her mother's pronouncement, she would have to choose an amulet.

"I can't. You don't understand what an amulet in my hands—"

Her father ignored her protests, and pulled her mother's arm, forcing her to look at him. "Desde, do you understand what you are saying? You can't take her to the ford. You cannot."

"I have no choice. I need every last Fal'kin in the province to turn back the Ken'nar. I cannot ask other mothers and fathers to give up their children while I hold my own back, even if it shatters my heart to do so. Our children must take up their amulets. Tonight. Including Mirana. I know what this means, *Ëi ama*, but I have no choice. She must choose her amulet and ride to the ford. I need her there. Kinderra needs her there."

Her mother's pronouncement drove like a pike through Mirana's mind. Turning back from an amulet had been her last refuge to prevent her destiny of destruction. Cold no longer surrounded her with an insidious comfort but became a lethal weight dragging her down.

"No. I must not choose. I told you. I will destroy Kinderra, not save her. I am the Dark Trine."

"Miri, stop this! Now!" Kaarl shouted, swiping his hand down like a sword. "You are not the Dark Trine!"

"Your father is right," Lord Garis said. "Listen to him."

"If you don't believe me, I will show you." She thrust out her hand and reached for the Trine's amulet to release the keep vision from her mind.

He grabbed her hand before she could touch the hematite crystal. ... *No, Mirana, stop ... Even if they see it, they will not understand its importance ... I can help you ...*

She tried to pull her hand back from his, but it remained locked in his grip. "No, you can't. Nobody can."

"Mirana, trust me. It will be all right."

She locked herself behind U'Nehíl, wanting not just her presence but her entire being to disappear. It would never be all right unless she made it right. One way or another.

CHAPTER 14

*"Oëa gemma pone com aste proxi Ëi pecta. Oëa servad
ísi gloriaé en nome il'Aspecta'e Alta hale!"*
("Thy crystal resteth like a star against my
breast. Thy servant is glorified in the name of
the holy Aspects Above!")
—*il'Exultantae (The Rejoice)*, Ora Fal'kinnen 12:3–4

Mirana stood unmoving, her feet a part of the slate pavers
on the floor. The central nave of the cavernous gathering hall
stretched before her, both impossibly long and frighteningly
short. As a very young child, she had been terrified of becoming
lost from her parents during convocations within the enormous
sanctuary. Now, the aisle that once appeared so lengthy was not
nearly long enough to give her time to find a path away from the
future she dreaded.

The line of Fal'kin *scholaire'e* slowly moved toward a dais at the aisle's end, one hundred brave youths, fear and expectation written on their faces.

"Go on, sweetling. I thought you'd be running up that aisle."

She turned toward the familiar voice. Gemma hadn't heard yet what happened at the war council, not everything. She would learn soon enough.

The boy in front of her was already five rows ahead. She nodded to the herbswoman and attempted to smile. Dragging one foot forward, she began walking in the Choosing Ceremony procession.

Hundreds of Fal'kin packed the hall's transepts and aisles. The heat from the packed bodies, the acrid scent of incense, and the smothering pall of emotion-laden minds pressed down on her.

Torchlight and candlelight quaked within the gathering hall in anemic mimicry of the storm's lightning outside. The amulets of hundreds of Fal'kin ebbed and glowed in the fretful light, reflecting the calls and emotions of their owners. She concentrated on the worn slate floor tiles to try and distance herself from the sensations of which she was all too keenly aware. A myriad of colors from the amulet crystals played strange shadows against lofty stone columns upholding a ceiling lost in darkness.

Mirana prayed as she stumbled forward on leaden feet. The one thing—the one thing!—she had promised herself was that she would never accept an amulet into her soul unless she could find a way to avoid her destructive fate at Jasal's Keep. Perhaps choosing an amulet was exactly what the Aspects Above had willed for her after all.

She lifted her head to the dark ceiling. "If I give myself to your divine directive and take up an amulet, will you take Jasal's Keep from me?" Only the thunder answered in reply. The leather pectoral armor constricted her chest like a prisoner's bonds as she walked. Thick animal-hide guards shackled her thighs over buckskin leggings.

She dimly recalled Binthe Lima and Niah Beltran securing her armor while her mother watched. The young il'Kin seer's face had remained stoic, belying the tears that brimmed in her eyes. *Matrua* Niah had tried to hold back her crying, odd guttural clicks in her throat. Mirana's hands had shaken violently as she struggled to fasten the buckle of her knife belt. Her mother held out two long knives. The weapons of battle seers. With numb fingers, she had placed them in the sheaths at her waist, nicking her unsteady thumb on one. Her mother had remained silent as she wound Mirana's hair into a coil at the nape of her neck where it would not interfere if she had to fight. Her hands had trembled as much as Mirana's own.

All at once, the emotions her mother had locked within her escaped in a cry. She had pulled Mirana to her fiercely and refused to let her go. Binthe and Niah had to pull her away, both women vowing to give their own lives to keep her safe.

Her mother was here now in the gathering hall, standing atop the dais at the end of that impossibly long, frighteningly short nave. Or was she? Tall and golden-haired, wrapped in silver mail and silver-plated leather, gleaming knives of her own caressing her hips. Her yellow topaz scintillated like the venomous eye of a serpent. That woman was not her *maithe*. She was not even a woman, but the incarnation of a heathen goddess of war.

The province's senior Fal'kin stood in the dark shadows of the dais behind her mother, an austere and foreboding pantheon of lesser gods.

"Kin il'Aspecta'e Alta biran derra u'kin voide. Kinderra Oëme nomé fár Id ísi Derra i'Kin." The ancient chant her mother sang reverberated in her ears.

The youth ahead of Mirana had a sword strapped to his waist, not long knives. Light glinted off the shiny metal of the cross guard. Its luster betrayed that the blade had yet to be tested. Like its owner. He would be elevated from a *scholaire* to a defender. And he would likely die at the ford.

"The Light of the Aspects Above called land forth from the dark void. Kinderra, They named it, for it was the Land of Light. May the Light of the Aspects shine on the land," the Fal'kin responded to the orison.

Her father stood near her mother on the altar, wearing the armor and mail he had shed only sevendays ago. His plain white livery was devoid of heraldics as the il'Kin were sworn to protect every province. She was a Trine. She was sworn to protect every province, too.

Her throat ached with the force of holding back yet another sob. "Please. I want to. You must know that," she whispered once more to the silent godhead.

His silver gaze tried to catch hers. ... *Mirana ... I will keep you safe ... You will be with Maithe and me ... You will be safe ...*

His mind was filled with enough frantic determination to do something rash. She had never known him to react this way.

She averted her eyes from his and shut out his mind. She focused instead on putting one awkward, heavy-booted foot in front of the other. The long knives brushed against her hips as she walked up the aisle, a constant reminder of their presence.

… I will take up an amulet if that is what you need me to do … she called to the Aspects Above. *… Answer me! … Is this what you have willed for me? …*

The minds of those gathered pressed in on her, mocking her prayer with the response of their meaningless din. She groaned as her empty stomach clenched again.

Her mother chanted another passage from the Ora Fal'kinnen in the Old Tongue.

"May the Light of the Aspects fill the land," the gathering responded in unison.

The Choosing Ceremony. The wedding of a Fal'kin's Aspect to the soul of a crystal. The consummation of a sacred bond conferring control over the release of the Light from Within.

If the keep vision had never been in her life, she would have run up the nave just like Gemma described, and grabbed the first amulet she could reach. She would have raced to Two Rivers Ford and brought down every single Ken'nar herself to protect these innocents.

These youths, boys and girls she had known since she was born, would die because of her negligence. There had to be a way to save them, even now when all looked so hopeless. There just had to be. She moaned and grabbed a heavy wrought iron candle stand to steady herself.

… They don't deserve to die … I do … Please, Aspects Above … Help me save these people …

Again, always, the Aspects Above were silent. They only spoke to her when they wished to torment her.

Three steps led up to the dais where her mother and the senior Fal'kin stood. Arrayed on the dais in front of them were hundreds of amulets. One would glow as its rightful owner drew near. Brilliant light would shine out in the darkness as the bond between crystal and Fal'kin took place. For her, however, not just one would sing to her soul. They all would.

Mirana staggered again. The boy in front of her whirled around with his defender's reflexes to catch her. The chain mail under his metal armor made a high-pitched shivering sound as he quaked in fear and excitement. He gave her a knowing smile as his nervousness flowed to her mind. He must have assumed she felt the same way. He was right, and so very wrong. Her anxiety had nothing to do with the impending battle at the ford.

It was not supposed to be like this. Joining with an amulet was supposed to be the most fulfilling experience of one's life. Her mother had once described choosing her amulet as a reunion with a part of herself she never knew she had lost. Her father wanted that union so badly, he broke into the gathering hall on the eve of a Choosing Ceremony when he was only fifteen and stole an amulet so he could bond with it three summers sooner than he should have.

The amulets on the dais would not want to bond with her. They would not want to join in holy union with her. They would possess her, devour her whole in their frantic need to fuse to her Trine Aspects. It would not be just one amulet that wailed to her as it would to other Fal'kin. All of them would. She was a Trine. Such was the miraculous and cruel gift of holding three Aspects. Every amulet, chosen or free, was open to her.

A powerful Aspected mind touched hers. Behind the Fal'kin on the dais towered Trine Tetric Garis. His black tunic appeared to absorb what little light surrounded him. The uniform's silver griffin seemed to float in the darkness. The hematite amulet about his neck washed silver and black, a strange inverse of light. He softened his mind's connection to hers, then closed himself from her. His amulet winked out. For a moment, that one less voice, that one less amulet to scrape at her soul, gave her relief. She took a deep breath and nodded to him. He inclined his head.

Outside, lightning flashed and thunder crashed. Mirana flinched as the stained-glass windows rattled in their frames.

Yenira, the seer girl with whom she shared so many of her mother's lessons, ascended the three steps of the dais. The fear of the imminent battle at the ford imprinted on her face washed away into beatified joy as a blue topaz gleamed in her hand. Moments later, an emerald glowed as a boy drew near. He released the white-knuckled grip on his battle seer's long knife and picked up the green gem. His face broke into a glorious smile even before he placed its chain over his head.

A familiar mind, a presence, rose above the rest. It didn't call out to her—it couldn't. She sensed it only because she was so closely attuned to it. Teague.

… Please don't let him die … she begged. *… Not Teague … I will take an amulet and use it to destroy myself if that is what you will for me … But please don't hurt him …*

Mirana wilted, overwhelmed with grief at the possibility of losing Teague. She fell against a cold marble column, clinging to it for support, only to sink to her knees.

Teague hauled her up and pulled her into the shadows of an aisle. "Mirana," he whispered as he held her. "I can't believe you're going through with this."

"I have to. It is my prime's order. These people. Our friends. The ford will be their death sentence." She peered through the dim light to the line of *scholaire'e.* "They are paying for my crimes. Maybe with an amulet, I can begin to make up for all of this." Or maybe she would be the only one punished.

"I should have taken you away when you asked." He pressed his cheek against hers. "I am so sorry. This is all my fault."

"How is any of this your fault? It's all mine. I allowed my fear to convince me I was wrong when I knew I was right. Now, so many of these—they will be killed."

Their blood. On her hands. Now, she understood Tetric Garis's words.

"You shouldn't be doing this yet. I should," he breathed, passion making his voice harsh. "I have the blood of defenders, seers, and healers in my veins. I should be going up to that dais. To take up an amulet to protect you. To keep that Ken'nar Dark Trine bastard away from you."

He was the only thing she wanted to choose, the only one she wanted to join her life to. "You cannot save me from this. No one can." Only the Aspects Above could save her now. Unless she wasn't meant to be saved.

"We're leaving. Now." He pulled her arm.

"No. It's too late for that." She struggled, freeing herself from his grip. "Teague, leave me. Never speak to me again. For your own sake."

Tears shimmered in his eyes, reflected by the candlelight. "Don't push me away. I love you."

"You can't love me. Leave me. Please." She turned once again to the procession.

The youth ahead of her climbed the three stairs.

"Who seeks communion with creation?" Mirana's mother intoned.

"Atan," the boy said. "Atan il'Badif il'Robaar."

"What gift have the Aspects Above bestowed upon thee?"

"The Light to Defend," he responded, his voice breathless with anticipation.

"Then, Defender, step forward and allow the living presence of the light of the Aspects to choose thy crystal as a testament to thy commitment to protect creation."

Off in a far corner, an amethyst glowed with a violet so deep it was hard to see in the darkness. The boy rushed over to it and placed the amulet around his neck with trembling fingers.

All too soon, the dais loomed in front of Mirana. Her mother awaited her, her face stern, Lord Garis and the other Fal'kin behind her. Her father stood on the top-most stair, his expression resolute. His thoughts, however, sparked and flashed with martial precision like bursts of amulet fire. His gaze now darted from her to the amulets to the gathering hall exits, a battlefield defender searching for routes of advancement. For routes of escape? Was he going to drag her bodily from the ceremony?

The amulets. There on the dais. Lying in wait. She had just three steps to wait for a miracle. She began to shake uncontrollably. The unfamiliar weight of her combat boots caught a stair. Her father grasped her arm and steadied her.

… Biraena, it will be all right … I will keep you safe …

"No, you can't. I am in the hands of the Aspects Above," she replied, shunning the intimacy of his mind's voice.

She pushed out of his arms and climbed to the top of the dais. Amulets surrounded her, trapped her. She gasped at the intense pull on her Aspects. They were too close.

"Who—" Her mother paused and pulled her shoulders back, steeling herself. "Who seeks communion with creation?"

… You will be wrapped in my love, biraena, as you were when the Aspects Above granted you life within me …

Mirana's throat constricted. For a moment, she could not make her tongue work. "Mirana il'Kellis il'Pinal." Her jaw moved, but she heard no sound.

Her mother nodded down at her, sending love and encouragement from her mind. "What gift have the Aspects Above bestowed upon thee?"

She simply had to reach for an amulet, a gem that spoke to her and only to her. But, as a Trine, they all spoke to her, needed her. They wanted all she was.

She lifted her head and searched the dark ceiling once more for a deity that empowered her yet left her a captive. ... *I surrender all that I am to you ... Use me as you will ...*

Her mother swallowed back her tears and nodded. ... *Speak, child ... It is time for the secrets to end ...*

Lord Garis came forward and stood close. His mind slipped past her feeble attempts to shut him out. ... *Choose any of these crystals and be at peace ... I will be with you ...*

Her eyes held his, and for a moment, determination replaced fear. "That is for the Aspects Above to decide."

"Step back, Garis," her father hissed.

She lifted her hand, stopping her father from further protests. "Enough." She raised her eyes to her mother's. "The Aspects Above have granted—" She fought for breath, but this time, it would not come. Everything, the people's minds, the amulets, her parents' deep concern, their pride—it was too much. "They have—"

Lord Garis turned to face the assembly. "The Aspects Above have granted all three gifts on their servant—the Light to See, the Light to Defend, and the Light to Heal. The Aspects Above have called Mirana il'Kellis il'Pinal as their Trine."

... *You bastard!* ... Her father's mind-voice turned venomous.

Shouts rose from the throng behind her. Questions and shock she could not deflect assaulted her mind.

"Then, Trine, step forward and allow the living presence of the Light of the Aspects to choose thy crystal as a testament to thy commitment to protect creation." Her mother's words rang in her ears.

Mirana knelt to grasp a red beryl encased in gold lying at her feet. It began to glow, a soft dawn-pink hue in the center, deepening at its edges to the color of blood. Her fingertips touched the gem and accidentally brushed a blue sapphire near it. The beryl gleamed, as did the sapphire. She hesitated. Touching her foot, an emerald set in silver brightened. When she pushed it from her, she set an adjacent amethyst aglow once the emerald came in contact with the purple gem. She drew her hand away as if stung. The harmonics of the scarlet beryl crystal clashed with her life's rhythms, pulling her into itself, drawing the Aspects from her. She couldn't breathe. The room swirled, and the floor heaved upward.

Jasal's Keep. Thunder crashes. She collapses on her hands and knees. Sleet beats down, biting at the back of her neck. Agony from her abdomen pulses with each heartbeat. Blood from the mortal wound rushes thick and hot over her hand. It drips into a grout line in the paving, rain diluting its thickness in the water. She has failed.

White light explodes.

"I'm getting her out of here before she is overcome." Her father reached down, snatched up the beryl, and began to place its chain over her head.

"No!" She shoved away her father's hand and the amulet he held. She stepped back from her parents and Lord Garis. "I will not let this happen. Forgive me."

Mirana flew down the three steps, out of the gathering hall, and into the storm-lashed night.

CHAPTER 15

*"But to harken unto Their Will requires a decision I
am loath to make."*

—The Codex of Jasal the Great

Mirana ran through the corridors of the learning hall, as
empty and unforgiving as a tomb. She sped across the rain-
drenched courtyard and stopped when she reached the hall's
library. Catching her breath, she laid her palms and forehead
against the great oak doors. She pulled her mind inward,
dissolving her presence into the life around her. She did not
want to be found. Ever.

The Aspects Above had shunned her. No saving grace had
come from on high, no absolution was granted, no expiation

given for the sins she had committed, nor the ones that awaited her. No hope remained, only one last choice.

She pulled back on the iron rings and went through the doors. The smell of dust and age filled her nostrils. Thunder crashed, and she cringed instinctively at the deafening crack. Lightning lashed at the tall stained-glass windows, illuminating in violent bursts the harsh colors of their facets. The intermittent light put the ceiling corbels in stark relief as they hid high up in barrel and groin vaults. The oil lamps flickered in meek imitation of the lightning outside.

She hurried deep into the sepulchral library. Thousands of volumes, parchments, linen scrolls, and preserved hides mouldered away on the shelving, corpses stacked within catacombs of knowledge, as useless and dead to her as cadavers. A few leather-bound books around the cavernous room stood tethered to stands by chains, prisoners of false wisdom. As was she.

Long tables sat before the shelves, great, dark planes of wood like so many altars ready for a sacrifice. Carved under one of those tables were her and Teague's names. He had cut their glyphs into the wood with his belt knife after she had kissed him for the first time. They were fourteen. She would never taste his kiss again.

"Teague."

Mirana sank against a heavy wooden chair. All of those memories of their primary lessons together in this place, all those dreams, that first timid kiss—they were lies. They were denials of a self she believed herself to be, only to be destroyed by the person she would become.

She crossed her arms on the leather seat and buried her face in them. Caresses touched her mind, insidious in their insistence, sickening in their supplication. She lifted her head, blinking through rain- and sweat-matted hair. Amulets. Statues of Fal'kin, most of whose names were lost to time, stood in niches and alcoves around the library. Amulets hung from their cold, stone necks and whispered to her now.

She bit back another cry, her chest constricting with the effort. She could choose every one of them. All she had to do was hold one and let it into her being. When she did, though, it would taunt her with its gleaming, a sign of the power she held but could not find a way to safely use.

She sat up and leaned against a statue plinth. She let her head fall back. Jasal Pinal's carved likeness stood over her, his chest devoid of an amulet. Once, the sculpture had been whole, but for as long as she could remember, great chunks of marble had been missing, leaving little more than a torso, chipped arms, and half a face. Scorch marks blemished the pure white marble. She traced the deep grooves and scratches marring the black onyx pedestal.

Before the statue on a stand sat an unadorned leather-covered book secured by a chain and locked by a simple metal clasp.

"The Codex of Jasal Pinal," she whispered.

She had read the journal many times. It once was a mischievous pleasure, browsing it with Teague because it was banned from their primary lessons. Later, she studied it, pored through its pages, scrutinized every quill stroke, hoping to find the answers to control her Trine Aspects. Filled with his teachings of the Fal'kin way, his love for his Tash-Hamari wife, Antiri, the book also told of the battles he fought against Ilrik the Black and other Ken'nar warlords, and the walls and gates he built to keep Deren safe. Of his keep, however, she had found almost nothing written. The last entries of his journal ended just before the completion of the watchtower. Fear, angst, and emotions far darker lived within his words but no answers.

Mirana pushed herself to her feet. As she had done so many times before, she laid her hand on the lock. She reached out to the mechanism with her mind, and the clasp released with an audible click. She gently opened the cover and turned back several blank pages of vellum to Jasal's first entry.

"'What mysterious things are the Aspects Above to choose me as their servant,'" she read aloud, her voice shaking. "'For I can see no talent, no strength real or designed by artifice, no skill in my life that separates me from any other man or woman.'"

And yet, they have chosen me their Trine.

She knew the words by heart. Jasal's quill strokes were bold, but the sense behind the words was not. The Codex of Jasal Pinal the Great was not a book she merely read, she lived it. Imbued within its pages was the reflection of her ancestor's presence, echoes of his thoughts and emotions as he wrote the passages. He spoke to her in his pages. Sometimes, she wished he did not.

He had been all but consumed by grief in his last writings. It was there, embedded in his words. Then, at the end of his Codex, his trapped, agonized emotions abruptly disappeared from the pages. No room remained for misinterpretation.

Jasal Pinal had committed suicide.

Wind-driven rain battered the windows, followed by a low rumble of thunder. Mirana shivered in a draft, her clothes and skin damp from the storm and sweat. The sword in the statue's broken and scarred hands gleamed in the lightning. The mighty blade which defeated the Dark Triumvirate: the Ken'nar defender Ilrik the Black, and the Ken'nar seer and the Ken'nar healer who both fought alongside him. The three had once stood, battling as one, as an evil counterpoint to Jasal's Trine Aspects. Thrice-cursed. Thrice-blessed.

Why would the Aspects Above even call forth someone cursed? It made no sense—unless they were so disgusted with their creation tearing itself apart for more than three thousand summers, they wanted to wipe the land clean of the stain of their Aspected people. Maybe the thrice-cursed would purge all of creation for the Aspects Above. Maybe the deity was just as ignorant and uncaring as the ocean she once believed would be her escape. Maybe there simply were no Aspects Above at all. Maybe Lord Garis was right, and prophecies were just meaningless words written by senile old men and women. Or maybe all the evil in Kinderra had been brought about, not by divine vengeance, but by the choices of men. Or of a girl.

Mirana hid her face in her hands. "Why did the Aspects Above choose you as their Trine, only to have you die in failure? What sense is there in that?"

Were the Trine powers too terrible for him to bear? To control? Was ending his own life the only answer to his grief and self-loathing? Why had the Aspects Above brought him to that?

No. Jasal's failure was not the fault of the Aspects Above. His failure was his own. As was hers. Jasal Pinal was right. This time, answers would be found in something other than books. She slid her back down the pedestal to sit heavily on the floor once more.

Mirana pulled one of the long knives from a scabbard at her waist, the soft, sinister song of its unsheathing reverberating up her arm and across her chest. The blade, the length of two hands, gleamed dully in the torchlight. No ornamentation decorated its steel. It was strictly utilitarian, forged for but one purpose.

She pressed the knife's edge against the hollow of her throat, the steel cold on her skin. She could not find a way to use her Aspects without destroying Kinderra, so she would make certain they were never released.

The library doors banged open against the stone walls.

"Stop! What do you think you're doing?" a voice rang through the vast building and her mind.

Tetric Garis rushed past the endless shelves and somber statues, frighteningly agile for a man of his size. Once he reached her, he fell to his knees and tried to pull the knife from her hand.

She struggled in his grip. "Leave me alone!"

"We have no time for these adolescent melodramatics." He wrestled with her for the blade. "Kinderra is too important. You are too important."

She refused to release the long knife. "Let me go."

He dug his thumb into the sinews of her wrist, and the blade fell from her grip. "I know what else it was you saw when we viewed the ford vision together. The images you tried to hide from me." … *You saw Jasal's Keep erupt in light* …

"If you saw it, then you know why this has to be." She fought him again, grappling for the long knife.

"You will end this nonsense now!" The Trine wrapped his long fingers around her arms, holding her fast. "We must understand the power we both saw unleashed by Jasal's Keep."

"What is there to understand? Because of me, our *scholaire'e* will have to fight at Two Rivers Ford and so many may die. Our troops. They will be decimated because of me."

He shook his head. "You had no way to know exactly what it was you were seeing in the first vision of Two Rivers Ford."

She tried once again to pull away from his grip, but his hands were like iron bonds. "You're wrong. I knew exactly what

I saw, what I sensed. I just didn't want to believe it. I must pay for my crime."

He released her and sat back on his heels. "Being frightened of one's powers is not a crime."

"Withholding the information I saw is." His hematite amulet hung too close to her. Could she choose it? Right off his neck? Fire it on herself? "Lord Garis, I didn't want to believe what I sensed. I lied to myself. I allowed myself to believe I was wrong when I knew, deep inside, I was right. Because of my fear and my cowardice, I didn't tell my parents of the first ford vision until it was too late. If anyone knew I was a Trine, they would have demanded I choose an amulet immediately. I was trying to save lives by keeping silent. I swear it."

She deflated against the base of Jasal's statue, her eyes on Lord Garis's amulet. "If you've seen Jasal's Keep exploding in light, then you know why I cannot choose an amulet. Stop me now before I truly become the Dark Trine. The only way I can save lives now is with my death."

He shook his head slowly. "You are not the Dark Trine."

"But the keep—"

"We don't know what the keep is." Lord Garis gestured toward a window and the watchtower looming outside. "*Ai,* there will be losses at the ford—that is unavoidable regardless of any vision—but if we can find out exactly what Jasal's Keep is, you won't have condemned Kinderra. In the end, you will have saved her."

A bead of grief-wrought sweat trailed down her temple and followed the curve of her jaw to her neck. Its salt stung the cut at the hollow of her throat. "You're wrong, my lord. Everything is falling apart because of me. You are the Light Trine. It is your duty to save Kinderra from me. Kill me!"

… Mirana— …

… Kill! … Me! …

He grabbed her arms again and pierced through the protective psychic walls she had raised. … *STOP!* … She gasped as his mind stormed through hers. "I need your help as much as you need mine," he said. "That is why I am here. I told you, I, too, saw the keep and the unimaginable power it contains. That was no nightmarish memory of yours. It was a vision. Your Aspects and mine were together at that moment. It was my vision, too. That keep could end this conflict that has plagued us for three thousand summers. We must understand what all of this means. But, to do that, I need your help."

"I can't possibly help you. Or Kinderra. Please, just go. Just. Go." She buried her face in her hands.

"Mirana, look at me." He gently pulled her hands down from her face. "Mirana."

She searched his face, his eyes like windows to the midnight sky.

"The Aspects Above have given both of us this keep vision for a reason. Your ancestor built the watchtower. You must be a key to understanding its power. I am here to help you unlock those secrets. As Trines, we are bound by the same fate to save Kinderra from destroying herself. Only together can we do this. I need you. Kinderra needs you. You need me, too. Do you understand…" he pointed to the knife, "*that* is not the path for you?"

She would never lie to herself again. She knew she was at the center of all the rage, the pain, the crushing failure, and the suffocating sense that thousands had perished.

She was so tired. So very tired of trying to find answers where there were none. She wanted it to be over. All of it. She stared at the long knife on the floor at her feet. "For summers,

I've searched for a way to prevent myself from becoming the Dark Trine."

He scowled, more from pity than from confusion. "Do you truly believe that is what you are?"

What else could she be? "*Ai*. Someday."

He hung his head for a moment and exhaled. "The Trine powers are blessed and terrible gifts. I know. Since I was a small boy, I, too, have seen unspeakable destruction from my own hands in events that had yet to take place. I can show you how even such a horror as that can be a gift. I can show how it can be used for knowledge, to find a way to stop even more violence. Or why it is necessary to let such damning actions continue for the greater good."

When she didn't respond, he frowned. He picked up the knife and set it on the table next to where he knelt. He took her hand and placed her palm on his chest over his heart. "What do you feel?" Her hand trembled beneath his. She did not want to reach out with her Healing gift. She wanted to destroy it.

"Mirana. Reach out to me with your Aspects and tell me what you feel."

She took a breath. "Your heartbeat. Your life."

He nodded. "*Ai*. Every heartbeat, every life, every single one feels like this. Every life note in Kinderra, just like this one, will be extinguished in this bloody civil war unless we stop it. Unless we can understand the power of Jasal's Keep and use it to save this land, all of this," he patted her hand over his heart, "will be gone. Do you understand?"

No. No, she did not understand. How could the salvation of everyone and everything she loved come from her when all she saw was destruction at her hand?

"The Aspects Above confer their gifts upon us, but it is we mortals who make the decision how to use them. You will not destroy anything unless you decide to do so."

She began to shake again. "I am frightened."

"I know you are." He took her other hand and now held them both in each of his. "But I will help you. You no longer have to bear these burdens alone. Not your fear. Not your Trine Aspects. Not the keep. We shall bear them together, and we shall find a way to save Kinderra. Together."

She could not speak, overcome by the possibility of a fate beyond destruction and death. Her heart banged in her chest. Tetric Garis said she was the key to understanding the keep. Was his belief in her worth risking Kinderra? Risking Teague?

Lord Garis's amulet glowed softly. It appeared to breathe in ebbs and pulses with a life-light of its own.

"Do you mean it?" she whispered, terrified to believe him.

He gripped her hands tighter, so she could not deny his conviction. … *Fear can make us do terrible things … And, ai, you made a terrible choice to lie to yourself … But your heart was pure … You meant to try and save Kinderra, even by withholding knowledge, even by lying to yourself … Those are not the actions of an evil one … Those are the choices of a Trine …* "If there's even the slightest chance the power in the keep will stop this war, we must find out how. Is that not worth living for?"

The Trine Prophecy came back to her once more. Was Tetric Garis the "hope that remained"? For her?

She drilled her gaze into his eyes. "Swear to me you won't let me destroy Kinderra."

"*Ai*, I swear it. With all my Aspects."

She rose and stepped over to the Codex. A link opened, and the chain fell away. She clutched the tome to her. "Then let us save Kinderra."

She and the Trine both turned at the sound of rushing footsteps.

"Mirana!" her father cried, her mother running just behind him. They rushed over and drew her into their arms.

Her mother kissed Mirana's forehead. "Thank the Aspects."

"Is she all right?" her father asked Lord Garis.

"I will be," Mirana answered for the Trine.

He retrieved the long knife from the table and held it out to her, his face set like flint.

"I will make this right. All of it. Somehow. I promise."

She sheathed the weapon with a determined thrust of her hand.

CHAPTER 16

*"A spent blade must be sharpened, or its metal used for
a new purpose."*

—The Book of Kinderra

Kaarl stood by the window in the prime's chambers. Dawn
cut a faintly brighter swath of sky on the eastern horizon than
the darkness above it. Below, in the courtyard, Desde gave
preliminary orders to the provincial troops. She still wore her
light armor and chain mail from the previous evening's
Choosing Ceremony. It glinted in the torchlight as she movved.
In another corner, Morgan Jord spoke with a small group of
white-uniformed men and women, the defenders of the il'Kin.
Yesterday, they had been Kaarl's to lead. Yesterday, he served

as a defender commander. Now, he was Steward of the Quorum of Light.

The role of the Quorum's steward was full of contradictions, and he hated them all. The Quorum itself comprised all of Kinderra's primes and seconds, and decided policies affecting the entire continent's Fal'kin. Its steward, however, was both the most and least powerful person in Kinderra, as far as he was concerned. *Ai*, he would serve as a proxy voter for absent provincial representatives, and he would also break a deadlock by casting a decisive vote in the rare instance it might occur. That was all well and good.

The steward, however, had no true vote in Quorum proceedings, giving up the needs of his or her province for the greater good of Kinderra. He would continue to direct the il'Kin strike force, but now as a noncombatant tactician, not as a battlefield commander.

He looked at his hands. The cuts and scrapes from the grynwen had healed. While he didn't bring down every Ken'nar he fought against, more times than not, he left them corpses if they dared confront him. Sometimes he did not even leave that much. With no vote of his own, how would he be able to keep Kin-Deren province safe, let alone the rest of Kinderra?

He caught his reflection in the glass of the window, the gray just beginning to silver his black hair, the silver eyes of his infamous ancestor staring back. The Quorum members would never let him remain steward on principle. It stood too close to Jasal Pinal's dictatorial status as Primus Magne, the sole governing leader over all of Kinderra's Fal'kin. The whole of the Fal'kinnen would never make that mistake again.

At some point, his transgressions would be found out. When they were, he could lose far more than just his role as steward. The Quorum could expel him from Kin-Deren province. He touched the garnet resting against his chest. He'd be lucky if his expulsion was the only sentence handed down. His amulet could be removed from him. He'd no longer be a Fal'kin, or even a defender. He'd be nothing. He let his hand fall.

The choice was obvious. When the Quorum convened in the autumn, its members would award the permanent steward's seat to Tetric Garis. As a Trine, Tetric already gave his Aspects in service to all of Kinderra. As steward, the il'Kin would be his to command. In one brilliant move, all that Kaarl had spent his lifetime building, serving, and bleeding for would be gone. Nothing would stop the man from enfolding the il'Kin's fighters into his Dar-Azûlan provincial ranks and effectively dissolving the strike force.

If Kaarl wished to remain as the leader of the elite unit, he would have to swear allegiance to Tetric Garis. Or he would have to step down from the il'Kin's ranks. He had no choice but to accept the mantle of stewardship, and maybe even fight to keep it. That was the contradiction he hated the most—to save the il'Kin, he had to leave it.

Kaarl held his sword. He hefted its familiar weight, noting again its exquisite balance. It was a fine instrument, forged true of hard Tash-Hamari steel. The cross guard of its hilt was crafted with two eagle's heads, the heraldic of Kin-Deren province. Pits and scratches etched the entire length of the blade, every mark delivered by a Ken'nar weapon. The grain of the leather wrapping the scabbard was worn smooth. The thin bands of silver once crisscrossing the sheath had since broken and were missing in places.

Toban had the sword made for him when he passed thirteen summers. It had been a bit too long, a bit too heavy for him then. He had taken it as a compliment that the old seer believed he had enough skill to master it. It had saved his life and the lives of those he protected more times than he could count.

"I know nothing of the way one must mince words just to gain sentences. This is insanity. I am a defender, Toban. A fighter, a warrior. Not a politician." He shook his head. What would Toban have said if he had called the old man such?

Why in the name of the Aspects Above had Toban Kellis named him his successor?

Privately, he knew the real reason, one he had not wanted to admit to himself. The seer prime knew Kaarl had all but lost the will to fight. Had Desde spoken to her father? After thirty summers of bloodshed, he was nearly beaten inside. The deaths of so many of the il'Kin over the recent summers had allowed hopelessness to creep into his heart. The old seer knew—with his Aspect, maybe he was even certain—Kaarl's next major campaign could be his last.

He placed the blade on the desk. For as long as he had known Desde's father, the seer had sat behind its ornately carved wood. He touched the surface, the dark walnut smooth with wax and use. There, on the front panel, was the chip in the wood from the heel of his boot when Toban had sat him on the desk's top to tell him his father had been killed. On the back leg of the chair, just below the mortise-and-tenon joint, was the nick where he'd flailed with his sword, showing off for the prime. On the far corner was the tiny groove he had made with his fingernail as he stood asking to be joined in union with Desde.

Kaarl had given command of the il'Kin to Morgan, his defender second, elevating him to defender commander. It was time. Perhaps a younger man with a fresh perspective could pull the elite troop back from the brink of extinction. Toban had probably felt the same about giving him the chair of stewardship.

He smiled. "You were always one step ahead of everyone, weren't you?" He hung his head. How could he even hope to fill the void left by that great man?

He could not. He would not even try. He would have to find his own path. He had wondered not all that long ago how one could avoid one's destiny. His wife, always so perceptive of his mind, told him he couldn't, but he could choose how to face it. Toban would not have named him to the post had he not been a capable man, even to save his life. He would strive to honor the man he loved as much as his own father, but he would not imitate him.

A knock interrupted his thoughts.

"I have come—" Tetric Garis began.

"I know why you are here."

Kaarl remained facing the window, away from the other man. As the Trine crossed the room, his heavy boots echoed unusually loud in the chamber, breaking the early morning's stillness.

"You're coming to the ford?" he asked, hefting Kaarl's sword. "I thought Defender Jord would be leading—"

"After Mirana's revelation, we have no idea what to expect now. We may need every defender we have," Kaarl replied, watching him from the corner of his eye. "I will be deliriously happy if my time is wasted. I intend to strategize a defense with Desde and lend my amulet to the battle seer's defense group, if it comes to that."

Tetric set the sword down on the desk, nodding with approval. "Or act as Mirana's bodyguard."

Kaarl turned to face him at last and frowned.

"She will be safe with me. It is for the best."

"Apparently, my wife agrees with you."

The Trine drew next to him to look through the window down at the courtyard. "Despite the law, even I don't think Desde would truly consider expelling Mirana."

He looked at Tetric in alarm. "Expulsion? What are you talking about? Mirana was traumatized by some damn nightmare she believes has her bringing about the end of time. That is why she left the Choosing Ceremony. Being terrified is not a crime."

The other man's gaze remained fixed on the courtyard below. "No. But refusing to choose an amulet is. A capital crime your daughter committed most publicly. To say nothing of possibly withholding information. The sentence for refusing an amulet is expulsion from the province, to be killed on sight if she ever steps foot back within Kin-Deren's borders." He lifted his face to take in Jasal's Keep.

Kaarl could not think of a single word that would adequately express his hatred of Tetric Garis at that moment.

"I doubt it will come to all that," the Trine said. "Mirana's situation is complicated. She is under the age of majority, although Desde's pronouncement elevating those fifteen and older to Fal'kin does call that into question. And she is now known to be a Trine." He turned to Kaarl. "I convinced Desde that your daughter's case should be heard by the Quorum when we meet in the autumn. There is no way your wife, even as a prime, could be impartial in such a situation. Furthermore, we Trines are dedicated to all provinces, so that makes provincial expulsion impractical, if not impossible."

Kaarl's eyes widened in disbelief. "We are about to march into war. We don't know if we will have an assured victory or a massacre. You dare speak of my daughter's expulsion and possible execution at a time like this?"

"I told you, she will be safe with me." Tetric raised his palms in apology. "Only I can make Mirana what she must become. You know this."

"What she must become?" he asked, desperation edging his words. "Aspects Above, man, we're dragging her to the ford. The Dark Trine will most certainly be there. He stands to lose too much by not being present."

"Or gain."

Kaarl curled his hands into fists, as much to keep them still as to answer the desire to use them. "If she goes to the ford, that black-hearted Ken'nar bastard will kill her."

"Desde has given her to me as my *scholaira*. I will complete her training. She will remain with me until she does choose an amulet." The Trine placed a hand on his shoulder. "No harm will come to her. I will guard her as if she were my own child."

"You decided my own child's future without me?" He looked down at the man's hand. His gaze slid back to the Trine, who prudently stepped back from his gesture. "Alone? With my wife?" His voice dropped to a menacing growl.

The tall Dar-Azûlan now held his ground, his eyes like shards of black ice. "So you could watch over her while she slept for a few hours. Your wife is prime of Kin-Deren province. She need not consult with anyone regarding her Fal'kin. Even you."

The tension in his fists spread up his arms and across his chest to settle within his vermilion garnet amulet. "You've all but taken my il'Kin from me. Now, you take my only child as well?"

Tetric made no move. "She tried to kill herself."

Kaarl froze. "Wh-What?"

"I barely had time to save her life."

"She-She didn't say a word." That hairline cut at the hollow of her throat. It hadn't been a buckle scratch from her armor.

"She just fell asleep in my arms. Holding that accursed book of Jasal's to her like the ragdoll she had when she was a babe. I just thought she was exhausted from the ceremony. I knew the amulets were overpowering her. That's why I grabbed the nearest one I could reach. I just wanted her to take the damned thing and leave before they drove her into a faint. She didn't say a word. Not one word."

A moist, burning sensation seared Kaarl's eyes. Something wet traveled down his cheek. ... *Oh, Miri ... What have I done? ...*

He hitched up his shoulder to wipe the dampness away from his face. "Do you believe—" He swallowed his emotions back under control. "Do you believe this nightmare of hers? Is it truly a vision?"

Tetric shrugged and sighed. "I have seen something of it. It is alarming, but I don't understand it. Yet."

"Does Desde know? What happened?" he asked.

The Trine shook his head.

"I'd like to keep this between us."

"Ëo comprende."

Kaarl and the Trine both stood silent for a long moment, observing the Fal'kin below out the window.

"The summers have not touched Desde," the Dar-Azûlan said at last.

He watched his wife in the courtyard. A smile briefly touched his face. Tetric was right. Desde was still a strikingly beautiful woman. He, however, felt older than Toban at the moment. "I know where all those summers went." His smile faded.

Was that what he had done to Mirana? Driven her to try to take her own life?

Tetric nodded. "I think we share some of those lost summers." He turned back to him. "I do not intend for your daughter to stay at the ford any more than you do. I also understand Desde's moral and, frankly, legal dilemma. As the prime, she cannot hold back her child while sending others' children to the ford when she has made such an order. But with Mirana as a Trine, I'm not sure it's worth the risk to have the girl at the front even in a support role."

He wanted to feel relieved. Shock, however, still held his emotions captive. "With Mirana as your *scholaira*, Desde's effectively taking her out from under her orders." His wife was just as cagey as her father. That did give him some relief.

The Trine smirked. "We are all painfully aware Mirana does not have an amulet. When was the last time she held a blade, anyway?"

Kaarl whipped his head to face him.

The tall man squeezed his eyes shut in a wince at his poor choice of words. "She may have to ride with us to the ford, but I will not have her stay."

Was she still in her room?

"What if the Dark Trine reaches the ford ahead of us? My daughter will be trapped." No, she would be in the stables by now, readying Ashtar for the ride. He'd told her to take his warhorse. She loved the beast. Ashtar would be as much a bodyguard as he would be. He'd find another horse to ride.

"I will see to it she makes it out," Tetric said resolutely. "It is best I do not tell you further about our plans. The fewer people who know of her whereabouts, the safer she is."

Kaarl dipped his chin in acquiescence. He laid his hand on the crosshatched glass of the window. In front of the great oak door of Jasal's Keep, Desde addressed the battle seer unit. Its ranks now swelled with the addition of newly elevated Fal'kin.

Jasal's Keep had protected Deren all those long summers ago, but it could do nothing now to keep his daughter safe. For that, he had no other choice than to release his beloved tiny girl from his protection to that of a man he hated as much as he respected.

"I did not come to discuss Mirana. I have come to ask you again to reconsider my offer."

"Tetric, please. Not now."

"We may not get another chance to discuss this. Let us combine our forces. You will be my defender commander. There will be none before you. If we work together, you and I, we could turn the tide of this war."

He shook his head. "Morgan rides at the head of the il'Kin now, not I."

"He is a good defender, but he is not you," Tetric replied. "The Ken'nar are growing. Their army is expanding. They are far better trained and better coordinated than ever before, more than most of the primes realize. I know it and you know it."

Kaarl frowned and nodded.

"We know because we have not just sat in halls watching visions and discussing hypotheticals," the Trine continued. "The blood of our defenders, our own blood, has been shed for Kinderra." He paused, his dark gaze boring into Kaarl. "It is time for this to end. I mean to stop this war, but I cannot without your help."

His first thought was for Mirana's safety. If the man had some insane vendetta against the Dark Trine, she could be killed at his side just as surely as at Two Rivers Ford.

When he did not reply, the Trine gestured with his chin to the keep looming in the blue dawn light. "What made Jasal Pinal so great?"

He scowled, confused. "Most do not share your opinion."

"He bore the title of 'Jasal the Great' for summers before he built that tower."

"He was a Trine. He saved Kinderra by stopping the Dark Triumvirate. He was a good man. A great man. Before that." He, too, gestured to the tower.

"*Ai*," Tetric nodded, "*ai*, he was all those things. However, his true power lay within the Aspected who served under him. Without them, his greatness would have amounted to next to nothing. They gave Kinderra the first glimpse of peace she had seen since before the Sundering."

"I understand what you are saying, but too much has passed between us. If you had only asked three summers ago instead of two."

"I did ask three summers ago, and every summer before and after that skirmish."

It was no skirmish. The memory of the fight had remained like an open wound in Kaarl's mind. The Ken'nar had surged across Thyre's Crossing on the border between Kana-Akün and Trak-Calan, a direction they had least expected. He and the il'Kin had set out to meet them, their forces augmented by some one hundred fighters from Kana-Akün and another hundred from Tash-Hamar. Tetric's advice, from his very Seeing Aspect, gave them time to form up, but no one expected the Ken'nar to come down in such numbers. Fifteen hundred of them. They had never before appeared in such numbers, usually striking unsuspecting farms and hamlets with mere hundreds, if that. The Trine had held back his forces to cut off any escape the Ken'nar could make back over the crossing. His presence had sent the Ken'nar into a panic. After a brief fight with five hundred of Tetric's Dar-Azûlan troops, the black-armored bastards broke ranks and made for the Trak-Calan highlands to the north, forcing their mounts to swim the Bherath River. The damage had been done, however. Fifteen il'Kin never breathed again, nor dozens of archers from Kana-Akün. Tash-Hamar took the brunt, with more than half of its defenders cut down.

Kaarl gave a small, hopeless laugh. "If we do our jobs at the ford, we might not even need to unite our forces."

"That is just the beginning," Tetric replied. "It will take more than that to save Kinderra. I mean for all of us to unite. It was the only way Jasal could truly stop Ilrik the Black. It is the only way to end the war now."

For the second time in as many moments, disbelief held Kaarl. One prime. Over all the provinces. "Primus Magne?" He could barely utter the words. "You can't be serious."

"We have no other choice." The Trine lifted his head, gazing back out the window. "I have no other choice."

He shook his head, aghast. "I couldn't possibly support you. I couldn't support anyone. Not even Toban." He shook his head again. "I'm not sure I could even support Desde if she asked me. We'd find another way."

The Dar-Azûlan stepped closer. "You would put our disagreements ahead of Kinderra? Ahead of your daughter?"

Kaarl gripped the other man's arm. "I love Mirana more than life itself."

"I know you do." The Trine returned the gesture. ... *She will never be safe until this war ends ... I need you ... I need you by my side ... As I said before, the Quorum will listen to you ... Desde will listen to you ... I saved your daughter's life ... Help me now give her a future ...*

He let his arm fall. "Tetric. Primus Magne?"

... I am Trine of Kinderra ... I already safeguard all the provinces ... Becoming Primus Magne merely formalizes it within the Quorum of Light ... I am only asking for your trust ... Is that so difficult? ...

Kaarl stepped back from him and walked over to Desde's primeship chair. He leaned on it, hanging his head. "It is not a matter of trust. There is nothing the Dark Trine could ever do that would make me believe elevating a Primus Magne and throwing away our Aspect-given right to govern ourselves was the answer. Regardless of our struggles, I have never once doubted your conviction to protect Kinderra." He raised his head. "*Ai*, as a Trine, you do give your life in service to all of Kinderra. But I am steward now. It is my duty as well to intercede on behalf of all Fal'kin in interprovincial conflicts. You asked me to work together with you to end this war. That I will agree to." He called to his sword, and it flew into his hand. He slid it into its sheath with a decisive snap. "As equals."

Tetric held his gaze a moment, nodded, and turned to leave.

The man had saved his daughter's life, and all he had asked for in return was trust. Tetric didn't want his trust, though, not really. He wanted his fealty, he wanted to take away his free will to act on his own terms when necessary. Kaarl's lips tightened. How could he keep his daughter safe if he were a glorified slave?

Tetric had made a unilateral decision that cost the lives of his il'Kin and so many more, despite the eventual victory it gave the Fal'kin. The man also saved his daughter's life. He would never count the Trine as a friend, but he owed him as much gratefulness as contempt. "I know it's not what you want, but my partnership is all I can give you." ... *That, and my undying gratitude* ...

The Trine hesitated by the door but did not turn around. "It is a brutal, depraved business, this war. Men and women do things that would be considered the most heinous of crimes in any other context. I have. You have. Things I hope Mirana never has to do." He opened the door. ... *Do not make yourself my enemy, Kaarl Pinal ... I beg of you* ...

CHAPTER 17

*"Like a storm gathering on the horizon, the Dark
Ones advanced. Our swords were sharpened. Our
arrows were nocked. But were we ready for battle?"*
                                    —The Book of Kinderra

The Ain Magne charged his stallion through the rain
toward Two Rivers Ford. He ignored the minds of the
thousands of riders who surrounded him, allowing instead the
images of the bridge complex to fill his mind. Great spans
stretched over the Garnath and Anarath Rivers. They would
serve as the swiftest way to move a massive fighting force from
the north into Kin-Deren province and farther south. Once he
controlled the bridges, he would make up any time lost at
Falantir. He would then descend on Deren like a maelstrom
borne of the Aspects Above themselves.

Another image, however, continued to nudge at his consciousness despite his attempt to focus on the upcoming battle. Mirana Pinal.

Her ability to find a single hidden mind had made him change his initial plan of attack on the ford to prevent the discovery of his tactics. His Sight now told him, however, his Ken'nar would take heavy losses because Kin-Deren province rode with many more Fal'kin to the ford instead of the few hundred he originally anticipated.

He gritted his teeth. The reason for the change in their response to his impending attack was obvious: Mirana had seen his plans with her Aspects, correctly interpreted the changes in the skeins of time, and warned Kin-Deren's leadership.

He had been right to be wary of her interpretation skills, but he hadn't been wary enough. Now, instead of the glorified skirmish he had been expecting, it would be a long, protracted, bloody battle. The jarring from each hoof strike of his mount clamped his jaws tighter.

He wrapped his presence with a thicker blanket of life-force reflections. Those around him were so intent on staying upright in the mud as they rode, to say nothing of the battle ahead, they would not feel the draw from themselves.

If Mirana forced his hand to change the skeins of time once, he would change them yet again. He still had the element of surprise in his favor, and he intended to use it to the fullest.

What if she gleaned this knowledge from the Aspects, too?

The Ain Magne gripped his reins as tightly as he clenched his teeth. His second wanted the Pinal girl dead. He reconsidered the idea once more.

No. She must remain alive. His Aspects had shown him the incomprehensible power of Jasal's Keep, and she somehow played a role in unlocking its mysteries.

If her oh-so-skilled interpretations were compelling enough to call an entire province to war, he more than needed her alive. He needed to control her, an amulet in human form. He needed to control her to control Jasal's Keep. He needed her as much as the ford. Maybe even more.

Mirana did not know him yet, but she would. By the time he was ready to reveal himself to her, she would understand the true gift of the Aspects Above. She would come to understand the Power from Without.

The Ain Magne eased the tension in his body and gave his horse free rein over the sodden ground. The beast was sure-footed, and he held no fear of falling in the treacherous mud.

He grasped his amulet, savoring the way the crystal's facets slid against his palm, its heat warming his hand.

… Hear me, my second …

… Ëo hac … his seer second returned.

… What is your location? …

… Two days from the ford, my lord …

He gripped his amulet tighter at his lieutenant's answer. His forces would arrive too late at that pace for this next phase.

… What are your orders, Great One? …

… Prepare for a much larger force …

… How much larger? … his second asked, unease edging his mind-words.

… Some two thousand Fal'kin now ride to the ford …

… Although our fight will be more difficult, my lord, our victory is still at hand … I have seen this can only help our ultimate cause … his seer second returned.

The Ain Magne raised an eyebrow. *… How so? …*

… My lord's own prescience held the answer … The Fal'kin were indeed more inclined to take this new bait … Kin-Deren will now be

emptied of her Fal'kin … Her provincial troops will be squandered at the ford … The citadel itself will lie all but defenseless …

The Ain Magne smiled. The boy was good. The boy was very good.

… You are correct, my second … Well done … We still have much to overcome, however … All must be ready by the time I reach the ford …

He called several images in rapid succession to the young seer's mind. His lieutenant grew silent. The Ain Magne waited for a response and wondered if his servant had dropped the connection to his mind.

He began to strengthen his hold on his second's mind when the seer returned … *I am not certain we can accomplish your orders in time …*

… You must if we are to gain the ford … I have every faith in you … His words were kind, as he meant them to be, but they also contained a note of warning. His second's mind lingered within his own. … *What is it? …*

… The girl rides to the ford … There is a danger with her there … I have seen this … She is a danger to our plans … A danger to you … The vision of Jasal's Keep preys on my mind and my Sight … She should be eliminated …

… I will deal with her myself … I have told you before, she is not your concern …

… We outnumber the Fal'kin excra and yet you have changed our battle plans because of her, now a second time … You would not think twice to kill one of your own if he or she interfered with your strategy this way, and yet you allow her to live … Kill her, my lord …

His servant was correct. However, the young seer, for all his skill, still did not understand what was at stake.

… You will give me Two Rivers Ford … Mirana Pinal will give me Kinderra …

… Am I not the one who rides at your vanguard? … Has not my blood been spilled on your behalf? … I owe all I am to you, but it is I who will lay Kinderra before you …

This was an interesting—and unexpected—development. His seer second had begun to view the girl as a rival. This development was as dangerous as it was beneficial. Dangerous, because such jealousies could become destructive. Beneficial, because those destructive jealousies could be used to eliminate problematic situations. If it should come to that.

… I will not remind you again … She is not your concern … the Ain Magne called.

… But you are … I put you before my own family and province … You and our conquest of Kinderra, they are the only things I live for … My lord, if you do not want her killed, let me capture her for you … A sense of feral desire washed through his second's mind. *… I will ensure she will remain compliant for harvesting …*

… Your only task is to get me the ford … The Ain Magne sent a scorching reprimand through the young seer's mind, nearly breaking their connection. *… Do you understand? …*

… Ai, Great One, ai … Ëo comprende … came his second's reply, faint with pain.

… You will move into position by midnight next … I will be at the ford soon …

The Ain Magne brought his awareness back to himself. The rain now came down in torrents. The horse of a battle seer who rode next to him slid in the mud, nearly throwing its rider. A young defender reached out with lightning-fast reflexes and grabbed the other mount's reins, steadying the steed and the seer.

"*Gratas Oë, Ëi cara. Gratas,*" the battle seer stammered, more than aware that, had she fallen, the surging horses behind her would have likely trampled her to death.

He smiled, noting the exchange. The defender showed promise despite his youth. For many, many summers now, the Ain Magne had captured Fal'kin fighters, or cornered disloyal Ken'nar, and obliterated their wills with his powers to make them more perfect warriors. It was painful, as much for the victims as it was for him. He sensed their agony through that same Aspect he used to cause their pain. He hated it, but it was necessary, for nothing great could be accomplished without sacrifice. Only when he had enough Ken'nar to quell any Fal'kin resistance would Kinderra finally be at peace. There was no agony he would not endure to see that accomplished.

The thousands who rode with him now. How many would see the dawn two days hence? What good had killing ever done the land? Death was the ultimate failure. Once dead, beings cherished by the Aspects Above, along with their sacred gifts, were gone forever. Not only did his harvested warriors still live, but they also ceased fighting against him and now obeyed his commands without question. Most important, though—even imperative to his plans—they continued to use their Aspects in service to Kinderra.

He would make certain the young defender's Aspect would continue to serve Kinderra.

The Ain Magne surged his stallion forward.

CHAPTER 18

"Aspecta il'Defende dam forte. Aspecta il'Sanarente dam ain. Aspecta il' Vidë ísi magne ken tuda fár Ida dam comprende."
("The Aspect of Defense gives strength. The Aspect of Healing gives wholeness. The Aspect of Sight, however, is the greatest of all powers for it gives knowledge.")

—Ora Fal'kinnen 38:5–7

Thank the Aspects.

Her mother finally called for them to camp for the night. The torrential downpours had made the blistering ride to Two Rivers Ford all the more exhausting.

Mirana reined in her horse Ashtar, slowing him to a trot. Her father insisted she ride his enormous warhorse even though she could barely straddle the chestnut destrier's back. Tetric coaxed his mount to a walk beside her as the two thousand Fal'kin from Kin-Deren province around her brought their steeds to a halt.

She swung her leg over Ashtar's back, grimacing. Dismounting after days in the saddle was painful. Her boots sank in the mud. She grimaced again. Standing was even more so.

She wiped the muck and water from her face. Sixthmonth had come, but the spring rains refused to yield to the summer sun. Her mother had set a grueling pace despite the saturated ground. At least they would be at the ford garrison in just two more days. She paused in untying her saddlebag. Then again, maybe that wasn't such a good thing, after all.

Lord Garis removed his helmet and set it down where he would make camp, clawing his fingers through his dark hair. He had no mud on his face. She frowned. Many Fal'kin wore helmets. Her father, however, hated them. He had worn one when he fought as part of the provincial forces, and the moment he became an il'Kin, he never wore one again. He had said it was hard enough to see straight ahead with one on, let alone use peripheral vision. He had said he believed his Aspect and his eyes were more than enough to keep his head on his shoulders.

Her frown deepened. She'd know soon enough if he was right.

She unpacked a goatskin tent and shook it out. It had taken her days to figure out how to erect the sad little thing. It was more mud than leather by now, and it had a few extra holes in it from misplaced anchor spikes. Still, it was better than sleeping in the rain. Maybe.

She glanced at the Trine. How in Kinderra would he fit within such a small shelter like hers when she could barely stretch out her own legs?

"Mirana, your horse," Lord Garis directed her as he removed the packs from his own mount.

She frowned and nodded. She let the tent fall into the sludge once more and uncinched Ashtar's saddle.

She watched Lord Garis as he finished settling his stallion for the night. He had been strangely quiet for some time. Not quiet, really, but distant, like he wasn't even there.

"Idiot," she muttered, chastising herself. Of course he was distant. He was under U'Nehîl. He didn't need to exactly advertise to the Ken'nar warlord that he was approaching. Had she not been riding next to him, she would have never known he was there.

He had hardly spoken two words since they had set out from Deren. She bit her lip. Was he having second thoughts about taking her as his *scholaira*? She had quite literally turned away from her duty. She had nearly turned away from everything. Was he having second thoughts about her, period?

Ashtar's heavy saddle slipped from her wet hands into the mire, and the Trine gave her a disapproving look. She answered with a wan smile of apology.

Lightning illuminated the clouds clinging to the backbone of the Dar-Anar Mountains far to the west. The wind picked up in answer, driving the rain into the tents.

Mirana shook her sopped hair out of her eyes as she fed Ashtar from a small feed bag from her pack. The grain looked more like gruel. Like her own dinner, come to think of it. By the Light, what she wouldn't do for some of Quartermaster Haarlen's roast chicken right now.

Lord Garis solved his shelter problem by spreading his cloak over his horse's back and securing the ends to the edges of the standard-issue tent with leather ties at the corners. While not exactly roomy, it was adequate for his stature.

A Kin-Deren red eagle within a gold circle proudly emblazoned the tent. She scowled. What happened to his tent?

"I gave it to one of my defenders after a campaign. He was dying. We couldn't take him with us," he said over his shoulder.

For some reason, that surprised her. She couldn't picture the stoic man so caring. "You couldn't heal him?"

He paused as he made camp. "Not all can be saved."

A cloudburst decided at that moment to empty itself upon her, drenching her and all but submerging her tent in the mud. Would it still be raining this hard when the Ken'nar attacked? Then again, the Ken'nar would have to fight in this deluge, too. Why wasn't that the least bit comforting?

As she set up the tent, she pulled deeper inward, where far more fearful concerns than the rain dwelt. Whether five hundred or five thousand Ken'nar ultimately attacked the Fal'kin at Two Rivers Ford, all the visions of the battle carried with them the unmistakable sense of peril. Specific. Hard. Real. Her parents would be stationed in the command tent. It might be located away from the battlefront, but no greater target existed.

"Do the Ken'nar strike first at the battle seer group or the command tent?" she asked the Trine.

Within his tent, he pulled a whetstone from his belt and began sharpening his longsword. The shelter's opening faced perpendicular to the gale-driven storm. She frowned and reoriented her tent.

"That is a very good question. What would you do?"

How could he even ask such a question? Wasn't the man starving? Wasn't he even tired? What would she do? Not envisioning herself as a warlord is what she would do. She threw a saddlebag into her waterlogged shelter. Couldn't he wait until later to fiddle with that ungodly long blade of his? It was an unsettling reminder that she, too, would be using her long knives soon. The last thing she needed was to imagine herself at the head of some marauding army.

She unfolded her bedroll and plopped down. Water and mud trickled in through a tear in the tent and struck her face. Irritated by more than the leak, she swiped it away. "I don't know."

"Think, Mirana."

She had had her fill of soggy grain meal. She pulled some hardtack—well, now *soft* tack—from her saddlebag and took a bite. "I would destroy the battle seer group."

"Interesting. Why?"

She clenched her jaw. She did not want to discuss this.

"Why?" he asked again.

"Without the battle seers, you can't predict enemy troop movements easily. That's the whole point, isn't it?" she answered, irritation clipping her words.

"And?"

And? What did he mean, "and"? "And without those in the command tent, coordination might suffer, but the battle seers can still call the attack directly to the legion commanders."

"Very good. Furthermore, if the attacking forces are any good, both targets will be eliminated at the same time."

The waybread stuck in her throat as she imagined her parents' bloody bodies splayed on the ground. At least she hoped it was an imagining.

She loosened the ties of her belt pouch and touched her pendant. The mica warmed her fingertips. Teague.

She glanced at Lord Garis. He was examining the cross guard of his sword. She quickly fished out the delicate gift and slipped it over her head, tucking it under her soggy linen shirt.

"The Ken'nar don't kill herbsfolk, do they?"

He drew his sharpening stone down to his sword's edge and shrugged. "Sometimes."

She threw him an angry glance. "You do not always have to be so honest, Lord Trine."

He made a sound like a chuckle. She could not hear it fully over the sound of the storm. She didn't think the Trine was capable of laughing.

"Your parents have fought in many battles."

"My mother hasn't. Not for a long time." Her glare turned into an intent plea. ... *What if I'm right, Lord Garis? ... What if the Ken'nar Dark Trine attacks with the five thousand I saw? ... How can we fight against that? ...*

... Maybe fighting isn't the best strategy in that case ...

She scowled in confusion. "What do you mean?"

... Think ... What would you do in the face of such superior numbers? ...

"I'm sorry I asked." She turned her back to him and pretended to fuss with her bedroll.

... I want an answer from you ...

She whirled around to face him. "Can we *please* talk about something else? I should have never brought this up," she added under her breath.

He gave a heavy sigh. That, she clearly heard. ... *You are a Trine ... Someday, all of Kinderra will look to you for answers ...*

The memory of thousands of Ken'nar cutting down the Fal'kin at the ford flew up in her mind. "If they attack with a force truly that large, we will have to retreat."

"Back to Deren."

"No. South. Sün-Kasal."

He frowned. "You would surrender the ford and leave Deren defenseless if you went south to Sün-Kasal."

She shrugged and returned her half-eaten hardtack to her pack. She no longer had an appetite. "Not for long."

"Go on." He looked down the length of his sword then sheathed it.

She glared at him and gave him a frustrated sigh of her own. "Our two thousand with Sün-Kasal's five thousand? It's the Ken'nar who would be outnumbered. We would return and take back the ford. We're not just going to give it up to them forever."

He blinked and was silent for a long moment. "There are good retreats and bad retreats. That would be a good one."

Surprise from his mind leaked to hers, then disappeared into pride. Pride? He was proud of her? She smiled. "Or a bad one. If you're a Ken'nar."

A series of shouts rose from the camp, startling the horses. In one lightning-fast movement, Lord Garis flew from his tent, grabbed his longsword, and put himself between her and the disturbance. His blade seemed to clear its sheath before the sound of its drawing rang.

"What? What is it?" Mirana asked as she dashed from her tent to stand behind him.

Had the Ken'nar already begun their attack? From their location in the middle of the camp, she could not see what had happened, nor had she sensed anything. Lord Garis did not answer her immediately. He held out his free hand, protective of her, while he watched and listened.

He made a low noise of disapproval and shoved his sword back into its scabbard. "One of the horses was not pleased about something." He turned to her. "Get some rest. Your mother will not keep us here long."

She searched the camp for the disturbance once more but sensed nothing other than a slight warming of Teague's pendant against her skin. She crawled back into the tent. The Trine had pulled a corner of his shelter down and had slipped behind U'Nehíl once more. She shook her head and huddled, shivering, in her saddle blanket. She sat within a camp of two thousand men and women, and had never felt so alone.

Lord Garis was right about their stay.

Mirana closed her eyes on the murky, rain-soaked night until he awakened her far too soon to another murky, rain-soaked dawn. She wasn't sure she had slept at all. Moments later, they and the Fal'kin army were off.

The gray day deepened into an even grayer evening when she finally heard the rushing of rivers rising above the drumming hoofbeats. It was a comforting and thoroughly incongruous sound to the noise of the fighting that would soon take place.

Somewhere in the gloom, the swift Garnath River and the wide Anarath River flowed out of the Dar-Anar Mountains. They bisected the apex of the landmass that made up Kin-Deren province's far western border like a wedge of Quartermaster Haarlen's meat pie. Her stomach growled at the thought.

The stone bridges of Two Rivers Ford itself were barely visible in the dank evening, but what she could see made her jaw drop. No image passed to her from seers did them justice. An enormous span arched across each river, upheld by massive buttresses sunk deep into the rock walls of the river gorges. One to the north over the Garnath River connected Varn-Erdal to Kin-Deren. The other, to the south, stood over the Anarath River, linking Kin-Deren to Sün-Kasal.

Her primary lessons said the bridges were ancient, built before the Sundering, before there even were Fal'kin and Ken'nar. Were they too old? She bit her lip. When was the last time they had supported this many riders at once? A warning drifted through her mind, soft like the sound of running water, though it was not at all soothing. Was it one of her Aspects whispering to her, or just plain anxiety? She shook her head. She had been riding for too long.

Farther in the distance, she spied pinpoints of light. The ford garrison. It was only a collection of sod and wooden buildings and semi-permanent tents to house the troops that guarded the ford, but she nearly wept with relief. To bed down in a bunkhouse after unending days in a leaky tent would be like sleeping in the arms of the Aspects Above themselves.

Mirana followed Lord Garis, letting Ashtar pick his way down into the shallow valley of the ford, to what she assumed was the command tent. Its wide canvas walls and pitched oilcloth roof were lit by tall torches at its entrance—and indistinguishable from any of the other tents. She smiled tightly. That was probably the idea.

Horses were already tethered outside. Her parents and some of the other senior Fal'kin must have arrived ahead of them. She hissed as she clambered off her horse and grabbed a stirrup to steady herself.

Seeing her grimace, Lord Garis asked, "When was the last time you rode a horse?"

"I ride all the time, my lord. Just never this far. Or this fast." She stretched painfully. "Or on such a gigantic beast."

His mouth thinned with a frown. "Help me see to the horses." He hefted the saddlebags from Ashtar's back and gave them to her. "Your horse must always come ahead of your own comfort. It is more than just a means of transportation; it is your companion, your defender, and *ai*, even your food or shelter."

"Food and shelt—" Mirana sucked in a breath as the Trine called to her mind a bleak notion of a snow-swept plain filled with wounded fighters, some staying alive by the only means possible. She eyed Ashtar, his ruddy coat glistening in the garrison torchlight, wet with flecks of foamy sweat from the demanding ride. She would rather starve than kill such a magnificent animal.

The tall Dar-Azûlan took the bags from his horse and draped them over her shoulder. She took one step toward the tent before she stumbled in the mud under all the weight. Then the mud disappeared.

The garrison at Two Rivers Ford. The undulating mass of the Dar-Anars looms in the distance, darker than the night. Shapes move in the blackness. Lightning flashes. A feral cry sounds in the gloom, gibbering yelps from mouths searching for blood. Grynwen. The sound of hoofbeats drums above the thunder. Lightning flares, revealing Ken'nar. They disappear in the darkness. The pounding of steeds remains. The Fal'kin charge to meet the Ken'nar. Men and women fall to the gnashing teeth. Amulets fire. The stench of burned flesh rises in the air, heedless of the storm. Swords clash. Cries of agony split the night. Terrified horses scream. The Fal'kin are pushed toward the southern stone bridge of the ford. Defenders from both armies fall shrieking into the raging waters a hundred feet below.

Her legs gave out and she collapsed in the muck, the saddlebags spilling some of their contents.

Lord Garis hauled her to her feet. He shook his head angrily. "If you cannot even bear a ride, how do you expect to fight someday?"

He stood over her, glowering down at her. Was he the tallest man in Kinderra?

"My lord, I think—" She staggered back and dropped down again into the sodden earth. Teague's pendant lay hot against her skin.

Fighting spills onto the fields near the southern bridge egress. Grynwen snap at each other, fighting for the flesh of fallen Fal'kin who have yet to die. Lightning. Blood coats their muzzles. Blood soaks armor. Blood sprays skin, faces. The sickening, coppery, sweet taste.

"Mirana?"

An eerie keening sings above the howls of the grynwen. Peculiar whistles shriek overhead.

"Mirana? Have you seen something?" the Trine asked as he crouched down. "Answer me."

"The ford will—"

The Fal'kin fighters in the rear guard of the forces turn their heads southward. And die.

Her breaths came in pants. What was she seeing? *When* was she seeing? Arrows? From the south? That couldn't be right. Every vision—hers and the other seers, even Tetric Garis's— had always shown the Ken'nar attacking the ford from the north. What had just happened?

The Trine's presence permeated her mind, cutting her off from her Seeing Aspect. ... *Mirana, come back to me* ... "What did you see?"

"The ford. I saw the ford again," she gasped. "Only, this time, I saw arrows. From behind us."

The command tent entrance flew open. "Mirana?" Her father rushed over to her, followed by her mother. Together they helped her up.

Her father laid his hand on Lord Garis's forearm and stared at him intently, apparently calling something private.

"She refuses to leave." He pulled his arm out from under her father's hand. "It appears she has quite a will of her own. I wonder from whom she gets it?"

"What happened?" her mother asked. "Is she all right?"

Mirana took a slow breath to calm her racing heart, ignoring the question. "Has our intelligence changed at all?" she asked instead.

"I thought we had an agreement, Garis," her father said.

She wiped some of the mud from her face. Agreement? What agreement? "Father?"

The Trine held his hands out at his sides. "What would you have me do?"

"The Ken'nar battle plan remains unchanged, although we see our troops shifting locations," her mother answered Mirana, but her eyes remained on the men.

"She cannot remain here." Her father's voice held less acid but remained just as emphatic.

"Kaarl, I don't like it any more than you do, but I need her. I need her insight," her mother said.

He gave the Trine a piercing glare.

Lord Garis's gaze was just as pointed. "I have not betrayed your trust. What must be done will be done."

Her father's jaw tightened, and he nodded brusquely.

"I need to speak with you and Mother," she said. "Now. I saw arrows."

Her mother nodded. "As have we."

"From the south."

Her parents and Lord Garis grew quiet.

"I saw something. Just now. The vision proceeds as we have seen it these past sevendays. Five hundred come from the north. But then a hail of arrows comes from the south. Many arrows. And grynwen." She held her mother's hand and called to her mind the images.

After a moment, Desde squeezed her hand and nodded. "I was hoping to stop them from advancing off the Garnath bridge, but now we might have two fronts to worry about." She covered her mouth, then her hand slipped to tug at her lower lip. "Forces from Varn-Erdal are expected tonight as well. Could the arrows be theirs?"

"No," Mirana replied. "We fall before those arrows."

"Ashtar can drink a waterskin dry by himself. Take the brute to the well," her father said and placed a hand on her shoulder. ... *Leave this place ... Now ...* She blinked at the intensity of his call. ... *Ride south and follow the river ... Do not stop until you are within Deren's gates ... Do you understand? ...*

... I can't leave ... If the ford falls, it's my fault ...

"*Biraena*," her father cautioned.

"Mirana, did I not just remind you of the importance of caring for the horses?" Lord Garis said. "Listen to your father and go." He enunciated each word. "Now."

She picked up one of the waterskins from the mud. "What is your horse's name, my lord?"

The Trine scowled. "What?" He shook his head. "He has no name. He answers to a call within the Aspects. Why?" He looked at her father, then back to her. He picked up the other waterskin and brushed her hand as he gave it to her. ... *I said leave ...*

"I wanted to call him something when I watered him." She slung the skins over her shoulder. "I will be right back."

She was not leaving the ford, no matter how much her father and Lord Garis wanted her to. If she could see some minor movement of the Ken'nar forces, sense some scrap of information, she had to try to give the Fal'kin any advantage she could. She would never make the mistake of silence again. And she did have her long knives.

CHAPTER 19

*"To see the skeins of the future is a gift of the most
terrible kind. In my heart, I long for blindness. But one
cannot embrace both ignorance and knowledge."*
—The Codex of Jasal the Great

Thunder rumbled in the distance as Mirana walked Ashtar
to the garrison's well. They had outridden the storm, but it now
caught up to them. The horse trotted over to the well and
slurped at the water, his nose nearly submerged.

If only she had believed her first viewing of the attack on
Two Rivers Ford, in which she had seen some five thousand
Ken'nar descending on the unsuspecting outpost, they would
have had at least some time to gather Fal'kin from neighboring
provinces. Surely, some would have arrived at the ford in time.
Anything would have helped. Lord Garis's reassurances may

have saved her life, but they did nothing to resolve her guilt. It preyed on her like grynwen on a blooded deer, relentless and unyielding.

Lightning forked overhead, its glare reflected in the water, looking all too much like the white light that flared from Jasal's Keep.

Her hand drifted to one of her long knives.

"Lord Garis needs my help to understand Jasal's Keep, Ashtar. He said it might be able to stop this war." She gripped the knife's hilt a moment longer, then released it.

"No. I will not leave. I will make this right." She clenched her fists. For the first time in a long, long time, she hoped her Seeing Aspect would give her the most graphic vision she was capable of receiving. Teague's pendant warmed against her skin. She wanted to know every step, every hoof fall the Ken'nar were making. Right. Now.

As she dipped a waterskin into the trough, the well disappeared from her mortal eyes.

"Mirana! Go! Now!"

Teague cries out in pain. His body collapses on the stone pavers. The blood from the wound in his side leaks out in slow pulses, trickles from his mouth, a red so dark it looks like a liquid bruise. It congeals in the icy rain.

"Teague!"

Lightning crashes overhead. The pinnacle of Jasal's Keep, a crowned skull in the garish light.

Light explodes, more brilliant than the inside of a thunderbolt.

Mirana sucked in her breath. No. Not this. Anything but this.

Teague approached the well with a pair of waterskins. He stopped and stood still, his eyes wide.

She blinked. Was he part of the vision or was he real?

He dropped the skins with a cry of relief, ran to her, and enveloped her in his arms. "Miri! I've looked everywhere for you. After you ran out of the Choosing Ceremony, I tried to see you, but they wouldn't let me. Even my parents wouldn't tell me what happened to you. I've looked for you every day and night since." He stood back and held her face in his hands. "Are you all right?"

No. No, she was not all right. She didn't think she'd ever be all right again. The sense of his peril had been present for sevendays but undefined. Now, her Aspects had given her a vision to make her fear concrete.

"*Ai*. I'm—" She took another breath, stifling the stronger emotions that threatened to break free. "*Ai*."

He still hadn't released her. "You don't look it. You look like you've seen a ghost."

She wouldn't let anything happen to him. Not Teague. If the Aspects Above refused to alter her destiny, could they not, in their infinite grace, spare his life at least?

She gently lowered his hands from her face. "I was with Lord Garis and—what happened to your chest?" She pointed to an angry purple contusion shaped like a horseshoe.

"It's just a bruise," he said and shook his head to dismiss her concern. "Listen, Mirana—"

She squinted at the bruise. "Were you the commotion in the camp the other night?"

"*Ai*, I guess. My horse—your mother gave me your *brepaithe*'s palfrey, Bankin—she doesn't like to be approached from behind." He fished her waterskin from the well and set it down on the ground. "Mirana, we still have time—"

"No horse does." Those were the words that came from her mouth because she could not speak the words her Aspects demanded she say. A trace of blood had dried by his nose. He was soaked, dirty, maimed, and he had never looked so perfect to her. How could she possibly live without him? "By the Light, Teague, you could have been killed! You could have broken your neck, you could have been trampled, or—"

"Mirana, listen to me. Please." He glanced over his shoulder. "There's still time. We can leave. Together. Before the Ken'nar arrive."

Oh, Aspects Above, no. He was willing to forsake his duty as an herbsman for her. She was destroying his life without lifting a finger. If she left with him, if he remained with her, he would die.

She shook her head. "No, Teague. I can't leave. But you should. I had hoped your parents would have talked some sense into you and you would have stayed home."

His shoulders fell, and he snatched up one of his waterskins. "I'm not leaving without you. If you're staying," he dredged it through the trough to fill it, "then I am, too."

Mirana gritted her teeth at his referred pain as he hefted the heavy skin and set it on the ground. She ached to hold him and take away his pain, to feel the warmth of his body next to hers. She longed for his kiss, to let into her mind the love he held in his.

"You're in pain." She reached out to him. Frustration. Desire. Longing. Hope. Anxiety. Pain. Of the body. Of the heart. Love. His emotions. And hers.

Teague took her hand from his chest and held it. "I know what you said at the Choosing Ceremony. About us not being together anymore. I know you didn't mean it."

She would not let Teague die. "I'm sorry. It has to be."

"I know you don't mean that."

"All of Kin-Deren province knows I am a Trine now. Soon, so will all of Kinderra. Including the Ken'nar. Even without an amulet, everything has changed."

He took her other hand and held them both. "Maybe so, but I know nothing has changed between us. We haven't changed."

To keep him safe, she would have to let him go. If she did not, he would be swept up in the maelstrom of her destiny. He could die. She knew it. She saw it.

"Lord Garis is my *patrua* and my prime. I ride with him and the Dar-Azûlans now." She pulled her hands from his. "I don't want it to be like this. It has to be."

Teague would want to come with her and Trine. Even if she eluded him and left him behind, he would try to follow her. Pushing him away would save his life, but in doing so, she would lose a part of hers. The part that mattered most. His life was worth denying her love. It was worth her own life. It was worth everything.

"Why? Because of your keep vision?" He plunged his other skin into the water. "I'm here now, Mirana. I'm living, breathing. I'm not some vision. I'm not some person who doesn't exist yet, and neither are you." He threw the skin down. "We are here, in this moment, not in a nightmare that might never happen. I've done everything I can to help you, and I'd do it all again a thousand times over, but you're the one who's letting your visions come between us. Not me."

Ai. He was right. She was. She had to.

"It's not some childish nightmare. You know that."

He threw his arms out at his sides. "What is there to see? Rain? Armies fighting? A white light?"

"There's more to it than that." She was afraid speaking any more words would make them true.

"You become the Dark Trine? That's utterly ridiculous!" He then exhaled, calming himself. "If you see something that horrific, then let me help you. The Aspects Above may have ignored me with their gifts, but I want Kinderra's peace as much as you do. I want to fight for it alongside you."

She shook her head, dismissing his foolhardy notion. "You're Unaspected and training as an herbsman. You cannot take up a sword. Unaspected do not fight, and certainly not herbsfolk. The Unaspected have never fought. We Fal'kin exist so you can exist."

He tried to draw her back into his embrace, but she leaned back from him. Again, a crushing blow from his heart leaped from his mind to hers. He let his arms fall heavily to his sides. "I don't care about any of that. I care about you. You are the only thing I care about. You're going to have to make a choice, Mirana. Do you want to believe in some vision that hasn't happened yet and may never happen? Or the reality of me standing here, in front of you, now?"

She searched his forest-green eyes for some other answer, any other answer. The Seeing Aspect, however, had already given her one. The only answer. To keep Teague alive, she would have to shatter his heart.

"We cannot be together. I am Aspected, Teague. I am a Trine." She clenched her teeth, catching her tongue, and tasted blood. "And you are not."

His shock slammed into her mind like a fist of stone. "Y-You said that never mattered to you. You've told me that our whole lives."

"It matters now," she said, her voice constricted by the emotion she fought to contain. "We've always known this. We've just been lying to ourselves. I can't lie anymore."

Disbelief flooded away his shock, drowning her. "Mirana, please. Don't do this."

Searing loss burned through him into her. "*Ben íre,* Teague."

He stood motionless for a moment. Something disappeared from his eyes, leaving them hollow, almost dead. He backed away from her, hefted his waterskins, and returned to the camp.

Mirana sank to her knees against the well and pulled out his pendant. She held it to her lips. A sob erupted from her so deep, so broken, it made no noise. No mortal grief could give voice to it.

Tears streamed down her face and dripped from her chin to the delicate mica sheets. They beaded like droplets of rain on the smooth surface.

"Oë tuda a Ëa." She clutched the pendant to her heart. He was everything to her. Her body spasmed, forcing the cries from her throat. She clutched Teague's pendant tighter, its crystalline sheets of mica growing hot against her skin. She had destroyed his love for her, the one thing above all else she was trying to save.

"Damn you, Tetric Garis. Why didn't you leave the knife in my hand?"

Mirana rubbed her chest. It ached just below her peda blossom pendant. Everything ached.

The sound of thunder came closer. A breath of warm, wet wind came from the south, unfurling the pennant flags atop the ford tents. It brought with it the smell of rain.

South. South was bad.

She wiped her cheek with the heel of her hand. Her breath shuddered as a warning sense fought for her attention over her anguish. She grabbed the sides of the well and hauled herself to her feet. Teague had disappeared into the camp toward the south. He should not go south.

She looked down at the delicate mica pendant in her hand. It burned her palm, turning it red. The mica sheets. Were the flawed crystal plates working as a crude amulet?

The Ken'nar were to attack the garrison at Two Rivers Ford from the north, crossing the Garnath River bridge just before dawn. That future skein, that direction, had never wavered—not in the seers' visions, not in hers.

Her mind snapped back to what she'd seen while unpacking Ashtar upon first arriving at the garrison. The arrows and the grynwen. They had come from the south. She whipped her head around to the west, facing the Dar-Anar Mountains. The star Gabrial. It hadn't been visible in the night sky in those images. It was not yet dawn.

"No. It can't be. Not yet."

She peered at the darkening fields outside the garrison.

A detachment of Ken'nar, thousands strong, would approach, not from the north—but from the south. The larger force. They were coming. Not at dawn.

Now.

Mirana vaulted onto Ashtar's back and raced for the command tent at a dead run.

CHAPTER 20

"Derranen fissura crear fár doma u'daingaen."
("A split foundation makes for an unstable house.")
—Ora Fal'kinnen 22:2

"The Ken'nar. They're coming now. From the south." Mirana dashed through the entrance of the command tent. "The Ken'nar are coming now."

Her parents, Tetric Garis, and the other senior Fal'kin looked up from a large map draped over two saddles.

Her mother rushed over and steadied her with a hand on her arm. "Slow down. What do you mean 'now'?"

"Thousands are on the move. Five—" She gulped a breath. "Five thousand. They're riding up from the south right now. The other five hundred—"

"Will come from the north, as in our vision," her mother said. Her face went white. "Tetric?"

"I was just about to inform you that I sensed an impression that the Ken'nar might be changing their timetable. Your daughter is most perceptive."

If the situation wasn't so urgent, Mirana would have hugged the man for corroborating what she had just seen. "Mother, we don't have much time." She thought back to Lord Garis's earlier question on superior forces and inferior odds. "Maybe we should consider a retreat."

Desde turned to the other Fal'kin. "We cannot fight a force that large. Mirana's right. We will have to retreat. We must prevent the northern phalanx from merging with the larger force. If they do, even the Aspects Above will not be able to save us. Tell the commanders to deploy their units to the Garnath bridge. Have the garrison troops form a perimeter on the ridge to safeguard our retreat. Go now." Men and women ran from the tent to carry out her orders.

Her mother turned back to her. "How soon will the Ken'nar be here?"

"I couldn't be certain, but soon."

Lord Garis closed his eyes briefly as he held his amulet. "Within the hour."

"There's no time to waste." Her father pointed out the tent. "Garis, get her out of here."

Her mother shook her head. "She can't leave now. She'll run right into them."

"She can head east, back to Deren, if she leaves now ahead of them. Mirana, go."

"No, Father. I will stay with Mother in the command tent and help relay communications to and from the battle seer unit. I can do that much."

"If you will not listen to your father, you will listen to me. I am your *patrua* now," the Trine demanded. "Leave. Immediately." His mind speared into hers. ... *Follow the Anarath south ... I will meet you by the trader's ferries near the Stairs of Anar rapids ...*

She winced at the sudden communication. "But—"

... *Do not stop until you reach the ferries ... I will meet you there ...*

Her mother closed her eyes and gripped her amulet, turning away from the group for a moment. "The battle seers say the northern phalanx is less than five leagues away." Mirana had never seen her so strong and so helpless at the same time. "Gather the il'Kin. They can guard our backs. We need to leave while we still can."

Her father gripped the hilt of his sword. "And sacrifice the ford? Desde—"

Her mother's shoulders fell. "Kaarl, we can't possibly repel a force of that size. We'll regroup. Return. We'll get fighters from Sün-Kasal, Tash-Hamar, even Jad-Anüna in the east. It's about time Defender Prime Nambre Dinir remembered Kinderra survives on mutual aid."

Mirana heard her father's curse with her ears and her Aspects. He gave an explosive exhale and nodded. "I'll call Dav and tell him to begin moving the provincials eastward out of the ford. Keep another two units to hold back the northern Ken'nar phalanx until the garrison has been evacuated."

"You'll never make it out of the river valley," Lord Garis said. "The Ken'nar were lying in wait. You lost the advantage of a retreat the moment you arrived. The southern phalanx will block any escape route eastward the minute they cross the Anarath bridge. You have no choice but to fight, my prime."

No retreat? Mirana's breath stilled in her chest. They were trapped.

Her mother lifted her chin. "Kaarl's plan is sound. We can at least try for one."

Her mother's topaz flared in her hand as Mirana overheard her urgent orders called to the minds of the provincial defenders.

The command tent flap flew open. Morgan Jord and Binthe Lima rushed in, followed by the Healers Tennen and Niah.

Teague? Where was Teague? Had he left the garrison, crushed by her words? Oh, Lights. He'd ride right into them and never know they were coming until it was too late. She started to ask the healers about him, but Morgan's hand on her shoulder interrupted her.

"Steward Pinal. The battle seers say Ken'nar are coming from the north and the south."

Lord Garis turned to the healers. "Tennen, Niah, move up into the foothills, out of the way of action."

"How will you bring us the wounded if the Ken'nar take the southern bridge?" Healer Niah asked.

"The battlefield will be too dangerous to heal during the conflict. If you leave now, you might be able to make it across ahead of the southern Ken'nar unit. Hurry. You have no time to waste," the Trine replied. The healers nodded and dashed from the tent. He then turned to the il'Kin. "Defender Commander Jord, have the il'Kin guard the healers. You will be the only protection they have to make it through."

"Halt, Morgan," her father said. "The northern phalanx will enter the garrison at any moment. We need to stop them before they can merge with the southern force. Go now."

"Hold." Lord Garis held up his hand. "You are too few. The provincials can handle the north. The healers must be kept clear from the fray. They are too important to lose."

When her father took a step toward Lord Garis, she moved quickly to stand between the men. "Father—"

"If they are not on the battlefield, they do not need a guard. The Ken'nar surely mean to box us in."

"If the healers die, so will others who could have been saved. Do you want that kind of blood on your hands? We are wasting time, Steward."

Her father glared at the Trine a moment longer. "Morgan, guard the healers."

Binthe shook her head in disbelief. "The Ken'nar will—"

"Do as I say before more people die needlessly," her father snapped, his silver eyes flashing in anger.

Morgan's gaze slid from her father to Lord Garis. "I will wait for your next call, my steward."

He and Binthe ran from the tent. Kaarl turned to the Trine. "Whatever has passed between us, please, save my daughter. I'm begging you."

"I promised you, no harm will come to her as long as I am alive. I stand by my word." Lord Garis's mouth curled into a most unpleasant smile. "In spite of what has passed between us."

What was going on here? Mirana glanced at the Trine, to her father, and back again.

"Garis." Her father's shoulders sagged. "I don't want you to protect her. I want you to get her out of here. She won't make it past the black bastards without you."

Her mother shook her head. "It's too late for that now."

Mirana held the hilt of a long knife. "I have to stay and help. It's my right—"

The sound of a galloping horse interrupted the rest of her reply. A fiercely beautiful young woman staggered into the command tent, cradling another, unconscious older woman in her arms. Their torn cloaks bore a red horse on a white field, the mark of the Varn-Erdal province. For a moment, Mirana didn't recognize them. Blood and grime covered both women, the younger woman's face contorted in grief. Liaonne Edaran and her mother Vallia, the province's defender prime. The few times Mirana had met them during Quorumtide had been brief. Her father once said they fought like Ken'nar, only not as mercifully.

"Expect no aid from Varn-Erdal, Prime Kellis Pinal," the young woman said, her voice hoarse with exhaustion. "I need help. My mother is dying."

Lord Garis took Vallia Edaran from Liaonne and laid her down on the tent floor to examine her injuries.

"Liaonne, what happened?" Desde helped the younger defender sit on a supply chest.

"We took a different route from Edara to come to the ford for our tour of duty." She clawed the mud and blood out of the braids in her pale-gold hair. "Traders reported Ken'nar on our eastern borders. We rode on the windward side of the Dar-Anars, making for the Kabaarh Pass. The Ken'nar were already there. More than I've ever seen."

Mirana never heard the rest of Liaonne Edaran's tale. The tent vanished from her eyes.

Pain. In the chest. In the stomach. A stabbing, burning agony, consuming all. Blood. Gushing away, away, away.

"She's bleeding." What was this she was seeing with her Healing Aspect? *Where* was this?

"Vallia is done for, Tetric," her father said. "The Ken'nar are coming. Please take Mirana away from here."

… I need your help … the Trine called to Mirana. *… The healers have left …*

She shook her head. "I've never done anything like this."

Lord Garis's amulet glowed as he put his hands on Vallia Edaran's injuries. *… You must help me stop the bleeding …*

… I hear it, but I don't know how to stop it … The screeching discord nearly drowned out the Trine's call.

… You do not need to … I need you to work in concert with me … I need you … Now … He reached up with a bloody hand to grab her wrist and pull her down to her knees with him. He forced her hand into wounds in the woman's chest.

She tried to pull away, but his grip on her was unbreakable. Vallia Edaran's wounds, the Trine's Healing Aspect, and the Trine's amulet pulled at her even stronger.

Chest muscles torn. Blood leaks from veins. Soft gray lobes, lungs, punctured. Filling with blood. Another artery, low in the abdomen, bleeds, bleeds, bleeds.

Mirana's consciousness slipped further from her control. The woman's injuries immobilized her, starved for her Aspects to heal them. Lord Garis's presence held her fast to Vallia's wounds. Her very life felt as though it were draining from her. He focused on the rent flesh in the woman's chest. In Vallia's abdomen, however, blood hemorrhaged unchecked in rhythmic, ever-weakening rushes. The Varn-Erdalan prime would bleed to death from the stomach wound before he would finish repairing her chest. Mirana knew this. Her Healing Aspect told her so. Her Seeing Aspect told her so.

Her Defending Aspect, however, rose in response to a warning, competing for her attention. The Ken'nar advanced ever closer.

Mirana's Healing powers welled up within her, demanding release. She wrested her hand from Lord Garis's grip and reached for his amulet. Her Aspects surged through her, through the Trine, through his amulet. They collided with the harmonics of the hematite crystal with brutal force, vying for control of the amulet over its owner. She sank her free hand deep into the Vallia Edaran's ruined abdomen. She needed to heal.

She. Must. Heal.

A large artery in the woman's abdomen leaked out her life with each fading heartbeat. The cacophony of the injuries resolved into a single unbearable note. She poured all her strength into silencing that note, trying to close the tear in the great vessel behind the woman's bowels.

The wound was suddenly torn from her mind's eye. She screamed—the separation was too abrupt, too profound.

"How dare you use my daughter like an accursed Ken'nar tool?" Her father dragged her back from the dying woman's body. The tent snapped into focus again.

Her mother rushed over. "Kaarl!"

Mirana gasped. Blood had spattered over her clothes, her chest, and her face. She began to shake with revulsion as she attempted to wipe the gore away from her cheek with the back of a bloody hand.

Liaonne Edaran ran to Vallia, holding her head. "Lord Trine, please save my mother."

"What in Aspects' name are you doing, man?" Lord Garis shouted. "Vallia Edaran will die without Mirana."

The raw notes from Vallia Edaran's body silenced abruptly.

"No!" Mirana pulled herself from her father's hold. She sank back to her knees and placed her hands on the Varn-Erdalan prime. "Oh, no." She frantically searched for the discord of agony that had been there a moment ago. All was silent. "No."

The Trine held his amulet a moment longer, then let it fall back against his chest. "You will regret this, Pinal." He sat back on his heels and glared at her father with raw hatred. Was he calling something to him—or was he going to attack him?

The Dar-Azûlan raised his face to Liaonne. "I am so sorry, Defender Second. Your mother is gone." He reverently lifted the prime's red beryl amulet over her neck and handed it to her daughter. "*Oë Primus*. Thou art prime, Liaonne il'Edaran. *Diu vide a Vallia il'Edaran*. Long live Vallia Edaran."

"Why, Father?" Mirana staggered to her feet. "Why?"

Lightning flashed outside the tent, illuminating the canvas, and her father's furious face riveted on Lord Garis. Thunder cracked in answer. The wind rose sharply, battering at the tent.

The Trine rose to his feet and wiped his hands on his cloak. "Mirana, leave it be."

She ignored him. "Is your hatred of Lord Garis so strong, you would let a prime die rather than let me work with him to save her?"

He shook his head. "He was stealing your Aspects from you."

"Stealing? He was directing me. I've never done this before. We were trying to save Prime Edaran's life. You would let a woman die in an act of revenge because our Trine did not answer your call for aid two summers ago? Did you ever think about how painful that decision was for *him* to make, knowing good men and women were going to die? Did you? And now you let another good woman die to spite him."

"Mirana, stop," the Trine said, breathing his words in futility.

Her father held up his hands, pleading. "No. Of course not. I was trying to protect you."

She curled her hands into fists. "You would rather a woman die because of a disagreement about the future of the il'Kin?"

"I was trying to protect you, Mirana. Don't you understand that?" Her father grabbed her arms. "I have not kept your Trine gifts a secret for sixteen summers only to have you killed!"

The tent went silent.

She froze in horrified astonishment. "You what?" Disbelief slammed into her like a battering ram made of amulet fire. She wrenched herself free. "You knew? All along?"

Her mother clutched her amulet. "We were trying to keep you safe, *biraena*. Please believe that. But now, we must retreat. The Ken'nar will be here at any moment. Please believe us."

"You both knew? Both of you?" Mirana looked from her mother to her father, ignoring the warning. "Why didn't you tell me?"

"Please understand, Miri," her mother said, "we never meant to deceive you. We knew you'd understand your powers someday, but we hoped you'd come to us before now. When you didn't, we thought you still didn't know. We decided to wait until you were ready to choose an amulet. That way, you could protect yourself—" She looked out the tent entrance. "—in case we no longer could. We were wrong. So very wrong."

Her father now held his amulet, red light spilling from between his fingers. "If the Dark Trine knew yet another Trine existed, he would have done everything in his power to kill you." He glanced out of the tent. "We did this to keep you safe. We have no time to discuss this now. We must hurry."

Mirana whirled around to face Tetric Garis. "Did you know, too?"

He shook his head. "I never knew for certain. They would never let me near you."

Had she only known when she was a young child, had she only been apprenticed to Lord Garis sooner, she might never have had her vision of the white light in the keep. Of Kinderra's destruction at her hands. Of Teague's death. Kinderra might have been free of what she was to become. If she had known summers ago, she might not have been so wrapped in fear that she lost trust in herself, and she could have saved these people at the ford. Had she only known sooner.

Anger consumed her like a wildfire burning tinder-dry grass. It filled her, validated her sense of betrayal. "Do you have any idea what you've done?"

Her father's face so often wore a determined expression, as if he never left his battles behind. Now, it sank into utter despondency, reflecting the desperation and despair in his mind. He deserved his pain. Maybe he would know something of what the Underworld her life had become felt like. "Mirana, please. We never meant to hurt you. You must go now."

She backed away from them. "It's more than me you've hurt. Kinderra will suffer, too."

She stormed out of the command tent. Thunder rolled through the cold, damp night, but this time it did not die away. It grew louder. Otherworldly cries filled the air followed by peculiar whistles and dull thuds. Grynwen. Arrows.

The Ken'nar had arrived.

CHAPTER 21

"Quen u'pace ve, Aspecta'e Alta ire."
("When war comes, the Aspects Above abandon.")
—Ora Fal'kinnen 95:16

Mirana stood, disbelief and fear adding to her rage at her parents' betrayal. A nightmare came to life before her. To the north, two battalions of Fal'kin clashed with an equal number of Ken'nar as lightning knifed overhead. Grynwen tore at the bellies of horses with claws and knife-long fangs, sending their riders falling into the amulet fire and swords of the black-armored warriors. An instant later, the lightning ceased and the fields were plunged back into the inky darkness, but the sounds of war drew inexorably closer. This was no longer a vision from the Seeing Aspect, no longer just moving pictures in her mind. This was real.

The Fal'kin leaders rushed from the tent behind her. Liaonne Edaran growled at the Ken'nar nearing the camp. "I will fight with you, Prime Kellis Pinal. And I will make every single one of those black bastards pay for what they've done to Varn-Erdal and to me!"

"I cannot express my sorrow or gratitude to you," her mother replied to Liaonne, but her eyes remained on Mirana. "Take Legion Three from Defender Second Niall Corran. I'll call him with the order."

The new prime nodded and raced to her horse. Mirana shook her head, breaking her daze. She fought the urge to follow the Varn-Erdalan and add her own inferno of fury to the defender woman's revenge.

Desde reached out to her. "Miri, Lightness, please—"

She pushed her mother away. "Don't. Just. Don't."

Her Seeing and Defending Aspects rose. She sucked in a raw breath. Without an amulet to focus them, they fought each other for supremacy within her. Her Defending Aspect surged, blotting out future skeins of time with the immediacy of need.

Dark-fletched arrows sang overhead, their flaming shafts making bright streaks in the night sky. A long, thick projectile tore through the command tent, setting it ablaze. She screamed, the fire tearing her awareness from her Aspects.

Tetric Garis tore his helmet from the saddlebag straps and slammed it down on his head. In one smooth movement, he swung his leg over his black stallion. … *Get on your horse, Mirana … Now …*

She ran for Ashtar and vaulted onto his saddle. She turned to her parents, more emotions boiling in her than she could ever identify. "I never want to see either of you again."

She dug her heels into Ashtar's sides and sent him into a run.

Mirana's Aspects were assaulted by the fury of the oncoming Ken'nar as she charged to the east with the Trine. Her Healing Aspect erupted in response to the abrupt ending of lives. Swift and relentless, images borne of her Seeing Aspect cut in and out before her mind's eye and her mortal eyes. A burning hunger welled up from deep in her chest. Her Defending Aspect begged to be released to stop the Ken'nar.

She stole a glance to the south. Through a flash of lightning, she saw the southern Ken'nar contingent riding toward the garrison. Like a black ocean, the warriors covered the plains just beyond the entrance to the ford valley. Thunder plunged the scene back into darkness.

Lord Garis charged his stallion alongside her. ... *Follow the Anarath River until you are well away from the ford ... I will meet you by the Stairs of Anar ... Go now ...* He sharply wheeled his horse away to charge south.

"My lord, wait—!"

Flares of multicolored lightning exploded around her. She screamed and ducked low over her saddle, covering her head with one arm. Fal'kin converged on the Ken'nar as they neared the installation. The clash of their swords cut through the night air.

The blood-soaked fury around her was far more terrifying than any vision ever could be. She fought to put the death that surrounded her, the agony, the rage into some sort of context, but no rationale could ever explain this. The Underworld had released itself before her and she was now one of the damned.

Panicked, she drew a long knife as Ashtar surged forward, frantically searching the battlefield for the Trine. ... *Lord Garis* ... No answer returned to her. Had he hidden under U'Nehíl, cloaking his presence from the Ken'nar Dark Trine? No Fal'kin could fight under U'Nehíl, and certainly not use an amulet while hidden. Lord Garis was no ordinary Fal'kin, however. Could his Trine Aspects uphold U'Nehíl while he fought? She couldn't possibly sift through Aspects amid the fighting to find his mind behind false duplications of life like she had her father. There was simply too much of…of everything.

Only Tetric Garis could help her find a new destiny, one that would save Kinderra and not destroy it. If the Ken'nar Dark Trine was here at the ford, he would try to kill him just as surely as he would try to kill her. Fervent determination welled up from her, no less powerful than a true Aspect.

Tetric Garis had saved her life. And she would save his.

"Ashtar, we have to find him before the Dark Trine does."

Mirana slapped the horse's reins on his shoulder with one hand, held out her long knife with the other, and charged south, farther into the embattled garrison.

CHAPTER 22

"The love I bear for my wife, and she for me, has been made incarnate. A son! The Aspects Above hath granted their servant a son!"

—The Codex of Jasal the Great

Teague raced toward the Dar-Anar foothills with his parents and the herbsfolk who had come with them from Deren. The il'Kin defenders surrounded them in a protective circle as they rode.

He glanced back over his shoulder and wished he hadn't. Flames within the garrison shot up into the sky, engulfing the canvas and wood tents. The battle was silhouetted against the bright orange of the fire. Thankfully the Ken'nar were so preoccupied with the Fal'kin, their little group hadn't been seen. He frowned at himself. Should he even be thankful for that?

Defender Commander Morgan Jord raised a fist in the air and brought the group to a halt. "We should be far enough away."

Battle Seer Binthe Lima cantered her horse up to them and squinted into the distance. She closed her eyes and held her amulet. A moment later, his mother and father exchanged confused expressions. Morgan nodded and frowned.

Teague had never witnessed a battle seer calling a fight before. It was unnerving. "What?" he asked Binthe. He winced. Did he do the wrong thing and break her concentration?

She opened her eyes, but they remained unfocused. "Our battalions are focused on the northern Ken'nar phalanx." Her words came slowly as she translated the visual language of her Seeing Aspect. "But the southern Ken'nar forces are holding their position." She jutted her chin in a direction beyond the Anarath bridge.

Teague squinted. Barely visible in the foggy murk was a long black line, darker than the night. Not seeing the warriors but knowing they were there was more frightening than actually having them apparent. Maybe. He swallowed.

"She means to prevent the northern Ken'nar force from regrouping with the south," Binthe continued, "but she will not have enough fighters. When the southern force comes."

His father gripped his horse's reins with white knuckles. "The provincial forces will be overrun. I will not sit here and watch our people be slaughtered."

"No, Tennen," his mother pleaded.

"I have the blood of defenders in my veins."

"*Ai*, but it is the Healing Aspect you hold. You cannot use a blade."

"I do not need a blade to stop them."

"Tennen, *Ëi cara*, listen to your wife," Morgan said. "If you were to be killed, who would heal us?"

"If I can stop the Ken'nar, no Fal'kin will need to be healed."

Alarm shot arrowlike through Teague. He had never seen his father like this. "Father, you're a healer. You cannot kill."

His father exhaled, releasing his anger. He hung his head. "*Ai*, son. I am sorry. I do not fight Ken'nar, I fight a much more terrible foe—death itself. My place is here." He turned to the defender and the seer. "But it is not yours. The il'Kin have done enough getting us out safely. Desde and Kaarl need you far more than we do. Go."

Binthe's fingers curled around the hilt of one of her long knives. "I sense danger to you here."

"There is danger everywhere," his mother replied. "If the il'Kin can help Kaarl stop the southern phalanx, we will be safe. Maybe we are too small a group to be noticed."

His father stared intently at Morgan and must have called something, as the il'Kin leader nodded after a moment.

The young defender commander returned a grim smile. "Remember the Light and the Keep, *Ëi cara. Rememore Kin e Forte.*"

Even Teague knew it would take more than a battle cry to save the Fal'kin.

As the il'Kin raced back toward the southern bridge and what was left of the garrison, Binthe paused. "Be careful. Please." She charged after the others.

His parents and the herbsfolk dismounted and began to check what supplies they had in their packs. Teague remained in his saddle, locked in horrified fascination at the battle. Jets of colored lightning flared. Was Mirana still somewhere in the garrison, trapped behind the lines?

She had told him she didn't want him in her life anymore. It was more than his heart could bear, a wound that would never stop bleeding. Every time one of the amulets loosed its deadly fire, frantic dread gripped him as he wondered if she had been struck down.

His father approached and put a hand on the broad neck of Teague's horse. "I want you to ride south. Do not stop until you reach Kasan." His eyes, too, remained on the il'Kin riding toward the distant battle. "Tell the defender prime there what has happened."

He shook his head. "I'm not leaving."

His father reached up and grabbed his arm so tightly he thought he'd snap it in two. "You will do as you're told."

"No. That is a massacre." He pulled himself free and pointed to the embattled garrison. "You'll need every herbsman, just like Seer Prime Kellis Pinal needs every Fal'kin."

Mirana. She didn't have an amulet.

"I don't know everything, but I can be of some help."

"Teague—"

"Tennen, the Ken'nar came from the south," his mother said, cutting off his father's warning. "There could be more."

His father blew out his breath and nodded. "Get down from your horse, son. You'll be less of a target for arrows. If any should come this way."

Teague climbed down and watched the distant il'Kin disappear into the rain and smoke and death.

CHAPTER 23

"Patientia ísi straitéis magne i'tuda"
("Patience is the best strategy of all.")
—Ora Fal'kinennen 95:29

The Ain Magne sat astride his stallion as he surveyed the fight from a river bluff south of the garrison and tightened a buckle on his chest plate. His armor was indistinguishable from every other Ken'nar, save for the fact he wore no livery, no surcoat with a heraldic. He was Trine for all of Kinderra, therefore no single provincial symbol would he prefer over another. After a gesture with his hand, an aide immediately handed him a gauntlet. He had young Aspected who had yet to choose an amulet bear for him the skeletal black plates of metal and dark chain mail of the Ken'nar, but he dressed himself.

More than one Ken warlord had died at the hands of an armor-bearer.

... First North artillery ... One more sortie ... Defenders ... At the ready ...

He allowed the myriad of sensations to wash through him, over him, every Aspect thrumming, every nerve alight with the heady maelstrom of war. When he was young, his first experience with battle had overwhelmed him as pain, fear, fury, bloodlust, past impressions, future tellings, and the raw need to release power from him all vied for his attention. He had long since learned to let such sensations run their course for a moment rather than fighting to beat them back. After decades of war, the onslaught of emotions no longer subdued him. Only when the shock of mayhem and death at the opening of a battle had receded did he clear his mind and take control of himself and the fray. He did not savor the experience, far from it, but he let the abrupt *endness* of death serve as a constant reminder of how much was at stake. How much there was to lose. To gain.

... Cease fire ... Archers pull back ... Defender Commander Staine, you have the field ...

... Ai, Lord ... his northern captain returned. *... What of the Varn-Erdalans? ... Our battle seers had divined a large unit in the Dar-Anars heading toward our location ...*

The Ain Magne smiled. Let his second take the credit he was due. He turned his head to face the thousands of Ken'nar behind him and the young, thin man at their head. "Seer Second?'

His lieutenant nodded, his pale-green amulet shining in the darkness. *... The Varn-Erdalan forces are no longer an issue for you, Commander ...* the young seer replied.

... Excellent! ... We will have the Garnath Bridge for you shortly, my Trine ...

From his vantage point, he could view the entirety of the battle. His northern phalanx had done its job, sending barrage after barrage of ignited naphtha-coated arrows into the installation. The heavy rain, of course, would have doused conventional fire. His second scoffed at the use of the Seeing Aspect to predict the weather. The young man would learn it was one of that particular Aspect's greatest uses.

Brilliant white fire consumed garrison tents, sending the Fal'kin scrambling for their horses. Greasy, acrid smoke, the odor perceptible even at his distance, mixed with fog and slowly spread a pall over what was left of the garrison. The Fal'kin battle seers had certainly predicted the presence of his southern contingent, but his troops had yet to enter the theater of battle. An immediate threat always took precedence over a less urgent one. So, Seer Prime Kellis Pinal had given the only order she could: form a line to prevent his northern units from coming any closer. Desde was a smart woman, though. More than likely, she, too, knew the futility of her order before she even gave it. And so, he had her right where he wanted her.

His second trotted his horse closer. He removed the steel, wolf-like skull of a helmet and shook the sweat from his light brown hair. "The troops grow restless, my lord. Give me the order."

It was a fair observation, but sending in the southern phalanx at this very moment would accomplish nothing but waste precious defenders—on both sides.

The boy was smarter than this and should be above letting bloodlust get the better of him. "The time is not yet right. Use your Aspect. Tell me what you see."

The seer stared at him a moment, not bothering to hide the frustration leaking from his mind. "I have, my lord. As always. If we move in now, we can wipe out the Kin-Deren bitch—"

"Show some respect. She is a prime."

The young seer bowed his head, acknowledging the reprimand, but his face reddened with anger, not contrition. "We can wipe out Kellis Pinal's north unit before her defenders have fully organized. We need to be bold and swift."

"And we will be. When I am ready."

His second leaned forward in his saddle and bounced his black armored forearm against the pommel of his saddle, an anxious gesture that had never disappeared despite training. "Staine won't be able to take the bridge without more troops. He's outnumbered two to one."

"*Ai*. He is. But not for long." He shifted in his saddle and sought his field commander's mind. … *Shore up your eastern flank and herd the Fal'kin down the ridge …*

His commander was far too engaged in fighting to call a mind-worded reply but instead sent an affirmative intent. The man was a seasoned defender, a veteran of many battles. He had been right to put Staine in a position of leadership. He was not insulted but grateful the man had not wasted time and effort on a more formal reply.

The Trine curled his armor-encased fingers around the dark crystal of his amulet and let the connection build between his Aspects and the gem. His northern phalanx was momentarily pushed back by the Fal'kin defending the Garnath Bridge. Soon, the Pinals would make another move, again the only one they could, again leading them closer to their downfall. His shoulders tensed with a surge of the Defending Aspect within him.

Beside him, his second inhaled sharply, pale light spilling from the amulet he held. "She's going to make a mistake. She will destroy herself with that order."

"Eventually. But it's not Desde's mistake, she will only accede to it. It will be her husband who will make the mistake."

The time had nearly come.

"I have an order for you. Make certain the girl remains alive. Make certain your men and women know this. If any of your troops try to harm her, kill that person. Personally."

Again, the seer faced him, but this time he withheld comment.

It was a sacrifice he was loath to make, but Mirana Pinal alone was worth more than every single Ken'nar on the face of the continent.

The Ain Magne set his grynwen-skull helmet over his head and adjusted the faceplate.

… Seer Second … Move the southern phalanx into position …

CHAPTER 24

"And the battle was joined. Like the fire of the
Aspects, all were consumed in their wake."

—The Book of Kinderra

Kaarl shrugged off the burning sensation in his shoulder and sucked in a lungful of air, vitality returning to him. He pulled his sword free from the Ken'nar's chest as the light from the dark warrior's amulet faded. The Ken'nar who died at the end of his blade had dared try to use Kaarl's own life to power his damned amulet, but his sword was even faster than the Power from Without.

He, Desde, her battle seers, and a unit of provincial defenders fought to hold the eastern ridge leading into the ford valley so the garrison could retreat. The fighting moved down the valley rim from them, giving him a moment to study the battle. The Fal'kin at the northern Garnath bridge had taken losses. The line was holding, but they would not be able to maintain it much longer. Death lay ahead and behind. Once the main Ken'nar host from the south arrived, they would be hopelessly outnumbered. They would lose. The Ken'nar would then march east and would take Deren with almost no resistance from the citadel. All of Desde's fighters had been deployed here at the ford. To save Deren, and the rest of the continent, they had to succeed at the ford. But how?

"How did they find the command tent so quickly?" Desde asked. "We barely escaped being burned alive." She shook off something from one of her long knives. Grynwen flesh. Disgusting, mangy beasts.

"They didn't find anything. They just set flames at will."

He would have never known his wife had not seen combat in nearly twenty summers. He wondered, not for the first time, if she had a touch of the Varn-Erdalan viciousness somewhere in her blood.

She held her amulet, then gasped and pointed southward. "Look."

A black wave swept toward the ford off to the south and emerged from the darkness between flashes of lightning. The Ken'nar southern phalanx. Five thousand of them.

A wash of grim dread flooded him. When all the Fal'kin intelligence spoke of an attack at dawn, the Dark Trine sent the Ken'nar under cover of night. When they expected a force of five hundred from the north, the Dark Trine split his troops into two units, with five thousand approaching from the south.

He searched the battlefield with his eyes and with senses more acute. "Where is Garis?"

"I do not know. I cannot sense him. He must be under U'Nehíl."

He tore his gaze away from the battle lines to look at his wife. "During a battle?"

"Maybe he's shielding her somehow as well." Desde wasn't watching the fighting but focused on the long knife in her hand.

"I hope he's not at the ford at all." He prayed the Trine was riding away with Mirana. He dared not reach for his daughter's mind. He would not be able to fight if the Aspects gave him silence.

He shut out his worry for his daughter, his determination a citadel gate slamming closed against a marauding horde. His Aspect and his amulet were the only things left to him to save her now that his silence no longer could. He studied the Ken'nar battle lines again. "They will attempt to surround us."

She nodded. "*Ai.* I've seen it in four out of five future skeins."

"Garis was right. We will not be able to get out." He gritted his teeth. "You'll have to order the provincials to split into two units, one to keep the southern phalanx from advancing and the other to try to finish off the northern unit."

Desde frowned. "It will turn our one weak army into two even weaker ones."

"Can you think of any better way to prevent being cut down between their two?"

His wife sighed in frustration. "No."

"By your order, my prime, I will take half and go south. Defender Commander Dav Koehl and Liaonne Edaran can have at these bastards."

She nodded, her face taut with concern. "We need a miracle, *Ëi ama.*"

Anger quickly replaced his defeat, his Defending Aspect rising to the need. He cast out a wide call. Hundreds of Kin-Deren defenders peeled off from the fighting and raced south.

Kaarl curled his lip into a fierce snarl. "I will be your damned miracle."

He dug his heels into the sides of his horse and charged into the fray.

CHAPTER 25

"The question is not what I would do for Kinderra but
what I would not do. To that, I reply, 'Nothing!'"
                                            —The Codex of Jasal the Great

"Father, Mirana's out there." Teague wiped the wet hair from his eyes. He blinked against the rain as the horror in the distance continued to unfold.

His mother stifled yet another moan. "There's so much death. I cannot keep it from me." His father put a hand on her, steadying her.

He had never seen her react this way. It frightened him. His parents had each other and were surrounded by the herbsfolk. Mirana might be all alone. If the Dark Trine found her, he would surely kill her.

He gritted his teeth as fire bit into something flammable in the garrison and flames exploded into the sky. "I have to find her."

"She is with her mother, one of Kinderra's most skilled battle seers," his father replied, not taking his eyes from the embattled garrison.

Teague clenched his teeth tighter. A skilled battle seer who hadn't fought since well before he was born. He tightened his hands into fists. He could not sense his father's emotions, but he was certain they now shared the same rage, which neither could use. "The garrison is overrun. They'll be out on the fields by now."

The flashes of amulet light in the north dwindled. The Fal'kin were dying. The ford was lost. Mirana. Panicked need welled up from the pit of his stomach like bile. He had to do something. Anything.

His father closed his eyes, his mouth working in a silent curse. As a child, he had been known as "the boy who could see death." The overwhelming sense of lives lost mustn't have been any easier for his father to bear than for his mother. "Mirana is clever. Her Trine Aspects—" He took a breath and swallowed before he opened his eyes. "Her Aspects will keep her safe."

Fire consumed another tent in the camp, sending bright orange flames high into the air.

"Mirana hasn't trained for something like this," Teague said, gesturing wide at the distant battle. "She hasn't even held a knife in more than six summers. Regardless of her Aspects, she's only one person against thousands. She will be killed. I have to help her."

His father whirled toward him. "No, you do not, *biraen.*"

"You can't protect me anymore. I'm not a child."

"*Ai*, you are. You are *my* child. I will protect you. No matter what I must do."

Teague clenched and unclenched his hands in useless anger. "You don't think I can protect myself? Or her? Because I'm not Aspected?"

"*Ai*, dammit, *ai*. Because she has not one but three Aspects. Because she has Sight to see those who will strike her down before they do. Because she has had at least some training with a blade. You do not have any of those."

Teague glanced at his mother as she drew in a sharp breath once more, trying to push away the omnipresent sense of death. He turned back to his father. "It does not matter whose hand holds a sword. It can still kill."

Instead of another reprimand, Teague's father pulled him into a fierce embrace. "You have always thought I was ashamed of you because were born without Aspects." He held him back, gripping his head to stare into his eyes. "I am grateful, Teague il'Sahli il'Beltran, so very grateful you do not have these burdens, because you will never be consigned to the madness of combat." He wrapped his arms around Teague once more. "You are my son. The greatest gift the Aspects Above could have ever bestowed on me. I will not lose you to the Ken'nar. I will not."

Teague returned his embrace with equal strength. "Father, why didn't you ever tell me this before—"

"Tennen." His mother pointed toward the blazing garrison. A detachment of riders separated from the embroiled fighting and rode in their direction.

Teague stepped from his father. "Do they have wounded with them?"

Tennen stood motionless, his eyes wide.

"Father?"

His mother's face had gone white. His parents looked at each other. Tennen nodded minutely. He slowly walked over to his horse and drew a sword from beneath the saddle blanket.

Teague's eyes widened in horror. "F-Father?" He hadn't meant for him to take his earlier words literally.

"Son, get on your horse. Now." His mother's voice was taut with her command. In her hand, she held a long knife.

"But—"

She swallowed noisily. "We have no choice now."

"Everyone, to your horses." His father swung up into his saddle as the other herbsfolk quickly scrambled to their mounts. "Ride south. Head for the Sün-Kasalan grasslands." He jabbed at the sides of his horse with his heels and broke into a dead run.

Teague shook himself and clambered onto Bankin's saddle. She immediately took off without any urging.

High-pitched whines shrieked through the air, rising above the din of the battle. He ducked instinctively. Two of the herbsfolk riding close to him screamed and fell off their horses, arrows protruding from their chests. Ken'nar flooded across the fields toward them.

He reined in his horse to avoid running into one of the dark-armored warriors. His father swung his sword. A Ken'nar fell, screaming, then was silent. He stared at his father. Blood smeared the sword the healer held in his hand, his face twisted in grief and rage. "Get down!"

Teague ducked, narrowly avoiding being decapitated by a Ken'nar sword. The movement, however, spilled him from the saddle. He landed hard. Dazed, he shook his head to clear it. A Ken'nar mount was coming down on top of him. He screamed and rolled away.

His mother turned her blood-spattered face toward him. "Teague. Run." A Ken'nar charged his mount, shrieking a war cry, and tried to pull his mother from her horse.

"Mother!"

She flung her arm, and the Ken'nar landed on the ground several feet away.

The dark warrior reached for his amulet, aiming it at Teague. Fire never left the amulet. The Ken'nar's head twisted with a wet crack and lolled to one side. He collapsed into a heap. His mother gripped her amulet, groaning in pain and anguish.

Teague shook with terrified understanding. She had used her Healing Aspect to break the Ken'nar's neck. She killed the dark warrior to save his life.

His father grabbed him and shoved him toward his horse. "Go!" He took a glancing blow to his shoulder from an amulet and cried out in pain.

Panicked, Teague looked for a weapon. "I—"

"Please, son."

He swung up into the saddle. He slapped at his horse with the reins and plowed through three Ken'nar. He had to find Lord Garis, someone, anyone. He had to get help.

Teague raced hard for the Anarath bridge.

CHAPTER 26

*"The Kin-Deren defenders met the Ken'nar on the field
of battle, mighty red eagles winging their way toward
accursed black crows."*

—The Book of Kinderra

Kaarl let loose another volley of vermilion fire from his
garnet amulet at a group of Ken'nar crossing the southern
bridge. The pouring rain hissed as it touched the crystal's heat.
The dark-armored warriors charged toward the garrison,
lightning reflecting off their wet protective plates.

He yanked the reins of the sleek, gray charger he rode,
dragging its head around and slipping out of a melee. This
animal—he hadn't had time to learn its name before marching
out of Deren—was much leaner than Ashtar. Lean and swift.

That might give him a few advantages fighting in such close quarters while mounted.

As they neared, he fired another strike with his amulet. They answered him with a hail of arrows. He thrust out his hands at the incoming projectiles. Arrows dropped from the sky at an oblique angle, hitting an invisible Aspected wall. Many, even most of them, fell. But not all. There were too many. He heard a scream behind him. His curse was lost as a Ken'nar mind clutched at him, grasping, the warrior trying to draw from his Aspects to feed his power. The pull released abruptly when the head flew from the Ken'nar's shoulders by a Fal'kin sword.

… *Legion Five … Advance left … Don't let them break the line* … he called to one of the battalions Desde had put under his command. He dug his heels into his horse and rode for a unit of Ken'nar trying to curl around to the west as they came off the bridge.

He had hoped they could keep the Ken'nar on the Sün-Kasalan side of the southern Anarath bridge. He must avoid fighting on the bridge itself. There would be no room to maneuver there, even for his slight horse. That had been his plan, anyway.

The Ken'nar bastards flew across the Anarath bridge and cut off any escape to the east. He and the provincial forces he commanded for Desde were caught between the Ken'nar in front of the southern bridge and the apex of the land's edge where it dropped away into the river gorge. His only choice now was to press them east once more into the shallow bowl of the valley and attack the enemy on the open fields. Ken'nar tangled with Fal'kin there, too, but at least he'd have room to fight. What was more, if he could hold the Ken'nar to that location, Desde and what was left of Dav Koehl's legions could try again for a retreat. He had to prevent his forces from being herded south onto the bridge or off the cliffs into the river ravine.

Kaarl whirled in his saddle and narrowly blocked the heavy blade of a Ken'nar warrior with his own sword. The clash sent jarring pain through his elbow and up his arm. He gripped the hilt of his blade with both hands and slid it out from under the Ken'nar's parry, bringing it down on his attacker's shoulder. The black-armored fighter howled in pain and rage but sidestepped his horse away. The Ken'nar swung the broadsword at his neck.

Kaarl ducked low over his saddle pommel, then thrust his blade through a chink in the rib plates of the Ken'nar's armor. The blow unseated his opponent. The dark warrior's horse screamed in terror at the sudden loss of its rider and bucked, pawing at the air. It came down hard on its master's chest, finishing Kaarl's grim work. Two grynwen slunk beneath the terrified horse and tore at its fallen rider. Even their strong jaws could not penetrate Ken'nar armor, so they simply shook their heads, rending his limbs from his torso. He hoped the man was already dead.

Another wave of dark riders raced toward him and the Fal'kin. He hammered at a Ken'nar with a jet of red lightning from his amulet. It met the Ken'nar's green flame, creating a tall column of deadly fire between them as each sought to repel the other. A wrenching pull within him nearly forced him from his saddle. He would not fall prey to the Power from Without so easily. He dug deep and poured out his Defending Aspect. Another Fal'kin slashed at his attacker and, at last, his amulet fire engulfed the Ken'nar.

An agonized scream lifted in the air. Not Kaarl's attacker— he was already a pile of greasy ash. It came from behind. He spared a glance behind him. Several combatants, Fal'kin and

Ken'nar both, slipped over the land's edge into the river gorge as the ground fell apart under the hooves of their mounts.

He gasped. The very earth was crumbling away. The ground, made soft and unstable by days of pounding rain, eroded under the weight of hundreds of fighters.

More fighters screamed as they plummeted over the edge of the land.

He had to break the Ken'nar line or the Fal'kin would be pressed off the cliff—and into the abyss.

CHAPTER 27

*"The Power from Without: An Aspect created by man
to do what man wishes with Life, not that which is the
will of the Aspects Above."*

—The Book of Kinderra

The Ain Magne grimaced behind the faceplate of his
grynwen-like helmet and ignored the heat reflecting in his face
from his breath against the steel. Ken'nar and Fal'kin alike
slipped over the edge of the ford, plunging to their deaths in the
ravine as the bluffs themselves gave way.

... Fall back! ... Fall back! ... he screamed through his call.

The damned rain. He had used it to his advantage. Now, it
was a weapon turned against him, one he was not prepared to
fight.

... Why dost thou test thy servant, O Aspects Above? ...

He swept his great sword at a group of Fal'kin who raced toward him, blood on their minds, and beheaded three at once. "Damn you!" There simply hadn't been time to harvest them.

... Ëi Seconde! ... Advance the archers toward the Fal'kin rear guard ... Move them away from the cliffs ...

An intent of consent reached his mind. Several hundred feet ahead of him, a wave of black-armored archers ebbed from the land's end, pushing the Fal'kin closer to the egress of the Anarath bridge.

The Trine lifted his bottom lip over the upper one, tasting the salt of his sweat as it trickled down his face. And smiled. His second had taken the first step toward creating the last step for the Fal'kin.

Before he could even think about connecting with his Seeing Aspect, blistering heat burned into his shoulder. He hissed a curse and yanked the head of his stallion around.

"I am not so easily defeated!" He loosed metallic-colored light from his amulet, filling the gem with the life force of his opponent. His Fal'kin foe erupted into screaming flames.

The Ain Magne glanced once more at his Ken'nar on the bridge. The Fal'kin would be hounded in the front and the rear by his troops when they made a play for his yet-unsupported southern phalanx. He would have the Fal'kin trapped.

A wall of red eagles-on-saffron fell upon his troops, driving them back toward the open fields of the river valley.

The Kin-Deren provincials.

Bright red amulet fire stuttered over a Ken'nar unit, five of his warriors erupting into flames as the tongues of fire caressed them.

Kaarl Pinal.

"Damn him!" He dug his heels into the sides of his mount and charged closer to the southern landing of the Anarath bridge.

His Seeing Aspect nudged him with no particular vision, just a knowing.

He was running out of time.

CHAPTER 28

"Te Aspecta'e Alta solis ísí Oë busquaer defendeo."
("From the Aspects Above alone shall you seek protection.")
—Ora Fal'kinnen 15:6

All around Mirana lay bodies—Fal'kin, Ken'nar, horses, grynwen—death contorting their limbs. Heaving bodies still locked in mortal combat whirled about her as she raced Ashtar past the battle lines. The faces of the dark forms struggling in the pounding rain only revealed themselves when lightning stabbed at the tormented sky or when amulets illuminated vanquishers and the vanquished. Rage, agony, terror, the brutality of war pierced her mind like lances.

… Lord Garis … Where are you? … Answer me … she called.

Her Defending Aspect flared. *What? Where?* She looked around frantically for the threat. Without an amulet, she had no way of knowing for certain.

Arrows soared over her head. Ashtar veered, trying to avoid the lethal missiles, and threw her from her saddle with his sudden movement. She landed on a dead Fal'kin, his blood and bowels staining her leather armor. She cried out in horrified disgust and flipped herself over, away from the corpse. Out of the storm and the swirling fighters, an enormous dark mass slammed into her, driving her back down into the offal and the mud.

A grynwen gnashed at her throat with fangs longer than her fingers. She screamed and tried to push the beast from her with her arms and her Aspects, but the vicious carnivore outweighed her by five times. Hot saliva dripped from its maw onto her throat as its blood-red eyes narrowed with each snap of its jaws.

"I'll not have you take another one of mine, you rackin' cur!" a woman screamed.

A sword took the beast's head from its haunches, spraying her with blood. She looked up.

Into the helmet of a Ken'nar warrior.

CHAPTER 29

"My help comes from the Aspects Above alone."
—The Codex of Jasal the Great

"Run, Bankin!"

Teague dug his heels into his mount's sides, willing her to charge faster. When he reached the southern causeway of the Anarath bridge, he found the far end packed with fighting bodies. There would be no crossing it.

Moments later, a hail of arrows shot through the air and pelted the ground around him. Bankin paced, terrified, uncertain in which direction to run.

Again, he raced toward the bridge, wildly dodging another flock of arrows. He searched for a Fal'kin unit fighting on the fringes of the Ken'nar column, intending to convince them to break off and save his parents and the herbsfolk. His horse stumbled, nearly throwing him again. He reined to a dead stop.

Bodies covered the entire southern plain. Torn standards of a red horse on a white field lay in the bloody mud. The guard from Varn-Erdal.

They had been killed. All one hundred of them. Their bodies, gray forms in the dim predawn light, lay contorted on the wet ground. Grynwen gibbered in ravenous glee as they fed on the dead. In the damp air, shreds of fog swirled and crept across the fields like wraiths. His stomach clenched. Hardtack didn't taste good coming up. Actually, it didn't taste good going down, either. He fought to get his stomach under control between heaves.

The bridge remained locked in the grip of the Ken'nar, cutting off any escape for the Fal'kin.

Teague turned in his saddle toward the foothills. His breath dragged itself from his lungs, weighted with helplessness.

There would be no help for his mother and father.

CHAPTER 30

"The light of the Aspects will be my shield! My amulet, my sword!"
—The Codex of Jasal the Great

Kaarl ducked another Ken'nar blade.

Where were Morgan and Binthe when he needed them? Garis had ordered them out of action. Damn Tetric Garis.

No. This time he could not blame the Trine. The healers were too important to lose.

… All units … Concentrate fire full front … Concentrate fire full front … he called wide.

A riot of colored Fal'kin amulet fire erupted, washing over the Ken'nar. The dark warriors fell by the dozen. Kaarl and the Fal'kin charged from the land's edge, pushing the Ken'nar line back east toward the open fields of the ford valley.

He spied the tight knot of Desde's Fal'kin battle seers on the ridge to the east. Her defender guard unit was embroiled in fighting. They would not last.

… Desde … Fall back … Fall back. …

… Kin-Deren north guard … Two enemy units … Moving south-southeast … His seer wife called to the Kin-Deren provincial army, ignoring his plea.

The unceasing onslaught of amulet fire from Kaarl's Fal'kin herded the Ken'nar forces away from the bridge toward the open fields. He didn't utter a prayer of gratitude yet.

A familiar presence brushed at his mind. "Steward Pinal." He turned to see Morgan Jord riding toward him, his sword drawn, followed by Binthe Lima and thirteen other il'Kin.

He wanted to be relieved. He wasn't. They had taken serious losses. "The healers?"

"Safe," Binthe said, shaking her hair away from her face with a spray of rain and blood. She sucked in a breath as her emerald amulet suddenly brightened. "Down!"

He and Morgan both ducked, evading a hail of arrows. Embers singed the back of his neck as the projectiles turned to cinders by Fal'kin defender amulets.

He raised his head to thank the seer, but Desde's mental cry cut off his response. He snapped his head up to the ridge. A dozen of her Fal'kin defenders attempted to stop the Ken'nar army as the monstrous infantry advanced from the south again, and this time, merged with the remnants of the northern phalanx. The sons of grynwen whores had allowed themselves to be pushed east and had circled the edge of his forces.

Kaarl searched the battlefield for a way to get to her, or for an escape route he could call to her. Several Ken'nar punched through the Fal'kin line and rode straight for him, death on their minds. He thrust out his hand, sending one warrior flying from his saddle into his comrades. Morgan and the other il'Kin turned them into ash.

The Ken'nar poured onto the battlefield on Kin-Deren soil toward Desde. They surged unheeded through the weakened Fal'kin line, armored and mounted black spears through parchment. Her group was overcome and forced southward.

... *Desde!* ... he called.

Morgan followed his gaze. ... *To the ridge* ... he ordered the il'Kin, brandishing his sword.

Kaarl jammed his heels into the sides of his mount, charging east toward his wife. He would run through the Ken'nar bodily if he must to save her.

... *All commands ... Ken'nar archers ... Moving north* ... Desde called, her mind's voice desperate.

He whipped his head around to look south. A column, one-thousand strong, rode toward him. Those racking maggots had split their unit yet again. The Ken'nar broke for the outside of the garrison to the west, along the land's edge overlooking the river gorge, and attempted to create a perimeter. They would move to surround Kaarl's forces.

The maneuver forced him to call off his charge toward Desde. ... *Morgan, get her out of there* ... he called to his friend and wheeled his mount around toward the surging southern phalanx.

If his Fal'kin could outrun the Ken'nar and make it south across the Anarath bridge, the southern Ken'nar might be drawn away from their northern phalanx—and Desde. It was more than risky. The bridge was exactly where he did not want to be. He couldn't make more amulets, but maybe he could leave fewer Ken'nar for Dav Koehl, Liaonne Edaran, and what was left of the Fal'kin northern provincial unit. He gritted his teeth. If nothing else, they could hold the bridge for a retreat. If they could pull it off. If he could hold out that long. If.

Kaarl regrouped his provincial forces and charged to meet the remainder of the southern Ken'nar phalanx head-on. He gripped his amulet and downed one Ken'nar. He aimed for another, but the Ken'nar repulsed the strike with amulet fire of his own. Two provincial Fal'kin fighters went down. Another defender incinerated several arrows at once with her amulet, but there were too many. A lethal projectile found its mark in her neck. Soon, the air was alive with arrows.

… Desde … Run … Run! … he called while deflecting the deadly missiles with his Aspect.

His wife and her dwindling guard raced toward his forces, the tattered remnants of the il'Kin guarding their backs. A blistering exchange from the Fal'kin opened the embroiled Ken'nar line for Desde and the others, but that frail victory only handed them another defeat. No one called the battle now. He cursed. Even if Desde and Binthe could handle all the communication for the harrowing fight themselves, they no longer had a vantage point.

Cold apprehension swallowed him as he searched the sodden, bloody battlefield for some advantage, some weakness in the Ken'nar lines he could use. The regrouped northern phalanx of the Ken'nar—now two thousand strong—curled around the western edge of the garrison, a wave in an ocean of black armor. Those from the east pushed back his line.

Searing pain scorched his back. He screamed in agony and fury as he wheeled his horse to face his attacker. The Ken'nar died from amulet fire and a pair of long knives.

Kaarl threw an arm around his wife as she reached him, nearly pulling her from her horse in his effort to embrace her. "Desde."

She brushed her lips on his cheek. "Dav Koehl—" She panted, trying to recover her breath from the strain of her Sight.

"He has fallen. Liaonne and Niall Corran are doing what they can with our northern provincial troops, but our line is gone."

Corran was a very smart defender second—or defender commander now—but he'd have his hands full. Kaarl could expect no aid from the other Fal'kin forces.

Her words chilled him, his blood oozing like mud in his veins. "The Ken'nar are going to merge and box us in."

… We will create a feint …

The air surrounding him became alive with Fal'kin arrows. He smiled. They were an illusion. But the Ken'nar didn't know that. … *We ride for Deren!* … He reached deep within himself, his power billowing in him, and his red amulet exploded in fury.

At a full gallop, his forces, at last, broke through the Ken'nar archer line as the dark warriors momentarily retreated against the image of an aerial barrage. Fal'kin amulets flashed like earthbound lightning to match the lightning in the heavens, and downed enemy fighters in waves. The diversion wavered as Desde and Binthe could no longer maintain the illusion of arrows. Real Ken'nar arrows forced them to focus on saving their own lives.

Kaarl dealt death for death with the dark-armored warriors, but for each one he cut down, another Ken'nar took his opponent's place. The Fal'kin around him began to falter under the might of their enemy. Already, defenders were being forced off the Kin-Deren plain between the two bridges into the river chasm. They plummeted to their deaths far below as whole sections of earth fell away from under their feet.

He swung his sword and fired unceasingly with his amulet, but he knew now it was useless. They were trapped.

CHAPTER 31

*"Hand in hand, Hafen and Halen together opened the
womb of their mother. Now, their hands hold swords,
opening the floodgates of their mother's heart."*

—The Book of Kinderra

This bloodbath had gone on long enough. It was time to
bring it to an end.

The Ain Magne was too experienced in the peculiar art of
war to acknowledge victory while an enemy was cornered.
Nothing fought more fiercely than trapped prey.

He reined his stallion to a canter behind the rear of his
southern phalanx. He had the Fal'kin surrounded on the
Anarath bridge. And in the center of his ever-tightening noose,
fought Kaarl Pinal. There was nowhere for him to run.

He clenched and relaxed the grip on his sword in an exceedingly rare moment of indecision. The steward would never accept his philosophy that both the Light from Within and the Power from Without merited benediction from the Aspects Above. No, Kaarl would not.

But his daughter would. He would make certain of it.

The Trine pulled in the essence of life from around him, savoring it as it filled him. He held onto it, letting it build and grow within him to the point where his chest felt on fire. The milky, metallic crystal at his chest burned bright like flaming mercury. The decision made him want to both weep and shout in triumph. Kaarl Pinal had to die.

A rumble like that of distant thunder reverberated across the battlefield. Tremors vibrated up from the ground, up through the iron-shod hooves of his stallion, his dark-patinaed greaves.

"No."

An unbidden vision exploded before his mind's eye, stealing the Power from Without from his Defending Aspect.

Stone falls. Earth slides. A red curtain of light. The Anarath bridge. Consumed.

"No, you little fool! What are you doing? You'll kill yourself!"

He dragged his horse's head around and charged downriver, searching for a way to cross the swollen course.

CHAPTER 32

"My visions have disheartened me once again."
—The Codex of Jasal the Great

... *Now you die, Fal'kin bitch* ... The Ken'nar defender woman called, her mind-words filled with bloodlust.

Mirana screamed. Before she could grapple for her long knives, the woman gurgled on a cry as a sword plunged through her neck and into her throat from behind.

Hot, red blood sprayed Mirana. She flailed to get out from under the ghastly shower as the Ken'nar's body collapsed on top of her. With a shove, she pushed the corpse from her. She spat out blood that found its way into her mouth and wretched on her hands and knees, seeing nothing more than the dark form of her savior as he rode away.

She collapses to her hands and knees. Blood from the deep gash in her side drips onto the paving, the rain and sleet creating little red rivulets in the grout. Teague lies, unmoving. A sob of pain, of desolation, escapes her mouth as she slowly lifts her head.

"It is over, child. Give it to me."

She shook her head to dispel the vision fragment. She had to move. She had to find Lord Garis. If she didn't, Two Rivers Ford would be just the beginning. The Ken'nar would march, unstoppable, across Kinderra. The saving power of Jasal's Keep, if it existed, would never be known. Teague would die. She would fail at the keep, at everything, if the ford fell to the Ken'nar.

If the ford fell.

She sucked in a breath. Her three Aspects rose sharply. They begged for release. Her heart was on fire. She swore she would not take an amulet and wreak the awful destruction she witnessed through her keep vision. But could she do something to save the Fal'kin? With an amulet? Now? If she did, would they remain alive by her hand, only to die by it later at Jasal's Keep?

If she didn't act now, the Fal'kin of an entire province would be wiped off the face of Kinderra. Her province. Her people. People whose lives she had already put in jeopardy.

Mirana scrambled back onto her horse, drawing his head toward the direction of the land's end. "Ashtar! Run!"

CHAPTER 33

"And it shall come to pass that Kinderra will cry out
in such agony as to deafen even Her birth."
	—The Trine Prophecy, The Book of Kinderra

Mirana raced toward the river gorge. The first rays of the dawning sun stroked the Dar-Anar Mountains with red far off to the west as the storm exhausted itself. A lone star, Gabrial, shivered above the range's crooked back.

Sharp metal cries of swords punctuated the agonized human cries of the wounded and the dying. Grynwen howls sang a brutal counterpoint to the hissing, pitched whistle of Ken'nar arrows. Horses and men and women screamed in rage, in terror. Her Defending, Seeing, and Healing Aspects rose, battling against one another for her control.

She charged Ashtar toward the apex of the Kin-Deren's landmass between the two bridges, willing him to run faster than he ever had before. The Fal'kin were trapped on the southern bridge, Ken'nar in front and behind. They could not get off. They would either be slain where they stood or fall over the ford's edge into the river gorge as the land crumbled away under their feet. The very earth was perishing.

She dug her heels into her horse's sides. An arrow screamed through the air. She cried out in pain as it raked down her back at an angle. The thick leather armor Binthe had lashed to her in those harrowing moments before her ill-fated Choosing Ceremony saved her life.

A deep groaning echoed through the ford as though the land itself was in agony. The ground between the bridge arches could no longer bear the weight of so many. Weakened by the rain, it was crumbling. Dying.

Around her, the amulets of the dead glinted in the fading lightning as the storm left the battle in its wake. For summers, the thought of choosing an amulet had paralyzed her. The sacred bond between crystal and Aspect, answering her birthright as a Fal'kin, would unleash a destiny of unimaginable destruction through her. Someday.

… Mirana, please be safe …

Father.

Hatred and love, both raw and pure, surged through her.

If she did nothing at this moment, the Fal'kin would be destroyed. She must act. Now.

Mirana thrust out her hand. A blood-red ruby amulet flung itself from the neck of a dead Fal'kin and hurtled through the air into her waiting palm. She caught it and threw the thick golden chain over her head. The amulet fell heavy against her breastbone, pressing the edges of Teague's delicate pendant into her skin.

The Trine Prophecy. She was the thrice-cursed, sent to destroy. She would turn the ford itself into a weapon of destruction. Maybe she would save the Fal'kin now so they would live to stop the Ken'nar once and for all in the future. Destroy. Rebuild. In one.

Maybe she was that one.

CHAPTER 34

"And thus Kinderra was sundered."
—The Book of Kinderra

Kaarl could not see. Thick black smoke from the blazing garrison billowed in the wind created by the flames themselves, obscuring his vision. The accursed Ken'nar had slathered their arrows with naphtha before lighting them. Even the rain would not put out that fire. He relied on his heightened defender's senses to pick out the nearest of the incoming arrows, listening for the *twang* of bowstrings and the peculiar whistles made by the black fletching.

Grim satisfaction curdled in his stomach. He had been right. Columns from the merged northern Ken'nar forces had indeed followed him and his troops south. The Fal'kin, however, failed in their attempt to rout the Ken'nar off the southern bridge to the Sün-Kasalan plains just beyond. There were simply too many. They fought too tenaciously, leaving humanity behind as they struck. The only dismal good he could see was that the grynwen preferred to stay off the bridge, relishing instead the feast of the killing fields on the ford valley's plains.

Again, the eerie scream of Ken'nar arrows split the air overhead. He could move only so far, however, to avoid them. One false step, one unanticipated shove by some Ken'nar's damned Aspect, and he'd fall off the southern Anarath bridge into the river chasm below.

Once more, Kaarl thrust his sword at a Ken'nar, dropping him from his mount, but he took a glancing blow on his own arm from the melee next to him. The bodies packed on the bridge made fighting all but impossible.

He wheeled his horse away from the combatants when a sharp pain drove through the back of his left shoulder. He cried as burning agony lanced through his arm. An arrow had found its mark, slicing through an opening in his chain mail rent by a Ken'nar broadsword. The arrow's head protruded forward from the thick part of his shoulder muscle. He turned to see more Ken'nar advancing behind him. Seething, he cursed and broke off the tip. He tried to reach back to pull out the remainder of the headless arrow, but the pain was too great. He would just have to cut down the damned Ken'nar with one hand.

Kaarl surged his horse forward, but his charger stumbled as its belly was cut open by the broadsword of a dying Ken'nar from beneath. He arched his body as he dropped to avoid slipping off the bridge. He screamed in pain and rage. Ignoring his wounds, he scrambled to his feet and released deadly fire from his amulet. Sawing agony sheared through his left shoulder as someone pulled the arrow shaft. He whirled around and gripped the vermilion garnet, centering himself to incinerate whoever dared to touch him. Part of the shaft broke as he turned, leaving a portion embedded.

Desde threw away the arrow fragment and reached down to him to help him onto her horse. He thrust away the thought that he had almost killed his wife.

"Keep to the middle—" Her words were lost as a Ken'nar tried to drag her from her horse's saddle. She slashed viciously at her attacker.

Binthe rode up behind the dark warrior and scissored both of her long knives under his helmet and across his throat. He choked a cry and fell over the bridge into the abyss below. A Ken'nar next to her made a wide, sweeping motion with her hand, throwing the seer from her mount. She screamed and disappeared under an onslaught of Ken'nar fighters.

Kaarl thrust out his good arm, wrapping his Aspect around the Ken'nar, and flung the warrior away from her as Morgan reeled his horse around.

"Binthe!" The young defender let out a cry of rage and released a wash of fire from his amethyst amulet.

Five Ken'nar ceased to exist. Binthe emerged from the ash, shaking, bleeding from a dozen cuts. Kaarl caught Morgan's fleeting call to her, no words, only emotion.

Kaarl's Defending Aspect again cried a sharp warning to him. "Morgan! Look out!" Two sets of hands pulled the il'Kin defender off his horse. Binthe swept wide with her hand, throwing one Ken'nar off the bridge, while Desde's lightning-fast movements slashed at the other. As the warrior's hands flew to his throat, she planted a booted foot into the Ken'nar's stomach, sending him sprawling. The Ken'nar reached out in the last instant for Morgan but snagged the reins of the il'Kin defender's horse instead. The women dragged Morgan away as the Ken'nar fell to his doom, taking the il'Kin defender's mount with him.

Kaarl had no time to embrace his friend. "Down!" he screamed and pushed his former lieutenant to his knees. Red fire arched from his amulet, striking a Ken'nar behind the younger defender.

Morgan rose wearily to his feet. "We need to get off the bridge. This is madness."

Kaarl scanned the span, the pain in his shoulder momentarily forgotten. The Fal'kin had to fight their way clear.

He swung his sword at the Ken'nar warriors impeding their way but could not advance. Morgan sprayed the Ken'nar line with deadly purple fire from his amethyst. Kaarl lent his amulet fire to the young defender commander's strike.

Ken'nar fell under their attack, but it was not enough. The southern phalanx kept coming and coming. The northern column herded all that was left of the Fal'kin forces onto the Anarath bridge and into the arms of the southern battalion. There was no room to move on the bridge, no room to fight, nowhere to run.

For the first time in a very, very long time, a tendril of fear wound its way through his mind. If they could not find a way off the bridge, they would die.

He was not afraid to die if it meant his daughter would live. That thought was the only thing that kept him going in the face of so much horror over the long summers. He'd be damned if the Dark Trine would take her while he still breathed.

"Diamond defense! Now!"

Standing back to back, he, Desde, Morgan, and Binthe created a defensive box. The defenders covered the seers with amulet fire while the seers slashed and stabbed at any who drew near.

Screams of terror rose above the battle as Fal'kin and Ken'nar fell off the bridge into the water far below. Even the very earth had turned against them, taking the Aspected of both sides with impunity as the soil washed away, down into the river gorge.

Kaarl slashed at an attacker, but she danced just outside his reach. She toyed with him, coyly, almost seductively, her mind reaching out to his as she tried to draw his Aspects from him. She attempted to coax him out of formation toward her, coming nearly within arm's reach of him. He pulled back, spitting an invective at her, and clamping down on his mind. She laughed in reply—her voice deep and rich and devoid of warmth—and taunted him now with her sword. That was a mistake. Her last. Morgan batted away her sword with his blade. Kaarl reached within himself and emptied his amulet on her. She died, screaming, in the shroud of the garnet's scarlet fire.

He had no time to catch a breath. More Ken'nar moved in to take her place.

Kaarl thrust and feinted with his sword, but it was of little use. The diamond tactic was a defensive move. It afforded no way to spread outward into an offense without breaking the pattern's security. It was a last stand. He was going to die.

... Mirana, please be safe ...

*   *   *

Mirana closed her eyes. The cries of the ruby around her neck became overwhelming as they shrieked against her own life's music. She could no longer feel her body sitting in Ashtar's saddle. Her reality became an all-encompassing resonance only her soul could hear. Her own life's music oscillated through the flawless crystal while its vibrations rippled back to her. Her life's song thrilled in harmony with the music of the ruby until the counterpoint fell away, note by note. At last, her life's harmonics adapted and blended themselves to those of the ruby and it to hers. Disparate chords merged, and she cried out as a single, pure tone, a glorious unison, rose to a crescendo within her.

Mirana's three Aspects joined together as one. Bloodred fire erupted from the amulet in a curtain of flame.

*   *   *

Teague felt it more than heard it—a rumbling from deep within the earth. It vibrated up through his mount's iron-shod hooves. Moments later, a massive wall of red fire erupted in the dim pre-dawn light and hammered at the Ken'nar blocking the southern landing of the Anarath River bridge.

Instinctively, he threw up an arm to shield himself from the brilliant light. When the light dimmed, he lowered his arm. Where fighters once stood, now there were columns of fire. Hundreds. He shook in fear and shock. Was it the Dark Trine? The human pyres collapsed, and the deafening screams were silenced. The Fal'kin surged forward off the bridge, the Ken'nar behind them in pursuit.

Again, a curtain of red flame swept across the Anarath bridge, and again, he shied away from the intense radiance. He blinked his watering eyes to clear them. The sounds of the battle died away as the rumbling grew louder. A great swath of Ken'nar dropped from view as the bridge span on which they stood disintegrated into the chasm. Slowly, inexorably, whole sections of earth slid away.

Grynwen turned from their grisly feast of human carcasses at the light and thunderous crash, and fled in terror around him, baying in primitive fear.

Once more, the scarlet brilliance engulfed the ford. He gasped. The northern Garnath bridge now curled away from its rock-hewn buttresses, dragging still more Ken'nar with it. Dust and screams rose from the ravine until they too disappeared.

He could not move, held captive by what he had just witnessed.

Two Rivers Ford was gone.

The massive wall of red fire. Was it the Dark Trine? Tetric Garis? No.

It was her.

"Mirana," Teague breathed.

* * *

The Ain Magne raced his mount down the sodden banks of the overflown Anarath River, searching for a place to cross over to the Kin-Deren side of the garrison. Somewhere amid the seething masses of combatants was Mirana Pinal. He had to find her before she could attempt her foolhardy plan. The massive power she needed to condense to pull off her reckless act could kill her before she had a chance to release it.

The girl was crucial to his conquest of Kinderra. She was linked to Jasal's Keep. Without her, the power that lay locked within would remain untapped. Kinderra would devolve into anarchy.

The Trine reined his stallion to a halt, the beast's sides heaving with labored breathing. He frowned at the muddy, bloody river. He had no choice but to swim across the raging torrent to get to her.

"You don't know what you're trying to do, child."

He clutched at his amulet and searched for the presence he had felt within her call in the Kana-Akün months ago.

Out of the waning night, a brilliant wall of red light enveloped the southern bridge.

… RETREAT! … RETREAT! … RETREAT! … He called the order with so much force, his stallion reared in fear. It no longer mattered if the Fal'kin heard his command as well or not.

The Ain Magne let the amulet fall against his chest.

"Mirana. What have you done?"

*   *   *

Kaarl gripped his blade with both hands, swinging wildly at anything that moved. Morgan's back pressed against his as the younger defender loosed violet flame over the encroaching Ken'nar.

… Desde … Binthe … Another seer's feint … Kaarl called. *… It might be our only hope …*

… I cannot spare— … His wife screamed in pain. A point-blank strike from a Ken'nar amulet melted the chain mail on her shoulder.

"Desde!" With a fierce cry and sweep of his good arm, he sent the Ken'nar flying into a group of dark-armored warriors and plunging off the bridge to their deaths.

A wall of pure red flame burst forth out of the gloom, brighter than the coming dawn. It washed over the Ken'nar, devouring entire companies whole and tearing at the bridge itself.

Kaarl fell to his knees and shielded himself from the brilliant light. Under his feet, the earth trembled. He and hundreds of fighters, Fal'kin and Ken'nar, paused from fighting. Did the Ken'nar have some sort of new war machine spawned from the Underworld?

The ground shook violently again. He and Desde crouched while Morgan dropped to his knees, clutching Binthe to him. Ken'nar and Fal'kin screamed as they were thrown from the Anarath bridge into the abyss.

He was not about to waste the slim advantage of the Ken'nar's distraction. "Forward!" he ordered as the bridge groaned, its buttress bones breaking.

He and the Fal'kin charged at the Ken'nar on the southern end of the bridge, determined to break their line and escape to the safety of solid ground.

Again, the scarlet wall of flame erupted out of the night. He dropped to his stomach and buried his face against his arms from the radiance. When he dared lift his head again, his eyes widened in fear and awe. Hundreds of Ken'nar had disappeared, instantly turned into ash.

… RETREAT! … RETREAT! … RETREAT! …

Kaarl snapped his head to look over at his wife. "Who—?"

Desde shook her head, and Binthe did likewise.

The remnants of the southern Ken'nar contingent broke ranks and fled off the Anarath bridge as it began to crumble beneath them. They rode west to vanish into the Dar-Anar foothills and the blue-gray light of early dawn. The northern phalanx of the Ken'nar surged at the backs of the Fal'kin, then broke into a panic at the sight of the curtain of flame.

Kaarl scrambled to his feet. A jarring beneath his boots sent a shockwave up his legs. Cracks and fissures appeared in the stone of the bridge. Pieces of carved granite buttresses and rock crumbled away, falling into the river gorge.

He, Desde, and the Fal'kin surged forward to flee the failing bridge. His wife stumbled as the death throes of the bridge made the way treacherous. He caught her with his Aspect and threw her from the bridge to the marginal safety of the landing. Morgan and Binthe grabbed Kaarl's arms and pulled him off the span as it broke apart.

He immediately turned to reach for another Fal'kin, but the woman's hand slipped through his. She fell, screaming, into the gorge.

"No!" Kaarl cried. He tried to reach out to her with his Aspect to stop her plummet and call her body back to him, but she had disappeared into the mists.

The ground trembled again. Strong hands pulled him back farther onto solid ground before he could plunge to his own death.

Again, the wall of pure red flame exploded, splitting the dim early morning light. The land holding the span disintegrated and fell into the chasm below. He reached for his amulet in terrified astonishment. The crimson gout of fire continued to beat against the land. The stone bridge gave one last death rattle, then slowly collapsed, struggling against its demise.

On and on, the massive red barrage of deadly light hammered into the ford. What was left of the apex of the Kin-Deren landmass sheared away in a titanic landslide. Enormous sections of rock and earth broke apart and slid, now peeling away the northern Garnath bridge in the distance. Hundreds of Ken'nar plunged to their deaths, their terrified voices rising above the moaning earth. Moments later, even the echoes of the dying were silenced.

His hand fell heavily from his chest to his thigh. "By the Light that surrounds all."

Desde knelt beside him. "Kaarl. What—?"

Fear snuffed out his overwhelmed wonder like a gale against a candle flame. The Dark Trine would stop at nothing to kill her now. She would become his obsession, and he would not rest until she was dead. His child. His tiny child.

Kaarl's eyes burned with the afterimage of the massive wall of flame, but all he could see in his mind were a pair of silver eyes, so like his own.

"Mirana."

CHAPTER 35

"I looked into the eyes of Death. And saw myself."
—The Codex of Jasal the Great

Mirana cried in exultation as she unleashed a wall of red fire from the ruby amulet at her chest.

By the hundreds, Ken'nar were transformed into human pyres, then disappeared into ash.

… RETREAT! … RETREAT! … RETREAT! …

The remnants of the southern Ken'nar phalanx broke ranks and ran for the Dar-Anar foothills.

She sensed the called order, but such mind-words no longer held any meaning. She no longer heard the screams of raging bloodlust. Her three Aspects became living powers submitting themselves to her supreme authority.

The Fal'kin charged, fleeing from the bridge, but the dark warriors at their heels cut them down as they tried to escape.

An enormous jet of red fire exploded again from her amulet. It writhed and snaked, hammering away at the stone buttresses supporting the southern Anarath bridge. They groaned and shuddered. Boulders and great portions of earth sheared away to fall into the rivers below. Raw power leaked around the ruby amulet onto her chest as she poured out more of herself than the crystal could contain. Her hands and the skin over her breastbone became streaked with burns. She cried out in pain and triumph. She was of the Aspects.

She was the Aspects.

Her Trine Aspects coursed through her and out of the ruby amulet onto the ford, Seeing, Defending, Healing coalescing as one within her. The Anarath stone bridge shook once more, then collapsed, the span falling away into the abyss. The landmass apex joining the two bridges crumbled away and fell, faster and faster, as the avalanche tumbled into the river below. Earth and rock continued to slide, dragging the northern Garnath River bridge with them.

The remnants of the ford fell tumbling into the twin river chasm below, carrying the Ken'nar to the same fate. The black-armored warriors who escaped her destruction rode north in a retreat, leaving their dead comrades to the coming dawn.

The amulet's crystal now vibrated, unable to withstand her demand. It splintered into thousands of shards. She screamed in agony as the union between her Aspects and the ruby shattered, the sudden loss of the sacred connection irrevocably sundered. She slid from Ashtar's saddle to the ground.

She tried to push herself up onto her forearms, then collapsed back to the wet, cold earth. The death of her amulet had shredded her soul. She writhed, her unfocused Aspects now immolating her from the inside, desperate to release themselves from the prison of her body.

A dark form moved within the flames of the garrison. It emerged toward her out of the fire. The spectral image appeared, a featureless black shade silhouetted against the swirling smoke and flames. It carried an impossibly long sword. It paused. Searching. Thinking.

The Ken'nar Dark Trine.

Mirana's terror seeped away, profound resignation taking its place. The very sword of the blessed thrice-cursed overlord himself would save Kinderra. At last, her beloved homeland would be spared from her becoming its instrument of death. She would now pay for the transgressions she had seen herself perpetrating before she could commit them. End and beginning, in one, in both.

Only two Trines would remain, as the prophecy had always foretold—Tetric Garis and this Dark demon. She was never meant to play a role in the ancient prediction but to be sacrificed so the prophecy could unfold as had been divined.

The shadow flew toward her, an avenging angel of the Underworld. She steeled herself for the sword's plunge into her body.

… *Without you, all is lost* …

She tried to respond when she convulsed once more in agony.

Strong arms lifted her as darkness took her.

CHAPTER 36

"U'isi sol kin scinane mor potem luveclae?"
("Does not the sun shine brighter after a storm?")
—Ora Fal'kinnen 123:30

Two Rivers Ford was gone.

The Ain Magne stood in the mud, the flooded riverbank before him. His helmet slipped from his grip to fall with a squelch in the filth. His hands hung limply at his sides. The newly torn edge of land lay raw in the distance, now visible in the soft light of morning. Bloody water and silt lapped at his boots. Exhaustion and a despondency far more debilitating than fatigue vied for his strength. The ford was destroyed, and no amulet, no sword, no fist would bring it back.

His plan had been perfect. His Ken'nar had outnumbered the Fal'kin more than two to one, and yet it was his own warriors who limped away, his regiments in tatters. He had split his forces and surrounded the Kin-Deren troops, yet he had lost three thousand men and women, a full one thousand when the bridges fell. Vallia Edaran should have been captured and harvested, using her viciousness for him, and yet her life's song echoed no more from within the Aspects. Her daughter Liaonne should have been killed, and yet her presence still returned to his mind.

His plan had indeed been perfect. Mirana Pinal, however, had been more perfect. He should have foreseen this, all of this. He should have foreseen *her*. Every time he made his plans, she and her Trine Aspects somehow divined them. *Ai*, she was a Trine. He knew that now for certain.

He wanted to be angry. Oh, how he wanted to be. He had every right to be. He should strike her down with his vengeance and the fullness of his Aspects, not even leaving ash behind. Anger, however, would not bring back the ford nor move his war machine to Deren.

Anger certainly wouldn't give him something even more important than a thousand fords: Jasal's Keep and its awesome and terrifying power. Only Mirana could give him that. Once he had the keep, Kinderra would be his, and this continuous slaughter would, at last, be over.

The Ain Magne stepped a few paces from the flood plain and sank to the muddy ground. He buried his face in his hands. He had pushed himself during the battle almost beyond even his limits, leaving him spent and empty inside. Calling a battle while hidden under the cloak of U'Nehíl to the minds of his field marshals was taxing. Healing was taxing. Harvesting Aspected warriors was taxing. The procedure had drained him to his core. He would soon have aid in harvesting, however. That was perhaps the one feeble success of this contemptible campaign.

He let his hands fall away. They were covered in blood, as was his armor, as was his sword. Some of it was his own. Most of it was not. Such a needless, senseless waste.

He reached for his amulet and pulled deep within himself for his Aspects. Not enough of the living surrounded him to allow him to draw upon the Power from Without.

Two Rivers Ford was gone, but the Aspects Above never took away anything without giving something back in return. That was an edict he believed in more fervently than the expectation that the sun would rise each morning. Had the Aspects Above taken the ford from him to guide him toward a new future?

He called to his Seeing Aspect—and this time he smiled.

Images flashed through his consciousness. His victory had not been stolen from him by a woman-child. No. Instead, she only brought it one step closer.

He still had thousands of men and women, siege towers, catapults, and battering rams. *Ai*, an easy land route for his war machine was gone, but another one still existed. It would be more difficult, *ai*, but far shorter in distance. He needed steeds for his Ken'nar, perhaps now more than ever, to make up for the time he would lose with the difficulty of this new crossing. The conquest of Deren, however, had not changed, only its timing. If he moved swiftly, the losses the Fal'kin took at the ford would work in his favor.

And if he left Mirana Pinal alive after this destruction, it could place a wedge further between his seer second and himself.

The Ain Magne pursed his lips. His servant wanted her dead, but the young seer had yet to realize her importance. He held his amulet tighter. His seer second remained critical to his plans. Though his most loyal servant, his second also posed his greatest risk. He knew his servant regarded him as a mentor, a *patrua*, even a father figure. He used those feelings to ensure that loyalty. But everyone, even his second, had a breaking point. If the seer continued to view the girl as a rival, this could become an issue, perhaps even a fatal one.

An even darker thought curled its way through his mind. The Ain Magne had come to power himself by earning the trust of one of the most dreaded Ken'nar warlords to have walked Kinderra—then killed him. The man was a despot and had cared nothing for Kinderra or for bringing peace to her.

What would happen when his second did finally come to understand Mirana as the key to conquering Kinderra? If his seer second and the Pinal girl united and conspired against him, he would have to make choices he did not even want to contemplate. For his plans to succeed, he needed both his second and the girl—and their undying loyalty. To him.

Jasal's Keep flared once again before his mind's eye, an otherworldly impression wrought by his Seeing Aspect. It exploded with unspeakable power and, once again, the image faded into Mirana's face. The young Trine was linked to the keep and, for that reason alone, he had allowed her to live. He had meant to use her to gain Jasal's Keep, then dispose of her. Her potential as a rival was too dangerous to allow her to remain alive forever.

He winced as a patch of skin on the side of his forearm pulled away from a bit of melted chain mail, leaving a raw wound.

What if the girl was not a rival, however? What if he, instead, shaped and forged her into a weapon to be used *for* him?

He rubbed his hand over the injury. The dark jewel at his chest glowed and the wound disappeared.

Another Trine by his side presented advantages he had not considered. An innocent, young Fal'kin girl who embraced his philosophy might be able to convince the Fal'kinnen to lay down their arms for the good of the land. If she could see that noble future herself and her place within it, she could show the Fal'kin the beauty and worthiness of his designs.

Legend said Deren could not be conquered. The Ain Magne did not believe in absolutes, save for the Aspects Above themselves. Despite the destruction of the ford, had he not cut down Kin-Deren's Fal'kin nearly to a man? Without the province's Fal'kin, the citadel's battlements would pose but a minor obstacle, and not even that if he held the keep.

He pursed his lips. *Ai*, controlling Jasal's Keep would not only give him Deren but the whole of Kinderra. For Kinderra to *remain* his, however, would require a force even more powerful than fear: love.

The Fal'kin would love Mirana Pinal, adore her as an instrument of peace. She would become the symbol of true unity in a new Kinderra. He would head a glorious new Aspected Triumvirate—he at the crown, Mirana on his right, his seer second on his left—leading Kinderra into a new age of enlightenment. That day, that age, however, was still far off, with many tenuous skeins needing to be woven before such a future could unfold.

The Ain Magne rose slowly out of the mud. Bodies surrounded him. Thousands of them, Ken'nar and Fal'kin, a rotting carpet of rent flesh. He finally gave in to the anger welling up in him. The waste! The needless, senseless waste! And for what? So one people's path to the Aspects could be proven superior over another's beliefs?

He looked down at the inert form by his feet and closed his eyes. A wave of sadness washed through him again, defeat threatening to return. So very much death.

The Trine girl did not know him yet. She did not understand the importance of her power, not truly. She would, in time. She must. Jasal's Keep was too important. Kinderra was too important.

The Ain Magne hated killing, detested it, but he hated failure most of all.

Mirana Pinal must come to understand him. She must. Or the ultimate failure of death would be the only fate left for Kinderra.

CHAPTER 37

"Nöc ten runh'e thet ain vidé bé dïe. Per the etís verdas u'len quen bia eta ain u'comprende len."

("The night holds secrets that can only be revealed by the dawn. But then there is hard truth when before there was only gentle ignorance.")

—Ora Fal'kinnen 123:56–57

Teague shivered despite the sweat that coated his limbs. The day had dawned clear, a beautiful one, really. Dewdrops on the grass glinted in the morning sunlight. After the night's storm, the air was balmy and fresh.

Except, that is, for the stench of death.

Five mutilated bodies lay on the ground below him, next to his horse, Bankin. They didn't look much like bodies anymore, but they were. He knew of such things now. Ash darkened the ground, too. Ash that had been bodies.

A strange numbness pervaded him, a sort of disassociation between his brain and his body. Nothing held any meaning or emotion. His stomach heaved now and then, but food had left him long ago. Not even much bile came up anymore. It struck him that all of his symptoms might be the slightest bit concerning. He might even be in shock.

He stared at the bodies. His parents were gone. Mirana was gone.

He thought he might have ridden in search of his beloved during the early hours before dawn, but he could have dreamt it. No, no, he had looked for her, he remembered now, traveling as far as the Great Anarath River itself. He had been on the Sün-Kasalan side of the river with no way to cross back over. The ford bridges were now gone, too, and the rains had swollen the already wide river. He had tried to find her, but she was gone.

He thought he might have tried to help a few wounded while searching for her. He was less sure of that. Those memories were fuzzier, more disjointed, like half-forgotten nightmares. He had never seen battle before. He had never seen what swords, knives, amulets, and hatred did to a body. Not this close, anyway. He had never held a dying person before, either. Sometimes they just slipped away. Other times, their deaths were less peaceful. Or had he just dreamt that? Surely, people who had once been living could not have made sounds of such abject agony? Or have done incomprehensible things like try to stuff their own bowels back into their bodies before they collapsed, unmoving? That couldn't have been real. Could it?

At some point, he must have decided to ride back west to the mouth of the Kabaarh Pass in the Dar-Anar foothills in search of his parents. He must have gotten back here somehow. It was the last place he had seen them. Maybe his parents were still waiting for him. There were bodies on the ground before him. Or not.

He had no idea which way they would have gone. His parents. Mirana. She left no trace, her or Lord Garis. There was no trace of anyone. Anyone living, that is. Nothing moved. Even the bodies in front of him now had stopped jerking. Sometimes corpses made movements, the normal but disturbing ones bodies made when passing from death to decay. He had read about that but had never seen it before. Until now.

Had she ridden off with Lord Trine Garis? She could have made it, escaped. Or not. No, no, she made it. Lord Garis knew how special she was. *Ai*, they escaped.

The massive wall of red fire. It was Mirana. It had to be. Maybe she had escaped that brilliant curtain of light.

He had tried to find a way across the river, to Mirana, but he could not. She was a Trine. He was anything but. He had no way to reach her now.

Mirana. She was gone.

Five bodies lay right there in front of him, three herbsfolk and two Ken'nar. Right there. He should get down from his horse and position their arms and legs in a more respectable repose. At this point, though, their limbs would probably be frozen stiff with death. His parents were gone. Some ash had clumped on the grass. A lot of ash. Probably the ash from several people.

Maybe this was his new life now, to be surrounded by endless death, stretching to the horizon. Ash, bodies, pieces of bodies, flesh not even recognizable as having been part of a body.

Teague leaned low over the saddle and wretched again, spitting out bitter saliva.

He listened for voices. All was still.

That wasn't completely true. Now and then, a raven crowed, and a moan lifted into the air from somewhere, echoing through the pass where he sat on Bankin. It could be the breeze through the wet grass. It could be a man or woman dying. It could even be coming from his own lips.

Gente'e morte u'dici u'bendicta. "Dead men cannot curse," battle-hardened defenders joked. Now, he got it. He huffed a laugh. It sounded more like a sob, but he'd call it a laugh anyway.

Teague slipped off Bankin's saddle. His legs crumpled under him, their strength abandoning him. He sat on the wet grass.

His stomach clenched again. Nothing came up, so he ended up making animalistic heaving sounds. Maybe the moaning had come from him?

He should dig a grave and bury the bodies, but he had nothing with which to dig. Build a funeral pyre? He had no way of starting a fire, and everything was still sodden from the night's rain. Well, rain, and blood. He certainly couldn't release amulet fire. He was Unaspected. Ungifted. Sightless. Worthless.

A raven landed nearby. He wobbled to his feet and dug through the ash for something to throw at the bird. His fingers touched a round object. One of their amulets. His heart banged in his chest as he grasped it.

It was a kneecap.

He let it fall.

Two more ravens flew in. He spied a small jar within the ash and picked it up. He cocked his arm, ready to throw it, then paused. It was a tiny alabaster medicine jar, not much larger than an egg. Etched into the jar's surface was a leopard. The standard of Tash-Hamar. *Maithe.*

How many of his cuts and scrapes had she gently daubed with some of the jar's numbweed salve because he hated being healed with the Aspects? She understood. Unless it was serious, she let him heal on his own. He had learned to bear pain, physical and otherwise, particularly well.

His mother had told him she'd carried the jar with her when she was a little girl sent from Tash-Hamar to Kana-Akün to learn to be a Fal'kin healer, and every day since. She would never leave it behind.

With his fortitude and Mirana by his side, he could withstand just about anything. But she had left his life. Only his resilience remained.

What did it matter? For summers and summers, their entire lives, she had said his lack of Aspects did not matter to her. He was foolish enough to have believed her. He was a fool to have believed they might have had a future together. That he could make her his wife, provide for her, care for her, protect her from the demons only she saw.

He'd been a fool to believe she loved him.

Had she lied to him all this time? Or had she, at last, come to her senses? She had finally seen him for what he truly was— a worthless, Sightless piece of *excra* the Aspects Above cared so little about they even forgot to end his life.

How many summers had he pleaded, begged the Aspects Above to give him just one ounce of their power? He was useless to her. She'd told him so. She had cut him off from her like a diseased limb. He was useless to everyone. His parents. They were gone.

No, that was a lie. His parents were not gone. They were dead. Like Mirana's love.

She had left him because she was a Trine and he was Unaspected—the river, the divide, the chasm between them was just too wide to cross. He had known it. He had always known it. All his life, he had hoped, somehow, that it wasn't true.

Hope. There was another word for hope. Denial.

A sob escaped his lips, a childlike, frustrated, angry, pathetic noise.

With leaden feet, Teague turned back to Bankin. "White Light," her name meant in the Old Tongue. What cruel irony that the horse he rode was named for the very thing that separated Mirana from him. She'd chosen to hold on to an insubstantial vision of terror instead of him and all his physical reality. His complete and utter lack of Aspects made it impossible for him to show her otherwise.

He stumbled. A Ken'nar broadsword.

The blood of defenders from his father's lineage flowed in his veins, if only a drop of it. His mother's family gave rise to some of the most powerful battle seers Kinderra had ever known. And his parents? His parents were healers, possessing the rarest, most precious Aspect of all. Only Trines were more treasured. The Aspects Above could have given him any one of these gifts. Instead, they chose to ignore him completely.

Something hot began to boil in his belly. Not battle trauma, not anymore. Not soul-wrenching grief. Anger? Maybe even rage? Was this what rage felt like?

Teague hefted the broadsword, gripping the hilt with both hands. It was very heavy. The dark metal did not gleam in the sunlight but seemed to absorb light into its patina. The particular alloy the Ken'nar used for their blades and armor made the metal dark and nearly impervious. He tested the blade with his thumb. Even scraping across it, it sliced his thumb. He sucked at the blood.

He could not heal, but he had the knowledge his parents gave him of how the body worked. He had no sight, but he could now tell Ken'nar from Fal'kin on the battlefield. He had no Defending Aspect, but he had a sword.

They said Ken'nar blades could cut through chain mail. He hoped they, whoever they were, were right. He would bring down the Dark Trine, somehow, even if he had to give his own sightless, defenseless, worthless life to do it.

CHAPTER 38

"Kin il'Aspecta'e Alta vidé ad gente Oëme crearé, per Oëme u'placreé, fár eta u'gente defende tuda il'Crearae."

("The Light of the Aspects Above looked at the people They created, but They were not pleased, for there was no one to protect all of Creation.")

—*il'Crearae* (The Creation), Ora Fal'kinnen 1:11

Kaarl squinted at the sky. It was approaching noon. They needed to move on.

Desde had regrouped what Fal'kin were still alive and immediately marched them to the Sün-Kasalan plains, south of what had been the Two Rivers Ford garrison. They would let their troops rest for a little while longer, then continue southeast along the river until nightfall.

They would try to cross the Anarath River into Kin-Deren over the shallows of the Stairs of Anar before it fell away into rapids. They didn't have much of a choice. It would take days to reach the trader ferries farther downstream. He must move the Fal'kin onto Kin-Deren soil as quickly as possible. Deren lay completely undefended at the moment. He prayed what Ken'nar had retreated from the ford hadn't made straight for the city. Like so many of the thoughts sliding through his mind, he thrust this one away, too, blocking it like a Ken'nar blade.

He began to fold his arms, but quickly released them as the pain in his left shoulder flared. Most of Desde's defenders had sustained wounds, but no one could find the healers. She sent a small patrol into the foothills where Morgan had said he had last seen them.

With any luck, the same number of Fal'kin that marched with them today would be with them when they reached home. Luck, however, was capricious in war. The only certainty in war was uncertainty.

He held the hand of his good arm across his brow against the bright sun and studied the swollen river's current. He hoped it would let up by the time they reached the shallows.

Now and then, arrows, a body, or some other detritus left from the battle would float past. Each time, stark terror would attempt to slash through his resolve.

… Mirana …

Still no call returned to him.

Ignoring his wounds and his fatigue, he had spent the remainder of the night and well into the morning searching for any sign of his daughter or Tetric Garis. They had somehow vanished into thin air.

Part of him wanted to give in to the almost giddy sensation of relief that his daughter had escaped the fray with Garis. Another part, a tiny yet terrifyingly tenacious part, embedded a question in his brain that would not leave him.

The memory of the wall of deadly red fire and the ford collapsing into the abyss swelled in his mind. It was Mirana. She saved their lives. Intuition as her father, not even born of his Aspect, told him so. The ford's destruction had to have been mediated with an amulet. She must have chosen one, at last, the courage he knew she possessed strengthening her in the end.

He had no proof, of course, that it was her. It could have been Garis. His amulet, however, was not red. It was hematite, an infernal thing that spat a jet of silver fire tinged with black. The Trine could have chosen another amulet to use for some reason. It could have been the Dark Trine himself, seeking to annihilate the Fal'kin on the ford bridges and ending up making a catastrophic mistake. Or, even more hideous, the warlord had so little regard for life, he had sacrificed his troops so no one could use Two Rivers Ford, rather than let it stay in Fal'kin hands.

Kaarl gripped his amulet, this time holding it to give him the strength to push back emotions threatening to overtake him.

For sixteen summers, he had done everything he could to keep his daughter's Trine Aspects a secret—he and Desde both—even hiding the knowledge from the girl herself. They had meant to protect her from the Dark Trine.

They should have known, in time, she would figure out her gifts. For so many summers, he had hoped she would not. He had dreaded the day when she would come to them with her revelation. When that day never came, he was as relieved as he was guilty. When she did finally admit to her Trine Aspects, the war and Garis took her from him, and there wasn't a damn thing he could do about it.

He would never let Desde share the blame. She had wanted to tell Mirana everything so many times. He'd refused, insisting on their silence. It was denial, plain and simple. He had been so terrified his precious child would be taken from him, like so much else in his life, he caused the very thing he had tried to prevent.

In the end, all their secrecy had amounted to nothing. Their lies only sent her to Garis, a man who sought to take his il'Kin from him, a man who sacrificed Kaarl's troops in the name of the greater good. A man who saved Mirana's life. A man whom Kaarl depended on still to keep her alive.

He gripped his amulet harder, feeling its edges press into his palm. Garis, as the Light Trine of the prophecy, was most likely a target of the Dark Trine as well. Yet only the Dar-Azûlan wielded enough power to protect Mirana from the Ken'nar overlord. That served as some consolation—if he could call it that.

The sunlight dappled on the fast water. It sparkled like his daughter's eyes when she laughed.

"Do not take my child from me. I beg thee, O Aspects Above."

He let go of his amulet, sank to his knees on the soft ground on the riverbank, and covered his face with his hands, letting the pain in his shoulder add to his grief.

A warm presence drew near him. Desde knelt beside him and rested her forehead on his uninjured shoulder, entwining her arm through his. He turned and brushed his lips on her head. Tears trailed down the curve of her face. For a long time, he simply held her hand.

He took a slow inhale and let it out just as slowly. "I have a gift for you." He reached into his belt pouch and held out the short stub of the arrow shaft that had remained in his shoulder.

She took it and groaned in disgust. "I can add it to the collection." Her eyes widened as a thought occurred to her. "Did she come back? Is Mirana back? Her Healing Aspect. Did she heal you?"

Kaarl shook his head. "Binthe. She can do nothing about wounds, but she can use her Seeing Aspect to find embedded arrowheads and sword tips to remove them. She has saved many il'Kin with her gentle hands when no other help could be found. I do think the Aspects Above gave her the wrong gift with her tender spirit."

"Her grandmother Eshe saved her life by sending her away from Rün-Taran. No one should have had to witness what happened to one's parents as she did." Desde tossed the arrow shaft stub into the river and watched it float in the water for a moment. "Eshe will need her back soon, I fear. She is old, older than my father. She did not look well last Quorumtide."

She sat back on her heels and rubbed her face with her hands. The perfection of her long, elegant fingers was marred by cuts, bleeding from Ken'nar blades and her own. She slid her hands down to hug her arms, wincing as they brushed against the burn on her shoulder.

Kaarl took one of her torn, elegant hands in his. … *She will be all right, Ëi ama …*

She laughed darkly. "You are telling a seer the future?"

"No, I am trying to comfort a mother."

"Did we make the right decision? All those summers of secrecy?"

He was no longer certain. "She's still alive, isn't she?" He meant the question to be a rhetorical one. Instead, he accidentally—or maybe not—had given voice to that terribly tenacious question in his mind. His wife avoided answering him for the same reason. "We would know it. We would know."

She nodded. "She was right, you know. About the Trine Prophecy. None of our scriptures, philosophies, or writings mention three Trines. Only once before in recorded history has there been two Trines in power at the same time. I fear for what this means."

He swallowed, the action sounding loud in his ears. "You don't actually believe she could become—?"

"No. Never. I fear it means Tetric may not last."

He frowned and nodded. As long as he lived long enough to see Mirana safe. His wife sat back from him, having heard his thought.

"I've never been so uncharitable as to wish him ill."

Mock surprise momentarily erased the worry on her face.

"Well, not truly, Desde, but I don't want the man to die." His expression turned serious. "If he does, there will be no one to protect her."

"Unless she has never been a part of the prophecy at all. What if it always has been about Tetric and that Ken'nar monster? What if she is the one who is meant to die so Tetric will live to vanquish him? What have we done? Oh, Kaarl!" His wife deflated into his embrace. Her body shook in his arms with racking sobs. "We pushed her away. We pushed her right into the Dark Trine's blade. My Lightness!"

He held Desde, rocking her gently. He let her vent the fear and the grief for both of them.

Binthe and Morgan approached. The fact that these two still breathed was about the only peace he could hold in his heart at the moment. He brushed his lips against Desde's hair and helped her to her feet.

"Any sign of Mirana?" Kaarl asked, while his wife turned from them to compose herself.

Binthe's eyes rested on Desde for a moment. "We looked everywhere. The riverbanks are flooded. We found no tracks."

"I tried to swim back over to the Kin-Deren shore to search there, but the current was uncooperative," Morgan said.

Kaarl suppressed a grin at his friend's attempt at humor. Binthe, however, apparently found his comment anything but humorous.

"You washed downstream and nearly drowned. I had to call you back with the Aspects."

The young defender commander gave her a wan smile, then shook his head. "I could find no sign of her, but I will keep looking."

Desde turned to face the il'Kin. Except for the moisture on her cheeks, no sign remained of her grief. "What of Niah and Tennen?"

"Nothing," Morgan said. "This might be a good sign, though. For all of them. We have no evidence whatsoever that anyone has been harmed. And Tetric Garis is—"

"Lord Garis is Lord Garis," Liaonne Edaran said. Kaarl turned as the Varn-Erdalan woman walked over to them. "I think he surprises even the Aspects Above themselves sometimes. Steward, Prime Kellis Pinal." She gripped his wife's forearm in greeting.

Desde held the defender woman's forearm. "Liaonne."

Kaarl did likewise. Liaonne had only seen twenty-five summers, but she fought like no defender he had ever known. The young woman who stood before him now, however, appeared more like a caricature of the strong-willed Varn-Erdalan he knew. A hollowness lay in her sienna-brown eyes, replacing the ferocious intensity which normally dwelt there.

"My heart weeps for the passing of your mother, noble Vallia," Desde said. "You now carry an enormous burden as prime, one which was handed to you by violence and not by a peaceful passing such as how my elevation was initiated."

"It is a difficult burden regardless of how one receives it. I have never had the privilege of watching you in battle, Desde. My estimation of battle seers has changed."

Kaarl glanced at his wife. She gave the defender woman a curt nod. Binthe's face remained placid with a faint smile, but he wasn't all that surprised. He knew the il'Kin battle seer well. It took far more than a vague insult to release her ire.

Liaonne fidgeted for a moment. "Forgive me, I do not have my mother's way with words, so I shall be direct. I need Kin-Deren's help."

"We will offer you whatever aid we can," Desde replied.

"I need defenders. Other than a handful of old seers who have never called a battle, I have no Fal'kin. Even my hall sentries are now dead. I have two defender *scholaire'e* who might be ready for Choosing, but the rest are children. Most have not even seen twelve summers. The unending skirmishes with the Ken'nar over the recent summers have left us weaker than we've ever been. We are a hall of *brepaithe'e* and *biraen'e*." She paused, then took a breath. "I am asking for a cleaving."

"A cleaving?" Desde blinked. "Take half my Fal'kin? Permanently? I have none to spare. Look around you." She spread her arms wide. "This is all that remains to safeguard my own province. Liaonne, you may ask anything of me but this."

"There is more to consider," Morgan said. "With a cleaving, you might as well have a clarion announce to the Dark Trine your vulnerable situation, and Kin-Deren's, too."

"He already knows," Liaonne replied, exasperation coloring her hard alto voice. "The Dark bastard had to have been at the ford. The calling of that massacre had to have been from his diseased mind. If it hadn't been for Lord Garis destroying the bridges, all of us would have been lost." She clenched her hands to calm herself.

Kaarl's eyes went wide. "Did you see him? Garis? Did you see him destroy the ford?"

Liaonne shook her head and straightened in surprise at his emphatic questions. "Well, no. But who else could have done that?"

His wife took a deep breath before she answered. "It was Mirana."

He stiffened at her response, then let his shoulders fall. There was no point in keeping the secret any longer.

Liaonne scowled. "Your daughter? I remember her bitter words in the command tent—it's true? She is a Trine?"

"*Ai.*" It was such a simple word, yet it was the most difficult one he had ever spoken.

"Then I need her. One does not have to be a seer to know Edara will be the Dark Trine's next target."

Binthe fingered her amulet. "We believe his true goal is Deren."

"That may be, but he won't get there without conquering Edara. Varn-Erdal province is the last point of resistance in the northern half of the continent."

"You may be correct, Liaonne," Desde said. "He has the forests of Kana-Akün to build his war machines. Without Two Rivers Ford, he will have a long, slow march overland, but he will not wait forever. He will need to mount his men now to make up for lost time and turn his infantry into a cavalry."

The young defender prime nodded. "Then you understand my situation. He means to go after my horses."

The seers were correct. Kaarl had expected the Dark Trine to make a play for Deren, and he would, but not yet. Varn-Erdal bred the most prized warhorses on the continent. With Vallia and most of Varn-Erdal's defenders now dead, the province's capital city of Edara and its fabled horses were ripe for conquest.

"Unless you honor my cleaving, I will not be able to turn him back. Protection of the south will then be on Kin-Deren's shoulders alone."

He cursed under his breath. Liaonne was not exaggerating. If Varn-Erdal fell, Kin-Deren would soon as well. Neither province had enough defenders to repel any serious attack. With Kana-Akün under Ken'nar control, and Trak-Calan too far and too small to send any substantive aid, the Dark Trine would effectively hold the entire northern half of the continent. Much of Kinderra's population, to say nothing of her food crops and resources, lay south of the Anarath River. Granted, the southern provinces had the largest complements of Fal'kin, but the collateral damage in the wake of a Ken'nar onslaught would be catastrophic. The whole continent could starve. If Kinderra was to survive, Edara and Deren would have to survive as well.

Kaarl sensed his wife's emotions spike then slip back under her control. She was in an untenable spot. If she gave away half her troops, they would be made even more vulnerable, if that was possible. It was unlikely Liaonne could withstand a direct assault of any sizable force even if she had five hundred defenders. The Fal'kin Deren needed so badly were likely to be sacrificed at Edara, yet Deren at least had its walls and gates. Edara had little more than wooden ramparts.

"I do not intend for Varn-Erdal province to be left defenseless," Desde said. She then turned from the group and walked a few steps away.

"Desde?" He went over to her. Eyes closed, she cupped her topaz amulet, and golden light leaked from between her fingers. "*Ama?*" He placed his hand on Desde's back. She was invisible from within the Aspects. Whatever she was thinking, she did not want even him to know.

"I cannot give you half of my Fal'kin, Liaonne," she said at last and turned back around.

Liaonne tensed as if an amulet had struck her. "What?"

Binthe shook her head in astonishment. "You cannot refuse her, *Ëi siba.* The other primes will take note. If you do, Kin-Deren may find herself alone when she needs aid."

The young defender prime stepped in close to Desde, standing toe to toe. "I am begging you, woman. Do you not understand both of our provinces are in mortal peril?"

"I will give you twenty-five," she replied.

"Twenty-five?" Liaonne laughed in disbelief. "Twenty-five? I need at least a hundred."

"No. You need at least three thousand. As do I. But we do not have that many. Only the southern provinces have those numbers, and they are too far to come to aid either of us. Time is short. Less than two hundred of my Fal'kin survived. I, too, have nothing left but children."

Kaarl now sensed Desde's resolve growing stronger, along with her dismay. Whatever she was planning, it terrified her. Very little frightened his wife like this, and that made him concerned. So much so, his Defending Aspect began to smolder within him. "We will send riders south. Perhaps Sün-Kasal or Tash-Hamar or even Jad-Anüna will help."

Liaonne gave a derisive laugh. "Sün-Kasal. I have sat in Quorum enough as a prime's second to know Sahm Klai is an obstinate isolationist. It would take me a sevenday of sevendays to convince the defender prime. It would take at least that long for any defenders from Tash-Hamar to reach Edara, even if Prime Fasen Aldi would agree to give them to me. I do not have that kind of time. Jad-Anüna lies so far east from Varn-Erdal, Prime Nambre Dinir has the luxury of pretending to be ignorant of what goes on in this land. The last time the Jad-Anünans came out in any sizable force, I had yet to hold an amulet. As much as I do not wish to take my mother's seat, Varn-Erdal lies leaderless, and the Ken'nar who attacked us here at the ford may already be planning their strike on my province. I need to move now."

"I can give you twenty-five now," Desde said, "but I will bring you more before the Ken'nar attack Edara. Many more."

"How? Do you intend to make Fal'kin out of clay?"

His wife gave the young defender prime an intense stare. "I am asking you to trust me."

"I trust you will try, *Ëi siba*. I do not trust you will succeed." Liaonne nodded a farewell and left to prepare for her ride north.

Kaarl witnessed the devastation on Liaonne's face at his wife's decision. He would not have wanted to wait for help either. He also knew the offer was the best Desde could make under the circumstances.

Tetric Garis's desire to become Primus Magne came back to him. Maybe Kinderra was that desperate. Even as Primus Magne, though, he would need fighters. Not even three hundred remained between the two provinces. Even the il'Kin were effectively gone. Well, almost gone. Morgan said something quietly to Binthe as he watched the Varn-Erdalan woman leave.

"I can give Varn-Erdal a few more Fal'kin." Kaarl smiled at the pair.

"Do you understand what you are doing if you order us to Varn-Erdal?" Binthe asked.

It was not a question at all. It was a protest, but since the il'Kin were bound by the Quorum steward's directives—his directives, now—it was as much of a protest as the young battle seer could make.

Desde shook her head. "By giving up Morgan and Binthe to Liaonne, you'll dissolve the il'Kin."

He nodded slowly. "*Ai*. The il'Kin have always served Kinderra whenever and wherever she needed them. That has not changed."

"He is right," Morgan said. "That duty hasn't changed even if I were to stand alone. And Varn-Erdal was my home. For five summers." Binthe touched the back of Morgan's hand with her fingertips.

Kaarl turned to the young seer woman. "Binthe?"

Desde held up her hand, silencing her before she could answer him. "Binthe needs to go home. Her *bremaithe* needs her."

"Maybe the il'Kin exists in little more than in name only, but we do exist," the young seer said, determination hardening her sea-green eyes. "The steward elevated Morgan as defender commander of the il'Kin. Where he goes, I go. Edara needs a battle seer. Rün-Taran does not. Not yet."

"Dav Koehl fell," Desde pointed out. "The Ken'nar swarmed him like vultures. They didn't even leave a body behind. I elevated Niall Corran to defender commander. He will need a good defender second at his side. Morgan was born to Kin-Deren province. I will need him to help lead what's left of my provincial troops."

Kaarl gave his wife a roguish grin. "Maybe I know of another defender born to Kin-Deren who is more or less unemployed at the moment."

Desde put her hands on her hips, not amused at all. "You cannot. You are Steward of the Quorum of Light."

"Even I have to accept the state of the il'Kin," he replied, serious this time. "Your father was steward and still held his role as prime and seer. I am a defender. I will defend. The steward's office is sworn to negotiate between provinces, assisting in their needs. I have done that. Varn-Erdal needs fighters. I have given her fighters. Kin-Deren needs a defender second, at least for the time being. I have given her one." His wife crossed her arms, eyeing the group, then nodded.

"Morgan and Binthe, go to Varn-Erdal," he continued. "Liaonne will need you more than Desde for the moment."

"However, you will go as il'Kin," Desde added, her dark eyes on Kaarl, "and you will return to Deren as il'Kin after this crisis has been resolved."

A group of five Kin-Deren Fal'kin riders approached. "Steward Pinal, Prime Kellis Pinal." Niall Corran nodded quickly to Kaarl and Desde.

Kaarl returned the gesture. "Defender Commander."

Niall frowned. "I didn't want it."

Desde reached up and held his hand for a moment. "I know. That is why you have the rank."

He gave her a spare smile. "We searched the foothills for the healers and the herbsfolk. We found the bodies of Ken'nar and some of the herbsfolk. And ash."

"Any amulets?" Kaarl asked.

He shook his head. "They were probably taken for bounty," he replied, hatred thick in his voice.

Kaarl cursed. The Ken'nar bastards often stole amulets still warm from the fight right off the necks of Fal'kin they had just killed as trophies.

His wife stiffened. "Teague."

That tenacious question fell hard in his brain once again. "Corran, the bodies. Was there a boy, sixteen summers?"

Niall Corran shook his head. "No. But there was a large amount of ash."

Kaarl nodded bleakly. "*Gratas Oë.* Get yourselves some food and water." The Kin-Deren commander nodded once more and trotted off with his fighters.

"I know how close Teague and Mirana were," Morgan said. "And I know Tennen was a good friend."

"You heard me accuse him and Niah of putting my daughter in harm's way to keep Teague and her apart." He looked to the mountain foothills on the western horizon. "I never had a chance to apologize. To either of them."

"Tennen knows you were frightened for Mirana's life. They both do."

Kaarl noted his friend's use of the present tense. He thanked the Aspects Above once again for having a man like Morgan Jord at his side. Even though the il'Kin were all but gone, Kinderra would need a leader like him.

With Kana-Akün province under Ken'nar control, Kaarl was all but certain Healer Prime Belessa Tir was dead. The enormity of the loss of Tennen and Niah now struck him. He wiped at his face. "Kinderra has no more healers."

"We don't know that any more than we know what happened to Teague," Desde said. "There are many possible reasons they haven't been found. Perhaps the three of them escaped together and are on their way home now. Maybe—" She reached for his hand. ... *Maybe they have Mirana with them ...*

"There is still Lord Garis," Binthe added. "And your daughter."

He did not answer her. Oh, that tenacious thought.

"As we ride with Liaonne, we will look for the Beltrans and Mirana," Morgan said. "If they are alive, we'll find them."

He nodded. "*Gratas.*"

His wife gave the young woman a warm embrace. "Be careful. Both of you."

"The future seems dark," Binthe said, "but the Aspects Above have yet to weave their skeins. Take comfort in that."

Kaarl likewise held the battle seer tightly. "You come back to us, Binthe of the Sea, do you hear?"

She kissed him lightly on the cheek, then left with Morgan to prepare for the journey to Edara.

Desde took a few steps closer to the river, holding her amulet. "I once met the artisan who made this. There are few higher acts of service for the Unaspected than crafting the amulets we bear to protect them." She let her amulet fall back to her chest and gave a ragged exhale. "Those twenty-five defenders will make little difference for Edara. Most will probably not survive. Our numbers will never recover. Varn-Erdal's future is clouded, but Kin-Deren's future is even darker unless I take a new course. I have only one choice now to guard both provinces."

Kaarl blanched as she opened her mind to him. What she planned would unlock the very gates of the Underworld.

"You cannot. Desde, you cannot. You must not."

"I can no easier prevent the Dark Trine from overrunning Edara than I can protect Deren. Yet, both must happen. For that, I need an army. There are no more Fal'kin left." She clenched her jaw and closed her eyes. "We have no other choice, *Ëi ama*. We must ask our Unaspected brothers and sisters to stand with us."

He grabbed her arms. "You can't do this. The very reason we breathe is to protect the Unaspected, not ask them to fight our wars for us."

She pulled out of his grip. "So, now you stand on principle? This would be a first, Kaarl il'Tern il'Pinal. This is the only way I can protect two provinces. It is the only way I can protect our daughter."

"Please listen to reason."

"I cannot even keep Kin-Deren safe, let alone aid Varn-Erdal. Kana-Akün has already fallen. It will only be a matter of time before the Dark Trine marches on Deren. I have no choice."

He shook his head in disbelief. "There is always a choice. We will ask every province on the continent for a cleaving. I will rebuild the il'Kin. I am steward, am I not? I will—"

"We do not have that kind of time. I have only time enough to do what needs to be done."

"But we are Fal'kin, Desde," he pleaded.

She held her amulet once more and studied it. "We were."

To ask the Unaspected to fight was anathema. "Jasal Pinal was in a more dire situation than we are when he faced the Ken'nar Triumvirate, and even he did not ask the Unaspected to fight."

"He had five thousand Fal'kin and the vantage of that watchtower on his side." Desde then frowned skyward. "The Aspects Above have abandoned us."

… I will find another way … he called.

She whirled to face him. "There is no other way. We have failed in our purpose." With effort, she composed herself once more. "Perhaps in our frailty, though, we can give one more act of service. To step aside for the good of Kinderra. No matter his strength, the Dark Trine's armies are no match for the millions of Unaspected who live on this continent. The Aspects Above created them first, gave them their breath first, gave them this land first. Kinderra is as much theirs to cherish and protect as it is ours. Perhaps the age of the Fal'kin was meant to fade away to keep Kinderra safe. I would rather see that than have Kinderra enslaved under the yoke of the Dark Trine's tyranny just to keep a failing grip on our amulets."

"I am begging you. Do not do this. I cannot let you do this."

"You cannot let me?" She laughed without humor. "I am prime of Kin-Deren province. It is my decision and mine alone. You may defend, but I see. Unless we do this, there will be nothing left for you to defend."

"If you do this, Kinderra will never be the same again. There has to be another choice, another solution. I will find one."

Desde placed her once-perfect porcelain fingers on his amulet. "And if you fail?"

Kaarl did not answer. If he failed, Kinderra could be destroyed without the firing of a single amulet. And his daughter would be no safer.

CHAPTER 39

"His hand is with all."
>   —The Codex of Jasal the Great

Mirana smelled the scent of wet grass. Clean. Fresh. Good. She inhaled the fragrant green aroma, then stopped quickly. Her breath burned her lungs, each inhale a hot coal. Her chest, her arms, her hands ached—raw, scorched, and shredded. She remembered and awoke with a start.

A dark-cloaked figure sat an arm's length away. She shouted and drew one of her long knives, scrambling backward.

"Oh! Lord Garis!" She put the knife away. "You're alive!"

"Quite." He lowered the cowl of his black cloak. "And so are you, despite your best efforts to the contrary."

In her relief, she ignored his admonition. "I tried to find you. I couldn't."

"*Ai*, the battle was a desperate one, but I have been in desperate battles before and will be again."

She sat in the middle of a prairie sea stretching from horizon to horizon. She did not see a single tree or shrub, just sky and grass. The sunlight warmed her skin. Insects droned in the tall blades. Small birds flew after them, chirping. She attempted to stretch, and instead winced at her sore muscles.

"Can you ride?"

No, but she would anyway. "*Ai*." Her insides felt like a side of Quorumtide beef roasted on a spit. Every muscle felt burned and shredded, but she wasn't about to admit it.

"Good." He nodded. "Here. Eat." He handed her some dried beef.

She took a bite, chewed, and shoved the rest in her mouth. When had she last eaten?

He held a slice back from her. "Slowly."

A bee flitted between tiny yellow flowers. The blooms dotted the landscape like bits of sunshine. Peda blossoms. Teague. The beef stuck in her throat.

Her hand flew to her chest. Teague's pendant still hung from her neck. The thin gold frame, however, was warped and discolored with a tarnished patina. The yellow flowers pressed between the fingernail-thin sheets of mica were now brown and shriveled. A faint red outline in the shape of its small rectangle scarred the skin over her breastbone. Its warmth, however, still reflected against her fingertips like sunlight. Like Teague. Like love.

She dared not reach out with her Aspects to know if he had survived the battle at Two Rivers Ford. She would rather remain in hope, in ignorance, if only for a little while longer.

Lord Garis's mind nudged hers. "You have no room in your life for him now. You would do well to forget him."

She could no easier forget Teague than she could forget how to breathe. Had a Ken'nar blade made the choice for her? The simple act of eating suddenly became more difficult. She worked the dried beef down in several swallows.

The Trine exhaled in disapproval. "He lives."

She wanted to weep with relief. "*Gratas Oë*, Lord Trine."

"As do your parents."

"*Gratas.*" She was grateful—and a thousand more conflicted things besides—to hear that, too.

He gestured to the dried meat in her hand. "Eat."

She took another bite as she looked around her. "Where are we?" she asked with a full mouth.

He rose and threw a furred animal skin over the back of his horse. "Sün-Kasal province, about two days' ride—" He sighed at her grimace as she tried to stretch again. "—three-days' ride north of Kasan."

She blinked. "Wait. Three days?" She nearly choked on her food. "How long have I been asleep?"

"You weren't asleep. I held you unconscious so you could heal."

That disturbed her. She would have rather awakened when she was ready, regardless of the pain. "I remember being on the Kin-Deren side of the ford, between the two bridges."

"You were. I had to swim across the Anarath."

Her eyes widened in disbelief. "How? With all the rain, the current should have been too strong for anyone to swim."

"Lucky for you, I am a strong swimmer." He inclined his head toward her horse. "Lucky for the both of us, your warhorse is a strong swimmer, too."

"He is a magnificent beast." She rose gingerly and patted Ashtar's powerful flank. It shone like copper in the sun. As she put the rest of the dried beef in her mouth, she pulled up a handful of grass and fed it to him. He lipped the blades from her hand.

"You could have drowned." She stroked the white blaze on Ashtar's nose. She had cost so many so much. "You risked your life for me. Why?"

He frowned. "Discovering the power in Jasal's Keep is paramount. I thought you understood that." He tossed something toward her. "Now. How are you feeling? Really?"

An amulet's empty gold casing lay in the grass at her feet, now a piece of melted, twisted metal. She said nothing.

"It is not easy to lose one's amulet." His voice sounded uncharacteristically soft.

Choosing the ruby amulet at the ford had been, what? Something so wondrous, yet so natural. It was nothing at all like the suffocating domination she had experienced during the Choosing Ceremony. When she'd released her Aspects through it, the glorious connection completed her, made her whole at last.

She picked up the amulet casing. It was bent beyond repair. With an amulet, she had experienced a connection to the Aspects deeper than she ever had before. Now, her perceptions without one were diluted and bereft by comparison.

"I feel…" She fought for a word. "Separated. Disconnected. Alone." She thought of her mother and father, and their betrayal. Abandoned.

He nodded. "Most Aspected never recover from the loss."

"But I am a Trine. I can choose any amulet, not just one. Why do I feel any loss at all?"

"Using and choosing an amulet are two different things. It is something only a very few have ever understood."

His emotions shifted, or rather, new ones surfaced and passed to her mind only to recede again. Was he annoyed with her? Resigned to her presence? Angry? Or was he worried? Even actually being kind?

"What in the name of the Aspects were you thinking?" he rebuked her at last.

Angry. He was angry. "My lord, I thought—"

He stabbed a long finger at her. "No. You absolutely did not think. You could have killed yourself by destroying Two Rivers Ford. Leveraging that kind of power from Within should have left you dead."

That victory, however, gave her small comfort. Thousands of her Kin-Deren provincemen died during the battle because of her, because she no longer trusted what she knew to be true.

That was the problem. She no longer knew right from wrong.

She traced the ruined amulet with a finger. "I had to do something."

He towered over her, balling those very large fists of his on his hips. He snatched the amulet casing from her hands, then shook it at her. "Do you have any idea what you've done?"

She didn't want to look into his hard, obsidian eyes. She would have hidden in the grass if she could have. "I know with the ford gone, it will make crossing the rivers more difficult, but the Dark Trine's armies will also be stopped in their tracks."

"It will also stop commerce, and any food coming from the bounty of the south to the northern provinces. These rains will have delayed crops in the north. If we have a harsh winter, provinces may starve. *Ai*, you've stopped something. You have stopped the continent." He threw the empty amulet back down at her feet.

Hundreds of miles away lay the ocean. She had Ashtar and a piece of food. What would it take to ride away to the sea? Probably more than one piece of tough jerked beef.

"The Fal'kin were being slaughtered. I couldn't let them die." She had saved a hundred Fal'kin, only to cripple Kinderra in the process. "You should have left me in the library."

He sighed and rubbed at his eyes. "I thought we were past this."

She caught a number of emotional shades from the Trine again. Anger, *ai*, but also concern, about her and for her. Frankly, that shocked her. She'd figured she was little more than a nuisance to him. After destroying the ford, she might even be a downright hindrance.

She massaged the tender red burns on one palm with her thumb, wanting to do anything but face his penetrating dark gaze. "How did you know I was in the library anyway? I was hidden under U'Nehîl."

"And very well, too." She looked up. A corner of the Trine's mouth finally curved upward into a grin, not so much in humor, but in acknowledgment of her cleverness. Or maybe his cleverness in finding her. She didn't know which. He was an enigma. "Where is the only place a young girl could go to face the creator of a nightmare that has preyed upon her for summers?" He was right.

He crouched and picked up her spent amulet once more, studying it. "*Ai*, you made egress across Kinderra much more difficult, but you did end the battle very effectively. Lives were indeed saved that most certainly would have been lost. I also have no doubt you knew it might cost you your own."

His words, or rather the emotions behind his words, were not so much complimentary as they were compassionate. She fought the urge to hug him.

Lord Garis laid the tarnished setting on the grass and leaned over to reach into one of Ashtar's saddlebags on the ground. He handed her another piece of beef and a wafer of waybread. "You need to eat more. Healing takes as much from the patient as the healer. Perhaps had you packed more food instead of Jasal's Codex, we could have traveled longer." He took out the tome.

She smiled sheepishly and took a bite of the hardtack. She chewed quickly and swallowed. "We will need it if we are to figure out how the keep works."

She reached for the Codex. Unlike the journals of so many other primes and learned Fal'kin, Jasal's journal was not much larger than an ordinary book. It was not inset with gems, nor leafed with gold. Other than the clasp, nothing about it indicated how incredibly unique it was.

"So, you stole it." He eased himself back down on the grass and took a bite of waybread.

"I didn't steal it. I just, um—" Mirana pursed her lips for a moment. "Borrowed it. Every book in Deren's library is available for those who seek knowledge." She sat down next to him.

He made a strange sound in the back of his throat. Had the Lord Trine Tetric Garis just laughed? "I suppose you're correct. What do you know about your ancestor's keep?"

She paused, thinking. "Jasal Pinal built the keep during the Siege of Deren some twelve hundred summers ago. He knew the citadel walls and the gates wouldn't be enough to stop the Ken'nar from entering the city. Instead of leading his armies against Ilrik the Black, it appears Jasal was focused on finishing the watchtower." She patted the cover of the Codex. "In the end, neither his body nor his amulet was found. All of Kinderra believes Jasal abandoned Deren and the Fal'kin at the height of the battle."

Lord Garis stroked his beard. "I have fought long enough to know that lack of an identifiable body is seldom proof of whether one is living or dead. But what of his keep, the very thing that saved Deren?"

She was too shocked to answer his question. She had one of her own. "You don't think Jasal was a coward?"

He shook his head. "I don't care if he was or was not."

Jasal Pinal had been branded a villain more despicable than even a traitor. Her family was still treated with a certain amount of mistrust more than a thousand summers later because of it. The Trine's dismissal of her family's curse stunned her.

"Well, um, his keep did work, according to the Book of Kinderra," she answered. "Passages from that time say Ilrik the Black was killed, and his Ken'nar were defeated. Deren was saved. Somehow."

"Somehow," the Trine repeated. He pointed to the journal in her hands. "Have you read the passage in his Codex—or in the Book of Kinderra, for that matter—that says how the keep accomplished this supposed miracle?"

She shook her head. "No."

"Why is that?"

"Because it is not there."

"*Ai*," he nodded. "Doesn't it strike you as odd that one of the most magnificent pieces of engineering on the continent has almost no mention in the very journal of its builder?" He gestured to the northeast, where Deren and the watchtower lay hundreds of leagues away.

"I've always wondered that, too." She shook her head slowly, thinking again. "Jasal must have had plans, drawings, something."

"I agree, but I don't recall ever reading anything like that."

He gestured for her to give him the book and flipped to the pages at the back. After searching a bit, he read, "'This is a time of great peril.'" He scanned the script. "'Thus, the Aspects

Above have revealed to me their divine plan. But to hearken unto their will requires a decision I am loath to make. My choice is before me. I could no easier ignore the need than I could ignore my beloved Antiri's call. Therefore, I have called upon the whole of the Fal'kinnen for a great sacrifice as demanded by the Aspects Above.' What do you make of this?"

Mirana leaned forward a bit to get a better view of the passage and bit off a groan as her muscles complained at the movement. "That part is a little strange to me. It's very direct, for one thing. Jasal is usually much more poetic. He sounds doubtful. Or terrified." She straightened—very slowly. "What's even more strange, the concluding ones afterward make no sense."

Lord Garis pursed his lips for a moment. "How so?"

"Well, the content doesn't flow. More than that, though, I think everything coming after this passage was written by another writer. Read this." She flipped a few pages and tapped on the flowing script. "'At great cost have we won. Deren lives, yet our Treasure has been lost to us. The Light from our greatest Jewel shines elsewhere.' Not only do the glyphs of the script look different, but this writer also used a prime glyph in the words 'treasure,' 'light,' and 'jewel.' I think whoever wrote this last passage was referring to Jasal himself, not amulets. Jasal never describes himself like this. He is a very humble man, really."

She knew without a doubt the final passage had been written by someone else. Jasal's sense was completely gone from those particular words. She suspected it was Antiri, Jasal's beloved wife and seer from the southern desert province of Tash-Hamar.

"Look here." Mirana took the book back and pointed to another paragraph whose black ink had faded to brown over time. "This verse reads, 'The Sisters shall be the guardians of the Keep.' Then it says, in the Old Tongue no less, '*Iës manë ísi cin tuda*.' His hand is with all. Jasal rarely uses the Old Tongue. He's always trying to move people's thinking forward, away from the old ways. What's more, this passage is written in the third person."

The Trine raised a dark eyebrow. "You can read this upside down?"

She gave him a bashful grin. "I've studied it. A lot."

A corner of his mouth twitched. "You are a singular girl, aren't you?"

By. The. Light. Was he not only smiling—or close to it— but *teasing* her? Maybe he was human, after all.

He sat back and toyed with his silvery black amulet. "If his hand is with us all, why can't we find it?"

"I think there are missing pages." She caressed the journal. "They could have been destroyed."

"That is quite possible. Yet the rest of his Codex remains." He gestured to the book.

"It's been in my family for generations. It's only been on display in Deren's library for a couple of decades. My *brepaithe*, when he was prime, placed it there shortly after my father joined in union with my mother."

A notion tickled at the back of her mind. She contemplated the glyphs on the page. *His hand is with all.*

"Wait a moment." She placed her palm on the page. "Hand. Handwriting, maybe?" She was so close to understanding. His handwriting is with all. All. All the people? The provinces? She read the passage again. "'The Sisters shall be the guardians—' Oh!" She jumped to her feet and the Codex fell to the grass, a startling notion overcoming her pain. It was so obvious. Why had she not seen it before?

Lord Garis sat back in surprise. "What?"

"The Sisters. He's hidden the missing passages in the learning halls."

He nodded, understanding. "His hand is with all. The Nine Sisters."

"No." She shook her head emphatically in her excitement. "It would only be in the learning halls of the provinces in existence during his time. Kin-Deren, Trak-Calan, Rün-Taran—"

"And Tash-Hamar, *ai*." He stroked his beard, dark eyes glittering.

Jasal's plan sent Mirana reeling. It was ingenious. "He split up the keep treatise and hid the passages at the four province learning halls so the secret of how it saved Deren would be safe from the Ken'nar. Even if one piece were found, no individual part would give away the entirety of its construction."

The Trine's dark brows furrowed even deeper. "Then, why write them at all if he feared they would be discovered by those he considered enemies?"

The brilliance of her ancestor's plan continued to unfold in her mind. "He wants them to be found. His keep saved Kinderra once. He may have known it would be needed again. At a 'time of great peril.'" Like now. But in her hands, his keep appeared to do anything but save the land.

"How can you be so sure?" he asked.

Jasal Pinal built the keep to save Kinderra. That was not the act of a criminal. What if he did not die a coward, forsaking his people? What if, all this time, everyone had been wrong?

She began to shake. If he died in shame, abandoning his wife and their newborn son to the swords of the Ken'nar and leaving Deren to destruction, would Antiri still have written about him in such tender terms in the last passage?

Her heart pounded. Had Jasal touched the white light when he died? Unlike the rest of the terrifying vision, the white light was magnificent. It was as rapturous as it was ruinous, like the Aspects Above themselves had come down from the heavens in that brilliance. If he died in shame, if she were to die filled with enraged evil, did it not stand to reason such a miraculous experience would be denied both of them for bringing doom upon Kinderra?

Unless Jasal Pinal did not die in shame.

"Mirana?"

She bit her lip. She knew unequivocally he had taken his own life. But was there more to Jasal's story?

What if her own destiny held more beyond all the ruin she saw at her hands? What if her ancestor had found a path of hope out of an end of failure?

If he could find such a way, could she?

"Mirana?" Lord Garis asked once more. "What else do you know about Jasal?"

"It's all there," she said at last. "His joy, his pain, his doubt. There. Captured within the pages." She knelt back down, took his hand, and placed it on the Codex. "You are a Trine. You must feel it as well." Her throat tightened when his expression did not change. "Can't you?"

He shook his head. "I feel nothing."

Her eyes widened. "I cannot be the only one to sense him."

"You sense his presence?" he asked, his voice hushed.

"Not exactly his presence, but his emotions. They are here. In these pages. Within his handwriting."

He sat silent for a long time. "You are his legacy, an heir to his Trine powers. Perhaps that explains why you can sense him and I cannot." He exhaled loudly and wiped at his face. "To think you nearly killed yourself. Twice."

She eyed the amulet casing in the grass. "Kinderra is more important than me. Far more."

"When are you going to start believing in your own importance?" he replied, his voice quiet, yet yielding none of its strength. He rose. "Do you not see who you are? What you are? There will be no Kinderra without you. You can sense a reflection of Jasal Pinal in the passages he wrote about his keep, a reflection I cannot. Without those writings, without you being able to find them in provinces that lie ahead, we will never understand how the keep saved Deren all those centuries ago. Without you, there will be no saving keep for us now.

"I know you fear what you have seen in your vision of the keep, but also know this: your ancestor built that keep for one purpose—to save Kinderra," he continued. "The fact that you want to help me use the keep to do so again means you have already chosen the right path."

Lord Garis took the Codex from her and set it back down in the grass. He grasped her hands and turned them over, her palms facing up. Traces of burns remained. "Mirana, I spent the better part of a day healing you. If you died, Kinderra would be lost. Do you understand that now?"

He had saved her life, twice, even risking his own, in the belief that she could somehow unlock the secrets to Jasal's Keep. What if those secrets, what if the power that lay hidden, would not save Kinderra?

"I can't hide who or what I am anymore, but I don't know how to go forward. What if I," she eyed her broken amulet on the ground, "fall from our path?"

He laid his large hand on her shoulder. "I never had anyone to show me how to be a Trine, and I paid for my ignorance. I will make sure you never do. I told you, you will not bear these burdens alone. We shall go forward together."

His words humbled her. With no way to express her gratitude, she simply nodded.

"We will head to Tash-Hamar. If you are correct, we shall find some of Jasal's writings there." The Trine finished readying his horse and lifted her saddle and packs onto Ashtar's back. "You must tell no one about the keep passages."

She scowled. It was not a request but an order. "Why?"

His mouth grew hard. "Think, Mirana. We have touched upon a secret so vast, it might very well change the course of history. Men and women would kill for this information. No one must find out what we've discovered. No one."

She nodded and slipped the Codex back into her saddlebag. Jasal Pinal had died by his own hand. That was certain. Had he been overwhelmed by his own Trine powers? Had he abandoned his people and died a coward's death? Or had he found a way through his own self-loathing? Had he sacrificed himself somehow for his people to die a hero? If he found a way to save his people by turning back from his fear of failure—emotions she sensed so strongly within his words—could she turn back from her own future of failure?

Jasal Pinal's fate was tied to the keep, and her fate was tied to Jasal.

Her ruined amulet lay dull in the grass, its luster burned away. An amulet without a crystal was useless. It could save no one. Until she knew the truth about her destiny, she could no more save Kinderra from the Ken'nar than an empty, useless amulet could.

"Come. We have a long journey ahead of us." Lord Garis swung up onto his horse and tapped his mount's sides.

Mirana climbed onto Ashtar's broad back and followed the Trine, leaving the empty amulet behind in the grass.

THE SAGA CONTINUES…
Trine Fallacy
The Kinderra Saga: Book 2

TRINE RISING

The Kinderra Saga: Book 1

Dramatis Personae

Kin-Deren—1st Hall. Standard: gold field with red eagle

ANTIRI il'Amil Pinal (2094–2127): Seer. Joined in union with Jasal Pinal. Son, Jasan (b. 2122). Born to Tash-Hamar province. Amulet: blue-green aquamarine.

ATAN Robaar (3350–): Fal'kin *scholaire* Defender. Chooses early to support the Battle of Two Rivers Ford. Amulet: red ruby.

DAV Koehl (3319–): Defender. Defender Commander of Kin-Deren provincial Fal'kin forces. Amulet: blue sapphire.

DESDE il'Kellis Pinal (3319–): Seer. Prime of Kin-Deren. Served as il'Kin battle seer before elevation as Prime's Second. Joined in union with Kaarl Pinal. Mother of Mirana Pinal. Amulet: yellow topaz.

GANNAH Tesabe (3345–3367): Defender. Member of the il'Kin. Born to Jad-Anüna Province. Killed in a grynwen ambush in the Kana-Akün forest in 3367. Amulet: yellow sapphire.

GEMMA il'Lakumbe Piaar (3318–): Unaspected. Senior herbswoman at the Healing Hostel of Kin-Deren. Born to Jad-Anüna province. Husband Baden Piaar (deceased). Mother to five children (three sons, two daughters) killed in a Ken'nar raid in 3350.

HAARLEN Lasen (3312–): Unaspected. Quartermaster of the Learning Hall of Kin-Deren province.

ILRIK Maldaar (2089–2122): Defender. Ken Defender of the Dark Triumvirate. Also known as "Ilrik the Black." Amulet: deep red-purple garnet.

ISEL, Wend (3317–): Defender. Horsemaster of Kin-Deren province. Oversees the stables in Deren and the province's warhorse herd. Amulet: yellow zircon.

JASAL Pinal (2092–2122): Trine. Primus Magne and Prime of Kin-Deren. Amulet: diamond.

KAARL Pinal (3314–): Defender. Defender Commander of the il'Kin. Named Steward of the Quorum of Light after the death of Toban Kellis. Joined in union with Desde il'Kellis Pinal. Father of Mirana Pinal. Amulet: red garnet.

MAARK Bedane (3352–): Unaspected. Orphaned when his parents were killed in a Ken'nar raid of their homestead and farm in 3365.

MIRANA Pinal (3351–): Fal'kin *scholaira*, training as a seer. Daughter of Kaarl and Desde Pinal.

MORGAN Jord (3334–): Defender. Commander's Second of the il'Kin. Amulet: purple amethyst.

NIAH il'Sahli Beltran (3325–): Healer. *Priora* of Healing Hostel of Kin-Deren. Born to Tash-Hamar province. Joined in union with Tennen Beltran. Mother of Teague Beltran. Amulet: rose quartz.

NIALL Corran (3318–): Defender. Commander's Second of the Kin-Deren provincial Fal'kin forces. Amulet: red beryl.

TADDIE (Taddeus) Egen (3362–): Fal'kin *scholaire* Seer. Apprenticed under Defender Wend Isel as a stable hand.

TARN Salka (3315–3365): Defender. Member of the il'Kin. Killed in a Ken'nar skirmish near Thyre's Crossing in the Trak-Calan highlands in 3365. Amulet: blue zircon.

TAUL Brandt (3320–): Unaspected. Magistrate of Deren.

TEAGUE Beltran (3351–): Unaspected. Son of Healers Tennen and Niah Beltran. Apprenticed as an herbsman in the Healing Hostel.

TENNEN Beltran (3322–): Healer. *Priore* of Healing Hostel of Kin-Deren. Joined in union with Niah il'Sahli Beltran. Father of Teague Beltran. Amulet: light-purple sapphire.

TOBAN Kellis (3272–3367): Seer. Former Prime of Kin-Deren, Steward of the Quorum of Light. Father of Desde il'Kellis Pinal. Amulet: light-yellow beryl.

YENIRA Irasda (3349–): Fal'kin *scholaira* Seer. Chooses early to support the Battle of Two Rivers Ford. Amulet: blue topaz.

Trak-Calan—2nd Hall. Standard: gold field with green tiger

HINSAH Parn (3348–): Defender. Commander's Second of Trak-Calan provincial Fal'kin forces. Amulet: medium-green peridot.

KOBEN Ryotan (3314–): Seer. Prime of Trak-Calan. Raised as a foster brother to Tetric Garis. Amulet: dark-orange garnet.

SHALAS Yutan (3245–3330): Seer. Prime of Trak-Calan. Foster father and *patrua* mentor of Tetric Garis. Amulet: golden topaz.

Rün-Taran—3rd Hall. Standard: white field with blue capricorn

BINTHE Lima (3343–): Seer. Battle seer of the il'Kin. Granddaughter of Eshe and Lindar Pashcot. Amulet: green emerald.

ESHE il'Bahane Pashcot (3270–): Seer. Prime of Rün-Taran. Joined in union with Lindar Pashcot (deceased). Grandmother to Binthe Lima. Amulet: pale-blue zircon.

LINDAR Pashcot (3268–3330): Defender. Defender Commander of Rün-Taran provincial Fal'kin forces and Prime's Second. Joined in union with Eshe il'Bahane Pashcot. Grandfather to Binthe Lima. Amulet: red-orange carnelian.

SYNE Develan (3289–): Defender. Prime's Second and Defender Commander of Rün-Taran provincial Fal'kin forces. Amulet: orange citrine.

Tash-Hamar—4th Hall. Standard: purple field with red leopard

FALANNAH il'Aldi Sadhi (3308–3350): Seer. Served as a battle seer in the Tash-Hamari provincial Fal'kin forces. Mother of Timir Sadhi. Sister of Fasen Aldi. Amulet: pink morganite.

FASEN Aldi (3303–): Defender. Prime of Tash-Hamar. Uncle of Timir Sadhi. Brother to Falannah il'Aldi Sadhi. Amulet: blue sapphire.

TIMIR Sadhi (3333–): Defender. Prime's Second and Defender Commander of Tash-Hamari Fal'kin provincial forces. Nephew of Fasen Aldi. Amulet: deep-orange citrine.

Kana-Akün—5th Hall. Standard: green field with gold hart

BELESSA il'Isofar Tir (3279–3367): Healer. Prime of Kana-Akün. Presumed killed in the Battle of Falantir, winter 3367. Amulet: green tourmaline.

THIEER Pannen (3321–3367): Seer. Prime's Second and Seer Commander of Kana-Akün provincial Fal'kin forces. Presumed killed in the Battle of Falantir, winter 3367. Amulet: yellow apatite.

Varn-Erdal—6th Hall. Standard: white field with red horse

CLARIENNE il'Hadten Jord (3336–3359): Unaspected. Shepherd and homesteader. Wife of Morgan Jord. Died with infant son, Pieter, in a Ken'nar raid in the Varn-Erdal plains in 3359.

DREI Carada (3348–3365): Defender. Son of Trein Carada and Marienne Tans. Attacked by Ken'nar, winter 3365, presumed dead. Amulet: deep-magenta rhodolite.

ERAN Talz (3315–): Unaspected. Horsemaster of Varn-Erdal province. Oversees the stables in Edara and the province's warhorse herd.

GRENNE Fadern (3325–): Seer. Elevated to Prime's Second of Varn-Erdal before the Battle of Edara. Two sons (deceased), one daughter (deceased) by Trein Carada. Previously coupled with Trein Carada until his death. Coupled with Liaonne Edaran. Amulet: deep-pink tourmaline.

ILLENNE Talz (3349–): Unaspected. Horse herd mistress and archer. Daughter of Eran Talz.

LIAONNE Edaran (3342–): Defender. Prime of Varn-Erdal, elevated after the Battle of Two Rivers Ford. Daughter of Vallia Edaran. Amulet: yellow topaz.

MARIENNE Tans (3318–): Unaspected. Learning hall attendant and laundress. Mother of Drei Carada. Coupled with Trein Carada until his death. Bore five other children (three sons, two daughters), all defenders, deceased.

NATHEN Keldir (3298–): Defender. Senior defender on Prime's Council. Father of Liaonne Edaran. Amulet: amber citrine.

PALEN Clar (3298–): Unaspected. Senior learning hall herbsman.

PIETER Jord (3358–3359, d. 6 months): Unaspected. Son of Morgan and Clarienne Jord. Died in a Ken'nar raid in the Varn-Erdal plains.

PIOL Lidan (3295–): Defender. Senior defender on Prime's Council. Amulet: green chrysoberyl.

TREIN Carada (3317–3365): Defender. Attacked by Ken'nar, winter 3365, presumed dead. Amulet: blue apatite.

WESAL Pettan (3293–): Defender. Senior defender on Prime's Council. Amulet: dark-pink zircon.

VALLIA Edaran (3317–3368): Defender. Prime of Varn-Erdal. Perished in an ambush during the Battle of Two Rivers Ford. Amulet: red ruby.

Jad-Anüna—7th Hall. Standard: blue field with gold lion

ABER Hebari (3328–): Defender. Prime's Second and Defender Commander of Jad-Anünan Fal'kin provincial forces. Amulet: green spinel.

NAMBRE Dinir (3302–): Defender. Prime of Jad-Anüna. Amulet: red-brown andalusite.

TILENATETE Nasta (2835–2867): Trine. Prime of Jad-Anüna. Elevated to Primus Magne during the Red Plague of 2864–2866. Killed by Ken'nar when she tried to offer aid during the pandemic. Amulet: pale-green chrysoberyl.

Sün-Kasal—8th Hall. Standard: red field with white bull

BYSTRA il'Tari Klai (3312–3350): Defender. Joined in union with Sahm Klai. Two sons (deceased), one daughter (deceased). Amulet: blue-gray cordierite.

RABB Plout (3328–): Seer. Prime's Second and Seer Commander of Sün-Kasal provincial Fal'kin forces, serves as battle seer. Amulet: red-brown topaz.

SAHM Klai (3308–): Defender. Prime of Sün-Kasal. Joined in union with Bystra il'Tari Klai (deceased). Two sons (deceased), one daughter (deceased) with Bystra il'Tari. Amulet: smoky-brown quartz.

Dar-Azûl—9ᵗʰ Hall. Standard: black field with argent silver griffin

SIDO Rendel (3345–): Seer. Prime's Second and Seer Commander of Dar-Azûlan Fal'kin provincial forces, serves as battle seer. Born to Kana-Akün province. Amulet: light-green peridot.

STAINE, Kev (3325–): Defender. Amulet: medium-blue kyanite.

TETRIC Garis (3313–): Trine. Prime of Dar-Azûl. Amulet: hematite.

TRINE RISING

The Kinderra Saga: Book 1

Glossary of Terms and Words

-á .... past-perfect tense; joined to the word it modifies. Example: had created = creará.

a .... to

a nehíl .... (you are) welcome; literally "a nothing;" not to be confused with a greeting "Ben ve" as in "good coming."

accepte, acceptem .... accept, acceptance

ad .... at

adam, adamé, adamá .... forget, forgot, forgotten

agen .... again

ai .... yes

ain .... one, whole, complete, only

aire .... air

alainne .... beautiful

alta .... above, high

ama .... love

amausar......................................steward, stewardship,
manage; literally "loving use"

amula......................................amulet; Amulets allow an
Aspected to further focus
and use their innate Aspects,
especially outside of
themselves. An Aspected's
life force harmonics will
resonate with one specific
crystal, except in the case of
a Trine. Because they possess
all three Aspects, Trines have
the innate ability to modulate
their life harmonics to adapt
to any amulet.

amulet......................................The sacred tool and relic
containing a gemstone used
by the Aspected to manifest
their powers outside of
themselves. While all
Aspected have certain
abilities without an amulet
(e.g. telekinesis, telepathy), to
produce major actions with
their Aspects requires the use
of an amulet. Typically, when
they've reached 18 summers
old, Aspected choose a single
amulet for life through a
mystical union of life
harmonics matching the

natural harmonics within the gemstone's crystal structure. The connection is unique and indelible. The loss or destruction of an amulet causes untold anguish for the Aspected individual, most committing suicide. Only Trines, those with all three Aspects, can choose more than one amulet. (see Aspects, Aspected, Choosing Ceremony, Trine)

an	an
anaíl, anaíle	breath, breathe
anelies	another
animale	animal
Anqa Lingua	literally "old tongue"; the ancient language of Kinderra
aonta	union
aquete, aqueté	water, watered
aquila	eagle
ár	on, upon
as	as
aspeca	life
aspecaem	soul, spirit

aspece, aspecae ....live, alive

Aspecta('e) ....Aspect(s)

Aspecta'e Alta ....Aspects Above; This is the trinity-like deity that Kinderrans believe created the universe and all living things. They are the source of life and the powers of the Aspects.

Aspected ....Generic term for one who possesses the powers of the Aspects. In the culture and beliefs of Kinderra, the Unaspected were the first peoples created by the Aspects Above. Some of these were chosen by the Aspects Above and touched with fingers of lightning, bestowing upon them the powers of the Aspects to become the Aspected, stewards, and protectors of all of Kinderra. The expression of Aspect powers occurs in about one of every 1,000 births.

Aspects, Powers of the ....The powers of the Aspects occur in three types: Defending, conferring extraordinary reflexes, speed, strength, and situational awareness, as well as the ability to manifest amulet fire from one's amulet; Seeing, conferring the ability to see into the past, present, and future; and Healing, conferring the ability to stimulate the healing of injury and illness thousands of times faster than normal. Major expressions of the Aspects require the focus of an amulet. For example, while it is possible for a healer without an amulet to suppress pain in another to a degree, to set a broken bone would require an amulet to focus the Healing Aspect. All Aspected have certain innate abilities that do not require an amulet, including telekinesis, telepathy, and some ability to shunt away pain and enhance endurance.

aste .... star

atuda .... together

aud, audé .... hear, heard avera ....long for, want

ban ....white

bath..both

bé ....by

ben...good, kind

Ben dië...good morning, good day

Ben iré...farewell, goodbye; literally
                                                    "good leaving"

Ben kin; B'kin ....hello, hi (informal); literally
                                                    "good light"

Ben nöc..good night

benedicta, benedictaé,
benedictan ....bless, blessed, blessing

besa..kiss

bhéth; bhéth en aonta.....................join; join in union (marry)

bia ....before

bir...bring

biraen, biraena, biraen'e ....child/son, daughter,
                                                    children; often used as a term
                                                    of endearment

biran ....birth; literally "bring forth"

Book of Kinderra, The...................Historical reference of
                                                    Kinderra written before the
                                                    Sundering by Aspected and

Unaspected scholars. Considered one of the two revered books of the Fal'kin, along with the Ora Fal'kinnen.

braith, braith ár .... depend/rely, depend/rely on

brea .... great, most (quantity); (see also magne)

bremaithe .... grandmother; also a term of respect for female elders

brepaithe .... grandfather; also a term of respect for male elders

buai.. win

caela .... sky

call.. telepathic communication ("He called a warning to her mind."); also the act of telekinesis ("He called a cup into his waiting hand.")

calora, calorae................................ warm, warming

cara, caran; Ëi cara('e) .... friend, friendship; my friend(s)

cëos; cëosan .... choose; chosen

cerebus.. brain, mind

Choosing Ceremony .... The sacrament where Aspected *scholaire'e* choose

their gemstone amulets
through the mystical union of
their life harmonics with the
harmonics of a gemstone's
crystal. The ceremony is held
annually for those who have
reached 18 summers old.

chosant...protect

cin ....with

cinen...within

cinstandan...withstand

clae...sword, weapon

Codex of Jasal
the Great, The ....The journal of Jasal Pinal.
Written between 2117–2132.
There have been several
attempts throughout history
to destroy the work, but
none have succeeded.

com...like (similar to)

comé...what

compre...know

comprende, comprendea ....understand, understanding

confian ....trust

consente..agree; Example: I agree, okay
= Ëo consente

corem .... face

covrir (v.) .... cover

crear, crearé, creará .... create(s), make; created, had created

il'Crearae (The Creation) .... The creation psalm from the Ora Fal'kinnen. Also a euphemism for Kinderra or the universe

culpa; Ëo ad culpa .... fault; "I'm sorry" (literally, "I am at fault")

cunaré (slang) .... derogatory term for female genitalia

daingaen .... stable, solid

dam .... give

dar .... mountain

defecta, defectim .... fail, failure

defende, defendeä, defendeo .... defend, fight, protect; defender; defense, protection

defender .... An Aspected individual who possesses the Defending Aspect

Defender Commander .... Highest-ranking officer in a Fal'kin provincial army; (see Second)

Defender's Second............Second-in-command of a Fal'kin provincial army; (see Second)

derra ....earth, land, world

derranen............foundation; based on the root word for "land"

dhái............past

dici............speak, say

dië............dawn, day, morning

digita............finger

diu............long (length)

doma............home, house

dúa............between

-'e............plural suffix (pronounced 'eh'); joined to the word it modifies. Example: friend/friends = cara/cara'e.

-é............past tense suffix; joined to the word it modifies. Example: created = crearé.

e............and (pronounced 'ee')

Ëa............me

Ëam............mine

Ëi............my

elies .... other

ëllenas .... fill(s)

empe, a'empe .... begin, had begun

emplecti .... embrace, hug

en .... in

engre (n.), engren (v.) .... anger

enigma .... puzzle, riddle

Ëo .... I, I am

Ëo anaíle; Ëo aspece .... "I breathe; I live." A defender's adage.

Ëome .... us

Ëomus .... we, we are

et .... there

eta(n) .... there was/were

etim .... still

etís .... there is/are

expel .... Punishment for a capital crime among the Fal'kin, where the condemned is forced to leave Fal'kin society and his/her province. In the most extreme circumstances, a Fal'kin's amulet is taken. Most Fal'kin would prefer death to being kept from their calling to the Aspects, their amulets, and their province.

il'Exultantae (The Rejoice) ....Psalm of praise from the Ora Fal'kinnen

exulte..exult, exalt, praise

fal...follow

Fal'kin; Fal'kinnen............................"They who follow the Light;" the whole body of the Fal'kin. These Aspected people believe in the philosophy of the Light from Within. They use their innate powers of the Aspects within themselves as their sole source of power. To draw in life forces to augment one's power is considered the most extreme crime one could commit. Fal'kin caught using the Power from Without are relieved of their amulets and expelled from the province.

fár..for

fárdam, fárdamen;
Ëo fárdam Oë................................forgive, forgiven; "I forgive you"

fhí, fhíagn, a fhí ....weave, weaving, to weave filam .... thread

fin .... at last, end, finished

fissura... crack, fissure, split

forma .... form

forte .... fort, keep (building), strong

fos... yet

fuádain .... fleeting

gainem .... sand (n.)

gemma .... crystal, jewel

gente, -n, -na...................................... people, man, woman

gháinn, gháinn'e .... grain, grains

gloria, gloriae, gloriaé .... glory, glorify, glorified

Gratas, Gratas Oë................................ thanks; thank you

grynwen .... Massive, wolflike carnivores known for their pupilless red eyes and their viciousness. It is believed they use some type of primitive Aspect-like senses to hunt.

gryphus... griffin

hac... here

hale.. holy

har .... hill healer..An Aspected individual who possesses the Healing Aspect

i'...of; joined to the word it modifies

-í...future tense suffix, joined to the word it modifies; Example: will create = crearí.

id (m.), ida (f.) ....it(s)

Iëa, Iëam Iëas..she, her, hers

Ië, Iëm, Iës ....he, him, his

il'-...of the; joined to the word it modifies. Often used as a prefix in formal surnames, especially matrilineal names.

il'Kin..The Fal'kin strike force comprises defenders and battle seers from all nine provinces. The il'Kin is a special operations unit serving all of Kinderra and augments provincial forces in times of need. It is under the direction of the Steward of the Quorum of Light and led by a defender commander. Historically, the il'Kin has served Kinderra in the absence of a Trine's provincial forces. Only the most highly accomplished Fal'kin are invited to join its ranks.

imbecilae, -t .... ignorance, stupidity; ignorant, stupid

impatientia .... impatience

inaspeca (n.) .... free will, will

incendio .... burn

infera .... below, under

inimica .... enemy

íre .... go, leave, journey

ísi(é) .... are, be, is; was (preposition); (see pronouns)

íuven; íuven sibe/siba .... young; younger ("little") brother/sister

ken .... power

Ken'nar; Ken'narren .... "They who use the Power;" The whole body of the Ken'nar. Ken'nar believe in the philosophy of the Power from Without. They use their innate Aspects and their amulets only to pull in the life forces around them and pour out that power back through their amulets,

	providing a seemingly limitless supply of power. They believe the use of the Aspects should not be limited by one's innate powers.
kin	light
Kin ísi Oëa	Light be yours; a formal greeting. The reply is "E Oë" (And you).
kinema	lightning
len	gentle, soft
leten	allow, let
locarae	location, place
luve	rain
luveclae	storm, tempest; literally "rain sword"
ma, maís	may, may be, maybe
maent	meant
magistrate	the highest-ranking government official of a province's Unaspected, akin to a Fal'kin prime
magne	great (honorable); (see also brea)

maithe .... mother; has the connotation of "mommy"

manë .... hand

marca .... brand

matrua .... aunt; also can mean "godmother," "teacher," or "mentor"

mer .... sea, ocean

mercare, mercaré .... buy, bought

minia .... little, small, tiny

mista .... mist

morte, mortea,
mortean, mortes .... dead, death, die

mor .... more

nome .... name, call; also a telepathic call of communication

necesit .... must

nefas, nefas'e .... sin, sins

nehíl .... nothing

nöc .... night

nubla .... cloud

numbers, 1-10
(cardinal, quantity) .... primus, seconda, trina, quatra, quinta, sexta, septa,

octa, nonta, decema (see also "ain")

nun...nor

nunqa...never

-ó..present-perfect tense; joined to the word it modifies. Example: have created = crearó

o ....or

obsca; Obsca Oëa osa ....close, shut; "Close your mouth" ("shut up")

Oë...you

Oëa ....your, yours

Oëma...who, whom

Oëme...they

Oëmea..those

Oëmus..them, their

onoír...honor

Ora Fal'kinnen...............................Literally "Prayer of the Fal'kin." The major religious work of the Fal'kin, detailing their relationship with the Aspects Above, the powers of the Aspects, and Kinderra. Considered one of the great

books of the Fal'kin along
with The Book of Kinderra.

osa .... mouth

oscuil, oscuil'e .... eye, eyes

pace.. peace

palibre.. word

passenae (n.), passen (v.) .... passage, hallway (n.); pass (v.)

paithe.. father; has the connotation
of "daddy"

patientia.. patience

patrua.. uncle; also "godfather,"
"teacher" or "mentor"

pecta.. breast, chest

penilaré (slang) .... derogatory term for male
genitalia

per .... but

periclaem... fear

pericul, periculus............................. danger, dangerous

pián .... pain, suffering

placre .... please (v.)

potest.. possible

pon, pone... lay/lay down, lies/rests potem..after

Prime..The Aspected leader of a
province's Fal'kin

Prime's Second...................................The Aspected next in line for
primeship (see Second)

Primus...Anqa Lingua for "prime;"
used as a formal reference

Primus Magne....................................A dictator-like role elevated
from among the Aspected to
lead the entire continent's
Fal'kin. This role is enacted
during times of extreme
duress in Kinderra, such as a
pandemic or other
widespread calamity.

priore (m.), priora (f.),
priore'e (pl.).......................................The head of a healing hostel
or infirmary, something akin
to the chief of staff

pronouns ....are capitalized; Ëo (I), Oë
(you), Ëomus (we), etc.; state
of being implied. Example: I
am here = Ëo hac.

proxi..against, close, near

qua ....which

quen...when

quet, quetís ....where, where is quis.. some

quistempre('e).................................. sometime(s)

quod.. because

Quorum of Light............................ The council comprises all the primes and seconds from the nine provinces of Kinderra. The Quorum discusses the state of affairs in Kinderra, and sets policy and laws affecting the Fal'kin of every province.

Quorumtide....................................... The major holiday time in Kinderra, marked by feasting and celebration, and often fewer military actions due to impending winter weather. It coincides with the Quorum meeting, which occurs in Deren for one sevenday each Reckoning in Fifthmonth.

reace.. reach

Reckoning... The literal number of the year. Example: Mirana Pinal was born in the Reckoning of 3352.

rememore.. remember

Rememore Kin en Forte................ Remember the Light in the Keep

Rememore Kin e Forte ....Remember the Light and the Keep

responara ....answer

requa...require

revelar...reveal

risa ....rise

rith ....run

robare..steal

runh ....secret, hide

sana..health

Sana e Kin a Oë..............................Health and Light to You; a formal greeting

sanare, sanarente, sanareä ....heal, healing, healer

sculpte ....sculpt, shape

scinane, scinané, scinaneá ....shine, shined, shone

scholaire (m.), scholaira (f.), scholaire'e (pl.)....................................Aspected students learning how to use their powers.

Second..The second-in-command of a province's Fal'kin (Prime's Second) or Fal'kin army (Commander's Second). This is an extremely influential and pivotal role, requiring much vetting and interviewing, and provides an immediate and seamless transition of power upon a prime's or defender commander's death or incapacitation. Final approval for either role rests with a province's prime, although in the case of a Commander's Second, the Defender Commander's choice strongly influences the decision.

Seconde...See Second

seer...An Aspected individual who possesses the Seeing Aspect

seer's ruse...A seer technique for projecting visions through an amulet to be viewed by others. (see also Visi Externa)

servad..servant

settan...set

siba, Ëi siba......................................sister, my sister

sibe, Ëi sibe......................................brother, my brother

siber (n.), sibere (v.)......................sieve (n.), sift (v.)

siniúint...destiny skene...skein

solis...alone, apart, separate

staíonnae, staíonne...........................need (n.), need (v.)

statam...now

standan...stand

Steward of the
Quorum of Light...........................The influential facilitator of
the Quorum of Light is
elected by the primes and
seconds of the Quorum. The
steward has no vote for
his/her province but can cast
a single vote by proxy for
another province unable to
attend Quorum meetings as
well as cast a tie-breaking
vote in the rare instance
when it occurs.

straitéis...strategy, plan

summer...Euphemism for a calendar
year, especially in reference
to age (I am sixteen summers
old; the man has seen thirty
summers); also the literal
summer season. (see also
Reckoning)

ta ....to

talus('e)...claw(s), talon(s) te .... from

tempre .... time

ten .... has, have

testus; Ëo testus .... swear (an oath); I swear

tha .... than

the .... then

thet .... that

toucha .... touch

todhái .... future

traiseh .... treasure

tré .... through

treor .... command, guide

trevia .... direction, way; (see also íre, passenae)

Trine .... One who possesses all three powers of the Aspects (i.e. Defending, Seeing, and Healing). These individuals are exceedingly rare, perhaps one born only once every several hundred summers. In Kinderran culture, it is believed the Aspects Above create a Trine to save

	Kinderra from some great impending calamity.
tuda	all
tudempre	always, eternal, forever; literally "all time"
tudsa	also
tuil, tuilé	earn, earned
u'-	not, un-; joined to the word it modifies. Example: u'kin meaning dark or "not light."
u'ai	no
u'ben	evil; literally "not good"
u'bendicta	curse; literally "un-blessing"
u'cin	without
u'gen, u'gente	none, no one
u'kin	dark; literally "not light"
u'len	hard
U'Nehíl	Literally "false nothing." The practice of masking one's presence from within the Aspects by manipulating one's Aspects to mimic or reflect the "life force" noise in the general vicinity.

u'pace .... battle, war; literally "not peace"

u'verdas .... falsehood, lie

u'vide .... blind, sightless, often derogatory; "u'vide vermihn" meaning "sightless maggot" as someone without the Aspects.

u'vide excra (slang) .... Unaspected; literally "sightless shit"

Unaspected .... those without the Aspects

upacaem .... destruction; based on the root word for "war"

usar .... use

ve .... come(s)

verda, verdas .... true, truth

vermihn .... maggot, worm, or any vermin or disgusting creature; often used as an insult

vide, vidé, Videä, Vidë .... look/see, looked/saw, Seer, Sight

virtú .... bravery, courage

visi .... vision

Visi Externa ....A seer technique for projecting visions through an amulet to be viewed by others; also known as a seer's ruse

voide..void

year ....see Reckoning; see summer

ABOUT THE AUTHOR

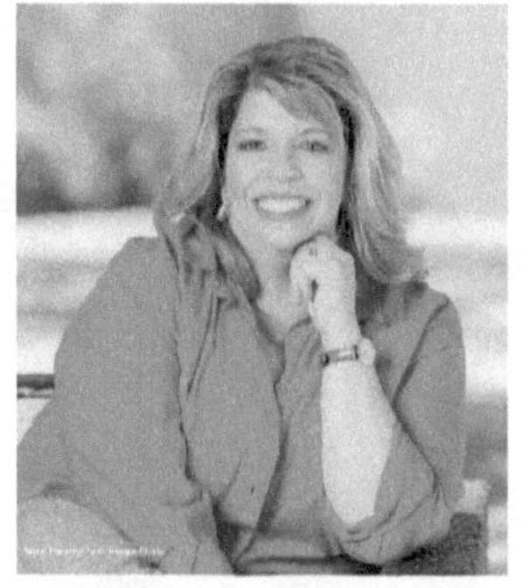

While other kids read comic books under the covers with a flashlight at bedtime, C.K. DONNELLY wrote fan fiction and fantasy stories.

She used her love of writing to pursue a career in journalism and was honored with several press awards for business and economic reporting. She has also held careers in healthcare, and currently runs a freelance writing and marketing support firm.

She resides in Arizona with her oh-so-patient husband and her little black dog (who is equally patient). She no longer writes under the covers by flashlight. Usually.

TEIL I

eter

»PAPA!« Dem schrillen Aufschrei folgt das Geräusch kleiner Füße, als mein Sohn durch die Tür stürmt und seine dunklen, welligen Haare dabei um sein glühendes Gesicht fliegen.

Ich lache, als ich seinen kleinen, robusten Körper auffange, der auf mich zufliegt. »Hast du mich vermisst, *Pupsik?*«

»Ja!« Seine kurzen Arme umfassen meinen Hals, und ich atme tief ein, um seinen süßen, kindlichen Duft aufzusaugen. Auch wenn Pasha schon fast drei Jahre alt ist, riecht er immer noch nach Milch – nach gesundem Baby und Unschuld.

Ich drücke ihn fest an mich und spüre, wie die Eiseskälte in mir schmilzt, als sich eine weiche, strah-

lende Wärme in meiner Brust ausbreitet. Es ist schmerzhaft, so wie wenn man in heißes Wasser eintaucht, nachdem man gefroren hat, aber es ist ein guter Schmerz. Ich fühle mich dadurch lebendig, die Leere in mir wird gefüllt, bis ich fast glauben kann, dass ich vollständig bin und die Liebe meines Sohnes verdiene.

»Er hat dich vermisst«, sagt Tamila, als sie in den Flur kommt. Wie immer bewegt sie sich leise, fast lautlos, und hat ihre Augen auf den Boden gerichtet. Sie blickt mich nicht direkt an. Seit ihrer Kindheit ist sie dazu erzogen worden, Augenkontakt mit Männern zu vermeiden, also sehe ich nur ihre langen Wimpern, während sie nach unten schaut. Sie trägt ein traditionelles Kopftuch, das ihre langen, dunklen Haare versteckt, und ihr graues Kleid ist lang und formlos. Trotzdem sieht sie wunderschön aus – so schön wie sie vor dreieinhalb Jahren, als sie sich in mein Bett geschlichen hatte, um der Hochzeit mit einem der älteren Männer aus dem Dorf zu entfliehen.

»Und ich habe euch beide vermisst«, erwidere ich, als mein Sohn gegen meine Schultern drückt, weil er herunter möchte. Grinsend setze ich ihn auf dem Boden ab, und er ergreift augenblicklich meine Hand und zieht an ihr.

»Papa, willst du meinen LKW sehen? Willst du, Papa?«

»Das will ich«, antworte ich und grinse noch breiter, während er mich ins Wohnzimmer zieht. »Was für ein LKW ist es?«

»Ein großer!«

»Okay, dann zeig mal her.«

Tamila kommt langsam hinter uns her, und ich bemerke, dass ich noch gar nichts zu ihr gesagt habe. Ich bleibe stehen, drehe mich herum und schaue meine Frau an. »Wie geht es dir?«

Sie blickt mich kurz durch ihre Wimpern an. »Mir geht es gut. Ich freue mich, dich zu sehen.«

»Und ich freue mich, dich zu sehen.« Ich möchte sie küssen, aber ich weiß, dass es ihr peinlich ist, wenn ich es vor Pasha tue, also halte ich mich zurück. Stattdessen berühre ich sanft ihre Wange und lasse mich dann von meinem Sohn zu seinem LKW führen, den ich als denjenigen wiedererkenne, den ich ihm vor drei Wochen aus Moskau geschickt habe.

Er führt mir stolz alle Funktionen des Fahrzeugs vor, während ich neben ihm hocke und sein lebhaftes Gesicht betrachte. Er hat Tamilas dunkle, exotische Schönheit einschließlich der Wimpern, aber er hat auch etwas von mir, selbst wenn ich nicht genau sagen kann, was.

»Er hat deine Furchtlosigkeit«, sagt Tamila leise, während sie sich neben mich kniet. »Und ich denke, dass er genauso groß werden wird wie du, auch wenn man das wahrscheinlich so früh noch nicht sagen kann.«

Ich blicke sie kurz an. Sie tut das häufig, mich so gründlich zu durchschauen, dass es scheint, als könne sie meine Gedanken lesen. Andererseits ist es auch keine Kunst, zu erahnen, was ich gerade denke. Ich

habe einen Vaterschaftstest gemacht, noch bevor Pasha geboren wurde.

»Papa. Papa.« Mein Sohn zieht wieder an meiner Hand. »Spiel mit mir.«

Ich lache und wende meine Aufmerksamkeit wieder ihm zu. In der nächsten Stunde spielen wir mit dem LKW und einem Dutzend weiterer Spielzeuge, die auch alle Autos sind. Pasha ist besessen von Spielzeugautos, angefangen von Krankenwagen bis hin zu Rennwagen. Es ist egal, wie viele andere Spielsachen er von mir bekommt, er spielt nur mit denjenigen, die Räder haben.

Nach dem Spielen essen wir Abendbrot, und Tamila badet Pasha, bevor er ins Bett geht. Ich bemerke, dass die Badewanne Risse hat, und speichere in meinem Hinterkopf ab, eine neue zu bestellen. Das kleine Dorf Daryevo liegt hoch oben im Kaukasus und ist schlecht zu erreichen, also kann ich nicht einfach in einem Geschäft bestellen. Trotzdem habe ich meine Möglichkeiten, Dinge hierherbringen zu lassen.

Als ich Tamila von meinem Vorhaben erzähle, schnellen ihre Wimpern in die Höhe, und sie schaut mir ausnahmsweise mit einem strahlenden Lächeln in die Augen. »Das wäre sehr schön, vielen Dank. Ich musste fast jeden Abend Wasser vom Boden aufwischen.«

Ich lächele zurück, und sie fährt damit fort, Pasha zu baden. Nachdem sie ihn abgetrocknet und ihm den Schlafanzug angezogen hat, trage ich ihn in sein Bett und lese ihm eine Geschichte aus seinem Lieblings-

buch vor. Er schläft fast augenblicklich ein, und ich küsse seine zarte Stirn, wobei sich mein Herz voller Gefühl zusammenzieht.

Das ist Liebe. Ich erkenne sie, auch wenn ich sie niemals zuvor gefühlt habe – auch wenn ein Mann wie ich kein Recht darauf hat, sie zu fühlen. Keines der Dinge, die ich jemals getan habe, zählt hier, in diesem kleinen Dorf in Dagestan.

Wenn ich bei meinem Sohn bin, verbrennt das Blut an meinen Händen nicht meine Seele.

Ich stehe vorsichtig auf, um Pasha nicht aufzuwecken, und verlasse den winzigen Raum, der sein Schlafzimmer ist. Tamila wartet bereits in unserem Schlafzimmer auf mich, also ziehe ich mich aus, begebe mich zu ihr ins Bett und liebe sie so zärtlich, wie ich kann.

Morgen werde ich den hässlichen Seiten dieser Welt ins Auge sehen, aber heute bin ich glücklich.

Heute kann ich lieben und geliebt werden.

»BITTE GEH NICHT, Papa.« Pashas Kinn zittert, als er versucht, nicht zu weinen. Tamila hat ihm vor einigen Wochen gesagt, dass große Jungs nicht weinen, und er hat alles versucht, um ein großer Junge zu sein. »Bitte, Papa. Kannst du nicht noch ein wenig bleiben?«

»Ich werde in ein paar Wochen wieder hier sein«, verspreche ich ihm und hocke mich hin, um auf

Augenhöhe mit ihm zu sein. »Ich muss arbeiten, verstehst du das?«

»Du musst immer arbeiten.« Sein Kinn zittert stärker, und in seinen großen, braunen Augen fließen die Tränen über. »Warum kann ich nicht mit dir zur Arbeit kommen?«

Bilder der Terroristen, die ich letzte Woche gefoltert habe, steigen in meinem Kopf auf, und ich muss mich anstrengen, meine Stimme ruhig zu halten, als ich sage: »Es tut mir leid, Pashen'ka. Mein Arbeitsplatz ist kein Ort für Kinder.« Oder für Erwachsene, aber das sage ich nicht. Tamila weiß einige Dinge der Sachen, die ich als Teil der Speznas, der russischen Spezialeinheiten, tue, aber selbst sie kennt die dunkle Realität meiner Welt nicht.

»Aber ich würde mich gut benehmen.« Jetzt weint er richtig. »Ich verspreche es, Papa. Ich würde mich gut benehmen.«

»Ich weiß, dass du das würdest.« Ich ziehe ihn an mich und umarme ihn fest, während ich spüre, wie sein kleiner Körper von Schluchzern erschüttert wird. »Du bist mein guter Junge, und du musst dich bei Mama gut benehmen, während ich weg bin, okay? Du musst auf sie aufpassen, so wie das große Jungen wie du machen.«

Das scheinen die magischen Worte zu sein, weil er nur noch einmal schnieft und sich dann aufrichtet. »Das werde ich.« Der Rotz läuft aus seiner Nase, und seine Wangen sind nass, aber sein Kinn wirkt

Veröffentlicht von Mozaika Publications, einer Druckmarke von Mozaika LLC.
www.mozaikallc.com

Aus dem Amerikanischen von Grit Schellenberg
Lektorat: Fehler-Haft.de

Cover Design von Najla Qamber Designs
najlaqamberdesigns.com

e-ISBN: 978-1-63142-275-1
ISBN: 978-1-63142-276-8

MEIN PEINIGER

ANNA ZAIRES

♠ MOZAIKA PUBLICATIONS ♠

innerlich, und ich kann kaum die Worte, die ich sagen muss, aus meinem Hals zwingen. »Tamila und Pasha?«

»Es tut mir leid, Peter. Einige der Dorfbewohner wurden während des Kreuzfeuers getötet, und …«, er schluckt hörbar, »die Vorberichte sagen aus, dass Tamila unter ihnen war.«

Meine Finger zerquetschen fast das Telefon. »Was ist mit Pasha?«

»Das wissen wir noch nicht. Es gab einige Explosionen und …«

»Ich bin auf dem Weg.«

»Peter, warte …«

Ich beende das Gespräch und eile aus der Tür.

———

BITTE, *bitte lass ihn am Leben sein. Bitte lass ihn am Leben sein. Bitte, ich werde alles tun, lass ihn einfach nur am Leben sein.*

Ich bin nie religiös gewesen, aber als der Militärhubschrauber über die Berge fliegt, erwische ich mich dabei, wie ich bete, darum bettele und flehe, ein kleines Wunder Wirklichkeit werden zu lassen, eine kleine Barmherzigkeit zu erleben. Das Leben eines Kindes ist bedeutungslos für die Welt, aber für mich bedeutet es alles.

Mein Sohn ist mein Leben, der Grund dafür, dass ich existiere.

Der Lärm des Hubschraubers ist ohrenbetäubend, aber er ist nichts im Vergleich zu dem Lärm in meinem entschlossen, als er mir in die Augen blickt. »Ich werde auf Mama aufpassen, das verspreche ich dir.«

»Er ist so intelligent«, meint Tamila, die sich neben mir hinkniet, um Pasha zu umarmen. »So als sei er fast fünf und nicht erst fast drei.«

»Ich weiß.« Meine Brust schwillt voller Stolz an. »Er ist fantastisch.«

Sie lächelt mich an und blickt zu mir hoch, so dass ich wieder in ihre großen, braunen Augen schaue, die Pashas so sehr ähneln. »Pass auf dich auf und sei bald wieder zu Hause, okay?«

»Das werde ich.« Ich beuge mich nach vorn, um ihre Stirn zu küssen, und streiche danach über Pashas seidige Haare. »Ich werde zurück sein, bevor ihr bemerkt, dass ich weg bin.«

———

ICH BIN IN GROSNY, Tschetschenien, und verfolge gerade die Spur einer neuen radikalen aufständischen Gruppe, als ich die Nachricht bekomme. Derjenige, der mich anruft, ist mein Boss aus Moskau, Ivan Polonsky.

»Peter.« Seine Stimme ist ungewöhnlich ernst, als ich das Gespräch annehme. »Es gab einen Zwischenfall in Daryevo.«

Mein Innerstes vereist. »Was für ein Zwischenfall?«

»Es gab eine Operation, von der wir nichts wussten. Die NATO war daran beteiligt. Und es gab ... Opfer.«

Eiseskälte breitet sich in mir aus, zerfetzt mich

Kopf. Ich kann nicht atmen, kann wegen der Wut und der Angst, die mich innerlich ersticken, nicht denken. Ich weiß nicht, wie Tamila gestorben ist, aber ich habe genügend Leichen gesehen, um mir ihren Körper vorstellen zu können, um ganz deutlich ihre wunderschönen Augen, die jetzt ausdruckslos und blind sein müssen, und ihren schlaffen und blutverkrusteten Mund zu sehen. Und Pasha …

Nein. Daran kann ich jetzt nicht denken. Nicht, bis ich es mit Sicherheit weiß.

Das hätte nicht passieren sollen. Daryevo liegt nicht in der Nähe der bekannten Krisenherde in Dagestan. Es ist eine kleine, friedliche Siedlung ohne Verbindungen zu Rebellengruppen. Sie hätten hier in Sicherheit sein müssen, weit weg von meiner gewalttätigen Welt.

Bitte lass ihn am Leben sein. Bitte lass ihn am Leben sein.

Der Flug scheint ewig zu dauern, aber endlich durchbrechen wir die Wolkendecke, und ich sehe das Dorf. Mein Hals wird eng, und ich kann nicht mehr atmen.

Rauch steigt von vielen Gebäuden im Zentrum auf, und bewaffnete Soldaten befinden sich vor Ort.

Ich springe aus dem Hubschrauber, sobald er den Boden berührt.

»Peter, warte. Du brauchst Deckung«, ruft der Pilot, aber ich renne bereits und stoße die Menschen, die mir im Weg stehen, einfach beiseite. Ein junger Soldat versucht, mich aufzuhalten, aber ich reiße ihm seine M16 aus den Händen und richte sie auf ihn.

»Führe mich zu den Leichen. Jetzt.«

Ich weiß nicht, ob es an der Waffe oder meinem tödlichen Ton liegt, aber der Soldat gehorcht und eilt zu einem Schuppen am anderen Ende der Straße. Ich folge ihm, während das Adrenalin wie Gift durch meine Adern fließt.

Bitte lass ihn am Leben sein. Bitte lass ihn am Leben sein.

Ich sehe die Leichen hinter dem Schuppen, einige ordentlich hingelegt, und andere aufeinandergestapelt auf dem schneebedeckten Gras. Niemand ist bei ihnen; die Soldaten müssen die Dorfbewohner bis jetzt von ihnen ferngehalten haben. Ich erkenne sofort einige der Toten – die älteren Menschen des Dorfes, mit denen Tamila auch zu tun hatte, die Frau des Bäckers, der Mann, von dem ich schon einmal Ziegenmilch gekauft habe – aber andere kann ich nicht identifizieren, einerseits wegen der Ausmaße ihrer Wunden und andererseits, weil ich nicht viel Zeit im Dorf verbracht habe.

Ich habe eigentlich *gar keine* Zeit hier verbracht, und jetzt ist meine Frau tot.

Ich bereite mich psychisch auf das vor, was jetzt kommen wird, knie mich neben einen schlanken Frauenkörper, lege die M16 ins Gras und ziehe das Tuch, das den Kopf bedeckt, zur Seite. Ein Teil des Kopfes ist von einer Kugel weggeschossen worden, aber ich kann genug von dem Gesicht erkennen, um zu wissen, dass es nicht Tamila ist.

Ich untersuche den nächsten Frauenkörper, der mehrere Einschusslöcher in der Brust hat. Es ist Tamilas Tante, eine schüchterne Frau in den Fünfzigern, die in den letzten drei Jahren weniger als fünf Worte mit mir gesprochen hat. Für sie und den Rest von Tamilas Familie bin ich immer ein Fremder gewesen, ein angst-einflößender Fremder aus einer anderen Welt. Sie haben Tamilas Entscheidung, mich zu heiraten, nicht verstanden, sie sogar verurteilt, aber Tamila war das egal.

Sie war immer unabhängig gewesen.

Ein weiterer Frauenkörper zieht meine Aufmerksamkeit auf sich. Die Frau liegt auf der Seite, aber die sanfte Kurve ihrer Schultern ist schmerzhaft vertraut. Meine Hand zittert, als ich sie umdrehe, und weißglühender Schmerz durchfährt mich, als ich ihr Gesicht sehe.

Tamilas Mund ist genauso locker, wie ich ihn mir vorgestellt hatte, aber ihre Augen sind nicht leer. Sie sind geschlossen, ihre langen Wimpern versengt und ihre Augenlider von Blut verklebt. Mehr Blut bedeckt ihre Brust und ihre Arme, und ihr graues Kleid ist fast schwarz davon.

Meine Frau, meine wunderschöne junge Frau, die den Mut hatte, ihr eigenes Schicksal zu wählen, ist tot. Sie ist gestorben, ohne jemals ihr Dorf verlassen zu haben, ohne jemals Moskau gesehen zu haben, wovon sie immer geträumt hatte. Ihr Leben wurde ausgelöscht, bevor sie eine Chance hatte, zu leben, und es ist meine Schuld. Ich hätte hier sein sollen, hätte sie und Pasha beschützen müssen. Zur Hölle, ich hätte über diese beschissene Operation Bescheid wissen müssen; niemand hätte hierherkommen sollen, ohne dass mein Team und ich darüber informiert wurden.

Wut steigt in mir auf, vermischt sich mit qualvollem Schmerz und Schuldgefühlen, aber ich verdränge das alles und zwinge mich dazu, mich weiter umzuschauen. Die Leichen, die in Reihen ausgebreitet wurden, sind ausschließlich Erwachsene, aber es gibt ja noch diesen anderen Haufen.

Bitte lass ihn am Leben sein. Ich werde alles tun, solange er nur lebt.

Meine Beine fühlen sich wie abgebrannte Streichhölzer an, als ich mich dem Haufen nähere. Er besteht aus einzelnen Gliedmaßen und Körpern, die bis zur Unkenntlichkeit verstümmelt sind. Das müssen die Opfer der Explosionen sein. Ich lege jeden Körperteil zur Seite, nachdem ich ihn betrachtet habe. Der Geruch nach altem Blut und verbranntem Fleisch hängt dick in der Luft. Ein normaler Mann würde sich bereits übergeben haben, aber ich bin noch nie normal gewesen.

Bitte lass ihn am Leben sein.

»Peter, warte. Eine Spezialeinheit ist auf dem Weg hierher, und sie wollen nicht, dass wir die Leichen anfassen.« Der Pilot, der mich hierhergebracht hat, Anton Rezov, kommt vom Schuppen aus zu mir. Wir arbeiten seit Jahren zusammen, und er ist ein enger

Freund, aber wenn er versuchen sollte, mich zu stoppen, werde ich ihn töten.

Ohne zu antworten, fahre ich mit meiner grausamen Aufgabe fort und betrachte alle Gliedmaßen und jeden verbrannten Rumpf, bevor ich alles zur Seite lege. Die meisten Körperteile scheinen zu Erwachsenen zu gehören, auch wenn ich auf einige wenige in Kindergröße stoße. Sie sind allerdings zu groß, um Pashas zu sein, und ich bin egoistisch genug, um darüber erleichtert zu sein.

Dann sehe ich es.

»Peter, hast du mich gehört? Du kannst das noch nicht tun.« Anton will meinen Arm ergreifen, aber bevor er mich berühren kann, wirbele ich herum, und meine Hand formt automatisch eine Faust. Diese Faust kracht auf seinen Kiefer, er wird durch die Wucht des Aufschlags zurückgeschleudert und seine Augen verdrehen sich. Ich schaue nicht dabei zu, wie er fällt; ich bewege mich bereits und wühle mich durch den restlichen Stapel der Körper, um die kleine Hand zu finden, die ich eben gesehen habe.

Eine kleine Hand, die ein kaputtes Spielzeugauto umklammert.

Bitte, bitte, bitte. Bitte, lass es eine Verwechslung sein. Bitte lass ihn am Leben sein. Bitte lass ihn am Leben sein.

Ich arbeite wie ein Besessener und konzentriere mich auf ein einziges Ziel: zu dieser Hand zu gelangen. Einige der Körper ganz oben auf dem Stapel sind beinahe intakt, aber trotzdem spüre ich ihr Gewicht nicht, als ich sie zur Seite lege. Ich fühle das Brennen meiner Muskeln durch die Anstrengungen nicht, genauso wenig wie ich den widerlichen Gestank des gewaltsamen Todes rieche. Ich beuge mich einfach immer wieder nach unten und werfe die Körperteile zur Seite, bis ich von ihnen umgeben und blutdurchtränkt bin.

Ich höre nicht auf, bis ich den kleinen Körper freigelegt habe und jeder Zweifel verschwunden ist.

Zitternd sinke ich auf die Knie, da meine Beine mich nicht mehr halten können.

Wie durch ein Wunder ist eine Gesichtshälfte Pashas unverletzt, seine weiche Babyhaut hat nur einen Kratzer abbekommen. Eines seiner Augen ist geschlossen, sein kleiner Mund ist geöffnet, und würde er wie Tamila auf der Seite liegen, könnte man ihn für ein schlafendes Kind halten. Aber er liegt nicht auf der Seite, und ich sehe das klaffende Loch, das die Explosion hinterlassen hat, als sie die Hälfte seines Schädels wegsprengte. Sein linker Arm fehlt ebenfalls, genauso wie sein linkes Bein ab dem Knie. Sein rechter Arm ist allerdings unversehrt, und seine Finger umklammern das Spielzeugauto.

Aus einiger Entfernung höre ich ein Heulen, ein verrücktes, gebrochenes Geräusch menschlicher Wut. Erst als mir auffällt, dass ich den kleinen Körper an meine Brust drücke, verstehe ich, dass ich dieses Geräusch von mir gebe. Ich verstumme, aber ich kann nicht damit aufhören, hin und her zu schaukeln.

Ich kann nicht aufhören, ihn zu umarmen.

Ich weiß nicht, wie lange ich so verharre, die Überreste meines Sohnes an mich drücke, aber als die Soldaten der Spezialeinheit ankommen, ist es bereits dunkel. Ich wehre mich nicht. Das wäre sinnlos. Mein Sohn ist von uns gegangen, bevor sein helles Licht die Gelegenheit hatte, zu scheinen.

»Es tut mir leid«, flüstere ich, als sie mich wegzerren. Mit jedem Meter Abstand zwischen uns wächst meine innere Kälte, und die letzten Reste von Menschlichkeit verlassen meine Seele. Ich kann nicht mehr Bitten, keine Verhandlungen mit irgendjemandem oder irgendetwas führen. Ich habe alle Hoffnung verloren, meine Liebe und Wärme ist mir genommen worden. Ich kann die Zeit nicht zurückstellen und meinen Sohn länger halten, ich kann nicht warten, so wie ich es sollte. Ich kann nicht nächstes Jahr mit Tamila nach Moskau reisen, so wie ich es ihr versprochen hatte.

Es gibt nur eine Sache, die ich für meine Frau und meinen Sohn tun kann, und deshalb lebe ich weiter.

Ich werde dafür sorgen, dass ihre Mörder bezahlen.

Jeder Einzelne von ihnen.

Sie werden für dieses Massaker mit ihrem Leben bezahlen.

S *ara*

»BIST DU SICHER, dass du nicht etwas mit mir und den Mädchen trinken gehen möchtest?«, fragt Marsha und kommt zu meinem Spind. Sie hat bereits ihren Schwesternkittel aus- und ein sexy Kleid angezogen. Mit ihrem leuchtend roten Lippenstift und ihren blonden Locken sieht sie wie eine ältere Version von Marilyn Monroe aus und liebt es auch genau wie sie, Party zu machen.

»Nein, danke. Ich kann nicht.« Ich versüße meine Abfuhr mit einem Lächeln. »Es war ein langer Tag, und ich bin müde.«

Sie rollt mit den Augen. »Natürlich bist du das. Du bist in letzter Zeit dauernd müde.«

»Arbeit bringt das mit sich.«

»Ja, wenn man neunzig Stunden in der Woche arbeitet. Wenn ich dich nicht besser kennen würde«, würde ich sagen, dass du dich zu Tode arbeitest. Du bist kein Assistenzarzt mehr. Du musst diesen Scheiß nicht mehr machen.«

Ich seufze und ergreife meine Tasche. »Jemand muss Rufbereitschaft haben.«

»Ja, aber das musst nicht immer du sein. Es ist Freitagnacht, und du hast die ganzen letzten Monate am Wochenende gearbeitet, von den Nachtschichten mal ganz abgesehen. Ich weiß, dass du der Neuzugang in eurer Praxis bist, aber …«

»Mir machen die Nachtschichten nichts aus«, unterbreche ich sie und gehe zum Spiegel. Die Wimperntusche, die ich heute Morgen aufgetragen habe, ist unter meinen Augen verwischt, und ich benutze ein feuchtes Papiertuch, um sie wegzubekommen. Das verbessert meine hagere Erscheinung nicht wirklich, aber ich nehme an, dass das sowieso egal ist, da ich auf direktem Weg nach Hause gehen werde.

»Genau, weil du nicht schläfst«, sagt Marsha und stellt sich hinter mich. Ich bereite mich darauf vor, ihr beliebtestes Thema über mich ergehen zu lassen. Auch wenn sie gute fünfzehn Jahre älter ist als ich, ist Marsha im Krankenhaus meine beste Freundin und hat ihre Bedenken in letzter Zeit immer deutlicher ausgesprochen.

»Marsha, bitte. Ich bin einfach zu müde dafür«, sage ich und binde meine widerspenstigen Wellen zu einem Pferdeschwanz. Ich brauche keine Vorhaltung, um zu wissen, dass ich mich gerade verausgabe. Meine braunen Augen sehen im Spiegel rot und trüb aus, und ich fühle mich wie sechzig und nicht wie achtundzwanzig.

»Ja, weil du überarbeitet bist und unter Schlafmangel leidest.« Sie verschränkt ihre Arme vor der Brust. »Ich weiß, dass du nach George Ablenkung brauchst, aber …«

»Aber nichts.« Ich wirbele herum und starre sie wütend an. »Ich will nicht über George reden.« …»Sara …« Sie legt die Stirn in Falten. »Du musst damit aufhören, dich selbst dafür zu bestrafen. Das war nicht dein Fehler. Er *wollte* ans Steuer, es war *seine* Entscheidung.«

Mein Hals wird eng, und meine Augen brennen. Zu meinem Entsetzen bin ich kurz davor zu weinen, und ich drehe mich weg, um mich wieder unter Kontrolle zu bringen. Aber ich kann mich nirgendwohin drehen, da vor mir der Spiegel ist und alles reflektiert, was ich gerade fühle.

»Es tut mir leid, Süße. Ich bin ein unsensibles Arschloch. Das hätte ich nicht sagen sollen.« Marsha sieht wirklich so aus, als würde sie es bereuen, als sie sich ausstreckt, um meinen Arm leicht zu drücken.

Ich atme tief durch und drehe mich herum, um sie wieder anzuschauen. Ich bin müde, was nicht gerade dabei hilft, die Gefühle zu kontrollieren, die mich überkommen.

»Das ist schon in Ordnung.« Ich zwinge mich dazu, zu lächeln. »Kein Problem. Du solltest dich langsam auf den Weg machen, die Mädchen warten wahrscheinlich schon auf dich.« Und ich muss nach Hause, bevor ich zusammenbreche und in aller Öffentlichkeit weine, was mehr als demütigend wäre.

»In Ordnung, Süße.« Marsha lächelt zurück, aber ich sehe das Mitleid in ihren Augen. »Aber sieh zu, dass du dieses Wochenende ein wenig Schlaf bekommst, okay? Versprich es mir.«

»Ja, *Mama*.«

Sie rollt mit den Augen. »Gut, dass du mich verstanden hast. Wir sehen uns am Montag.« Sie verlässt den Umkleideraum, und ich warte eine Minute, bevor ich ihr folge, um im Fahrstuhl nicht auf die Gruppe ihrer Freundinnen zu stoßen.

Noch mehr Mitleid halte ich nicht aus.

———

ALS ICH DEN Parkplatz des Krankenhauses betrete, kontrolliere ich aus reiner Gewohnheit mein Handy, und mein Herz setzt einen Schlag aus, als ich eine Textnachricht von einer blockierten Nummer sehe.

Ich bleibe stehen und fahre mit meinem zittrigen Finger über das Display.

Es ist alles in Ordnung, aber wir müssen den Besuch diese Woche verschieben, steht in der Nachricht. *Wichtige Termine.*

Ich atme erleichtert aus, und sofort verspüre ich das vertraute Schuldgefühl. Ich sollte nicht erleichtert sein. Diese Besuche sollten etwas sein, was ich möchte, und keine unangenehme Pflicht. Aber ich kann das, was ich fühle, nicht ändern. Jedes Mal, wenn ich George besuche, werden Erinnerungen an jene Nacht wach, und ich kann einige Nächte lang nicht schlafen.

Wenn Marsha denkt, dass ich jetzt gerade an Schlafmangel leide, sollte sie mich nach diesen Besuchen sehen.

Ich stecke mein Handy wieder in die Tasche und gehe zu meinem Auto. Es ist ein Toyota Camry, den ich seit fünf Jahren habe. Jetzt, nachdem ich mein Darlehen für das Studium abbezahlt und einige Ersparnisse habe, könnte ich mir etwas Besseres leisten, aber ich sehe keinen Grund dafür.

George hatte eine Schwäche für Autos, nicht ich.

Der Schmerz überkommt mich vertraut und stark, und ich weiß, dass der Grund dafür diese Textnachricht ist. Na ja, sie und die Unterhaltung mit Marsha. In letzter Zeit gab es Tage, an denen ich überhaupt nicht an den Unfall gedacht habe, an denen ich meinen Aufgaben nachgegangen bin, ohne erdrückende Schuldgefühle zu haben, aber heute ist keiner dieser Tage.

Er war erwachsen, erinnere ich mich selbst in Gedanken und wiederhole dabei das, was alle sagen. *Es war seine Entscheidung, sich an jenem Tag hinter das Steuer zu setzen.*

Rational gesehen weiß ich, dass diese Worte wahr sind, aber egal, wie oft ich sie höre, ich kann sie nicht verinnerlichen. Meine Gedanken sind in einer Schleife gefangen, die immer wieder jenen Abend abspielt, und egal, wie sehr ich es auch versuche, ich kann diese Gedanken einfach nicht unterbrechen.

Es reicht, Sara. Konzentrier dich auf die Straße.

Ich atme tief durch und fahre vom Parkplatz Richtung Zuhause. Vom Krankenhaus aus ist es etwa eine Fahrt von vierzig Minuten, was in diesem Moment vierzig Minuten zu viel für mich sind. Mein Bauch beginnt zu krampfen, und ich bemerke, dass einer der Gründe dafür, dass ich heute so emotional bin, der ist, dass ich meine Tage bekomme. Als Frauenärztin weiß ich am besten, wie stark die Auswirkungen der Hormone sein können, und wenn sich zum PMS auch noch lange Arbeitsstunden und Erinnerungen an George gesellen …

Ja, das ist es. Ich bin einfach nur hormongeladen und müde. Ich muss nach Hause, und dann wird alles wieder gut.

Da ich fest entschlossen bin, mich wieder in den Griff zu bekommen, schalte ich das Radio ein, suche einen Sender mit Neunziger-Jahre-Popmusik und singe zu einem Lied von Britney Spears. Das ist jetzt vielleicht nicht die anspruchsvollste Musik, aber sie hebt die Stimmung, und das ist genau das, was ich gerade brauche.

Ich werde nicht zerbrechen. Heute *werde* ich schlafen, selbst wenn ich Zolpidem nehmen muss, damit das passiert.

———

MEIN HAUS BEFINDET sich in einer von Bäumen gesäumten Sackgasse, die von einer zweispurigen Straße abgeht, die sich durch Felder windet. Wie viele andere in dieser besseren Gegend in Homer Glen, Illinois, ist es riesig – fünf Schlafzimmer und vier Badezimmer plus einen voll ausgebauten Keller. Es hat einen großen Garten und ist von so vielen Eichen umgeben, dass es sich anfühlt, als befände es sich mitten im Wald.

Es ist perfekt für die große Familie, die George wollte, und schrecklich einsam für mich.

Nach dem Unfall habe ich darüber nachgedacht, das Haus zu verkaufen und näher an das Krankenhaus zu ziehen, aber ich konnte es einfach nicht über mich bringen. Das kann ich immer noch nicht. George und ich haben das Haus zusammen renoviert, die Küche und die Badezimmer modernisiert und sorgfältig jeden Raum dekoriert, um eine gemütliche und einladende Atmosphäre zu schaffen. Eine Familienatmosphäre. Ich weiß, dass die Chancen auf diese Familie jetzt inexistent sind, aber ein Teil von mir hängt an diesem alten Traum, dem perfekten Leben, das wir haben sollten.

»Mindestens drei Kinder«, hatte George mir bei unserem fünften Date gesagt. »Zwei Jungen und ein Mädchen.«

»Warum nicht zwei Mädchen und einen Jungen?«, hatte ich ihn grinsend gefragt. »Was ist mit Gleichberechtigung und so?«

»Wie soll zwei gegen einen denn gleichberechtigt sein? Jeder weiß, dass Mädchen dich um ihre kleinen, hübschen Finger wickeln, und wenn man zwei von ihnen hat …« Er erschauderte theatralisch. »Nein, wir brauchen zwei Jungen, damit die Balance in der Familie stimmt. Ansonsten ist Papa verloren.«

Ich habe gelacht und ihn auf die Schulter geboxt, aber insgeheim mochte ich den Gedanken an zwei Jungen, die laut herumrennen und ihre kleine Schwester beschützen. Ich bin ein Einzelkind, aber ich wollte immer einen großen Bruder, weshalb es einfach für mich gewesen war, Georges Traum zu meinem eigenen zu machen.

Nein. Denk nicht darüber nach. Mit Mühe verdränge ich diese Erinnerungen aus meinem Kopf, weil – egal, ob sie gut oder schlecht sind – sie immer zu jenem Abend führen, und damit kann ich gerade nicht umgehen. Die Krämpfe sind schlimmer geworden, und ich kann nur mit Mühe meine Hände am Lenkrad lassen, als ich in meine Garage für drei Autos fahre. Ich brauche Ibuprofen, ein Heizkissen und mein Bett, genau in dieser Reihenfolge, und wenn ich ganz viel Glück habe, werde ich sofort einschlafen, ohne dass ich Zolpidem benötige.

Ich unterdrücke ein Stöhnen, schließe das Garagentor, gebe den Sicherheitscode ein, um den Alarm auszuschalten, und schleppe mich ins Haus. Die Krämpfe sind so schlimm, dass ich kaum gehen kann, ohne mich zu krümmen, also gehe ich ohne Umwege zum Medizinschrank in der Küche. Ich schalte nicht einmal das Licht an; der Lichtschalter ist weit von der Garagentür entfernt, und ich kenne die Küche außerdem gut genug, um mich auch im Dunkeln in ihr zurechtzufinden.

Ich öffne den Medizinschrank, ertaste die Ibuprofenpackung, nehme mir zwei Tabletten und schiebe sie mir in den Mund. Dann gehe ich zur Spüle, lasse Wasser in meine Hand laufen und schlucke die beiden Tabletten damit hinunter. Keuchend halte ich mich am Küchentresen fest und warte darauf, dass die Medizin zu wirken beginnt, bevor ich versuche, etwas so Ehrgeiziges zu tun wie zum Schlafzimmer im ersten Stock zu gehen.

Ich spüre ihn erst eine Sekunde, bevor es passiert. Ganz unterschwellig bemerke ich einen Luftzug hinter mir, einen Hauch von etwas Fremdem … ein Gefühl plötzlicher Gefahr.

Die Haare in meinem Nacken stellen sich auf, aber da ist es bereits zu spät. In einem Moment stehe ich noch neben der Küchenspüle, und im nächsten bedeckt eine große Hand meinen Mund, und ein harter Körper drängt mich von hinten gegen die Theke.

»Nicht schreien«, flüstert eine tiefe Stimme in mein Ohr, und etwas Kaltes und Scharfes drückt gegen meinen Hals. »Du willst doch nicht, dass mein Messer abrutscht.«

3

ara

ICH SCHREIE NICHT. Nicht, weil es das Cleverste in dieser Situation ist, sondern weil ich kein Geräusch von mir geben kann. Ich bin vor Entsetzen wie versteinert und ganz und gar gelähmt. Meine Muskeln, einschließlich meiner Stimmbänder, haben sich verkrampft, und meine Lunge hat aufgehört zu arbeiten.

»Ich werde meine Hand von deinem Mund nehmen«, flüstert er in mein Ohr, und sein Atem fühlt sich auf meiner feuchten Haut warm an. »Und du wirst ruhig bleiben. Verstanden?«

Ich kann nicht einmal ein wimmerndes Geräusch von mir geben, aber ich schaffe es, leicht zu nicken.

Er nimmt seine Hand weg, legt seinen Arm stattdessen um meine Rippen, und meine Lungen fangen genau in diesem Moment wieder an zu funktionieren. Ohne es zu wollen, atme ich pfeifend ein. Sofort drückt sich das Messer tiefer in meine Haut, und ich versteinere erneut, als ich spüre, wie warmes Blut an meinem Hals hinunterläuft.

Ich werde sterben. Oh mein Gott, ich werde hier sterben, in meiner eigenen Küche. Das Entsetzen in mir ist ein monströses Etwas, das mich mit eisigen Nadeln sticht. Ich war noch nie so kurz davor, zu sterben. Nur einen Zentimeter nach rechts und …

»Du musst mir zuhören, Sara.« Die Stimme des Eindringlings ist sanft, straft das Messer, das in meinen Hals schneidet, Lügen. »Wenn du kooperierst, wirst du das hier lebendig überstehen. Wenn nicht, wirst du in einem Leichensack enden. Du hast die Wahl.«

Lebendig? Ein Hoffnungsschimmer dringt durch den panischen Nebel in meinem Gehirn, und mir fällt auf, dass der Mann einen leichten Akzent hat. Einen exotischen. Naher Osten vielleicht, oder osteuropäisch.

Eigenartigerweise sammele ich mich durch dieses Detail, das meinem Gehirn etwas Konkretes bietet, auf das es sich konzentrieren kann, ein wenig. »W-was wollen Sie?« Diese Worte sind ein bebendes Flüstern, aber es ist schon ein Wunder, dass ich überhaupt sprechen kann. Ich fühle mich wie ein Reh im Scheinwerferlicht, betäubt und überwältigt, und meine Denkprozesse sind seltsam verlangsamt.

»Nur einige Antworten«, antwortet er und zieht sein Messer ein wenig zurück. Ohne den kalten Stahl, der in meine Haut schneidet, verschwindet ein Teil meiner Panik, und ich bemerke weitere Details wie die Tatsache, dass mein Angreifer mindestens einen Kopf größer als ich und muskelbepackt ist. Der Arm um meinen Brustkorb ist wie ein Stahlband, und der große Körper, der sich gegen meinen Rücken presst, gibt nicht einen Millimeter nach, lässt keine Weichheit spüren. Ich bin eine durchschnittlich große Frau, aber schlank und zierlich, und er ist so muskulös, dass ich vermute, dass er fast das Doppelte wiegt wie ich.

Selbst wenn er kein Messer hätte, könnte ich ihm nicht entkommen.

»Was für Antworten?« Meine Stimme ist jetzt ein wenig ruhiger. Vielleicht ist er nur hier, um mich auszurauben, und alles, was er braucht, ist meine Safekombination. Er riecht sauber, nach Waschmittel und gesunder, männlicher Haut, also ist er kein Meth-Süchtiger oder Penner von der Straße. Vielleicht ein professioneller Einbrecher? Falls ja, verzichte ich gerne auf den Schmuck und das Notfall-Bargeld, das George hier im Haus versteckt hat.

»Ich möchte, dass du mir von deinem Mann erzählst. Ganz besonders bin ich an seinem Aufenthaltsort interessiert.«

»George?« Mein Kopf wird leer, als mich eine neue Angstwelle überkommt. »W-was ... warum?«

Das Messer drückt sich in meine Haut. »Ich stelle hier die Fragen.«

»B-bitte«, presse ich heraus. Ich kann nicht denken, kann mich auf nichts anderes als das Messer konzentrieren. Heiße Tränen laufen mein Gesicht hinunter, und ich zittere am ganzen Körper. »Bitte nicht …«

»Beantworte einfach meine Frage. Wo ist dein Mann?«

»Ich …« Oh Gott, was soll ich ihm nur sagen? Er muss einer von *ihnen* sein, dem Grund für die ganzen Vorsichtsmaßnahmen. Mein Herz schlägt so schnell, dass ich fast hyperventiliere. »Bitte, ich weiß nicht … ich habe keine …«

»Lüg mich nicht an, Sara. Ich brauche seinen … Aufenthaltsort. Jetzt.«

»Ich weiß es nicht, ich schwöre es. Bitte, wir sind …« Meine Stimme wird brüchig. »Wir haben uns getrennt.«

Der Arm um meinen Brustkorb legt sich fester um mich, und das Messer dringt ein wenig tiefer in meine Haut ein. »Möchtest du sterben?«

»Nein. Nein, das möchte ich nicht. Bitte …« Ich zittere stärker, und die Tränen strömen unkontrolliert meine Wangen hinunter. Nach dem Unfall gab es Tage, an denen ich dachte, dass ich sterben möchte, als die Schuldgefühle und das schmerzhafte Bedauern überwältigend waren, aber jetzt mit dem Messer an meiner Kehle will ich leben. Das will ich unbedingt.

»Dann sage mir, wo dein Mann ist.«

»Ich weiß es nicht!« Meine Knie drohen damit, nachzugeben, aber ich kann George nicht einfach so verraten. Ich kann ihn nicht diesem Monster aussetzen.

»Du lügst.« Die Stimme meines Angreifers ist so

kalt wie Eis. »Ich habe deine Nachrichten gelesen. Du weißt genau, wo er sich befindet.«

»Nein, ich …« Ich versuche, eine plausible Lüge zu finden, aber mir fällt keine ein. Ich kann die Panik auf meiner Zunge schmecken, als mir hektische Fragen durch den Kopf gehen. Wie konnte er die Nachrichten lesen? Wann? Wie lange verfolgt er mich schon? Ist er einer von *ihnen*? »Ich – ich weiß nicht, wovon Sie sprechen.«

Das Messer schneidet noch eine Spur tiefer ein, und ich kneife die Augen zusammen, während mein Atmen zu einem schluchzenden Keuchen wird. Ich bin dem Tod so nahe, dass ich ihn schmecken, riechen … ihn mit jeder Faser meines Körpers fühlen kann. Er ist in dem metallischen Geruch meines Blutes, dem kalten Schweiß, der meinen Rücken hinunterläuft, dem Dröhnen meines Pulses in meinen Schläfen und in der Anspannung meiner zuckenden Muskeln. Noch eine Sekunde länger, und er wird meine Halsschlagader aufschneiden und ich werde ausbluten, genau hier auf dem Fußboden meiner Küche.

Habe ich das verdient? Werde ich so für meine Sünden zahlen?

Ich beiße die Zähne zusammen, damit sie nicht klappern. *Bitte verzeih mir, George. Wenn es das ist, was du brauchst …*

Ich höre, wie mein Angreifer seufzt, und im nächsten Moment ist sein Messer verschwunden und ich liege umgedreht auf der Theke. Mein Rücken trifft auf den harten Granit, und mein Kopf fällt nach hinten in die Spüle, wobei meine Nackenmuskeln vor Belastung schreien. Keuchend trete ich aus und versuche, ihn zu schlagen, aber er ist zu stark und schnell. Wie ein Blitz springt er auf die Theke, spreizt meine Beine und fixiert mich mit seinem Gewicht. Er sichert meine Handgelenke mit etwas Hartem und Unzerbrechlichem, bevor er sie mit einer Hand ergreift, und ich sie nicht befreien kann, egal, wie sehr ich es versuche. Meine Fersen rutschen nutzlos über den glatten Tresen, und meine Nackenmuskeln brennen davon, meinen Kopf oben halten zu müssen. Ich bin hilflos, werde festgehalten, und eine neue Art von Panik überkommt mich.

Bitte nicht das, oh Gott. Alles, aber keine Vergewaltigung.

»Wir werden etwas anderes ausprobieren«, sagt er, und ein Stück Stoff fällt über mein Gesicht. »Mal schauen, ob du wirklich für diesen Bastard sterben willst.«

Keuchend werfe ich meinen Kopf von einer Seite zur anderen und versuche, den Stofffetzen loszuwerden, aber er ist zu lang, und ich kann unter ihm kaum atmen. Versucht er, mich zu ersticken? Ist das der Plan?

Dann quietscht der Griff des Wasserhahns, und ich verstehe, was er vorhat.

»Nein!« Ich werfe mich stärker hin und her, aber er ergreift meine Haare mit seiner freien Hand und hält meinen zurückgeworfenen Kopf unter den Wasserhahn.

Der anfängliche Schock über die Nässe ist nicht so

schlimm, aber innerhalb weniger Sekunden wandert das Wasser meine Nase hinauf. Mein Hals verengt sich, meine Lungen verkrampfen sich und mein ganzer Körper versucht, sich aufzurichten, während ich würge und nach Luft schnappen will. Die Panik ist instinktiv und unkontrollierbar. Der Stofffetzen fühlt sich wie eine nasse Pfote an, die über meiner Nase liegt und sie zusammendrückt. Das Wasser ist in meiner Nase und in meinem Hals. Ich ersticke, ertrinke. Ich kann nicht atmen, kann nicht atmen …

Der Wasserhahn wird abgestellt und der Stofffetzen von meinem Gesicht gerissen. Hustend atme ich Luft ein, während ich gleichzeitig schluchze und keuche. Mein ganzer Körper ist ein zuckendes, zitterndes Etwas, und weiße Punkte tanzen vor meinen Augen. Bevor ich mich erholen kann, wird der Stofffetzen erneut auf mein Gesicht gelegt, und das Wasser wird wieder angestellt.

Dieses Mal ist es noch schlimmer. Meine Nasenhöhlen brennen von dem Wasser, und meine Lungen schreien nach Luft. Ich zucke und würge, ersticke und weine. Ich kann nicht atmen. *Oh mein Gott, ich sterbe; ich kann nicht atmen …*

Im nächsten Moment ist das Tuch verschwunden, und ich schnappe krampfhaft nach Luft.

»Sag mir, wo er ist, und ich höre damit auf.« Seine Stimme ist ein dunkles Flüstern über mir.

»Ich weiß es nicht! Bitte!« Ich kann das Erbrochene in meinem Hals schmecken, und das Wissen, dass er das noch einmal tun wird, verwandelt mein Blut in

Säure. Es war leicht, bei dem Messer mutig zu sein, aber nicht bei dem hier. Ich kann nicht so sterben.

»Letzte Chance«, meint mein Peiniger leise, und der nasse Stofffetzen fällt erneut auf mein Gesicht.

Der Griff des Wasserhahns beginnt zu quietschen.

»Stopp! Bitte!«, bricht ein Schrei aus mir heraus. »Ich sage es Ihnen! Ich sage es Ihnen!«

Das Wasser wird ausgestellt, und der Stofffetzen wird von meinem Gesicht gezogen. »Sag es mir.«

Ich schluchze und huste zu sehr, um einen zusammenhängenden Satz herauszubekommen, also zieht der Mann mich vom Tresen auf den Boden und kniet sich hin, um mich in seine Arme zu schließen. Auf einen Außenstehenden könnte es gerade so wirken wie eine tröstende Umarmung oder die beschützende Geste eines Liebhabers. Diese Illusion wird durch die weiche und sanfte Stimme meines Peinigers verstärkt, der beruhigend in mein Ohr flüstert: »Sag es mir, Sara. Sag mir, was ich wissen will, und ich gehe.«

»Er ist …« Ich halte eine Sekunde vor dem Herausplatzen der Wahrheit inne. Das panische Tier in mir fordert das Überleben um jeden Preis, aber ich kann das nicht tun. Ich kann dieses Monster nicht zu George führen. »Er ist im Advocate Christ Hospital«, presse ich heraus. »In der Langzeitpflege.«

Das ist eine Lüge und offensichtlich keine gute, weil die Arme, die mich halten, ihren Griff verstärken und fast meine Knochen brechen. »Verarsch mich nicht.« Der beruhigende Ton seiner Stimme ist verschwunden, und an seiner Stelle höre ich beißende

Wut. »Er hat sie verlassen – vor Monaten. Wo versteckt er sich?«

Ich schluchze stärker. »Ich … Ich weiß nicht …«

Mein Angreifer stellt sich hin, zieht mich nach oben, und ich schreie und wehre mich, als er mich zur Spüle zieht. »Nein! Bitte nicht!« Ich bin hysterisch, als er mich auf die Theke hebt, und meine gefesselten Hände schwingen hin und her, als ich versuche, ihm das Gesicht zu zerkratzen. Meine Fersen schlagen auf dem Granit auf, als er meine Beine spreizt und mich erneut an Ort und Stelle festhält, und Galle steigt in meinem Hals auf, als er mein Haar ergreift und meinen Kopf in die Spüle drückt. »Stopp!«

»Sag mir die Wahrheit – und ich werde aufhören.«

»Ich … ich kann nicht. Bitte, das kann ich nicht tun!« Das kann ich George nach allem, was passiert ist, nicht antun. »Bitte hören Sie auf!«

Der nasse Stofffetzen legt sich über mein Gesicht, und mein Hals verschließt sich voller Panik. Das Wasser ist noch nicht angestellt, aber ich ertrinke bereits; ich kann nicht atmen, kann nicht atmen …

»Scheiße!«

Ich werde plötzlich mit einem Ruck vom Tresen auf den Boden gerissen, wo ich schluchzend zu einem Häufchen zusammensacke. Aber dieses Mal gibt es keine Arme, die mich halten, und ich bemerke benebelt, dass er weggegangen ist.

Ich sollte aufstehen und weglaufen, aber meine Hände sind gefesselt und meine Beine wollen einfach nicht funktionieren. Alles, was ich tun kann, ist, erbärmlich auf die Seite zu rollen und zu versuchen, wegzukriechen. Die Angst macht mich blind, verwirrt mich, und ich kann in der Dunkelheit nichts sehen.

Ich kann *ihn* nicht sehen.

Lauft, versuche ich meinen schlaffen, zitternden Muskeln zu befehlen. *Steht auf und lauft.*

Ich hole tief Luft, bekomme etwas zu greifen – eine Ecke der Arbeitsplatte – und ziehe mich hoch, bis ich stehe. Aber es ist zu spät: Er ist bereits bei mir, und sein Arm umgreift meine Rippen von hinten wie ein Stahlband.

»Mal sehen, ob das besser funktioniert«, flüstert er, und etwas Kaltes und Scharfes sticht mir in den Hals.

Eine Nadel, wird mir voller Entsetzen klar, und mein Bewusstsein schwindet.

———

ICH SEHE ein verschwommenes Gesicht vor meinen Augen. Ein hübsches Gesicht, ein sehr schönes sogar, trotz der Narbe, die die linke Augenbraue halbiert. Hohe, schräge Wangenknochen, stahlgraue Augen, die von schwarzen Wimpern eingerahmt werden, ein hartes Kinn mit Bartstoppeln – das Gesicht eines Mannes, lässt mich mein Gehirn verschwommen wissen. Sein Haar ist dick und oben länger als an den Seiten. Kein alter Mann, aber auch kein Teenager. Ein Mann in seinen besten Jahren.

Seine Stirn ist gerunzelt, und sein Gesicht weist raue, düstere Züge auf. »George Cobakis«, sagt der harte, gemeißelte Mund. Es ist ein sexy Mund, gut geformt, aber ich höre die Worte wie aus einem Megaphon in einigem Abstand zu mir. »Weißt du, wo er sich aufhält?«

Ich nicke, oder zumindest versuche ich es. Mein Kopf fühlt sich schwer an und mein Hals eigenartig wund. »Ja, ich weiß, wo er ist. Ich dachte auch, ich würde ihn kennen, aber eigentlich tue ich es nicht. Kann man jemanden wirklich richtig kennen? Ich denke nicht, oder zumindest kannte ich *ihn* nicht. Ich dachte, dass ich ihn kennen würde, aber das tat ich nicht. Die ganzen Jahre, die wir zusammen verbracht haben, dachte ich, wir seien perfekt. Das perfekte Paar, so haben sie uns genannt. Können Sie das glauben? Das perfekte Paar. Wir waren die Crème de la Crème, die junge Ärztin und der aufsteigende Starjournalist. Sie haben gesagt, dass er eines Tages einen Pulitzer-Preis gewinnen würde.« Ich bemerke am Rande, dass ich einfach rede, aber ich kann nicht aufhören. Die Worte schießen aus mir heraus, all die angestaute Bitterkeit und der Schmerz. »Meine Eltern waren an unserem Hochzeitstag so stolz, so glücklich. Sie hatten keine Ahnung, was kommen würde, was passieren würde.«

»Sara. Konzentriere dich auf mich«, sagt die Megaphon-Stimme, und ich höre einen leichten ausländischen Akzent. Dieser Akzent gefällt mir, führt dazu, dass ich mich vorbeugen und meine Hand auf diese gemeißelten Lippen legen möchte, mit meinen Fingern über dieses …harte Kinn fahren möchte, um zu sehen, ob es kratzig ist. Ich mag kratzig. George kam häufig von seinen Reisen nach Hause und war kratzig, und ich mochte es. Ich mochte es, auch wenn ich ihm immer gesagt habe, er solle sich rasieren. Er sah rasiert besser aus, aber manchmal mochte ich das kratzige Gefühl, mochte es, das Kratzen auf meinen Schenkeln zu spüren, wenn er …

»Sara, hör auf«, unterbricht mich die Stimme, und das Stirnrunzeln des exotisch hübschen Gesichts vertieft sich.

Ich habe laut gesprochen, wird mir klar, aber es ist mir überhaupt nicht peinlich. Die Worte gehören nicht zu mir; sie platzen einfach beliebig heraus. Meine Hände tun auch das, was sie wollen, und versuchen, dieses Gesicht zu berühren, bevor etwas sie innehalten lässt. Ich senke meinen schweren Kopf, um nachzuschauen, was es ist, und erblicke Kabelbinder an meinen Handgelenken und eine große Männerhand über meinen Handflächen. Diese Hand ist warm, und sie fixiert meine Hände auf meinem Schoß. Warum tut sie das? Woher kam diese Hand? Als ich verwirrt nach oben schaue, befindet sich das Gesicht näher an mir, und graue Augen starren in meine.

»Du musst mir sagen, wo dein Mann ist«, sagt der Mann, und das Megaphon kommt näher. Es hört sich so an, als befände es sich genau neben meinem Ohr. Ich zucke zusammen, aber gleichzeitig fasziniert mich dieser Mund. Ich will diese Lippen berühren, sie lecken, sie auf meinen – Moment. Sie fragen mich etwas.

»Wo mein Mann ist?« Meine Stimme hört sich so an, als halle sie von den Wänden wider.

»Ja, George Cobakis, dein Mann.« Die Lippen sehen verlockend aus, als sie die Worte formen, und der Akzent ist trotz dieses Megaphon-Effekts wie eine Streicheleinheit für mich. »Sag mir, wo er ist.«

»In Sicherheit. Er ist in einer geheimen Unterkunft«, antworte ich. »Sie könnten ihn suchen. Sie wollten nicht, dass er über diese Sache schreibt, aber er tat es trotzdem. Er war so mutig, oder dumm – wahrscheinlich dumm, stimmt's? Und dann ist der Unfall passiert, aber sie könnten immer noch hinter ihm her sein, weil sie genau das tun. Die Mafia interessiert es nicht, dass er jetzt den IQ eines Gemüses hat, einer Gurke, einer Tomate, einer Zucchini. Na ja, Tomate ist eine Frucht, aber er ist wie ein Gemüse. Ein Brokkoli vielleicht? Ich weiß es nicht. Aber das ist auch nicht wichtig. Es ist einfach so, dass sie an ihm ein Exempel statuieren wollen, anderen Journalisten, die an seiner Seite stehen, Angst einjagen wollen. Das tun sie; so funktionieren sie. Es geht immer um Bestechungen, und wenn man das ans Licht bringt ...«

»Wo ist sein Versteck?« Ich sehe ein dunkles Glitzern in diesen stählernen Augen. »Sag mir die Adresse seines geheimen Unterschlupfes.«

»Ich kenne die Adresse nicht, aber es befindet sich an der Ecke Ricky's Laundromat in Evanston«, erzähle ich diesen Augen. »Sie bringen mich immer in einem Auto dorthin, also kenne ich die genaue Adresse nicht, aber ich habe das Gebäude von einem Fenster aus gesehen. Es sind mindestens zwei Männer in diesem Auto, und sie fahren ewig umher, manchmal wechseln sie sogar das Auto. Der Grund dafür ist die Mafia, weil sie alles beobachten könnte. Sie schicken immer ein Auto, das mich abholt, aber dieses Wochenende konnten sie nicht kommen. Wichtige Termine, haben sie gesagt. Das passiert manchmal; die Schichten der Wächter passen nicht und ...« ...»Wie viele Wächter gibt es dort?«

»Drei, manchmal vier. Es sind diese großen Militärtypen. Oder Ex-Militär, das weiß ich nicht. Sie sehen einfach danach aus. Ich weiß nicht, warum, aber sie sehen alle so aus. Das ist wie ein Kronzeugenschutz, aber irgendwie auch nicht, weil er spezielle Pflege benötigt, aber ich meinen Job nicht verlassen kann. Ich will meinen Job nicht verlassen. Sie haben gesagt, sie könnten mich versetzen, mich verschwinden lassen, aber ich möchte nicht verschwinden. Meine Patienten brauchen mich, und meine Eltern. Was sollte ich mit meinen Eltern tun? Sie nie wiedersehen oder anrufen? Nein, das ist verrückt. Also haben sie das Gemüse verschwinden lassen, die Gurke, den Brokkoli ...«

»Sara, schscht.« Finger legen sich auf meinen Mund, lassen den Strom der Worte verstummen, und das Gesicht kommt noch näher. »Du kannst jetzt damit aufhören. Es ist vorbei«, flüstert der sexy Mund, und ich öffne meine Lippen, um an diesen Fingern zu saugen. Ich schmecke Salz und Haut, und ich will mehr, also lege ich meine Zunge um seine Finger, fühle die Rauheit seiner Schwielen und die stumpfen Kanten seiner kurzen Nägel. Es ist schon so lange her, seit ich jemanden berührt habe, und mein Körper erwärmt sich bei diesem kleinen Vorgeschmack, bei diesem Blick in diese silberfarbenen Augen.

»Sara ...« Seine Stimme mit diesem Akzent ist jetzt leiser, tiefer und weicher. Sie gleicht keinem Megaphon mehr, sondern ist eher wie ein sinnliches Echo, wie Musik von einem Synthesizer. »Das möchtest du nicht tun, *ptichka*.«

Doch, genau das will ich. Und zwar unbedingt. Ich fahre weiterhin mit meiner Zunge um die Finger und sehe, wie sich die grauen Augen verdunkeln, wie sich die Pupillen sichtbar weiten. Ich weiß, dass das ein Zeichen von Erregung ist, und es bringt mich dazu, mehr tun zu wollen. Ich will seine gemeißelten Lippen küssen, will meine Wange an diesem stacheligen Kinn reiben. Und dann sind da noch diese Haare, diese dunklen, vollen Haare. Fühlen sie sich weich oder eher hart an? Ich will es wissen, aber ich kann meine Hände nicht bewegen, also nehme ich seine Finger einfach tiefer in meinen Mund, liebe sie mit meinen Lippen und meiner Zunge, sauge an ihnen, so als seien sie ein Lutscher.

»Sara.« Die Stimme ist belegt und rau, das Gesicht voll kaum zurückgehaltenem Hunger. »Du musst damit aufhören, Ptichka. Du wirst es morgen bereuen.«

Bereuen? Ja, wahrscheinlich werde ich das. Ich bereue alles, so viele Dinge, und ich lasse die Finger los, um genau das zu sagen. Aber bevor ich ein Wort sagen kann, ziehen sich die Finger zurück, und auch das Gesicht entfernt sich von mir.

»Geh nicht.« Dieser Ausruf ist kläglich, hört sich an, als käme er von einem anhänglichen Kind. Ich will mehr von dieser menschlichen Berührung, dieser Verbindung. Mein Kopf fühlt sich leer an, und alles an mir schmerzt, besonders mein Nacken und meine Schultern. Außerdem krampft mein Bauch. Ich will, dass jemand meine Haare kämmt, meinen Nacken massiert und mich wie ein Baby hin und her schaukelt. »Bitte, geh nicht.«

Etwas, das vage an Schmerz erinnert, flackert kurz auf dem Gesicht des Mannes auf, bevor ich erneut den kalten Einstich der Nadel in meinem Hals spüre.

»Auf Wiedersehen, Sara«, murmelt die Stimme, und schon bin ich weg, da mein Verstand dahinweht wie ein gefallenes Blatt.

4

S ara

DIE KOPFSCHMERZEN. Als Erstes bemerke ich die Kopfschmerzen. Mein Schädel fühlt sich an, als wolle er zerspringen, und die Schmerzwellen sind wie Trommelschläge in meinem Kopf.

»Dr. Cobakis ... Sara, können Sie mich hören?« Die weibliche Stimme ist weich und sanft, aber sie jagt mir Angst ein. In dieser Stimme liegt eine Mischung aus Besorgnis und unterdrückter Dringlichkeit. Ich höre diesen Ton die ganze Zeit im Krankenhaus, und er ... bedeutet nie etwas Gutes.

Ich versuche, meinen pochenden Schädel nicht zu bewegen, zwinge mich dazu, meine Augen zu öffnen und muss wegen des grellen Lichts blinzeln. »Was ...

wo …?« Meine Zunge ist dick und unbeweglich, und mein Mund ist schmerzhaft trocken.

»Hier, trinken Sie das.« Ein Strohhalm wird an meinen Mund gehalten, und ich nehme ihn und sauge gierig das Wasser ein. Meine Augen beginnen, sich an das Licht zu gewöhnen, und ich kann den Raum erkennen. Ich bin in einem Krankenhaus, aber nicht in meinem Krankenhaus, wie ich an der Zimmereinrichtung erkennen kann. Außerdem bin ich nicht dort, wo ich eigentlich bin. Ich stehe nicht an einem Krankenhausbett; ich liege in einem.

»Was ist passiert?«, frage ich heiser. Als ich etwas klarer im Kopf werde, bemerke ich, dass mir übel ist und ich weitere Beschwerden und Schmerzen habe. Mein Rücken fühlt sich wie ein riesiger Bluterguss an, und mein Hals ist steif und wund. Meine Kehle fühlt sich auch rau an, so als hätte ich geschrien oder mich übergeben, und als ich meine Hand anhebe, um sie zu berühren, fühle ich eine dicke Bandage auf der rechten Seite meines Halses.

»Sie wurden überfallen, Dr. Cobakis,« sagt eine Frau mittleren Alters sanft, und ich erkenne ihre Stimme als dieselbe wieder, die eben gesprochen hat. Sie ist mit einem Schwesternkittel bekleidet, aber irgendwie sieht sie nicht wie eine Krankenschwester aus. Als ich sie verständnislos anstarre, fährt sie fort: »In Ihrem Haus. Ein Mann kam zu Ihnen. Können Sie sich an irgendetwas erinnern?«

Ich blinzele und versuche, diese verwirrende Aussage zu verstehen. Ich fühle mich, als sei ein riesiger Wattebausch in mein Gehirn gestopft worden – zusammen mit einer dröhnenden Trommel. »Mein Haus? Überfallen?«

»Ja, Dr. Cobakis«, antwortet eine männliche Stimme, und ich zucke instinktiv zusammen, und mein Puls rast, noch bevor ich die Stimme erkenne. Vorsichtig drehe ich meinen schmerzenden Kopf, blicke Agent Ryson an, und mein Magen zieht sich bei dem Ausdruck seines blassen, wettergegerbtem Gesichts zusammen. Bruchstücke meiner Qualen steigen in meinen Erinnerungen auf, und mit ihnen überkommt mich eine Welle von Entsetzen.

»George, ist er …«

»Es tut mir leid.« Die Falten auf Rysons Stirn vertiefen sich. »Letzte Nacht wurde auch eines unserer Geheimverstecke überfallen. George … hat nicht überlebt. Genauso wenig wie die drei Wächter.«

»Was?« Es fühlt sich an, als punktierte ein Skalpell meine Lunge. Ich kann seine Worte nicht aufnehmen, das Unfassbare, was sie sagen, nicht verarbeiten. »Er … er ist tot?« Dann fällt mir der Rest der Aussage ein. »Und die drei Wächter? Was … wie …?«

»Dr. Cobakis – Sara.« Ryson tritt näher an mich heran. »Ich muss ganz genau wissen, was letzte Nacht geschehen ist, damit wir ihn verstehen können.«

»Ihn? Wer ist *ihn*?« Bis jetzt ist es immer *sie* gewesen, die Mafia, und ich bin zu benommen für den plötzlichen Wechsel des Pronomens. George ist tot. George und drei Wächter. Das will mir nicht in den Kopf, und ich erzwinge es auch nicht. Noch nicht, zumindest. Bevor ich Trauer und Schmerz zulassen kann, muss ich weitere Erinnerungen freilegen, das schreckliche Puzzle zusammensetzen.

»Sie kann sich vielleicht nicht erinnern. Der Drogencocktail in ihrem Blut war ziemlich stark«, meint die Krankenschwester, und mir wird klar, dass sie zu Agent Ryson gehören muss. Das würde erklären, warum er so offen vor ihr spricht, obwohl er normalerweise so diskret ist, dass es an Paranoia grenzt.

Während ich das verarbeite, tritt die Frau näher an mich heran. Ich bin mit einem Monitor verbunden, der die Vitalfunktionen überwacht, und sie überprüft die Blutdruckmanschette an meinem Arm, bevor sie leicht meinen Unterarm drückt. Ich blicke auf meinen Arm, und Kälte breitet sich in meiner Brust aus, als ich eine dünne, rote Linie um mein Handgelenk sehe. Mein anderes Handgelenk weist sie ebenfalls auf.

Kabelbinder. Diese Erinnerung überkommt mich mit plötzlicher Klarheit. Ich hatte Kabelbinder um meine Handgelenke.

»Er hat mich gewaterboarded. Als ich ihm trotzdem nicht sagen wollte, wo George ist, hat er mir eine Nadel in den Hals gestochen.«

Ich bemerke nicht, dass ich das laut gesagt habe, bis ich das Entsetzen auf dem Gesicht der Schwester sehe. Agent Rysons Gesicht ist gefasster, aber ich weiß trotzdem, dass er auch entsetzt ist.

»Das tut mir leid.« Seine Stimme ist angespannt. »Wir hätten das vorhersehen müssen, aber da er die Familien der anderen nicht verfolgt hat, und Sie nicht wegziehen wollten ... Trotzdem hätten wir wissen müssen, dass er auf keinen Fall aufhören würde ...«

»Welche anderen? Wer ist er?« Meine Stimme wird lauter, als weitere Erinnerungen in meinem Kopf hochkommen. *Messer an meiner Kehle, nasser Stofffetzen auf meinem Gesicht, Nadel in meinem Hals, kann nicht atmen, kann nicht atmen ...*

»Karen, sie hat eine Panikattacke! Tu etwas.« Rysons Stimme ist hektisch, als die Monitore zu piepen beginnen. Ich hyperventiliere und zittere, aber trotzdem finde ich die Kraft, auf diese Monitore zu schauen. Mein Blutdruck ist in die Höhe geschnellt, und mein Puls ist gefährlich schnell, aber diese Zahlen zu sehen beruhigt mich. Ich bin eine Ärztin. Das ist meine Umgebung, die Umgebung, in der ich mich wohlfühle.

Ich schaffe das. *Einatmen. Ausatmen.* Ich bin nicht schwach. *Einatmen. Ausatmen.*

»So ist es gut, Sara. Atmen Sie einfach weiter.« Karens Stimme ist sanft und beruhigend, während sie meinen Arm streichelt. »Sie schaffen das. Atmen Sie einfach tief ein und aus. Genau so. So ist es gut. Und noch einmal. Und noch einmal ...«

Ich folge ihren sanften Anweisungen, während ich die Zahlen auf den Monitoren verfolge, und langsam lässt das Gefühl, zu ersticken, nach, und meine Vitalfunktionen stabilisieren sich. Weitere dunkle Erinnerungen dringen an die Oberfläche, aber ich bin noch nicht bereit, mich ihnen zu stellen. Ich schiebe sie beiseite und schlage so fest ich kann eine geistige Tür vor ihnen zu.

»Wer ist er?«, frage ich, als ich wieder sprechen kann. »Was meinen Sie mit ›die anderen‹? George hat diesen Artikel allein geschrieben. Warum ist die Mafia hinter jemand anderem her?«

Agent Ryson wechselt einen Blick mit Karen, bevor er sich zu mir dreht. »Dr. Cobakis, es tut mir leid, aber wir haben Ihnen nicht ganz die Wahrheit gesagt. Wir haben Ihnen die wirkliche Lage nicht erklärt, weil wir Sie schützen wollten, aber offensichtlich haben wir in diesem Punkt versagt.« Er atmet tief ein. »Es war nicht die örtliche Mafia, die hinter Ihrem Mann her war. Es war ein international gesuchter Flüchtling, ein gefährlicher Krimineller, auf den Ihr Mann bei einem Auslandsauftrag getroffen ist.«

»Was?« Mein Kopf pocht schmerzhaft, und die Enthüllungen sind fast zu viel, um sie verarbeiten zu können. George hat als Auslandskorrespondent ange-fangen, aber in den letzten fünf Jahren hatte er sich mehr und mehr um inländische Geschichten geküm-mert. Ich habe mich darüber gewundert, da auswärtige Angelegenheiten seine Leidenschaft waren, aber als ich ihn gefragt habe, hat er mir geantwortet, dass er mehr Zeit mit mir zu Hause verbringen möchte, und ich habe das Thema fallengelassen.

»Dieser Mann hat eine Liste von Menschen, die ihn verraten haben – oder von denen er denkt, dass sie es getan haben«, meint Ryson. »Ich befürchte, dass George auf dieser Liste stand. Die genauen Umstände und die Identität des Flüchtlings sind geheim, aber nach dem, was passiert ist, verdienen Sie es, die Wahrheit zu erfahren – zumindest so viel, wie ich preisgeben darf.«

Ich starre ihn an. »Das war ein Mann? Ein Deserteur?« Ein Gesicht erscheint in meinem Kopf, ein hartes, wunderschönes männliches Gesicht. Es ist verschwommen, wie ein Bild aus einem Traum, aber aus irgendeinem Grund weiß ich, dass er es ist, der Mann, der in mein Zuhause eingebrochen ist und mir diese schrecklichen Dinge angetan hat.

Ryson nickt. »Ja. Er ist hervorragend ausgebildet und verfügt über umfangreiche Ressourcen, wodurch er in der Lage war, uns so lange einen Schritt voraus zu sein. Er hat überall Verbindungen, angefangen in Osteuropa über Südamerika bis hin zum Nahen Osten. Als wir erfahren haben, dass der Name Ihres Mannes auf dieser Liste stand, haben wir George in die geheime Unterkunft gebracht, und dasselbe hätten wir auch mit Ihnen tun sollen. Wir haben einfach gedacht …« Er hält inne und schüttelt den Kopf. »Ich nehme an, dass es nicht wichtig ist, was wir dachten. Wir haben ihn unterschätzt, und jetzt sind vier Männer tot.«

Tot. Vier Männer sind tot. Dann trifft es mich wie ein Schlag, das Wissen, dass George tot ist. Ich hatte es davor nicht verstanden, nicht wirklich. Meine Augen beginnen zu brennen, und meine Brust fühlt sich an, als würde sie in einem Schraubstock zusammengedrückt werden. In einem Moment der Klarheit setzen sich alle Teile des Puzzles zusammen.

»Ich war es, stimmt's?« Ich setze mich hin und ignoriere den Schwindel und die Schmerzen. »Ich habe das getan. Ich habe irgendwie die Lage des Geheimverstecks verraten.«

Ryson und die Schwester tauschen erneut einen Blick aus, und meine letzte Hoffnung verschwindet. Ich bekomme keine Antwort, aber ihre Körpersprache spricht Bände.

Ich bin verantwortlich für Georges Tod. Für alle vier Tode.

»Das ist nicht Ihre Schuld, Dr. Cobakis.« Karen berührt erneut meinen Arm, und ihre braunen Augen sind voller Mitleid. »Die Droge, die er Ihnen verabreicht hat, hätte jeden gebrochen. Sagt Ihnen Thiopental etwas?«

»Das Barbiturat?« Ich blinzele sie an. »Natürlich. Es wurde häufig für Narkosen verwendet, bevor Propofol zum Standardmittel wurde. Was hat … oh.«

»Ja«, sagt Agent Ryson. »Ich sehe, Sie wissen auch über seine andere Verwendung Bescheid. Es wird selten dafür benutzt, zumindest außerhalb der Geheimdienste, aber es ist ein sehr wirkungsvolles Wahrheitsserum. Es senkt die höheren kortikalen Gehirnfunktionen und macht das Opfer gesprächig und kooperativ. Und in Ihrem Fall war es eine Designerversion, Thiopental gemischt mit anderen Verbindungen, die wir noch nie gesehen haben.«

»Er hat mich unter Drogen gesetzt, um mich zum

Reden zu bringen?« Mein Magen brennt durch die Galle. Das erklärt die Kopfschmerzen und den benebelten Kopf, und das Wissen, dass mir so etwas angetan wurde – dass ich auf diese Art und Weise benutzt wurde –, weckt in mir das Verlangen, meinen Kopf innen mit Chlor zu schrubben. Dieser Mann ist nicht nur in mein Zuhause eingedrungen; er ist in meinen Kopf eingedrungen, ist in ihn eingebrochen wie ein Dieb.

»Das nehmen wir an, ja«, antwortet Ryson. »Sie hatten eine große Menge dieser Droge in ihrem Körper, als unsere Agenten Sie gefesselt in Ihrem Wohnzimmer fanden. Sie hatten außerdem Blut an ihrem Hals und den Oberschenkeln, so dass sie anfänglich dachten, dass …«

»Blut auf meinen Oberschenkeln?« Ich bereite mich auf eine neue schreckliche Enthüllung vor. »Hat er …«

»Nein, keine Angst, er hat nichts dergleichen getan«, erklärt mir Karen und wirft Ryson einen düsteren Blick zu. »Wir haben Ihren ganzen Körper untersucht, als Sie eingeliefert wurden, und es handelte sich dabei um Ihr Menstruationsblut, nichts weiter. Es gab keine Anzeichen für einen sexuellen Übergriff. Abgesehen von einigen blauen Flecken und den leichten Einschnitten am Hals geht es Ihnen gut – oder zumindest wird es Ihnen gut gehen, sobald die Wirkung der Drogen abgeklungen ist.«

Gut. Hysterisches Gelächter steigt in meinem Hals auf, und ich muss meine ganze Kraft aufwenden, es nicht herauszulassen. Mein Mann und drei weitere

Männer sind meinetwegen tot. In mein Haus wurde eingebrochen; in meinen *Kopf* wurde eingebrochen. Und sie denkt, dass es mir gut gehen wird?

»Warum haben Sie sich die Lüge über die Mafia ausgedacht?«, frage ich und habe Schwierigkeiten, die Schmerzen, die sich in meiner Brust ausbreiten, zu unterdrücken. »Wieso hätte sie mich schützen sollen?«

»Weil dieser Deserteur in der Vergangenheit niemals auf Unschuldige losgegangen ist – die Frauen und Kinder der Menschen auf seiner Liste wurden auf keinste Weise in die Sache hineingezogen«, antwortet Ryson. »Aber er hat die Schwester eines Mannes getötet, weil der Mann sich ihr anvertraut hatte und sie für sein Untertauchen benutzt hat. Je weniger Sie wussten, desto sicherer waren Sie, besonders deshalb, weil Sie nicht umziehen und mit Ihrem Mann verschwinden wollten.«

»Ryson, bitte«, sagt Karen scharf, aber es ist zu spät. Diese neue Enthüllung hat mich bereits aus der Bahn geworfen. Selbst wenn man mir verzeihen könnte, dass ich unter Drogeneinfluss geredet habe, ist es allein meine Schuld, dass ich nicht umziehen wollte. Ich war egoistisch gewesen, hatte an meine Eltern und meine Karriere gedacht, anstatt an die Gefahr, die ich für meinen Mann darstellen könnte. Ich hatte geglaubt, dass es dabei um *meine* Sicherheit ging, nicht seine, aber das ist keine Entschuldigung. Ich habe Georges Tod auf dem Gewissen, genauso wie den Unfall, der sein Gehirn geschädigt hat.

»Hat er …« Ich schlucke belegt. »Hat er gelitten? Ich meine … wie ist es passiert?«

»Ein Kopfschuss«, antwortet Ryson mit gedämpfter Stimme. »Genau wie bei den drei Männern, die ihn bewacht haben. Ich glaube, dass es alles zu schnell ging, als dass irgendjemand noch gelitten hat.«

»Oh Gott.« Mein Magen krampft plötzlich heftig, und Erbrochenes steigt in meinem Hals auf.

Karen muss gesehen haben, dass mein Gesicht die Farbe verloren hat, weil sie schnell reagiert, eine Metallschale von einem Tisch in der Nähe ergreift und sie mir in die Hand drückt – gerade noch rechtzeitig. Ich kann meinen Mageninhalt nicht länger zurückhalten, und die Säure brennt in meiner Speiseröhre, während ich mit zitternden Händen die Schale halte.

»Das ist völlig in Ordnung. Das ist überhaupt nicht schlimm. Wir machen Sie einfach wieder sauber.« Karen hat die gleiche zügige Effizienz wie eine richtige Krankenschwester. Welche Rolle sie auch immer beim FBI spielt, sie weiß, was sie in einer solchen Situation zu tun hat. »Kommen Sie, ich helfe Ihnen ins Badezimmer. Sie werden sich gleich besser fühlen.«

Sie stellt die Schale auf den Nachttisch, legt ihren Arm um meinen Rücken, um mir aus dem Bett zu helfen, und führt mich zum Badezimmer. Meine Beine zittern so stark, dass ich kaum gehen kann; wenn sie mich nicht stützen würde, hätte ich es nicht geschafft.

Trotzdem, ich brauche einen Moment für mich, also sage ich zu Karen: »Können Sie mich bitte einen Moment allein lassen? Mir geht es jetzt wieder besser.«

Ich muss mich überzeugend genug anhören, weil Karen mir antwortet »Ich bin gleich vor der Tür, falls Sie mich brauchen« und die Tür hinter sich schließt.

Ich schwitze, und ich zittere, aber ich schaffe es, mir den Mund auszuspülen und meine Zähne zu putzen. Danach erledige ich ein anderes dringendes Bedürfnis, wasche meine Hände und spritze mir kaltes Wasser ins Gesicht. Als Karen an die Tür klopft, fühle ich mich schon ein wenig menschlicher.

Ich versuche, an nichts zu denken. Wenn ich darüber nachdenke, wie George und die anderen gestorben sind, werde ich mich erneut übergeben. Ich habe während meiner Ausbildung im OP einige Schusswunden gesehen, und ich weiß, welche verheerenden Wunden Kugeln zufügen.

Denke nicht darüber nach. Noch nicht.

»Sind meine Eltern benachrichtigt worden?«, frage ich, nachdem Karen mir dabei geholfen hat, wieder ins Bett zurückzugehen. Sie hat die Schüssel bereits entfernt, und Agent Ryson sitzt in einem Stuhl neben dem Bett, und sein zerfurchtes Gesicht sieht müde und angespannt aus.

»Nein«, sagt Karen leise. »Noch nicht. Wir wollten das zuerst mit Ihnen besprechen.«

Ich schaue erst sie und danach Ryson an. »Was besprechen?«

»Dr. Cobakis – Sara – wir denken, dass es das Beste wäre, wenn die genauen Todesumstände Ihres Mannes und auch der Überfall auf Sie geheim bleiben würden«, erklärt Ryson. »Das würde Ihnen eine

Menge unangenehme Aufmerksamkeit der Medien und …«

»Sie meinen, es würde *Ihnen* eine Menge unangenehmer Aufmerksamkeit der Medien ersparen.« Aufwallende Wut verjagt einen Teil des Nebels in meinem Kopf. »Deshalb bin ich auch hier und nicht in einem normalen Krankenhaus. Sie wollen das vertuschen, so tun, als sei es niemals geschehen.«

»Wir möchten Sie in Sicherheit wissen und Ihnen dabei helfen, das Geschehene zu verarbeiten«, sagt Karen, und ihre braunen Augen blicken ernst auf mein Gesicht. »Diese Geschichte in die Zeitungen zu bringen wäre nicht gut. Was passiert ist, war eine schreckliche Tragödie, aber Ihr Mann wurde bereits künstlich am Leben erhalten. Sie wissen am besten, dass es nur eine Frage der Zeit war, bevor …«

»Was ist mit den anderen drei Männern?«, unterbreche ich schneidend. »Wurden sie auch künstlich am Leben erhalten?«

»Sie sind während ihres Dienstes gestorben«, sagt Ryson. »Ihre Familien sind bereits unterrichtet worden, also müssen Sie sich darüber keine Gedanken machen. Sie waren Georges einzige Familie, also …«

»Also bin ich jetzt auch informiert worden.« Mein Mund zuckt. »Ihr Gewissen ist beruhigt, und jetzt ist es Zeit für Schadensbegrenzung. Oder sollte ich sagen, Zeit, ›um Ihren Arsch zu retten‹?«

Sein Gesicht spannt sich an. »Diese Angelegenheit wird immer noch als geheim eingestuft, Dr. Cobakis. Wenn Sie sich an die Medien wenden, werden Sie in ein Wespennest stechen, und glauben Sie mir, das wollen Sie nicht. Das würde Ihr Ehemann auch nicht wollen, wenn er noch am Leben wäre. Er wollte nicht, dass irgendjemand etwas darüber weiß, nicht einmal Sie.«

»Was?« Ich starre den Agenten an. »George wusste es? Aber …«

»Er wusste nicht, dass er auf der Liste stand, und das wussten wir auch nicht«, sagt Karen und legt ihre Hand auf die Lehne von Rysons Stuhl. »Wir haben das erst nach dem Unfall erfahren, und ab diesem Zeitpunkt haben wir alles getan, was wir konnten, um ihn zu beschützen.«

Mein Kopf pocht, aber ich ignoriere den Schmerz und versuche, mich auf das zu konzentrieren, was sie mir sagen. »Ich verstehe das nicht ganz. Was ist bei diesem Auslandsaufenthalt passiert? Wie konnte George auf diesen Deserteur treffen? Und wann?«

»Das ist der geheime Teil«, antwortet Ryson. »Es tut mir leid, aber es ist das Beste, wenn Sie sich keine Gedanken darüber machen. Wir suchen gerade nach dem Mörder Ihres Mannes, und wir versuchen, die restlichen Personen auf dieser Liste zu schützen. Wenn man seine Ressourcen bedenkt, ist das keine leichte Aufgabe. Wenn wir die Medien an uns kleben haben würden, könnten wir unseren Job nicht so effektiv ausführen, und weitere Menschen würden sterben. Verstehen Sie, was ich sage, Dr. Cobakis? Für Ihre Sicherheit und die der anderen Menschen müssen Sie dieses Thema fallenlassen.«

Ich spanne mich an und erinnere mich an das, was der Agent über die anderen gesagt hat. »Wie viele hat er bereits getötet?«

»Leider zu viele«, meint Karen düster. »Wir wussten nichts über diese Liste, bis er einige Menschen in Europa getötet hat, und als wir in der Lage waren, die richtigen Schutzmaßnahmen zu ergreifen, waren nur noch wenige Personen übrig.«

Ich atme zitternd ein, und mein Kopf dreht sich. Ich hatte natürlich gewusst, was George als Auslandskorrespondent getan hat, und ich habe viele seiner Artikel und Berichte gelesen, aber diese Geschichten hatten sich nie ganz echt angefühlt. Selbst als Agent Ryson vor neun Monaten auf mich zugekommen ist und mir von der Bedrohung durch die Mafia berichtet hat, war meine Angst eher akademisch als gefühlt gewesen. Abgesehen von Georges Unfall und den schmerzhaften Jahren bis dorthin hatte ich ein bezauberndes Leben voller vorstädtischer Sorgen um Schule, Arbeit und Familie. Internationale Deserteure, die Menschen, die auf einer mysteriösen Liste stehen, foltern und töten, liegen so weit außerhalb meiner persönlichen Erfahrungen, dass ich mich fühle, als sei ich in das Leben einer anderen Person gestoßen worden.

»Wir wissen, dass das eine Menge zu verarbeiten ist«, meint Karen sanft, und ich verstehe, dass sich meine Gefühle auf meinem Gesicht widerspiegeln müssen. »Sie stehen wegen des Überfalls immer noch unter Schock, und zusätzlich diese Dinge zu erfahren …« Sie holt Luft. »Wenn Sie jemanden zum Reden brauchen, ich kenne einen guten Therapeuten, der mit Soldaten mit posttraumatischen Belastungsstörungen und Ähnlichem gearbeitet hat.

»Nein ...« Ich will ablehnen, ihr sagen, dass ich niemanden brauche, aber ich kann meinen Mund nicht dazu bringen, diese Lüge zu formulieren. Der Schmerz in meiner Brust erstickt mich, und trotz meiner psychischen Mauer kommen immer mehr Erinnerungen hoch, voller Dunkelheit, Hilflosigkeit und Entsetzen.

»Ich gebe Ihnen einfach seine Karte«, meint Karen, kommt zu mir ans Bett, und ich sehe den besorgen Blick, den sie den piependen Monitoren zuwirft. Ich muss nicht auf sie schauen, um zu wissen, dass mein Herzschlag wieder extrem schnell ist, und mein Körper in diesem Kämpfen-oder-Wegrennen-Modus ist.

Mein Eidechsenhirn weiß nicht, dass die Erinnerungen mir keinen Schaden zufügen können, dass das Schlimmste bereits geschehen ist. Außer ...

»Werde ich untertauchen müssen?«, presse ich aus meinem engen Hals. »Denken Sie, er wird ...«

»Nein«, antwortet Ryson, der meine Angst sofort versteht. »Er wird Sie nicht noch einmal aufsuchen. Er hat das bekommen, was er wollte; er hat keinen Grund dafür, zurückzukommen. Wenn Sie es wollen, können wir einen Umzug für sie organisieren, aber ...«

»Hören Sie auf, Ryson. Können Sie nicht sehen, dass sie hyperventiliert?«, sagt Karen nachdrücklich und ergreift seinen Arm. »Atmen Sie, Sara«, sagt sie zu mir in einem beruhigenden Ton. »Machen Sie schon, meine Liebe, atmen Sie einfach tief ein. Und noch einmal. Genau so ...«

Ich folge ihrer Stimme, bis mein Herzschlag sich wieder beruhigt hat und die schlimmsten Erinnerungen hinter der Metallwand verschlossen sind. Ich zittere allerdings immer noch, also wickelt Karen mich in eine Decke, setzt sich neben mich auf das Bett und umarmt mich fest.

»Es wird alles gut werden, Sara«, murmelt sie, als der Schmerz mich überwältigt, und ich beginne zu weinen, die Tränen laufen wie Lavaströme über meine Wangen. »Es ist vorbei. Es wird alles wieder gut werden. Er ist weg und wird Ihnen nie wieder wehtun.«

5

Peter

»*ASCHE ZU ASCHE, Staub zu Staub …*«

Die dröhnende Stimme des Priesters erreicht meine Ohren, und ich blende sie aus, während ich mit meinen Augen die Trauergäste abfahre. Es sind über zweihundert Menschen hier, alle in dunkler Kleidung und mit düsteren Gesichtsausdrücken. Unter dem Meer aus schwarzen Regenschirmen erblicke ich viele rot geränderte und geschwollene Augen, und einige Frauen weinen hörbar.

George Cobakis war zu seinen Lebzeiten beliebt gewesen.

Dieser Gedanke sollte mich wütend machen, aber das tut er nicht. Ich fühle gar nichts, wenn ich an ihn

60

denke, ich bin nicht einmal zufrieden, dass er tot ist. Die Wut, die

mich jahrelang aufgefressen hat, hat sich im Moment beruhigt und mich eigenartig leer zurückgelassen.

Ich stehe am Ende der Trauergemeinschaft, und mit meinem schwarzen Mantel und meinem Regenschirm sehe ich aus wie alle anderen. Eine hellbraune Perücke und ein dünner Bart verschleiern mein Aussehen, genauso wie meine schlurfende Haltung und ein flaches Kissen, das meine Körpermitte polstert.

Ich weiß nicht, warum ich hier bin. Ich bin noch nie bei einer der Beerdigungen gewesen. Sobald ein Name von meiner Liste gestrichen wird, bewegen mein Team und ich uns zum nächsten, kalt und methodisch. Ich bin ein gesuchter Mann; es hat keinen Sinn, dass ich mich hier länger aufhalte, in dieser kleinen Vorstadt, aber trotzdem kann ich einfach nicht gehen.

Nicht, ohne sie noch einmal zu sehen.

Mein Blick wandert von einer Person zur nächsten, als ich die schlanke Gestalt suche, und endlich sehe ich sie, ganz vorn, dort, wo es sich für die Frau des Verstorbenen gehört. Sie steht neben einem älteren Paar, hält einen großen Schirm über sie und sich selbst, und auch in dieser Menschenmenge schafft sie es, unnahbar auszusehen, irgendwie distanziert.

Sie sieht aus, als existiere sie auf einer anderen Ebene, so wie ich.

Ich erkenne sie an den kastanienbraunen Wellen, die unter ihrem kleinen, schwarzen Hut hervor-schauen. Sie trägt ihre Haare heute offen, und trotz des grauen, regnerischen Himmels sehe ich rötliche Reflexe in der dunkelbraunen Masse, die ihr bis einige Zentimeter über die Schultern fällt. Ich kann nicht viel mehr sehen – es befinden sich zu viele Menschen und Regenschirme zwischen uns –, aber ich betrachte sie trotzdem, genauso wie ich sie den ganzen letzten Monat betrachtet habe. Nur dass mein Interesse an ihr jetzt anders ist, unendlich persönlicher.

Kollateralschaden. Als das habe ich sie am Anfang gesehen. Sie war keine Person für mich, sondern ein Anhang ihres Mannes. Ein mit Sicherheit intelligenter und hübscher Anhang, aber das war mir egal. Ich wollte sie nicht unbedingt umbringen, aber ich hätte das getan, was nötig war, um mein Ziel zu erreichen.

Ich *habe* getan, was nötig war.

Sie war vor Entsetzen versteinert, als ich sie ergriffen habe, und ihre Reaktion war die Antwort einer Person, die nicht für solche Situationen ausgebildet wurde, der primitive Instinkt einer hilflosen Beute. An dieser Stelle hätte es leicht sein müssen – einige leichte Schnitte und fertig. Dass mein Messer sie nicht sofort gebrochen hat, war beeindruckend und gleichzeitig ärgerlich; ich habe schon professionelle Mörder gesehen, die sich bei weniger Anreiz eingepisst und gesungen haben.

Ich hätte ihr zu diesem Zeitpunkt mehr antun können, sie wirklich mit meinem Messer bearbeiten können, aber stattdessen habe ich mich für eine

Verhörmethode entschieden, die weniger Schaden zufügt.

Ich habe sie unter den Wasserhahn gehalten.

Es hat hervorragend funktioniert – und genau da habe ich den Fehler gemacht. Sie hat nach der ersten Runde so sehr gezittert und geschluchzt, dass ich sie auf den Boden gezogen und sie in meine Arme genommen habe, sie festgehalten und gleichzeitig beruhigt habe. Ich habe das getan, damit sie wieder reden konnte, aber ich habe nicht mit meiner Reaktion auf sie gerechnet.

Sie hat sich so klein und zerbrechlich, so unglaublich hilflos angefühlt, als sie in meiner Umarmung gehustet und geschluchzt hat, und aus irgendeinem Grund habe ich mich daran erinnert, meinen Sohn auf diese Weise gehalten zu haben, ihn getröstet zu haben, wenn er weinte. Aber Sara ist kein Kind, und mein Körper hat auf ihre schlanken Kurven mit überraschendem Hunger reagiert, mit einer Begierde, die genauso primitiv wie irrational war.

Ich begehrte diese Frau, die ich eigentlich befragen wollte, die Frau, deren Mann ich umbringen wollte.

Ich habe versucht, meine ungewollte Reaktion zu ignorieren, einfach so weiterzumachen wie zuvor, aber als sie wieder auf dem Tresen lag, konnte ich das Wasser einfach nicht wieder anstellen. Ich war mir ihrer zu bewusst; sie war eine Person für mich geworden, eine lebendige, atmende Frau statt eines Werkzeugs, das ich benutzen wollte.

Deshalb blieb mir nur noch die Droge. Ich hatte

nicht vorgehabt, sie bei ihr zu benutzen, da es erstens Zeit kostet, bis sie richtig wirkt, und weil es die letzte Dosis war, die wir noch hatten. Der Chemiker, der sie hergestellt hatte, wurde kürzlich umgebracht, und Anton hat mich gewarnt, dass es einige Zeit dauern würde, einen anderen Lieferanten zu finden. Ich habe diese letzte Dosis für einen Notfall aufgehoben, aber ich hatte keine Wahl.

Ich, der Hunderte gefoltert und getötet hat, konnte es einfach nicht über mich bringen, dieser Frau wehzutun.

»Er war ein freundlicher und großzügiger Mann, ein talentierter Journalist. Sein Tod ist ein unermesslicher Verlust für seine Familie und sein Arbeitsumfeld ...«

Ich zwinge meine Augen, sich von Sara zu trennen und sich auf den Sprecher zu konzentrieren. Es ist eine Frau mittleren Alters, und ihr Gesicht ist tränenüberströmt. Ich erkenne, dass sie eine von Cobakis' Kolleginnen der Zeitung ist. Ich habe zu allen von ihnen Nachforschungen angestellt, um herauszufinden, ob sie etwas mit der Sache zu tun hatten, aber zu ihrem Glück war Cobakis der Einzige.

Die Stimme fährt mit Cobakis' herausragenden Qualitäten fort, aber ich blende sie erneut aus, und mein Blick wandert zu der schlanken Gestalt unter dem riesigen Schirm zurück. Alles, was ich von Sara sehen kann, ist ihr Rücken, aber ich kann mir leicht ihr blasses, herzförmiges Gesicht vorstellen. Seine Züge sind in meinen Kopf gebrannt, jeder einzelne, angefangen von den weit auseinanderstehenden braunen

Augen und der kleinen geraden Nase bis hin zu ihren weichen, vollen Lippen. Sara Cobakis hat etwas, was mich an Audrey Hepburn denken lässt, eine Art altmodische Schönheit wie die der Filmstars aus den Vierzigern und Fünfzigern. Das verstärkt das Gefühl, dass sie nicht hierhergehört, dass sie irgendwie anders ist als die Menschen, die sie umgeben.

Dass sie sich irgendwie über ihnen befindet.

Ich frage mich, ob sie weint, ob sie um den Mann trauert, den sie, wie sie zugegeben hat, kaum gekannt hat. Als mir Sara erzählt hat, dass sie und ihr Mann sich getrennt hätten, habe ich ihr nicht geglaubt, aber einige der Dinge, die sie mir unter Drogeneinfluss gesagt hat, haben meine Meinung geändert. Irgendetwas ist in dieser vermeintlich perfekten Ehe unglaublich schiefgelaufen, etwas, was eine unauslöschliche Spur bei ihr hinterlassen hat.

Sie hat Schmerz kennengelernt; sie hat mit ihm gelebt. Ich konnte das in ihren Augen, in der weichen, zitternden Linie ihres Mundes sehen. Er hat mich fasziniert, dieser kurze Einblick in ihren Kopf, und das hat dazu geführt, dass ich tiefer in ihre Geheimnisse eindringen wollte. Als sie ihre Lippen um meinen Finger gelegt und an ihnen gesaugt hat, ist der Hunger, den ich unterdrücken wollte, zurückgekommen, und mein Schwanz hat sich unkontrollierbar versteift.

Ich hätte sie nehmen können, und sie hätte es zugelassen. Scheiße, sie hätte mich mit offenen Armen empfangen. Die Droge hatte ihre Hemmungen gesenkt, ihre ganze Abwehr zerstört. Sie war so offen und verletzlich, auf gewisse Weise so bedürftig, dass sie mein Innerstes berührt hat.

Bitte, geh nicht. Bitte, geh nicht.

Selbst jetzt kann ich ihre Bitte immer noch hören, die mich so sehr an Pashas Bitte erinnert, als ich ihn das letzte Mal gesehen habe. Sie wusste nicht, um was sie mich da bat, wusste nicht, wer ich war oder was ich tun würde, aber ihre Worte haben mich aufgerüttelt, und jetzt sehne ich mich nach etwas völlig Unmöglichem. Ich hatte meine ganze Willenskraft aufwenden müssen, um wegzugehen und sie an den Stuhl gefesselt zurückzulassen, damit das FBI sie finden kann.

Es hat meine letzten Kraftreserven gefordert, zu gehen und meine Mission fortzuführen.

Meine Aufmerksamkeit wendet sich wieder der Gegenwart zu, in der Cobakis' Kollegin ihre Ansprache beendet, und Sara zum Podium geht. Ihre schlanke, dunkel gekleidete Gestalt bewegt sich mit unbewusster Anmut, und ich verspüre eine gewisse Vorfreude, als sie sich herumdreht und sich dem Publikum zuwendet.

Sie hat sich einen schwarzen Schal um den Hals gelegt, der sie vor dem kühlen Oktoberwind schützt und den Verband verdeckt, der sich dort befinden muss. Ihr herzförmiges Gesicht über dem Schal ist bleich wie das eines Geistes, aber ihre Augen sind trocken – zumindest soweit ich das aus dieser Entfernung sagen kann. Ich würde liebend gerne näher bei ihr stehen, aber das ist zu riskant. Es ist bereits ein Risiko, überhaupt hier zu sein. Unter den Anwesenden befinden sich mindestens zwei FBI-Agenten, und einige weitere sitzen unauffällig in den Regierungsfahrzeugen auf der Straße. Sie rechnen nicht damit, dass ich hier bin – würden sie das tun, wäre mehr Sicherheitsdienst hier vertreten – aber das bedeutet nicht, dass ich nicht vorsichtig sein muss. Anton und die anderen denken, dass ich verrückt bin, hier aufzutauchen.

Normalerweise verlassen wir nach einem erfolgreichen Einsatz innerhalb weniger Stunden die Stadt.

»Wie Sie alle wissen, haben George und ich uns an der Uni getroffen«, spricht Sara ins Mikrofon, und ein Schauer fährt mir bei dem Klang ihrer weichen, melodiösen Stimme über den Rücken. Ich habe sie lange genug beobachtet, um zu wissen, dass sie singen kann. Sie singt oft zu Popmusik, wenn sie allein in ihrem Auto ist oder Hausarbeit erledigt.

Die meiste Zeit klingt sie besser als der eigentliche Sänger.

»Wir haben uns in einem Chemielabor kennengelernt«, fährt sie fort, »weil George, auch wenn man es sich kaum vorstellen kann, damals darüber nachgedacht hat, Medizin zu studieren.« Ich höre einige Menschen in der Menge auflachen, und Saras Lippen lächeln leicht, als sie sagt: »Ja, George, der den Anblick von Blut nicht ertragen konnte, hat ernsthaft darüber nachgedacht, Arzt zu werden. Glücklicherweise hat er schnell seine wirkliche Leidenschaft entdeckt – Journalismus –, und der Rest ist Geschichte.«

Sie fährt damit fort, über die verschiedenen Gewohnheiten und Eigenarten ihres Mannes zu reden, einschließlich seiner Leidenschaft für Käsesandwiches mit Honig, bevor sie zu dem kommt, was er erreicht hat, und zu seinen guten Taten, einschließlich seiner unerschütterlichen Unterstützung für Kriegsveteranen und Obdachlose. Während sie spricht, fällt mir auf, dass alles, was sie sagt, mit *ihm* zu tun hat, und nicht mit den beiden. Abgesehen von der anfänglichen Geschichte, wie sie sich getroffen haben, hätte Saras Rede auch von einem Mitbewohner oder einem Freund kommen können – eigentlich irgendjemandem, der Cobakis kannte. Sogar ihre Stimme ist fest und ruhig, ohne einen Hinweis auf die Angst, die ich in jener Nacht in ihren Augen erblickt habe.

Erst als sie zu dem Unfall kommt, sehe ich echte Gefühle in ihrem Gesicht. »George hatte viele wunderschöne Seiten«, sagt sie und blickt über die Menge. »Aber sie alle endeten vor achtzehn Monaten, als sein Auto gegen eine Leitplanke fuhr und sie durchbrach. Alles, was er gewesen war, starb an diesem Tag. Was übrigblieb, war nicht George. Es war seine Schale, ein Körper ohne ein Gehirn. Als ihn der Tod am frühen Samstagmorgen holte, bekam er nicht meinen Ehemann. Er bekam nur diese Schale. George war zu diesem Zeitpunkt schon lange von uns gegangen, und nichts konnte ihm Leid zufügen.«

Sie hebt ihr Kinn bei diesem letzten Teil an, und ich blicke sie eindringlich an. Sie weiß nicht, dass ich hier bin – das FBI wäre schon bei mir, wenn sie es täte –, aber ich fühle mich, als würde sie direkt mich ansprechen, mir sagen, dass ich versagt habe. Fühlt sie mich auf einer bestimmten Ebene? Spürt sie, dass ich sie beobachte?

Weiß sie, dass ich vor zwei Nächten, als ich mich über das Bett ihres Mannes gebeugt habe, für einen kurzen Moment in Betracht gezogen habe, *nicht* abzudrücken?

Sie beendet ihre Ansprache mit den traditionellen Worten darüber, wie sehr man George vermissen wird, und verlässt das Podium, um den Priester die letzten Worte sagen zu lassen. Ich sehe ihr dabei zu, wie sie zu dem älteren Paar zurückgeht, und als die Menge beginnt, sich aufzulösen, folge ich den anderen Trauergästen ruhig aus dem Friedhof.

Die Beerdigung ist vorbei, und meine Faszination mit Sara muss das auch sein.

Es stehen noch weitere Menschen auf der Liste, und zu ihrem Glück ist Sara keiner davon.

TEIL II

6
____

 ara

»LIEBLING, isst du schon wieder nichts?«, fragt meine Mutter mit einem besorgten Stirnrunzeln. Auch wenn sie gerade durchgesaugt hat, als ich vorbeikam, ist ihr Make-up genauso perfekt wie immer, ihr kurzes, weißes Haar in hübsche Locken gelegt, und ihre Ohrringe passen zu ihrer stilvollen Halskette. »Du siehst in letzter Zeit so dünn aus.«

»Die meisten Menschen würden das als etwas Gutes ansehen«, entgegne ich trocken, aber um ihr einen Gefallen zu tun, strecke ich mich nach ihrem selbstgebackenen Apfelkuchen aus, um mir ein zweites Stück zu nehmen.

»Nicht, wenn du so aussiehst, als könne dich ein Chihuahua hinter sich herziehen«, antwortet meine

Mutter und schiebt den Kuchen zu mir. »Du musst auf dich aufpassen, oder du wirst deinen Patienten bald nicht mehr helfen können.«

»Das weiß ich, Mama«, sage ich zwischen zwei Bissen. »Mach dir keine Sorgen, okay? Es war ein anstrengender Winter, aber bald sollte es wieder ruhiger werden.«

»Sara, mein Liebling …« Die Sorgenfalten auf ihrem Gesicht vertiefen sich. »Es sind sechs Monate seit Georges …« Sie hält inne und holt tief Luft. »Schau mal, was ich sagen will, ist, dass du dich nicht weiterhin totarbeiten …kannst. Das ist zu viel für dich, dein reguläres Arbeitspensum plus diese ganze neue freiwillige Arbeit. Schläfst du überhaupt?«

»Natürlich, Mama. Ich schlafe wie ein Stein.« Das ist keine Lüge; ich schlafe ein, sobald mein Kopf das Kopfkissen berührt, und wache erst auf, wenn mein Wecker klingelt. Oder zumindest passiert genau das, wenn ich völlig erschöpft bin. An den Tagen, an denen ich so etwas wie einen normalen Arbeitsplan habe, wache ich zitternd und schweißüberströmt aus Albträumen auf, also gebe ich mein Bestes, jeden Tag erschöpft zu sein.

»Wie geht der Verkauf des Hauses voran? Hast du schon Angebote bekommen?«, will mein Vater wissen, der sich gerade in das Esszimmer schiebt. Er benutzt wieder einen Gehwagen, also muss sich seine Arthritis bemerkbar machen, aber ich freue mich, zu sehen, dass seine Haltung etwas gerader ist. Er folgt dieses Mal wirklich den Anweisungen seines Physiotherapeuten und geht jeden Tag im Fitnessstudio schwimmen.

»Der Makler macht nächste Woche einen Tag der offenen Tür«, antworte ich und unterdrücke meinen Drang, meinen Vater dafür zu loben, dass er das Richtige tut. Er mag es nicht, an sein Alter erinnert zu werden, also ist alles, was mit seiner oder der Gesundheit meiner Mutter zu tun hat, kein Thema für den Esstisch. Das macht mich verrückt, aber gleichzeitig muss ich seine Entschlossenheit einfach bewundern.

Mit seinen fast achtundsiebzig Jahren ist mein Vater noch genauso hartnäckig wie eh und je.

»Oh, gut«, meint meine Mutter. »Ich hoffe, dass sich daraus ein paar Angebote ergeben. Vergiss nicht, an diesem Tag morgens Kekse zu backen; dadurch riecht das Haus gut.«

»Ich kann vielleicht meinen Makler bitten, welche mitzubringen, und sie in der Mikrowelle zu erwärmen, bevor die ersten Besucher kommen«, sage ich lächelnd zu ihr. »Ich glaube nicht, dass ich Zeit haben werde, zu backen.«

»Natürlich wird sie das nicht, Lorna.« Mein Vater setzt sich neben meine Mutter und greift nach einem Stück Kuchen. Er blickt mich kurz an und meint: »Du wirst wahrscheinlich gar nicht zu Hause sein, stimmt's?«

Ich nicke. »Ich muss an dem Tag von der Klinik direkt ins Krankenhaus gehen.«

Er runzelt die Stirn. »Du tust das immer noch?«

»Diese Frauen brauchen mich, Papa.« Ich versuche,

die Verzweiflung in meiner Stimme zu unterdrücken. »Du kannst dir nicht vorstellen, wie das in dieser Gegend ist.«

»Aber Liebling, diese Gegend ist genau der Grund, weshalb wir nicht wollen, dass du dorthin gehst«, mischt sich meine Mutter ein. »Kannst du nicht woanders freiwilligen Dienst leisten? Und dann auch noch nachts nach einer deiner langen Schichten …«

»Mama, ich habe niemals Bargeld oder Wertsachen bei mir, und ich bin nur einige Stunden am Abend da«, entgegne ich, und meine Geduld hängt an einem seidenen Faden. Wir hatten dieses Gespräch mindestens fünfmal in den letzten drei Monaten, und jedes Mal tun meine Eltern so, als hätten wir noch nie darüber gesprochen. »Ich parke genau vor dem Gebäude und gehe ohne Umwege hinein. Sicherer geht es nicht.«

Meine Mutter seufzt und schüttelt den Kopf, aber diskutiert nicht weiter. Mein Vater schaut mich allerdings immer noch stirnrunzelnd über sein Stück Kuchen an. Um ihn abzulenken, stehe ich auf und frage: »Möchte jemand Kaffee oder Tee?«

»Koffeinfreien Kaffee für deinen Vater«, antwortet meine Mutter. »Und einen Kamillentee für mich, bitte.«

»Ein entkoffeinierter Kaffee und ein Kamillentee sind schon unterwegs«, sage ich und gehe zu der schicken Kaffeemaschine, die ich ihnen letztes Weihnachten geschenkt habe. Nachdem ich ihnen die gewünschten Getränke zubereitet und sie ihnen an den

Tisch gebracht habe, gehe ich zurück, um mir eine Tasse echten Java zu holen.

Nach diesem Abendessen habe ich Bereitschaft und kann das Koffein gebrauchen.

»Und weißt du was, Liebling?«, sagt meine Mutter, als ich mich wieder zu ihnen an den Tisch setze. »Am Samstag kommen die Levinsons zum Abendessen zu uns.«

Ich trinke einen Schluck von meinem Kaffee. Er ist heiß und stark, genau so, wie ich ihn mag. »Das ist schön.«

»Sie haben nach dir gefragt«, meint mein Vater und verrührt den Zucker in seinem Kaffee.

»Aha.« Ich halte meinen Gesichtsausdruck neutral. »Grüßt sie bitte von mir.«

»Warum kommst du nicht auch vorbei, mein Liebling?«, fragt meine Mutter, so als sei sie gerade erst auf diesen Gedanken gekommen. »Sie würden sich freuen, dich zu sehen, und ich werde dein Lieblings …«

»Mami, ich habe im Moment kein Interesse daran, mich mit Joe zu verabreden – oder mit irgendjemand anderem«, unterbreche ich sie und lächele, damit meine Ablehnung nicht so hart wirkt. »Es tut mir leid, aber ich bin noch nicht so weit. Ich weiß, dass ihr Joes Eltern liebt und dass er ein toller Anwalt und netter Mann ist, aber ich bin einfach noch nicht bereit dafür.«

»Du wirst auch nicht herausfinden, ob du schon bereit dafür bist, wenn du nicht ausgehst und es versuchst«, entgegnet mein Vater, während meine

Mutter seufzt und in ihre Teetasse blickt. »Du kannst nicht mit George sterben, Sara. Du bist stärker als das.«

Ich schütte meinen Kaffee hinunter, anstatt zu antworten. Er hat Unrecht. Ich bin nicht stark. Ich kann einfach nur hier sitzen und so tun, als ginge es mir gut, als sei ich immer noch intakt, gesund und funktionierte. Meine Eltern, genau wie alle anderen, wissen nicht, was in jener Freitagnacht passiert ist. Sie denken, dass George im Schlaf gestorben ist, dass sein Tod eine verspätete Folge des Autounfalls war, durch den er achtzehn Monate davor ins Koma gefallen war. Ich habe die Beerdigung mit einem geschlossenen Sarg damit erklärt, dass ich nur so mit meiner Trauer umgehen könnte, und niemand hat es hinterfragt. Wenn meine Eltern die Wahrheit wüssten, wären sie am Boden zerstört, und das würde ich ihnen niemals antun.

Niemand, außer dem FBI und meinem Therapeuten, weiß, welche Rolle der Deserteur und ich bei Georges Tod gespielt haben.

»Denk einfach darüber nach«, meint meine Mutter, als ich weiterhin schweige. »Du musst dich auf nichts festlegen oder tun, was du nicht tun möchtest. Aber denke bitte darüber nach, ob du vielleicht am Samstag kommen möchtest.«

Ich schaue sie an, und zum ersten Mal bemerke ich die Anspannung, die sie unter ihrem perfekten Make-up und den stilvollen Accessoires versteckt. Meine Mutter ist neun Jahre jünger als mein Vater und sie ist so gepflegt und energiegeladen, dass ich manchmal vergesse, dass das Alter auch bei ihr seinen Tribut fordert, dass ihre Sorge um mich nicht gut für ihre Gesundheit sein kann.

»Ich werde darüber nachdenken, Mama«, verspreche ich ihr und stehe auf, um die Teller abzuräumen. »Wenn ich Samstag nicht arbeiten muss, versuche ich, zum Abendessen zu kommen.«

7

MEIN BEREITSCHAFTSDIENST VERGEHT mit einer
Ansammlung aus Notfällen, angefangen von einer Frau
mit schweren Blutungen im fünften Schwangerschafts-
monat bis hin zu einer meiner Patientinnen, deren Wehen
sieben Wochen zu früh einsetzen. Letztendlich führe ich
bei ihr einen Kaiserschnitt durch, und das Baby – ein kleiner, aber perfekt entwickelter Junge – kann allein atmen
und saugen. Die Frau und ihr Ehemann weinen vor Glück
und bedanken sich überschwänglich bei mir, und als ich
endlich im Umkleideraum ankomme, um meine Arbeits-
kleidung auszuziehen, bin ich körperlich und emotional
ausgelaugt. Trotzdem bin ich auch unglaublich zufrieden.

Jedes Kind, das ich auf diese Welt hole, jede Frau,

80

deren Körper ich heile, lässt mich ein wenig besser fühlen, erleichtert das Schuldgefühl, das mich wie ein nasser Lappen erstickt.

Nein, denk nicht darüber nach. Hör auf. Aber es ist bereits zu spät, und die Erinnerungen überkommen mich, dunkel und exotisch. Keuchend lasse ich mich auf die Bank neben meinem Spind sinken, und meine Hände umklammern das harte, hölzerne Brett.

Eine Hand über meinem Mund. Ein Messer an meiner Kehle. Ein nasses Stofftuch auf meinem Gesicht. Wasser in meiner Nase, in meinen Lungen …

»Hey, Sara.« Sanfte Hände ergreifen meine Arme. »Sara, was ist los? Geht es dir gut?«

Ich keuche, mein Hals ist unglaublich eng, aber ich schaffe es, leicht zu nicken. Ich schließe die Augen und konzentriere mich darauf, langsamer zu atmen, genau so, wie mein Therapeut es mir beigebracht hat, und nach einigen Momenten lässt das Gefühl, zu ersticken, ein wenig nach.

Ich öffne meine Augen und erblicke Marsha, die mich besorgt ansieht.

»Es geht mir gut«, sage ich zitternd und stehe auf, um meinen Schrank zu öffnen. Meine Haut ist kalt und klamm, und meine Knie fühlen sich an, als würden sie gleich einknicken, aber ich möchte nicht, dass irgendjemand im Krankenhaus über meine Panikattacken Bescheid weiß. »Ich habe wieder vergessen, etwas zu essen, also ist mein Blutzuckerspiegel wahrscheinlich zu niedrig.«

Marshas blaue Augen weiten sich. »Du bist doch nicht schwanger, oder?«

»Was?« Auch wenn ich immer noch nicht gleichmäßig atme, muss ich vor Überraschung lachen. »Nein, natürlich nicht.«

»Oh, okay.« Sie grinst mich an. »Und ich dachte schon, dass du endlich wieder angefangen hast zu leben.«

Ich werfe ihr einen *Na-toll*-Blick zu. »Selbst wenn, meinst du nicht, dass ich weiß, wie man eine Schwangerschaft verhindert?«

»Hey, man kann nie wissen. Unfälle passieren.« Sie öffnet ihren Spind und beginnt, sich den Kittel auszuziehen. »Aber du solltest wirklich einen Happen mit mir und den Mädchen essen gehen. Wir wollen jetzt gleich zu Patty's.«

Ich ziehe die Augenbrauen in die Höhe. »Eine Bar um fünf Uhr morgens?«

»Ja, warum nicht? Wir wollen sie ja nicht leersaufen. Sie haben jeden Tag ganztägig Frühstück, und es ist um Längen besser als in der Cafeteria. Du solltest es mal probieren.«

Ich will gerade ablehnen, als ich mich daran erinnere, dass ich so gut wie nichts in meinem Kühlschrank habe. Ich habe nicht gelogen, als ich gesagt habe, dass ich heute nichts gegessen habe. Das Abendessen im Haus meiner Eltern ist schon zehn Stunden her, und ich bin am Verhungern.

»Okay«, meine ich und überrasche Marsha damit fast genauso sehr wie mich selbst. »Ich komme mit.«

Ich ignoriere das aufgeregte Kreischen meiner Freundin, ziehe meine Straßenbekleidung an und gehe zum Waschbecken, um mich frischzumachen.

———

ALS WIR BEI Patty's ankommen, überrascht es mich nicht, dort viele bekannte Gesichter zu sehen. Ein großer Teil des Krankenhauspersonals kommt in diese Bar, um sich nach der Arbeit zu entspannen und soziale Kontakte zu pflegen. Ich hatte nicht erwartet, dass der Ort zu dieser Uhrzeit mitten in der Nacht – oder am Morgen, je nachdem, wie man es nimmt – so voll sein würde, aber wenn sie neben Alkohol auch Frühstück servieren, macht das durchaus Sinn.

Marsha, zwei Schwestern aus der Notaufnahme und ich bahnen uns unseren Weg zu einem Tisch in der Ecke, und eine gestresst wirkende Kellnerin nimmt unsere Bestellung auf. In dem Moment, in dem sie unseren Tisch verlässt, beginnt Marsha, eine Geschichte über ihr verrücktes Wochenende in einem Klub in Chicago zu erzählen, und die beiden Krankenschwestern – Andy und Tonya – lachen und ziehen sie mit dem Typ auf, den sie fast abgeschleppt hätte. Danach berichtet Andy allen von der Besessenheit ihres Freundes von lilafarbenen Kondomen, und als unser Essen kommt, lachen die drei so sehr, dass die Kellnerin uns böse anschaut.

Ich lache ebenfalls, weil die Geschichte lustig *ist*, aber ich kann die Fröhlichkeit nicht spüren, die normalerweise beim Lachen aufkommt. Ich habe sie seit langer Zeit nicht mehr gefühlt. Es ist so, als sei etwas in mir erfroren, und meine Gefühle und Empfindungen seien gedämpft. Mein Therapeut sagt, dass es eine der Arten ist, auf die sich meine posttraumatische Belastungsstörung zeigt, aber ich weiß nicht, ob er recht hat. Schon lange bevor der Fremde in mein Haus eingedrungen ist – sogar vor dem Unfall –, habe ich mich gefühlt, als gäbe es eine Barriere zwischen mir und dem Rest der Welt, eine Mauer aus falschem Anschein und Lügen.

Seit Jahren trage ich eine Maske, und jetzt fühlt es sich an, als sei ich zu dieser Maske geworden, so, als ob darunter nichts real sei.

»Was ist mit dir, Sara?«, fragt Tonya, und mir fällt auf, dass ich in meine eigenen Gedanken versunken gewesen bin und meine Eier wie ferngesteuert gegessen habe. »Wie war dein Wochenende?«

»Es war gut, danke.« Ich lege meine Gabel ab und versuche, ein Lächeln aufzusetzen. »Nichts Aufregendes. Ich verkaufe gerade mein Haus, also musste ich meine Garage säubern und andere langweilige Dinge tun.« Außerdem hatte ich achtzehn Stunden lang Bereitschaftsdienst und habe weitere fünf Stunden freiwillig in der Klinik verbracht, aber das erzähle ich Tonya nicht. Marsha denkt sowieso schon, dass ich ein Workaholic bin, und wenn sie erfahren würde, dass ich für andere Ärzte in der Praxis des Krankenhauses einspringe und zu meiner normalen Arbeit auch noch in der Klinik aushelfe, würde ich das bis zu meinem Lebensende zu hören bekommen.

»Du solltest nächsten Freitag mit uns mitkommen«, sagt Tonya und streckt ihren schlanken, braunen Arm aus, um sich den Salzstreuer zu nehmen. Mit ihren vierundzwanzig Jahren ist sie eine der jüngsten Schwestern bei uns, und laut dem, was Marsha mir erzählt hat, ist sie ein schlimmeres Partygirl als meine Freundin und macht mit ihren Grübchen beim Lachen und dem schlanken Körper Männer jeden Alters wahnsinnig. »Wir werden zuerst im Patty's etwas trinken gehen und danach in die Stadt fahren. Ich kenne einen Promoter des neuen Klubs in der Innenstadt, also müssen wir uns nicht einmal anstellen.«

Ich blinzele wegen des unerwarteten Angebots. »Oh, ich weiß nicht … ich bin mir nicht sicher, ob …«

»Freitagnacht musst du nicht arbeiten«, meint Marsha. »Ich weiß es, weil ich mir deinen Dienstplan angesehen habe.«

»Ja, aber du weißt ja, wie es ist.« Ich spieße mit meiner Gabel Ei auf. »Babys kommen nicht immer planmäßig.«

»Jetzt komm schon, Marsha, lass sie in Ruhe«, meint Andy und streicht sich eine rote Locke hinter das Ohr. »Siehst du nicht, dass das arme Mädchen gerade müde ist? Wenn sie gehen will, wird sie gehen. Du musst sie nirgendwo hinschleifen.«

Sie zwinkert mir zu, und ich lächele sie dankbar an. Das ist das erste Mal, dass ich etwas mit Andy außerhalb der Krankenhausflure zu tun habe, und mir fällt auf, dass ich sie wirklich gerne mag. Genau wie ich ist sie Ende zwanzig und hat laut Marsha seit fünf Jahren einen festen Freund. Der Freund – der mit den lilafarbenen Kondomen – ist offensichtlich ein egozentrisches Arschloch, aber Andy liebt ihn trotzdem.

»Du bist von Michigan hierhergezogen, stimmt's?«, frage ich sie, und Andy nickt grinsend und erzählt mir, dass Larry, ihr Freund, einen Job hier bekommen hat, der sie beide gezwungen hat, umzuziehen. Während ich ihr zuhöre, entscheide ich, dass Marshas Meinung von Andys Freund nicht wirklich falsch ist.

Larry wirkt wie ein egozentrisches Arschloch.

Der Rest des Essens vergeht dank der ungezwungenen und unterhaltsamen Gespräche wie im Flug, und als wir bezahlen und die Bar verlassen, fühle ich mich unbeschwerter als seit Monaten. Vielleicht hat mein Vater recht, und ausgehen und Freunde treffen könnte gut für mich sein. Vielleicht werde ich wirklich zu dem Abendessen mit den Levinsons gehen und vielleicht sogar in den Klub mit Tonya.

Meine verbesserte Stimmung hält auch noch an, als ich den drei Frauen gute Nacht sage und die zwei Straßen bis zum Parkplatz des Krankenhauses gehe, auf dem mein Auto steht. Lady Gaga singt in meinen Kopfhörern, und der Himmel erhellt sich gerade. Ich fühle mich, als würde der Sonnenaufgang zu mir sprechen und mir versprechen, dass die Dunkelheit in mir in einer nicht allzu entfernten Zukunft auch verschwindet.

Er fühlt sich gut an, dieser winzige Hoffnungsschimmer. Es fühlt sich gut an, einen Schritt nach vorn zu machen.

Ich bin bereits auf dem Parkplatz, als es erneut passiert.

Es beginnt mit einem leichten Prickeln auf meiner Haut … einer leichten Überreizung meiner Nervenbahnen. Danach kommt der Adrenalinschub, der von einer Welle lähmenden Entsetzens begleitet wird. Meine Herzfrequenz schießt in die Höhe, und mein Körper spannt sich für einen Angriff an. Keuchend wirbele ich herum, reiße mir die Kopfhörer aus den Ohren, während ich in meiner Tasche nach dem Pfefferspray wühle, aber hier ist niemand.

Es ist einfach dieses Gefühl, als befände ich mich in Gefahr, ein Gefühl, beobachtet zu werden. Keuchend bewege ich mich im Kreis und umklammere dabei das Pfefferspray, aber ich kann niemanden sehen.

Ich sehe niemals jemanden, wenn mein Gehirn diese Kurzschlüsse hat.

Zitternd gehe ich zu meinem Auto und steige ein. Ich muss einige Minuten lang meine Atemübungen machen, bis ich mich ausreichend beruhigt habe, um fahren zu können, und ich weiß, dass ich heute trotz meiner Müdigkeit nicht schlafen können werde.

Ich verlasse den Parkplatz und fahre anstatt nach rechts nach links.

Ich kann genauso gut zur Klinik fahren. Sie erwarten mich zwar nicht vor morgen, aber sie sind für jede Hilfe dankbar.

8

S*ara*

»ERZÄHLEN Sie mir von dem letzten Vorfall, Sara«, sagt Dr. Evans und schlägt seine langen Beine übereinander.

»Warum haben Sie gedacht, dass Sie beobachtet wurden?«

»Ich weiß es nicht. Es war einfach …« Ich hole Luft und versuche, die richtigen Worte zu finden, aber schließlich schüttele ich den Kopf. »Es war nichts Konkretes. Ich weiß es ehrlich gesagt nicht.«

»Okay, gehen wir mal einen Schritt zurück.« Sein Ton ist warm und gleichzeitig professionell. Das ist ein Teil dessen, was ihn zu einem guten Therapeuten macht, diese Fähigkeit, sich Sorgen zu machen und gleichzeitig Abstand zu halten. »Sie haben gesagt, dass

Sie mit einigen Kollegen frühstücken gegangen sind, und danach sind Sie zu ihrem Auto zurückgegangen, richtig?«

»Richtig.«

»Haben Sie irgendetwas gehört? Oder etwas gesehen? Irgendetwas, was Ihre Reaktion ausgelöst haben könnte? Eine zuschlagende Autotür, umherfliegende Blätter … vielleicht ein Vogel?«

»Nein, ich kann mich an nichts Bestimmtes erinnern. Ich bin einfach gegangen und habe dabei Musik gehört, als ich es gespürt habe. Ich weiß nicht, wie ich es beschreiben soll. Es war wie …« Ich schlucke, und mein Herz beginnt zu rasen, als ich mich daran erinnere. »Es war so wie jenes Mal in der Küche, als ich ihn eine Sekunde, bevor er mich ergriff, spürte. Das gleiche Gefühl.«

Das schmale, intelligente Gesicht des Therapeuten nimmt einen besorgten Ausdruck an. »Wie oft geht ihnen das jetzt so?«

»Es war das dritte Mal diese Woche«, gebe ich zu, und meine Wangen erröten vor Verlegenheit, als er etwas auf seinen Notizblock schreibt. Ich hasse dieses Gefühl, nicht alles unter Kontrolle zu haben, das Wissen, dass mein Gehirn mir Streiche spielt. »Zum ersten Mal ist es im Supermarkt passiert, danach, als ich in die Klinik gegangen bin, und jetzt auf dem Parkplatz des Krankenhauses. Ich weiß nicht, warum das passiert. Ich dachte wirklich, dass es mir langsam besser geht. Ich hatte in den letzten zwei Wochen nur eine kleine Panikattacke, und nach dem Frühstück gestern hatte ich richtig Hoffnung geschöpft. Das ergibt keinen Sinn.«

»Unsere Köpfe brauchen Zeit, um zu heilen, Sara, genau wie unsere Körper. Manchmal hat man einen Rückfall, und manchmal schlägt die Krankheit eine andere Richtung ein. Sie wissen das genauso gut wie ich.« Er schreibt erneut etwas auf seinen Block, bevor er hochschaut. »Haben Sie darüber nachgedacht, noch einmal mit dem FBI zu sprechen?

»Nein, die werden denken, dass ich verrückt geworden bin.«

Nach meinem ersten paranoiden Anfall vor einem Monat habe ich mit Agent Ryson gesprochen, und er hat mir erklärt, dass Interpol gerade die Spur des Mörders meines Mannes in Südafrika verfolgt. Trotzdem hat er mir vorsichtshalber einen Personen-schutz zugeteilt. Nachdem er mir einige Tage lang gefolgt war, war er sicher, dass es nichts Bedrohliches gibt, und Agent Ryson hat die Beamten wieder abge-zogen und dabei Entschuldigungen wie »begrenzte Mittel und Personal« gemurmelt. Er hat mir nicht vorgeworfen, dass ich paranoid sei, aber ich weiß, dass er es insgeheim getan hat.

»Weil der Mann, vor dem sie sich fürchten, weit weg ist«, sagt Dr. Evans, und ich nicke.

»Ja. Er ist weg und hat keinen Grund zurück-zukommen.«

»Gut. Rational gesehen wissen Sie das. Wir werden daran arbeiten, auch Ihr Unterbewusstsein davon zu überzeugen. Zuerst müssen Sie allerdings herausfinden, was diese Paranoia auslöst, damit Sie lernen können, wie Sie diese Auslöser erkennen und Ihre Reaktion auf sie kontrollieren. Das nächste Mal, wenn es geschieht, achten Sie darauf, was Sie gerade tun und wie Sie sich fühlen, wenn diese Reaktion beginnt. Befinden Sie sich in der Öffentlichkeit oder sind Sie allein? Ist es ruhig oder laut? Sind Sie drin oder draußen?«

»Okay, ich werde sicherstellen, alles aufzuschreiben, während ich ausflippe und mein Pfefferspray umklammere.«

Dr. Evans lächelt. » Ich habe Vertrauen in Sie, Sara. Sie haben bereits riesige Fortschritte gemacht. Sie können wieder zu Ihrer Küchenspüle gehen, stimmt's?«

»Ja, aber ich kann den Wasserhahn immer noch nicht anfassen«, antworte ich, und meine Hände auf meinem Schoß spannen sich an. »Das macht es irgendwie sinnlos.«

Meine Küchenspüle ist einer der vielen Gründe, aus denen ich das Haus verkaufe. Zuerst konnte ich nicht einmal in die Küche gehen, aber nach Monaten intensiver Therapie bin ich an einem Punkt, an dem ich mich der Spüle ohne eine Panikattacke nähern kann – auch wenn ich das Wasser noch nicht anstellen kann.

»Ein Schritt nach dem anderen «, sagt Dr. Evans. »Eines Tages werden Sie auch den Wasserhahn anstellen können. Außer natürlich, sie verkaufen das Haus vorher. Haben Sie das immer noch vor?«

»Ja, mein Makler veranstaltet sogar in einigen Tagen einen Tag der offenen Tür.«

»Okay, gut.« Er lächelt mich erneut an und legt seinen Notizblock zur Seite. »Unsere Sitzung ist für heute vorbei, und ich werde für die nächsten eineinhalb Wochen im Urlaub sein, aber wir sehen uns danach wieder. In der Zwischenzeit machen Sie bitte einfach mit dem weiter, was Sie tun, und schreiben Sie detailliert auf, wenn Sie weitere paranoide Anfälle haben. Wir werden das und Ihre Gefühle, was den Hausverkauf betrifft, in der nächsten Sitzung besprechen, okay?«

»Hört sich gut an.« Ich stehe auf und schüttele die Hand des Arztes. »Wir sehen uns. Genießen Sie ihren Urlaub.«

Ich verlasse seine Praxis, gehe zu meinem Auto und zwinge meine Hand, an meiner Seite herunterzuhängen und nicht das Pfefferspray in meiner Tasche zu umklammern.

———

IN DIESER NACHT schlafe ich gut, und in der darauffolgenden auch. Der Grund dafür ist, dass ich so viel arbeite, dass ich abends einfach buchstäblich umfalle. Wenn ich so müde bin, kann ich überall schlafen, sogar in meinem großen, von Eichen umgebenen Haus. Das FBI hat nicht herausbekommen, wie der Deserteur in mein Haus eindringen konnte, ohne den Alarm auszulösen oder Schlösser zu knacken, also fühle ich mich hier so sicher, als würde ich auf der Straße schlafen, auch wenn ich mein Sicherheitssystem aufgerüstet habe.

Es ist die dritte Nacht, in der ich diese Albträume habe. Ich weiß nicht, ob sie kommen, weil ich früher am gleichen Tag einen paranoiden Anfall hatte – dieses Mal auf einer belebten Straße neben einem Coffeeshop – oder weil ich nur zwölf Stunden gearbeitet habe, aber in dieser Nacht träume ich von *ihm*.

Wie immer ist sein Gesicht in meinem Kopf unscharf; ich kann nur seine grauen Augen erkennen und die Narbe, die seine linke Augenbraue teilt. Diese Augen halten mich fest, während er ein Messer an meine Kehle hält, und sein Blick ist genauso schneidend und grausam wie die Klinge. Dann taucht George auch dort auf und kommt mit braunen, leeren Augen auf mich zu.

»Tu das nicht«, flüstere ich, aber George kommt näher, und ich sehe, dass Blut aus seiner Stirn läuft. Eine kleine, saubere Wunde, nichts wie das klaffende Loch, das die echte Kugel in seinem Kopf hinterlassen hatte, und obwohl ein Teil von mir weiß, dass ich träume, schluchze und zittere ich immer noch, als der Mann mit den grauen Augen mich hochhebt und mich zur Spüle trägt.

»Bitte nicht«, flehe ich den Mann an, aber er ist unerbittlich und hält meinen Kopf über die Spüle, während George weiterhin mit hassverzerrtem Gesicht auf mich zu schlurft.

»Das ist für das, was du mir angetan hast«, sagt

mein Ehemann und dreht den Wasserhahn auf. »Für alles, was du getan hast.«

Ich wache schreiend und keuchend auf, und meine Bettwäsche ist schweißnass. Als ich mich ein wenig beruhigt habe, gehe ich nach unten und mache mir eine Tasse koffeinfreien Tee, wobei ich das Wasser aus dem Filter des Kühlschranks benutze. Während ich meinen Tee trinke, starre ich die Uhr der Mikrowelle an, und die blinkenden grünen Nummern informieren mich darüber, dass es noch nicht einmal drei Uhr ist – also viel zu früh, um aufzustehen, wenn ich die extralange Schicht, die mir heute bevorsteht, durchhalten möchte. Am Nachmittag wartet eine Operation auf mich, und dafür muss ich fit sein, da ich ansonsten meine Patienten in Gefahr bringe.

Ich überlege einen Moment lang hin und her, bevor ich schließlich aufstehe und mir Zolpidem aus dem Medizinschrank hole. Ich halbiere eine Tablette, spüle sie mit meinem restlichen Tee herunter und gehe wieder nach oben.

So sehr ich es auch hasse, Tabletten zu nehmen, heute habe ich keine andere Wahl. Ich hoffe nur, dass ich nicht wieder von dem Deserteur träumen werde. Nicht, weil ich Angst vor diesem Albtraum mit dem Waterboarding habe – ich habe ihn nie zweimal in der gleichen Nacht –, sondern weil er mich in meinen Träumen nicht immer foltert.

Manchmal fickt er mich, und ich ihn.

9

———

eter

ICH STEHE über sie gebeugt an ihrem Bett und betrachte sie im Schlaf. Ich gehe ein Risiko dabei ein, hierherzukommen, anstatt sie über die Kameras zu beobachten, die meine Männer in ihrem ganzen Haus installiert haben, aber das Zolpidem sollte verhindern, dass sie aufwacht. Trotzdem sehe ich mich vor, kein Geräusch zu machen. Sara reagiert auf meine Gegenwart empfindlich, kann meine Nähe auf eine eigenartige Weise spüren. Deshalb trägt sie jetzt auch ein Pfefferspray bei sich und sieht aus wie ein gejagtes Reh, jedes Mal, wenn ich in ihre Nähe komme.

Unterbewusst weiß sie, dass ich zurückgekommen bin. Sie spürt, dass ich hinter ihr her bin.

Ich weiß immer noch nicht, wieso ich das tue, aber

95

ich habe es aufgegeben, meine Besessenheit zu analysieren. Ich habe versucht, ihr fernzubleiben, mich auf meine Mission zu konzentrieren, aber selbst als ich alle bis auf einen Namen meiner Liste gefunden und ausgelöscht hatte, dachte ich immer noch an Sara, daran, wie sie am Tag der Beerdigung ausgesehen hat, und erinnere mich an den Schmerz in ihren warmen, braunen Augen.

Ich erinnere mich daran, wie sie ihre Lippen um meine Finger gelegt und mich gebeten hat, zu bleiben.

Nichts an meiner Besessenheit von ihr ist normal. Ich bin gesund genug, um das zuzugeben. Sie ist die Frau eines Mannes, den ich getötet habe, eine Frau, die ich gefoltert habe wie einst verdächtige Terroristen. Ich sollte nichts für sie fühlen, genauso, wie ich nichts für meine anderen Opfer gefühlt habe, aber ich kann sie mir nicht aus dem Kopf schlagen.

Ich will sie. Das ist völlig irrational und auf so vielen Ebenen völlig falsch, aber ich will sie. Ich will diese weichen Lippen schmecken und die Weichheit ihrer blassen Haut spüren, will meine Finger in ihrem dicken, braunen Haar vergraben und ihren Geruch einatmen. Ich will, dass sie mich anbettelt, sie zu ficken, und dann will ich sie festhalten und genau das tun, immer wieder.

Ich will die Wunden heilen, die ich ihr zugefügt habe, und sie dazu bringen, dass sie sich genauso stark nach mir sehnt wie ich mich nach ihr.

Sie schläft weiter, während ich sie betrachte, und meine Finger wollen sie berühren, ihre Haut fühlen, auch wenn es nur für einen kurzen Augenblick ist. Aber wenn ich das täte, könnte sie aufwachen, und ich bin noch nicht bereit dafür.

Wenn Sara mich das nächste Mal sieht, soll es anders sein.

Ich möchte, dass sie mich als etwas anderes kennenlernt, nicht als ihren Angreifer.

10

S*ara*

IN DEN NÄCHSTEN Tagen verstärkt sich meine Paranoia. Ich fühle mich ständig so, als würde ich beobachtet werden. Selbst wenn ich allein zu Hause bin, alle Vorhänge zugezogen und alle Türen geschlossen habe, fühle ich unsichtbare Blicke auf mir. Ich habe es mir angewöhnt, mit meinem Pfefferspray unter dem Kissen zu schlafen, und nehme es sogar mit ins Badezimmer, aber das reicht nicht.

Ich fühle mich nirgendwo in Sicherheit.

Donnerstag breche ich schließlich zusammen und rufe Agent Ryson an.

»Dr. Cobakis.« Er hört sich vorsichtig und gleichzeitig überrascht an. »Wie kann ich Ihnen helfen?«

»Ich würde gern mit Ihnen reden«, antworte ich. »Persönlich, wenn das möglich ist.«

»Ach? Worüber?«

»Das würde ich lieber nicht am Telefon besprechen.«

»Ich verstehe.« Einen kurzen Augenblick lang herrscht Stille. »In Ordnung. Ich denke, dass ich mich heute Nachmittag auf einen schnellen Kaffee mit Ihnen treffen kann. Wäre Ihnen das recht?«

Ich schaue auf meinen Arbeitsplan auf meinem Laptop. »Ja. Könnten wir uns im Snacktime Café beim Krankenhaus treffen? So gegen drei?«

»Ich werde dort sein.«

———

AM ENDE WERDE ich von einem Patienten aufgehalten, und es ist schon zehn nach drei, als ich in das Café eile.

»Ich wollte gerade gehen«, meint Ryson und steht von seinem Stuhl an einem kleinen Ecktisch auf.

»Es tut mir wirklich leid.« Außer Atem lasse ich mich auf den Stuhl ihm gegenüber fallen. »Ich verspreche, ich mache es kurz.«

Ryson setzt sich wieder hin. Die Bedienung kommt, und wir geben unsere Bestellung auf: einen Espresso für ihn und eine Tasse entkoffeinierten Kaffee für mich. Meine Nerven brauchen heute kein zusätzliches Koffein.

»In Ordnung«, meint er, als die Bedienung wieder gegangen ist. »Schießen Sie los.«

»Ich muss mehr über diesen Deserteur wissen«, komme ich sofort auf den Punkt. »Wer ist er? Warum war er hinter George her?«

Rysons buschige Augenbrauen ziehen sich zusammen. »Sie wissen, dass diese Informationen geheim sind.«

»Das weiß ich, aber ich weiß auch, dass dieser Mann mich gewaterboarded, unter Drogen gesetzt und meinen Ehemann getötet hat«, sage ich ruhig. »Und Sie wussten, dass er kommen würde, und haben sich nicht die Mühe gemacht, mich darüber zu informieren. Das sind die Dinge, die ich weiß – eigentlich die einzigen Dinge, die ich weiß. Wenn ich mehr wüsste – sagen wir seinen Namen und seinen Beweggrund –, könnte es mir dabei helfen, zu verstehen, was geschehen ist, und darüber hinwegzukommen. Ansonsten ist es wie eine offene Wunde oder vielleicht wie eine Blase, die nicht aufgestochen wird. Sie wächst einfach vor sich hin und ist immer in meinem Kopf. Irgendwann kann ich sie vielleicht nicht mehr aufhalten, und die Blase könnte von alleine aufplatzen. Verstehen Sie mein Dilemma?«

Rysons Kiefer spannt sich an. »Drohen Sie uns nicht, Sara. Sie würden das Ergebnis nicht mögen.«

»Für Sie Dr. Cobakis, Agent Ryson.« Ich erwidere seinen harten, wütenden Blick. »Und ich mag das Ergebnis schon jetzt nicht. Georges Kollegen von der Zeitung würden es auch nicht mögen – sollten sie Wind davon bekommen. Deshalb haben Sie mir von dem Deserteur erzählt, stimmt's? Damit ich meinen Mund halte und bei diesem ganzen ›Er starb friedlich in seinem Schlaf‹-Scheiß mitspiele. Sie wussten, Georges Kollegen hätten diesen vermeintlichen Schlag der Mafia gründlich untersucht, und das wollten Sie nicht. Das wollen Sie immer noch nicht, habe ich recht?«

Er starrt mich wütend an, und ich kann seinen inneren Kampf sehen. Vertrauliche Informationen zu teilen und vielleicht in Schwierigkeiten geraten – oder sie nicht teilen und auf jeden Fall in Schwierigkeiten geraten? Sein Selbsterhaltungstrieb muss gewinnen, denn er sagt grimmig: »In Ordnung. Was möchten Sie wissen?«

»Fangen wir bei seinem Namen und seiner Identität an.«

»Ryson sieht sich um und beugt sich weiter nach vorn. »Er hat viele Namen, aber wir glauben, dass sein wirklicher Name Peter Sokolov ist.« Er spricht mit extrem leiser Stimme, obwohl die Tische um uns herum leer sind. »Unseren Aufzeichnungen nach kommt er ursprünglich aus einer kleinen Stadt bei Moskau, in Russland.«

Das erklärt den Akzent. »Was ist sein Hintergrund? Wieso ist er flüchtig?«

Ryson lehnt sich nach hinten. »Ich kenne die Antwort auf die letzte Frage nicht. Ich habe keine ausreichende Sicherheitsfreigabe.« Er schweigt, als sich die Bedienung mit unseren Getränken nähert. Nachdem sie gegangen ist, fährt er fort: »Was ich Ihnen sagen kann, ist, dass er ein Spatsnaz, ein Teil der russischen Spezialeinheiten war, bevor er ein Deserteur wurde. Sein Job war es, jeden aufzuspüren und zu verhören, der eine Bedrohung für die russische Sicherheit darstellte – Terroristen, Aufständische aus den Republiken der ehemaligen Sowjetunion, Spione usw. Man sagt, dass er sehr gut darin war. Vor fünf Jahren hat er auf einmal die Seiten gewechselt und damit begonnen, für die schlimmsten Individuen der kriminellen Unterwelt zu arbeiten – Diktatoren, die wegen Kriegsverbrechen verurteilt waren, Bosse mexikanischer Drogenkartelle, illegale Waffendealer … Während dieser Zeit hat er sich eine Liste mit Namen ausgedacht – Menschen, von denen er glaubte, sie hätten ihm irgendwie Schaden zugefügt – und seitdem tötet er sie systematisch.«

Meine Hand zittert, als ich nach meiner Kaffeetasse greife. »Und George war auf dieser Liste?«

Ryson nickt und trinkt seinen Espresso in einem großen Schluck aus. Er stellt seine Tasse ab und sagt: »Es tut mir leid, Dr. Cobakis. Ich habe keine Ahnung, was Ihr Ehemann oder die anderen getan haben, um auf dieser Liste zu enden. Ich verstehe, dass Sie gern mehr Antworten hätten, und glauben Sie mir, die hätten wir auch gern, aber ein großer Teil von Sokolovs Akte ist zensiert.« Er hält inne, um die Bedienung erneut vorbeigehen zu lassen, und fügt danach leise hinzu: »Sie müssen diesen Mann vergessen, für Ihre Sicherheit und unsere.« Sie möchten nicht noch einmal seine Aufmerksamkeit auf sich ziehen, glauben Sie mir.«

Ich nicke und habe einen Knoten im Magen. Ich

weiß nicht, warum ich dachte, dass es besser wäre, einige Dinge über den Mann zu wissen, der mich in meinen Träumen verfolgt, als weiterhin im Dunklen zu tappen. Wenn überhaupt bin ich jetzt noch besorgter, und meine Hände und Füße sind vor Angst ganz eisig.

»Sind Sie sicher, dass er von hier verschwunden ist?«, frage ich den Beamten, als er aufsteht. »Sind Sie sicher, dass er nicht mehr in der Nähe ist?«

»Niemand kann sich irgendeiner Sache sicher sein, was diesen Psychopathen betrifft, aber auf jeden Fall hat er vor etwas über sechs Wochen eine andere Person von seiner Liste getötet – in Südafrika«, antwortet Ryson düster. »Und davor zwei weitere in Kanada, trotz unserer besten Bemühungen, sie zu schützen. Also ja, soweit wir wissen, befindet er sich weit entfernt vom Territorium der USA.«

Ich starre ihn einfach nur an, weil ich vor Entsetzen nichts sagen kann. Drei weitere Opfer in den letzten sechs Monaten. Drei weitere verlorene Leben, während ich gegen Albträume und Paranoia angekämpft habe.

»Viel Glück, Dr. Cobakis«, meint Ryson nicht unfreundlich und legt einige Dollarscheine auf den Tisch. »Die Zeit heilt wirklich alle Wunden, und eines Tages werden Sie auch über das hier hinweg sein. Da bin ich mir sicher.«

»Danke«, sage ich mit erstickter Stimme, aber er geht bereits weg, und seine gedrungene Gestalt verschwindet durch die Glastür des Cafés.

—

IN DIESER NACHT träume ich erneut von Peter Sokolovs Überfall, und der Albtraum nimmt die Wende, vor der ich mich am meisten fürchte. Anstatt mich unter den Wasserhahn zu halten, hält er mich unter sich auf dem Bett fest, und seine Stahlfinger fesseln meine Handgelenke. Ich spüre, wie er sich in mir bewegt, wie lang und dick sein Schwanz ist, als er in meinen Körper eindringt, und die Hitze pocht unter meiner Haut, meine Nippel sind hart und schmerzen, als sie gegen seine muskulöse Brust reiben.

»Bitte«, bettele ich und umschlinge seine Hüften mit meinen Beinen, während seine metallischen Augen in meine blicken. »Bitte härter. Ich brauche dich.«

Ich bin nass durch dieses Bedürfnis; es brennt in mir, heiß und dunkel, und er weiß das. Er fühlt es. Ich kann es in der Kälte seines silbernen Blickes sehen, in den grausamen Linien seines sinnlichen Mundes. Seine Finger festigen ihren Griff um meine Handgelenke, schneiden wie Kabelbinder in meine Haut, und sein Schwanz verwandelt sich in ein Messer, reißt mich auf und lässt mich bluten.

»Härter«, bettele ich, und meine Hüften heben sich seinen messerartigen Stößen entgegen. »Geh nicht. Nimm mich härter.«

Genau das tut er, jeder Stoß zerreißt mich, und ich schreie vor Schmerzen und abartigem Genuss, vor Erleichterung und süßer Qual.

Ich schreie, während ich in seinen Armen sterbe, und es ist der beste Tod, den ich mir vorstellen kann.

———

ICH WACHE mit einem nassen und pochenden Geschlecht auf, und mein Magen zieht sich vor Übelkeit zusammen. Von allen Streichen, die mir mein Gehirn spielt, sind diese perversen Träume die schlimmsten. Ich kann die Panikattacken und die Paranoia verstehen – sie sind eine natürliche Folge dessen, was ich durchgemacht habe –, aber es ist nichts Natürliches an den sexuellen Tendenzen dieser Albträume. Allein der Gedanke an sie macht mich vor Scham körperlich krank.

Ich stehe auf, ziehe mir einen Bademantel über den Schlafanzug und gehe nach unten in die Küche. Ich atme ungleichmäßig, und mein Herz rast, aber dieses Mal nicht aus Angst. Ich bin errötet und feucht, und mein Körper schmerzt vor frustrierter Erregung.

Ich bin während dieses Traumes fast gekommen. Noch einige Sekunden mehr, und der Orgasmus hätte mich überrollt – so wie bereits zweimal zuvor in dieser Woche.

Der Ekel vor mir selbst liegt wie eine schwerer Stein in meinem Magen, als ich mir meinen entkoffeinierten Tee aufbrühe. Was für eine abartige Person hat schon erotische Träume mit dem Mörder ihres Ehemanns? Wie krank muss man sein, um es zu genießen, in den Armen des besagten Mörders zu sterben?

Ich habe darüber nachgedacht, mit Dr. Evans über diese Träume zu sprechen, aber wann immer ich versuche, dieses Thema in unseren Sitzungen anzusprechen, mache ich dicht. Ich bringe es einfach nicht fertig, diese Worte auszusprechen. Diese Träume auszusprechen würde ihnen eine Substanz geben, sie von einem vernebelten Produkt meines schlafenden Unterbewusstseins in etwas verwandeln, über was ich nachdenke und rede, wenn ich wach bin, und das will ich nicht.

Ich weiß sowieso, was mein Therapeut mir sagen würde. Er würde sagen, dass ich eine junge, gesunde Frau bin, die seit Langem keinen Sex mehr gehabt hat, und dass es normal ist, diese Triebe zu verspüren. Dass es meine Schuldgefühle und mein Selbsthass sind, die meine sexuellen Fantasien in etwas Dunkles und Anrüchiges verwandeln, und dass die Träume nicht bedeuten, dass ich mich wirklich zu dem Mann hingezogen fühle, der mich gefoltert und George umgebracht hat.

Dr. Evans würde versuchen, meine Schuld- und Schamgefühle zu lindern, und das ist nichts, was ich verdient habe.

Als der Tee fertig ist, trage ich ihn zum Küchentisch und setze mich hin. Ich will gerade den ersten Schluck trinken, als ich wieder das Gefühl bekomme, als würde ich beobachtet. Rational weiß ich, dass ich allein bin, aber mein Herz beginnt zu rasen, und meine Handflächen werden schweißnass.

Mein Pfefferspray ist oben, also stehe ich so ruhig ich kann auf und gehe zu dem Messerblock auf dem

Tresen. Ich nehme das größte und schärfste Messer heraus und bringe es mit zum Küchentisch. Ich weiß, dass es gegen jemanden wie Peter Sokolov nutzlos wäre, aber es ist besser als nichts. Nach einigen tiefen Atemzügen habe ich mich genug beruhigt, um meinen Tee trinken zu können, aber dieses beunruhigende Gefühl unsichtbarer Augen verschwindet nicht.

Wenn sich das Haus nicht bald verkauft, ziehe ich einfach aus, beschließe ich, als ich zurück ins Bett gehe.

Ich kann mir eine Zweitwohnung leisten, und selbst ein übles Studio wäre besser als das hier.

S*ara*

»Na, wie ist der Tag der offenen Tür gestern gelaufen?«, ruft Marsha über die Musik hinweg, als wir auf unsere vierte Runde Drinks an der Bar warten.

»Der Makler hat gesagt, dass er gut war«, schreie ich zurück und versuche, nicht zu nuscheln. Ich habe das seit Ewigkeiten nicht mehr getan, und der Alkohol steigt mir schnell zu Kopf. »Mal sehen, ob Angebote kommen werden.«

»Ich kann gar nicht glauben, dass dir ein Haus gehört und du es verkaufst«, sagt Tonya, als der nächste Song beginnt, und die Lautstärke von betäubend laut auf nur noch laut sinkt. »Ich würde mir eines Tages so gern ein Haus kaufen, aber es wird ewig dauern, bis ich genug gespart haben werde.«

»Na ja, wenn du auch die Hälfte deines Gehalts für Klamotten und Schuhe ausgibst«, erwidert Andy grinsend, und ihre roten Locken wippen, als sie ihre kurvige Hüfte im Takte der Musik bewegt. »Außerdem ist Sara eine Ärztin. Sie verdient das dicke Geld, auch wenn sie sich nicht so abgehoben benimmt wie der Rest von ihnen.«

Tonya lacht, und ihre Ohrringe wackeln. »Das stimmt. Du siehst so jung aus, Sara, dass ich immer vergesse, dass du ein echter Arzt bist.«

»Sie *ist* jung«, meint Marsha, bevor ich antworten kann. »Sie ist unser persönlicher kleiner Doogie Howser.«

»Ey, halt den Mund.« Ich verpasse Marsha eine mit meinem Ellenbogen, und meine Wangen brennen vor Verlegenheit, als ich sehe, dass mich der tätowierte Barkeeper angrinst. Er mixt gerade unsere Lemon Drops mit geübten Bewegungen, und seine braunen Augen blicken mich mit unverkennbarem Interesse an.

»Bitte, Ladys«, sagt er, als er uns unsere Getränke zuschiebt, und Andy zwinkert mir zu, als sie mir eines der Gläser reicht.

»Prost«, sagt sie, und wir kippen die Shots herunter, bevor wir wieder zur Tanzfläche gehen, auf der bereits der nächste Song aus den Lautsprechern zu dröhnen beginnt.

Nach der beschissenen Woche, die ich hatte, wollte ich diesen Freitag eigentlich nicht ausgehen, aber in letzter Minute habe ich dann gedacht, dass ausgehen und sich betrinken besser sein würde, als früh einzuschlafen und einen weiteren abartigen erotischen Traum zu riskieren. Zum Glück habe ich ein Paar niedliche, silberfarbene Ballerinas in meinem Spind auf der Arbeit, und Tonya hat mir ein kurzes, schwarzes Kleid geliehen, das mir erstaunlich gut passt.

»H&M, Baby«, hatte sie stolz geantwortet, als ich von ihr wissen wollte, woher sie das Kleid hat, und ich habe mir im Hinterkopf abgespeichert, bei dem trendigen Laden vorbeizuschauen und mir etwas Ähnliches zu kaufen – für den Fall, dass ich jemals in Versuchung geführt werden sollte, diese verrückte Aktion noch einmal zu wiederholen.

Wir haben mit ein paar Drinks bei Patty's angefangen und uns danach von einem Taxi zu dem Klub bringen lassen, von dem Tonya erzählt hatte. Genau wie sie gesagt hatte, konnte uns der Promoter ohne anzustehen hereinlassen, und wir haben die letzten zwei Stunden durchgetanzt. Ich schwitze, meine Füße tun weh, und ich werde wahrscheinlich morgen den Kater aller Kater haben, aber so viel Spaß hatte ich seit … na ja, Jahren nicht mehr.

Vielleicht seit mehr als fünf Jahren.

Die Gäste des Klubs sind gemischt, angefangen bei Studenten bis hin zu heißen Mittvierzigern wie Marsha, aber die Mehrheit sieht aus, als sei sie genau wie ich Ende zwanzig. Der DJ ist hervorragend, mischt die besten neuesten Hits mit Hip-Hop-Klassikern, und ich singe mit, während wir tanzen, schmettere meine Lieblingslieder hingebungsvoll mit. Ich habe Musik und Tanz schon immer geliebt – in der

Grund- und Mittelschule habe ich Ballett getanzt, und auf der Uni habe ich Salsaunterricht gehabt – und mit meinem leichten Schwips fühle ich mich sexy und sorgenfrei, endlich einmal wie jede andere junge Frau in dem Klub. Heute bin ich nicht die ernsthafte Studentin, die überarbeitete Ärztin, die pflichtbewusste Tochter oder die perfekte Ehefrau. Ich bin nicht einmal die Witwe mit Paranoia und kranken Träumen.

Heute Nacht bin ich einfach nur ich.

Zuerst tanzen wir vier allein, bevor einige Jungs zu uns kommen und Tonya und Marsha antanzen. Ich werde von Andy mit zur Toilette geschleift, und als wir zurückkommen, flirten Tonya und Marsha heftig mit den Jungen.

»Nimmst du noch einen Drink?«, schreit Andy über die Musik, und ich nicke und folge ihr zur Bar. Der Raum um mich herum dreht sich, also denke ich mir, dass ich wohl nur ein Wasser nehmen werde.

In der letzten Stunde ist der Klub voller geworden, die Tanzfläche erstreckt sich mittlerweile bis zur Bar und dem Loungebereich, und als eine Gruppe lachender Frauen sich vor mich schiebt, verliere ich Andy aus den Augen. Ich mache mir nicht wirklich Sorgen – ich kann sie ja an der Bar treffen –, also gehe ich um die Gruppe herum, um mich nicht hindurchdrängeln zu müssen.

Ich bin fast an der Bar, als sich starke Finger um meinen Oberarm legen, und eine tiefe, männliche Stimme in mein Ohr flüstert: »Tanz mit mir, Sara.«

Ich versteinere, und das Blut in meinen Adern erstarrt.

Ich kenne diese Stimme, diesen leichten russischen Akzent.

Langsam drehe ich meinen Kopf um und treffe auf diese metallischen Augen, die mich in meinen Träumen verfolgen.

Peter Sokolov steht vor mir, und sein gemeißelter Mund lächelt leicht.

12

SIE SCHWANKT, ihr Gesicht ist kreidebleich, und ich ergreife ihren anderen Arm, um ihr Halt zu geben. Sie weiß ganz offensichtlich, wer ich bin, erkennt mich wieder.

»Nicht schreien«, sage ich. »Ich bin nicht hier, um dir wehzutun.«

Ihre braunen Augen sehen wild aus, und ich weiß, dass sie nicht wirklich versteht, was ich sage. Alles, was sie gerade erblickt, ist eine tödliche Bedrohung, und sie reagiert entsprechend. In einigen wenigen Sekunden wird sie entweder in Ohnmacht fallen oder hysterisch werden, und beides wäre nicht gut.

»Sara.« Ich benutze meine harte Stimme. »Ich bin nicht hier, um irgendjemandem wehzutun, aber ich werde es tun, wenn ich muss. Verstehst du mich? Wenn du irgendetwas tust, was Aufmerksamkeit auf uns lenkt, werden Menschen sterben.«

Die verständnislose Panik auf ihrem Gesicht lässt leicht nach und wird von einer rationaleren Angst ersetzt, die allerdings nicht weniger intensiv ist. Ich dringe zu ihr durch.

Es hilft auch, dass ich nicht bluffe.

»W–was wollen Sie?« Trotz des Lipgloss, den sie heute Abend trägt, sind ihre zitternden Lippen blass. »Warum sind Sie hier?«

»Ich wollte dich sehen«, antworte ich und ziehe sie mit mir durch die Menge, um mich von den Kameras zu entfernen, die rund um die Bar angebracht sind. Saras nackte Arme in meinem Griff sind angespannt, ihre Haut fühlt sich kalt an, aber wie ich erwartet hatte, schreit sie nicht.

Nach allem, was ich über sie weiß, würde die kleine Ärztin lieber sterben, als einen Haufen Fremder in Gefahr zu bringen.

»Tanz mit mir«, wiederhole ich, als ich sie dort habe, wo ich möchte – neben einer Wand im schummrig beleuchteten Teil der Tanzfläche, wo die Massen einen menschlichen Schild um uns formen. Damit sie meiner Bitte besser nachkommen kann, lasse ich ihre Arme los und ergreife ihre Hüften, wobei ich darauf achte, sie ganz sanft anzufassen.

Ihr Körper ist so steif wie ein Eisblock, als ich sie so eng bei mir halte, aber für jeden um uns herum sehen wir wie jedes andere Paar aus, das sich zur Musik bewegt. Diese Illusion wird dadurch verstärkt, dass sie ihre Hände hebt, und ihre Handflächen auf meiner Brust ablegt. Sie versucht, mich wegzuschieben, aber sie ist zu entsetzt, um besonders viel Stärke in diese Bewegung zu legen. Nicht, dass es helfen würde, wenn sie mit ihrer *ganzen* Kraft zudrücken würde.

Ich kann die meisten Männer mit minimalem Aufwand überwältigen, ganz zu schweigen von Frauen, die so leicht sind wie sie.

»Hab keine Angst«, flüstere ich und schaue ihr dabei in die Augen. Selbst auf dieser überfüllten Tanzfläche kann ich ihren Duft riechen, der zart und blumig ist, und mein Körper reagiert auf ihre Nähe damit, dass sich mein Schwanz versteift, als ich ihre schlanke Taille zwischen meinen Handflächen spüre. Ich will sie näher an mich heranziehen, ihren Körper an meinem spüren, aber ich zwinge mich dazu, einen kleinen Abstand einzuhalten. Ich will sie nicht durch die Intensität meines Verlangens verschrecken. Allerdings sehen Saras Augen wie die eines in einer Falle gefangenen Tieres aus, sind vor Angst und Verzweiflung völlig blind. Ich will sie hochnehmen und sie an meine Brust drücken, aber das würde sie nur noch mehr verschrecken. Es gibt nichts, was ich gerade tun kann, was ihr keine Angst einjagen würde; ich könnte sie bitten, mit mir Karaoke zu singen, und sie würde eine Panikattacke bekommen.

»Was wollen Sie von mir?« Sie atmet schnell und flach, als sie zu mir hochschaut. »Ich weiß nichts …«

»Ich weiß.« Ich achte darauf, dass meine Stimme

sanft ist. »Mach dir keine Sorgen Sara. Dieser Teil ist vorbei.«

Verwirrung verdrängt einen Teil des Entsetzens in ihren Augen. »Aber, warum sind Sie dann ...«

»Warum ich hier bin?«

Sie nickt vorsichtig.

»Ich bin mir nicht sicher«, antworte ich, und das ist die reine Wahrheit.

In den letzten fünfeinhalb Jahren hat Rache mein Leben regiert. Alles, was ich tat, diente dazu, dieses Ziel zu verfolgen, aber jetzt habe ich meine Liste fast abgearbeitet, und die Zukunft liegt dumpf und leer vor mir, der Weg, der mir bevorsteht, wird von einem düsteren Nebel verdeckt. Sobald ich die letzte Person getötet haben werde, die für den Tod meiner Familie verantwortlich ist, habe ich kein Ziel mehr. Meine Existenzgrundlage wird einfach verschwunden sein.

Das habe ich zumindest gedacht, bis ich sie getroffen und den Schmerz in ihren Rehaugen gesehen habe. Jetzt füllt *sie* meine Träume aus und verfolgt mich, wenn ich wach bin. Wenn ich an Sara denke, sehe ich nicht den zerfetzten Körper meines Sohnes und Tamilas blutiges Gesicht.

Ich sehe einzig und allein sie.

»Werden Sie mich umbringen?«

Sie versucht – erfolglos –, ihre Stimme ruhig zu halten. Trotzdem bewundere ich ihren Versuch, gelassen zu bleiben. Ich habe mich ihr an einem öffentlichen Ort genähert, damit sie sich sicherer fühlt, aber sie ist zu clever, um darauf hereinzufallen. Wenn sie ihr etwas über mich erzählt haben, muss sie wissen, dass ich ihr schneller den Hals umdrehe, als sie nach Hilfe rufen kann.

»Nein«, antworte ich und beuge mich dabei weiter nach vorn, da ein lauterer Song beginnt. »Ich werde dich nicht töten.«

»Was wollen Sie dann von mir?«

Sie zittert in meinen Armen, und etwas an dieser Tatsache fasziniert mich und stört mich gleichzeitig. Ich will nicht, dass sie Angst vor mir hat, aber gleichzeitig mag ich es, dass sie mir ausgeliefert ist. Ihre Angst spricht das Raubtier in mir an, verwandelt mein Verlangen nach ihr in etwas Dunkleres.

Sie ist eine gefangene Beute, weich und süß und meine, die ich verschlingen kann.

Ich beuge meinen Kopf nach unten, vergrabe meine Nase in ihrem gut riechenden Haar und flüstere ihr ins Ohr: »Triff mich morgen um zwölf in dem Starbucks in der Nähe deines Hauses, und dort werden wir reden. Ich werde dir alles erzählen, was du wissen möchtest.«

Ich ziehe mich zurück, und sie starrt mich mit riesigen Augen in ihrem herzförmigen Gesicht an. Ich weiß, was sie denkt, also beuge ich mich erneut nach vorn, bis mein Mund sich neben ihrem Ohr befindet.

»Wenn du das FBI kontaktierst, werden sie versuchen, dich vor mir zu verstecken. Genauso wie sie versucht haben, deinen Ehemann und die anderen auf meiner Liste zu verstecken. Sie werden dich entwurzeln, dich von deinen Eltern und deiner Karriere trennen, und das alles wird nichts bringen. Ich werde dich finden, egal, wohin du gehst, Sara … egal, was sie tun, um dich von mir fernzuhalten.« Meine Lippen fahren auf dem Rand ihres Ohres entlang, und ich spüre, wie ihre Atmung stockt. »Alternativ könnten sie dich als Köder nutzen wollen. Sollte das der Fall sein, sollten sie mir eine Falle stellen, werde ich das herausfinden, und unser nächstes Treffen wird nicht bei einem Kaffee sein.«

Sie erschaudert, und ich atme tief ein, nehme ein letztes Mal ihren zarten Duft in mich auf, bevor ich sie loslasse.

Ich trete zurück, verschwinde in der Menge und schreibe Anton eine Nachricht, dass sich die Mannschaft auf ihre Positionen begeben soll.

Ich muss sicherstellen, dass sie wohlbehalten nach Hause kommt, ohne von jemand anderem außer mir belästigt zu werden.

13

———

ICH WEIß NICHT, wie ich es nach Hause schaffe, aber irgendwie finde ich mich in meiner Dusche wieder, nackt und zitternd unter dem heißen Wasser. Ich habe nur eine vage Erinnerung daran, dass ich mich mit einer blöden Ausrede bei Andy entschuldigt habe und dann aus dem Klub gestolpert bin, um mir ein Taxi zu nehmen; der Rest des Wegs ist eine verschwommene Mischung aus geschockter Taubheit und Alkoholnebel.

Pater Sokolov hat mit mir gesprochen. Er hat mich *in seinen Armen gehalten.*

Der Mörder meines Ehemanns, der Mann, der mich gefoltert und mein Leben zerstört hat, hat mit mir getanzt.

Meine Knie geben nach, und ich sinke keuchend zu

Boden. Die Duschkabine um mich herum dreht sich, als mir schwindelig wird, und alles, was ich in dem Klub getrunken habe, damit droht, wieder hochzukommen.

Peter Sokolov war mit mir in dem Klub. Es war nicht mein Kopf, der mir Streiche gespielt hat, er war wirklich da.

Ich schlucke krampfhaft, als sich meine Übelkeit verschlimmert. Das Wasser läuft fast schmerzhaft heiß auf mich, aber ich kann nicht aufhören zu zittern.

Das Monster aus meinen Albträumen ist echt.

Es verfolgt mich.

Mein Schwindelgefühl verstärkt sich, und ich lege mich hin, rolle mich auf den Fliesen wie ein Embryo zusammen. Meine Haare liegen nass und dick auf meinem Gesicht, und mein Hals verengt sich, als Erinnerungen an jene Nacht hochkommen. Die ersten Tage nach dem Überfall habe ich mir meine Haare nicht gewaschen, weil ich das Gefühl nicht ertragen konnte, dass Wasser über meinen Kopf fließt, aber irgendwann hat mein Bedürfnis, sauber zu sein, die Angst besiegt.

Einatmen. Ausatmen. Langsam und gleichmäßig.

Langsam lässt das Gefühl, zu ersticken, nach, und übrig bleibt nur noch Elend. Ich fühle mich betrunken, mir ist schlecht, und ich muss meine ganze Kraft aufwenden, um mich hinzustellen und das Wasser abzustellen.

Warum ist er hier? Warum ist er zurückgekommen? Was will er von mir?

Diese Fragen gehen mir durch den Kopf, als ich

mich abtrockne, aber ich bin den Antworten nicht näher als ich es im Klub war. Mein Kopf fühlt sich schwammig an, und ich denke träge und langsam.

Ich wickele das Handtuch um meine nassen Haare, stolpere ins Schlafzimmer und falle auf mein Kingsize-Bett. Die Decke schaukelt hin und her, so als befände ich mich auf einem Schiff, und ich weiß, dass ich morgen einen üblen Kater haben werde. Ich bin seit der Uni nicht mehr so betrunken gewesen, und mein Körper weiß nicht, wie er damit umgehen soll.

Ich atme flach ein und aus, rolle mich auf der Seite zusammen und ziehe mir die Decke über die Brust. Der Alkohol zieht mich runter, aber ausnahmsweise kämpfe ich gegen die Verlockung des Schlafens an. Ich muss nachdenken, verstehen, was passiert ist, und herausfinden, was ich tun soll.

Der Mörder, der mich gewaterboarded hat, will sich morgen mit mir zum Kaffeetrinken treffen.

Das wäre komisch, wenn es nicht so schrecklich wäre. Ich verstehe nicht, was er will. Warum ist er in dem Klub zu mir gekommen? Warum will er mich noch einmal in aller Öffentlichkeit treffen? Er wird von allen Strafverfolgungsbehörden gesucht, das weiß er mit Sicherheit auch. Warum geht er dieses Risiko ein?

Außer … außer er denkt, dass es kein Risiko ist.

Vielleicht ist er arrogant genug, zu denken, dass er sich der Justiz für immer entziehen kann.

Wut steigt in mir auf und vertreibt einen Teil des Nebels in meinem Gehirn. Ich setze mich hin, kämpfe gegen eine erneute Übelkeitswelle an und greife nach dem Telefon auf dem Nachttisch. Es ist uralt, klobig und mit Kabelanschluss und im Zeitalter der Handys überflüssig, aber George hatte darauf bestanden, einen Festnetzanschluss im Haus zu haben.

»Man kann nie wissen«, hatte er auf meine Einwände geantwortet. »Handys können auch mal nicht funktionieren. Wenn es während eines Wintersturms einen Stromausfall gibt, was wirst du tun?«

Meine Augen fangen bei dieser Erinnerung an zu brennen, und ich ergreife das Telefon mit einer zitterigen Hand. Ich habe ein gutes Zahlengedächtnis, also wähle ich Agent Rysons Nummer aus dem Kopf, drücke einen Knopf nach dem anderen.

Ich habe fast alle Zahlen eingegeben, als ein plötzlicher Gedanke mich versteinern lässt.

Könnte Peter mein Telefon angezapft haben? Hat er das gemeint, als er gesagt hat, dass er es herausfinden würde, wenn sie ihm eine Falle stellen würden?

Eine weitere Möglichkeit kommt mir in den Sinn.

Könnte er mich gerade beobachten?

Meine Atmung wird schneller, und meine Haut kribbelt vor Adrenalin. Vor dem Klub hätte ich diesen Gedanken auf meine Paranoia geschoben, aber es ist keine Paranoia, wenn es echt ist.

Ich bin nicht verrückt, wenn es wirklich passiert.

Peter hat Ressourcen, hat Ryson gesagt. Könnte er Zugang zu Hightech-Überwachungsequipment haben?

Befinden sich in meinem Haus Kameras und Abhörgeräte?

Mein Herz hämmert, ich lege den Hörer auf die Gabel zurück und schnappe mir meine Decke, um sie über meine nackten Brüste zu ziehen. In meinem Schlafzimmer ziehe ich mir nur selten etwas an, selbst im Winter schlafe ich nackt unter der Decke. Ich war nie prüde – George hat es geliebt, wenn ich nackt umhergelaufen bin –, aber bei dem Gedanken, dass sein Mörder mich nackt gesehen haben könnte, fühle ich mich vergewaltigt und schmerzhaft ausgesetzt.

Außerdem erinnere ich mich dadurch an meine kranken Träume.

Nein. Nein, Nein, Nein. Keuchend wickele ich die Decke um mich und stolpere aus dem Bett zum Schrank, um mir ein T-Shirt und Unterwäsche zu holen. Ich kann nicht an diese Träume denken. Ich weigere mich. Ich bin betrunken; das ist der einzige Grund, warum mein Kopf diese Verbindung mit dem Monster hergestellt hat.

Aber er sieht nicht aus wie ein Monster. Selbst mit der Narbe durch die Augenbraue ist er ein umwerfend gutaussehender Mann, einer, auf den die Frauen stehen. Wenn ich ihn in dem Klub getroffen hätte, ohne zu wissen, wer er ist, hätte ich mit ihm getanzt.

Ich hätte seine starken Arme um mich und seinen harten Körper an mich geschmiegt haben wollen.

Meine Hände zittern, als ich die Unterwäsche anziehe, und ich fühle einen feuchten Fleck an der Stelle, an der mein Geschlecht die Baumwolle berührt.

Nein. Das passiert nicht gerade. Ich bin nicht erregt.

Während ich das erste T-Shirt anziehe, das ich

finde, taumele ich zum Bett zurück, lasse mich drauf-
fallen und wickele mich in die Decke. Das Zimmer
dreht sich, und mein Magen mit ihm. Ich atme gegen
die Übelkeit an und bemerke, dass meine Augenlider
schwer werden und meine Gedanken anfangen zu
wandern.

Ich beiße die Zähne zusammen und zwinge meine
Augen, geöffnet zu bleiben. Ich kann nicht einschlafen,
bis ich entschieden habe, was ich morgen machen soll.

Ich starre an die sich drehende Decke und gehe in
Gedanken meine Möglichkeiten durch.

Das Vernünftigste wäre, Ryson davon zu erzählen
und zu hoffen, dass er mich beschützen kann. Außer
wenn meine Vermutungen stimmen und Peter Sokolov
mich wirklich beobachtet, da er in diesem Fall wissen
wird, wenn ich das FBI kontaktiere, und ich überlebe
vielleicht nicht, bis die Beamten bei mir sind.

Natürlich würde ich nicht einmal unter dem Schutz
des FBIs überleben, sollte er beschließen, mich umzubringen. Die Menschen auf seiner Liste haben es definitiv nicht getan, und er hat mir gesagt, dass er mich
verfolgen würde.

Er hat geschworen, mich aufzuspüren, egal, wohin
ich gehe.

Aber vielleicht ist es trotzdem einen Versuch wert,
weil die Alternative ist, Peters grausames Spiel mitzuspielen. Ich weiß nicht, was er von mir will, aber was es
auch ist, es kann nichts Gutes sein. Vielleicht hat er
George so sehr gehasst, dass er jetzt seine Witwe
quälen möchte, oder vielleicht denkt er, auch wenn er

das abgestritten hat, dass ich etwas weiß – so wie die Schwester dieses armen Mannes, den er getötet hat.

In diesem Moment könnte er sich eine neue, exotische Foltermethode für mich überlegen, etwas besonders Schreckliches, was etwas mit Kaffee zu tun hat.

Meine Augenlider fallen erneut zu, und ich reibe mit meinen Händen über mein Gesicht und versuche, die Augen offen zu halten. Ich weiß, dass ich gerade nicht klar denke, aber ich kann nicht schlafen, ohne diese Entscheidung getroffen zu haben.

Rufe ich das FBI an oder nicht? Und wenn nicht, gehe ich dann wirklich zu diesem Starbucks?

Ein heftiger Schauer durchfährt mich, als ich mir vorstelle, mich mit dem Mörder meines Mannes auf einen Kaffee zu treffen. Ich glaube nicht, dass ich das tun kann. Allein bei dem Gedanken daran zieht sich alles in mir zusammen. Aber was sollte ich stattdessen tun? Mich den ganzen Tag im Bett verstecken, und dann wie versprochen für das Abendessen mit den Levinsons zu meinen Eltern fahren? So tun, als ob das Monster, das mein Leben zerstört hat, nicht hinter mir her sei?

Es ist der Gedanke an meine Eltern, der mich eine Entscheidung treffen lässt. Wenn ich allein wäre, könnte ich mich auf den fragwürdigen Schutz durch das FBI einlassen, aber ich kann meine Eltern nicht in Gefahr bringen. Ich kann sie nicht zwingen, ihr Haus und alle, die sie kennen, zu verlassen, nur weil die unwahrscheinliche Möglichkeit besteht, dass Ryson und seine Kollegen uns besser beschützen könnten, als sie es bei den anderen getan haben. Und meine Eltern zu verlassen kommt für mich nicht in Frage. Selbst wenn ihr Alter kein Problem wäre, könnte ich es nicht riskieren, dass Peter sie so befragt, wie er mich zu George befragt hat.

Es gibt nur eine Sache, die ich tun kann.

Ich muss mich morgen mit meinem Peiniger treffen und hoffen, dass er das, was er mit mir vorhat, nicht auf den Rest meiner Familie ausdehnt.

Als ich endlich meine Augen schließe und einschlafe, träume ich erneut von ihm. Aber diesmal foltert er mich nicht und fickt mich auch nicht.

Er sitzt neben meinem Bett und betrachtet mich mit einem warmen und eigenartig besitzergreifenden Blick.

14

ara

ALS ICH UM zwölf bei dem Starbucks ankomme, ist aus dem stechenden Schmerz in meinem Schädel ein dumpfes Pochen geworden, und mein Magen droht mir auch nicht mehr pausenlos damit, zu rebellieren. Trotzdem sind meine Handflächen vor Angst feucht, und meine Hände zittern so sehr, dass ich fast den Schlüssel fallen lasse, als ich aus dem Auto steige.

Als ich den Parkplatz überquere, fühle ich mich, als ginge ich zu meiner eigenen Hinrichtung. Die Angst wird mit jedem meiner schnellen Herzschläge durch mich gepumpt. Er könnte mich genau jetzt umbringen, mich einfach mit einem Präzisionsgewehr erschießen. Vielleicht hat er mich deshalb hierhergelockt: um mich an einem öffentlichen Ort zu ermorden und meinen Körper liegenzulassen, um alle zu terrorisieren.

Aber ich werde von keiner Kugel getroffen, und als ich den Coffeeshop betrete, erblicke ich ihn sofort. Er sitzt an einem der leeren Tische in der Ecke, und seine große Hand umfasst einen Pappbecher.

Als sich unsere Blicke treffen, zucke ich zusammen, so als hätte mir jemand mit einem Defibrillator einen Schock verpasst. Zum ersten Mal sehe ich ihn im Tageslicht, ohne Alkohol oder Drogen im Blut.

Und zum ersten Mal verstehe ich, wie gefährlich er wirklich ist.

Er hat sich in seinem Stuhl zurückgelehnt, seine langen, jeansbedeckten Beine sind ausgestreckt, und seine Knöchel unter dem Tisch überschlagen. Das ist eine entspannte Haltung, aber es gibt nichts Entspanntes an der dunklen Macht, die er in Wellen abgibt. Er ist nicht nur gefährlich; er ist tödlich. Ich sehe das an seinem eisigen Blick und der bereiten Anspannung in seinem Körper, seinem arroganten Kinn und der grausamen Linie seiner Lippen.

Das ist ein Mann, der Gewalt lebt und atmet, der durch und durch ein gefährliches Raubtier ist, für das die Regeln der Gesellschaft nicht existieren.

Ein Monster, das unzählige Menschen gefoltert und getötet hat.

Die Welle aus Wut und Hass, die diesem Gedanken folgt, durchdringt meine Angst, und ich gehe einen Schritt nach vorn, dann noch einen und noch einen, bis ich auf beinahe sicheren Beinen auf ihn zugehe. Wenn er mich töten wollte, hätte er das bereits auf eine Million andere Arten tun können, also was auch immer er heute möchte, muss etwas anderes sein.

Etwas Bösartigeres.

»Hallo Sara«, sagt er und steht auf, als ich fast bei ihm bin. »Es freut mich, dich wiederzusehen.«

Seine tiefe Stimme legt sich warm um mich, und sein weicher russischer Akzent liebkost meine Ohren. Sie sollte sich hässlich anhören, diese Stimme aus meinen Albträumen, aber wie alles an ihm ist sie trügerisch anziehend.

»Was wollen Sie?« Ich bin unhöflich, aber das ist mir egal. Wir haben Höflichkeit und gutes Benehmen bereits hinter uns gelassen. Es ist sinnlos, so zu tun, als sei das ein normales Treffen.

Der einzige Grund, aus dem ich hier bin, ist der, dass ich ansonsten meine Eltern in Gefahr bringen könnte.

»Bitte, setz dich.« Er deutet auf den Stuhl ihm gegenüber und setzt sich hin. »Ich habe mir die Freiheit genommen, einen Kaffee für dich zu bestellen. Schwarz, ohne Zucker … und entkoffeiniert, da du ja heute nicht arbeitest.«

Ich werfe einen Blick auf den zweiten Becher, der genauso ist, wie ich ihn bestellt hätte, und schaue ihn danach wieder an. Mein Herz schlägt mir bis zum Hals, aber meine Stimme ist ruhig, als ich sage: »Sie *haben* mich beobachtet.«

»Ja, natürlich. Aber das ist dir bereits letzte Nacht aufgefallen, stimmt's?«

Ich zucke zusammen. Ich kann nichts dagegen tun. Wenn er gesehen hat, dass ich versucht habe, den Anruf zu tätigen, dann hat er mich auch sturzbetrunken ins Badezimmer und nackt aus ihm herauskommen sehen.

Wenn er mich bereits seit einer Weile beobachtet, hat er mich in allen möglichen privaten Momenten gesehen.

»Setz dich, Sara.« Er deutet erneut auf den Stuhl, und dieses Mal gehorche ich – wenn auch nur, um mir die Gelegenheit zu geben, mich zu beruhigen. Wut und Angst sind wie verhedderte Stromkabel in meiner Brust, und ich fühle mich, als stünde ich nur einen Atemzug vorm Explodieren.

Ich bin nie eine gewalttätige Person gewesen, aber wenn ich eine Waffe bei mir hätte, würde ich ihn erschießen. Ich würde sein Gehirn auf diese trendige Starbuckswand spritzen lassen.

»Du hasst mich.« Er sagt es ruhig, eher wie die Feststellung einer Tatsache als eine Frage, und ich starre ihn überrascht an.

Kann er Gedanken lesen, oder bin ich so durchschaubar?

»Das ist schon in Ordnung«, meint er, und ich kann einen Hauch von Belustigung in seinen Augen erkennen. »Du kannst es ruhig zugeben. Ich verspreche dir, dass ich dir heute nicht wehtun werde.«

Heute? Was ist mit übermorgen und überübermorgen? Meine Hände ballen sich unter dem Tisch zu Fäusten, und meine Nägel graben sich in meine Haut.

»Natürlich hasse ich Sie«, antworte ich, so ruhig ich kann. »Ist das eine Überraschung?«

»Nein, natürlich nicht.« Er lächelt, und meine Lungen ziehen sich zusammen und verhindern, dass ich atmen kann. Es ist kein perfektes Lächeln – seine Zähne sind weiß, aber einer unten ist ein wenig schief, und auf seiner Unterlippe befindet sich eine kleine Narbe, die bis jetzt nicht zu sehen war – aber es ist trotzdem anziehend.

Es ist ein Lächeln, das nur für einen Zweck geschaffen wurde: unvorsichtige Frauen anzulocken und sie das Monster dahinter vergessen zu lassen.

Meine Nägel schneiden tiefer in meine Handflächen, und der Schmerz verfestigt sich, als er sagt: »Sie haben alles Recht der Welt, mich für das zu hassen, was ich getan habe.«

Ich starre ihn mit offenem Mund an. »Versuchen Sie gerade, sich zu *entschuldigen*? Denken Sie wirklich, dass ...«

»Du hast mich missverstanden.« Das Lächeln verschwindet, und in seinen silberfarbenen Augen blitzt plötzlich Wut auf. »Dein Ehemann hatte es verdient. Wäre er nicht hirntot gewesen, hätte ich ihn viel mehr leiden lassen.«

Ich ziehe mich instinktiv zurück, schiebe meinen Stuhl nach hinten, aber bevor ich aufspringen kann, fängt seine Hand mein Handgelenk ein und hält es am Tisch fest.

»Ich habe nicht gesagt, dass du gehen kannst, Sara.«

Seine Stimme ist dunkel und eisig. »Wir sind noch nicht fertig.«

Seine Finger liegen wie Handschellen aus geschmolzenem Eisen um mein Handgelenk – sein Griff ist brennend heiß und unzerbrechlich. Ich bleibe sitzen und blicke mich instinktiv um. Die nächsten Gäste sitzen etwa dreieinhalb Meter von uns entfernt, und niemand schenkt uns Aufmerksamkeit. Panik schlägt in meiner Brust, aber ich erinnere mich daran, dass mangelnde Aufmerksamkeit gut ist. Ich habe nicht vergessen, dass er im Klub eine Drohung gegen die anderen ausgesprochen hat.

Ich unterdrücke meine Angst und konzentriere mich auf meine Atmung. »Was wollen Sie von mir?«

»Das versuche ich gerade zu entscheiden«, antwortet er, und sein Gesicht glättet sich. Er lässt mein Handgelenk los, nimmt seinen Becher in die Hand und trinkt einen Schluck. »Du solltest wissen, Sara, dass ich *dich* nicht hasse.«

Ich blinzele ihn an, weil er mich erneut überrascht hat. »Nicht?«

»Nein.« Er stellt den Becher ab und betrachtet mich mit kalten, grauen Augen. »Wahrscheinlich wirkt das nach dem, was ich mit dir angetan habe, so auf dich, aber ich habe nichts gegen dich. Eigentlich ganz im Gegenteil.«

Mein Puls setzt aus, bevor er einen hektischen, neuen Rhythmus annimmt. »Wie meinen Sie das?«

Seine Mundwinkel gehen nach oben. »Was denkst du denn, Sara? Du interessierst mich. Eigentlich faszinierst du mich sogar.« Er beugt sich nach vorn, und sein Blick hypnotisiert mich. »Du erinnerst dich nicht an das, was du mir gesagt hast, als du unter Drogen standst, stimmt's?«

Eine Hitzewallung breitet sich von meinem Nacken aus und zieht über mein Gesicht. Ich kann mich nicht an alles aus jener Nacht erinnern, aber ich erinnere mich an genug. Bruchstücke dessen, was ich ihm gesagt habe, als ich unter Drogeneinfluss stand, steigen manchmal in meinem Kopf auf, wenn ich wach bin, und dringen auch in meine Träume ein, wenn ich schlafe.

In meine *krankhaftesten* Träume, in diejenigen, über die ich nicht nachdenken möchte.

»Ich sehe, du erinnerst dich.« Seine Stimme wird leise und rau, und seine Lider schließen sich zur Hälfte, während seine warme Hand sich auf meine zitternde Handfläche legt. »Ich habe mich gefragt, was passiert wäre, wenn ich in jener Nacht geblieben wäre … Wenn ich deiner Bitte nachgekommen wäre.«

Seine Berührung verbrennt mich, bevor ich meine Hand wegreißen kann und sie unter dem Tisch zu einer Faust balle. »Das war kein Wunsch.« Mein Herz dröhnt in meinen Ohren, und meine Stimme ist durch die Demütigung angespannt. »Ich war high. Ich wusste nicht, was ich sagte.«

»Ich weiß. Drogen, die die Hemmungen senken, haben diesen Effekt.« Er lehnt sich zurück, erlöst mich von der starken Wirkung seiner Nähe, und meine Lungen holen zum ersten Mal seit zwei Minuten tief

Luft. »Du wusstest nicht, wer ich war oder was ich tat. Du hättest genauso auf jeden anderen halbwegs attraktiven Mann reagiert, der sich in dieser Situation bei dir befunden hätte.«

»Das … das stimmt.« Mein Gesicht ist glühend heiß, aber die rationale Erklärung beruhigt mich ein wenig. »Es hätte jeder gewesen sein können. Das war nichts Persönliches.«

Aber weißt du, Sara«, er beugt sich wieder nach vorn, und seine Augen leuchten dunkel und intensiv, »meine Reaktion *war* persönlich. *Ich* stand nicht unter Drogeneinfluss, und als du mich angefleht hast, wollte ich dich. Ich will dich *immer noch*.«

Entsetzen lässt mein Blut gefrieren, auch wenn mein Geschlecht als Antwort auf seine Aussage zuckt. Er kann mir nicht gerade das sagen, was er mir sagt. »Sie … Sie sind verrückt.« Ich fühle mich, als würde ich ohne einen Fallschirm aus einem Flugzeug fallen. »Ich bin nicht … Das ist einfach nur krank.« Ich will aufspringen und weglaufen, aber ich halte durch, atme mich durch diese Panikattacke. Ich muss ihm das klarmachen, diesen Wahnsinn ein für alle Mal beenden. »Es ist mir egal, was Sie möchten oder was Ihre Reaktion war. Ich werde nicht mit Ihnen schlafen, nachdem Sie meinen Ehemann und wer weiß wie viele andere getötet haben. Nachdem Sie mich gefoltert und …«

»Ich weiß, Sara,« Seine Hand findet mein Knie unter dem Tisch und legt sich darauf. »Ich wünschte, ich könnte die Zeit zurückdrehen, weil ich einen anderen Weg finden würde.«

Überrascht schiebe ich meinen Stuhl zur Seite, um seiner Reichweite zu entkommen. »Sie hätten George nicht getötet?«

»Ich hätte dich nicht gefoltert«, erklärt er mir und legt seine Hand wieder auf den Tisch. »Ich hätte dieses *sookin syn* auf einem anderen Weg finden können. Es hätte länger gedauert, aber das wäre es mir wert gewesen, um dir nicht wehzutun.«

Mein freier Fall aus dem Flugzeug geht weiter, und die Luft rauscht an meinen Ohren vorbei. Von welchem Planeten kommt dieser Mann? »Sie denken, dass es ein Problem ist, mich zu foltern, aber dass es in Ordnung ist, *meinen Ehemann zu töten?*«

»Der Ehemann, der dich angelogen hat? Derjenige, über den du gesagt hast, dass du ihn nicht wirklich kanntest?« Erneut flammt Wut in seinen Augen auf. »Du kannst dir einreden, was du möchtest, Sara, aber ich habe dir einen Gefallen getan. Ich habe dieser ganzen beschissenen Welt mit seinem Ableben einen Gefallen getan.«

»Einen Gefallen?« Jetzt werde auch ich von einer Wutwelle erfasst, die alle Vorsicht verbrennt. »Er war ein guter Mann, Sie ... Sie *Psycho*! Ich weiß nicht, was Sie denken, was er getan hat, aber ...«

»Er hat meine Frau und meinen Sohn abgeschlachtet.«

Schock lähmt meine Stimmbänder. »Was?«, presse ich heraus, als ich endlich wieder sprechen kann.

Ein Muskel in Peters Kiefer zuckt. »Weißt, du,

womit dein Ehemann sein Geld verdient hat, Sara? Was er *wirklich* gemacht hat?«

Eine übelkeitserregende Vorahnung erfüllt mich. »Er war ein … ein Auslandskorrespondent.«

»Das war seine Tarnung, ja.« Die Oberlippe des Russen zieht sich nach oben, während er seinen Oberkörper aufrichtet. »Ich habe mir schon gedacht, dass du es nicht wusstest. Die Ehefrauen wissen es selten, auch wenn sie die Lügen spüren.

Meine Welt fällt aus den Angeln. »Was meinen Sie mit Tarnung? Er *war* ein Journalist. Er hat Artikel für …«

»Ja, das hat er. Und während er diese Geschichten verfolgt hat, hat er Informationen für die CIA gesammelt und verdeckte Missionen für sie durchgeführt.«

»Was? Nein.« Ich schüttle verzweifelt den Kopf. »Sie haben unrecht. Sie haben einen Fehler gemacht. Sie haben den falschen Mann erwischt. Ich *wusste*, dass Sie den falschen Mann erwischt hatten. George war kein Spion. Das ist unmöglich. Er wusste nicht einmal, wie man einen Reifen wechselt. »Er …«

»Er wurde auf der Uni rekrutiert«, sagt Peter leise. »An der University of Chicago, die ihr beide besucht habt. Das tun *sie* häufig, sich auf den Unis umsehen, um die Besten und Intelligentesten zu bekommen. Sie halten nach bestimmten Dingen Ausschau: wenige familiäre Verbindungen, clever und ehrgeizig, aber fehlende Zielstrebigkeit … Hört sich das nach deinem Ehemann an?«

Ich starre ihn an, während meine Brust sich immer

mehr zusammenzieht. Georges Mutter war in seinem letzten Jahr an der Highschool bei einem Autounfall gestorben, und sein Vater, ein Marine, wurde in Afghanistan getötet, als George noch ein Baby war. Sein recht alter Onkel hat ihm durch die Zeit an der Uni geholfen, aber auch er starb vor einigen Jahren, weshalb jetzt nur noch eine entfernte Cousine übrig war, um zu Georges Beerdigung vor sechs Monaten zu kommen.

Nein. Das kann nicht stimmen. Das hätte ich gewusst.

»Nur, wenn er es dir gesagt hätte«, entgegnet Peter, und mir fällt auf, dass ich meinen letzten Gedanken laut ausgesprochen habe. »Sie bringen ihnen bei, wie sie ihren echten Job vor allen, selbst vor ihren Familien, geheim halten. Fandst du es nicht verdächtig, dass Cobakis seine Leidenschaft für den Journalismus über Nacht entdeckt hat? Dass er an einem Tag noch Biologie studieren wollte, bevor er am nächsten Praktika bei Zeitschriften im Ausland absolviert hat?«

»Nein, ich …« Meine Brust ist so eng, dass ich kaum Luft holen kann. »Das ist eben Uni. Man soll sich selbst entdecken, seine Leidenschaft finden.«

»Und das hat er auch: für die Regierung zu arbeiten.« In dem silbernen Blick des Russen ist keine Gnade. »Sie haben ihn trainiert, ihm die Zielstrebigkeit gegeben, die ihm gefehlt hatte. Sie haben ihm beigebracht, wie er dich und alle anderen anlügen muss. Als er das Studium abgeschlossen hat, haben sie ihm einen Job bei einer Zeitung besorgt, damit er eine Entschuldigung hatte, zu allen Brennpunkten weltweit reisen zu können.«

Ich springe auf, da ich nicht weiter zuhören kann. »Sie haben unrecht. Sie wissen nicht, worüber Sie reden.«

Es steht ebenfalls auf, und sein großer Körper ragt über mich. »Weiß ich das nicht? Denke zurück, Sara. Denke zurück an den Mann, den du geheiratet hast, zurück an das Leben, das ihr *wirklich* zusammen hattet. Nicht das perfekte, das du der Welt gezeigt hast, sondern das, was ihr hinter geschlossenen Türen geführt habt. Wer war dein Ehemann? Wie gut kanntest du ihn wirklich?«

Es fühlt sich an, als habe sich mein Inneres in Eisen verwandelt, als ich einen Schritt zurücktrete und meinen Kopf unablässig schüttele, um seiner Aussage zu widersprechen. »Sie haben unrecht«, wiederhole ich mit erstickter Stimme, wirbele herum und renne aus dem Coffeeshop zu meinem Auto.

Erst als ich an einer roten Ampel in der Nähe meines Hauses anhalte, fällt mir auf, dass Peter Sokolov nichts getan hat, um mich aufzuhalten.

Er stand einfach nur da und hat mir dabei zugesehen, wie ich gegangen bin.

15

Peter

ICH SEHE durch mein Fernglas dabei zu, wie Sara das Haus ihrer Eltern betritt; dann öffne ich meinen Laptop und rufe die Übertragung der Kamera im Hausflur auf.

Saras Eltern wohnen in einem kleinen, hübschen Haus, das einige Ausbesserungen vertragen könnte, aber ansonsten warm und gemütlich ist. Selbst ich kann sehen, dass es ein Zuhause ist und nicht einfach ein Platz zum Leben. Aus irgendeinem eigenartigen Grund erinnert es mich an Tamilas Haus in Daryevo, auch wenn dieses amerikanische Zuhause in einer Vorstadt nichts mit einer Hütte in einem Bergdorf gemeinsam hat.

Sara küsst ihre Eltern im Flur und folgt ihnen

danach ins Esszimmer. Ich wechsele auf die Kamera, die sich dort befindet, und zoome auf ihr Gesicht, als sie die anderen Gäste begrüßt – ein älteres Ehepaar und einen großen, schlanken Mann Mitte dreißig.

Es sind die Levinsons, und ihr Sohn Joe, der Rechtsanwalt, von dem sich Saras Eltern wünschen, dass sie mit ihm ausgeht.

Etwas Hässliches rührt sich in mir, als Sara die Hand des Anwalts mit einem höflichen Lächeln schüttelt. Ich will sie nicht mit ihm sehen; allein der Gedanke daran erweckt in mir den Wunsch, ihm mein Messer in die Rippen zu rammen. Gestern, als der Barkeeper sie angelächelt hat, wollte ich meine Faust in seine grinsende Visage schlagen, und dieser gewalttätige Drang ist heute noch stärker.

Ich habe sie noch nicht erobert, aber sie wird mein sein.

Sara hilft ihren Eltern dabei, die Vorspeisen aufzutragen, und setzt sich danach neben den Anwalt. Ich stelle die Audioübertragung an und höre dem Smalltalk der beiden zu. Für jemanden, der gerade etwas über das Doppelleben seines Ehemannes herausgefunden hat, ist die kleine Ärztin erstaunlich gefasst, und ihre lächelnde Maske sitzt fest auf dem Gesicht. Niemand, der sie ansieht, würde vermuten, dass sie sich, bevor sie hierhergekommen ist, stundenlang in ihrem Wandschrank versteckt hat und erst vor vierzig Minuten mit roten und geschwollenen Augen herausgekommen ist.

Niemand würde vermuten, dass sie Angst hat, weil ich sie will.

Ich musste meine ganze Kraft aufbringen, sie in dem Wandschrank sitzen und allein weinen zu lassen. Sie ist in ihn gegangen, um sich vor meinen Kameras zu verstecken, und ich habe ihr diese Zeit für sich gegeben. Sie wäre mehr als wütend gewesen, wenn ich hineingegangen wäre und sie umarmt hätte – wenn ich versucht hätte, sie auf die Art zu trösten, die ich wollte.

Ich muss ihr mehr Zeit geben, sich an den Gedanken an uns beide zu gewöhnen – und mir zu vertrauen, dass ich ihr nicht wehtun werde.

Das Abendessen dauert einige Stunden, bevor Sara ihrer Mutter hilft, den Tisch abzuräumen, und sich danach mit einer Entschuldigung verabschiedet. Der Anwalt fragt sie nach ihrer Telefonnummer, und sie gibt sie ihm, aber ich kann sehen, dass das eher eine höfliche Geste ist. Ihre Wangen sind völlig blass – sie zeigen nicht einmal einen Hauch der Farbe, die sie in meiner Gegenwart haben – und ihre Körpersprache verrät ihre Gleichgültigkeit. Joe Levinson begeistert sie nicht, und das ist etwas Gutes.

Es bedeutet, dass er lebendig zu Hause ankommt.

Ich folge Sara in einigem Abstand, als sie zur Klinik fährt, und warte dann in meinem Auto, bis sie wieder herauskommt, wobei ich die Wartezeit damit überbrücke, sie durch die Kameras zu beobachten, die ich in der Klinik angebracht habe. Ich weiß, dass mein Verhalten Stalking auf höchstem Niveau ist, aber ich kann nicht anders.

Ich muss wissen, wo sie ist und was sie tut.

Ich muss sicherstellen, dass sie sich in Sicherheit befindet.

Ich könnte die Überwachung vor Ort auch Anton und meinen anderen Männern überlassen – sie beobachten sie immer dann, wenn ich nicht kann –, aber ich will persönlich hier sein. Ich will sie mit meinen eigenen Augen sehen. Mit jedem Tag, der vergeht, wird mein Verlangen nach ihr stärker, und jetzt, nachdem ich eine wirkliche Unterhaltung mit ihr hatte, verwandelt sich meine Faszination schnell in eine Besessenheit.

Ich muss sie haben. Bald.

Etwa drei Stunden später verlässt sie die Klinik, und ich folge ihr, als sie zu einem Hotel fährt. Wahrscheinlich denkt sie, dass es hier für sie sicherer ist als in ihrem Haus mit den ganzen Kameras, aber sie hat unrecht.

Ich warte, bis sie in das Hotel eingecheckt hat und auf ihrem Zimmer ist, bevor ich aus dem Auto steige und ebenfalls hineingehe.

16
———

 *ara*

DIE SCHICHT in der Klinik war heute besonders hart. Ich hatte eine vierzehnjährige Patientin, die nach der Pille danach gefragt hat, weil sie von ihrem Bruder vergewaltigt wurde, und eine andere Anfang zwanzig, die bereits das dritte Mal eine Fehlgeburt erlitten hat. Ich habe getan, was ich konnte, aber ich weiß, dass das nicht genug ist.

Nichts, was ich für diese Mädchen tue, wird jemals genug sein.

Ich bin emotional so ausgelaugt, dass es mich meine ganze Kraft kostet, zu duschen und meine Zähne mit der kleinen Zahnbürste zu putzen, die ich am Empfang bekommen habe. Die Nacht hier zu verbringen war eine spontane Entscheidung, also habe ich nicht einmal

Unterwäsche zum Wechseln dabei. Ich werde morgen früh an meinem Haus vorbeifahren müssen, bevor ich zur Arbeit gehe, aber das ist besser, als zu Hause zu sein und zu wissen, dass mein tödlicher Stalker mich gerade beobachten könnte.

Mich beobachtet und mich will. Sich vielleicht sogar bei dem Anblick meines nackten Körpers einen runterholt.

Das ist krank, aber bei diesem Gedanken steigt Hitze zwischen meinen Schenkeln auf.

Ich steige aus der Dusche, wickele ein Handtuch um meine Brust und betrachte mich selbst im Spiegel. Die Visine-Augentropfen haben meine geröteten Augen hervorragend verschwinden lassen, aber meine Lider sind von meinem Heulkrampf vorhin immer noch geschwollen, und mein Gesicht ist von der heißen Dusche gerötet. Außerdem habe ich Spannungskopfschmerzen, die mich nicht denken lassen, aber das ist auch gut so.

Ich habe vorhin zu viel nachgedacht.

George als Spion. George führt ein Doppelleben. Das scheint unmöglich zu sein, aber es würde so vieles erklären. Der Schutz durch FBI-Agenten, der plötzlich da war. Seine langen Abwesenheiten, wenn er eigentlich einer Geschichte nachjagte, aber trotzdem häufig ohne nach Hause kam. Seine Stimmungswechsel, die kurz nach unserer Hochzeit vor sechs Jahren begannen. Ist etwas auf einer seiner geheimen Missionen schiefgelaufen?

Könnte sein wahrer Job der Grund dafür sein, dass

er sich in den letzten Jahren vor dem Unfall so sehr verändert hat?

Meine Kopfschmerzen verstärken sich, und mir wird klar, dass ich es schon wieder tue. Ich denke über George nach, quäle mich mit der Vergangenheit, die ich nicht ändern kann, anstatt mich auf die Zukunft zu konzentrieren, die ich noch unter Kontrolle habe. Ich sollte versuchen, herauszufinden, was ich mit dem Mörder tun soll, der mich verfolgt, aber mein Kopf will nicht darüber nachdenken.

Ich werde später über ihn nachdenken, wenn ich geschlafen habe und mein Gehirn nicht mehr so matschig ist.

Ich wickele ein zweites Handtuch um meine tropfnassen Haare, öffne die Badezimmertür, trete heraus und springe mit einem überraschten Aufschrei zurück.

Peter Sokolov sitzt auf meinem Bett, und seine halb geschlossenen Augen ruhen auf meinem Gesicht.

»NICHT SCHREIEN, Sara.« Er steht mit einer geschmeidigen Bewegung auf. »Wir müssen keine anderen Gäste mit hineinziehen.«

Ich schnappe nach Luft, und Adrenalinnadeln stechen auf meiner Haut, als er auf mich zukommt, und sein großer Körper sich mit der Leichtigkeit eines Raubtiers bewegt.

»Sie … Sie sind mir hierher gefolgt.« Meine Knie geben nach, als ich instinktiv zurückweiche und das dünne Handtuch umklammere, das meinen Körper bedeckt.

»Ja.« Er bleibt einen Meter vor mir stehen, und seine grauen Augen leuchten. »Du hättest nicht hierherkommen sollen. Dein Alarmsystem zu Hause ist zumindest eine kleine Herausforderung. Hier kann ich einfach reinkommen.«

»Wieso sind Sie hier?« Mein Herz fühlt sich an, als würde es gleich aus meiner Brust springen. »Was wollen Sie?«

Seine Lippen zucken voller dunkler Belustigung. »Du bist eine Ärztin, die mit den Folgen dieser Aktivität arbeitet. Du kannst dir wahrscheinlich denken, was ich will.«

Oh Gott. Meine Haut fühlt sich gleichzeitig heiß und kalt an, und mein Puls rast noch schneller. »Verschwinden Sie. Ich … Ich werde schreien, ich schwöre es.«

Er neigt seinen Kopf fragend zur Seite. »Wirst du? Warum hast du es dann noch nicht getan?«

Ich weiche noch einen Schritt zurück, und mein Blick fällt für den Bruchteil einer Sekunde auf die Zimmertür. *Könnte ich es schaffen, bevor er mich fängt?*

»Versuch es gar nicht erst, Sara. Wenn du rennst, *werde* ich dich einholen.«

Ich weiche weiter zurück. »Ich habe Ihnen bereits gesagt, dass ich nicht mit Ihnen schlafen werde.«

»Nein? Das werden wir sehen.«

Er kommt auf mich zu, ich weiche noch weiter zurück, und mein Magen krampft. Ich weiß, was eine Vergewaltigung mit Frauen macht; ich habe die Folgen gesehen, das körperliche und emotionale Wrack, das sie zurücklässt. Ich weiß nicht, ob ich das nach all den anderen Sachen überleben kann.

Ich weiß nicht, ob ich es bei *ihm* überleben kann.

Meine zitternde Hand berührt die Tür, aber bevor ich die Klinke nach unten drücken kann, schlagen seine Handflächen rechts und links neben mir auf der Tür auf und sperren mich zwischen seinen kräftigen Armen ein.

»Du kannst mir nicht entkommen, Ptichka«, sagt er leise und blickt zu mir herunter. »Jetzt nicht, und nie mehr. Du kannst dich genauso gut daran gewöhnen.«

Er berührt mich nicht, aber er ist so nah, dass ich die Hitze spüren kann, die sein großer Körper abgibt, und einige weitere Narben auf seinem symmetrischen Gesicht sehen kann. Die Unvollkommenheiten geben seiner Anziehungskraft einen tödlichen Hauch und verstärken ihre Wirkung auf meine Sinne. Mein Herzschlag ist ein wildes Dröhnen in meinen Ohren, aber trotzdem spannt sich mein Körper auf eine Art und Weise an, die nichts mit Angst zu tun hat. Ich sollte wie eine Verrückte schreien oder zumindest versuchen, gegen ihn anzukämpfen, aber ich kann mich nicht bewegen. Ich kann nichts anderes tun, als den tödlich schönen Mörder, der mich gefangen hält, anzustarren.

»Komm, Sara.« Seine Hand gleitet nach unten, um sich vertraut eisern um mein Handgelenk zu legen. »Ich werde dir nicht wehtun.«

Ich atme zitternd ein. »Werden Sie nicht?« Vielleicht wird er sanft sein. *Bitte, lass ihn wenigstens sanft sein.* Ich habe Gewalt durch seine Hände erlebt, und sie macht mir noch mehr Angst als der Gedanke an eine Vergewaltigung.

»Nein. Jetzt komm.«

Er drückt sich von der Tür weg, aber anstatt mich zum Bett zu führen, gehen wir zu dem Stuhl vor dem Frisierspiegel.

»Setz dich.« Er drückt meine Schultern nach unten, und ich sinke auf den Stuhl, wobei ich versuche, meine abgehackte Atmung zu beruhigen. Was tut er? Warum greift er mich nicht an? Mein Gesicht ist im Spiegel leichenblass, und meine Augen weit aufgerissen, als er hinter mich tritt und etwas aus der Innentasche seiner Jacke zieht.

Es ist eine kleine in Plastik verpackte Haarbüste – eine dieser billigen, die man manchmal in Hotels oder bei besseren Fluggesellschaften bekommt.

»Das ist alles, was sie im Kiosk unten hatten«, sagt er und nimmt die Bürste aus der Plastikhülle, bevor er mich über den Spiegel anschaut. »Ich habe mir gedacht, dass das besser ist als nichts.«

Besser als nichts für was? Irgendein eigenartiges perverses Spielchen? Meine Kehle verengt sich, aber bevor mich die Panik überkommt, nimmt er das Handtuch von meinem Kopf und lässt es auf den Boden fallen. Seine starke, sonnengebräunte Hand sieht neben meinem Kopf riesig aus, als er mein Haar zu einem nassen Pferdeschwanz zusammennimmt und beginnt, sich mit der Bürste durch die Knoten zu arbeiten.

Der Schock lässt die ganze Luft aus meinen Lungen entweichen. Der Mörder meines Ehemanns – der Mann, der mich verfolgt – *bürstet gerade meine Haare.*

Seine Berührung ist sanft, aber sicher, zeigt keine Spur eines Zögerns. Es fühlt sich an, als habe er das bereits ein Dutzend Male getan. Zuerst fährt er mit der Bürste durch die Enden, damit sie glatt und ohne Knoten sind, bevor er sich systematisch nach oben vorarbeitet, bevor die Bürste durch alle meine Haare gleiten kann, ohne hängenzubleiben. Und während dieses ganzen Prozesses verspüre ich keine Schmerzen – eigentlich ganz im Gegenteil. Die Kunststoffborsten massieren meine Kopfhaut, wenn sie über sie hinwegfahren, und wohlige Schauer laufen mir jedes Mal über den Rücken, wenn seine warmen Finger über die empfindliche Haut meines Nackens fahren.

Angst hin oder her, das ist das sinnlichste Erlebnis meines Lebens.

Ein eigenartiges Gefühl von Unwirklichkeit überkommt mich, während ich hier sitze, und ihm im Spiegel dabei zusehe, wie er mein Haar kämmt. Bei jedem unserer vorangegangenen Treffen war ich so konzentriert darauf gewesen, welche Gefahr er darstellt, dass ich den wichtigeren Dingen wie seiner Kleidung keine Aufmerksamkeit geschenkt habe. Jetzt bemerke ich zum ersten Mal, dass er eine graue Lederjacke über einem schwarzen Thermo-Shirt, dunkle Jeans und ein Paar schwarze Boots trägt. Seine Kleidung ist *casual*, etwas, was jeder Mann zum Frühlingsanfang in Illinois tragen könnte, aber trotzdem kann man meinen Peiniger nicht für einen normalen Mann von der Straße halten.

Peter Sokolov ist eine Naturgewalt, rücksichtslos und nicht aufzuhalten.

Er bürstet meine Haare einige Minuten lang,

während ich so still dasitze wie ich kann, weil ich mich nicht traue, auch nur einen Muskel zu bewegen, damit er nicht damit aufhört. Jeder Bürstenstrich fühlt sich wie eine Liebkosung an, jede Berührung seiner rauen Hände ist beruhigend und gleichzeitig aufregend. Was noch viel wichtiger ist, ist, dass er, während er meine Haare kämmt, nichts anderes mit mir tun kann – keines der Dinge, vor denen ich mich fürchte.

Viel zu früh legt er die Büste allerdings auf den Schminktisch, und seine Augen treffen im Spiegel auf meine. »Steh auf«, befiehlt er, und seine Hände legen sich um meine nackten Schultern und ziehen mich hoch.

Ich schlucke belegt, drehe mich um, um ihn anzublicken, wenn er mich loslässt, aber er ist bereits weggetreten und zieht seine Jacke aus.

Schweren Herzens sehe ich ihm dabei zu, wie er seine Jacke über den Stuhl hängt und nach dem Saum seines langärmeligen Thermo-Shirts greift. Mit einer geschmeidigen Bewegung zieht er das T-Shirt über seinen Kopf, und mein Atem stockt, als er es auf seiner Jacke ablegt.

Seine Schultern sind breit, seine Arme mit dicken, klar definierten Muskelschichten überzogen. Weitere Muskeln bedecken seinen schlanken, V-förmigen Oberkörper, und sein flacher, geriffelter Bauch zeigt nicht ein Gramm Fett. Wie seine Hände sind seine Brust und seine Schultern gebräunt, so als wenn er eine Menge Zeit in der Sonne verbringen würde, und sein linker Arm ist fast komplett mit Tattoos bedeckt, die von seiner Schulter bis zu seinem Handgelenk reichen. Zwischen einem Hauch dunkler Haare auf seiner Brust sehe ich weitere verblichene Narben, und ich erwische mich selbst dabei, wie ich auf die sexy Linie aus Haaren starre, die an seinem Nabel beginnt und in dem Bund seiner tief sitzenden Jeans verschwindet.

Als Nächstes wendet er sich der Jeans zu, macht den Reißverschluss auf, und ich zwinge mich dazu, wegzuschauen. Trotz seiner urmännlichen Schönheit bedeckt eine Schicht kalten Schweißes meinen Körper, und mein Puls ist übelkeitserregend schnell. Er mag vielleicht ein umwerfend schönes Ungeheuer sein, aber das ist auch schon alles: ein Ungeheuer, ein kaltherziges Monster. Es ist egal, dass ich mich unter anderen Umständen unglaublich von ihm angezogen gefühlt hätte. Ich will das, was gerade passiert, nicht. Es würde mich zerstören.

Aus meinem Augenwinkel sehe ich, wie er seine Stiefel auszieht und seine Jeans nach unten schiebt, wobei er einen blauen Slip mit einer dicken, langen Wölbung und kräftige Beine mit einem Hauch dunkler Haare freilegt. Er beugt sich nach vorn, um die Jeans ganz auszuziehen, und mein Entsetzen erreicht einen neuen Höchststand.

Ich vergesse seine Warnung und schieße zur Tür.

Diesmal komme ich nicht einmal in die Nähe meines Ziels. Er fängt mich einen halben Meter vor der Tür ab, indem sich ein starker Arm um meinen Brustkorb legt und mich in die Luft hebt, während seine andere Hand sich auf meinen Mund legt und meinen instinktiven Schrei dämpft.

Ich kralle mich an seinen Oberarmen fest, und meine Füße treten gegen seine Schienbeine, während er mich zum Bett trägt, aber es ist sinnlos. Alles, was ich erreiche, ist, dass sich das Handtuch auf meinem Rücken löst. Sein Arm um meinem Brustkorb verhindert, dass es zu Boden fällt, aber mein Rücken, mein Po und die rechte Seite meines Körpers liegen völlig frei. Ich kann fühlen, wie seine nackte Brust gegen meinen Rücken reibt, den sauberen, männlichen Moschusgeruch seiner Haut riechen, und die unerwünschte Intimität verstärkt meine Panik und meine Gegenwehr.

»Scheiße«, knurrt er, als meine Ferse auf sein Knie trifft, und ich verspüre einen leichten Triumph.

Er dauert nicht lange an. Eine Sekunde später fällt er mit dem Rücken zuerst aufs Bett, zieht mich mit sich, und bevor ich reagieren kann, rollt er sich herum und fixiert mich unter sich. Ich ende mit dem Gesicht auf der Matratze, meine Hände kratzen nutzlos über die weiche Oberfläche, und meine Beine werden durch seinen schweren, muskulösen Unterschenkel festgehalten. Mit seiner Handfläche auf meinem Mund kann ich außer gedämpften Geräuschen nichts von mir geben, und Paniktränen brennen in meinen Augen, als ich seine harte Erektion gegen die Rundung meines Pos drücken spüre. Nur seine Unterhose trennt uns jetzt noch, und ich verdoppele meine Anstrengungen, auch wenn das sinnlos ist.

Es vergehen einige Minuten, bis ich meine Kraft

aufgebraucht habe – und bemerke, dass er sich nicht bewegt.

Er hält mich fest, aber er macht keine Anstalten, mich zu nehmen.

»Bist du jetzt fertig?«, murmelt er, als ich erschlaffe, weil meine Muskeln vor Anstrengung zittern und meine Lungen nach Luft schreien. »Oder möchtest du noch ein wenig kämpfen? Ich kann das die ganze Nacht lang tun.«

Ich glaube ihm. Er ist so viel größer als ich, dass er einfach nur auf mir liegen muss und ich ihm weder wehtun noch fliehen kann. Die Anstrengungen auf seiner Seite sind minimal, während ich meine ganze Kraft ohne irgendeinen Erfolg aufbrauche.

»Wirst du dich benehmen, wenn ich meine Hand wegnehme?« Seine Lippen schweben über meinem Ohr und sein Atem erhitzt meine Haut.

Meine Schultern drücken sich nach oben, um meinen Nacken vor diesen missbrauchenden Lippen zu schützen, und er seufzt hörbar. »In Ordnung, dann muss ich dich wohl knebeln und meine Handschellen holen, nehme ich an.«

Ich gebe einen gedämpften Laut hinter seiner Handfläche von mir, und er lacht. »Nein? Also wirst du dich benehmen?«

Ich schaffe es, leicht zu nicken. Diese Niederlage ist wie ein beißendes Brennen in meinem Hals, aber ich will nicht geknebelt und in Handschellen gelegt werden.

»Braves Mädchen.« Er schiebt sich von mir

herunter und nimmt seine Hand von meinem Mund, wodurch ich Luft in meine unter Sauerstoffmangel leidenden Lungen ziehen kann. »Jetzt, nachdem du das alles rausgelassen hast, was hältst du davon, wenn wir schlafen gehen? Ich weiß, dass morgen ein langer Tag vor dir liegt, und vor mir auch.«

»Was?« Ich bin so überrascht, dass ich mich auf den Rücken rolle und meine Nacktheit völlig vergesse.

Ein leichtes, anzügliches Lächeln erscheint auf seinem Mund, als sein Blick über meinen Körper wandert, bevor er wieder zu meinem Gesicht zurückkehrt. »Schlaf, Ptichka. Wir beide brauchen ihn.«

Ich setze mich hin, schnappe mir ein Kissen, drücke es gegen meine Brust und rücke zum Kopfende – so weit weg von ihm, wie es das Bett zulässt. Was er sagt, ergibt keinen Sinn. Er will mich ganz offensichtlich; seine Erektion zerfetzt beinahe seine Unterhose. »Sie ... Sie wollen mit mir *schlafen*? Einfach nur *schlafen*?«

Das Lächeln verschwindet von seinem Gesicht, und in seinen Augen glüht eine dunkle Hitze. »Offensichtlich will ich mehr, aber heute Nacht gebe ich mich mit Schlafen zufrieden. Ich habe es dir doch gesagt, Sara – ich werde dir nicht noch einmal wehtun. Ich werde warten, bis du bereit bist ... bis du mich genauso möchtest wie ich dich.«

Ihn wollen? Ich will schreien, dass das verrückt ist, dass ich niemals freiwillig Sex mit ihm haben werde, aber ich schlucke meine Antwort hinunter. Ich bin im Moment zu verletzlich, und er ist zu unberechenbar.

Davon abgesehen, wenn er schläft, werde ich die Möglichkeit haben, zu fliehen – ihn vielleicht sogar niederschlagen und die Polizei rufen können.

»In Ordnung.« Ich versuche, noch hilfloser auszusehen, als ich in Wirklichkeit bin. »Wenn Sie versprechen, mir nicht wehzutun …«

Seine Lippen zucken. »Ich verspreche.« Er steigt aus dem Bett, zieht die Decke mit einem festen Ruck unter mir hervor und breitet sie aus, bevor er die Kopfkissen aufschüttelt. Er klopft auf die freiliegende Matratze und sagt: »Komm her.«

Ich rücke einige Zentimeter näher an ihn heran, während ich mein Kissen weiterhin gegen meine Brust gedrückt halte.

»Näher.«

Ich wiederhole mein Manöver, und mein Herz rast plötzlich vor Angst. Ich traue ihm nicht ein bisschen. Er könnte mit mir spielen, aus irgendeinem komischen Grund über seine Absichten hinwegtäuschen.

»Geh unter die Decke«, sagt er, und ich gehorche, da ich froh bin, mich mit mehr als nur einem Kissen zu bedecken. Leider ist meine Erleichterung nur von kurzer Dauer. Sobald ich mich hinlege, macht er die Lichter über uns aus, kommt neben mich unter die Decke, und sein langer, muskulöser Körper streckt sich neben mir aus, als sei das sein Platz.

»Leg dich auf die Seite«, meint er und tut dasselbe, nachdem er auch die Nachttischlampe ausgeschaltet hat – unsere letzte Lichtquelle.

Mein Brustkorb zieht sich zusammen, als ich verstehe, was er vorhat.

Der Mörder meines Mannes will in Löffelchenstellung mit mir schlafen.

Ich ignoriere die verwirrende Dunkelheit und das erstickende Gefühl in meinem Hals, drehe mich auf die Seite und versuche, gleichmäßig zu atmen, als sich ein muskulöser Arm unter mein Kissen schiebt, während der andere sich besitzergreifend um meinen Brustkorb legt und mich an seinen großen Körper zieht. Auf jeden Fall kann ich unmöglich ruhig atmen. Mein nackter Po schmiegt sich an seinen harten, langen Schwanz, sein warmer, minziger Atem bewegt das feine Haar an meinen Schläfen, und seine Beine schmiegen sich von hinten an meine. Ich bin von seiner Größe und Kraft umgeben und völlig eingenommen. Und Hitze. Gott, sein Körper erzeugt so viel Hitze. Wo immer sein warmes Fleisch gegen meins drückt, brenne ich, so als ob er heißer wäre als ein normaler Mensch. Aber das ist nicht er – das liegt an mir. Nachdem der kalte Schweiß auf meiner Haut getrocknet ist, ist mir so kalt, dass ich zittere.

Ich weiß nicht, wie lange wir so daliegen, aber irgendwann dringt seine Wärme in mich ein und verwandelt sich dort in eine andere Art von Hitze, die tückische, die in meinen Träumen auftaucht und mich vor Scham brennen lässt. Jetzt, da ich nicht mehr so verängstigt bin, wird mir bewusst, dass sein Körper mehr ist als eine Bedrohung ... jetzt nehme ich seinen harten Schwanz als etwas anderes wahr, als ein Werkzeug zum Vergewaltigen. Sein warmer, männlicher Geruch umgibt mich, und meine Brüste fühlen sich über seinem Arm schwer und empfindlich an. Meine Nippel sind hart, und mein Geschlecht schmerzt durch seine nasse, pochende Leere. Wie lange ist es her, dass ich das letzte Mal so umarmt wurde? Zwei Jahre? Drei? Ich kann mich nicht an das letzte Mal erinnern, an dem George und ich Sex hatten, und noch weniger daran, wann wir das letzte Mal so zusammenlagen. Obwohl diese Situation so falsch ist, genießt ein Teil von mir es, die Wärme eines männlichen Körpers und das pulsierende Brummen von Erregung in meinem Unterleib zu spüren.

Es ist gut, dass ich nicht vorhabe einzuschlafen, weil es unmöglich ist, dass ich diese Situation mögen könnte – nicht, wenn mein Herz mit über hundert Schlägen pro Minute rast und die Gedanken in meinem Kopf noch schneller umherschwirren. Angst und Wut, Erregung und Scham – das alles vermischt sich, beschleunigt meinen Herzschlag und übersäuert meinen Magen. Was will Peter wirklich? Was hat er von diesem eigenartigen Kuscheln? Diese riesige Erektion muss unangenehm sein, wenn nicht sogar schmerzhaft, aber er scheint zufrieden zu sein, einfach hier zu liegen und nichts weiter zu tun, als mich zu halten. Warum? Was hat er vor? Warum hat er es auf mich abgesehen?

Und könnte das, was er über George gesagt hat, wahr sein? Könnte mein Ehemann seiner Familie etwas angetan haben?

Das ist der schlimmste Gedanke der ganzen Welt, aber ich kann nicht aufhören, darüber nachzudenken. Mein Mund scheint sich unabhängig von meinem Gehirn zu bewegen, als ich flüstere, »Ähm, Peter ... kannst du mir etwas über dich erzählen?«

Ich kann seine Überraschung daran spüren, dass sich seine Muskeln sofort anspannen und seine Atmung sich ändert. Ich habe ihn bis jetzt nie mit seinem Vornamen angesprochen, aber es wäre eigenartig, ihn zu siezen, wenn ich nackt in seinen Armen liege. Außerdem könnte ein wenig emotionale Intimität ihn eher dazu bringen, meine Fragen zu beantworten – und ihn davon abhalten, mir wehzutun, weil ich sie überhaupt stelle.

»Was möchtest du wissen?«, fragt er nach einer Sekunde leise und bewegt mich leicht, damit ich bequemer an ihm liege.

Warum denkst du, dass mein Mann deine Familie abge- schlachtet hat? Ich brenne darauf, genau das zu fragen, aber ich bin nicht so dumm, das gleich anzusprechen. Ich erinnere mich an seine Wut, als ich das letzte Mal dieses Thema angesprochen habe. Stattdessen antworte ich leise: »Sie haben mir erzählt, dass du in Russland geboren wurdest. Stimmt das?«

»Ja.« Seine tiefe Stimme hört sich leicht belustigt an. »Hörst du das nicht an dem Akzent?«

»Er ist sehr schwach, also nein. Du könntest von überall aus Europa oder dem Nahen Osten kommen. Dein Englisch ist hervorragend.« Wegen meiner Nervosität spreche ich zu schnell, also zwinge ich mich dazu, Luft zu holen und langsamer zu reden. »Hast du es in der Schule gelernt?«

»Nein, bei meiner Arbeit.«

Der Arbeit, bei der du mutmaßliche Bedrohungen für Russland aufgespürt und verhört hast? Ich unterdrücke einen Schauer und versuche, nicht an seine Befragungstechniken zu denken. *Leichte Konversation,* sage ich mir. *Und dann langsam hocharbeiten.* In einem entspannten Ton frage ich: »Als Erwachsener? Das ist beeindruckend. Normalerweise muss man eine Sprache als Kind lernen, um sie so gut sprechen zu können wie du.«

Ja, das ist gut. Ein wenig schmeicheln, ein wenig wirkliche Bewunderung. Das muss man tun, wenn man sich in einer verletzlichen Lage befindet: Eine Beziehung mit dem Angreifer herstellen, damit er dich als ein fühlendes, menschliches Lebewesen sieht, sich in dich hineinfühlen kann. Natürlich hängt der Erfolg dieser Strategie vom Einfühlungsvermögen des betreffenden Angreifers ab – etwas, von dem ich vermute, dass es der Psychopath, der mich gerade umarmt, nicht besitzt.

»Na ja, ich habe einige englische Worte und Sätze als Kind gelernt«, meint er. »Ich nehme an, dass das geholfen hat.«

»Ach? Wo hast du sie gelernt? In der Schule oder von deinen Eltern?«

Er lacht, und seine muskulöse Brust drückt gegen meinen Rücken. »Weder noch. Aus amerikanischen

Filmen. Das ist euer wichtigster Exportartikel – neben Hamburgern.«

»Stimmt.« Ich hole Luft und versuche, den schweren Arm zu ignorieren, der über meinem Brustkorb liegt, und den harten Hinweis auf seine Erregung, den ich an meinem Po spüre. Er beschäftigt mich auf eine Art und Weise, über die ich nicht nachdenken möchte. »Und was hat dich dazu gebracht, dich für deinen … na ja, Beruf, zu entscheiden?«

Er vergräbt seine Nase in meinem Haar und zieht tief Luft ein, so als wollte er mich einatmen. »Was genau hat Ryson dir erzählt?«

Ich spanne mich wegen seines vertrauten Umgangs mit dem Nachnamen des FBI-Agenten an, zwinge mich dann aber dazu, mich zu entspannen. Natürlich würde er wissen, wer Ryson ist, wahrscheinlich hat er auch gesehen, dass wir uns in dem Café getroffen haben. »Er hat mir erzählt, dass du in der russischen Spezialeinheit warst. Stimmt das?«

»Ja.« Seine Stimme hört sich heiser an, als er sich erneut hinter mir bewegt und sein Schwanz wie eine Stahlstange gegen mich drückt. »Ich habe eine kleine, geheime Einheit angeführt, die auf Anti-Terror-Maßnahmen und Aufstandsbekämpfung spezialisiert war.«

»Das ist … ungewöhnlich.« Mit ihm zu reden – und ihn in seinem erregten Zustand wachzuhalten – ist wahrscheinlich keine so gute Idee, aber ich kann einfach nicht damit aufhören. »Wie kommt jemand dazu? Bist du zur Armee gegangen und sie haben dich dort rekrutiert?«

»Nein.« Er fährt damit fort, sein Gesicht an meinen Haaren zu reiben. »Sie haben mich in einem Jugendknast gefunden.«

»Einem Gefängnis für jugendliche Straftäter?«

»Es war eher ein Arbeitslager, aber ja.«

»Was …« Ich schlucke, versuche mich eher auf seine Worte als die Auswirkungen zu konzentrieren, die sein offensichtliches Begehren für mich auf meinen Körper hat. »Was hat du getan, um dort zu landen?«

Das hat nichts mit George zu tun, aber ich kann meine Neugier nicht unterdrücken. Ich nehme an, dass das, was ich erfahren werde, mir nur noch mehr Angst machen wird, aber ich möchte wissen, wie mein Feind tickt.

Ich will seine Schwächen kennen, damit ich sie gegen ihn benutzen kann.

»Ich habe den Leiter des Waisenhauses getötet, in dem ich aufgewachsen bin.« In Peters Worten gibt es keine Spur eines Bedauerns, keine Gefühle außer der Lust, die seine Stimme belegt. Er könnte mir auch gerade erklärt haben, was er zum Abendbrot gegessen hat. »Ich nehme an, dass man sagen könnte, dass ich meine Karriere früh begonnen habe.«

»Ich verstehe.« Meine Haut prickelt, aber ich versuche angestrengt, mich ruhig anzuhören. »Wie alt warst du?«

»Elf, fast zwölf.«

»Was hat er dir angetan?«

Er seufzt und rückt leicht von mir ab. »Ist das wirklich wichtig, Ptichka? Du hast dir deine Meinung über mich doch bereits gebildet, und keine rührselige Geschichte aus meiner Vergangenheit wird sie ändern können. Jetzt gerade hasst du mich zu sehr, um etwas anderes als Freude über irgendwelche schlechten Dinge zu verspüren, die ich erlebt haben könnte.«

So viel dazu, eine emotionale Verbindung aufzubauen. »Was hast du denn erwartet?«, frage ich bitter und höre sofort auf, vorzugeben, ein verständnisvoller Zuhörer zu sein. »Dass du mich foltern und meinen Ehemann umbringen könntest und wir danach beste Freunde werden?«

»Nein, Ptichka. Trotz allem, was du vielleicht denkst, bin ich nicht wahnsinnig. Deine negativen Gefühle mir gegenüber sind rational und waren zu erwarten. Ich hoffe einfach, sie im Laufe der Zeit ändern zu können.«

Er *ist* wahnsinnig, wenn er denkt, dass ich jemals etwas anderes als Hass für ihn empfinden könnte, aber ich habe keine Lust, mich jetzt zu streiten. »Was bedeutet das Wort, was du für mich benutzt? Pti... und so weiter?«

»Ptichka.« Er vergräbt erneut sein Gesicht in meinem Haar und riecht an ihm, oder was zum Henker er auch immer tut. »Es ist das russische Wort für ›Vögelchen‹.«

Meine Hände krallen sich in die Decke vor mir. »Vögelchen?«

»Ja. Ein kleiner Singvogel, hübsch und anmutig wie

du.« Er macht eine kurze Pause, bevor er leise hinzufügt: »Und eingesperrt, genau wie du.«

Dieses Arschloch. Ich beiße meine Zähne zusammen und versuche, von ihm wegzurücken, soweit das der starke Arm um meine Taille zulässt. »Das ist eine vorübergehende Situation.«

»Oh, ich habe nicht gemeint, dass ich dich einsperre.« Ich kann das Lächeln in seiner Stimme hören, als er seinen Griff verstärkt und mich daran hindert, von ihm abzurücken. »Ich halte dich vielleicht in diesem Moment fest, aber du warst schon lange bevor ich in dein Leben getreten bin eingesperrt.«

Ich versteinere vor Überraschung. »Was?«

»Oh ja. Tu nicht so, als wüsstest du nicht, wovon ich rede, Sara. Ich weiß, dass du es gefühlt hast: all diese gesellschaftlichen Erwartungen, von deinen Eltern, deinem Ehemann und deinen Freunden … Der Erfolgsdruck, weil du clever und hübsch geboren wurdest, der Wunsch, perfekt zu sein, das Bedürfnis, für jeden immer alles zu sein …« Seine Stimme ist leise und dunkel, umhüllt mich wie ein seidenes, verführerisches Netz. »Ich habe es gestern im Klub gesehen: dein Verlangen nach Freiheit, deinen Wunsch, ohne die Einschränkungen zu leben, die dir auferlegt wurden. Einige Momente lang hast du auf der Tanzfläche die Fesseln abgelegt, und ich habe den hübschen Vogel seinen goldenen Käfig verlassen und frei fliegen sehen. Ich habe *dich* gesehen, Sara, und das war wunderschön.«

Einige Augenblicke lang kann ich nur bewegungslos daliegen, meine Brust schmerzt und meine Augen brennen in der Dunkelheit. Ich will lachen, und seine Worte leugnen, aber ich habe Angst, dass ich zusammenbrechen und schreien werde, wenn ich versuche, etwas zu sagen. Wie kann dieser Mann, dieser gewalttätige Fremde, etwas so Privates wissen – etwas, was ich gerade selbst erst über mich herausgefunden habe?

Und woher weiß er, dass mich mein nettes, komfortables Leben nicht länger glücklich macht ... es vielleicht nie getan hat?

Ich unterdrücke den Frosch in meinem Hals, schnaube höhnisch und sage: »Und was wirst du jetzt tun? Mich aus meinem eingeschränkten Leben befreien? Mich freilassen und mir beim Fliegen zuschauen?«

»Nein, Ptichka.« Seine Stimme ist voller sanftem Spott. »Nichts so Edles.«

»Was dann?«

»Ich werde dich in meinen Käfig sperren und dich zum Singen bringen.«

18

 eter

SIE ZITTERT IN MEINEN ARMEN, und ich kann spüren, wie die Angst sie überkommt. Ein Teil von mir bedauert meine brutale Ehrlichkeit, aber ich kann sie einfach nicht anlügen. Mein Verlangen nach ihr ist nicht die zärtliche Zuneigung, die ich für Tamila empfunden habe, oder die einfache Lust, die ich bei anderen Frauen erlebt habe.

Mein Verlangen nach Sara ist dunkler, beschmutzt durch das, was zwischen uns vorgefallen ist, und dem Wissen, dass sie meinem Feind gehört hat. Ich will ihr nicht wehtun, aber ich kann nicht abstreiten, dass mich ihr Leiden auf eine perverse Art und Weise anmacht. Sie zu quälen kühlt meine brennende Wut ab, befriedigt meinen Drang, zu bestrafen und Rache zu nehmen, auch wenn ich mir einrede, dass ich sie heilen will, den Schmerz, den ich ihr zugefügt habe, wiedergutmachen möchte.

Was Sara betrifft, bin ich ein Chaos aus Widersprüchen, und das Einzige, was ich ganz genau weiß, ist, dass es nicht ausreichen wird, sie nur zu ficken.

Ich will mehr.

Ich will, dass sie mir gehört.

Es ist verlockend, mein Versprechen zu brechen und sie jetzt zu nehmen, sie in Besitz zu nehmen und den Hunger zu stillen, der mich bei lebendigem Leib auffrisst. Sie liegt völlig nackt in meiner Umarmung, ihre Haut reibt bei jedem ihrer Atemzüge gegen meine. Ich kann das blumige Shampoo in ihrem feuchten Haar riechen, die Weichheit ihrer Brüste spüren, die auf meinem Arm liegen, und mein Schwanz pocht schmerzhaft an der Wölbung ihres Hinterns, weil mein Körper sich danach sehnt, in sie zu stoßen. Zuerst würde sie sich wehren, aber ich könnte sie dazu bringen, es zu mögen.

Sie ist mir gegenüber nicht immun. Ich weiß es. Ich kann es spüren.

Bevor der dunkle Drang gewinnen kann, hole ich tief Luft und atme sie wieder aus. So gut es sich auch anfühlen würde, Sara zu ficken, ich will ihr Vertrauen genauso sehr wie ihren Körper.

Ich will, dass sie von selbst für mich singt.

»Schlaf, Ptichka«, flüstere ich, als sie weiterhin

schweigt, und alle ihre Fragen für heute verstummt sind. »Heute Nacht bist du in Sicherheit.«

Ich ignoriere den Hunger, der in meinem Körper wütet, schließe die Augen und sinke in einen leichten, aber erholsamen Schlaf.

———

IN DIESER NACHT wache ich dreimal auf, zweimal, als Sara versucht, sich aus meiner Umarmung zu befreien – zweifellos, um zu fliehen und mir etwas Schmerzhaftes anzutun –, und einmal, als sie aus einem Albtraum aufwacht. Ich umarme sie in allen Fällen fester, und irgendwann schläft sie wieder ein. Nach einer Weile tue ich dasselbe, auch wenn die Lust in mir im Laufe der Nacht immer intensiver wird. Gegen Morgen bin ich kurz davor, zu explodieren, und ich brauche nur zwanzig Sekunden, bis ich komme, als ich kurz zur Toilette gehe.

Sie schläft immer noch, als ich aus dem Bad zurückkomme, und ich überlege einen Moment, ob ich mich noch einmal zu ihr unter die Decke legen sollte. Allerdings ist es schon fast sieben Uhr, und ich will mit Anton reden, bevor er seinen Dienst beginnt. Ich bin mir auch nicht sicher, wie gut meine Selbstkontrolle ist, da die schnelle Erleichterung mein gewaltiges Verlangen nach ihr nur leicht abgeschwächt hat.

Wenn ich wieder zu Sara ins Bett steige, riskiere ich es, mein Versprechen zu brechen.

Ich entscheide mich gegen dieses verlockende Schicksal, ziehe mich leise an und verlasse das Zimmer.

Ich werde Sara bald wiedersehen. In der Zwischenzeit muss Arbeit erledigt werden.

Sara

ICH HABE einen geplanten Kaiserschnitt am Morgen und einen ungeplanten am Nachmittag. Dazwischen behandele ich eine Frau, die schmerzhafte Menstruationsbeschwerden hat, aber keine hormonelle Empfängnisverhütung verträgt, die die Symptome lindern würde – etwas, was ich sehr gut nachempfinden kann –, und eine andere, die seit zwei Jahren erfolglos versucht, schwanger zu werden. Ich mache einen Termin für eine Ultraschalluntersuchung mit der ersten Patientin, um sie auf Endometriose zu untersuchen, und überweise die zweite zu einem Spezialisten für Reproduktionsmedizin. Sobald ich das erledigt habe, werde ich in die Notaufnahme gerufen, um eine Frau, die im sechsten Monat schwanger ist und in einen Verkehrsunfall verwickelt war, zu untersuchen. Zum Glück kann ich ihr mitteilen, dass ihr Baby gesund ist und tritt – das Beste, was bei einem so schlimmen frontalen Zusammenstoß passieren konnte.

Es überrascht mich, dass ich mich nach letzter Nacht auf meine Arbeit konzentrieren kann, aber zum ersten Mal seit Monaten kommen nicht andauernd dunkle Erinnerungen hoch, und die Paranoia der letzten Monate ist verschwunden. Es ist pervers, aber da ich jetzt *weiß*, dass ich beobachtet werde, ist dieser Gedanke weniger angsteinflößend als vorher, als ich dieses beunruhigende Gefühl hatte.

Außerdem fühle ich mich trotz minimalem Koffein-Konsum ausgeruht und wach, und ich vermute, dass es an den neun Stunden Schlaf liegt, die ich trotz des harten Körpers, der mich die ganze Nacht lang umgeben hat, bekommen habe.

Oder vielleicht gerade seinetwegen. Egal, wie sehr ich letzte Nacht versucht habe, wach zu bleiben, die animalische Wärme, die Peters Haut abgegeben hat, und seine gleichmäßige Atmung haben mich in den Schlaf gewiegt. Ich bin in der Nacht einige Male aufgewacht und habe versucht, mich aus seinem Griff zu befreien, aber das war unmöglich. Er hat mich so stark festgehalten wie ein Kind, das seinen Lieblingsteddy-bären umklammert, und irgendwann habe ich aufgegeben und geschlafen, da mein Unterbewusstsein sich nicht darüber bewusst war, dass die Quelle meiner Albträume genau neben mir lag.

Aus welchem Grund auch immer bleibe ich meine

gesamte Schicht lang ruhig und konzentriert. Es hilft mir, dass ich es geschafft habe, alle Gedanken an Peter und seine Absichten zu unterdrücken, sie zu verdrängen, während ich mich auf meine Patientinnen konzentriere. Wenn ich über seine Absichten nachdenken würde, würde ich schreiend aus dem Krankenhaus rennen, und wer weiß, was mein Stalker dann tun würde. Als ich heute Morgen lebendig und unverletzt aufgewacht bin, habe ich beschlossen, dass es das Beste ist, einfach einen Tag nach dem anderen zu überleben und Peter so wenig wie möglich zu provozieren.

Vielleicht wird er noch eine Weile nett zu mir sein, und ich habe Zeit, mir zu überlegen, was ich tun muss.

Als mein Dienst vorbei ist, gehe ich zum Umkleideraum und renne auf dem Flur in Andy. Sie muss gerade anfangen, weil ihr Kittel noch perfekt gebügelt ist und ihre Locken zu einem sauberen Dutt zusammengebunden sind, in dem es keine lockere Strähne gibt.

Am Ende einer Schicht sehen die meisten Schwestern und Ärzte, ich eingeschlossen, um einiges mitgenommener aus.

»Hey«, sagt sie und bleibt vor mir stehen. »Ist alles in Ordnung?«

Ich blinzele. »Ähm, ja.« Sie kann nichts über Peter wissen, oder doch? »Warum?«

»Als wir in dem Klub waren, hast du gesagt, dass du dich nicht gut fühlst«, meint Andy und runzelt leicht ihre Stirn. »Kurz bevor du verschwunden bist.«

»Ach ja, das tut mir leid.« Ich versuche ein verlegenes Lächeln aufzusetzen. »Ich habe zu viel getrunken und es nicht vertragen. Ich glaube, ich habe mich zu Hause übergeben, aber meine Erinnerungen sind etwas verschwommen.«

»Ah, ich verstehe.« Ein erleichtertes Grinsen verdrängt ihren besorgten Gesichtsausdruck von eben. »Ich dachte, dass dich vielleicht irgendetwas gestört hat. Du hast ausgesehen, als hätte jemand dein Lieblingspony vor deinen Augen erschossen.«

Ich lache und schüttele den Kopf, auch wenn sie fast den Nagel auf den Kopf getroffen hat. »Das einzige Opfer war meine Leber.«

Andy lacht und fragt: »Was machst du nächsten Samstag? Tony und Marsha planen einen weiteren Mädelsabend, aber ich dachte eher an ein Abendessen und einen Film mit Larry – beides zu einer vernünftigen Uhrzeit, weil ich am Sonntag Frühdienst habe. Willst du mitkommen?«

»Mit dir und deinem Freund?« Ich schaue sie überrascht an. »Wäre ich dann nicht das fünfte Rad am Wagen?«

»Na ja …« Ein verschmitztes Grinsen erhellt ihr sommersprossiges Gesicht. »Zufälligerweise hat Larry einen sehr gutaussehenden – und sehr erfolgreichen – Freund, der unbedingt ein nettes Mädchen kennenlernen möchte. Er ist ein Immobilien-Mogul und hat eine unendlich lange Liste von Anforderungen, aber«, sie hebt einen Finger, als ich sie unterbrechen will, »du erfüllst sie alle. Wenn das für dich in Ordnung ist, wird Larry ihn auch einladen, und wir könnten ein nettes Double-Date haben.«

Ich kräusele meine Nase. »Ich weiß nicht …«

»Er ist ein gutaussehender Kerl. Hier.« Sie zieht ihr Telefon aus der Tasche, wischt einige Male über das Display und zeigt mir ein Bild von einem Mann, der wie ein blonder Tom Cruise aussieht. »Siehst du? Es könnte wirklich schlimmer sein.«

Ich muss lachen. »Mit Sicherheit, aber …«

»Kein Aber.« Sie hält ihre Hand hoch, als ich etwas erwidern möchte. »Komm einfach, und wir werden Spaß haben. Kein Druck oder sonst etwas. Wenn du Larrys Freund magst, toll. Wenn nicht, verschwinden wir, um die Mädels zu treffen, und Larry kann einen Männerabend machen – das will er schon seit Ewigkeiten.«

Ich zögere, schüttele dann aber bedauernd den Kopf. »Danke, aber ich kann nicht.« Ich weiß nicht, ob Peter eine Gefahr für Andy oder ihren Freund ist, aber ich will es nicht riskieren. Mit einem russischen Killer, der jeden meiner Schritte überwacht, könnte jede Person in meiner Nähe ein Ziel werden.

Bis die Situation mit meinem Stalker nicht gelöst ist, bleibe ich lieber allein.

Andy lässt den Kopf hängen. »Oh, okay. Solltest du deine Meinung ändern, sag mir einfach Bescheid. Marsha hat meine Nummer.«

»Das mache ich, danke«, antworte ich, aber Andy eilt bereits, so schnell sie ihre weißen Turnschuhe tragen, weg.

———

AUF MEINEM WEG nach Hause höre ich Kelly Clarksons »Stronger« und kämpfe gegen meinen Drang an, einfach so lange weiterzufahren, bis ich mich in einem anderen Bundesstaat befinde. Oder vielleicht sogar in einem anderen Land. Kanada und Mexiko hören sich beide verlockend an, genauso wie die Antarktis oder Timbuktu. Statt zu meinem kameraverseuchten Haus könnte ich zum Flughafen fahren und in ein Flugzeug nach irgendwohin steigen – egal wohin.

Ich würde zum Nordpol fliegen, wenn ich die Garantie hätte, dass Peter mir nicht folgt.

Leider habe ich diese Garantie nicht. Eigentlich ganz im Gegenteil. Wenn ich weglaufe, wird er mir folgen. Da bin ich mir sicher. Er ist ein Jäger, ein Spurenleser, und er wird nicht aufgeben, bis er mich findet, genauso wie die ganzen Personen auf seiner Liste. Ich könnte in ein anderes Hotel oder auf einen anderen Kontinent gehen, und es würde keinen Unterschied machen.

Er wird mich nicht in Ruhe lassen, bis er bekommen hat, was er will, was auch immer das sein mag.

Meine Handflächen auf dem Lenkrad sind verschwitzt, und ich bemerke, dass ich schnell atme, weil meine Ruhe verschwindet, als Gedanken an letzte Nacht durch meinen Kopf schießen. Ich bin mir nicht sicher, was er will, aber es scheint etwas anderes als einfach nur Sex zu sein.

Etwas Dunkleres und viel Krankhafteres.

Als ich spüre, dass ich kurz vor einer Panikattacke

stehe, wechsele ich von Kelly Clarkson auf klassische Musik und konzentriere mich auf meine Atemübungen. Vielleicht mache ich einen Fehler, wenn ich nicht zum FBI gehe. Dort besteht wenigstens die Möglichkeit, dass sie mich beschützen könnten, während ich allein überhaupt keine Chance habe. Ich kann einfach nur hoffen, dass ihm bald langweilig mit mir wird, er sich das nächste Opfer sucht und mich verlässt, solange ich noch am Leben bin und meinen Verstand nicht komplett verloren habe.

Ich bin schon dabei, mein Telefon herauszuholen, als ich mich daran erinnere, warum ich Ryson nicht sofort angerufen habe: meine Eltern. Ich kann nicht verschwinden und sie zurücklassen, und es wäre egoistisch, sie wegen der kleinen Chance zu entwurzeln, dass das FBI sie schützen könnte. Um ihnen zu erklären, warum ein solcher Schritt nötig ist, müsste ich meinen Eltern alles erzählen, und ich weiß nicht, ob das Herz meines Vaters diesen Stress überstehen würde. Vor einigen Jahren hat er einen dreifachen Bypass bekommen, und die Ärzte haben ihm geraten, den Stress auf einem Minimum zu halten. Von einem mörderischen Stalker zu erfahren, der mich gefoltert und George getötet hat, könnte meinen Vater im wahrsten Sinne des Wortes umbringen und vielleicht sogar gefährlich für meine Mutter sein.

Nein. Das werde ich ihnen nicht antun. Ich bekomme meine Atmung in den Griff und mache wieder Kelly Clarkson an. Meine Eltern führen ein glückliches, normales Leben, und ich werde alles tun, damit das auch so bleibt. Wenn das bedeutet, dass ich allein mit Peter fertigwerden muss, dann ist das eben so.

Hoffentlich bin ich stark genug, das zu überleben, was er für mich vorbereitet hat.

S*ara*

WAS ER VORBEREITET HAT, ist Essen. Eine Menge köstlich riechendes Essen.

Überrascht starre ich auf meinen gedeckten Esstisch. Auf ihm steht ein gebratenes Hühnchen, eine Schüssel mit Kartoffelbrei und eine große Schüssel Blattsalat – alles hübsch angerichtet mit brennenden Kerzen und einer Flasche Weißwein.

Ich hatte mich darauf vorbereitet, heute Abend in meinem Haus überfallen zu werden, aber damit hatte ich nicht gerechnet.

»Hast du Hunger?«, fragt eine tiefe Stimme mit einem leichten Akzent hinter mir, und ich wirbele herum, und mein Herz setzt einen Schlag aus, als Peter Sokolov aus dem Flur kommt. Die Haare auf seiner

Stirn sind nass, so als habe er sich gerade das Gesicht gewaschen, und obwohl er ein blaues Hemd und dunkle Jeans trägt, hat er keine Schuhe an, sondern nur Socken.

Er sieht umwerfend aus – und gefährlicher als je zuvor.

»Was …« Meine Stimme ist zu hoch, also hole ich Luft und versuche es noch einmal. »Was ist das?«

»Abendessen«, antwortet er und sieht belustigt aus. »Nach was sieht es denn aus?«

»Ich …« Die Luft im Raum wird dünn, als er kurz vor mir stehen bleibt, und der vertraute Ausdruck in seinen Augen erinnert mich daran, dass ich nackt in seinen Armen geschlafen habe. »Ich habe keinen Hunger.«

»Nicht?« Er zieht seine dunklen Augenbrauen in die Höhe. »In Ordnung. Dann lass uns ins Bett gehen.« Er bewegt sich, so als wolle er zu mir kommen, und ich springe zurück.

»Nein, warte! Ich könnte etwas zu Essen vertragen.«

Ein Lächeln erscheint auf seinen Lippen. »Das habe ich mir gedacht. Nach dir.«

Er bewegt seinen Arm in einem höfischen Halbkreis, und ich gehe zum Tisch, während ich versuche, mein Herz wieder an seinen richtigen Platz zu drücken, als er die Lampe ausmacht, so dass das Kerzenlicht die einzige Beleuchtung ist, und mir zum Tisch folgt.

Er zieht einen Stuhl zurück, und ich setze mich hin.

Dann geht er zu dem Stuhl mir gegenüber und nimmt ebenfalls Platz. Mir fällt auf, dass der Tisch mit zwei Tellern und meinem guten Besteck gedeckt ist – jenes Besteck, von dem George wollte, dass ich es nur an Feiertagen und für Partys benutze.

Schweigend sehe ich Georges Mörder dabei zu, wie er fachmännisch das Hühnchen zerlegt und eine der Keulen – mein Lieblingsstück vom Huhn – auf meinen Teller legt, bevor er einige Löffel Kartoffelbrei und eine große Portion Salat hinzufügt.

»Wo hast du das ganze Essen her?«, frage ich ihn, als er seinen Teller füllt.

»Ich habe es gemacht.« Er schaut von seinem Teller auf. »Du magst Hühnchen doch, oder nicht?«

Das tue ich, aber das werde ich ihm nicht sagen. »Du kochst?«

»Ich versuche es.« Er nimmt seine Gabel und sein Messer. »Na los, probier schon.«

Ich schiebe meinen Stuhl nach hinten und stehe auf. »Ich muss mir die Hände waschen.« Ich bin gerade aus der Garage gekommen, und der Arzt in mir lässt es nicht zu, dass ich Essen anfasse, ohne vorher die Krankenhauskeime abzuwaschen.

»In Ordnung«, erwidert er, legt sein Besteck wieder ab, und ich verstehe, dass er vorhat, auf mich zu warten.

Mein Stalker hat hervorragende Tischmanieren.

Ich gehe ins Badezimmer und wasche meine Hände, schrubbe zwischen jedem Finger und um mein Handgelenk, so wie ich es immer mache. Als ich zum Tisch zurückkomme, hat er uns bereits Wein eingeschenkt, und der trockene Geruch des Pinot Grigio vermischt sich mit den köstlichen Aromen des Essens, was die Situation nur noch bizarrer macht.

Wenn ich es nicht besser wüsste, würde ich denken, dass wir ein Date haben.

»Woher wusstest du, dass ich hierherkommen würde, anstatt in ein Hotel zu gehen?«, frage ich, als ich mich wieder hingesetzt habe.

Er zuckt mit den Schultern. »Es war eine Vermutung. Du bist ein helles Köpfchen, also wirst du den gleichen Fehler wahrscheinlich nicht zweimal machen.«

»Aha.« Ich nehme meine Gabel in die Hand und probiere den Kartoffelbrei. Der volle, butterige Geschmack auf meiner Zunge ist umwerfend und kurbelt meinen Appetit trotz der Angst, durch die mein Magen sich zusammenzieht, an. »Das ist eine Menge Kochen für eine Vermutung.«

»Ja, schon, aber ohne Risiko keine Belohnung, stimmt's? Außerdem habe ich gesehen, wie du denkst, Sara. Du tust keine dummen, sinnlosen Dinge, und zu einem anderen Hotel zu gehen, wäre genau das gewesen.«

Meine Hand mit der Gabel spannt sich an. »Habe ich das richtig verstanden? Du denkst, dass du mich kennst, weil du mich einige Wochen lang verfolgt hast?«

»Nein.« Seine Augen glänzen im Kerzenlicht. »Ich

kenne dich nicht, Ptichka – zumindest nicht ansatzweise so gut, wie ich es gerne tun würde.«

Ich ignoriere diese provokante Aussage und konzentriere mich auf meinen Teller. Jetzt, nach dem ersten Bissen, giert mein Mund nach mehr. Trotzdem, was ich Peter vorhin gesagt habe, bin ich am Verhungern und freue mich über das köstliche Essen auf meinem Teller. Das Hühnchen ist perfekt gewürzt, der Kartoffelbrei großzügig mit Butter verfeinert und der grüne Salat erfrischend durch ein ungewöhnlich zitroniges Dressing. Ich bin so in das Essen vertieft, dass ich meinen Teller bereits halb aufgegessen habe, als mir ein beängstigender Gedanke in den Kopf schießt.

Ich lege die Gabel weg und schaue meinen Peiniger an. »Du hast keine Drogen oder so etwas hineingetan, oder?«

»Wenn ich es getan hätte, wäre es bereits zu spät für dich«, entgegnet er amüsiert. »Aber nein. Du kannst dich entspannen. Wenn ich dich unter Drogen setzen oder vergiften wollte, würde ich eine Spritze benutzen. Dafür muss ich kein gutes Essen verschwenden.«

Ich versuche, keine Reaktion zu zeigen, aber meine Hand zittert, als ich nach meinem Weinglas greife. »Schön. Es freut mich, das zu hören.«

Er lächelt mich an, und ich fühle ein warmes, feuchtes Gefühl zwischen meinen Beinen. Um mein Unbehagen nicht zu zeigen, trinke ich einige Schlucke Wein und setze das Glas wieder ab, bevor ich mich erneut meinem Teller zuwende.

Ich fühle mich *nicht* zu ihm hingezogen. Ich weigere mich, das zu tun.

Wir essen schweigend, bis unsere Teller leer sind, dann legt Peter seine Gabel ab und nimmt sein Weinglas in die Hand. »Erkläre mir etwas, Sara«, sagt er. »Du bist jetzt achtundzwanzig Jahre und seit zweieinhalb eine vollwertige Ärztin. Wie hast du das geschafft? Warst du eines dieser Kindergenies mit einem super hohen Intelligenzquotienten?«

Ich schiebe meinen leeren Teller zur Seite. »Hast du das bei deinem Stalking nicht herausgefunden?«

»Ich bin nicht tief in deinen Hintergrund eingedrungen.« Er trinkt einen Schluck Wein und stellt sein Glas wieder ab. »Wenn es dir lieber ist, kann ich das gerne tun – oder du kannst einfach mit mir reden, und wir lernen uns auf eine traditionellere Art und Weise kennen.«

Ich zögere, bevor ich entscheide, dass es nicht schadet, wenn ich mit ihm rede. Je länger wir am Tisch sitzen, desto länger kann ich das Zubettgehen und alles, was das zur Folge haben könnte, hinauszögern.

»Ich bin kein Genie«, erkläre ich ihm und trinke einen kleinen Schluck Wein. »Ich meine, ich bin nicht dumm, aber mein IQ ist im normalen Bereich.«

»Aber wie konntest du dann mit sechsundzwanzig Jahren schon ein fertig ausgebildeter Arzt sein, wenn das nach dem College mindestens acht Jahre dauert.«

»Ich war ein Unfall«, sage ich. Als er mich weiterhin fragend anschaut, erkläre ich ihm: »Ich wurde drei Jahre vor der Menopause meiner Mutter geboren. Sie war fast fünfzig, als sie schwanger wurde, und mein Vater war achtundfünfzig. Sie waren beide Professoren – sie haben sich kennengelernt, als er ihr Doktorvater wurde, auch wenn sie erst später zusammengekommen sind, und keiner von beiden wollte Kinder. Sie hatten ihre Karrieren, sie hatten einen tollen Freundeskreis und sie hatten sich. In jenem Jahr haben sie Pläne gemacht, sich zur Ruhe zu setzen, aber stattdessen bin ich passiert.«

»Wie?«

Ich zucke mit den Schultern. »Ein paar Drinks und die Überzeugung, dass sie zu alt wären, um sich über ein geplatztes Kondom Gedanken machen zu müssen.«

»Also wollten sie dich nicht?« Seine grauen Augen verdunkeln sich, aus Stahlgrau wird Blaugrau, und sein Mund spannt sich an.

Wenn ich es nicht besser wüsste, würde ich denken, dass er wütend auf meine Eltern ist.

Ich schüttele diesen lächerlichen Gedanken ab und sage: »Doch, sie wollten mich. Zumindest, als sie den anfänglichen Schock über die Schwangerschaft über-wunden hatten. Sie hatten das weder gewollt noch erwartet, aber als ich erst einmal da war, trotz allem gesund zur Welt gekommen war, haben sie mir alles gegeben. Ich wurde der Mittelpunkt ihrer Welt, ihr persönliches, kleines Wunder. Sie hatten eine Festan-stellung, sie hatten Ersparnisse und sie haben ihre neue Elternrolle mit derselben Hingabe erfüllt wie ihre Karrieren. Ich wurde mit Aufmerksamkeit über-schüttet und konnte lesen und bis einhundert zählen, bevor ich gehen konnte. Als ich im Kindergarten angefangen habe, konnte ich lesen wie ein Kind in der fünften Klasse und hatte mathematisches Grundwissen.

Die harte Linie seines Mundes wird weicher. »Ich verstehe. Also warst du der Konkurrenz um Längen voraus.«

»Ja. Ich habe zwei Klassen in der Grundschule übersprungen und hätte das auch bei weiteren machen können, aber meine Eltern dachten, dass es nicht gut für meine soziale Entwicklung sein würde, wenn ich sehr viel jünger als meine Klassenkameraden wäre. Letztendlich hatte ich Schwierigkeiten, in der Schule Freunde zu finden, aber das tut jetzt nichts zur Sache.« Ich mache eine Pause, um noch einen Schluck Wein zu trinken. »Ich habe die Highschool schließlich in drei Jahren abgeschlossen, weil sie einfach für mich war und ich anfangen wollte, zu studieren, und dann habe ich die Uni in drei Jahren abgeschlossen, weil ich viele Credits dafür bekommen habe, dass ich auf der Highschool viele Seminare auf Uni-Niveau besucht habe.

»Das sind also die vier Jahre.«

Ich nicke. »Ja, das sind die vier Jahre.«

Er betrachtet mich eindringlich, und ich rutsche auf meinem Stuhl hin und her, da mir die Wärme in seinen Augen unangenehm ist. Mein Weinglas ist jetzt fast leer, und ich beginne die Wirkung zu spüren, die leichte Gelöstheit durch den Alkohol, der den Großteil meiner Angst verjagt und mich solche unwichtigen Dinge wahrnehmen lässt, wie dass sein Haar so aussieht, als würde es sich dick und seidig anfühlen, und dass sein Mund gleichzeitig hart und weich ist. Er sieht mich voller Bewunderung … und etwas anderem an, etwas, wodurch sich meine Haut heiß und angespannt anfühlt, so als hätte ich Fieber.

Als würde er es spüren, lehnt Peter sich nach vorn, und seine Augen schließen sich leicht. »Sara …« Seine Stimme ist leise, tief und gefährlich verführerisch. Ich kann spüren, dass ich schneller atme, als er mit seiner großen Hand meine kleine bedeckt und flüstert: »Ptichka, du bist …«

»Warum denkst du, dass George deiner Familie wehgetan hat?« Ich ziehe meine Hand weg, weil ich verzweifelt versuche, meine wachsende Erregung zu bekämpfen. »Was ist mit ihr passiert?«

Meine Frage ist wie eine Bombe in der sexuell aufgeladenen Atmosphäre. Sein Blick wird verschlossen und hart, und die Wärme verwandelt sich in eisige Wut.

»Meine Familie?« Er ballt seine Hand auf dem Tisch zu einer Faust. »Du willst wissen, was mit ihr geschehen ist?«

Ich nicke vorsichtig und kämpfe gegen meinen Instinkt an, aufzuspringen und Abstand zu nehmen. Ich habe das furchtbare Gefühl, ein verwundetes Raubtier provoziert zu haben, eines, das mich mühelos zerreißen könnte, ohne es zu wollen.

»In Ordnung.« Sein Stuhl schabt über den Boden, als er aufsteht. »Komm her, und ich zeige es dir.

21

eter

SIE BLEIBT WIE VERSTEINERT SITZEN. Ein Reh, gefangen im Fadenkreuz der Waffe des Jägers. Ich weiß, dass ich ihr Angst mache, aber ich kann gerade nichts dagegen tun – nicht mit dem Schmerz und der Wut, die von tief innen heraus aufsteigen.

Selbst nach fünfeinhalb Jahren hat der Gedanke an Pashas und Tamilas Tod die Macht, mich zu zerstören.

»Komm her«, wiederhole ich und gehe um den Tisch herum. Ich ergreife Saras Arm, ziehe sie nach oben und ignoriere, wie steif sie ist. »Du willst es wissen? Du willst sehen, was dein Ehemann und seine Kohorte getan haben?«

Ihr schlanker Arm in meinem Griff ist angespannt, als ich mit meiner freien Hand in meine Tasche greife und mein altes Smartphone heraushole. Ich habe es immer bei mir, auch wenn es nicht mit einem Netzwerk verbunden werden kann und ich keine Telefonate damit tätigen kann. Ich wische mit meinem Daumen über das Display, um zu den ältesten Bildern zu gelangen.

»Hier.« Ich lege ihr das Telefon in ihre freie Hand. »Schau es dir ganz genau an.«

Saras Hand zittert, als sie das Telefon näher an ihr Gesicht hält, und ich kann den genauen Moment erkennen, in dem sie das erste Foto erblickt. Ihr Gesicht wird blass, und sie schluckt krampfhaft, bevor sie über das Display wischt, um die restlichen Bilder zu betrachten.

Ich selbst blicke nicht auf das Telefon – das muss ich nicht. Die Bilder sind in meine Netzhaut gebrannt, wie ein grausiges Tattoo in mein Gehirn.

Ich habe diese Fotos einen Tag nach meiner Flucht vor den Soldaten gemacht, die mich vom Tatort weggezogen haben. Sie hatten die verbliebenen Dorfbewohner bereits umgesiedelt, aber die Untersuchung begann gerade erst, und sie hatten die Leichen noch nicht weggebracht. Als ich zurückkam, lagen sie immer noch da, von Fliegen und auf ihnen krabbelnden Insekten bedeckt. Ich habe alles fotografiert: die ausgebrannten Gebäude, die dunklen Blutflecken auf dem Gras, die verwesenden Leichen und die abgerissenen Gliedmaßen, Pashas kleine Hand, die das Spielzeugauto umklammert ... es gab Dinge, die ich nicht einfangen konnte, wie den Gestank des verwesenden

Fleisches, der dick in der Luft hing, und die hoffnungslose Leere des verlassenen Dorfes, aber was ich aufgenommen habe, ist genug.

Sara lässt ihre Hand mit dem Telefon sinken, und ich nehme es aus ihren blutleeren Fingern, um es zurück in meine Tasche zu schieben.

»Das war Daryevo.« Ich lasse ihren Arm los, und jedes Wort fühlt sich wie Sandpapier auf meiner Kehle an. »Ein kleines Dorf in Dagestan, in dem meine Frau und mein Sohn lebten.«

Sara tritt einen Schritt zurück. »Was …« Sie schluckt hörbar. »Was ist dort passiert? Warum wurden sie umgebracht?«

Ich hole tief Luft, um die gewaltige Wut, die in mir kocht, zu kontrollieren. »Weil manche Menschen arrogant und voller blindem Ehrgeiz sind.«

Sara schaut mich verständnislos an.

»Es war eine geheime Mission, um eine kleine, aber sehr effektive Terroristenzelle im Kaukasus zu fassen«, fahre ich hart fort. »Eine Gruppe NATO-Soldaten hat nach Informationen von einem Bündnis der westlichen Geheimdienste gehandelt. Alles wurde heimlich gemacht, damit sie ihren Ruhm nicht mit den lokalen Antiterrorgruppen wie der, die ich für Russland angeführt habe, teilen mussten.«

Sara bedeckt ihren zitternden Mund, und ich kann sehen, dass sie beginnt, zu verstehen.

»Das stimmt, Ptichka.« Ich gehe zu ihr, ergreife ihr schlankes Handgelenk und ziehe ihre Hand von ihrem Gesicht weg. »Du kannst dir denken, wer damit zu tun hatte, den Soldaten die falschen Informationen zukommen zu lassen.«

Ihre Augen sind voller Entsetzen. »Die Terroristenzelle war nicht dort?«

»Nein.« Mein Griff um ihr Handgelenk ist bestrafend fest, aber ich kann meine Finger gerade nicht entspannen. Mit den Erinnerungen frisch in meinem Kopf kann ich nichts dagegen tun, sie als die Frau meines toten Feindes zu sehen. »Ein Dorf voller Zivilisten, und wenn dein Ehemann und die anderen, die in dem Team gearbeitet haben, *mein* Team kontaktiert hätten, hätten sie das wissen können.« Meine Stimme wird rauer und meine Worte beißender. »Wenn sie nicht so beschissen arrogant, so gierig auf Ruhm gewesen wären, hätten sie Hilfe gesucht, anstatt zu denken, dass sie alles wüssten – und sie hätten erfahren, dass ihre Informationsquelle die Terroristen selbst gewesen waren, und meine Frau und mein Sohn wären noch am Leben.«

Ich kann das schnelle Flattern von Saras Puls spüren, als sie zu mir hochblickt, und ich sehe, dass sie mir nicht glaubt, zumindest nicht ganz. Sie denkt, dass ich verrückt bin, oder bestenfalls falsch informiert. Ihr Zweifel verstärkt meine Wut, und ich zwinge mich dazu, ihr Handgelenk loszulassen, bevor ich ihre zerbrechlichen Knochen zerdrücke.

Sie geht sofort auf Abstand, und ich weiß, dass sie die Gewalt unter meiner Haut pulsieren spüren kann. In dem Moment, in dem ich erfahren habe, was wirklich passiert war, konnte ich die anderen NATO-

Soldaten oder die beteiligten Geheimagenten nicht bestrafen – die Aufräumaktion war unglaublich schnell und gründlich –, also habe ich meine Wut an der Terroristenzelle ausgelassen, die die falsche Information gestreut hatte, gefolgt von allen, die dumm genug waren, sich mir in den Weg zu stellen.

Der Tod meines Sohnes hat das Monster in mir entfesselt, und es läuft immer noch frei herum.

Als wir einen Meter Abstand zueinander haben, hört Sara auf, sich weiter zurückzuziehen und betrachtet mich vorsichtig. »Ist das der Grund, weshalb ...« Sie beißt sich auf die Lippe. »Bist du deshalb zum Deserteur geworden? Wegen dem, was damals passiert ist?«

Meine Hände ballen sich zu Fäusten, und ich drehe mich weg, um zum Tisch zurückzugehen. Ich kann nicht eine Sekunde länger darüber reden. Jeder Satz ist wie ein Säureregen auf mein Herz. Ich bin an dem Punkt angelangt, an dem ich einige Stunden verbringen kann, ohne permanent an den gewaltsamen Tod meiner Familie denken zu müssen, aber darüber zu reden, was passiert ist, bringt die Zerstörung jenes Tages zurück – und die Wut, die mich aufgefressen hat.

Wenn wir weiter bei diesem Thema bleiben, könnte ich meine Kontrolle verlieren und Sara wehtun.

Ein Schritt nach dem anderen. Eine Sache nach der anderen. Ich verdränge alles aus meinem Gehirn, so wie wenn ich einen Job erledige, und konzentriere mich auf das, was getan werden muss. In diesem Fall ist es, den Tisch abzudecken, die Reste in den Kühlschrank zu stellen und das Geschirr in den Geschirrspüler zu räumen. Ich konzentriere mich auf diese weltlichen Aktivitäten, und langsam lässt meine kochende Wut nach, genauso wie mein Drang, etwas Gewalttätiges zu tun.

Als ich den Geschirrspüler anstelle und mich wieder zu Sara umdrehe, sehe ich, dass sie mich vorsichtig betrachtet. Sie sieht aus, als würde sie jeden Moment flüchten wollen, und die Tatsache, dass sie es noch nicht getan hat, bedeutet, dass sie ihre Lage versteht.

Wenn sie jetzt rennt, werde ich nicht sanft sein, wenn ich sie fange.

»Gehen wir nach oben«, sage ich und gehe auf sie zu. »Es ist an der Zeit, ins Bett zu gehen.«

———

IHRE HAND IST EISIG in meiner, als ich sie die Treppe hinaufführe, und ihr wunderschönes Gesicht blass. Wenn ich mich innerlich nicht so roh fühlen würde, würde ich sie beruhigen, ihr sagen, dass ich ihr auch heute Nacht nicht wehtun werde, aber ich will nichts versprechen, was ich vielleicht nicht halten kann.

Das Monster ist zu nahe an der Oberfläche, zu sehr außer Kontrolle.

»Zieh dich aus«, befehle ich und lasse ihre Hand los, als wir an ihrem Schlafzimmer ankommen. Sie trägt Skinny-Jeans und ein weites, elfenbeinfarbenes Sweatshirt, und auch wenn sie in diesem schlichten

Outfit phänomenal aussieht, will ich, dass es verschwindet.

Ich will nicht, dass es Barrieren zwischen uns gibt.

Anstatt zu gehorchen, geht Sara auf Abstand. »Bitte …« Sie bleibt auf halbem Weg zwischen mir und dem Bett stehen. »Bitte tu das nicht. Es tut mir leid, was mit deiner Familie geschehen ist, und falls George auf irgendeine Art und Weise dafür verantwortlich war …«

»Das war er.« Mein Ton ist schneidend. »Es hat Jahre gedauert, aber ich habe die Namen aller Soldaten und Geheimdienstler bekommen, die an diesem Massaker beteiligt waren. Das ist kein Missverständnis, Sara, meine Liste kam direkt von eurem eigenen CIA.«

Sie sieht fassungslos aus. »Du hast sie vom CIA bekommen? Aber … wie? Ich dachte, du hättest gesagt, dass sie daran beteiligt waren, dass George einer von ihnen war.«

»Es gibt viele Divisionen und Fraktionen in der Organisation. Eine Hand weiß nicht immer oder interessiert sich nicht immer für das, was die andere tut. Ich kenne einen Waffenhändler, der einen Kontakt dort hat, und er, besser gesagt seine Frau, hat mir die Liste gegeben. Aber das ist irrelevant.« Ich verschränke meine Arme vor der Brust. »Zieh dich aus.«

Seine Augen richten sich auf das Bett und danach auf die Tür hinter mir.

»Tu das nicht. Du willst mich heute Nacht nicht testen, vertraue mir.«

Ihr Blick richtet sich wieder auf mein Gesicht, und

ich kann ihre Verzweiflung spüren. »Bitte, Peter. Bitte tu das nicht. Was deiner Familie zugestoßen ist, war furchtbar, aber das hier wird sie nicht zurückbringen. Es tut mir leid für sie, aber ich hatte nichts zu tun mit …«

»Das hat damit nichts zu tun.« Ich nehme meine Arme herunter. »Was ich von dir möchte, hat nichts mit dem zu tun, was passiert ist.« Aber als ich es ausspreche, weiß ich, dass es eine Lüge ist. Ich handele nicht wie ein Mann, der eine Frau umwirbt, sondern wie ein Raubtier, das seine Beute verfolgt. Wenn sie nicht diejenige wäre, die sie ist, wenn sie einfach eine zufällige Begegnung wäre, würde ich mich nicht derart in ihr Leben drängen.

Mein Verlangen nach ihr wäre sanft und kontrolliert gewesen, und nicht gefährlich besessen.

Sara wirft mir einen ungläubigen Blick zu, und mir wird klar, dass sie das auch weiß. Ich mache niemandem etwas vor. Was zwischen uns geschieht, hat definitiv mit der dunklen Vergangenheit zu tun, die wir gemeinsam haben.

Also gut.

Ich gehe auf sie zu. »Zieh dich aus, Sara. Ich werde dich nicht noch einmal bitten.«

Sie weicht wieder zurück, hält dann allerdings inne, wahrscheinlich, weil sie bemerkt, dass sie sich dem Bett nähert. Selbst mit ihrem dicken Sweatshirt, das ihre Rundungen verbirgt, kann ich ihre schmale Brust beben sehen, während ihre Hände an ihren Seiten sich abwechselnd zu Fäusten ballen und sich wieder entspannen.

»In Ordnung. Wenn du es so möchtest …« Ich beginne, zu ihr zu gehen, aber sie hebt ihre Arme mit den Handflächen in meine Richtung an.

»Warte!« Ihre Hände zittern, als sie nach ihrem Sweatshirt greift. »Ich werde es tun.«

Ich bleibe stehen und beobachte sie dabei, wie sie sich den Pullover über den Kopf zieht. Darunter trägt sie ein enges, blaues Tanktop, das ihre Schultern unbedeckt lässt und die weichen Kurven ihrer Brüste betont. Sie sind nicht die größten, die ich jemals gesehen habe, aber sie passen zu ihrer ballerinaartigen Figur, und mein Schwanz versteift sich, als ich mich daran erinnere, wie sich diese hübschen Brüste angefühlt haben, als sie letzte Nacht auf meinem Arm lagen.

Bald werde ich wissen, wie sie sich in meinen Händen anfühlen – und wie sie schmecken.

»Weiter«, sage ich, als Sara erneut zögert und ihr Blick an mir vorbei zur Tür schweift. »Tanktop, dann Jeans.«

Ihre Hände zittern, als sie meiner Aufforderung nachkommt und sich ihr Tanktop über den Kopf zieht, bevor sie nach dem Reißverschluss ihrer Jeans greift. Unter ihrem Top trägt sie einen zweckmäßigen weißen BH, und ich muss mich dazu zwingen, ruhig stehenzubleiben, als sie ihre Jeans nach unten zieht und einen hellblauen Slip freilegt. Auch wenn ich letzte Nacht ihre nackte Haut an meiner gespürt habe und sie mehrere Male unbekleidet in den Kameras gesehen habe, ist das hier das erste Mal, dass ich sie aus dieser Nähe nackt sehe, und mein Herzschlag wird schneller, als ich hungrig jede anmutige Linie und Wölbung ihres Körpers aufsauge.

Sie ist nur durchschnittlich groß, aber ihre Beine sind lang und haben die wohlgeformten Muskeln einer Tänzerin. Ihr Bauch ist flach und straff, ihre schmale Taille geht in weibliche Hüften über, und ihre Haut ist überall glatt und blass, ohne Anzeichen einer Sonnenbräune.

Sie ist wunderschön, meine neue Besessenheit. Wunderschön und verängstigt.

»Und jetzt den Rest«, sage ich rau, als sie ihre Jeans ganz ausgezogen hat und zitternd nur mit BH und Slip bekleidet dasteht. Ich weiß, dass ich gerade grausam bin, aber die rohe, schmerzende Wunde, die sie freigelegt hat, braucht meinen ganzen Anstand und mein Mitgefühl auf und hinterlässt nur Lust mit einem Hauch irrationalem Verlangen, zu bestrafen.

Ich möchte ihr vielleicht nicht wehtun, aber in diesem Moment muss ich sie leiden sehen.

Sie greift nach dem Verschluss ihres BHs auf dem Rücken, öffnet ihn mit ruckartigen Bewegungen, und ich hole scharf Luft, als der Schmerz in meiner Brust von einer noch intensiveren Lustwelle erstickt wird. Ich habe ihre Brüste letzte Nacht gesehen, also weiß ich, dass sie umwerfend sind, aber der Anblick ihrer straffen rosa Nippel und des weißen Fleisches trifft mich wie ein Faustschlag. Mein Herz schlägt in einem schnellen, harten Rhythmus, und ich kann kaum an meinem Platz stehen bleiben und sie nicht ergreifen, als sie ihren Slip auszieht. Ihre Muschi ist glatt und haarlos – entweder sie wachst sie regelmäßig oder hat sich irgendwann einer Laserbehandlung unterzogen – und mir läuft das Wasser im Munde zusammen, als ich mir vorstelle, wie meine Zunge durch diese zarten Falten fährt.

Ich kann es kaum erwarten, sie zu schmecken und sie kommen zu lassen.

Während ich mir das vorstelle, stellt sich Sara gerade hin und streckt trotzig ihr Kinn nach vorn. »Bist du jetzt glücklich?« Auch wenn ihre Wangen knallrot sind, versucht sie nicht, ihren Körper zu verstecken, und ihre Hände bleiben zu Fäusten geballt an ihren Seiten.

Perverserweise dämpft diese kleine mutige Geste die dunkle Lust, die in mir wütet, und mein Mund verzieht sich zu einem amüsierten Lächeln.

»Noch nicht, aber bald«, antworte ich und ziehe mich ebenfalls aus. Meine Bewegungen sind schnell und effektiv, um mein Ziel so schnell wie möglich zu erreichen, und ihr Gesicht brennt noch mehr und ihre Brust bebt, während sie mich anstarrt.

»Komm«, sage ich und gehe zu ihr, als ich komplett ausgezogen bin. »Ich weiß, dass du gern duschst, bevor du ins Bett gehst.«

Sie blinzelt, ihre Augen suchen mein Gesicht, und ich verstehe, dass sie meinen Schwanz angestarrt hat, der so hart ist, dass er sich in Richtung meines Bauchnabels biegt.

»Du kannst ihn unter der Dusche anfassen, wenn du möchtest«, sage ich, und mein Lächeln wird wegen ihrer offensichtlichen Verlegenheit noch breiter. »Komm, Ptichka. Du wirst es genießen.«

Ich umfasse ihr Handgelenk und führe sie zum Badezimmer.

22

———

 ara

ICH VERSUCHE, Haltung zu bewahren – oder zumindest den Anschein –, als Peter mich in das Bad schleift, und seine langen Finger dabei fest um meinem Handgelenk liegen. So habe ich mir diese Nacht definitiv nicht vorgestellt, als ich die Treppen nach oben gegangen bin. Trotz der unterschwelligen Dunkelheit in seinen Augen scheint mein Peiniger in einer unbeschwerten, fast spielerischen Stimmung zu sein – ein starker Gegensatz zu der furchtbaren Wut, die ich vorhin auf seinem Gesicht gesehen habe.

Es ist, als hätte mein erzwungener kleiner Striptease die Dämonen beruhigt, die die entsetzlichen Bilder entfesselt hatten.

Übelkeit breitet sich erneut in mir aus, als ich an die

Bilder denke, den Tod und die Zerstörung, die so grausam detailliert gezeigt wurden. Ich habe sie nur einige Sekunden lang angeschaut, aber ich weiß, dass ich sie nie wieder vergessen werde. Ich kann mir nicht vorstellen, wie es sein muss, persönlich dort zu sein und diese Fotos zu schießen, noch weniger, wenn es sich um meine Familie handeln würde, die dort läge – dass die verwesenden Leichen Menschen wären, die ich geliebt hätte. Allein der Gedanke daran erfüllt mich mit solchen Qualen, dass ich für einen herzzerreißenden Moment verstehe, was meinen Angreifer antreibt.

Das entschuldigt nicht das, was er tut, aber ich verstehe es, und Mitleid kämpft in meiner Brust gegen Entsetzen an.

Wenn Peter glaubt, dass mein Ehemann für diese Tode verantwortlich ist, hatte er keine andere Wahl, als ihn zu jagen. So viel ist mir klar. Selbst bevor er abtrünnig wurde, hatte der Russe durch seinen Job die dunkelsten Seiten der Menschlichkeit gesehen, gelernt, dass Gewalt eine Lösung ist, und das schließt noch nicht einmal seine Erfahrungen davor ein, die ihn im Alter von zwölf Jahren zu einem Mörder werden ließen. Ein Mann wie er würde nicht auch noch die andere Wange hinhalten, sondern ein Auge für ein Auge nehmen. Es wäre ihm egal, wie viele Unschuldige er bei seinem Streben nach Rache verletzt, und mit Sicherheit würde er nicht mit der Wimper zucken, die Frau seines Feindes zu foltern, um ihn zu finden.

Wenn George *irgendetwas* mit dem, was geschehen

ist, zu tun hatte, habe ich Glück, dass ich noch am Leben bin. Als wir vor der gläsernen Duschkabine stehen, lässt mein Gefängniswärter mein Handgelenk los, tritt hinein und macht das Wasser an. Als er den Wasserhahn bedient, um die richtige Wassertemperatur einzustellen, werfe ich einen Blick auf die Badezimmertür. Er ist nass und abgelenkt, also bin ich mir beinahe sicher, dass ich es die Treppen nach unten und in mein Auto schaffen kann, bevor er mich einholt. Aber was dann? Soll ich nackt zu irgendeinem Hotel fahren und hoffen, dass er mich heute Nacht nicht findet? Soll ich auf dem kürzesten Weg zum FBI fahren und sie anbetteln, mich zu verstecken?

Bevor ich diese innerliche Debatte erneut beginnen kann, tritt Peter aus der Dusche, und Wassertropfen glänzen auf seiner kräftigen Brust. »Komm rein«, sagt er, greift nach meinem Arm, und ich stolpere fast, als er mich in die Kabine zieht.

»Vorsichtig«, murmelt er, hält mich fest, und als ich aufschaue, sehe ich, dass er mich mit einer Mischung aus Verlangen und dunkler Belustigung anschaut. »Es ist feucht hier.«

Diese Anspielung erweckt die Röte, die mein Gesicht nie ganz verlassen hatte, zu neuem Leben. Ich hasse es, dass er über die Reaktion meines Körpers auf ihn Bescheid weiß – dass er mich vor einigen Momenten dabei erwischt hat, wie ich seine Erektion wie ein Teenager, der zum ersten Mal einen Porno sieht, betrachtet habe. Zugegeben, mit so einem Schwanz könnte er ein erfolgreicher Pornostar sein, aber das ist nicht der Punkt. Es sollte mir egal sein, dass er ein umwerfendes männliches Tier ist, und ich sollte Angst vor seinem kräftigen Körper haben, anstatt ihn zu begehren.

Er ist gefährlich, vielleicht ein verrückter Mörder, und als solchen sollte ich ihn auch sehen.

Und das tue ich auch, also rational zumindest. Aber als er die Dusche in meine Richtung dreht, damit das warme Wasser auf meinen Rücken spritzen kann, wird mir klar, dass ich nicht ansatzweise so verängstigt bin wie letzte Nacht, auch wenn ich das nach diesen Bildern sein sollte. Wenn Peter das glaubt, was er mir erzählt hat, dann hat er allen Grund dafür, mich zu hassen, und die Anziehung, die er mir gegenüber verspürt, ist wahrscheinlich eine vergiftete. Ich weiß nicht, warum er mich letzte Nacht nicht vergewaltigt hat, aber ich bin mir fast sicher, dass er es heute Nacht tun wird. Dieser Gedanke sollte mich mit Angst erfüllen, und das tut er auch, aber die instinktive Panik, die ich in jenem Hotel verspürt habe, fehlt. Es ist, als habe das Schlafen in seinen Armen mich unempfindlich dafür gemacht, wie falsch das ist, was er mir antut, dass er sich in meinem Haus und unter meiner Dusche befindet.

Zum zweiten Mal in genauso vielen Tagen sind wir beide nackt zusammen, und ich finde das nicht ansatzweise so verstörend, wie ich es finden sollte.

»Schließe deine Augen«, sagt Peter, als er die Shampooflasche hochnimmt, und ich gehorche und lasse ihn die flüssige Seife auf meinem Haar verteilen. Trotz seiner wechselhaften Stimmung von eben sind seine starken Finger sanft, als er das Shampoo auf meinem Kopf einmassiert, und mir wird klar, dass er mich erneut verwöhnt, mich weiter mit seiner eigenartig zärtlichen Fürsorge entwaffnet. Ich verspüre den unangebrachten Wunsch, meinen Kopf nach hinten fallen zu lassen, mich wie eine Katze, die eine Streicheleinheit einfordert, an seine Hände zu schmiegen, aber ich bleibe unbeweglich stehen, weil ich nicht will, dass er weiß, dass ich irgendetwas von dem, was er mit mir tut, genieße.

Welches Spiel mein Peiniger auch mit mir spielt, ich weigere mich, mitzuspielen.

Meine Entschlossenheit dauert an, bis er beginnt, meinen Nacken zu massieren, sich gekonnt durch die Knoten an meinem Schädelansatz arbeitet. Mir war nicht aufgefallen, wie verspannt ich gewesen war, bis sich die Verspannungen durch seine Berührungen und das heiße Wasser lösen und ich mich auf einmal so warm und entspannt fühle, wie ich es seit einer sehr langen Zeit nicht mehr getan habe.

Ich versuche, mich daran zu erinnern, ob George jemals mein Haar auf diese Weise gewaschen hat, aber mir fällt nichts ein. Ich kann mich, abgesehen von einigen Malen am Anfang unserer Beziehung, als wir im Bett noch relativ abenteuerlustig waren, nicht einmal daran erinnern, überhaupt mit ihm zusammen geduscht zu haben. Nachdem wir ein Jahr lang zusammen waren, war unser Sexleben zu einer Routine geworden, und George berührte mich kaum, ohne mich schnell kommen lassen zu wollen – und am Ende hat er mich kaum berührt, Punkt.

In den letzten Tagen hatte ich mehr körperliche Intimität mit dem Mörder meines Mannes als mit meinem Ehemann während eines Großteils unserer Ehe.

Als meine Haare sauber sind, führt Peter meinen Kopf unter den Wasserstrahl, spült das Shampoo aus und massiert die Spülung ein. Während er das tut, tritt er näher an mich heran, so dass seine Brust einen Augenblick lang meine berührt. Meine Nippel verhärten sich unter dem heißen Wasser, und mein Geschlecht wird weich und feucht, als die Eichel seines harten Schwanzes gegen meinen Bauch drückt.

Einen Moment später tritt er zurück, aber da ist es bereits zu spät. Das warme, entspannte Gefühl geht so schnell in Erregung über, dass ich keine Chance habe, mich dagegen zu wappnen. Auch wenn er mich kaum berührt hat, bin ich atemlos und zittere vor Begehren nach ihm. Das ist eine rein körperliche Reaktion, aber trotzdem schäme ich mich dafür. Ich sollte ihn oder diese aufgezwungene Intimität nicht wollen, nichts davon sollte mich auf irgendeiner Ebene ansprechen.

Ich beiße auf die Innenseiten meiner Wangen, um mich mit Schmerzen abzulenken, öffne meine Augen und sehe, dass er Duschgel in seine Handfläche gießt.

»Lass mich das tun«, sage ich angespannt und will ihm die Seife abnehmen, aber er schüttelt den Kopf, und ein sinnliches Lächeln erscheint auf seinen Lippen, als er die Flasche außerhalb meiner Reichweite abstellt.

»Noch nicht, Ptichka. Du musst warten, bis du dran bist.«

Er tritt hinter mich und beginnt, meinen Rücken zu waschen. Trotz der Wärme des Wassers brennt seine Berührung heiß auf mir, und jede Bewegung seiner rauen Hände lässt die Flammen meiner Erregung, die in meinem Unterleib lodern, höher schlagen. Ich versuche, mich auf etwas anderes zu konzentrieren, irgendetwas, aber mein Herz rast zu schnell, und mein Körper brennt zu gleichen Teilen vor Scham und Verlangen.

Und Angst. Auch wenn sie in diesem Augenblick schweigt, lauert sie heimtückisch in meinem Hinterkopf. Ich habe nicht vergessen, was dieser Mann, der mich gerade berührt, getan hat, und wozu er fähig ist. Vielleicht würde eine andere Frau in meiner Situation sich wehren, anstatt das zuzulassen, aber ich möchte nicht, dass er mir ernsthaft wehtut. Gestern hat er mich mit pathetischer Leichtigkeit unterworfen, und ich weiß, dass dasselbe heute geschehen würde. Allerdings mit dem kleinen Unterschied, dass er heute vielleicht nicht aufhören würde, wenn ich unter ihm liege.

Er könnte der Dunkelheit nachgeben, die ich heute in seinen Augen aufblitzen sehen habe, und das Spiel, wie auch immer es funktioniert, würde entsetzlich enden.

Also stehe ich bewegungslos da und starre geradeaus, sehe den Wassertropfen dabei zu, wie sie das beschlagene Glas hinuntergleiten, während seine seifigen Hände über meinen Rücken gleiten, über meine Schultern, über meine Arme … meine Seiten. Es ist eine andere Art von Folter, und als seine Hände sich nach vorn bewegen, Seife auf meinem zitternden Bauch verteilen, bevor sie an meinem Brustkorb nach oben fahren, kann ich es nicht mehr ertragen.

»Hör auf«, flüstere ich atemlos, und meine Nägel graben sich in meine Oberschenkel, als seine Finger über die Unterseite meiner Brüste streichen. »Bitte, Peter, hör auf.«

Zu meiner Überraschung hört er auf mich und bewegt seine Hände wieder zu meinen Hüftknochen. »Warum?«, murmelt er und zieht mich an sich. Seine Brust schmiegt sich an meinen Rücken, während seine Erektion sich in meinen Po drückt. »Weil du es hasst?« Er beugt seinen Kopf nach unten, und seine Stoppeln kratzen an meinen Schläfen, als er mit seiner Zunge den äußeren Rand meines Ohres abfährt. »Oder weil du es magst?«

Weder noch. Beides. Ich kann nicht klar genug denken, um mich zu entscheiden. Meine Augen schließen sich, und ich bekomme eine Gänsehaut, als seine Zunge in die Wölbung hinter meinem Ohr eintaucht und ich innerlich schmelze. Ich will ihn wegschieben, aber ich traue mich nicht, mich zu bewegen, falls ich etwas Dummes mache, wie meinen Kopf nach hinten fallen zu lassen, zur quälenden Hitze dieses bösen Mundes.

»Vor was hast du Angst, Ptichka?«, fährt er mit einer leisen, dunklen Stimme fort. »Schmerzen?« Er beißt sanft in mein Ohrläppchen. »Oder Lust?« Seine rechte Hand schiebt sich schräg über meinen Bauch, mit heimtückischer Langsamkeit in Richtung des nach ihm verlangenden Dreiecks. Er gibt mir mehr als nur eine Chance, ihn aufzuhalten, aber ich kann nicht – nicht einmal, als ich sein Ziel erkenne. Alles, was ich tun kann, ist, flach zu atmen, als seine rauen Finger den Anfang meines Schlitzes erreichen und gemächlich meine Falten auseinanderschieben, um das empfindliche Fleisch freizulegen.

»Keine Antwort?« Sein Atem bläst warm gegen meine Schläfen. »Ich nehme an, dass ich es selbst herausfinden muss.«

Die Spitze seines Fingers umkreist meine Klitoris, und mein Atem stockt in meiner Brust, während mein Kopf eigenartig leer wird. Es ist, als seien alle Nervenenden in meinem Körper auf einen Schlag zum Leben erweckt worden. Ich bin mir seines großen, harten Körpers, der sich gegen meinen Rücken drückt, seiner Stoppeln, die über mein Ohr reiben, seiner großen Hand, die auf meinem Unterleib liegt, und des heißen Wassers, das auf uns fällt, mehr als bewusst. Und dieses Fingers, dieses rauen und doch zärtlichen Fingers. Er berührt mich kaum, und trotzdem fühlt sich mein Körper wie aufgezogen an, jeder Muskel vibriert voller Vorfreude.

Ich nehme ganz schwach ein eigenartiges Geräusch wahr, und mir wird klar, dass es von mir kommt. Es ist ein Stöhnen, vermischt mit einer Art keuchendem Wimmern. Ich schäme mich, aber diese Scham verstärkt meine Erregung nur, und alle meine Sinne konzentrieren sich auf das pulsierende Verlangen in diesem Nervenbündel, mit dem er so grausam spielt. Ich kann die Nässe zwischen meinen Schenkeln spüren, und als seine Finger stärker auf das überempfindliche Fleisch drücken, wird aus dem Verlangen eine unerträgliche Anspannung, die mit jeder Sekunde wächst und intensiver wird. Es ist gleichzeitig ein Genuss und eine Qual, und es ist so heftig, dass ich vibriere und Hitzewellen über meine Haut rollen. Ich versuche, es aufzuhalten, die Anspannung davon abzuhalten, ihren Höhepunkt zu erreichen, aber es ist unmöglich, diese Flut abzuwenden.

Mit einem erstickten Aufschrei komme ich, und die Entladung ist so intensiv, dass mein ganzer Körper sich derart zusammenzieht, dass ich hinter meinen geschlossenen Augenlidern Weiß sehe. Mein Orgasmus scheint unendlich lange anzudauern, die Lust sendet pulsierende Wellen aus meinem Unterleib, die mich so benebelt und zitternd zurücklassen, dass ich kaum stehen kann. Ich versuche, meinen Peiniger wegzuschieben, um dieses entsetzliche Lustgefühl zu beenden, aber er hält mich nur noch fester, und ich habe keine andere Wahl, als es bis zum Ende zu durchleben, jeden einzelnen Schauer, den er meinem Körper abringt, zu spüren.

»Genau so, Ptichka«, haucht er, als ich endlich gegen ihn sacke, keuchend und ausgelaugt. »Das war so wunderschön.«

Seine Hand zieht sich von meinem Geschlecht zurück, und ich öffne meine Augen, da die postorgastische Lethargie sich in Luft auflöst, als mir dämmert, was gerade Entsetzliches geschehen ist.

Ich bin gekommen. Ich bin durch die Hände des Mannes gekommen, der das Leben meines Ehemanns beendet hat.

Er beginnt, mich herumzudrehen, damit ich ihn ansehen kann, und endlich finde ich die Stärke, etwas zu tun. Mit einem gequälten Stöhnen winde ich mich aus seinem Griff und stolpere nach hinten, wobei ich fast in die Glaswand hinter mir krache. »Nein!« Meine Stimme ist hoch und dünn, fast schon hysterisch. »Fass mich nicht an!«

Zu meiner Überraschung bleibt Peter still stehen, auch wenn ich sehen kann, dass er immer noch erregt ist, mich immer noch will. Er legt seinen Kopf auf die Seite und betrachtet mich einige Sekunden lang schweigend, bevor er sich ausstreckt und die Dusche abstellt.

»Komm raus«, sagt er sanft und macht die Tür der Duschkabine auf. »Ich denke, dass wir sauber genug sind.«

23

eter

ICH TROCKNE mich mit einem weichen, weißen Handtuch ab und nehme danach ein anderes, um es um Sara zu wickeln, als sie aus der Dusche tritt. Sie sieht aus, als würde sie gleich zerbrechen, ihre braunen Augen glitzern schmerzhaft hell, und trotz der Lust, die mich auffrisst, fühle ich so etwas wie Mitleid.

Sie muss sich in diesem Moment hassen. Fast so sehr wie sie mich hasst.

Ich reibe das Handtuch über ihren Körper, um sie abzutrocknen, bevor ich es um ihr nasses Haar wickele. Ich weiß, dass ich sie wie ein Kind und nicht wie eine erwachsene Frau behandele, aber mich um sie zu kümmern beruhigt mich, hilft mir dabei, die dunkleren Impulse zu kontrollieren.

Hilft mir dabei, daran zu denken, dass ich ihr nicht wirklich wehtun möchte.

Ich bücke mich, hebe sie in meine Arme, und sie schnappt überrascht nach Luft. »Was tust du?« Sie drückt gegen meine Brust. »Lass mich runter!«

»Gleich.« Ich ignoriere ihre Versuche, sich aus meinen Armen zu winden, als ich sie aus dem Bad trage. Sie ist leicht, einfach zu tragen. Es fühlt sich an, als seien ihre Knochen hohl, so wie die eines echten Vogels. Sie ist zerbrechlich, meine Sara, aber gleichzeitig belastbar.

Wenn ich vorsichtig vorgehe, könnte sie mir nachgeben, anstatt zu brechen.

Als wir am Bett ankommen, setze ich sie darauf ab, und sie schnappt sich die Decke, um ihre Nacktheit zu bedecken. Ihr Blick ist voller Verzweiflung, als sie nach hinten rutscht, weg von mir.

»Warum tust du mir das an? Warum kannst du keine andere Frau zum Quälen finden?«

»Du weißt, warum, Ptichka.« Ich klettere auf das Bett und ziehe ihr die Decke weg. »Ich bin an keiner anderen interessiert.«

Sie springt vom Bett, da sie offensichtlich völlig vergessen hat, dass es sinnlos ist, vor mir wegzulaufen, und ich bin mit einem Satz bei ihr und fange sie ein, noch bevor sie an der Tür ist. Mein Blut pumpt dickflüssig in meinen Venen, als das Monster sich aufbäumt, während sie in meinen Armen gegen mich ankämpft, und ich muss meine ganze Selbstkontrolle aufbringen, um sie nicht gegen die Wand zu drücken und sie ohne Vorspiel zu ficken.

Wenn es mir nicht so wichtig wäre, dass unser erstes Mal nicht auf so eine Art stattfindet, wäre ich bereits in ihr.

»Hör auf, dich zu wehren«, knirsche ich hervor, als sie damit fortfährt, sich in meinen Armen zu winden und zu versuchen, ihnen zu entkommen. Ich spüre, wie ich langsam die Kontrolle verliere, wie mein Schwanz auf ihre Bewegungen reagiert, als führe sie einen Lapdance auf. »Ich warne dich, Sara …«

Sie versteinert, da ihr klar wird, in welcher Gefahr sie sich befindet.

Ich hole langsam Luft, bevor ich sie loslasse und von ihr abrücke, um die Versuchung zu minimieren. »Geh ins Bett«, sage ich hart, als sie einfach nur keuchend dasteht. »Wir gehen schlafen, verstanden?«

Sie bekommt große Augen. »Du wirst mich nicht …«

»Nein«, antworte ich grimmig. Ich gehe nach vorn, ergreife ihren Arm und führe sie zum Bett. »Nicht heute Nacht.«

Egal, was für eine Qual es sein wird, ich werde Sara mehr Zeit geben, um sich an mich zu gewöhnen. Das ist das Mindeste, was ich tun kann, um unseren gewalttätigen Anfang wiedergutzumachen.

Sie wird bald mir gehören, aber noch nicht jetzt.

Nicht, bis ich sicher bin, dass ich sie nicht zerstöre.

»BIST DU WACH, Papa? Komm, spiel mit mir.« Eine kleine Hand zieht an meinem Handgelenk. »Bitte, Papa, komm spielen.«

»Lass deinen Vater schlafen«, rügt Tamila und stützt sich auf der anderen Seite des Bettes auf ihrem Ellenbogen auf. »Er ist gestern Abend erst spät nach Hause gekommen.«

Ich rolle mich auf den Rücken und setze mich gähnend hin. »Das ist in Ordnung, Tamilochka. Ich bin wach.« Ich beuge mich nach unten, nehme meinen Sohn hoch und stehe auf, wobei ich ihn gleichzeitig hochhebe. Pasha quietscht vor Vergnügen, und seine kleinen Beine treten in die Luft, als ich ihn über meinen Kopf halte.

»Du bist viel zu nachsichtig mit ihm«, murmelt Tamila, bevor sie ebenfalls aufsteht und sich einen Bademantel über ihren Schlafanzug zieht. »Ich gehe das Frühstück machen.«

Sie verschwindet im Badezimmer, und ich grinse Pasha an. »Du willst spielen, Pupsik?« Ich werfe ihn in die Luft und fange ihn wieder auf, wobei er lachend aufschreit. »So?« Ich werfe ihn erneut hoch.

»Ja!« Er lacht jetzt so sehr, dass er schon gluckst. »Mehr! Höher!«

Ich lache und werfe ihn dann noch einige weitere Male, wobei ich die Schmerzen in meinen geprellten Rippen ignoriere. Ich habe die letzte Woche damit verbracht, eine Gruppe von Aufständischen zu jagen, und gestern haben wir sie endlich gefunden. In der anschließenden Schießerei habe ich einige Kugeln in meine Weste bekommen. Nichts Ernstes, aber ich könnte ein paar ruhige Tage gebrauchen. Trotzdem würde ich diese Spielzeit um nichts auf der Welt missen wollen.

Mein Sohn wächst sowieso schon viel zu schnell.

ICH WACHE mit einem bittersüßen Schmerz in meiner Brust auf. Ich muss meine Augen nicht öffnen, um zu wissen, wo ich bin, oder zu verstehen, dass ich geträumt habe. Der Schmerz, Pasha verloren zu haben, sitzt zu tief in mir, als dass ich eine Erinnerung in einem Traum für etwas anderes halten könnte, auch wenn es das erste Mal *ist*, dass ich einen so lebhaften schönen Traum hatte.

Normalerweise sind meine Träume über meine Familie weich und verschwommen – zumindest bis sie zu bildhaften Albträumen werden.

Ich liege einige Momente still da, lausche Saras gleichmäßiger Atmung und nehme das Gefühl ihres schlanken Körpers in meiner Umarmung in mich auf. Endlich ist sie eingeschlafen, und ihr überaktiver Kopf ruht sich aus. Sie hat heute Abend nicht mehr mit mir geredet, hat einfach eine Stunde lang dagelegen, und ich wusste, dass sie sich wegen dem Vorwürfe gemacht hat, was unter der Dusche passiert ist. Ich habe darüber nachgedacht, mit ihr zu reden, sie von ihren Gedanken abzulenken, aber mit den frischen Erinnerungen in meinem Kopf und meinem harten und verlangenden Körper wollte ich es nicht riskieren, dass die Unterhaltung auf ein schmerzhaftes Terrain gelenkt wird.

Hätte sie begonnen, ihren Ehemann zu verteidigen, hätte ich die Kontrolle verlieren und ihr wehtun können.

Ich hole Luft, atme den süßen Duft ihres Haares ein und lasse die vertraute Lustwelle die restliche Anspannung in meiner Brust vertreiben. Es ergibt kaum einen Sinn, aber ich bin mir sicher, dass Sara der Grund dafür ist, dass ich zum ersten Mal in fünfeinhalb Jahren von meinem Sohn geträumt habe, ohne gleichzeitig von seinem Tod zu träumen. Auch wenn es eine Art Selbstfolter ist, ihren nackten Körper in meinen Armen zu halten, ohne sie zu ficken, hat Saras Gegenwart in meinem Bett dieselbe Wirkung auf mich wie ihre Nähe, wenn ich wach bin.

Wenn ich bei ihr bin, ist der Schmerz über meinen Verlust weniger stark, fast erträglich.

Ich schließe die Augen, versuche, an nichts zu denken, und lasse mich wieder in den Schlaf sinken.

Wenn ich Glück habe, werde ich Pasha noch einmal im Traum begegnen.

24

S*ara*

WIE GESTERN IST Peter bereits verschwunden, als ich aufwache. Ich bin froh, dass es so ist, weil ich nicht weiß, wie ich mich ihm gegenüber heute Morgen verhalten hätte. Jedes Mal, wenn ich an das denke, was in der Dusche geschehen ist, sterbe ich innerlich ein wenig.

Ich habe George betrogen, die Erinnerung an ihn auf die schlimmste vorstellbare Weise betrogen. Ich habe meinen Mann getroffen, als ich gerade achtzehn Jahre alt war. Er war mein erster fester Freund, mein erster Ein und Alles. Und selbst als die Dinge den Bach runtergingen, habe ich treu zu ihm und unserer Hochzeit gestanden.

Bis letzte Nacht war George der einzige Mann

gewesen, mit dem ich jemals Sex hatte, der Einzige, bei dem ich jemals gekommen bin.

Der Schmerz überrollt mich, die Trauer ist so durchdringend und plötzlich, dass sie sich wie ein Schlag ins Gesicht anfühlt. Keuchend beuge ich mich über die Spüle und umklammere meine Zahnbürste dabei mit der Faust. In den letzten sechs Monaten war ich mit meiner Angst, meinen Panikattacken und meinen Schuldgefühlen, weil ich für Georges Tod verantwortlich bin, so beschäftigt gewesen, dass ich keine Gelegenheit hatte, wirklich um meinen Ehemann zu trauern. Ich habe das leere Loch, das seine Abwesenheit in meinem Leben hinterlassen hat, noch gar nicht verarbeitet, habe mich noch nicht mit der Tatsache beschäftigt, dass der Mann, mit dem ich für fast ein Jahrzehnt zusammen gewesen bin, gegangen ist.

George ist tot, und ich hatte einen Orgasmus durch seinen Mörder.

Mein Magen krampft sich vor Übelkeit zusammen, während ich mich im Badezimmerspiegel anstarre und das Gesicht hasse, das zurückschaut. Die Leichtigkeit, mit der ich letzte Nacht gekommen bin, erfüllt mich mit einem heißen, roten Schamgefühl. Peter hat mich kaum berührt, hat kaum irgendetwas getan. Er hat mich nicht einmal wirklich festgehalten. Wenn ich es versucht hätte, hätte ich ihn vielleicht sogar wegschieben können, aber ich habe es nicht versucht.

Ich habe einfach nur dagestanden und der Lust nachgegeben, bevor ich die zweite Nacht hintereinander in den Armen meines Peinigers geschlafen habe.

Der Schmerz erstarrt zu einem dicken Knoten aus Ekel vor mir selbst, und ich blicke von meinem Spiegelbild weg, da ich die Kritik in den braunen Augen, die mich anblicken, nicht ertragen kann. Ich kann das nicht tun, kann dieses kranke und abartige Spiel, das Peter mir aufzwingt, nicht spielen. Es ist mir egal, ob er seine Gründe dafür hat oder denkt, er habe sie. Kein Leid dieser Welt entschuldigt das, was er George angetan hat, oder was er mir immer noch antut.

Mein Peiniger mag verletzt sein, aber das macht ihn nur noch gefährlicher – für meinen gesunden Verstand und meine Sicherheit.

Ich muss einen Ausweg aus dieser Sache finden.

Egal, mit welchen Mitteln, ich muss ihn loswerden.

———

ICH VERBRINGE den Großteil meiner Schicht wie ferngesteuert. Zum Glück stehen keine Operationen oder andere kritische Dinge an, ansonsten hätte ich vielleicht einen anderen Arzt bitten müssen, einzuspringen. Zum ersten Mal drehen sich meine Gedanken nicht um die Bedürfnisse meiner Patienten, sondern darum, was ich tun muss, um mit meinem Stalker fertigzuwerden.

Es wird nicht einfach werden und mit Sicherheit gefährlich, aber ich habe keine Wahl.

Ich kann nicht noch eine weitere Nacht in den Armen eines Mannes verbringen, den ich hasse.

Ich bin fast fertig mit meiner Schicht, als ich auf

dem Gang in Joe Levinson renne. Zuerst gehe ich an ihm vorbei, aber er ruft mich, und ich erkenne den großen, schlanken Mann mit den sandfarbenen Haaren wieder.

»Joe, hallo«, erwidere ich lächelnd. Es war nett gewesen, sich mit ihm bei dem Abendessen am Samstag bei meinen Eltern zu unterhalten, genauso wie eigentlich jedes andere Mal, an dem wir uns im Laufe der Jahre durch die Freundschaft unserer Eltern getroffen haben. Unter anderen Umständen – also wenn ich nicht erst verheiratet und dann plötzlich gewaltsam zur Witwe geworden wäre – hätte ich vielleicht darüber nachgedacht, mich auf ein Date mit Joe einzulassen, um meinen Eltern eine Freude zu machen und weil ich ihn wirklich gerne mag. Mein Puls fängt nicht an zu rasen, wenn ich ihn sehe, aber er ist ein netter Kerl, und für mich zählt das eine Menge. »Was tust du hier?«

»Das«, antwortet er reumütig und hebt seine rechte Hand, um einen dick bandagierten Finger zu zeigen.

»Oh nein! Wie ist das denn passiert?«

Er verzieht das Gesicht. »Ich habe gegen eine Küchenmaschine gekämpft, und die Maschine hat gewonnen.«

»Autsch.« Ich zucke zusammen, als ich mir das bildlich vorstelle. »Wie schlimm ist es?«

»So schlimm, dass sie es nicht nähen können. Ich werde warten müssen, bis es von alleine aufhört zu bluten.«

»Das tut mir so leid. Also bist du damit in die

Notaufnahme gegangen?«

»Ja, aber ich habe offensichtlich überreagiert. Ich meine, überall war Blut, und meine Fingerspitze besteht nur noch aus rohem Fleisch, aber sie haben gesagt, es würde von allein heilen und vielleicht nicht einmal eine schlimme Narbe hinterlassen.«

»Oh, das freut mich. Ich hoffe, dass es schnell heilt.«

Er grinst mich an, und seine blauen Augen funkeln. »Danke, ich auch.«

Ich lächele zurück und will gerade weitergehen, als er sagt: »Hey, Sara …«

Bei seinem zögerlichen Gesichtsausdruck zucke ich innerlich zusammen. »Ja?« Ich hoffe nur, dass er mich nicht fragen will, ob wir …

»Ich wollte dich eigentlich anrufen, aber da wir uns ja jetzt getroffen haben … Was machst du am Freitag?«, fragt er und bestätigt damit meine Vermutung. »Im Zentrum gibt es eine wirklich tolle Kunstausstellung, und …«

»Es tut mir leid. Ich kann nicht.« Ich lehne ganz automatisch ab, und erst als ich den enttäuschten Gesichtsausdruck von Joe sehe, fällt mir auf, wie unhöflich ich gewesen bin. Weil ich mich schrecklich fühle, mache ich einen Rückzieher. »Es ist nicht so, dass ich nicht möchte, aber ich habe Freitag wahrscheinlich Bereitschaftsdienst und weiß nicht, ob …«

»Ist schon in Ordnung. Mach dir keine Gedanken.« Er lächelt, und ich sehe sofort, dass es nur aufgesetzt ist. Ich tue dasselbe, wenn ich versuche, meine wahren Gefühle zu verbergen.

Scheiße. Er muss mich lieber mögen, als mir klar war.

»Möchtest du stattdessen etwas anderes tun?«, frage ich ihn, ohne nachzudenken. »Nicht diesen Freitag, aber vielleicht später?«

Joes Lächeln verwandelt sich in ein echtes, und er bekommt attraktive Fältchen an den Augenwinkeln. »Natürlich. Wie wäre es mit Abendessen übernächstes Wochenende? Ich kenne einen kleinen Italiener, der die beste Lasagne überhaupt macht.«

»Das hört sich gut an«, antworte ich und bereue bereits meine Spontaneität. Was ist, wenn ich meinen Stalker bis dahin nicht los bin? Aber da es bereits zu spät ist, um alles zurückzunehmen, sage ich: »Können wir den genauen Tag und die Uhrzeit später abmachen? Mein Arbeitsplan ändert sich andauernd, und ...«

»Du musst nichts weiter erklären. Ich verstehe das.« Er schenkt mir ein breites Lächeln. »Ich habe deine Nummer, also werde ich dich einfach nächste Woche anrufen, und du sagst mir, wann es dir am besten passt, okay?«

»Okay. Wir hören uns«, antworte ich und verschwinde den Gang hinunter, bevor ich meinen Mund noch einmal zu weit aufreiße.

Ich muss noch zu einem letzten Patienten gehen, und dann kann ich meine Mission ausführen.

Wenn alles klappt wie geplant, werde ich morgen wieder frei sein.

»WIRST du sie heute Nacht wiedersehen?«, fragt Anton mich auf Russisch, als ich den Raum betrete, und schaut von seinem Laptop auf. Wie immer ist der ehemalige Pilot von Kopf bis Fuß in Schwarz gekleidet und bis zu den Zähnen bewaffnet, auch wenn unser Versteck in der Vorstadt so sicher wie möglich ist. Wie der Rest meiner Mannschaft ist er ein tödlicher Bastard, und auch wenn wir ihn oft wegen seines hippen langen Haares und seinem dicken, schwarzen Bart aufziehen, sieht er genau nach dem aus, was er ist: ein ehemaliger Mörder des Speznas.

»Natürlich«, antworte ich, ebenfalls auf Russisch.

Ich bleibe neben dem kleinen Tisch neben dem Sofa, auf dem Anton sitzt, stehen, ziehe meine Lederjacke aus und nehme das Waffenarsenal ab, das an meiner Brust befestigt ist. Wenn ich zu Sara gehe, nehme ich nur eine Pistole und einige Messer mit, die ich strategisch in den Innentaschen meiner Jacke unterbringe, damit sie sie nicht sieht, wenn ich mich an- oder ausziehe. Ich will ihr keine Angst einjagen oder sie an das erinnern, was ich bin; sie weiß sowieso schon zu gut über meine Fähigkeiten Bescheid. Außerdem wäre ich ein Idiot, wenn ich ihr vertrauen würde, wenn Waffen in der Nähe sind.

Selbst jemand ohne Erfahrungen kann eine Waffe abfeuern und einen Glückstreffer landen.

»Yan übernimmt die erste Schicht heute Nacht«, sagt Anton, bevor er seine Aufmerksamkeit wieder dem Laptop auf seinem Schoß zuwendet. »Ich muss noch einige logistische Dinge für den Einsatz in Mexiko ausarbeiten.«

Ich runzele die Stirn, während ich meine kugelsichere Weste ablege. »Ich dachte, es sei bereits alles fertig.«

»Ja, das dachte ich auch, aber es sieht so aus, als sei er in einen kleinen Streit mit deinem alten Kumpel Esguerra geraten, und jetzt verschärft er wie ein Irrer seine Sicherheitsmaßnahmen. Ich denke, er erwartet, dass Esguerra ihn angreifen wird. Das hat offensichtlich nichts mit uns zu tun, aber trotzdem. Es erschwert unser Vorhaben.«

»Scheiße.« Dass Julian Esguerra mit der Sache zu tun hat, wie indirekt auch immer, erschwert definitiv mein Vorhaben, und nicht nur, weil er ungewollt unser

Opfer verschreckt hat. Dieser kolumbianische Waffenhändler ist ernsthaft wütend auf mich. Auch wenn ich das Leben dieses Bastards gerettet habe, habe ich dabei das Leben seiner Frau in Gefahr gebracht, und das wird er mir niemals verzeihen. Er verfolgt mich zwar nicht, aber sollte er erfahren, dass ich in Mexiko bin, so nahe bei ihm, könnte er sein Versprechen, mich zu töten, wahrmachen wollen.

Jetzt, da ich darüber nachdenke, wird mir klar, dass ich hier, in Illinois, auch in der Nähe seines Hoheitsgebiets bin. Die Eltern seiner Frau leben in Oak Lawn, nicht allzu weit entfernt von Saras Haus in Homer Glen. Ich glaube nicht, dass er ihnen in der nächsten Zeit einen Besuch abstatten wird, aber sollte er es tun und sollten sich unsere Wege irgendwie kreuzen, werde ich nicht darum herumkommen, mich mit ihm auseinanderzusetzen.

Aber gut. Darüber werde ich mir Gedanken machen, wenn es so weit ist. Ich werde auf keinen Fall von hier weggehen, bevor ich mit Sara fertig bin.

»Ja«, murmelt Anton, während er auf seinen Computer starrt. »Das ist wirklich scheiße.«

Ich lasse ihn in Ruhe arbeiten und gehe in die Küche, um mir ein Bier aus dem Kühlschrank zu nehmen. Heute habe ich einen Job hier in der Nähe erledigt, während Yans Zwillingsbruder, Ilya, Sara überwacht hat, und ich bin immer noch voller Adrenalin, so dass meine Sinne besonders scharf sind und mein Kopf besonders klar. Es ist eigenartig, dass man sich so lebendig fühlen kann, wenn man jemanden tötet, aber so ist es.

Wie jeder weiß, der im gleichen Bereich wie ich arbeitet, liegen Leben und Tod nur eine Messerklinge voneinander entfernt, und dieses Messer zu schwingen ist einer der größten Nervenkitzel, die es gibt.

Ich trinke eine halbe Flasche Bier, esse eine Handvoll Nüsse aus einer Schale auf dem Tresen und gehe zurück ins Wohnzimmer. Bald werde ich zu Saras Haus fahren, um uns Abendessen zu kochen, und der Snack sollte mich bis dahin über Wasser halten. Bevor es so weit ist, müssen Anton und ich aber reden.

Dieses Mexiko-Ding ist groß, und wir können es uns nicht erlauben, es zu versauen.

»Also, was gibt's Neues?«, frage ich und setze mich neben Anton aufs Sofa. Ich stelle mein Bier auf dem kleinen Tisch ab und schaue auf das Display. »Wie viel unseres Planes können wir vergessen?«

»So ziemlich alles«, knurrt Anton. »Die Einsatzpläne der Wächter sind chaotisch, überall gibt es neue Sicherheitskameras, und Velazquez lässt Patrouillen das gesamte Anwesen kontrollieren.«

»In Ordnung. Schauen wir mal.«

In der nächsten Stunde entwickeln wir einen neuen Plan, um Velazquez anzugreifen, einen, der die erhöhten Sicherheitsmaßnahmen auf seinem Anwesen berücksichtigt. Anstatt ihn nachts umzubringen, wie wir es eigentlich geplant hatten, werden wir zur Mittagszeit hineingehen, weil dann nur einige Anfänger auf den Wachposten stehen. Es ist dumm, aber die meisten Menschen, einschließlich mexikanischer Drogenbosse, die es eigentlich besser wissen sollten, fühlen sich tagsüber sicherer. Das ist eines der am häufigsten vorkommenden Probleme, auf die ich während meiner jahrelangen Tätigkeit als Sicherheitsberater gestoßen bin, und ich habe meinen Kunden immer geraten, die Vorkehrungen zu allen Zeiten gleich stark zu treffen, egal, ob die Sonne scheint oder nicht.

»Ist die Überweisung angekommen?«, frage ich, als wir fertig sind, und Anton nickt.

»Sieben Millionen Euro, wie abgesprochen, und die andere Hälfte nach Beendigung des Jobs. Das sollte uns eine Weile über Wasser halten.«

Ich lache trocken auf. Anton und die andere beiden Mitglieder meines alten Teams – die Ivanov-Zwillinge – haben sich mir vor zwei Jahren angeschlossen, nachdem ich meine Liste bekommen und sie mit dem Versprechen um Hilfe gebeten habe, sie reich zu machen. Sie haben zugestimmt, weil wir Freunde sind und sie immer enttäuschter von der russischen Regierung waren. Als die Mannschaft komplett war, habe ich von Sicherheitsberatungen auf etwas Lukrativeres und Flexibleres umgesattelt und meine Kontakte dazu genutzt, hochbezahlte Aufträge für uns an Land zu ziehen. Ich brauchte das Geld, um meinen Rachefeldzug zu finanzieren und den Behörden immer einen Schritt voraus zu sein, und meine Männer brauchten eine neue Herausforderung. Die Menschen auf meiner Liste umzubringen hatte zwar Priorität, aber nebenbei konnten wir einige Aufträge ausführen und uns einen Ruf in der Unterwelt aufbauen. Jetzt haben wir uns darauf spezialisiert, schwierige Opfer auf der ganzen Welt zu töten, und bekommen riesige Geldsummen für Aufträge, die aus Angst niemand anderes ausführen möchte. Meistens sind unsere Kunden gefährliche, wahnsinnig reiche Kriminelle, und unsere Opfer ebenfalls, genau wie Carlos Velazquez, der Kopf des Juarez-Kartells.

Was mein Team betrifft, macht es für sie keinen großen Unterschied, Terroristen aufzuspüren oder Verbrecherbosse hochzunehmen. Oder alle umzubringen, die sich uns in den Weg stellen. Wir haben bereits vor Jahren all das verloren, was auch nur ansatzweise mit Gewissen und Moral zu tun hat.

»Gehst du?«, fragt Anton und klappt seinen Laptop zu, während ich aufstehe und mir meine Jacke überziehe. »Bleibst du wieder die ganze Nacht bei ihr?«

»Wahrscheinlich.« Ich taste meine Jacke ab, um sicherzustellen, dass meine Waffen alle gut versteckt sind. »Höchstwahrscheinlich.«

Anton seufzt, steht auf und lässt den Laptop auf dem Sofa liegen. »Du weißt, dass das verrückt ist, stimmt's? Wenn du sie so sehr möchtest, dann nimm sie dir einfach – und gut ist. Ich habe diese lokalen Zehntausender-Aufträge satt; diese dämlichen Schlägertypen wehren sich nicht einmal. Wenn wir keinen echten Job bekommen, bevor wir nach Mexiko fliegen, werde ich noch verrückt.«

»Du kannst gerne auf eigene Faust losziehen«,

merke ich an und unterdrücke ein Lachen, als Anton mir den Mittelfinger zeigt. Selbst wenn wir keine Freunde wären, würde er das Team nicht verlassen. Meine Verbindungen sind der Grund dafür, dass wir diese ganzen lukrativen Aufträge bekommen. Während der Zeit, in der ich versucht habe, die Liste zu bekommen, bin ich tief in die kriminelle Unterwelt eingetaucht und habe viele ihrer Hauptakteure kennengelernt. So gut meine Männer auch sind, sie wären ohne mich nicht halb so erfolgreich, und das wissen sie auch.

»Viel Spaß«, ruft Anton, als ich zur Tür gehe, und ich tue so, als würde ich nicht hören, dass er etwas über besessene Stalker und arme, gefolterte Frauen vor sich hin murmelt.

Er versteht nicht, warum ich Sara das antue, und ich habe nicht vor, es ihm zu erklären.

Besonders deshalb nicht, weil ich es selbst nicht verstehe.

*S*ara

DER LECKERE GERUCH von butterigen Meeresfrüchten und geröstetem Knoblauch begrüßt mich, als ich mein Haus betrete, und meine Handtasche wie zufällig über der Schulter hängen habe. Wie ich gehofft hatte, ist der Esstisch erneut mit Kerzen dekoriert, und eine Flasche Weißwein steht in einem Kühleimer mit Eis. Der einzige Unterschied ist das Essen. Es sieht so aus, als gäbe es heute Linguini mit Meeresfrüchten als Hauptgang und Tintenfisch und Tomaten-Mozzarella-Salat als Vorspeise.

Ich hätte es nicht besser vorbereiten können.

Verhalte dich normal. Bleib ruhig. Er kann nicht wissen, was du vorhast.

»Italienische Nacht?«, frage ich, als Peter sich am

Küchentresen umdreht, an dem er irgendetwas hackt, was nach Basilikum aussieht. Mein Herz schlägt ungleichmäßig in meiner Brust, aber ich schaffe es, meinen Ton kühl und sarkastisch zu halten. »Was wird es denn morgen? Japanisch? Chinesisch?«

»Wenn du das möchtest«, antwortet er und geht zum Tisch, um das gehackte Basilikum über den Mozzarella zu streuen. »Allerdings kenne ich mich in beiden Küchen nicht so gut aus, also werden wir vielleicht etwas bestellen müssen.«

»Aha.« Mein Blick fällt auf seine Hände, als er die Basilikumreste von seinen Fingern streicht. Ein warmer Schauer durchfährt mich, als ich mich an mein verheerendes Lustgefühl erinnere, als diese Finger mich berührt haben, und ich mich in seinen Armen verloren habe.

Nein. Denk nicht darüber nach.

Da ich mich verzweifelt ablenken möchte, konzentriere ich mich auf seine Kleidung. Heute trägt er ein schwarzes Hemd mit hochgerollten Ärmeln, und ich bekomme bei dem Anblick seiner gebräunten, muskulösen Unterarme, von denen der linke bis zum Handgelenk mit Tattoos übersät ist, einen trockenen Mund. Tätowierte Männer sind normalerweise nicht mein Fall, aber diese kunstvollen Tattoos stehen ihm, betonen die Kraft, die unter dieser glatten, leicht behaarten Haut ruht. Kräftige, männliche Unterarme haben mich schon immer angezogen, und Peter hat die besten, die ich jemals gesehen habe. George hat Kraftsport getrieben, also hatte er auch nette Arme, aber sie waren nicht ansatzweise so kraftvoll wie diese.

Pfui, hör auf. Ekel vor mir selbst brennt in meinem Hals, als ich bemerke, was ich tue. Ich sollte niemals meinen Ehemann, einen normalen, friedlichen Mann, mit einem Mörder vergleichen, dessen Leben sich um Gewalt und Rache dreht. Natürlich ist Peter Sokolov besser in Form, das muss er sein, um diese ganzen Menschen zu töten und den Behörden zu entkommen. Sein Körper ist eine Waffe, geschliffen durch jahrelanges Kämpfen, während George ein Journalist war, ein Autor, der seine meiste Zeit am Computer verbracht hat.

Allerdings ... würde ich Peter Glauben schenken, wäre mein Mann *kein* Journalist gewesen. Er war ein Spion, der in der gleichen Schattenwelt wie das Monster gearbeitet hat, das in meiner Küche werkelt.

Hinter meiner Stirn macht sich Anspannung bemerkbar, und ich schiebe alle Gedanken an eine mögliche Täuschung durch meinen Ehemann beiseite und konzentriere mich stattdessen auf die restliche Bekleidung meines Stalkers: wieder ein Paar dunkle Jeans und schwarze Socken ohne Schuhe. Einen Augenblick lang frage ich mich, ob Peter ein Problem damit hat, Schuhe zu tragen, aber dann erinnere ich mich daran, dass es in einigen Kulturen als respektlos und unsauber angesehen wird, Straßenschuhe im Haus zu tragen.

Ist das in der russischen Kultur der Fall? Und wenn ja, zeigt mir dann der Mann, der mich in genau dieser

Küche gefoltert hat, auf einem sehr indirekten Weg, dass er mich respektiert?

»Los, wasch deine Hände oder was auch immer du machen musst«, sagt er und dimmt das Licht, bevor er sich an den Tisch setzt und den Wein öffnet. »Das Essen wird kalt.«

»Du hättest nicht auf mich warten müssen«, sage ich und gehe ins Badezimmer, um meine Hände zu waschen. Ich hasse es, dass er sich so benimmt, als würde er meine Gewohnheiten kennen, aber ich werde nicht aus Trotz meine Gesundheit aufs Spiel setzen.

»Ich meine das ernst«, sage ich, als ich zurückkomme. »Du hättest überhaupt nicht herkommen müssen. Du weißt, dass es nicht deine Pflicht als Stalker ist, mich mit Essen zu versorgen, stimmt's?«

Er grinst, als ich mich ihm gegenüber hinsetze und meine Handtasche über die Stuhllehne hänge. »Ist das so?«

»Das sagen zumindest alle Jobangebote für Stalker.« Ich spieße mit der Gabel ein Stück Tomate mit Mozzarella auf und lege beides auf meinen Teller. Meine Hand ist ruhig und verrät die Angst nicht, die mich innerlich auffrisst. Ich will meine Handtasche an mich drücken, sie auf meinem Schoß liegen haben, so dass ich leicht an sie herankomme, aber wenn ich das täte, würde er misstrauisch werden. Ich gehe schon ein Risiko damit ein, sie über meinen Stuhl zu hängen, da ich sie normalerweise einfach auf dem Sofa im Wohnzimmer liegen lasse. Ich hoffe, dass er das der Tatsache zuschreibt, dass ich direkt in die Küche gekommen bin, anstatt wie sonst zuerst zum Sofa zu gehen.

»Also wenn sie das sagen, muss es wohl so sein.« Peter schenkt uns beiden ein Glas Wein ein, bevor er ein wenig von dem Tomaten-Mozzarella-Salat auf seinen Teller legt. »Ich bin kein Experte auf diesem Gebiet.«

»Du hast noch nie andere Frauen derart verfolgt?«

Er schneidet ein Stück Mozzarella ab, schiebt es sich in den Mund und kaut langsam. »Nein, so nicht«, antwortet er, nachdem er heruntergeschluckt hat.

»Ach?« Mir fällt auf, dass ich krankhaft neugierig bin. »Wie hast du sie dann verfolgt?«

Er blickt mich ruhig an. »Vertraue mir, das willst du nicht wissen.«

Wahrscheinlich hat er recht, aber da die Möglichkeit besteht, dass ich ihn nach dieser Nacht nie wiedersehen werde, verspüre ich den eigenartigen Drang, mehr über ihn herauszufinden. »Doch, das möchte ich«, entgegne ich, und es beruhigt mich, den Riemen der Handtasche an meinem Rücken zu spüren. »Ich möchte es wissen. Erkläre es mir.«

Er zögert einen Moment, bevor er sagt: »Die Mehrzahl meiner Aufträge waren Männer, aber als Teil meines Jobs bin ich auch Frauen gefolgt. Unterschiedliche Jobs, unterschiedliche Frauen, unterschiedliche Gründe. Damals in Russland waren es oft die Ehefrauen und Freundinnen der Männer, die mein Land bedrohten, und wir haben sie verfolgt und befragt, um die Aufenthaltsorte unserer eigentlichen

Zielpersonen herauszufinden. Später, als ich ein Deserteur wurde, habe ich einige Frauen als Teil meiner Arbeit für verschiedene Kartellbosse, Waffendealer und Ähnliches aufgespürt, normalerweise weil sie irgendeine Bedrohung darstellten oder die Männer betrogen hatten, für die ich arbeitete.«

Das Tomatenstück, das ich gerade gegessen habe, scheint in meinem Hals festzustecken. »Du hast sie … nur aufgespürt?«

»Nicht immer.« Er greift nach den Linguini, dreht eine Gabel in ihnen ein und hebt eine große Portion auf seinen Teller, ohne dabei mit der butterigen Soße zu kleckern. »Manchmal musste ich auch mehr tun.«

Meine Fingerspitzen beginnen, sich kalt anzufühlen. Ich weiß, dass ich das Thema fallenlassen sollte, aber stattdessen höre ich mich fragen: »Was musstest du tun?«

»Das kam auf die Situation an. Einmal war mein Auftrag eine Krankenschwester, die einen meiner Auftraggeber, den Waffenhändler, den ich eben erwähnt habe, an einen Terroristen verraten hatte. Deshalb wurde damals seine jetzige Ehefrau entführt, und er wurde beinahe umgebracht, als er sie retten wollte. Das war eine hässliche Situation, und als ich die Schwester gefunden habe, musste ich auch auf eine hässliche Lösung zurückgreifen.« Er macht eine Pause, und seine grauen Augen leuchten. »Möchtest du die Einzelheiten wissen?«

»Nein, das …« Ich ergreife mein Weinglas und nehme einen großen Schluck. »Das reicht schon.«

Er nickt und beginnt zu essen. Ich habe keinen Appetit mehr, aber ich zwinge mich, seinem Beispiel zu folgen, und hebe etwas von der Pasta auf meinen Teller. Sie ist köstlich. Die Meeresfrüchte und die Pasta sind auf den Punkt gegart und mit der reichhaltigen, würzigen Soße bedeckt, aber ich schmecke das alles nur unterschwellig. Ich kann es kaum ertragen, darauf zu warten, endlich in meine Handtasche fassen zu können und die kleine Viole herauszunehmen, die dort auf mich wartet, aber dafür muss Peter abgelenkt sein, mindestens zwanzig Sekunden lang nicht auf sein Weinglas schauen. Ich weiß, dass es mindestens zwanzig Sekunden sein müssen, weil ich es im Krankenhaus mit Wasser geübt habe: fünf Sekunden, um die Viole aufzumachen, weitere fünf, um mich über den Tisch zu beugen und den Inhalt in das Weinglas zu schütten, und drei weitere, um meine Hand zurückzuziehen und unauffällig auszusehen. Das sind etwa dreizehn Sekunden und keine zwanzig, aber er darf keinen Verdacht schöpfen, also brauche ich einen Puffer.

»Also, erzähle mir von deinem Tag, Sara«, sagt er, nachdem der Großteil seiner Linguini verschwunden ist. Ich schaue auf, und er hält mich mit seinem kalten, silbernen Blick fest. »Ist irgendetwas Interessantes passiert?«

Mein Magen zieht sich zusammen, bildet einen Knoten um die Linguini, die ich mir gerade hinuntergewürgt habe. Peter kann nichts davon wissen, dass ich Joe heute getroffen habe, oder doch? Mein Peiniger hat nichts gesagt, aber falls in seinem Kopf dieses eigenartige Ding, das wir haben, eine Art Anbändeln ist, könnte er etwas dagegen haben, dass ich mich mit anderen Männern unterhalte und mich mit ihnen verabrede.

»Ähm, nein.« Zu meiner Erleichterung klingt meine Stimme relativ normal. Ich werde besser darin, unter extremem Stress zu funktionieren. »Eine junge Frau kam mit schweren Schmierblutungen, und es stellte sich heraus, dass sie eine Fehlgeburt von Zwillingen hatte, und wir hatten ein fünfzehn Jahre altes Mädchen mit einer *geplanten* Schwangerschaft – sie hat gesagt, dass sie schon immer Mutter sein wollte –, aber das ist für dich mit Sicherheit nicht besonders interessant.«

»Das stimmt nicht.« Er legt seine Gabel weg und lehnt sich zurück. »Ich finde deine Arbeit faszinierend.«

»Wirklich?«

Er nickt. »Du bist ein Arzt, aber nicht nur jemand, der Leben rettet und Krankheiten heilt. Du *bringst* Leben in diese Welt, Sara, und hilfst Frauen, wenn sie am verletzlichsten sind – und am schönsten.«

Ich hole Luft und starre ihn an. Dieser Mann – dieser *Mörder* – kann das nicht wirklich verstehen, oder doch? »Du findest … dass schwangere Frauen schön sind?«

»Nicht nur schwangere Frauen. Der ganze Prozess ist wunderschön«, antwortet er, und mir wird klar, dass er es versteht. »Findest du nicht?«, fragt er, als ich ihn stumm vor Schock einfach nur weiter anstarre.

»Wie Leben entsteht, wie ein kleiner Haufen Zellen wächst und sich verändert, bevor er auf die Welt kommt? Findest du das nicht wunderschön, Sara? Sogar wunderbar?«

Ich hebe mein Weinglas an und trinke einen Schluck, bevor ich antworte. »Das tue ich.« Meine Stimme hört sich belegt an, als ich endlich wieder sprechen kann. »Natürlich tue ich das. Ich hatte einfach nicht erwartet, dass *du* das so empfinden würdest.«

»Warum?«

»Ist das nicht offensichtlich?« Ich stelle mein Glas ab. »Du nimmst Leben. Du verletzt Menschen.«

»Ja, das tue ich«, stimmt er zu, ohne mit der Wimper zu zucken. »Aber das verstärkt meine Bewunderung nur. Wenn man die Zerbrechlichkeit des *Seins*, seine schiere Vergänglichkeit versteht, wenn man sieht, wie leicht es ist, eine Existenz auszulöschen, weiß man das Leben mehr zu schätzen, nicht weniger.«

»Also, warum tust du es dann? Warum zerstörst du etwas, was du schätzt? Wie kannst du ein Mörder sein, wenn du …«

»Wenn ich menschliches Leben wunderschön finde? Das ist einfach.« Er beugt sich nach vorn, und seine Augen funkeln düster im Kerzenlicht. »Du musst verstehen, Sara, dass der Tod Teil des Lebens ist. Ein hässlicher Teil, mit Sicherheit, aber es gibt keine Schönheit ohne Hässlichkeit, genauso wie es kein Glück ohne Trauer gibt. Wir leben in einer Welt voller Kontraste, nicht des Absoluten. Unsere Köpfe sind dafür gedacht, zu vergleichen, Veränderungen wahrzunehmen. Alles, was wir sind, alles, was wir als menschliche Wesen tun, beruht auf der einfachen Tatsache, dass X sich von Y unterscheidet – besser, schlechter, heißer, kälter, dunkler, heller, was auch immer es ist – aber nur im Vergleich. In einem Vakuum besitzt X keine Schönheit, genauso wie Y nicht hässlich ist. Es ist ihr Kontrast, der es uns ermöglicht, das eine mehr zu schätzen als das andere, eine Wahl zu treffen, um glücklich zu sein.«

Mein Hals fühlt sich unerklärlich eng an. »Also tust du was? Durch deine Arbeit Freude in die Welt bringen? Alle glücklich machen?«

»Nein, natürlich nicht.« Peter ergreift sein Weinglas und schwenkt es leicht. »Ich habe keine falschen Vorstellungen von dem, was ich bin und was ich tue. Aber das bedeutet nicht, dass ich die Schönheit *deiner* Arbeit nicht sehe, Sara. Jemand kann in der Dunkelheit leben und das Licht der Sonne sehen, auf diese Weise ist es sogar noch heller.«

»Ich …« Meine Handflächen sind feucht, als ich mein Weinglas anhebe und mit meiner freien Hand verstohlen in meine Tasche greife. So faszinierend das auch ist, ich muss handeln, bevor es zu spät ist. Es gibt keine Garantie dafür, dass er sich ein zweites Glas einschenken wird. »Ich habe das noch nie auf diese Weise betrachtet.«

»Es gibt keinen Grund dafür, warum du es tun solltest.« Er stellt sein Glas ab und lächelt mich an. Es ist sein dunkles, magnetisches Lächeln, dieses, was Hitzewellen in meinen Unterleib sendet. »Du hast ein sehr anderes Leben geführt, Ptichka. Ein netteres Leben.«

»Stimmt.« Ich atme nur flach, während ich mein Glas hochnehme und es zu meinen Lippen führe. »Ich nehme an, dass ich das habe – bis du hineingeplatzt bist.«

Sein Gesichtsausdruck wird düster. »Das stimmt. Falls es dich tröstet …«

Mein Glas rutscht mir aus der Hand, und sein Inhalt ergießt sich vor mir auf dem Tisch. »Mist.« Ich springe auf und tue so, als sei mir das unangenehm. »Das tut mir leid. Ich gehe schnell …«

»Nein, bleib sitzen.« Er steht auf, genau wie ich es gehofft hatte. Auch wenn er sich in meinem Haus befindet, mag er es, einen guten Gastgeber zu spielen. »Ich mache das weg.«

Er braucht nur wenige Schritte bis zu dem Küchenrollenhalter auf dem Tresen, aber das ist genügend Zeit für mich, um die Viole zu öffnen. *Sechs. sieben, acht, neun …* Ich zähle in Gedanken mit, während ich die Flüssigkeit in sein Glas schütte. *Zehn, elf, zwölf.* Er kommt mit der Küchenrolle in der Hand zurück, und ich lächele ihn verlegen an, während ich mich in meinen Stuhl sinken lasse, nachdem ich die Glasviole wieder in meine Tasche geschoben habe. Mein Rücken ist klatschnass von kaltem Schweiß, und meine Hände zittern vom Adrenalin, aber meine Aufgabe ist ausgeführt.

Jetzt muss ich ihn nur noch dazu bringen, den Wein zu trinken.

»Lass mich helfen«, sage ich und greife nach einem Tuch, während er den verschütteten Wein auf dem Tisch aufwischt, aber er winkt mich weg.

»Es ist alles in Ordnung, mach dir keine Sorgen.« Er trägt meinen mit Wein überschwemmten Teller zum Mülleimer und schmeißt die Reste meiner Pasta weg – was eine weitere Gelegenheit gewesen wäre, stelle ich nebenbei fest – und kommt danach mit einem sauberen Teller zurück.

»Danke«, sage ich und versuche, mich auch dankbar anstatt frohlockend anzuhören, als er mein Weinglas gegen ein neues austauscht und mir einschenkt, bevor er sich selbst auffüllt. »Tut mir leid, manchmal bin ich wirklich ein Tollpatsch.«

»Macht nichts.« Er sieht leicht amüsiert aus, als er sich wieder hinsetzt. »Normalerweise bist du sehr anmutig. Das ist eines der Dinge, die ich am liebsten an dir mag: wie genau und kontrolliert deine Bewegungen sind. Liegt das an deiner medizinischen Ausbildung? Eine ruhige Hand für Operationen?«

Verhalte dich nicht so, als seist du nervös. Was auch immer du machst, verhalte dich nicht so, als seist du nervös.

»Ja, das ist ein Teil davon«, antworte ich und versuche, eine ruhige Stimme beizubehalten. »Ich habe als Kind auch Ballettstunden gehabt, und meine Lehrerin war pedantisch, was Präzision und eine gute Technik betraf. Unsere Hände mussten genau so positioniert sein, unsere Füße genau so. Sie hat uns jede Position und jeden Schritt üben lassen, bis wir ihn beherrschten, und wenn wir unsere gute Haltung auch nur einmal verloren, mussten wir wieder von vorn beginnen und das üben, was wir erneut falsch gemacht hatten, manchmal eine ganze Unterrichtsstunde lang.

Er nimmt sein Glas hoch und schwenkt wieder die Flüssigkeit darin. »Das ist interessant. Ich habe immer gedacht, dass du wie eine Tänzerin aussiehst. Du hast die Haltung und die Figur.«

»Findest du?« *Trink. Bitte, trink.*

Er stellt sein Glas ab und betrachtet mich eindringlich mit einem rätselhaften Gesichtsausdruck. »Auf jeden Fall. Aber du tanzt nicht mehr, oder?«

»Nein.« *Komm schon, nimm dein Glas wieder in die Hand.* »Ich habe mit dem Ballett aufgehört, als ich in die Highschool kam, aber auf der Uni habe ich ein wenig Salsa getanzt.«

»Warum hast du mit dem Ballett aufgehört?« Seine Hand bewegt sich auf das Glas zu, so als würde er es wieder nehmen wollen. »Ich kann mir vorstellen, dass du gut warst.«

»Nicht gut genug, um es professionell zu machen, zumindest nicht, ohne zusätzliches Training. Und das wollten meine Eltern nicht.« Mein Puls steigt voller Vorfreude an, als sich seine Finger um den Stiel des Glases legen. »Das potentielle Gehalt eines Tänzers ist nicht besonders hoch, genauso wenig wie die Länge seiner Karriere. Die meisten Tänzer hören Mitte zwanzig auf und müssen etwas anderes finden, was sie machen können.«

»Wie praktisch«, erwidert er und hebt sein Glas an. »War das dir oder deinen Eltern wichtig?«

»Was war wichtig?« Ich versuche, nicht auf das Weinglas zu starren, als es wenige Zentimeter vor seinen Lippen schwebt. *Jetzt komm schon, trink einfach.*

»Das potentielle Gehalt.« Er schwenkt erneut sein Weinglas, und etwas scheint ihn am Anblick der hellen Flüssigkeit, die sich in ihm bewegt, zu erfreuen. »Wolltest du eine reiche, erfolgreiche Ärztin werden?«

Ich zwinge mich, meinen Blick von der hypnotisierenden Bewegung des Weines abzuwenden. »Natürlich. Wer würde das nicht?« Die Anspannung frisst mich auf, also lenke ich mich ab, indem ich mein Weinglas nehme und einen großen Schluck trinke. *Bitte mache es mir unbewusst nach und trinke. Komm schon, nur einen Schluck.*

»Ich weiß nicht«, murmelt er. »Vielleicht ein kleines Mädchen, das lieber eine Ballerina oder eine Sängerin wäre?«

Ich blinzele und bin einen Augenblick lang davon abgelenkt, dass er nicht trinkt. »Eine Sängerin?« Warum sagt er das? Niemand, abgesehen von meinem Berater in der siebten Klasse, wusste von diesem Plan.

Auch mit zehn Jahren wusste ich es bereits besser, als etwas so Abwegiges bei meinen Eltern anzusprechen – besonders nachdem sie mir ihre Ansichten über das Ballett gesagt hatten.

»Du hast eine wunderschöne Singstimme«, sagt Peter, der immer noch mit seinem Weinglas spielt. »Es wäre nur logisch, wenn du irgendwann darüber nachgedacht hättest, aufzutreten. Und im Gegensatz zum Tanzen muss eine erfolgreiche Gesangskarriere nicht früh enden. Viele ältere Sänger werden immer noch sehr respektiert.«

»Das stimmt wohl.« Ich werfe erneut einen Blick auf sein Glas und werde immer frustrierter. Es ist, als wollte er mich quälen und sehen, wie lange ich brauche, um mich zu verraten. Um meine Ungeduld zu zähmen, nehme ich einen weiteren Schluck Wein und frage: »Woher weißt du überhaupt, was für eine Singstimme ich habe? Warte, vergiss es. Deine Abhörgeräte, stimmt's?«

Er nickt und sieht kein bisschen reumütig aus. »Ja, du singst oft, wenn du allein bist.«

Ich nehme noch mehr Wein. Zu jedem anderen Zeitpunkt wäre ich über seine Missachtung meiner Privatsphäre wütend geworden, aber in diesem Moment gilt all meine Aufmerksamkeit dem blöden Wein. *Warum trinkt er ihn nicht?*

»Also denkst du wirklich, dass ich eine schöne Singstimme habe?«, frage ich, und mir fällt auf, dass ich mich wütender anhören sollte. In einem säuerlicheren Ton füge ich hinzu: »Da ich ja sowieso schon, ohne es zu wissen, für dich gesungen habe, kannst du mir auch deine ehrliche Meinung sagen.«

Seine Augenwinkel legen sich in Falten, während er das Glas wieder senkt. »Deine Stimme ist wunderschön, Ptichka. Das habe ich dir bereits gesagt, und ich habe keinen Grund zu lügen.«

Mein Gott, trink einfach den verdammten Wein! Um mich davon abzuhalten, das laut hinauszuschreien, atme ich tief ein und zwinge ein hübsches Lächeln auf meine Lippen. »Na ja, du *hast* einen Grund, schließlich willst du mich ja ins Bett bekommen. Und wie jede Frau dir bestätigen kann, helfen Komplimente dabei.«

Er lacht und nimmt sein Glas wieder in die Hand. »Das stimmt. Aber ich habe das Gefühl, dass ich dir bis in alle Ewigkeit Komplimente machen könnte, ohne dass es etwas ändern würde.«

»Man kann nie wissen.« Ich behalte einen leicht flirtenden Ton bei, obwohl mir kalter Schweiß den Rücken hinunterläuft. Wenn er nicht von allein trinkt, werde ich seiner Hand nachhelfen müssen.

Wir können dieses Essen nicht beenden, bis er nicht wenigstens einige Schlucke getrunken hat.

Ich hebe mein Glas, lächele breiter und sage: »Warum trinken wir nicht darauf? Auf die Eitelkeit der Frauen und deine Komplimente für mich.«

»Warum eigentlich nicht?« Er hebt sein Glas und stößt damit gegen meines. »Auf dich, Ptichka, und deine wunderschöne Stimme.«

Wir führen die Gläser an unsere Lippen, aber bevor ich einen Schluck trinken kann, rutscht ihm das Glas aus den Fingern.

»Ups«, murmelt er, als das Glas nach vorn kippt und der Wein sich vor ihm ergießt, genauso wie das bei mir vorhin der Fall war. Seine Augen funkeln dunkel. »Mein Fehler.«

Ich höre auf zu atmen, und mein Blut gefriert in meinen Adern. »Du ... du ...«

»Ob ich wusste, dass du etwas in mein Getränk geschüttet hast? Ja, natürlich.« Seine Stimme bleibt weich, aber ich kann jetzt einen tödlichen Unterton heraushören. »Denkst du, dass noch nie jemand versucht hat, mich zu vergiften?«

Mein Puls rast, aber trotzdem schaffe ich es nicht, mich zu bewegen, als er aufsteht, um den Tisch herumgeht und mit der Anmut eines Raubtiers zu mir kommt. Alles, was ich tun kann, ist, ihn anzustarren und die Wut zu sehen, die in diesen metallischen Augen kocht.

Jetzt wird er mich umbringen. Dafür wird er mich umbringen. »Ich wollte dich nicht ...« Entsetzen brennt giftig in meinen Adern. »Ich wollte dich nicht ...«

»Nein?« Er bleibt neben mir stehen, greift in meine Handtasche und zieht die leere Viole hervor. Ich sollte wegrennen oder es zumindest versuchen, aber ich bin nicht mutig genug, um ihn noch mehr zu provozieren. Also bleibe ich still sitzen und atme kaum, als er die Viole unter seine Nase hält und an ihr riecht.

»Ach so«, murmelt er und lässt seine Hand sinken. »Ein wenig Diazepam. Ich konnte es in dem Wein nicht riechen, aber jetzt ist es eindeutig.« Er stellt die Viole vor mir auf den Tisch. »Ich nehme an, das hast du aus dem Krankenhaus?«

»Ich ... ja.« Es ist sinnlos, das abzustreiten. Der Beweis steht schließlich vor mir.

»Hm.« Er lehnt seine Hüfte gegen den Tisch und schaut auf mich herunter. »Und was wolltest du mit mir machen, wenn ich bewusstlos bin, Ptichka? Mich dem FBI ausliefern?«

Ich nicke nur und schaue ihn an, da die Worte in meinem Hals eingefroren sind. Durch seinen Körper, der über mir ragt, fühle ich mich wie der kleine Vogel, mit dem er mich vergleicht: klein und verängstigt im Schatten eines Falken.

Sein sinnlicher Mund verzieht sich zur Parodie eines Lächelns. »Ich verstehe. Und du hast gedacht, dass es so einfach sein würde? Mich bewusstlos machen und fertig?«

Ich blinzele ihn verständnislos an.

»Denkst du, dass ich keinen Notfallplan für eine solche Situation habe?«, verdeutlicht er, und ich zucke zusammen, als er seine Hand anhebt. Aber alles, was er macht, ist eine meiner Locken anzuheben und mit ihr an meinem Kinn entlangzufahren, eine zärtliche Geste, die gleichzeitig spöttisch ist. »Falls du mich töten oder anderweitig außer Gefecht setzen möchtest?«

»Das ... das hast du?«

Seine Lider schließen sich ein wenig, und sein Blick fällt auf meinen Mund. »Natürlich.« Die Locke fährt über meine Lippen, und ihre Enden kitzeln auf dem empfindlichen Fleisch, mein Magen zieht sich zu einem harten Ball zusammen, als er sanft sagt: »In diesem Moment beobachten meine Männer nicht nur dein Haus und alles in einem Radius von zehn Straßen, sondern auch den kleinen Bildschirm, der meine Vitalzeichen überträgt.« Er schaut mir in die Augen. »Möchtest du raten, was sie getan hätten, wäre mein Blutdruck unerwartet abgefallen?«

Ich schüttele schweigend den Kopf. Wenn Peters

Männer wie er sind – und das müssen sie, um für ihn zu arbeiten –, würde ich lieber nicht im Detail wissen, was gerade an mir vorbeigezogen ist.

Er lächelt dunkel. »Ja, das ist wahrscheinlich besser, Ptichka. Unwissenheit macht glücklich und so.«

Ich nehme meinen ganzen verbliebenen Mut zusammen. »Was wirst du jetzt mit mir tun?«

»Was denkst du, werde ich tun?« Er legt seinen Kopf schief, und sein Lächeln wird noch ein wenig düsterer. »Dich bestrafen? Dir wehtun?«

Mein Herz klopft mir bis zum Hals. »Wirst du?«

Er schaut mich für einige lange Augenblicke an, sein Lächeln verschwindet, und er schüttelt den Kopf. »Nein, Sara.« Seine Stimme hat einen eigenartig müden Unterton. »Nicht heute.«

Er stößt sich vom Tisch weg, beginnt, die Teller zusammenzuräumen, und ich sinke in meinen Stuhl, da ich zwar erleichtert bin, aber dennoch jede Hoffnung verloren habe.

Wenn er nicht lügt, was seine Männer betrifft – und ich denke nicht, dass er das tut –, sitze ich noch mehr in der Falle, als ich gedacht habe.

*P*eter

ES SOLLTE NICHT SO WEHTUN, das Wissen, dass sie mich loswerden will. Es sollte sich nicht so anfühlen, als würden Feuerklingen meine Brust aufschlitzen. Jede Person in Saras Situation würde sich wehren, das ist nur logisch und zu erwarten.

Es sollte nicht wehtun, aber genau das tut es, und egal, was ich mir einrede, während ich Sara nach oben führe, das Monster in mir faucht und heult, fordert, dass ich genau das tue, wovor sie Angst hat, und sie für ihr Vergehen bestrafe.

Als wir im Schlafzimmer ankommen, zwinge ich sie nicht wieder dazu, sich vor mir auszuziehen, da ich zu nahe daran bin, die Kontrolle zu verlieren. Ich habe sie bereits zu lange während des Abendessens getestet, als ich bei ihrem Ich-habe-nicht-gerade-etwas-in-deinen-Wein-gekippt-Spielchen mitgespielt habe. Ich wusste sofort, was sie tat – es war zu abwegig bei ihr, dass sie ihren Wein verschüttet –, aber ich wollte sehen, ob sie eine gute Schauspielerin ist, und deshalb habe ich mich weiter mit ihr unterhalten, habe vorgegeben, keine Ahnung zu haben und leichtgläubig zu sein, ein Idiot, der auf einen der ältesten Tricks der Welt hereinfällt.

»Du kannst duschen gehen«, sage ich und nicke in Richtung Badezimmertür, als sie neben das Bett tritt und ihr Blick nervös zwischen mir und dem Bett hin und her wandert. »Ich werde hier auf dich warten.«

Erleichterung blitzt kurz auf ihrem Gesicht auf, und sie verschwindet im Bad. Ich nutze die Gelegenheit, um nach unten zu gehen und mich schnell in einem der anderen Badezimmer abzuduschen.

Auch wenn ich nach dem heutigen Auftrag bereits geduscht habe, möchte ich für sie besonders sauber sein.

Sie ist immer noch unter der Dusche, als ich ins Schlafzimmer zurückkehre, also falte ich sorgfältig meine Sachen zusammen und lege sie auf die Kommode, bevor ich ins Bett gehe. Ich habe mich vorhin schnell mit der Hand befriedigt, aber mein Verlangen nach Sara ist nicht weniger geworden, und ich weiß, dass ich nicht in der Lage sein werde, dieses Spiel noch viel länger zu spielen.

Ich werde sie nehmen und sie zu der meinen machen.

Wenn nicht heute Nacht, dann sehr bald.

Sara duscht lange, so lange, dass ich weiß, dass sie das Duschen als Vorwand nutzt, mich zu meiden, aber das ist mir egal. Ich nutze die Zeit, um einen leeren Kopf zu bekommen und den restlichen Ärger in mir abzukühlen, der in mir brennt. Als sie endlich in ein Handtuch eingewickelt aus dem Badezimmer kommt, habe ich das Monster unter Kontrolle und kann sie kühl anlächeln.

»Komm«, sage ich und klopfe neben mir auf das Bett. Ich versuche angestrengt, nicht daran zu denken, wie feucht und weich ihre Muschi sich gestern angefühlt hat, aber das ist unmöglich. Ich will diese seidige Nässe um meinen Schwanz spüren, will sie aufstöhnen hören, während ich in sie eindringe. Ich will diesen vollen Mund küssen und sehen, wie ihre braunen Augen weich werden und ins Leere blicken, während ich sie immer wieder zum Höhepunkt bringe.

Ich will sie und ich kann sie nicht haben.

Noch nicht, zumindest.

Sie kommt unsicher näher, so skeptisch wie eine wilde Gazelle und genauso anmutig. Ich will sie ergreifen und sie ins Bett zerren, aber ich bleibe still liegen und lasse sie von allein zu mir kommen. Auf diese Weise kann ich so tun, als würde sie mich nicht hassen, dass es nicht ihre größte Freude wäre, mich im Gefängnis oder tot zu sehen.

Auf diese Weise kann ich mir vorstellen, dass sie irgendwann *wählen* wird, mit mir zusammen zu sein.

»Nimm das Handtuch ab und komm her«, befehle

ich ihr, als sie einen halben Meter vor dem Bett stehenbleibt, aber sie bewegt sich nicht, sondern umklammert das Handtuch mit den Händen vor ihrer Brust.

»Werden wir schlafen? Einfach nur schlafen?«, fragt sie mit zitternder Stimme, und ich nicke, auch wenn mein Schwanz allein von ihrem Anblick schmerzhaft hart ist. Wenn ich mir sicher wäre, die ganze Zeit lang die Kontrolle zu behalten, würde ich sie heute Nacht nehmen oder ihr zumindest einen weiteren Orgasmus verschaffen, aber so wie die Dinge stehen, halte ich sie am besten nur in meinen Armen und versuche, einzuschlafen. Selbst das wird eine Qual sein, aber die kann ich aushalten. Ich werde sie nicht zwingen, wenn sie erwartet, dass ich ihr wehtue. Egal, wie schwer es ist, ich werde ihre Ängste nicht bestätigen.

»Einfach nur schlafen«, verspreche ich und hoffe, dass sie den kaum unterdrückten Hunger in meiner Stimme nicht hören kann. »Wir gehen einfach nur schlafen.«

Sie zögert eine weitere Sekunde lang, bevor sie zum Bett kommt, das nasse Handtuch auf den Boden fallen lässt und unter die Decke kriecht. Ich sehe nur kurz ein Stück nackte Haut, aber das reicht dafür, dass meine Lust ungebremst zuschlägt. Ich bereite mich geistig auf das vor, was jetzt kommt, ziehe sie an mich und muss ein Stöhnen unterdrücken, als ihr weicher Po sich gegen meine Lende schmiegt und ihre Haut noch feucht und warm von der langen Dusche ist. Sie hat einen wunderschönen Po, meine kleine Ärztin, fest und wohlgeformt, und mein Schwanz pocht vor Verlangen, in ihr zu sein, zu spüren, wie diese weichen Backen gegen meine Eier drücken, während ich in sie stoße, sie immer wieder nehme.

Ich schließe meine Augen, atme den süßen Duft ihres Shampoos ein und konzentriere mich darauf, meine Atmung zu kontrollieren. Nach einer Weile spüre ich, wie die Anspannung in ihren Muskeln nachlässt, und ich weiß, dass sie beginnt, sich zu entspannen, zu glauben, dass ich sie trotz des harten Schwanzes, den sie gegen sich drücken fühlen muss, zu nichts zwingen werde.

Ganz langsam, sage ich mir, während ich ein- und ausatme. *Kontrolliere und konzentriere dich. Schmerz ist bedeutungslos. Leid ist bedeutungslos.* Das ist ein Mantra, das ich mir selbst während meiner Zeit in Camp Largo ausgedacht habe, und es stimmt. Schmerz, Hunger, Durst, Lust – das alles sind chemische Vorgänge und elektrische Impulse, ein Weg des Gehirns, mit dem Körper zu kommunizieren. Sara zu begehren wird mich nicht umbringen, nicht mehr als die sechs Monate, die ich in Einzelhaft verbracht habe, als ich vierzehn war. Die Qualen unerfüllten Begehrens sind nichts im Vergleich zu der Hölle, in einem Raum eingesperrt zu sein, der kaum groß genug war, um die Bezeichnung Käfig zu verdienen, mit niemandem zum Reden und nichts, um sich zu beschäftigen. Sie sind nichts im Vergleich zu den Qualen, wenn eine Klinge durch deine Niere fährt oder eine gigantische Faust fast dein Auge herausschlägt.

Wenn ich das Jugendgefängnis in Sibirien überlebt habe, werde ich es auch überleben, Sara nicht zu haben. Zumindest für noch ein wenig länger.

28

S*ara*

»WAS IST MIT DIR, Sara?«

»Was?« Ich blicke von meinem Teller auf und starre Marsha, die mich gerade etwas gefragt haben muss, verständnislos an.

Andy verdreht ihre Augen. »Sie ist wieder im La-la-land. Lass sie in Ruhe, Marsha.«

»Entschuldigt, ich war gerade mit meinen Gedanken woanders«, sage ich und streiche eine Locke zurück, die sich aus meinem Pferdeschwanz gelöst hat. Ich bin mir ziemlich sicher, dass meine Haare völlig durcheinander sind, aber ich vergesse andauernd, zu einem Spiegel zu gehen, um sie zu richten. Überhaupt ist alles, an was ich heute Morgen denken kann, der Moment, wenn ich heute Abend nach Hause komme und *er* dort bereits auf mich warten wird.

Peter Sokolov, der Mann, dem ich nicht entkommen kann.

»Ich habe dich gefragt, ob du am Samstag mit mir und Tonya mitkommen möchtest«, erklärt mir Marsha und sieht eher belustigt als wütend aus. »Andy hat gerade gemeint, dass sie auch mitkommt. Sie wird einen anderen Abend mit ihrem Freund verbringen. Was ist mit dir, Sara?«

»Oh, tut mir leid, ich kann nicht«, antworte ich und schiebe meinen Teller zur Seite. Ich habe die Krankenschwestern in der Cafeteria getroffen, als ich mir gerade ein schnelles Frühstück genommen habe, und sie haben mich überredet, mich einen Moment zu ihnen zu setzen. »Ich habe meinen Eltern versprochen, sie zu besuchen.«

Der letzte Teil ist eine Lüge, aber ich denke mir, dass das besser ist, als ihnen zu erklären, dass ich meine Freunde lieber nicht auf das Radar eines bestimmten russischen Killers bringen möchte – oder wen auch immer er schickt, um mich zu überwachen.

»Das ist wirklich schade«, meint Marsha. »Tonya wird uns wieder in den Klub bringen. Du schienst es dort zu mögen. Tonya hat gesagt, dass der niedliche Barkeeper nach dir gefragt hat.«

Ich runzele die Stirn. »Hat er?«

»Ja«, bestätigt Tonya. »Er hat aber etwas Eigenartiges gesagt. Er dachte, er hätte dich mit einem Typen gesehen, der sich sehr besitzergreifend aufgeführt hat, so als sei er dein Freund. Ich habe ihm gesagt, dass er sich irren muss, weil du in jener Nacht definitiv allein nach Hause gegangen bist. Stimmt doch, oder? Du versteckst doch nicht irgendwo einen geheimen Freund?«

Eis läuft über meinen Rücken, während mein Gesicht unangenehm heiß wird. »Nein, definitiv nicht.«

»Wirklich nicht?«, fragt Marsha und hört sich fasziniert an. »Warum wirst du dann rot? Und umklammerst die Gabel, als wolltest du jemanden erstechen?«

Ich blicke auf meine Hand und sehe, dass sie recht hat. Ich umklammere das Besteck so fest, dass meine Knöchel weiß sind. Ich zwinge meine Finger dazu, sich zu entspannen, lache unangenehm berührt und sage: »Sorry. In jener Nacht war ich betrunken, und das ist mir immer noch unangenehm. Ich glaube, ich habe mit irgendeinem Typen getanzt, und das hat der Barkeeper wahrscheinlich gesehen.«

Andy runzelt ihre Stirn. »Ist dieser Kerl der Grund dafür, dass du so überstürzt verschwunden bist? Du hast fast … verängstigt ausgesehen.«

»Was? Nein, ich war einfach nur betrunken.« Ich zwinge mich dazu, noch einmal unangenehm berührt aufzulachen. »Ihr wisst doch wie das ist, wenn man kurz davor ist, sich jeden Moment zu übergeben? In jener Nacht ging es mir so.«

»Okay«, sagt Tonya. »Ich werde Rick, das ist der Barkeeper, sagen, dass du noch zu haben bist. Falls du wieder mal mit uns in den Klub kommen solltest.«

»Oh, ich …« Mein Gesicht wird wieder heiß. »Nein, lieber nicht. Ich bin noch nicht bereit für Dates und …«

»Mach dir keine Sorgen.« Tonya legt ihre Hand auf meine, und ihre schlanken Finger fühlen sich kalt auf meiner Hand an. »Ich werde ihm deine Nummer nicht geben. Du kannst deinen Prinzessin-im-Turm-Zauber beibehalten. Das macht sie nur noch heißer, wenn du mich fragst.«

»Was?« Ich starre sie mit offenem Mund an. »Was meinst du damit?«

»Sie meint, dass du gerade diese unnahbare Aura hast«, meint Andy mit vollem Mund. »Es ist schwer zu beschreiben, aber es ist so, als wenn du diese Eisprinzessin-Vibrationen ausstrahlst, nur dass sie nicht kalt sind, verstehst du? Solche, wie wenn Jackie O. und Prinzessin Diana beschließen würden, sich bei der Arbeit unter das gemeine Volk zu mischen, wenn das Sinn ergibt.«

»Nein, nicht wirklich.« Ich runzele die Stirn, während ich das rothaarige Mädchen anschaue. »Willst du mir sagen, dass ich eingebildet wirke?«

»Nein, nicht eingebildet, einfach anders«, meint Marsha. »Andy hat es nicht gut erklärt. Du … hast einfach Klasse. Vielleicht sind es deine Ballettstunden als junges Mädchen, aber du siehst aus wie jemand, dem man beigebracht hat, einen Knicks zu machen und mit einem Buch auf dem Kopf zu gehen. So als ob du weißt, welche Gabel man wann bei einem formellen Essen benutzt und wie man Smalltalk mit irgendeinem Botschafter betreibt.«

»Was?« Ich breche in Gelächter aus. »Das ist lächerlich. Ich meine, George und ich waren bei einigen formellen Benefizveranstaltungen, aber das war sein Ding, nicht meins. Wenn ich die Wahl hätte, würde ich immer in Yogahosen und Sneakers herumlaufen, und du weißt das ganz genau, Marsha. Mein Gott, ich höre Britney Spears und tanze zu Hip-Hop und R&B.«

»Ich weiß, Süße, aber so siehst du nun mal aus, auch wenn du nicht so bist«, sagt Marsha und nimmt einen kleinen Spiegel hervor, um ihren Lippenstift aufzufrischen. Sie fährt mit einer geübten Hand über ihre Lippen, steckt den Spiegel und den Lippenstift wieder weg und meint: »Das ist etwas Gutes, glaub mir. Nimm doch zum Beispiel einmal mich. Ich könnte so viel ich wollte versuchen, mehr Klasse auszustrahlen, aber die Männer schauen mich an und entscheiden, dass ich leicht zu haben bin. Es ist egal, was ich anhabe oder wie ich mich verhalte, sie sehen nur meine Haare, meine Titten und meinen Arsch und nehmen an, dass ich verfügbar bin.«

»Und du bist ja auch verfügbar«, merkt Tonya grinsend an.

Marsha schnaubt und wirft ihre blonden Haare nach hinten. »Ja, aber das ist ja nicht der Punkt. Der Punkt ist, dass *sie*«, sie zeigt mit dem Daumen auf mich, »nicht einmal so aussehen könnte, als wäre sie leicht zu haben, wenn sie es darauf anlegen würde. Jeder Typ, der sie anschaut, weiß – er *weiß* es einfach –, dass er dafür arbeiten muss. Solche Dinge tun muss wie Abendessen mit Eltern und Ring am Finger.«

»Das stimmt nicht«, widerspreche ich. »Ich habe bereits lange bevor wir verheiratet waren mit George geschlafen.«

Andy verdreht die Augen. »Ja, aber wie lange wart ihr schon zusammen, bevor du mit ihm geschlafen hast?«

»Einige Monate«, antworte ich mit gerunzelter Stirn. »Aber ich war erst achtzehn und …«

»Siehst du? Einige Monate«, sagt Tonya und stößt Marsha mit ihrem Ellenbogen an. »Und wie lange lässt *du* sie warten?«

Marsha lacht. »Mindestens einige Stunden.«

»Na bitte«, meint Andy. »Und dann wunderst du dich, warum diese Arschlöcher dich nie wieder anrufen? Meine Mutter hat immer gesagt: ›Der schnellste Weg, einen Mann loszuwerden, ist, mit ihm zu schlafen.‹ Sara macht es richtig: verhalte dich kühl und distanziert, damit der Typ sein Glück kaum fassen kann, wenn du ihn nur einmal anlächelst.«

»Ach bitte.« Ich beschäftige mich mit den Überresten meines Frühstücks. »Wir leben im einundzwanzigsten Jahrhundert. Ich glaube, Männer wissen es besser, als …«

»Nein«, sagt Marsha fröhlich. »Das tun sie nicht. Wenn etwas leicht zu haben ist, schätzen sie es nicht so sehr. Ich weiß das, und es macht mir nichts aus, nur ein Mädchen für einen netten Abend zu sein. Meistens *möchte* ich auch gar nicht, dass mich diese Typen anrufen, und die wenigen Male, die ich es möchte …« Sie seufzt.» Na ja, es soll wohl einfach nicht sein, nehme ich an. Auf jeden Fall ist das Leben zu kurz, um es damit zu verschwenden, etwas anderes sein zu wollen, als man ist. Wenn du erst einmal in mein Alter kommst, wirst du das verstehen.«

»Ja klar.« Tonya schiebt sich den Rest ihres Bagels in den Mund. »Erzähle uns mehr, alte, weise Frau.«

»Halt den Mund«, murrt Marsha und wirft eine zusammengeknüllte Serviette nach ihr. Sie trifft Andy, die sich sofort mit einem eigenen Serviettengeschoss revanchiert, und ich ducke mich lachend, als das Frühstück sich in eine Serviettenschlacht verwandelt.

Erst als ich immer noch darüber lachend die Cafeteria verlasse, fällt mir auf, dass die Krankenschwestern nicht nur meine Laune verbessert und meine Gedanken von Peter abgelenkt haben.

Sie haben mir auch einen Denkanstoß gegeben.

———

MEINE RUFBEREITSCHAFT ENDET NICHT vor dem späten Abend, aber ich gehe danach trotzdem noch in die Klinik. Sie ist vierundzwanzig Stunden lang geöffnet, und sie können mich immer gebrauchen. Ich dagegen will es so lange wie möglich hinauszögern, nach Hause zu gehen. Von der Idee, die in meinem Kopf herumschwirrt, bekomme ich Magenkrämpfe, und das Letzte, was ich möchte, ist, meinen Stalker zu sehen.

Wie immer freuen sie sich in der Klinik, mich zu sehen. Obwohl es schon so spät ist, ist der Warteraum voller Frauen aller Altersgruppen, von denen viele schreiende Kinder dabeihaben. Neben den gynäkologischen Behandlungen kümmert sich das Klinikpersonal auch um kleinere Krankheiten der Kinder, was die Patienten und die nahegelegene Notaufnahme sehr zu schätzen wissen.

»Viel los heute Nacht?«, frage ich Lydia, die Empfangsdame mittleren Alters, und sie nickt abgehetzt. Sie ist eine der beiden bezahlten Angestellten, alle anderen in der Klinik, einschließlich der Ärzte und Schwestern, sind auf freiwilliger Basis hier. Das führt zu unvorhersehbaren Arbeitszeiten, aber nur so kann die Klinik, die von Spenden lebt, der Gemeinschaft kostenlose Hilfe anbieten.

»Hier«, sagt Lydia und drückt mir eine Liste in die Hand. »Beginne mit den fünf Namen unten.«

Ich nehme das Blatt und gehe in den kleinen Raum, der mir als Büro und Untersuchungszimmer dient. Ich lege meine Sachen ab, wasche meine Hände, spritze mir etwas kaltes Wasser ins Gesicht und gehe in das Wartezimmer, um meine erste Patientin aufzurufen.

Meine ersten drei Patienten sind einfach – eine braucht Verhütungsmittel, eine andere will auf Geschlechtskrankheiten getestet werden und die dritte will eine Bestätigung ihrer Schwangerschaft – aber die vierte, eine hübsche Siebzehnjährige namens Monica Jackson, beklagt sich über eine zu lange Menstruation. Als ich sie untersuche, finde ich vaginale Verletzungen und andere Zeichen sexueller Gewalteinwirkungen, und als ich sie darauf anspreche, bricht sie weinend

zusammen und gibt zu, dass ihr Stiefvater sie vergewaltigt hat.

Ich beruhige sie, schnappe mir ein Vergewalti-
gungs-Kit, behandele ihre Verletzungen und gebe ihr
die Telefonnummer eines Frauenhauses, in dem sie
bleiben kann, sollte sie sich zu Hause nicht sicher
fühlen. Ich schlage ihr außerdem vor, die Polizei einzu-
schalten, aber sie ist entschlossen, keine Anzeige zu
stellen.

»Meine Mutter würde mich umbringen«, sagt sie
mit rot umrandeten und hoffnungslosen Augen. »Sie
sagt, er ist ein guter Versorger und wir haben Glück,
dass wir ihn haben. Er hat Vorstrafen, also wenn ich
irgendetwas sage, werden sie ihn einsperren, und wir
werden wieder auf der Straße enden. Mir ist das egal,
ich würde lieber auf den Strich gehen, als mit diesem
Arschloch zu leben, aber mein Bruder ist erst fünf, und
er würde in eine Pflegefamilie kommen. Im Moment
kümmere ich mich um ihn, wenn meine Mutter es
nicht kann, und ich möchte nicht, dass er mir wegge-
nommen wird.«

Sie beginnt erneut zu weinen, und ich drücke ihre
kleine Hand, während sich mein Herz voller Mitgefühl
zusammenzieht. Auch wenn in den Papieren, die
Monica ausgefüllt hat, steht, dass sie siebzehn ist, sieht
sie mit ihrer zierlichen Figur und den runden Wangen
kaum alt genug aus, um in der Highschool zu sein. Ich
sehe hier häufig Mädchen wie sie, und jedes Mal lässt
mich das Wissen verzweifeln, dass ich kaum etwas tun
kann. Wenn sie allein wäre, könnte ich sie leicht aus

dieser Situation befreien, aber mit ihrem Bruder kann ich nur das Jugendamt benachrichtigen, und das könnte zu dem führen, vor dem sie sich am meisten fürchtet: dass ihr Bruder ohne sie in eine Pflegefamilie kommt.

»Es tut mir so leid, Monica«, sage ich zu ihr, als sie sich etwas beruhigt hat. »Ich denke immer noch, dass die Polizei die beste Option für dich und deinen Bruder ist. Gibt es niemand anderes, an den du dich wenden könntest? Einen Freund der Familie? Vielleicht einen Verwandten?«

Der Gesichtsausdruck des Mädchens wird leer. »Nein.« Sie springt vom Stuhl und zieht sich ihre Kleidung an. »Vielen Dank für Ihre Zeit, Dr. Cobakis. Machen Sie es gut.«

Sie geht aus dem Zimmer, und ich schaue ihr hinterher, während ich einfach nur weinen möchte. Das Mädchen befindet sich in einer schrecklichen Situation, und ich kann ihr nicht helfen. Ich kann den Mädchen wie ihr nie helfen. Außer …

»Warte!« Ich schnappe mir meine Tasche und renne hinter ihr her. »Monica, warte!«

»Sie ist schon gegangen«, sagt Lydia, als ich in den Empfangsbereich laufe. »Was ist passiert? Hat sie etwas vergessen?«

»So etwas in der Art.« Ich halte mich nicht mit weiteren Erklärungen auf. Ich stürme zur Tür, trete hinaus und betrachte die dunkle, menschenleere Straße. Monicas kleine, dunkelhaarige Gestalt ist bereits am Ende der Straße, und sie geht so schnell, dass ich rennen muss, weil ich verzweifelt etwas tun will, wenigstens dieses eine Mal.

»Monica, warte!«

Sie muss mich gehört haben, denn sie bleibt stehen und dreht sich herum.

»Dr. Cobakis?«, fragt sie überrascht, als ich sie eingeholt habe.

Ich bleibe vor Anstrengung keuchend stehen und wühle in meiner Tasche. »Wie viel brauchst du, um überleben zu können?«, frage ich atemlos und ziehe mein Scheckbuch und einen Stift hervor.

»Was?« Sie starrt mich an, als hätte ich mich in einen Alien verwandelt.

»Wenn du zur Polizei gehst und sie deinen Stiefvater verhaften, wie viel werden deine Mutter und du brauchen, um *nicht* auf der Straße zu enden?«

Sie blinzelt. »Wir bezahlen eintausendzweihundert Dollar Miete pro Monat, und die Erwerbsunfähigkeitsrente meiner Mutter deckt über die Hälfte ab. Wenn wir bis diesen Sommer durchhalten, könnte ich einen Vollzeitjob bekommen und einspringen, aber ...«

»Okay, das reicht.« Ich halte das Scheckbuch gegen eine Hauswand und schreibe einen Scheck über fünftausend Dollar aus. Ich hatte eigentlich geplant, dieses Geld zu benutzen, um meine Eltern zu ihrem Jahrestag auf eine Kreuzfahrt zu schicken, aber ich werde mir ein günstigeres Geschenk einfallen lassen.

Ich bin mir sicher, dass es meinen Eltern nichts ausmacht.

Ich reiße den Scheck aus dem Buch, gebe ihn dem

Mädchen und sage: »Nimm ihn und geh zur Polizei. Er hat es verdient, ins Gefängnis zu wandern.«

Ihr rundes Kinn bebt, und einen Moment lang habe ich Angst, dass sie wieder anfängt zu weinen. Aber sie nimmt einfach den Scheck mit zitternden Fingern. »Ich … ich weiß nicht einmal, wie ich Ihnen danken soll. Das ist …« Ihre junge Stimme bricht. »Das ist einfach …«

»Das ist schon in Ordnung.« Ich stecke mein Scheckbuch wieder weg und lächele das Mädchen an. »Geh ihn einlösen und schaff den Bastard aus dem Weg, okay? Versprich es mir.«

»Ich verspreche es«, sagt das Mädchen und steckt den Scheck in die Tasche ihrer Jeans. »Ich verspreche es, Dr. Cobakis. Vielen Dank.«

»Ist schon in Ordnung. Jetzt geh. Es ist spät, und du solltest um diese Uhrzeit nicht allein draußen sein.«

Das Mädchen zögert, bevor es seine Arme um mich legt und mich kurz drückt. »Danke«, flüstert es erneut, bevor es sich auf den Weg macht, und seine zarte Gestalt ab und an zwischen den Straßenlaternen auftaucht, bis sie ganz verschwunden ist.

Ich stehe da, bis ich Monica nicht mehr sehen kann, und dann drehe ich mich herum, um zurück zur Klinik zu gehen. Mein Kontostand hat gerade einen ernsthaften Rückschlag erlitten, aber ich bin so glücklich, als hätte ich im Lotto gewonnen. Zum ersten Mal, seit ich in der Klinik angefangen habe, habe ich wirklich jemandem geholfen, und es fühlt sich umwerfend an.

Der kalte Wind schlägt mir ins Gesicht, als ich

zurückgehe, und mir fällt auf, dass ich meinen Mantel in der Klinik vergessen habe. Das macht mir aber nichts aus. Ich glühe mit einer inneren Freude, für die ein kühler Märzabend kein Gegner ist.

Ich kann mein eigenes Leben nicht in den Griff bekommen, aber vielleicht habe ich gerade dem Mädchen geholfen, seines in Ordnung zu bringen.

Ich bin nur noch die halbe Straßenlänge von der Klinik entfernt, als mir ein Schatten auf der rechten Seite auffällt. Mein Herz hämmert, und Adrenalin überschwemmt meinen Körper, als zwei Männer, die wie Obdachlose aussehen, aus einer Art schmalen Gasse zwischen zwei Häusern heraustreten und das Straßenlicht sich in den glänzenden Klingen ihrer Messer spiegelt.

»Deine Tasche«, zischt der Größere und zeigt mit seinem Messer auf mich, und auch aus dieser Entfernung kann ich den übelkeitserregenden Gestank nach Schweiß, Alkohol und Erbrochenem riechen. »Gib sie her, Schlampe. Jetzt.«

Ich greife schon nach der Tasche, bevor er zu Ende gesprochen hat, aber meine eisigen Finger sind so steif, dass die Tasche von meiner Schulter rutscht und auf den Boden fällt.

»Du verdammte Schlampe! Gib sie her, habe ich gesagt!«, faucht er immer aggressiver, und ich verstehe, dass er etwas genommen hat. Meth? Koks? Wie auch immer, er ist instabil, und sein Partner, der angefangen hat, wie eine Hyäne zu kichern, muss es auch sein.

Ich muss sie beruhigen. Schnell.

»Einen Moment, ich gebe sie euch, versprochen.« Zitternd knie ich mich hin, um die Tasche aufzuheben, damit ich sie ihnen geben kann, aber bevor ich wieder aufstehen kann, sehe ich vor mir eine blitzschnelle Bewegung.

Keuchend falle ich nach hinten und fange mich mit meinen Handflächen ab, als eine große, dunkle Gestalt meine Angreifer rammt und sich dabei mit einer Geschwindigkeit und Geschicklichkeit bewegt, die fast übermenschlich zu sein scheint. Alle drei verschwinden wieder in der dunklen Gasse, und ich höre zwei panische Schreie, denen ein eigenartiges nasses Gurgeln folgt. Danach fällt scheppernd etwas Metallisches auf den Boden. Zweimal.

Oh Gott. Oh Gott, oh Gott, oh Gott.

Ich stolpere zurück und bemerke kaum, dass ich mir auf dem Asphalt die Haut von meinen Handflächen schabe, als mein Retter aus der Gasse tritt, und den Blick auf die beiden Männer hinter ihm freigibt, die gerade zusammensacken wie Marionetten, deren Fäden durchgeschnitten wurden. Eine dunkle Flüssigkeit breitet sich unter ihren auf dem Bauch liegenden Körpern aus, und der metallische Geruch von Blut, gemischt mit etwas noch Übelriechenderem, erfüllt die Luft.

Er hat sie getötet, wird mir benommen klar. Er hat sie verdammt nochmal *getötet.*

Entsetzen explodiert in mir, versorgt mich mit frischem Adrenalin, und ich springe auf, während ein Schrei in meinem Hals aufsteigt. Aber bevor er entweichen kann, tritt die dunkle Gestalt auf mich zu, und die Straßenlaterne beleuchtet ihr Gesicht.

Besser gesagt sein vertrautes, wunderschönes Gesicht.

»Haben sie dir wehgetan?« Peter Sokolovs Stimme ist genauso hart wie sein metallischer Blick, und wieder einmal bin ich wie gelähmt, verängstigt, aber trotzdem unfähig, mich auch nur einen Zentimeter zu bewegen, als er auf mich zukommt und seine Augenbrauen zu einem furchteinflößenden Stirnrunzeln zusammengezogen sind. Es ist das Antlitz eines Mörders, das Gesicht eines Monsters unter der menschlichen Maske, aber trotzdem gibt es dort mehr.

Etwas, das fast wie Besorgnis aussieht.

»Ich …« Ich weiß nicht, was ich sagen wollte, weil ich mich im nächsten Augenblick in seiner Umarmung wiederfinde, so fest gegen seine kräftige Brust gehalten werde, dass ich kaum atmen kann. Die Hitze seines großen Körpers umgibt mich, schützt mich vor dem eisigen Wind, und ich bemerke, wie kalt mir ist, wie sehr ich innerlich friere. Das ganze Entsetzen über das, was ich gerade gesehen habe, ist noch nicht angekommen, aber ich beginne bereits, mich taub zu fühlen, und meine Gedanken sind wirr und benebelt, als die Kälte sich weiter in mir ausbreitet und mich gegen das Trauma betäubt.

Schock, diagnostiziere ich automatisch. Ich falle gerade in einen Schock.

»Schscht, Ptichka. Es ist alles in Ordnung. Es wird alles gut werden.« Peters Stimme ist leise und beruhigend, sein Griff lockert sich, bis er mich mit einer überraschenden Zärtlichkeit wiegt, und mir wird klar, dass diese eigenartigen keuchenden Geräusche von mir kommen. Ich habe Schwierigkeiten, zu atmen, mein Hals schließt sich, als hätte ich eine Panikattacke.

Nicht so als ob – ich *habe* eine Panikattacke.

Er muss das ebenfalls erkennen, weil er ein Stück von mir abrückt und mit besorgten Augen auf mich herabblickt. »Atme«, befiehlt er, und seine Hände auf meinen Schultern verstärken ihren Griff. »Atme, Sara. Langsam und tief. Genau so, Ptichka. Und noch einmal. Atme ...«

Ich folge seiner Stimme, lasse ihn als meinen Therapeuten agieren, und langsam lässt das Gefühl, zu ersticken, nach, und meine Atmung beruhigt sich. Ich konzentriere mich darauf, normal zu atmen und nicht zu denken, weil wenn ich über das, was geschehen ist, nachdenke, wenn ich in die Gasse rechts von mir blicke und die marionettenartigen Körper sehe, könnte ich in Ohnmacht fallen.

»Ja, so ist es gut.« Er zieht mich wieder an sich, und seine große Hand streicht über mein Haar, während ich mit meinem Gesicht an seiner Brust einfach nur dastehe. »Es geht dir gut, Ptichka. Alles ist in Ordnung.«

In Ordnung? Ich will gleichzeitig lachen und weinen. In was für einer Welt sind zwei Leichen in einer Gasse denn »in Ordnung«? Jetzt zittere ich in dem kalten Wind und durch den Schock, und ich weiß, dass ich kurz davor bin, wieder die Kontrolle zu verlieren. Blut und Verletzungen sind mir nicht fremd, und ich habe im Krankenhaus auch schon Erfahrungen mit dem Tod gemacht, aber die Art und Weise, wie diese beiden Männer zusammengesackt sind, so als seien sie Säcke aus Fleisch und Knochen …

Ich halte inne, bevor meine Gedanken zu weit in diese Richtung abschweifen können, aber meine Kehle fühlt sich schon wieder eng an, und mein Zittern verstärkt sich.

»Schscht«, beruhigt mich Peter erneut und schaukelt mich sanft hin und her. Er muss mein Zittern spüren. »Sie können dir nichts tun. Es ist vorbei. Es ist alles vorbei. Komm, bringen wir dich nach Hause.«

Ich öffne meinen Mund, um zu protestieren, darauf zu bestehen, die Polizei oder einen Krankenwagen oder irgendwen zu rufen, aber bevor ich auch nur ein Wort herauspressen kann, beugt er sich nach unten und hebt mich in seine Arme. Er tut das mühelos, so als würde ich nichts wiegen. So als sei es normal, eine Frau, die gegen eine Panikattacke ankämpft, von dem Tatort eines doppelten Mordes wegzutragen.

So als täte er das jeden Tag, was, soweit ich weiß, auch der Fall sein könnte.

Endlich finde ich meine Stimme wieder. »Stell mich ab.« Es ist ein dünnes, hohles Flüstern, kaum ein Geräusch, aber es ist besser als nichts. Meine Hände schaffen es ebenfalls, sich zu bewegen, und drücken gegen seine Schultern, während er die Straße hinabgeht. »Bitte. Ich … ich kann gehen.«

»Das ist schon in Ordnung.« Er schaut mich beruhigend an. »Wir sind fast da.«

»Fast wo?«, frage ich, aber da sehe ich sein Ziel bereits.

Es ist ein schwarzer Geländewagen, der an einer Straßenecke eine Straße von meiner Klinik entfernt parkt. Ein großer Mann mit einem dicken schwarzen Bart lehnt an einer Seite, und als wir uns nähern, sagt Peter mit einem leisen und dringlichen Ton etwas in einer fremden Sprache zu ihm.

Der Mann antwortet in derselben Sprache – höchstwahrscheinlich Russisch, wird mir benommen klar –, bevor er ein schmales Smartphone hervorzieht und mit schnellen, wütenden Bewegungen über das Display wischt. Er hebt es an sein Ohr und spricht wieder auf schnellem Russisch, während Peter die Tür des Wagens öffnet und mich vorsichtig auf die Rückbank setzt.

Mein Peiniger hat nicht gelogen, als er mir gesagt hat, er habe ein Team. Dieser Mann muss einer seiner Helfer sein.

»Ich bin sofort bei dir, Ptichka«, murmelt Peter auf Englisch und streicht mein Haar mit der gleichen eigenartigen Zärtlichkeit aus meinem Gesicht, bevor er sich zurückzieht, die Tür hinter sich schließt und mich allein im warmen Inneren des Autos zurücklässt.

Ich sitze einige Sekunden lang still da und beobachte, wie er mit dem bärtigen Mann spricht, bevor ich reagiere.

Ich rutsche über die Rückbank, greife nach dem

Türgriff auf der gegenüberliegenden Seite von den beiden Männern und stoße die Tür auf, wobei ich fast aus dem Auto falle, weil ich es so eilig habe, wegzukommen. Meine Gedanken und Reaktionen sind durch meinen Schock immer noch langsam, aber ich habe mich genug erholt, um eine wichtige Tatsache zu verstehen.

Zwei Männer wurden vor meinen Augen getötet, und wenn ich nichts dagegen unternehme, bin ich ein Mittäter.

Der kalte Wind ist beißend, und meine Lungen brennen, als ich zur Klinik renne. Hinter mir höre ich einen Schrei, dem schnelle Schritte folgen, und ich weiß, dass sie hinter mir her sind. Meine einzige Hoffnung ist, in die Klinik zu gelangen, bevor sie mich fangen. Als ein gesuchter Mann sollte Peter es nicht riskieren wollen, erkannt zu werden. Sobald ich drinnen in Sicherheit bin, kann ich zu Atem kommen und mir überlegen, was ich tun soll, wie ich am besten die Polizei über das informiere, was geschehen ist.

Ich bin nur noch zweihundert Meter von meinem Ziel entfernt, als sich ein kräftiger Arm um meinen Brustkorb legt und eine große Hand meinen Mund bedeckt und meinen Schrei verstummen lässt. »Du magst es, wenn ich dich jage, stimmt's?«, knurrt eine vertraute Stimme in mein Ohr, bevor ich höre, dass sich ein Auto nähert.

Ich verdoppele meine Anstrengungen, trete gegen Peters Schienbeine und kratze seine Hand, die auf meinem Gesicht liegt, aber es ist sinnlos. Ich höre, wie sich eine Autotür öffnet, und dann schiebt Peter mich hinein, allerdings viel weniger vorsichtig als das letzte Mal.

»*Yezhay*«, ruft er dem bärtigen Fahrer zu, und dann rasen wir auch schon los, lassen die Klinik und den Tatort hinter uns zurück.

29

 *eter*

»YAN UND ILYA KÜMMERN SICH DARUM«, informiert Anton mich auf Russisch, als er auf die Straße einbiegt, die zu Saras Haus führt. »Sie waren dort, bevor jemand die Leichen entdeckt hat.«

»Gut.« Ich blicke auf Sara, die schweigend und leichenblass neben mir auf dem Rücksitz sitzt. »Sag ihnen, dass sie die Reste gründlich entsorgen sollen. Wir wollen nicht, dass irgendwo Körperteile auftauchen. Außerdem sollen sie ihr Auto zu ihrem Haus zurückbringen.

»Ja, das wissen sie.« Unsere Blicke treffen sich im Rückspiegel. »Was wirst du mit ihr tun? Du hast ihr wirklich Angst eingejagt.«

»Ich werde mir etwas einfallen lassen.«

Ich bin froh, dass Sara nicht versteht, was ich sage, weil sie ansonsten noch entsetzter wäre. Ich hätte diese Methheads nicht vor ihr töten sollen, aber sie haben sie mit Messern bedroht, und ich bin durchgedreht. Alles, was ich sehen konnte, war Tamilas Leiche, gebrochen und blutüberströmt, und der Gedanke, dass es Sara sein könnte, dass einer dieser zugedröhnten Obdachlosen sie getötet haben könnte, wenn ich nicht dagewesen wäre, hat mein Blut in vulkanisches Eis verwandelt. Ich kann mich nicht einmal daran erinnern, eine bewusste Entscheidung getroffen zu haben, ich habe rein instinktiv gehandelt. Innerhalb weniger Sekunden hatte ich sie entwaffnet und ihre Kehlen durchgeschnitten, und als ihre Körper auf dem Boden aufschlugen, war es bereits zu spät.

Sara hat sie sterben sehen.

Sie hat gesehen, dass ich sie getötet habe.

»Kannst du die restliche Nacht Ilyas Schicht übernehmen?«, frage ich Anton, als wir vor Saras Haus halten. Mit den hohen Eichen, die die Einfahrt umsäumen, und dem recht großen Abstand zu den nächsten Nachbarn ist dieser Ort schön und abgeschieden – hervorragend in Situationen wie dieser. Es ist schade, dass sie dieses Haus verkauft, ich mag es mittlerweile wirklich gern.

»Kein Problem«, antwortet Anton. »Ich werde in der Nähe bleiben. Wirst du bis zum Morgen dort bleiben?«

»Ja.« Ich blicke auf Sara, die immer noch einfach geradeaus starrt und nicht mitbekommen zu haben scheint, dass wir angekommen sind. »Ich werde bei ihr bleiben.«

Ich ergreife Saras Hand und sage ihr auf Englisch: »Wir sind da, Ptichka. Komm, wir gehen nach Hause.«

Ihre schlanken Finger fühlen sich in meiner Hand eisig an – sie steht immer noch unter Schock. Als ich ihr aus dem Auto helfe, schaut sie mich allerdings an und fragt rau: »Was ist mit der Klinik?«

»Was soll damit sein?«

»Sie werden sich fragen, was aus mir geworden ist.«

»Nein, das werden sie nicht.« Ich fahre mit meiner Hand in meine Tasche und ziehe ihr Handy hervor, das ich während der Fahrt aus ihrer Handtasche genommen habe. »Ich habe ihnen das geschickt.« Ich zeige ihr die Textnachricht, in der steht, dass sie sich um einen Notfall im Krankenhaus kümmern muss.

»Oh.« Sie sieht mich überrascht an. »Du hast das geschrieben?«

Ich nicke und lasse das Handy wieder in meiner Hosentasche verschwinden, während ich sie vom Auto wegführe. »Du warst auf der Fahrt ein wenig abwesend.« In Wirklichkeit ist das eine Untertreibung, da sie, als ich sie erst einmal im Auto hatte, aufgehört hat, sich zu wehren und fast katatonisch wurde.

Sie blinzelt. »Aber … was ist mit den Leichen?«

»Darum habe ich mich auch gekümmert«, beruhige ich sie. »Niemand wird dich damit in Verbindung bringen. Du bist in Sicherheit.«

Sara erschaudert sichtlich, also bringe ich sie schnell ins Haus, nachdem ich die Tür mit den Schlüsseln geöffnet habe, die ich auch aus ihrer Tasche genommen habe. Ich habe meine eigenen Schlüssel – ich habe sie mir vor Monaten machen lassen, als ich zu ihr zurückkam –, aber mir ist es lieber, wenn Sara das nicht weiß. Sollte sie die Schlösser noch einmal austauschen lassen, müsste ich den ganzen nervigen Aufwand noch einmal betreiben.

»Hier, setz dich«, sage ich, als ich sie zum Sofa führe. »Ich gehe dir einen Kamillentee machen.«

»Nein, ich …« Sie windet sich aus meinem Griff. »Ich muss mir die Hände waschen.«

»In Ordnung.« Ich erinnere mich daran, dass sie diese Eigenart hat. »Geh.«

Sie verschwindet um die Ecke im Badezimmer, und ich gehe zur Spüle in der Küche, um meine Hände ebenfalls zu waschen. Ich habe mich vorgesehen, nichts von dem Blut abzubekommen, als ich die Kehlen dieser Männer aufgeschnitten habe, aber trotzdem entdecke ich einige kleine rote Blutspuren auf meinen Unterarmen.

Hoffentlich hat Sara sie nicht gesehen.

Ich wasche meine Hände und meine Unterarme, bevor ich den Wasserkocher anstelle. Als das Wasser kocht, bereite ich zwei Tassen Tee zu und trage sie zum Tisch. Sara ist noch nicht zurück, also beschließe ich, nach ihr zu sehen.

Ich gehe zum Badezimmer und klopfe an die Tür. »Ist alles in Ordnung?«

Ich bekomme keine Antwort, sondern höre nur das Geräusch laufenden Wassers. Weil ich mir Sorgen mache, versuche ich, die Tür zu öffnen, aber sie ist verschlossen.

»Sara?«

Keine Antwort.

»Sara, mach die Tür auf.«

Nichts.

Ich atme tief ein, um mich zu beruhigen, und sage in einer sanfteren Stimme: »Ptichka, ich weiß, dass du aufgebracht bist, aber wenn du die Tür jetzt nicht öffnest, habe ich keine andere Wahl, als sie aufzubrechen.« Oder das Schloss zu knacken, aber das sage ich ihr nicht. Die Tür aufzubrechen hört sich viel bedrohlicher an.

Das Wasser wird abgestellt, aber die Tür bleibt verschlossen.

»Sara. Ich werde jetzt bis fünf zählen. Eins. Zwei. Drei –«

Die Tür klickt.

Erleichtert mache ich die Tür auf und mir wird klar, dass ich zu Recht besorgt war. Sara sitzt mit dem Rücken gegen die Wanne auf dem Boden und hat ihre Knie an die Brust gezogen. Sie gibt keinen Laut von sich, aber ihr Gesicht ist tränenüberströmt, und sie zittert.

Scheiße. Ich hätte sie wirklich nicht vor ihr töten sollen.

»Sara ...« Ich knie mich neben ihr hin, und sie rutscht zur Seite, weg von mir. Ich ignoriere ihre Reaktion, ergreife sanft ihren Arm und ziehe sie in eine Umarmung. »Ich werde dir nicht wehtun, Ptichka«, flüstere ich in ihr Haar, als ich spüre, dass sich ihr Zittern verstärkt. »Du bist bei mir in Sicherheit.«

Ein erstickter Schluchzer entweicht ihrem Mund, dann noch einer und noch einer, und plötzlich klammert sie sich an mir fest, ihre schlanken Arme umschlingen meinen Nacken, während sie beginnt, richtig zu weinen. Ich streiche ihr mit kreisförmigen Bewegungen beruhigend über den Rücken, während sie von unkontrolliertem Schluchzen geschüttelt wird, und sie umfasst mich fester, vergräbt ihr Gesicht an meinem Hals. Ich spüre die Nässe ihrer Tränen, was mich an jenes Mal in der Küche erinnert, als ich versucht habe, sie nach dem Waterboarding zu beruhigen. Von dieser Erinnerung wird mir schlecht, da ich mir jetzt nicht mehr vorstellen kann, ihr so etwas anzutun, mir nicht vorstellen kann, ihr jemals aus irgendeinem Grund wehzutun.

Sie ist für mich jetzt nicht nur eine Person, sie ist meine Welt, und ich werde sie vor allen und allem schützen.

Es dauert lange, bis sie weniger schluchzt, so lange, dass meine Beine steif sind, als ich endlich aufstehe und sie hochziehe.

»Komm«, flüstere ich und lege ihr stützend meinen Arm um den Rücken, als ich sie aus dem Badezimmer führe. »Trinken wir noch einen Tee, bevor wir ins Bett gehen. Du musst erschöpft sein.«

»Sie schnieft und flüstert rau: »Keinen Tee.«

»Okay, keinen Tee. Gehen wir einfach schlafen.«

Ich beuge mich nach unten, um sie auf den Arm zu nehmen.

Sie wehrt sich nicht dagegen, dass ich sie trage, sondern legt einfach ihren Kopf auf meine Schulter und schlingt ihre Arme um meinen Hals. Ihre Atmung ist von dem vielen Weinen immer noch abgehackt, aber sie ist dabei, sich zu beruhigen. Das freut mich, genauso wie die bedürftige Art und Weise, mit der sie an mir hängt. Ich weiß nicht, ob das die Nachwirkungen des Traumas sind, oder ob ich endlich ihren Widerstand brechen kann, aber dass sie sich so an mir festhält, ohne ein Anzeichen von Misstrauen, erfüllt meine Brust mit einer speziellen Wärme, einer, die die eisige Leere um mein Herz zum Schmelzen bringt.

Mit Sara werde ich wieder lebendig, und ich will mehr von diesem Gefühl.

30

Sara

IN DER DUSCHE ist er sehr sanft zu mir, seine Berührung ist zärtlich und unerwartet platonisch, als er mich von Kopf bis Fuß wäscht. Ich stehe still da, das ist alles, was ich in diesem Moment tun kann – einfach dastehen. Nichts interessiert mich in diesem Moment, weder meine Nacktheit noch seine. Jetzt, da der emotionale Sturm vorüber ist, fühle ich mich leer, und ein erschöpfter Nebel betäubt meine Gedanken und Gefühle. Ich bin jenseits von Verlangen, von Angst und Furcht, und alles, was existiert, sind Schuldgefühle.

Furchtbare, zerstörerische Schuldgefühle wegen des Wissens, dass zwei Männer meinetwegen gestorben sind.

Sie sind gestorben, weil ich einen Mörder in mein Leben gelassen und seine Besessenheit genährt habe.

Das ist mir jetzt klar, so offensichtlich, dass ich nicht weiß, warum ich es vorher nicht gesehen habe. Ich bin gefährlich – eine Bedrohung für alle um mich herum. Heute waren die Opfer zwei Drogenabhängige, morgen könnten es meine Freunde oder meine Familie treffen. Niemand um mich herum ist in Sicherheit, solange Peter mich will, und alles, was ich getan habe, hat seine Besessenheit nur angeheizt.

Von Anfang an habe ich das Spiel falsch gespielt, und jetzt haben zwei Männer dafür mit ihrem Leben bezahlt.

»Hier, komm heraus«, befiehlt Peter, und ich trete aus der Dusche und lasse mich von ihm in ein dickes Handtuch einwickeln. Er trocknet mich damit ab und behandelt mich ein weiteres Mal wie ein Kind. Ich lasse es zu, weil ich zu erschöpft bin, um etwas anderes zu tun. Und außerdem ist das alles, das Weinen in seinen Armen, an ihm zu hängen und es zuzulassen, dass er sich um mich kümmert, gut für meine neue Strategie.

Da er mich haben will, kann er mich haben.

Das ist keine besonders brillante Strategie, und es gibt auch keine Garantie dafür, dass sie funktionieren wird. Sie könnte sogar nach hinten losgehen. Aber an diesem Punkt habe ich bereits nichts mehr zu verlieren. Ich habe versucht, ihn abzuwehren, und er ist immer noch da, immer noch eine Bedrohung. Also muss ich jetzt etwas anderes versuchen.

Ich muss erreichen, dass er das Interesse an mir verliert.

Es war die Frühstücksunterhaltung, die mich auf diese Idee gebracht hat. Was, wenn die Schwestern recht haben und ich so etwas wie eine Eisprinzessin-Ausstrahlung habe, die meinen Stalker anspricht? Was ist, wenn er mich nur noch mehr will, je länger ich mich weigere?

Der schnellste Weg, einen Mann loszuwerden, ist, mit ihm zu schlafen. Das ist ein dummes Sprichwort, aber Andys Mutter ist nicht die Einzige, die daran glaubt.

Ich habe es schon tausendmal gehört, normalerweise von Eltern, die Teenager haben, die schwanger geworden sind, weil ihre Eltern darauf bestanden haben, mit ihnen lieber über Abstinenz als Geburtenkontrolle zu reden. Es ist ein altes, sexistisches Klischee über diese Dynamik zwischen Männern und Frauen, eines, das auf der beleidigenden Annahme beruht, dass Frauen wie Klopapier sind, ein Gegenstand, den man benutzen und dann wegwerfen kann.

Ich habe mich immer über solche Dinge lustig gemacht, aber gleichzeitig weiß ich, dass es Männer gibt, die sich genau so benehmen, die hinter Frauen her sind, bis sie sie ins Bett bekommen, und danach schnell das Interesse verlieren. Aber der Grund dafür ist nicht, dass sie denken, dass Frauen unberührt sein sollten, zumindest nicht normalerweise. Die Eroberung ist einfach das, was ihnen am meisten Spaß macht. Sie genießen die Vorfreude mehr als den eigentlichen Akt, und wenn sie einmal am Ziel sind, ziehen sie weiter und suchen nach neuen Jagdgebieten.

Ich weiß nicht, ob mein Stalker in diese Kategorie fällt, aber es ist möglich – sogar wahrscheinlich. Er ist ein umwerfend gutaussehender Mann und zweifellos an Frauen gewöhnt, die sich Hals über Kopf in seine gefährliche Alphatier-Ausstrahlung verlieben. Ich habe nie jemanden wie ihn kennengelernt, aber ich habe Schatten dieser Arroganz bei beliebten Sportlern auf der Uni, bei Wall-Street-Managern und überbezahlten männlichen Chirurgen gesehen. Männer wie diese – die am Anfang der Nahrungskette stehen – nehmen einen Hauch von Zögern als eine Herausforderung auf, es fesselt sie und bringt sie dazu, die betreffende Frau nur noch mehr zu verfolgen anstatt weniger.

Wenn das der Fall ist, und ich hoffe verzweifelt, dass er es ist, dann ist der einfachste Weg, Peter Sokolov loszuwerden, ihm genau das zu geben, was er möchte: mich freiwillig in seinem Bett. Aus irgendeinem Grund scheint der russische Killer bei Vergewaltigung eine Grenze zu ziehen und sich stattdessen lieber in mein Leben zu drängen, also muss ich ihm grünes Licht geben.

Wenn ich will, dass dieser Albtraum endet, muss ich freiwillig Sex mit meinem Peiniger haben.

»Komm her, leg dich hin«, drängt Peter, als wir am Bett ankommen. Er nimmt mir das Handtuch ab und führt mich sanft unter die Decke. »Morgen früh wirst du dich besser fühlen, versprochen.« Und erneut ist seine Berührung platonisch, fast klinisch, aber ich weiß, dass er mich will. Ich sehe, wie steif er ist, als er neben mir unter die Decke kriecht, spüre ich die Anspannung, die von ihm abstrahlt, als er sich herumdreht, um das Licht auszumachen, bevor er mich in seine Umarmung zieht und mich in der vertrauten Löffelchenstellung gegen seinen warmen Körper schmiegt.

Er will mich, aber er wird mich nicht nehmen – nicht, bis ich nicht zustimme.

Ich liege einige Augenblicke still da, während ich versuche, mich davon zu überzeugen, es wirklich zu tun. Mein Magen fühlt sich an, als würden in ihm ein Waschbär und ein Hamster kämpfen, und die Erschöpfung hat sich wie ein dickes, alles einhüllendes Tuch um meinen Kopf gelegt. Mit meinen wunden Augen und den Kopfschmerzen vom Weinen ist das Letzte, wonach mir gerade ist, Sex, aber vielleicht sollte ich es genau deswegen jetzt tun.

Vielleicht fühle ich mich nicht ganz so schlecht, wenn ich es nicht genieße.

Ich bereite mich psychisch darauf vor und bewege mich leicht, um meinen Po näher an Peters Lende zu schieben. Er versteift, atmet schwerer, und ich wiederhole das Manöver, reibe mich an ihm, während ich mich unter dem Vorwand hin und her bewege, eine bequemere Position zu finden. Da sein muskelbepackter Arm um meinen Brustkorb liegt, kann ich mich kaum bewegen, aber das ist egal. Wir sind beide nackt, und die kleinste Berührung seiner Haut an meiner ist elektrisierend, so voller Empfindungen, dass jedes meiner Nervenenden strammsteht. Ich kann in der rabenschwarzen Dunkelheit des Raumes nichts sehen, aber ich kann seine raue Beinbehaarung auf der Rückseite meiner Oberschenkel spüren, seinen sauberen männlichen Duft riechen, und ich atme schneller, während mein Herz wie wild in meiner Brust schlägt, als sein Schwanz noch härter wird und wie ein Gewehrlauf gegen meinen Po drückt.

Das ist es, komm schon. Ich ignoriere die Angst, die meinen Hals verengt, und bewege meine Hüften noch ein wenig mehr. Ich bringe es nicht über mich, mich umzudrehen und ihn zu umarmen, aber vielleicht wird er mit einer kleinen Ermutigung seine Kontrolle verlieren und mich anfassen. Ich werde nicht protestieren, werde nichts tun, um ihn aufzuhalten. Ich werde mich von ihm ficken lassen, vielleicht sogar vorgeben, es zu genießen, damit ich auch in diesem Punkt keine Herausforderung darstelle. Ich werde einfach daliegen und es über mich ergehen lassen, und danach wird alles vorbei sein.

Ich werde willig, aber langweilig sein, und er wird meiner müde werden.

Das ist zumindest der Plan, aber während ich mich bewege, bemerke ich, dass ein Teil meiner Müdigkeit verschwindet und von einem warmen, feuchten Gefühl ersetzt wird, das seinen Ursprung tief in meinem Unterleib hat. Da die Dunkelheit alles verdeckt, ist es leicht, so zu tun, als sei nichts davon real, als habe ich einen weiteren dieser abartigen Träume.

»Sara, Ptichka ...« Sein raues Flüstern klingt angespannt. »Wenn du schlafen möchtest, solltest du aufhören, dich zu bewegen.«

Ich liege einen Moment lang still, bevor ich mich langsam und absichtlich ein weiteres Mal an ihm reibe. »Was, wenn ...« Ich lecke über meine trockenen Lippen. »Was ist, wenn ich nicht schlafen möchte?«

Peters Körper hinter mir versteinert, und sein Arm um meinen Brustkorb spannt sich an. Für einen kurzen, irrationalen Augenblick befürchte ich, dass er ablehnen könnte, dass er mich trotz aller Hinweise nicht wirklich will, aber dann werde ich auf den Rücken gedreht, und sein schweres Gewicht drückt mich nach unten, während die Nachttischlampe angemacht wird.

Ich blinzele, da mich das Licht kurz blendet, bevor ich sein Gesicht erkenne und ich sehe, dass seine grauen Augen verengt sind und sein Kinn angespannt ist, während er sich auf einem Ellenbogen abstützt. Er sieht wütend aus, und eine schreckliche Sekunde lang frage ich mich, ob ich alles falsch verstanden habe, ob ich einen riesigen Fehler gemacht habe.

»Spielst du mit mir, Sara?« Seine Stimme ist leise und hart, und sein Akzent stärker als sonst, als er meine Handgelenke ergreift und sie über meinem Kopf mit einer großen Hand auf dem Kissen festhält. »Versuchst du herauszufinden, wie weit du bei mir gehen kannst?«

Ich starre ihn an, und ein dunkles Kribbeln überzieht meine Haut. Es ist unheimlich, wie viel Ähnlichkeit diese Situation mit meinen Träumen hat. Und trotzdem ist es gleichzeitig anders. Mein von Drogen benebeltes Gehirn hatte ihn hart und grausam dargestellt, eher wie ein Monster als einen Mann, aber das war falsch. Dieses tödliche, umwerfend schöne Gesicht, das mich anblickt, hat nichts von einem Monster. Die Träume hatten die Stärke seiner magnetischen Anziehung unterschätzt, die sinnliche Weichheit seiner Lippen, die starke, noble Form seiner Nase, die Art und Weise, wie sich seine Augenbrauen über den intensiven, metallischen Augen zusammenziehen und vieles mehr. Er ist hinreißend, mein angsteinflößender Stalker, und während ich hier unter seinem kräftigen, warmen Körper liege, verstärkt sich das dunkle Kribbeln und verwandelt sich in etwas Gefährliches und Verbotenes. Meine Nippel verhärten sich, und eine Hitzewelle überrollt mich, während sich meine inneren Muskeln voller Begehren zusammenziehen.

Ich will diesen Mann nicht. Ich *kann* ihn nicht wollen. Aber während ich mir das einrede, weiß ich, dass es eine Lüge ist, ein Wunschdenken. Was auch immer ihn zu mir zieht, tut dasselbe bei mir, diese Verbindung zwischen uns ist genauso stark wie irrational. Ich will ihn. Mehr als das, ich *brauche* ihn. Meinen Körper interessiert es nicht, dass er gerade zwei Menschen vor meinen Augen getötet hat, dass ich ihn mit meinem ganzen Wesen verachte. Seine Berührung stößt mich nicht ab, sie erregt mich, mein Verlangen wurde durch die erzwungene Intimität der letzten Tage und die perverse Lust, die ich in seinen Armen erfahren habe, nur verstärkt.

Durch diese unnatürliche, abartige Zärtlichkeit, die keinen Platz in unserer Beziehung hat.

Er wartet immer noch mit verengten Augen auf meine Antwort, und ich weiß, dass ich einfach aus der Sache herauskomme, indem ich so tue, als sei das Ganze ein großes Missverständnis. Aber wenn ich das mache, wird er mich weiterhin verfolgen, versuchen, meinen Widerstand Tag für Tag zu brechen, bis ich mich nach ihm sehne, und in der Zwischenzeit werden alle um mich herum sich in Gefahr befinden.

»Keine Spiele«, flüstere ich in die angespannte Stille. »Die Kondome sind im Nachttisch.«

Er holt tief Luft, seine Finger auf mir spannen sich an, und ich kann den genauen Moment erkennen, in dem er versteht, was ich sage. Seine Nasenlöcher blähen sich, seine Pupillen werden größer, und die Wut auf seinem Gesicht wird zu einem dunklen, unbändigen Hunger. Er greift mit seiner freien Hand in den Nachttisch, zieht ein verpacktes Kondom heraus, öffnet es mit seinen Zähnen und zieht es sich über seinen großen, hervorragenden Schwanz.

Mein Herz rast, und mein Brustkorb zieht sich angsterfüllt zusammen, aber es ist zu spät.

Peter senkt seinen Kopf und nimmt meine Lippen mit seinen gefangen.

31

Sara

ICH WEIß NICHT, warum, aber ich hatte nicht erwartet, dass er mich küssen würde, dass er seinen Mund auf meinen legen und ihn in Besitz nehmen würde, als sei er am Verhungern. Aber genauso fühlt es sich an: so als verspeise er mich, als nähme er alles, was mein Wesen ausmacht. Seine Lippen auf meinem Mund sind rau und wild, verschlingen mich und entziehen meinen Lungen ihre Luft. Seine freie Hand ist in meinem Haar vergraben und hält mich während des vereinnahmenden Kusses bewegungslos, weshalb ich nichts weiter tun kann, als dahinzuschmelzen. Weil er nicht nur nimmt, er gibt. Er gibt so viel Lust, dass ich überwältigt bin, überwältigt von seinem Geschmack und davon, wie er sich anfühlt.

Er küsst mich, bis ich errötet bin und brenne, bis ich mich kaum noch daran erinnern kann, wie es sich angefühlt hat, ihn nicht zu küssen, nicht seinen warmen, minzigen Atem zu riechen. Bis alle Gedanken daran, was wir sind, verschwunden sind, und ich mich ihm gedankenlos voller Begehren entgegenbiege, da ich verzweifelt mehr von seinen Berührungen und dieser prickelnden, heißen Lust will. Meine Fingerspitzen kribbeln wegen seines festen Griffs um meine Handgelenke, und sein Körper liegt schwer auf mir, aber ich will mehr.

Ich will mich in seiner erbarmungslosen Umarmung verlieren, mich in ihm auflösen und verschwinden.

Er löst sich von meinen Lippen, um eine brennende Spur auf meinem Gesicht und meinem Hals zu hinterlassen, und ich schnappe nach Luft, während mein Herz rast und ich von der elektrisierenden Lust Gänsehaut habe. Bei jedem Einatmen reiben meine Nippel gegen seine Brustmuskeln, und Nässe befeuchtet meine inneren Oberschenkel, da mein Körper sich auf ihn vorbereitet, auf diesen Akt, den ich nicht wollen sollte, nach dem ich mich nicht derart intensiv sehnen sollte.

Er atmet abgehackt, hebt seinen Kopf, und ich kann den gleichen Hunger in seinem silbernen Blick sehen, ein dunkles Begehren, vermischt mit etwas erschreckend Besitzergreifendem. Seine Hand löst sich von meinem Haar und bewegt sich an meinem Körper hinab, um meine Brust zu bedecken. »Sara …« Mein Name ist ein raues Ausatmen auf seinen Lippen, als sein Daumen über meinen vor Lust schmerzenden Nippel fährt. »Du bist so wunderschön, Ptichka ... alles, von dem ich jemals geträumt habe, und mehr.«

Seine glühenden Worte brennen sich in mich, erfüllen mich mit einer Wärme, die sich bis in meinen Unterleib ausbreitet – und Alarmglocken in meinem Kopf läuten lässt. Das hört sich zu sehr nach der Vollziehung einer Liebesbeziehung an, und als sein Knie sich zwischen meine Oberschenkel schiebt, löst sich der sinnliche Nebel, der mich einhüllt, einen Augenblick lang. Mit einer klaren Eingebung verstehe ich, was gerade geschieht, und Entsetzen dämpft mein Verlangen.

Was tue ich gerade? Wie kann ich das überhaupt auf irgendeine Weise genießen? Es ist eine Sache, für einen guten Zweck stoisch die Berührung eines Monsters zu ertragen, aber es wirklich zu begehren – es sich so benehmen zu lassen, als seien wir Liebhaber – ist krank, vollkommen verrückt. Auch wenn er meine Handgelenke festhält, ist es sinnlos, vorzugeben, dass ich unwillig bin, dass mein Körper sich nicht auf die perversesten Arten und Weisen nach ihm sehnt.

Der große Kopf seines Schwanzes berührt meine Falten, und meine Atmung wird flach, meine Muskeln ziehen sich plötzlich panisch zusammen. Ich kann das nicht tun – nicht so. Das ist zu sehr wie Liebemachen. Er schaut mich immer noch an, seine grauen Augen sind voller brennender Hitze, und ich weiß, dass ich ihm sagen muss, damit aufzuhören, das zu beenden ...

Er dringt mit einem einzigen kräftigen Stoß in

mich ein, und ich vergesse, was ich gerade sagen wollte. Ich vergesse alles, außer der Stärke und Brutalität seines Schwanzes, der sich in meinen Körper schiebt. Seine kompromisslose Härte zwingt meine enge Höhle auseinander, und trotz meiner Erregung fühle ich ein stechendes Brennen, als er sich tiefer hineindrückt und dabei den Widerstand meiner angespannten Muskeln ignoriert. Mein letztes Mal ist schon sehr lange her, und er ist groß, dicker und länger als Georges. Mein Herz schlägt heftig in meiner Brust, während mein Körper sich seiner rauen Penetration widerwillig beugt, und mit einer Mischung aus Enttäuschung und bitterer Erleichterung erkenne ich, dass meine Ängste vergebens waren.

Das ist ganz und gar nicht wie Liebemachen.

Als er vollständig in mir ist, hält er inne, seine Augen glänzen mit einem dunklen Hunger, und eine andere Art der Anspannung breitet sich in meinem Körper aus, verbannt den letzten Rest der unwillkommenen Erregung und festigt meinen Entschluss. Die sinnliche Anziehung seines Aussehens ist immer noch da, aber jetzt sehe ich das Monster hinter dem hübschen Gesicht, den Mörder, der mich gefoltert und mein Leben zerstört hat. Meine Gefühle sind nicht mehr widersprüchlich, sondern völlig klar. Mein Stalker, der Mann, den ich hasse, vergewaltigt meinen Körper, und ich bin froh darüber. Ich bin froh, weil seine Grausamkeit weniger schmerzt als seine Zärtlichkeit, seine Rücksichtslosigkeit weniger angsteinflößend ist als seine Gnade.

Ich hole beruhigend Luft und bereite mich darauf vor, einen harten und rauen Fick zu ertragen, aber er bewegt sich nicht. Sein Gesicht ist vor Lust verzogen, sein Körper ist so angespannt, dass er vibriert, aber er stößt nicht zu, und mir wird klar, dass er mein Unbehagen bemerkt hat und mir Zeit gibt, mich anzupassen.

Auf seine eigene Art und Weise versucht er, sanft zu sein – was das Letzte ist, das ich will.

Ich nehme meinen ganzen Mut zusammen, fahre mit meiner Zunge über meine Lippen und beobachte, wie sich der Hunger in seinen Augen intensiviert.

»Tu es«, flüstere ich, während sich meine inneren Muskeln zusammenziehen. Ich kann ihn hart und dick und gefährlich in mir pochen spüren. »Tu es, verdammt noch mal.«

Er starrt mich an, und ich kann seinen Kampf spüren, kann das Monster fühlen, das gegen den Mann kämpft. Ich bin nicht die Einzige mit gemischten Gefühlen hier. Es gibt einen Teil von Peter, der mich hasst, der mich als eine Erinnerung an seine persönliche Tragödie sieht. Er will mich, aber er will mir gleichzeitig wehtun und mich für das bezahlen lassen, was seiner Frau und seinem Sohn zugestoßen ist. Vielleicht ist es ihm selbst nicht klar, aber ich weiß es. Ich fühle es. Unsere Verbindung wurde mit Verlust und Schmerzen geschmiedet, unsere Intimität mit Folter. Nichts an seiner Anziehungskraft auf mich ist normal, sie ist genauso krank wie meine Reaktion auf ihn.

Seine Rache verbindet uns, und keine Zärtlichkeit dieser Welt kann diese Tatsache ändern.

Ich kann den genauen Moment sehen, in dem das Monster den Kampf gewinnt. Peters Kinn spannt sich an, als er sich ein Stück zurückzieht, bevor er mit einem harten Stoß erneut eindringt. »Willst du das von mir?« Seine Stimme ist leise und rau, und seine Augen werden von einer wachsenden Dunkelheit erfüllt. Er spannt seine Hüften an, und ich ziehe scharf Luft ein, als er tiefer in mich eindringt und seine Hände meine Handgelenke fester umfassen. »Sag es mir, Sara. Willst du das?«

Ich kann immer noch nein sagen, den Mann das Biest zurückhalten lassen, aber ich habe meinen Weg gewählt und werde nicht von ihm abweichen. Vielleicht ist dieser letzte Racheakt genau das, was wir beide brauchen, die Bestrafung, die ich für meine Absolution ertragen muss.

Wenn er seine Dunkelheit auf mich loslässt, können wir beide vielleicht endlich frei sein.

»Ja«, flüstere ich und mache mich auf das Schlimmste gefasst. »Genau das möchte ich.«

eter

ICH WEISS NICHT, was ich erwartet hatte, aber als ich in Saras braune Augen schaue und den Hass in ihnen sehe, lösen sich meine Fantasien, die Lügen, die ich mir eingeredet habe, im Angesicht der Wahrheit in Luft auf. Ihr Körper reagiert vielleicht auf mich, aber ich bin immer noch ihr Feind – und sie ist meiner. Auch wenn ihre seidige Muschi meinen pochenden Schwanz umklammert, ist das Verlangen in meinem Blut mit Gewalt vermischt, mein Verlangen nach ihr dunkler als alles, was ich kenne.

Ich will sie nicht einfach nur ficken; ich will sie aufbrechen, meine Rache an ihrem zarten Fleisch nehmen.

»Sara ...« Ich suche verzweifelt nach den letzten Überresten meines gesunden Verstandes, nach etwas, an dem ich mich festhalten kann, während die gedankenlose, rote Flut mich überrollt, die grausame Macht des Hungers meine Kontrolle untergräbt. »Du weißt nicht, um was du ...«

»Tu es einfach, verdammt noch mal«, flüstert sie erneut, während sie meinen Blick trotzig erwidert, und der seidene Faden, an dem meine Beherrschung hängt, reißt.

Mit einem leisen, rauen Stöhnen ziehe ich mich zurück und versenke mich in ihr, nehme kaum die Art und Weise wahr, auf die sich ihre Muschi in panischem Widerstand um mich zusammenzieht, ihr weicher Tunnel meinem Angriff nachgibt. Sie ist nass, aber sie ist eng, fast so klein wie eine Jungfrau, und selbst durch meinen Lustnebel hindurch verstehe ich, was das bedeutet.

Sie hat seit längerer Zeit keinen Sex gehabt – wahrscheinlich nicht nach ihrem Ehemann.

Dem Mann, dessen Arroganz meinen Sohn umgebracht hat.

Mein Verlangen wird noch dunkler, wird durch eine Welle aus Qualen geborener Wut angeheizt, und ich beuge meinen Kopf nach unten, um Saras Mund erneut in Besitz zu nehmen. Aber dieses Mal kann ich mich nicht zurückhalten, und der Kuss ist hart und wild, so gewalttätig wie die Gefühle, die mich zerreißen. Sie fühlt sich so zart an, riecht so süß und ihr

Mund ist so seidig – das alles macht mich verrückt, und ich schmecke den metallischen Geschmack ihres Blutes, als meine Zähne in ihrer Unterlippe versinken und ihre zarte Haut durchbrechen. Das sollte mich stoppen oder zumindest innehalten lassen, aber stattdessen regt es nur meinen Appetit an. Ich brauche das von ihr: ihren Schmerz, ihr Leiden. Es ist, als habe ein Fremder meinen Körper übernommen und mein Verlangen nach ihr in ein Bedürfnis sie zu bestrafen verwandelt, ein Bedürfnis, sie für die Sünden ihres Ehemanns zahlen zu lassen. Sara in Besitz zu nehmen ist gleichzeitig Himmel und Hölle, das intensive Vergnügen, sie zu ficken, vermischt sich mit dem bitteren Wissen, dass ich mein Versprechen gebrochen habe.

Ich verletze gerade die Frau, die ich heilen wollte, diejenige, durch die ich mich so lebendig fühle.

Ich weiß nicht, ob es diese Erkenntnis ist oder die Tränen, die ich auf ihrem Gesicht sehen kann, als ich meinen Kopf anhebe, aber die Wut beginnt, abzuschwächen und der rote Nebel zieht sich zurück, obwohl mein Verlangen eine neue Ebene erreicht. Meine Eier ziehen sich an meinen Körper und die präorgastische Anspannung sammelt sich am Anfang meiner Wirbelsäule, aber trotzdem bin ich mir der vogelartigen Zierlichkeit ihrer Handgelenke in meinem Griff und der verängstigten Steifheit ihres Körpers, während ich mich an ihrem Fleisch vergehe, schmerzhaft bewusst.

Unsere Blicke treffen sich, und ich sehe Schmerzen in den braunen Tiefen, die sich mit einer perversen Befriedigung vermischen. Ich mache es ihr zu leicht, gieße Benzin in das Feuer ihres Hasses. Das ist genau das, was sie die ganze Zeit von mir erwartet hat, wovor sie sich gefürchtet hat, obwohl sie es gleichzeitig wollte.

Nach heute Nacht werde ich nie wieder mehr sein als der Mann, der ihr wehgetan hat, der sie auf die grausamste Art und Weise benutzt hat.

Scheiße, nein. Ich beiße die Zähne zusammen und zwinge mich dazu, aufzuhören, gegen den aufsteigenden Orgasmus anzukämpfen. Ich lasse ihre Handgelenke los, ziehe mich aus ihr zurück und bewege mich an ihrem Körper hinunter, wobei ich die quälende Härte meines Schwanzes ignoriere. Ich stoppe zwischen ihren gespreizten Schenkeln, ergreife ihre Knie und beuge meinen Kopf nach unten.

»Was tust du …« beginnt sie benebelt, aber da lecke ich bereits ihre weiche Muschi, fahre mit meiner Zunge über ihre rosafarbenen, geschwollenen Falten. Sie ist nass, aber nicht so nass, wie ich sie gern hätte, also habe ich beschlossen, etwas dagegen zu unternehmen und dazu alle meine Fertigkeiten einzusetzen, die ich mir in meinen mehr als fünfunddreißig Jahren angeeignet habe.

»Warte, Peter, nicht …« Sie greift nach unten und versucht, mich wegzuschieben, während ich mit meiner Zunge ihre Klitoris umfahre, und als ihr das nicht gelingt, will sie ihre Beine schließen. »Das ist nicht …«

»Schscht.« Ich benutze meine Hände an ihren Knien dazu, ihre Schenkel geöffnet zu halten. »Leg dich einfach hin und entspanne dich.«

»Nein, ich …« Sie stöhnt auf und klammert sich in meinen Haaren fest, als ich ihre Klitoris in meinen Mund nehme. Ich beginne, mit starken, rhythmischen Bewegungen an ihr zu saugen, und die Anspannung ihrer Beinmuskulatur lässt nach, während ihre Atmung hörbar unregelmäßig wird. Ich kann spüren, wie sie unter meiner Zunge immer feuchter wird, und nutze ihre Abgelenktheit, um meine rechte Hand zu ihrer Muschi zu bewegen.

»Genau so, Ptichka, entspanne dich einfach …« Ich blase kühle Luft auf ihre Klitoris und werde mit einem leisen Aufstöhnen belohnt, bevor sich ihre Schenkel erneut anspannen. Sie versucht, sich zu wehren, das Vergnügen zurückzuweisen, aber ich habe meinen Ellenbogen bereits so positioniert, dass sie meinen Kopf nicht mit ihren Schenkeln zerquetschen kann. Sie atmet jetzt schwerer, und sie umklammert meine Haare fester, als ich wieder an ihrer Klitoris sauge und gleichzeitig mit zwei Fingern in ihre enge, nasse Öffnung eintauche und sie in ihr krümme, bis ich die schwammige Wand ihres G-Punktes spüre. Ihre Muschi zieht sich fest zusammen, erschaudert um meine Finger, und ihre Hüften heben sich vom Bett ab, als ich mein Saugen verstärke. Sie ist nahe dran, das kann ich fühlen. Mein Herz klopft stark in meiner

Brust, und meine Atmung ist schnell, während der Schmerz in meinen Eiern unerträglich wird, aber ich beherrsche mich, bis ich sicher bin, dass sie kurz davor ist. Dann, und erst dann, gebe ich meinem eigenen Verlangen nach.

Ich ziehe meine Finger aus ihr heraus, bewege mich nach oben, bedecke ihren Körper mit meinem und lege meinen Schwanz vor ihren geschwollenen Eingang.

»Komm mit mir zusammen«, sage ich rau und schaue ihr in die Augen, als ich mit einem harten Stoß in sie eindringe, und ihr Körper gehorcht mir, ihr enges, nasses Fleisch zieht sich um mich zusammen, melkt meinen Schwanz in dem Moment, in dem der Orgasmus mich überwältigt. Ihre wunderschönen Augen werden weich und abwesend, auf ihrem Gesicht spiegelt sich Ekstase wieder, während sich ihre Finger in meinen Seiten vergraben, und ich ihren erstickten Schrei in dem Moment höre, in dem mein Samen herausspritzt. Es fühlt sich an, als würden alle Muskeln meines Körpers gleichzeitig vibrieren, und meine Lungen arbeiten auf Hochtouren, während die Lust mich in heißen Wellen überrollt, und als ich auf ihr zusammenbreche, weiß ich, dass es das war.

Ich werde nie wieder eine andere Frau begehren.

Ich weiß nicht, wie lange es dauert, bis die Nachbeben abgeklungen sind, aber als ich endlich die Kraft finde, mich auf meine Ellenbogen abzustützen, hat sich Sara genug erholt, um zu verstehen, was passiert ist, und Entsetzen macht sich auf ihrem Gesicht breit. Wie ich atmet sie schwer, ihre Wangen sind rot und leuchten postkoital, aber in ihrem Blick ist keine Freude, sondern nur das Glitzern ihrer Tränen.

Sie bedauert das, macht sich erneut Vorwürfe, und das werde ich nicht zulassen.

»Tu das nicht.« Ich senke meinen Kopf, um ihre Wangen zu küssen, während die Tränen aufsteigen und über ihre Schläfen hinunterlaufen. »Tu das nicht, Ptichka. Fühl dich nicht schlecht. Du hast nichts Falsches getan. Ich habe das alles gemacht. Ich habe dir wehgetan, erinnerst du dich? Ich habe dir keine Wahl gelassen.«

Ihre Atmung ist abgehackt und ihre Lippen zittern, als ich Küsse auf ihrem Gesicht niederregnen lasse, und ich kann sie unter mir erschaudern fühlen, während immer mehr Tränen aufsteigen. Ich bin immer noch in ihr, mein weicher werdender Schwanz ist in ihrem Körper vergraben, aber trotzdem versucht sie nicht, mich zu berühren, sondern will sich zusammenrollen und die Verbindung zwischen uns ablehnen.

Ich wollte ihren Schmerz, und ich habe ihn bekommen – und jetzt zerreißt er mich innerlich.

Ich weiß nicht, was ich tun soll, wie ich sie beruhigen kann, also küsse ich sie einfach immer weiter und streichele sie, so sanft ich kann. Meine Rachegelüste sind verschwunden, und alles, was geblieben ist, ist Bedauern. Wieder einmal bin ich der Grund dafür, dass Sara leidet, und dieses Mal ist es unendlich viel schlimmer. Dieses Mal kenne ich sie.

Ich kenne sie, und sie bedeutet mir etwas.

Sie weint immer noch, als ich mich aus ihr zurückziehe und aufstehe, um das Kondom im Badezimmer zu entsorgen. Als ich mit einem nassen Handtuch zurückkommen, liegt sie zusammengerollt auf einer Seite und hat sich die Decke bis zum Hals hochgezogen.

»Lass dich von mir sauber machen«, murmele ich, während ich die Decke von ihrem nackten Körper ziehe, und als sie nicht protestiert, fahre ich mit dem Handtuch über ihre weichen Falten, um das wunde, geschwollene Fleisch zu beruhigen und den Beweis ihres Verlangens wegzuwischen. Sie weint nicht länger, aber ihre Augen sind immer noch nass, und in dem Augenblick, in dem ich fertig bin, kriecht sie wieder unter die Decke und zieht sie sich über den Kopf.

Ich will gerade zu ihr ins Bett steigen, als ich höre, dass mein Telefon auf dem Nachttisch vibriert, wo ich es für Notfälle abgelegt hatte.

Ich runzele die Stirn, nehme es in die Hand und schaue auf das Display.

Planänderung, steht in der Nachricht von Anton. *Velazquez wird sich in zwei Tagen zum Guadalajara-Anwesen begeben. Es ist entweder morgen oder nie.*

Ich schlucke einen Fluch hinunter und kämpfe gegen den Drang an, das Telefon durch den Raum zu werfen. Beschissener hätte das Timing nicht sein können … Wir hatten gerade den ganzen Plan ausgearbeitet und wollten in sechs Tagen zuschlagen. Aber wenn unser Opfer seinen Aufenthaltsort ändert, müssten wir die Planung komplett von vorn beginnen. Es könnte mehrere Wochen dauern, Velazquez

Anwesen in Guadalajara auszukundschaften, und unser Kunde, ein rivalisierender Drogenboss, ist bereits ungeduldig. Er will Velazquez lieber gestern als heute tot wissen und wird eine Verspätung nicht gut aufnehmen.

Anton hat recht. Wir müssen jetzt zuschlagen.

Bereite das Flugzeug und die Ladung vor, schreibe ich zurück. *Wir fliegen morgen früh.*

Verstanden, antwortet Anton. *Ich nehme an, dass du die Amerikaner bei ihr willst?*

Ja, schreibe ich. *Sag ihnen, sie sollen sich bei der Klinik immer in ihrer Nähe befinden.*

Das letzte Mal, als mein Team und ich das Land für einen Job verlassen mussten, habe ich einige Männer von hier dafür angeheuert, Sara während unserer Abwesenheit zu überwachen und über jeden ihrer Schritte zu berichten. Sie sind aufs Gründlichste sicherheitsüberprüft, und auch wenn ich ihnen nicht ansatzweise so sehr vertraue wie meinen Männern, war ich bis jetzt mit ihren Diensten zufrieden.

Sie sollten in der Lage sein, sie zu beschützen, solange ich weg bin.

Ich stelle meinen Wecker auf in vier Stunden, krieche zu Sara unter die Bettdecke und ziehe sie in meine Umarmung, um meinen Körper von hinten um ihren zu legen. Sie versteift, aber rückt nicht ab, und ich schließe meine Augen, atme ihren Duft ein und spüre, wie sich über mir der Frieden ausbreitet.

Nichts zwischen uns ist gelöst, aber aus irgendeinem Grund bin ich mir sicher, dass es das irgendwann sein wird, zuversichtlich, dass wir es hinbekommen, dass es funktionieren wird, was auch immer »es« sein mag. Das ist der einzige Weg, weil ich mir ein Leben ohne sie nicht mehr vorstellen kann.

Sara gehört mir, und ich würde eher sterben, als sie gehen zu lassen.

33

Sara

Ein hartnäckiges Summen reißt mich aus dem Schlaf. Einen Augenblick lang bin ich so desorientiert, dass ich denke, dass es mitten in der Nacht ist.

Ich rolle mich auf die Seite und taste blind nach meinem vibrierenden Telefon. »Hallo«, krächze ich, als ich es, ohne die Augen zu öffnen, von meinem Nachttisch genommen habe. Meine Augenlider fühlen sich an, als seien sie zusammengeklebt, und mein Kopf ist so schwer, dass ich ihn kaum vom Kissen loseisen kann.

»Dr. Cobakis, wir haben eine Patientin mit einer Frühgeburt, und Dr. Tomlinson musste wegen einer Familienangelegenheit gehen. Sie sind die Nächste auf der Bereitschaftsliste. Können Sie schnell hier sein?«

Ich setze mich hin, da der Adrenalinanstieg das Schlimmste meiner Müdigkeit verjagt. »Ähm …« Ich blinzele den Schlaf weg und bemerke, dass Sonnenlicht durch die Schlitze meiner Jalousie hereinfällt. Der Wecker neben dem Bett zeigt 6.45 Uhr an, was weniger als eine Stunde vor meiner eigentlichen Weckzeit ist. »Ja. Ich kann in etwa einer Stunde da sein.«

»Danke. Bis gleich.«

Sobald der Koordinator aufhängt, springe ich aus dem Bett, um schnell unter die Dusche zu springen – und halte abrupt inne, als ich spüre, wie wund ich tief drinnen bin. Erinnerungen an letzte Nacht steigen auf, glühend heiß und giftig, und alle Überreste von Müdigkeit verschwinden.

Letzte Nacht hatte ich Sex mit Peter Sokolov.

Er hat mir wehgetan, und ich bin in seinen Armen gekommen.

Einen Moment lang scheinen diese beiden Tatsachen unvereinbar zu sein, so wie ein Eissturm im Juli. Ich habe niemals auf Schmerz gestanden, ganz im Gegenteil. Die wenigen Male. die George und ich etwas andere Dinge ausprobiert haben, hat mich sein leichtes Spanking von meinem Orgasmus abgehalten, anstatt mich anzuheizen. Ich verstehe nicht, wie ich nach so grobem Sex kommen konnte, wie ich ein so intensives Lustgefühl verspüren konnte, als mein Körper sich zerrissen und angeschlagen gefühlt hat.

Und dieser Orgasmus war nicht der einzige. Mein Peiniger hat mich mitten in der Nacht aufgeweckt, als er in mich geglitten ist, während seine Finger gleichzeitig geschickt meine Klitoris verwöhnt haben, so dass ich trotz meines Wundseins innerhalb weniger Minuten gekommen bin, da mein Körper auf ihn reagiert hat, obwohl mein Kopf lautstark protestiert hat. Danach habe ich mich wieder in den Schlaf geweint, während er mich umarmt und meinen Rücken gestreichelt hat, so als würde er sich Sorgen machen.

Kein Wunder, dass ich so kaputt bin, durch den Sex und das Weinen habe ich nur wenige Stunden Schlaf bekommen.

Ich schlucke meine Beschämung herunter und zwinge mich dazu, mit dem weiterzumachen, was ich zu tun habe. Ich muss mich anziehen und zum Krankenhaus fahren. Egal, wie es sich gerade anfühlen mag, mein Leben hat letzte Nacht nicht geendet. Ich habe keine Ahnung, ob ich das Richtige getan habe, als ich Peter ermutigt habe, mit mir zu schlafen, aber was geschehen ist, ist geschehen, und ich muss nach vorn schauen.

Die gute Nachricht ist, dass ich ihn bis heute Abend nicht mehr sehen muss.

Vielleicht wünsche ich mir bei dem Gedanken daran, ihn zu sehen, nicht mehr, am liebsten zu sterben.

———

DER TAG VERFLIEGT durch einen Haufen Arbeit, und als ich endlich nach Hause komme, bin ich erschöpft und am Verhungern. Ich hatte so viel zu tun, dass ich kein Mittag gegessen habe, und auch wenn ich mich vor einer weiteren Nacht mit meinem Stalker fürchte, muss ich zugeben, dass ich mich auf sein Essen freue.

Peter Sokolov ist vielleicht ein Psychopath, aber er ist ein hervorragender Koch.

Zu meiner Überraschung – und meiner klitzekleinen Enttäuschung – begrüßt mich kein köstlicher Essensduft, als ich aus der Garage hineintrete. Das Haus ist dunkel und leer, und ich weiß, auch ohne alle Räume zu kontrollieren, dass er nicht hier ist. Ich kann es spüren. Mein Zuhause fühlt sich kälter an, weniger lebendig, so als ob die dunkle Energie, die Peter Sokolov ausstrahlt, ihm eine Art Lebensfreude gibt.

Trotzdem rufe ich: »Hallo? Peter?«

Nichts.

»Bist du hier?«

Keine Antwort.

Sollte mein Plan so schnell funktioniert haben? Ist es möglich, dass diese eine Nacht bereits das krankhafte Verlangen meines Stalkers befriedigt hat?

Verwirrt gehe ich zum Gefrierschrank und nehme eine Mahlzeit heraus, um sie in die Mikrowelle zu legen. Es ist eines dieser gesunden, organischen Fertiggerichte, Thai-Nudeln mit Gemüse und einer Sauce ohne zu viel Zucker, aber es ist immer noch ein Fertiggericht. Leider habe ich heute Nacht keine Energie für mehr. Ich hätte etwas aus der Cafeteria des Krankenhauses mitnehmen sollen, aber ich denke, ich habe mich unbewusst darauf verlassen, zu Hause bekocht zu werden.

Ich schüttele den Kopf, weil diese Tatsache so lächerlich ist, stelle die Mikrowelle an und gehe Hände waschen.

Mein Peiniger ist verschwunden, und das ist eine gute Sache.

Ich muss nur noch meinen Magen davon überzeugen.

———

ALS ICH AUFWACHE, ist er immer noch nicht da, und auch wenn ich den unterschwelligen Eindruck habe, überwacht zu werden, als ich zur Arbeit fahre, kann ich niemanden entdecken, der mir folgt. Das gleiche Gefühl habe ich auch den ganzen Tag über im Krankenhaus. Ich bin paranoid genug, um die ganze Zeit über Augen auf mir zu spüren, aber dieses Gefühl ist nicht ansatzweise so intensiv, wie es vorher war.

Wenn ich nicht wüsste, dass ich wirklich einen Stalker habe, könnte ich mir einreden, dass ich es mir nur einbilde.

Meine Eltern rufen während meiner Mittagspause an, um mich für Freitag zum Abendessen einzuladen. Ich gebe ihnen eine unverbindliche Antwort – ich will sie keiner Gefahr aussetzen – und rufe danach in der Klinik an.

»Hallo Lydia, alles in Ordnung?«, frage ich und

versuche, mich nicht zu nervös anzuhören. »Wie läuft es?«

»Hallo Dr. Cobakis.« Die Stimme der Rezeptionistin wird besonders warm. »Ich freue mich, von Ihnen zu hören. Hier ist alles in Ordnung. Im Moment ist nicht allzu viel los, aber wahrscheinlich wird es am Nachmittag mehr werden. Werden Sie es schaffen, diese Woche noch einmal zu kommen?«

»Ja, ich denke schon. Ähm, Lydia …?« Ich zögere, da ich nicht weiß, wie ich sie das fragen soll, was ich wissen möchte. In den Nachrichten habe ich nichts über die Morde gehört, aber das bedeutet ja nicht, dass die Leichen nicht gefunden wurden. »Sie haben nicht zufällig etwas … Ungewöhnliches gesehen oder gehört?«

»Etwas Ungewöhnliches?« Lydia hört sich verwirrt an. »Wie was?«

»Oh, nichts Bestimmtes.« Um nicht verdächtig zu wirken, füge ich hinzu: »Ich habe nur gerade an diese eine Patientin gedacht, Monica Jackson … Sie haben nicht zufällig etwas von ihr gehört? Dieses dunkelhaarige Mädchen, das ich gestern behandelt habe?«

Zu meiner Überraschung antwortet Lydia: »Ach das. Doch, habe ich sogar. Sie ist vor einigen Stunden vorbeigekommen und hat eine Nachricht für Sie hinterlassen. Irgendetwas wie ›Vielen Dank, er sitzt jetzt hinter Gittern‹. Sie hat es nicht weiter erklärt, weil sie meinte, Sie würden es verstehen. Ergibt diese Nachricht für Sie irgendeinen Sinn?«

»Ja.« Trotz meiner Anspannung breitet sich auf

meinem Gesicht ein breites Grinsen aus. »Ja, definitiv. Danke, dass Sie es mir ausgerichtet haben. Wir sehen uns die Tage.«

Ich lege immer noch grinsend auf und gehe mich für meinen Kaiserschnitt am Nachmittag waschen.

Ich habe keine Ahnung, wie Peter den Beweis für das Verbrechen verschwinden lassen hat, aber das hat er, und jetzt sieht es so aus, als habe dieser furchtbare Abend auch sein Gutes gehabt.

Ich mag keinen Fluchtweg haben, aber Monica ist frei.

———

MEIN HAUS IST ERNEUT DUNKEL und leer, als ich an diesem Abend zurückkomme, und als ich mich fertig mache, um ins Bett zu gehen, fällt mir auf, dass ich eigenartig melancholisch bin. Es war beängstigend, Peter in meinem Haus zu haben, aber immerhin war er eine menschliche Gegenwart. Jetzt bin ich wieder allein, genauso wie in den letzten zwei Jahren, und das Gefühl der Einsamkeit ist sogar noch stärker, mein Bett kälter und leerer, als ich es in Erinnerung hatte.

Vielleicht sollte ich mir einen Hund zulegen. Einen großen, den ich dadurch verziehen würde, dass er bei mir im Bett schlafen darf. Auf diese Weise hätte ich jemanden, der mich begrüßt, wenn ich nach Hause komme, und ich würde nicht so etwas Perverses vermissen wie die nächtliche Umarmung durch den Mörder meines Mannes.

Ja, ich werde mir einen Hund anschaffen, beschließe ich, steige in mein Bett und ziehe die Decke über mich. Sobald ich das Haus verkauft habe, werde ich mir etwas mieten, was näher am Krankenhaus liegt, und darauf achten, dass es hundefreundlich ist, vielleicht einen Park in der Nähe hat.

Ein Hund wird mir das geben, was ich brauche, und ich werde in der Lage sein, Peter Sokolov zu vergessen.

Zumindest, wenn er mich vergessen haben sollte.

34

S*ara*

AM MONTAG BIN ich beinahe davon überzeugt, dass
Peter für immer weg ist. Am Wochenende habe ich
mein ganzes Haus von oben bis unten abgesucht, um
die versteckten Kameras zu finden, aber entweder sind
sie alle verschwunden oder auf eine Art und Weise
verborgen, dass ein Laie wie ich keine Chance hat, sie
zu finden. Natürlich könnten sie auch nie existiert
haben, und mein Stalker hat die Dinge, die er wusste,
auf andere Art und Weise herausgefunden. Wie dem
auch sei, es gibt kein Zeichen von ihm, keinerlei
Kontakt. Ich habe den Großteil des Wochenendes in
der Klinik verbracht, und auch wenn ich Blicke auf mir
gespürt habe, als ich zum Auto gegangen bin, könnte es

sich dabei genauso gut um meine Paranoia gehandelt haben.

Vielleicht ist mein Albtraum endlich vorbei.

Es ist dumm, aber das Wissen, dass ich Peter mit so einem bisschen Sex verjagt habe, schmerzt ein wenig. Ich hatte gehofft, dass er mich in Ruhe lassen würde, wenn ich aufhöre, die unnahbare »Eisprinzessin« zu sein, aber ich hatte nicht damit gerechnet, dass es sofort geschehen würde. Vielleicht bin ich schlecht im Bett? Das muss ich wohl sein, wenn eine Nacht ausgereicht hat, um Peter klarzumachen, dass ich den Fantasien in seinem Kopf nicht gerecht werden kann.

Nachdem er mich wochenlang verfolgt hat, hat mich mein Peiniger nach nur einer Nacht verlassen.

Das ist natürlich gut so. Es gibt keine Abendessen mehr, keine Duschen, bei denen ich wie ein Kind umsorgt werde. Keine gefährlichen Mörder mehr, die mich nachts umarmen, mich verwirren und meinen Körper verführen. Ich verbringe meine Tage genauso wie die vergangenen Monate, nur dass ich mich stärker fühle, innerlich weniger zerbrochen. Mich mit der Quelle meiner Albträume auseinanderzusetzen hat mehr für meine geistige Gesundheit getan als monatelange Therapie, und dafür bin ich einfach dankbar.

Auch wenn ich mich schäme, wenn ich an die Orgasmen denke, die er mir beschert hat, fühle ich mich besser, mehr wie mein altes Ich.

»Also, Sara, erzählen Sie mir, wie es Ihnen geht«, sagt Dr. Evans, als ich ihn endlich nach seinem Urlaub wiedersehe. Er ist sonnengebräunt, und sein Gesicht strahlt vor Gesundheit. »Wie ist der Tag der offenen Tür gelaufen?«

»Mein Makler begutachtet gerade einige Angebote«, antworte ich und schlage die Beine übereinander. Aus irgendeinem Grund fühle ich mich heute unwohl in seinem Büro, so als gehöre ich nicht mehr hierher. Ich schüttele dieses Gefühl ab und fahre fort: »Sie sind allerdings beide niedriger, als uns das recht ist, also versuchen wir, sie gegeneinander auszuspielen.«

»Ah, gut. Das ist doch schon einmal ein Fortschritt an dieser Front.« Er legt seinen Kopf schief. »An den anderen Fronten vielleicht auch?«

Ich nicke, da mich die Wahrnehmungsgabe meines Therapeuten nicht überrascht. »Ja, meine Paranoia hat sich gebessert und meine Albträume auch. Samstag habe ich es sogar geschafft, den Wasserhahn in der Küche zu benutzen.«

»Wirklich?« Er zieht seine Augenbrauen nach oben. »Das sind tolle Neuigkeiten. Ist das durch etwas Bestimmtes ausgelöst worden?«

Ach, wissen Sie, der Mann, der mich gefoltert und meinen Ehemann umgebracht hat, ist wieder in meinem Leben aufgetaucht.

»Ich weiß es nicht«, sage ich und zucke mit den Schultern. »Vielleicht ist es die Zeit. Es ist jetzt bereits fast sieben Monate her.«

»Ja«, meint Dr. Evans sanft, »aber Sie sollten wissen, dass das nichts auf der Zeitleiste menschlicher

Trauer und posttraumatischer Verhaltensstörungen ist.«

»Okay.« Ich blicke auf meine Hände und bemerke einen ausgefransten Nietnagel an meinem linken Daumen. Es könnte Zeit für eine Maniküre sein. »Dann habe ich wohl Glück gehabt.«

»Das haben Sie.«

Als ich aufschaue, betrachtet mich Dr. Evans mit dem gleichen besorgten Gesichtsausdruck.

»Wie ist Ihr Sozialleben?«, fragt er, und ich spüre, wie ich erröte.

»Ich verstehe«, meint Dr. Evans, als ich nicht sofort antworte. »Gibt es etwas, über das Sie reden möchten?«

»Nein … nichts.« Mein Gesicht wird noch heißer, als er mir einen ungläubigen Blick zuwirft. Ich kann ihm nichts von Peter erzählen, also suche ich nach etwas anderem, was sich plausibel anhört. »Also, ich bin vor einigen Wochen mit ein paar Arbeitskolleginnen ausgegangen und hatte viel Spaß …«

»Ah.« Er scheint meine Antwort sofort zu akzeptieren. »Und wie hat es sich angefühlt, ›Spaß zu haben‹?«

»Ich habe mich … großartig gefühlt.« Ich denke an das Tanzen im Klub zurück, daran, wie der Rhythmus der Musik mich durchströmt hat. »Ich habe mich lebendig gefühlt.«

»Hervorragend.« Dr. Evans macht sich einige Notizen. »Und sind Sie danach noch einmal ausgegangen?«

»Nein, ich hatte noch keine Gelegenheit dazu.« Das ist eine Lüge, ich hätte letzten Samstag mit Marsha und den Mädchen ausgehen können, aber ich kann dem Therapeuten nicht erklären, dass ich versuche, meine Freundinnen zu beschützen, indem ich möglichst wenig Kontakt zu ihnen habe. Die Schweigepflicht eines Arztes hat ihre Grenzen, und zu enthüllen, dass ich Kontakt zu einem gesuchten Kriminellen hatte – und letzte Woche zwei Morde beobachtet habe –, könnte Dr. Evans dazu bringen, zur Polizei zu gehen und uns beide in Gefahr zu bringen.

Es war überhaupt eine schlechte Idee, heute hierherzukommen. Ich kann nicht über die Dinge reden, die ich eigentlich besprechen muss, und er kann mir nicht dabei helfen, mich durch meine komplizierten Gefühle zu arbeiten, wenn er nicht die ganze Geschichte kennt. Das ist der Grund dafür, warum ich mich unwohl fühle, wird mir klar: Ich kann Dr. Evans nicht mehr in mich schauen lassen. In meiner Tasche vibriert mein Handy, und ich stürze mich erleichtert auf diese Ablenkung. Ich ziehe das Telefon hervor und sehe, dass ich eine Textnachricht vom Krankenhaus bekommen habe.

»Bitte entschuldigen Sie mich«, sage ich, stehe auf und lasse das Handy wieder in die Tasche gleiten. »Bei einer meiner Patientinnen haben gerade vorzeitige Wehen eingesetzt, und sie braucht meine Hilfe.«

»Natürlich.« Dr. Evans richtet seinen schlaksigen Körper auf, um sich hinzustellen, und schüttelt meine Hand.

»Wir machen nächste Woche weiter. Es war mir wie immer ein Vergnügen.«

»Danke. Für mich auch«, antworte ich und vermerke im Hinterkopf, den Termin für nächste Woche abzusagen. »Ich wünsche Ihnen noch einen schönen Tag!«

Damit verlasse ich die Praxis des Therapeuten, eile zum Krankenhaus und bin dieses Mal wirklich dankbar für die Unberechenbarkeit meiner Arbeit.

———

ICH WEISS NICHT, ob es die Sitzung mit Dr. Evans oder der bessere Schlaf der letzten Tage ist, aber in dieser Nacht werfe ich mich hin und her und schlafe ein, nur um mit hämmerndem Herzen und einem undefinierbaren Angstgefühl aufzuschrecken. Die Leere meines Bettes zehrt an mir, und meine Einsamkeit ist ein schmerzhaftes Loch in meiner Brust. Ich möchte glauben, dass ich George vermisse, dass ich mich nach seinen Armen sehne, aber als mich endlich ein unruhiger Schlaf überkommt, sind es stahlgraue Augen, die in meinen Träumen auftauchen, keine sanften, braunen.

In den Träumen tanze ich vor meinem Peiniger wie eine professionelle Tänzerin. Ich bin mit dem hellgelben Kostüm mit steifen Federflügeln auch genauso angezogen. Als ich über die Bühne wirbele, fühle ich mich leichter als Nebel, anmutiger als eine Rauchschwade. Aber innerlich brenne ich vor Leidenschaft. Meine Bewegungen kommen aus den Tiefen meiner Seele, und mein Körper drückt sich über den

Tanz mit der ungefilterten Ehrlichkeit der Schönheit aus.

Ich vermisse dich, sagt dieser Plié. *Ich will dich,* bestätigt jene Pirouette. Ich sage mit meinem Körper, was ich nicht mit Worten sagen kann, und er betrachtet mich mit einem dunklen und mysteriösen Gesichtsausdruck. Rote Tröpfchen schmücken seine Hände, und ich weiß, auch ohne zu fragen, dass es sich dabei um Blut handelt, dass er heute ein weiteres Leben genommen hat. Das sollte mich anekeln, aber alles, was mich interessiert, ist, ob er mich möchte, ob er die Hitze spürt, die mich von innen heraus auffrisst.

Bitte, bettele ich mit meinen Bewegungen, während ich mich anmutig vor ihm drehe. *Bitte, sag es mir. Ich muss die Wahrheit wissen. Bitte.*

Aber er sagt nichts. Er betrachtet mich einfach nur, und ich weiß, dass ich nichts tun kann, dass es keinen Weg gibt, ihn zu überzeugen. Also tanze ich näher an ihn heran, da ich von seiner dunklen Ausstrahlung angezogen werde, und als ich mich in seiner Reichweite befinde, hebt er seine Arme, und seine blutbespritzten Hände umfassen meine Schultern.

»Peter ...« Ich biege mich ihm entgegen, da diese schreckliche Sehnsucht mich innerlich auffrisst, aber seine Augen sind kalt, so kalt, dass sie brennen.

Er will mich nicht mehr. Ich weiß es. Ich sehe es.

Trotzdem strecke ich mich nach ihm aus und hebe meine Hand zu seinem harten, kantigen Gesicht. Ich will ihn – ich brauche ihn – so sehr. Aber bevor ich ihn berühren kann, sagt er leise: »Auf Wiedersehen, Ptichka«, und schiebt mich weg.

Ich stolpere nach hinten und falle von der Bühne. Mein Kleid flattert einen kurzen Augenblick lang in der Luft, und dann werden meine Flügel zerquetscht, als ich auf dem Boden aufkomme. Noch bevor der Schock des Aufschlags durch mich vibriert, weiß ich, dass es das war.

Mein Körper ist gebrochen, genauso wie meine Seele.

»Peter«, stöhne ich mit meinem letzten Atemzug, aber es ist zu spät.

Er ist für immer weg.

Ich wache mit einem nassen Gesicht und einem Herzen voller Trauer auf. In dem Zimmer ist es rabenschwarz, und in der Dunkelheit ist es egal, dass ich nicht rational einen Mann vermissen kann, den ich hasse. Der Traum ist so lebhaft in meinem Kopf, dass ich mich fühle, als hätte ich ihn wirklich verloren ... als sei ich durch seine Zurückweisung gestorben. Ich weiß, dass meine Trauer durch meine wirklichen Verluste – George und das Leben, was ich eigentlich haben sollte – hervorgerufen worden sein muss, aber wegen meines leeren Betts und meines Körpers, der sich nach einer kräftigen und warmen Umarmung sehnt, fühlt es sich an, als vermisste ich *ihn*.

Peter.

Der Mann, der mir alle Gründe geliefert hat, ihn zu verabscheuen.

Ich kneife die Augen fest zusammen, rolle mich

unter meiner Decke zu einem kleinen Ball zusammen und kuschele mit einem Kissen. Ich brauche Dr. Evans nicht, um zu wissen, dass das, was ich fühle, unmöglich echt sein kann, dass es bestenfalls eine eigenartige Version des Stockholm-Syndroms ist. Man verliebt sich *nicht* in seinen Stalker, das geschieht einfach nicht. Ich kenne Peter noch gar nicht so lange. Wie lange gibt es ihn jetzt schon in meinem Leben? Eine Woche? Zwei? Die Tage seit dem Klub haben sich wie Jahre angefühlt, aber in Wirklichkeit ist kaum Zeit vergangen.

Natürlich hat er schon länger in meinen Albträumen existiert.

Zum ersten Mal erlaube ich mir, richtig über meinen Peiniger nachzudenken – mich zu fragen, was für ein Mann er ist. Wie war er bei seiner Familie? Es sollte schwierig sein, sich einen so rücksichtslosen Mörder in einer häuslichen Umgebung vorzustellen, aber aus irgendeinem Grund habe ich kein Problem damit, ihn mir dabei vorzustellen, wie er mit einem Kind spielt oder mit seiner Frau Essen kocht. Vielleicht ist es die sanfte Art, auf die er sich um mich gekümmert hat, dass ich das Gefühl habe, dass es etwas in ihm gibt, was über die monströsen Dinge hinausgeht, die er getan hat, etwas Verletzliches und durch und durch Menschliches.

Er muss seine Familie geliebt haben, um sich der Rache so vollständig zu verschreiben.

Die Bilder auf seinem Telefon steigen in meinem Kopf auf, und meine Brust zieht sich schmerzhaft zusammen. Falsche Informationen sollen laut Peter an diesen Gräueltaten schuld sein. Ist es möglich, dass George derjenige war, der diese Informationen zur Verfügung gestellt hat? Dass mein hübscher, friedlicher Ehemann, der gerne grillte und im Bett Zeitung las, wirklich ein Spion gewesen ist, dem ein so schrecklicher Fehler unterlaufen ist? Das scheint unglaublich zu sein, aber es muss einen Grund dafür geben, dass Peter hinter George her war, warum er so weit gegangen ist, um ihn zu töten.

Außer wenn Peter selbst einen riesigen Fehler gemacht hat, war George nicht derjenige, der er zu sein schien.

Ich drücke das Kissen noch fester an mich, als ich diese Erkenntnis vergegenwärtige und das Wissen in mich hineinsickern lasse. In den letzten eineinhalb Wochen habe ich es vermieden, über die Enthüllungen meines Stalkers nachzudenken, aber ich kann die Wahrheit nicht länger verdrängen.

Wenn man den Schutz durch das FBI, der aus dem Nichts kam, und die plötzliche Distanz, die es nach der Hochzeit zwischen George und mir gab, bedenkt, ist es durchaus möglich, dass mein Ehemann mich getäuscht hatte – dass er den Großteil einer Dekade mich und alle anderen angelogen hat.

Mein Leben war noch illusorischer gewesen, als mir bewusst war.

Als ich eine Stunde später einschlafe, habe ich auf meiner Zunge den bitteren Geschmack des Betrugs und in meinem Kopf einen neuen Entschluss.

Morgen früh werde ich eines der Angebote für mein Haus akzeptieren. Ich brauche einen Neuanfang, und ich werde ihn bekommen. Vielleicht werde ich an einem neuen Ort Georges Doppelleben und *ihn* vergessen.

Wenn Peter Sokolov für immer verschwunden ist, könnte ich endlich anfangen zu leben.

35

AM DONNERSTAG unterschreibe ich die Papiere und verkaufe mein Haus einem Anwaltspaar, das aus Chicago in diese Gegend zieht. Sie haben zwei Kinder in der Grundschule und eins ist unterwegs, weshalb sie die fünf Schlafzimmer brauchen. Auch wenn ihr Angebot drei Prozent unter dem Marktwert und einige tausend Dollar unter dem anderen Angebot lag, habe ich mich für die Anwälte entschieden, weil sie in bar bezahlen und ich somit den Hausverkauf schnell abschließen kann.

Wenn es bei der Überprüfung keine Probleme gibt, werde ich in weniger als drei Wochen ausziehen.

Da ich mich danach energiegeladen fühle, bitte ich

einen anderen Arzt, am Freitag für mich einzuspringen, und verbringe den Tag damit, mich nach Mietwohnungen umzusehen. Ich entscheide mich für ein kleines Apartment mit einem Schlafzimmer in einem tierfreundlichen Mehrfamilienhaus mit Eigentumswohnungen, von dem aus ich zu Fuß zum Krankenhaus gehen kann. Es ist ein wenig veraltet, und Stauraum gibt es auch fast keinen, aber da ich alles loswerden möchte, das mich an mein altes Leben erinnert, stört es mich nicht.

Neuanfang, ich komme.

Meine gute Laune hält bis zum Abend an, bis zu dem Augenblick, in dem ich nach Hause komme und erneut die Leere fühle. Mein Abendessen ist einmal wieder eine Packung aus dem Tiefkühlschrank, und trotz meiner besten Versuche, es nicht zu tun, muss ich die ganze Zeit an Peter denken und frage mich, wo er ist. Gestern ist mir aufgefallen, dass es auch einen anderen Grund für seine Abwesenheit geben könnte, und seitdem lässt mich dieser Gedanke nicht mehr los.

Die Behörden könnten ihn eingesperrt oder getötet haben.

Ich weiß nicht, wieso ich bis gestern nicht an diese Möglichkeit gedacht habe, aber jetzt bekomme ich sie nicht mehr aus dem Kopf. Das wäre offensichtlich etwas Gutes – ich wäre wirklich in Sicherheit, wenn er tot oder in Verwahrung wäre –, aber jedes Mal, wenn ich darüber nachdenke, fühlt sich meine Brust schwer und eng an, und etwas Unerklärliches wie Tränen brennt in meinen Augen.

Ich will Peter Sokolov nicht in meinem Leben, aber ich kann den Gedanken, dass er tot sein könnte, auch nicht ertragen.

Das ist dumm, so unglaublich dumm. Ja, wir hatten letzte Nacht Sex, und ja, er hat mich mehr als einmal kommen lassen, aber ich bin doch nicht irgend so ein jungfräulicher Teenager, der daran glaubt, dass Miteinanderschlafen unendliche Liebe bedeutet. Das einzige Gefühl zwischen uns, abgesehen von Hass, ist animalische Lust, die primitivste Ebene der Anziehung. So viel kann ich akzeptieren. Als Ärztin weiß ich, wie stark Biologie sich bemerkbar machen kann, da ich die Beweise gesehen habe, dass auch intelligente Menschen aus leidenschaftlichen Gründen dumme Sachen machen. Es ist beunruhigend, dass ich den Mörder meines Ehemanns überhaupt auf irgendeine Art und Weise will, aber mir darüber Gedanken zu machen, ob es ihm gutgeht, ist etwas völlig anderes.

Etwas viel Krankeres.

Ich vermisse Peter nicht, rede ich mir ein, während ich mich in meinem leeren Bett hin und her werfe. Die Einsamkeit, die ich spüre, ist das Resultat von zu viel Stress und nicht ausreichend Zeit mit meinen Freunden und meiner Familie. Wenn ein wenig mehr Zeit verstrichen sein wird und die Bedrohung durch meinen Stalker der Vergangenheit angehört, werde ich mit Marsha und den Krankenschwestern ausgehen und sogar in Betracht ziehen, mich mit Joe zu treffen.

Okay, Letzteres vielleicht nicht, da ich ihn abgewimmelt habe, als er vor einigen Tagen angerufen hat, und mir das bis jetzt nicht leidtut, aber ich will definitiv noch einmal tanzen gehen.

So oder so wird mein neues Leben bald beginnen.

36

Peter

SIE SCHLÄFT, als ich das Zimmer betrete, und ihr schlanker Körper ist von Kopf bis Fuß in die Decke gewickelt. Leise mache ich die Lichter an, bleibe stehen, und mein Atem stockt in der Brust. Während der letzten zwei Wochen, in denen ich mich von einer Stichwunde erholen musste, die ich in Mexiko erhalten habe, habe ich mich damit unterhalten, sie über ihre Hauskameras zu beobachten und die Berichte der Amerikaner über sie zu verschlingen. Ich weiß alles, was sie getan hat, mit wem sie gesprochen hat und wohin sie gegangen ist. Das sollte die Trennung erträglicher gemacht haben, aber sie so zu sehen, mit ihrem glänzenden, braunen Haar auf ihrem Kissen, nimmt mir die Luft und löst ein schlagartiges Verlangen aus.

Meine Sara. Ich habe sie unglaublich vermisst.

Ich nähere mich dem Bett, balle meine Hände zu Fäusten, um meinem Verlangen, sie anzufassen, sie in den Arm zu nehmen und sie nie wieder loszulassen, nicht nachzugeben.

Zwei Wochen. Für zwei unglaublich lange Wochen konnte ich nicht zu ihr zurückkommen, weil ich das Messer, das im Stiefel von einem der Wächter versteckt gewesen war, übersehen hatte. Zugegebenermaßen hatte ich gerade mit einem anderen Kerl zu tun, der eine AR15 auf mich gerichtet hatte, aber das ist keine Entschuldigung für Schlamperei.

Ich war bei meiner Arbeit abgelenkt, und das hat mich beinahe das Leben gekostet. Zwei Zentimeter weiter rechts, und ich hätte länger als zwei Wochen flachgelegen. Vielleicht für immer.

»Was soll der Scheiß, Mann?«, hatte Ilya gebrummt, als er und sein Bruder mich nach der Ausführung der Mission zusammengeflickt haben. »Er hätte fast deine Niere erwischt. Du musst verdammt noch mal besser aufpassen.«

»Dafür habe ich ja euch beide«, konnte ich gerade noch so sagen, bevor der Blutverlust Wirkung zeigte und mich davon abhielt, den Grund für meine Ablenkung zu erklären. Das war auch gut so. Die Wahrheit ist, dass ich das Messer nicht auf mich zukommen sehen habe, weil ich, während ich auf den Lauf der AR15 gestarrt habe, nicht an mein Team oder meine Mission, sondern an Sara gedacht habe und daran, sie nie mehr wiederzusehen.

Meine Besessenheit von ihr wäre fast mein Untergang gewesen.

Ich setze mich auf die Bettkante und ziehe vorsichtig die Decke von ihr herunter. Sie schläft wie immer nackt, und Lust dröhnt beim Anblick ihrer schlanken und anmutigen Kurven in meinen Venen. Sie wacht nicht auf, sondern schnauft wegen der fehlenden Decke nur wie ein beleidigtes Kätzchen, und ich fühle, wie etwas Sanftes in meine Brust eindringt. Mein Herz erfüllt sich mit einem warmen Glühen, auch wenn mein Schwanz noch härter wird und mein Puls ansteigt.

Ich muss sie haben. Jetzt.

Ich stehe auf, ziehe mir schnell die Kleidung aus, lege sie auf die Kommode und kontrolliere, dass meine Waffen gut versteckt sind. Die ruckartigen Bewegungen reißen an der frischen Narbe auf meinem Bauch, aber ich will sie so sehr, dass ich den Schmerz kaum bemerke. Ich streife mir ein Kondom über, steige zu ihr ins Bett, rolle sie auf den Rücken und begebe mich zwischen ihre Beine.

Meine Berührung weckt sie auf. Sie reißt ihre Lider auf, zeigt ihre braunen Augen, die gleichzeitig panisch und benebelt sind, und ich lächele, während ich ihre Handgelenke ergreife und sie neben ihren Schultern auf die Matratze drücke. Es ist das Lächeln eines Raubtiers, das weiß ich, aber ich kann es mir nicht verkneifen.

Selbst mit dem warmen Gefühl in meiner Brust ist

mein Hunger auf sie dunkel, genauso gewaltig wie vereinnahmend.

»Hallo, Ptichka«, sage ich leise und sehe dabei zu, wie sich das Entsetzen in ihren Augen ausbreitet, als ihr Blick sich klärt. »Es tut mir leid, dass ich so lange weg war. Ich konnte es nicht ändern.«

»Du bist … du bist zurück.« Ihre Brust hebt und senkt sich in einem ungleichmäßigen Rhythmus, und ihre Nippel sind wie harte, pinkfarbene Beeren auf ihren köstlichen, runden Brüsten. »Was machst du – warum bist du zurückgekommen?«

»Weil ich dich niemals verlassen würde.« Ich beuge mich nach unten, atme ihren Duft ein, der zart und warm und genauso fesselnd wie Sara selbst ist. Ich knabbere leicht an ihrem Ohr und flüstere an ihren Hals: »Denkst du, dass ich einfach weggehen würde?«

Sie erschaudert unter mir, ihre Atmung wird schneller, und ich weiß, dass sie zwischen den Beinen heiß und feucht sein wird, wenn ich sie jetzt dort anfasse. Sie will mich – oder zumindest tut ihr Körper das – und mein Schwanz pocht durch dieses Wissen, kann es nicht erwarten, die enge, feuchte Umarmung ihrer Muschi zu spüren. Zuerst möchte ich allerdings eine Antwort auf meine Frage.

Ich hebe meinen Kopf an und halte sie mit meinem Blick fest. »Hast du gedacht, dass ich gehen würde, Sara?«

Ihr Gesicht ist eine Maske der Verwirrung, als sie mich anblinzelt. »Na ja, schon. Ich meine, du warst weg, und ich habe gedacht – ich habe gehofft …« Sie hält stirnrunzelnd inne. »Warum bist du gegangen, wenn du nicht von mir gelangweilt warst?«

»Von dir gelangweilt?« Versteht sie nicht, dass ich tatsächlich die ganze Zeit an sie denke, selbst in der Hitze des Gefechts? Dass ich es nicht eine Stunde lang aushalte, ohne zu überprüfen, wo sie ist, oder auch nur eine Nacht verbringe, ohne sie in meinen Träumen zu sehen? Ich schaue ihr in die Augen und schüttele langsam den Kopf. »Nein, Ptichka. Ich war nicht gelangweilt von dir – und das werde ich auch nie sein.«

Aus dem Augenwinkel sehe ich, wie ihre schlanken Finger sich bewegen, und ich bemerke, dass ich ihre Handgelenke immer noch so fest neben ihren Schultern festhalte, als hätte ich Angst, dass sie mir entkommt. Das würde sie natürlich nicht – nicht einmal trotz meiner frischen Verletzung, da sie weder meine Reflexe noch meine Kraft besitzt – aber ich mag es, sie so zu sehen: unter mir, nackt und hilflos. Das ist Teil meiner kranken Gefühle für sie, dieses Bedürfnis, sie zu dominieren, sie immer meiner Gnade ausgesetzt zu sehen.

»Tu das nicht«, flüstert sie, aber ihre Zunge benetzt ihre weichen, rosafarbenen Lippen, und mein Hunger verstärkt sich, meine Eier ziehen sich zusammen, als mehr Blut in meine Lenden fließt. Sie hat etwas so Reines an sich, etwas so Sanftes und Unschuldiges in den anmutigen Linien ihres herzförmigen Gesichts. Es ist, als habe das Leben sie noch nicht berührt, als sei sie nicht von der Widerwärtigkeit verdorben, mit der ich täglich zu tun habe. Das macht die Dinge, die ich mit ihr anstellen möchte, so viel schmutziger, so viel falscher, aber trotzdem weiß ich, dass ich sie alle tun werde.

Richtig und Falsch war noch nie meine starke Seite.

Ich senke meinen Kopf und koste ihre Lippen, wobei mein Kuss trotz der schmerzenden Steifheit meines Schwanzes sanft bleibt. Trotz der dunklen Verlangen, die mich gerade überkommen, will ich ihr heute nicht wehtun – nicht nach dem letzten Mal. Ich kann immer noch nicht genau sagen, was sie für mich ist, aber ich weiß, dass sie mir gehört, dass ich mich um sie kümmern, sie verwöhnen und beschützen will. Ich will nicht, dass sie Angst hat, dass meine Berührung ihr Schmerzen zufügt – auch wenn ich ihn ihr manchmal zufügen möchte.

Ich weiß nicht, was ich von ihr will, aber ich weiß, dass es mehr als das ist.

Zuerst reagiert sie nicht, verschließt ihre Lippen vor den Versuchen meiner Zunge, sich hindurchzuschieben, aber ich küsse sie weiter, und irgendwann werden ihre Lippen weicher und sie lässt mich in ihren warmen Mund. Sie schmeckt köstlich, nach einem Hauch Minzzahnpasta und sich selbst, und ich kann ein Stöhnen nicht unterdrücken, als meine Eichel ihren inneren Oberschenkel streift. Ich will in ihr sein, will spüren, wie ihre heißen, feuchten Wände mich zerquetschen, aber ich widerstehe der Versuchung und konzentriere mich darauf, sie zu verführen, ihr so viel Lust zu bereiten, dass sie den Schmerz vergessen wird, den ich ihr zugefügt habe.

Ich weiß nicht, wie lange ich ihre Lippen liebkose, aber nach einer Weile fühle ich eine vorsichtige Berührung ihrer Zunge. Sie reagiert auf mich, küsst mich zurück, und als sich ihr Körper unter mir entspannt, schlägt mein Herz schneller, so als ob das Bedürfnis, sie zu haben, in meiner Brust hämmert. Ich atme abgehackt, als ich mich von ihren Lippen zu der zarten Haut ihres Halses bewege, danach zu ihrem Schlüsselbein und schließlich zur glatten Weichheit ihrer Brüste. Sie stöhnt, als meine Lippen sich über ihrem Nippel schließen, und ich spüre, dass sie sich mir entgegenbiegt, dass sie ihre Hüfte vom Bett hebt, um ihre Muschi an mich zu drücken.

Ich knurre leise in meiner Kehle, wende meine Aufmerksamkeit ihrer anderen Brust zu und sauge so lange an ihr, bis Saras Stöhnen lauter wird, sie sich unter mir windet und ihre Hände zucken, während ich ihre Handgelenke festhalte. Als ich meinen Kopf hebe, sehe ich, dass ihr Gesicht gerötet ist, sie ihre Augen zusammenkneift und ihr Kopf in sinnlicher Hingabe nach hinten gelegt ist.

Es ist Zeit. Scheiße, es ist schon lange nach der Zeit.

Ich gebe ihren Nippel frei, bewege mich nach oben und lege meinen harten Schwanz an den Eingang zu ihrem Körper.

»Willst du das?«, frage ich sie rau, als ihre Augenlider sich öffnen und ihre Augen, die vor Verlangen ganz benebelt sind, freilegen. »Sag mir, dass du das willst, Ptichka. Sag mir, dass du mich vermisst hast, als ich weg war.«

Saras Lippen öffnen sich, aber ohne Worte zu formen, und ich weiß, dass sie noch nicht bereit ist, es zuzugeben, die Verbindung, die zwischen uns existiert, zu akzeptieren. Ich mag ihren Körper haben, aber ich werde härter um ihren Kopf und ihr Herz kämpfen müssen. Und das werde ich, weil ich genau das von ihr brauche, bemerke ich: sie muss ganz mir gehören, sie muss mich genauso wollen und brauchen wie ich sie.

Ich senke meinen Kopf, küsse erneut ihre Lippen und lasse eines ihrer Handgelenke los, um meinen Schwanz in ihre heiße, feuchte Öffnung zu führen. Sie ist immer noch unglaublich eng, aber dieses Mal schaffe ich es, langsam voranzugehen, mich Zentimeter für Zentimeter vorzuarbeiten, bis ich vollständig in ihr bin. Sie krallt sich mit ihrer freien Hand an meiner Seite fest, und ihre Nägel drücken sich in meine Haut, während sie in mein Ohr stöhnt, und ich fühle, wie sich ihre inneren Wände zusammenziehen, als ich mich in ihr bewege, in einem vorsichtigen Rhythmus hinein und hinaus gleite. Mein eigenes Verlangen ist nahezu unkontrollierbar, und ich muss mich anstrengen, weiterhin langsam zuzustoßen und mich jedes Mal an ihrer Klitoris zu reiben, wenn ich bis zum Anschlag in ihr stecke.

»Ja, genau so«, stöhne ich, als ich spüre, dass sich ihre Muskeln anspannen und ihre Atmung schneller wird. »Komm für mich, Ptichka. Lass mich spüren, dass du kommst.«

Sie schreit auf, als ich mich schneller bewege, ihre Hüfte ergreife und das feste Fleisch ihres Pos drücke, während ich in sie hämmere und sie so hart ficke, dass das Bett unter uns knarrt. Ich kann nicht genug von ihr bekommen, von der seidigen Weichheit und ihrem süßen Duft, und ich fahre tiefer in ihren Körper, will mit ihr verschmelzen, so tief in ihrem Fleisch versinken, dass ich für immer in ihm eingebrannt bin.

Ihre Schreie werden lauter, hektischer, und ich spüre, wie ihre Muschi sich zusammenzieht, während sie sich vom Bett hochdrückt, als sie ihren Höhepunkt erreicht. Ihr Zucken ist der Tropfen, der das Fass zum Überlaufen bringt, und ich explodiere mit einem rauen Schrei, reibe mein Becken an ihrem, während mein Schwanz bei meiner Entladung bebt und pulsiert und das Kondom mit meinem Samen gefüllt wird.

Keuchend rolle ich von ihr herunter und ziehe sie an mich, um sie festzuhalten, während sich unser Atem beruhigt. Da mein Hunger jetzt gestillt ist, nehme ich das dumpfe Pochen meiner heilenden Wunde am Bauch wahr. Die Ärzte hatten mir ausdrücklich geraten, einige Wochen kürzerzutreten, aber das hatte ich vergessen, da ich zu sehr mit Sara und der glühenden Lust, sie zu besitzen, beschäftigt gewesen war.

Nach einer Minute stehe ich auf, um das Kondom zu entsorgen, und als ich zurückkomme, sitzt Sara auf dem Bett, und ihre schlanke Gestalt ist wie das letzte Mal in die Decke gewickelt. Allerdings gibt es heute keine Tränen, ihre Augen sind trocken, und sie schaut mir trotzig in die Augen, als ich den Raum durchquere. Vielleicht beginnt sie, unsere Realität zu akzeptieren, zu verstehen, dass es keine Schande ist, mich zu wollen?

»Warum bist du zurückgekommen?«, fragt sie mich, als ich mich neben sie setze, und ich höre hinter dem mutigen Ton ihre Verzweiflung heraus.

Ich habe mich geirrt. Sie ist noch weit davon entfernt, mich zu akzeptieren.

Ich hebe meine Hand und streiche eine glänzende Haarsträhne hinter ihr Ohr. Mit der um sie gewickelten Decke und den zerzausten braunen Wellen sieht meine hübsche Ärztin jung und verletzlich aus, eher wie ein Mädchen als eine Frau. Dieser Anblick setzt in mir den Wunsch frei, sie zu beschützen, die Grausamkeit meiner Welt von ihr fernzuhalten.

Leider bin ich auch Teil dieser Welt – und vielleicht sogar der grausamste in ihr.

»Ich bin niemals weggegangen«, antworte ich und lasse meine Hand sinken. »Zumindest hatte ich nicht vor, wegzugehen – nicht so lange. Ich musste einen Job erledigen, aber der hätte nur einen oder zwei Tage dauern sollen.«

»Einen Job?« Sie blinzelt. »Was für einen Job?«

Ich überlege kurz, es ihr nicht zu sagen, oder zumindest einige der grausameren Wirklichkeiten meiner Arbeit zu beschönigen, aber ich entscheide mich dagegen. Saras Meinung von mir kann nicht viel schlimmer werden, also kann sie auch ruhig die ganze Wahrheit erfahren.

»Mein Team führt bestimmte Aufträge aus«, erkläre ich vorsichtig und beobachte ihre Reaktion. »Aufträge, die nur wenige andere genauso gut und diskret erledigen können. Unsere Kunden arbeiten in der Regel im Verborgenen, genau wie die Opfer, für deren Ermordung wir bezahlt werden.«

Die postkoitale Röte verschwindet aus ihrem Gesicht, so dass sie plötzlich kreidebleich aussieht. »Du bist ein Mörder? Dein Team … tötet Menschen gegen Bezahlung?«

Ich nicke. »Nicht einfach jeden, aber ja. Unsere Zielpersonen sind meistens selbst hochgefährlich, oft von mehreren Sicherheitsebenen umgeben, die wir durchbrechen müssen. Deshalb ist mir auch das passiert.« Ich zeige auf die frische Narbe an meinem Bauch und sehe, dass ihre Augen riesig werden, als sie sie betrachtet – wahrscheinlich zum ersten Mal sieht. Ich bezweifle, dass sie einen guten Blick auf mich hatte, als ich sie gefickt habe.

»Wie ist das passiert?«, fragt sie und schaut von meinem Bauch hoch. Jetzt ist ihr Gesicht noch blasser, und ihre Porzellanhaut sieht grünlich aus. »Ist das eine Messerwunde?«

»Ja. Was das Wie betrifft, muss ich zugeben, dass ich einen Augenblick lang nicht aufgepasst habe.« Es macht mich immer noch wütend, dass ich nicht gesehen habe, dass der Wächter hinter mir nach seinem Messer gegriffen hat, als ich mich um seinen pistolenschwingenden Partner gekümmert habe. »Ich hätte vorsichtiger sein müssen.«

Sie schluckt und wendet sich wieder meiner Narbe zu. »Wenn es so gefährlich ist, wieso tust du es dann?«, fragt sie mich nach einem Augenblick, und ihre Augen richten sich wieder auf mein Gesicht.

»Weil es nicht billig ist, sich vor den Behörden zu verstecken«, antworte ich. Bis jetzt nimmt Sara meine Enthüllungen besser auf, als ich erwartet hatte, auch wenn ich annehme, dass sie vielleicht auf so etwas vorbereitet war, nachdem sie gesehen hat, wie ich die beiden Drogenabhängigen getötet habe. »Die Arbeit ist extrem gut bezahlt, und sie entspricht genau meinen Fähigkeiten. Bevor ich damit angefangen habe, habe ich einige unserer Klienten in Sicherheitsfragen beraten, aber mein eigenes Geschäft zu haben ist besser. Ich habe mehr Freiraum und bin flexibler – etwas, was wichtig wurde, nachdem ich meine Liste erhalten hatte.«

Sie presst ihre Lippen zusammen. »Die Liste, auf der mein Ehemann war?«

»Ja.«

Ihr Blick fällt auf ihren Schoß, aber nicht, bevor ich die Wut in ihren tiefen, braunen Augen gesehen habe. Es beschäftigt sie, dass ich keine Reue zeige, aber ich werde nicht so tun als ob. Dieser *ublyudok* – dieser Bastard von einem Ehemann – hatte einen viel schlimmeren Tod verdient gehabt als den, den er bekam, und das Einzige, was ich bereue, ist, dass er schon nur noch ein Stück Fleisch war, als ich zu ihm kam.

Das und die Tatsache, dass ich für einen kurzen Augenblick gezögert habe, abzudrücken.

Ich habe gezögert, weil ich an Sara anstatt an meine tote Familie gedacht habe.

Diese Erinnerung erfüllt mich mit der vertrauten Wut, und ich zwinge mich dazu, langsam und tief einzuatmen. Wenn ich mich nach dem Sex mit ihr nicht so entspannt fühlen würde, wäre es fast unmöglich gewesen, den Schmerz, der mein Herz ergriffen hat, zurückzuhalten, aber jetzt bin ich in der Lage, mich zu kontrollieren – selbst als Sara sich entschuldigt und immer noch in die Decke eingehüllt zum Bad geht.

Sie straft mich mit Schweigen, aber das ist mir egal. Es ist bereits nach Mitternacht, und wir werden morgen genügend Zeit zum Reden haben.

Ich strecke mich auf dem Bett aus und warte darauf, dass Sara zurückkommt. Es ist mir recht, dass sie unsere kleine Unterhaltung so kurz halten will. Auch wenn ich mich heute kaum bewegt habe, bin ich genauso müde wie nach einem Auftrag. Mein Körper muss sich immer noch erholen, eine Tatsache, die mich frustriert. Ich hasse es, wenn ich nicht kampfbereit bin und eine Schwäche habe, weil ich mich dann kribbelig und unruhig fühle.

Sara lässt sich im Badezimmer Zeit, aber irgendwann kommt sie zurück und legt sich neben mich, absichtlich ohne ihre Decke mit mir zu teilen. Ich bin gleichzeitig verärgert und amüsiert, ziehe ihr die Decke weg und lege sie über uns beide, sobald ich sie dort habe, wo ich sie haben möchte: in meinen Armen und mit ihrem festen, kleinen Arsch an meiner Lende.

»Gute Nacht«, flüstere ich, während ich ihren Nacken küsse, und als sie nicht antwortet, schließe ich die Augen und ignoriere das Zucken meines Schwanzes, der schon wieder steif wird.

So gern ich sie noch einmal ficken würde, ich muss schlafen, und sie auch.

Ich kann geduldig sein. Schließlich werde ich sie morgen wieder haben – und jeden Tag danach.

ICH WACHE von dem Duft nach Kaffee und Bacon und dem Sonnenlicht auf meinem Gesicht auf. Verwirrt öffne ich die Augen und sehe, dass es noch eine halbe Stunde bis zum Klingeln meines Weckers dauert. Während ich versuche, das zu verstehen, steigen die Erinnerungen an letzte Nacht in meinem Kopf auf, und ich ziehe mir stöhnend die Bettdecke über den Kopf.

Mein russischer Stalker ist zurück und macht in meinem Haus Frühstück.

Nach einer Minute überrede ich mich dazu, aufzustehen und meiner gewöhnlichen Morgenroutine nachzugehen. Ja, der Mörder meines Ehemanns hat mich letzte Nacht erneut gefickt, und ich bin gekommen, aber das war nicht das Ende der Welt, und ich muss mich dementsprechend verhalten.

Ich muss meinen Selbsthass ignorieren und zur Arbeit gehen.

Zehn Minuten später gehe ich frisch geduscht und angezogen nach unten. Es ist eigenartig, aber meine Gefühle für Peter haben sich nicht geändert, jetzt da ich weiß, womit er sein Geld verdient. Ich habe ihn schon so lange als einen Mörder betrachtet, dass das Wissen, dass er und sein Team das für Geld machen, mich kaum berührt. Allerdings bestärkt es meine Überzeugung, dass er gefährlich ist und dass ich vorsichtig vorgehen muss, damit ich diejenigen, die ich liebe, nicht auf sein Radar bringe.

»Ich hoffe, du magst Bacon und Rühreier«, meint er, als ich die Küche betrete. Wie ich ist er abgesehen von den Schuhen bereits angezogen, und seine Lederjacke hängt über einem der Küchenstühle. Seine Kleidung ist wieder einmal dunkel, und sein Anblick am Herd, so männlich stark und tödlich, lässt meinen Puls ansteigen, und mein Magen zieht sich durch etwas Beunruhigendes zusammen.

Etwas, was sich verdächtig nach freudiger Erregung anfühlt.

Ich verdränge diesen Gedanken, verschränke meine Arme vor der Brust und lehne meine Hüfte gegen den Tresen. »Natürlich«, sage ich ruhig und ignoriere mein rasendes Herz. »Wer tut das nicht?«

So gut es sich auch anfühlen würde, ihm das Essen ins Gesicht zu klatschen, ich will ihn nicht provozieren bis ich nicht eine neue Strategie gefunden habe.

»Das habe ich mir auch gedacht.« Er verteilt die Eier und den Bacon geschickt auf den Tellern, bevor er uns Kaffee einschenkt.

Ich denke mir, dass ich genauso gut helfen kann, und nehme die Becher und trage sie zum Tisch. Er bringt die Teller, und wir setzen uns hin, um zu frühstücken.

Die Eier sind hervorragend, aromatisch und locker, und der Bacon ist durchgängig knusprig. Selbst der Kaffee ist außergewöhnlich gut, so als habe er ein Geheimrezept bei meiner Keurig. Nicht, dass ich etwas anderes erwartet habe, da jede Mahlzeit, die er mir bis jetzt vorgesetzt hat, unglaublich gut war.

Wenn dieses Mörder- oder Stalker-Zeug nicht funktioniert, könnte mein Peiniger über eine Karriere als Koch nachdenken.

Dieser Gedanke ist so lächerlich, dass ich in meinen Kaffee lache, woraufhin Peter von seinem Teller hochschaut und seine Augenbrauen fragend in die Höhe zieht.

»Ich habe nur gerade gedacht, dass du das professionell tun könntest«, erkläre ich ihm, bevor ich mir eine weitere Gabel mit Rührei in den Mund schiebe. Vielleicht betrüge ich schon wieder die Erinnerungen an George, aber mir kommt gerade der Gedanke, dass mein Ehemann mir nicht ein einziges Mal Frühstück gemacht hat. In unserer Anfangszeit hat er es einige Male mit einem romantischen Abendessen versucht –

chinesisches Essen zum Mitnehmen und Kerzen –, aber ansonsten habe immer ich gekocht oder wir sind essen gegangen.

»Danke.« Ein leichtes Lächeln erscheint bei meinem Kompliment auf Peters Lippen. »Ich freue mich, dass es dir schmeckt.«

»Ja.« Ich konzentriere mich auf das Essen auf meinem Teller und versuche, nicht zu erröten, als ich mich daran erinnere, wie sich seine gemeißelten Lippen auf meinen Brüsten, meinen Nippeln und meinem restlichen Körper angefühlt haben. Ich will glauben, dass er mich letzte Nacht einfach unvorbereitet erwischt hat, dass meine Reaktion auf ihn das Ergebnis meines schlaftrunkenen Kopfes war, aber die freudige Erregung, die heute Morgen in meinen Adern vibriert, widerspricht dieser Annahme.

Ein kranker Teil von mir freut sich darüber, ihn zu sehen – und ist erleichtert, dass er am Leben ist.

Idiot, schimpfe ich mit mir. Peter Sokolov ist ein gesuchter Deserteur, ein Monster, das vor meinen Augen zwei Leben genommen hat, nachdem es mich gefoltert und George getötet hat. Ein Stalker, dessen Existenz mein Leben unglaublich verkompliziert hat und der eine Bedrohung für alle in meiner Nähe ist.

Es ist nicht nur falsch, ihn hier haben zu wollen, es ist geradezu pathologisch.

Aber trotzdem bemerke ich eine besondere Leichtigkeit in meiner Brust, als ich meine Eier aufesse und meinen Kaffee austrinke. Das Haus fühlt sich nicht länger riesig und erdrückend an, und die Küche ist hell und warm, anstatt kalt und bedrohlich. *Er* füllt den Platz jetzt mit seinem großen Körper und der beängstigenden Stärke seiner Persönlichkeit aus, und auch wenn er die letzte Person ist, deren Gesellschaft ich wollte, verschwindet die erdrückende Einsamkeit, wenn ich mit ihm zusammen bin.

Ein Hund, erinnere ich mich. *Alles, was du brauchst, ist ein Hund.* Und im nächsten Atemzug begreife ich, dass es damit ein Problem geben könnte – und generell mit meinem neuen Lebensplan.

»Du weißt, dass ich in einigen Wochen ausziehe, stimmt's?«, frage ich und stelle meinen leeren Becher ab. »Ich habe die Papiere zum Hausverkauf unterschrieben.«

Peters Gesichtsausdruck verändert sich nicht. »Ja, ich weiß.«

»Natürlich weißt du das.« Meine Hände ballen sich auf dem Tisch zu Fäusten, und meine Nägel graben sich in meine Handflächen. »Wahrscheinlich hast du mich überwachen lassen, während du weg warst. Diese Augen, die ich immer auf mir gespürt habe, die habe ich mir nicht eingebildet, richtig?«

»Ich konnte dich ja nicht ungeschützt zurücklassen«, sagt er mit einem ungerührten Schulterzucken.

»Stimmt.« Ich hole tief Luft und entspanne bewusst meine Hände. »Also, ich ziehe bald in ein Apartment, und ich bin mir ziemlich sicher, dass du nicht so einfach wie jetzt kommen und gehen kannst, zumindest nicht, ohne dass die Nachbarn dich dann täglich sehen. Du könntest also genauso gut eine andere Frau zum Foltern und Verfolgen finden. Es gibt viele, die in halb ländlichen Gegenden leben.«

Seine Mundwinkel zucken. »Ich bin mir sicher, dass es die gibt. Zu schade, dass ich keine von ihnen will.«

Ich trommele mit meinen Fingern auf den Tisch. »Wirklich nicht? Was ist mit den restlichen Menschen auf deiner Liste? Oder hast du sie schon alle umgebracht?«

»Eine Person ist noch übrig, aber die hat sich bis jetzt als sehr schwierig erwiesen«, erwidert er, und ich starre ihn verständnislos an, bevor ich meinen Kopf schüttele.

Ich bin nicht bereit dafür, dieses Thema heute weiterzuführen.

»Schön«, sage ich, um mich zu sammeln. »Also, wann wirst du *mich* in Ruhe lassen?«

»Wenn ich eine Kugel in meinem Kopf oder meinem Herzen habe«, erwidert er ohne zu blinzeln, und mein Magen zieht sich zusammen, als ich verstehe, dass er das völlig ernst meint.

Er hat nicht vor, mich zu verlassen. Niemals.

Die ganze Leichtigkeit und die Aufregung verschwinden und lassen nur das überwältigende Entsetzen über meine Wirklichkeit zurück. Nicht alle köstlichen Mahlzeiten, überwältigende Orgasmen oder zärtliche Umarmungen der Welt können die Tatsache ausblenden, dass ich praktisch eine Gefangene dieses tödlichen Mannes bin, für den Gewalt und Folter alltäglich sind. Seine Besessenheit von mir ist genauso gefährlich wie der Mann selbst, seine Gefühle sind genauso krank wie die dunkle Vergangenheit, die wir teilen.

Ein Monster, das auf mich fixiert ist, und es gibt keinen Ausweg.

Meine Beine sind wackelig, als ich aufstehe und meinen Stuhl nach hinten schiebe. Ich muss zur Arbeit«, sage ich angespannt, und bevor er mir widersprechen kann, schnappe ich mir meine Tasche und gehe schnell in die Garage.

Peter tut nichts, um mich aufzuhalten, aber als ich in das Auto steige, steht er im Türrahmen, und sein dunkles, wunderschönes Gesicht ist unleserlich.

»Wir sehen uns, wenn du von der Arbeit kommst«, sagt er, als ich das Auto anlasse, und ich weiß, dass er es ernst meint.

Mein Peiniger ist zurück, und er wird nicht weggehen.

38

———

Peter hält sein Wort und ist da, als ich an diesem
Abend von der Arbeit komme. Ich bin so müde und
gestresst, dass ich Lust habe, einfach nachzugeben und
das Abendessen zu essen, das er gekocht hat, ein
aromatisch riechendes Pilaw mit Champignons und
Erbsen. Aber ich kann nicht. Ich kann nicht einfach bei
dieser verrückten Geschichte mitspielen und so tun, als
sei das irgendwie normal.

Wenn mein Stalker mich sowieso nicht allein lassen
wird, macht es keinen Sinn, wenn ich so tue, als sei ich
einverstanden. Ich kann die Dinge auch so schwierig
wie möglich für ihn machen.

Ich ignoriere den gedeckten Tisch und gehe nach
oben, während er uns Wein einschenkt. Ich betrete das

Schlafzimmer, verschließe die Tür und spritze mir kaltes Wasser ins Gesicht.

Ich habe alles außer direktem Widerstand ausprobiert und ich bin verzweifelt genug, um genau das jetzt zu tun.

Als ich mir das Gesicht gewaschen habe, komme ich wieder heraus und setze mich auf das Bett, um zu sehen, was als Nächstes passieren wird. Ich habe nicht vor, diese Tür aufzuschließen und ihn hereinzulassen oder auf irgendeine andere Art und Weise zu kooperieren.

Ich habe genug davon, mit einem Monster Familie zu spielen. Wenn er mich will, wird er mich zwingen müssen.

Mein Magen knurrt vor Hunger, und ich trete mich selbst dafür in den Hintern, nicht gegessen zu haben, bevor ich nach Hause gekommen bin. Ich war so abgelenkt, weil ich den ganzen Tag an Peter denken musste, dass ich wie ferngesteuert nach Hause gefahren bin, während mein Kopf mit dieser unmöglichen Situation beschäftigt war. Jetzt, da ich über sein Team und ihre Auftragsmorde Bescheid weiß, bin ich noch weniger davon überzeugt, dass das FBI mich beschützen könnte, wenn ich zu ihm ginge.

Ich glaube nicht, dass es *irgendjemanden* gibt, der mich vor ihm beschützen kann. Ein Klopfen an der Schlafzimmertür reißt mich aus meinen deprimierenden Überlegungen.

»Komm runter, Ptichka«, sagt Peter von der anderen Seite. »Das Abendessen wird kalt.«

Mein ganzer Körper spannt sich an, aber ich antworte ihm nicht.

Noch ein Klopfen. Dann wackelt die Türklinke. »Sara.« Peters Stimme wird härter. »Öffne die Tür.«

Ich stehe auf, da ich zu unruhig bin, um stillzusitzen, aber ich mache keinen einzigen Schritt in Richtung Tür.

»Sara. Öffne diese Tür. Jetzt!«

Ich bleibe stehen, und meine Hände formen sich an meinen Seiten zu Fäusten. Bevor ich nach Hause kam, hatte ich darüber nachgedacht, mir eine Waffe zu besorgen, aber dann habe ich mich an das erinnert, was er mir über seine Männer erzählt hat, die seine Lebenszeichen überwachen, und habe diese Idee fallengelassen. Ich weiß nicht, wie diese Überwachung abläuft, aber es ist durchaus möglich, dass er eine Art Apparat trägt, der seinen Puls oder auch seinen Blutdruck misst. Vielleicht sogar ein Implantat. Ich habe von solchen Dingen gehört, auch wenn ich sie noch nie gesehen habe. Auf jeden Fall kann ich Peter, sollte das, was er mir erzählt hat, stimmen, nicht wirklich verletzen, ohne mein eigenes Leben und eventuell das derjenigen, die mir nahestehen, zu riskieren.

Männer, die für Geld töten, würden nicht zögern, ihren Boss auf die brutalsten Arten zu rächen.

»Du hast fünf Sekunden, um diese Tür zu öffnen.«

Ich kämpfe gegen das Gefühl an, ein Déjà-vu zu haben, beiße mir auf die Unterlippe und bleibe unbeweglich stehen, auch wenn mein Herz krankhaft schnell in meiner Brust schlägt und mir kalter Schweiß den Rücken hinunterläuft. Auch wenn ich nicht möchte, dass er mir wehtut, will ich auf keinen Fall so leben, will nicht zu verängstigt sein, meine Meinung zu vertreten und stattdessen widerspruchslos den Forderungen eines Irren zu folgen. Das letzte Mal, als ich ihn ausgeschlossen habe, war ich in einem Schockzustand gewesen, war so überwältigt und verängstigt gewesen, nachdem ich gesehen hatte, wie er diese beiden Männer umgebracht hat, dass ich ohne nachzudenken gehandelt habe. Jetzt allerdings tue ich es absichtlich.

Ich muss wissen, wie weit er gehen wird, was er alles tun wird, um es so zu haben, wie er es möchte.

Diesmal zählt er nicht laut, also zähle ich im Kopf. *Eins, zwei, drei, vier, fünf ...* Ich warte darauf, dass sein Tritt die Tür erschüttert, aber stattdessen höre ich Schritte, die sich nach unten entfernen. Erleichtert atme ich meinen angehaltenen Atem aus. Ist das möglich? Hat er wirklich aufgegeben und beschlossen, mich heute Abend allein zu lassen? Das habe ich nicht erwartet, aber er hat mich schon häufiger überrascht. Vielleicht hat er immer noch ein Problem damit, mir wehzutun; vielleicht geht es ihm zu weit, die Schlafzimmertür einzutreten und ...

Die Schritte kehren zurück, und die Türklinke bewegt sich erneut, bevor etwas Metallisches am Schloss schabt. Mein Herz setzt einen Schlag aus, bevor es wieder wütend schlägt.

Er knackt das Türschloss.

Die kühle Besonnenheit dieser Handlung ist irgendwie furchteinflößender, als wenn er einfach die

Tür eingetreten hätte. Mein Peiniger handelt nicht aus Wut, er hat sich vollkommen unter Kontrolle und weiß ganz genau, was er tut.

Das metallische Kratzen dauert weniger als eine Minute an. Ich weiß das, weil ich die blinkenden Zahlen auf dem Wecker, der auf meinem Nachttisch steht, betrachte. Dann geht die Tür auf, und Peters Gesichtsausdruck ist hart und kalt, als er mit Schritten eintritt, die unterdrückte Wut ausstrahlen.

Ich kämpfe gegen meinen Drang, wegzulaufen, an, erhebe mein Kinn und starre ihn an, als er vor mir stehen bleibt und sein großer Körper über meine viel kleinere Gestalt ragt.

»Komm essen.« Seine Stimme ist ruhig, sogar sanft, aber ich kann die pulsierende Dunkelheit dahinter heraushören. Seine Kontrolle hängt an einem seidenen Faden, und hätte ich noch Hoffnung, würde ich jetzt einen Rückzieher machen und meinem Selbsterhaltungstrieb nachgeben. Aber ich habe keine Strategien mehr, und irgendwann kommt der Punkt, an dem der Selbsterhaltungstrieb der Selbstachtung den Vortritt lassen muss.

Waghalsig schüttele ich meinen Kopf. »Ich werde das nicht tun.«

Seine Nasenlöcher beben. »Was? Essen?«

Mein Magen knurrt genau in diesem Moment erneut, und ich erröte wegen des schlechten Timings. »Ich werde nicht mit *dir* essen«, sage ich, so ruhig ich kann. »Oder mit dir schlafen oder überhaupt irgendetwas mit dir tun.«

»Nein?« Dunkle Belustigung erscheint in seinem grauen, eisigen Blick. »Bist du dir da sicher, Ptichka?«

Meine Hände ballen sich an meinen Seiten zu Fäusten. »Ich will, dass du mein Haus verlässt. Jetzt.«

»Oder was?« Er tritt näher an mich heran und bedrängt mich mit seinem großen Körper, bis ich keine andere Wahl habe, als mich in Richtung Bett zurückzuziehen. »Oder was, Sara?«

Ich will ihm mit der Polizei oder dem FBI drohen, aber wir wissen beide, dass ich mich bereits an sie gewandt hätte, hätte ich die Gelegenheit dazu bekommen. Es gibt nichts, was ich tun kann, um ihn aus meinem Leben zu vertreiben, und das ist das Problem an dieser Sache.

Ich ignoriere den Schweiß, der meinen Rücken hinunterläuft, und hebe mein Kinn weiter in die Höhe. »Ich habe genug davon, Peter.«

»Davon?« Er kommt noch näher und legt seinen Kopf auf die Seite.

»Diese kranke Beziehungsfantasie, die du hast«, verdeutliche ich. Er ist zu nahe bei mir, dringt in meinen persönlichen Bereich ein, als gehöre er dorthin. Sein männlicher Geruch umgibt mich, die Hitze, die sein Körper abgibt, erwärmt mich innerlich, und ich trete noch einen Schritt zurück, während ich versuche, das feuchte Gefühl in meinem Schritt und meine empfindlichen Nippel zu ignorieren.

Ich kann nicht so nahe bei ihm sein, ohne daran zu denken, wie es sich anfühlt, ihm noch näher zu sein, sich mit ihm auf die intimste Art und Weise zu verbinden.

»Eine kranke Beziehungsfantasie?« Seine Augenbrauen ziehen sich belustigt in die Höhe. »Das ist ein wenig hart, meinst du nicht?«

»Ich. Habe. Genug«, wiederhole ich und betone dabei jedes Wort. Mein Herz schlägt voller Angst gegen meinen Brustkorb, aber ich bin entschlossen, nicht nachzugeben oder mich mit einer Diskussion über unsere verworrene Beziehung ablenken zu lassen. »Wenn du in meiner Küche kochen möchtest, dann bitte schön, aber vergiss das erzwungene gemeinsame Essen. Ich werde nicht mit dir essen oder irgendetwas anderes aus freien Stücken mit dir tun.«

»Ach, Ptichka.« Peters Stimme ist weich, und sein Blick fast mitleidig. »Du hast keine Ahnung, wie falsch du damit liegst.«

Auf seinen Lippen erscheint dieses unvollkommene, magnetische Lächeln, und mein Magen zieht sich zusammen, als er noch näher kommt. Ich brauche verzweifelt Abstand und gehe einen weiteren Schritt nach hinten, aber da spüre ich bereits, dass die Rückseiten meiner Knie das Bett berühren.

Ich stecke fest, wieder einmal hat er mich gefangen.

Er tritt gnadenlos näher, und mein Geschlecht zuckt, als seine Hände sich um meine Schultern legen. »Komm mit mir nach unten, Sara«, sagt er sanft. »Du hast Hunger und wirst dich besser fühlen, wenn du erst einmal etwas im Magen hast. Und während du isst, können wir reden.«

»Worüber?«, frage ich mit angespannter Stimme. Die Hitze seiner Handflächen brennt sich sogar durch meinen dicken Pulli, und ich habe wegen der bösartigen Erregung in meinem Unterleib Probleme, gleichmäßig zu atmen. »Es gibt nichts, worüber wir reden sollten.«

»Ich denke, das gibt es«, entgegnet er, und ich sehe das Monster tief in seinen dunkelsilbrigen Augen. »Weißt du, Sara, wenn du nicht hier mit mir zusammen sein möchtest, können wir auch irgendwo anders hingehen. Die Fantasie kann Wirklichkeit werden – aber nur zu meinen Bedingungen.«

SIE ZITTERT, als ich sie nach unten führe, und ich weiß, dass es genauso sehr aus Wut wie aus Angst ist. Ich nehme an, dass mich ihre Reaktion beunruhigen sollte, aber ich bin selbst zu wütend. Gestern, und auch heute beim Frühstück, hätte ich schwören können, dass sie froh war, mich zu sehen, erleichtert, dass ich wieder da bin. Aber heute Abend ist sie wieder kalt und distanziert, und das werde ich nicht zulassen.

Es ist an der Zeit, die Samthandschuhe auszuziehen.

»Setz dich«, sage ich ihr, als wir am Küchentisch ankommen, und sie lässt sich mit einem trotzigen Ausdruck auf ihrem schönen Gesicht auf den Stuhl fallen. Sie ist entschlossen, die Dinge zu erschweren, und ich bin genauso entschlossen, das nicht zuzulassen.

Ich hole Luft, um mich zu beruhigen, mache das Licht aus und zünde die Kerzen an. Dann gebe ich Risotto auf einen Teller und bringe es zu ihr, bevor ich meinen Teller hole. Ich bin genauso hungrig wie sie und beginne zu essen, sobald ich sitze, da ich mir denke, dass die Unterhaltung über unsere Beziehung einige Minuten warten kann.

Leider teilt Sara diese Meinung nicht. »Was hast du mit ›die Fantasie kann Wirklichkeit werden‹ gemeint?«, fragt sie mit angespannter Stimme, während sie mit ihrer Gabel spielt. »Was genau willst du mir damit sagen?«

Ich lasse sie warten, bis ich meinen Bissen gekaut und heruntergeschluckt habe, bevor ich meine Gabel ablege und sie ruhig anschaue. »Ich will damit sagen, dass die Tatsache, dass du in diesem Haus lebst, zur Arbeit gehst und was mit deinen Freunden machen kannst, ein Privileg ist, das ich dir zugestehe«, sage ich ruhig und beobachte, wie sie erblasst. »Andere Männer in meiner Position wären nicht ansatzweise so entgegenkommend gewesen – und ich muss das auch nicht sein. Ich will dich, und ich habe die Macht, dich zu nehmen. So einfach ist das. Wenn du die Dynamik unserer derzeitigen Beziehung nicht magst, werde ich sie ändern, aber nicht auf eine Art und Weise, die du mögen wirst.

Ihre Hand zittert, als sie nach dem Glas Wein greift, das ich ihr vorhin eingeschenkt habe. »Also wirst du was? Mich entführen? Mich von jedem und allem fernhalten?«

»Ja, Ptichka. Das ist genau das, was ich tun werde, wenn du es nicht schaffst, dass die derzeitige Situation funktioniert.« Ich esse weiter, um ihr Zeit zu geben, meine Worte zu verarbeiten. Ich weiß, dass ich hart bin, aber ich muss diese kleine Rebellion niederschlagen und ihr klarmachen, wie gefährlich ihre Situation ist.

Es gibt keine Grenze, die ich nicht überschreiten würde, wenn es um sie geht. Sie wird so oder so mir gehören.

Sara starrt mich an, das Glas in ihrer Hand zittert, und dann stellt sie es ab, ohne einen Schluck getrunken zu haben. »Also warum hast du es dann nicht schon getan? Warum all das hier?« Sie macht eine ausladende Geste, wobei sie beinahe das Weinglas und einen der Kerzenständer umwirft.

»Vorsicht«, sage ich und stelle beide Objekte weiter von ihr weg. »Wenn ich es nicht besser wüsste, würde ich sagen, dass du wieder versuchst, mir Betäubungsmittel unterzuschieben.«

Ihre Zähne knirschen hörbar. »Sag es mir«, fordert sie, und ihre Hände ballen sich neben ihrem unberührten Teller zu Fäusten. »Warum hast du mich nicht bereits entführt? Mit Sicherheit hast du keine moralischen Bedenken.«

Ich seufze und lege meine Gabel ab. Vielleicht hätte ich ihr eine Unterhaltung nach und nicht während des Essens versprechen sollen. »Weil ich mag, was du tust«, antworte ich und nehme mein Weinglas, um einen Schluck zu trinken. »Mit Babys und Frauen arbeiten. Ich denke, deine Arbeit ist bewundernswert, und ich will dich davon nicht fernhalten – und von deinen Eltern auch nicht.«

»Aber du wirst es, wenn du musst.«

»Ja.« Ich stelle das Glas ab und nehme meine Gabel wieder in die Hand. »Das werde ich.«

Sie betrachtet mich einige Sekunden lang, bevor sie ihre Gabel nimmt und wir einige Minuten lang in bedrückendem Schweigen essen. Ich kann sie fast denken hören, als ihr kluger Kopf versucht, eine Lösung zu finden.

Es ist Pech für sie, dass es keine gibt.

Als Saras Teller halb leer ist, schiebt sie ihn weg und fragt mit angespannter Stimme: »Hast du sie auch verfolgt?«

Meine Augenbraue zieht sich nach oben, als ich das Weinglas hochnehme. »Wen?«

»Deine Frau«, antwortet Sara, und meine Hand spannt sich so stark an, dass ich beinahe das zarte Glas zerbreche. Instinktiv bereite ich mich auf den quälenden Schmerz und die Wut vor, aber alles, was ich spüre, ist ein dumpfes Echo von Verlust, das von einem bittersüßen Schmerz bei den Erinnerungen begleitet wird.

»Nein«, erwidere ich und bin selbst davon überrascht, dass ich liebevoll lächele. »Das habe ich nicht. Wenn überhaupt, hat sie mich verfolgt.«

40

———

S*ara*

SCHOCKIERT STARRE ICH MEINEN PEINIGER AN, weil mich sein sanftes, fast zärtliches Lächeln überrascht. Ich hatte erwartet, dass er bei dieser Frage explodieren würde, und als ich gesehen habe, dass sich seine Finger am Stiel des Glases anspannten, war ich sicher, dass er es tun würde.

Stattdessen hat er gelächelt.

Ich kaue auf meiner Unterlippe und überlege, ob ich das Thema fallenlasse, aber trotz der angedrohten Entführung kann ich mir die Gelegenheit, mehr über ihn zu erfahren, einfach nicht entgehen lassen.

»Wie meinst du das?«, frage ich und nehme mein Weinglas in die Hand. Das Risotto ist unglaublich gut, aber mein Magen hat sich zu einem Knoten zusammengezogen, und ich kann nicht mehr essen. Wein könnte ich allerdings vertragen.

Wenn ich genug trinke, vergesse ich vielleicht sein beängstigendes Versprechen.

»Wir haben uns getroffen, als ich vor fast neun Jahren durch ihr Dorf kam.« Peter lehnt sich mit dem Weinglas in seiner großen Hand in seinem Stuhl zurück. Das Kerzenlicht wirft ein sanftes, warmes Glühen über seine hübschen Gesichtszüge, und wenn ich nicht so viel Adrenalin durch den ganzen Stress in meinen Adern hätte, hätte ich der Illusion eines romantischen Dinners und der Fantasie, die er unbedingt umsetzen möchte, nachgeben können.

»Mein Team hat eine Gruppe von Aufständischen in den Bergen aufgespürt«, fährt er fort, und sein Blick wird abwesend, als die Erinnerungen in ihm aufsteigen. »Es war Winter und es war kalt. Unglaublich kalt. Ich wusste, dass wir uns für die Nacht ein warmes Plätzchen suchen mussten, also habe ich die Dorfbewohner gebeten, uns einige Zimmer zu vermieten. Nur eine Frau war mutig genug, das zu tun, und das war Tamila.«

Ich nehme einen Schluck Wein und bin völlig fasziniert. »Sie hat allein gelebt?«

Peter nickt. »Sie war damals erst zwanzig, aber sie hatte ein eigenes kleines Haus. Ihre Tante war gestorben und hatte es ihr vererbt. Es war in dem Dorf noch nie vorgekommen, dass eine junge Frau allein lebte, aber Tamila hat sich noch nie viel aus Traditionen gemacht. Ihre Eltern wollten sie mit einem der

Dorfältesten verheiraten, einem Mann, der ihnen eine Mitgift von fünf Ziegen geben konnte, aber Tamila fand ihn abstoßend und zögerte die Hochzeit so lange wie möglich hinaus. Natürlich hat ihren Eltern das nicht gefallen, und als meine Männer und ich ins Dorf kamen, suchte sie bereits verzweifelt nach einer Lösung, ihre Lage zu ändern.«

Ich trinke schnell den Rest meines Weins, während er fortfährt. »Von alledem wusste ich natürlich nichts. Ich habe einfach nur eine wunderschöne junge Frau gesehen, die aus irgendeinem Grund drei halberfrorene Speznas-Soldaten bei sich aufnahm. Sie hat meinen Männern ihr Schlafzimmer überlassen und mir den zweiten, kleineren Raum mit der Erklärung gegeben, dass sie auf dem Sofa schlafen würde.«

»Aber das hat sie nicht«, rate ich, als er sich nach vorn beugt, um mir Wein nachzuschenken. Mein Magen fühlt sich wie zugeschnürt an, da etwas Unangenehmes wie Eifersucht sich in meinen Eingeweiden ausbreitet. »Sie ist zu dir gekommen.«

»Ja, das ist sie.« Er lächelt erneut, und ich verstecke mein Unwohlsein, indem ich mehr Wein trinke. Ich weiß nicht, warum es mich stört, ihn mir mit dieser »wunderschönen jungen Frau« vorzustellen, aber das tut es, und ich schaffe es kaum, ihm ruhig zuzuhören, als er sagt: »Ich habe sie natürlich nicht weggeschickt. Kein Mann, der auf Frauen steht, hätte das getan. Sie war schüchtern und recht unerfahren, aber keine Jungfrau mehr, und als ich am nächsten Morgen weiterzog, versprach ich ihr, auf dem Rückweg wieder durch das

Dorf zu kommen. Das habe ich zwei Monate später auch getan und erfahren, dass sie von mir schwanger war.«

Ich blinzele. »Du hast nicht verhütet?«

»Doch, das erste Mal. Das zweite Mal habe ich geschlafen, als sie damit begann, sich an mir zu reiben, und als ich endlich richtig wach war, war ich bereits in ihr und habe nicht mehr an das Kondom gedacht.«

Meine Kinnlade klappt nach unten. »Sie ist absichtlich schwanger geworden?«

Er zuckt mit den Schultern. »Sie hat behauptet, das sei sie nicht, aber ich nehme an, dass sie es wollte. Sie lebte in einem konservativen, muslimischen Dorf, und sie hatte schon einen Liebhaber vor mir gehabt. Sie hat mir nie gesagt, wer er war, aber hätte sie einen der Ältesten geheiratet oder hätte sie ihn abgelehnt, um jemand anderen aus dem Dorf zu heiraten, hätte sie sich öffentlich zur Schau gestellt und hätte von ihrem Ehemann verstoßen werden können. Ein nicht-muslimischer Ausländer wie ich war das Beste, um diesem Schicksal zu entgehen, und sie hat die Gelegenheit ergriffen, als sie sie erkannte. Das ist wirklich bewundernswert. Sie ist ein Risiko eingegangen, und es hat sich gelohnt.«

»Weil du sie geheiratet hast.«

Er nickt. »Das habe ich – nachdem ein Vaterschaftstest ihre Aussage bestätigt hat.«

»Das ist … sehr anständig von dir gewesen.« Ich bin unglaublich erleichtert, dass er sich nicht Hals über Kopf in dieses Mädchen verliebt hatte. »Nicht viele

Männer wären bereit gewesen, eine Frau zu heiraten, die sie nicht lieben, weil sie ein Kind von ihnen bekommt.«

Peter zuckt erneut mit den Schultern. »Ich wollte nicht, dass mein Sohn dem Spott ausgesetzt ist, ohne Vater aufzuwachsen, und seine Mutter zu heiraten war der beste Weg, um das sicherzustellen. Außerdem habe ich Tamila wirklich lieben gelernt, nachdem mein Sohn geboren wurde.«

»Ich verstehe.« Erneut überkommt mich Eifersucht. Um mich abzulenken, trinke ich mein zweites Glas Wein aus und nehme mir die Flasche, um mir mehr einzuschenken. »Also hat sie dich in eine Falle gelockt, und es hat funktioniert.« Meine Handflächen sind feucht, die Flasche rutscht mir fast aus der Hand, und ich gieße den Wein mit so viel Schwung in das Glas, dass etwas über den Rand schwappt.

»Durstig?« Peters graue Augen glänzen amüsiert, während er seinen Arm ausstreckt, um mir die Flasche abzunehmen. »Vielleicht sollte ich dir lieber Wasser oder Tee holen?«

Ich schüttele vehement den Kopf, nur um zu bemerken, dass sich nach dieser Bewegung der Raum ein wenig dreht. Er könnte recht haben. Ich habe nicht viel gegessen und sollte meinen Wein wahrscheinlich langsamer trinken. Aber meine Angst schmilzt mit jedem Schluck dahin, und das fühlt sich zu gut an, um aufzuhören.

»Mir geht es gut«, sage ich und ergreife erneut mein Glas. Wahrscheinlich werde ich das morgen auf der Arbeit bereuen, aber ich brauche den warmen Rausch, den der Alkohol hervorruft. »Also hast du dich in Tamila verliebt. Und sie hat weiterhin in dem Dorf gelebt?«

»Ja.« Sein Gesicht spannt sich an, wahrscheinlich, weil wir uns den schmerzlichen Erinnerungen nähern. Er bestätigt meine Vermutung, indem er rau sagt: »Ich habe mir gedacht, dass sie und Pasha – so haben wir meinen Sohn genannt – dort sicherer sein würden. Sie wollte mit mir in meinem Apartment in Moskau leben, aber ich war wegen meiner Arbeit immer auf Reisen und wollte sie nicht allein in einer unbekannten Stadt lassen. Ich hatte ihr versprochen, mit ihr Moskau zu besuchen, wenn Pasha älter wäre, aber bis dahin dachte ich, dass es besser wäre, wenn sie in der Nähe ihrer Familie bliebe und mein Sohn mit frischer Bergluft anstatt mit Stadtsmog aufwächst.

Der Schluck Wein, den ich herunterschlucke, brennt in meinem Hals, der sich immer weiter zusammenzieht. »Das tut mir leid«, murmele ich und stelle mein Glas ab. Und es *tut* mir leid für ihn. Ich verachte Peter für das, was er mir antut, aber sein Leiden und sein Verlust, die ihn auf diesen dunklen Weg gebracht haben, schmerzen in meinem Herzen. Ich kann seine Schuldgefühle und die Qualen darüber, dass er versehentlich die falsche Wahl getroffen hat und sein Wunsch, seine Familie zu schützen, ihr Untergang war, sehr gut nachfühlen.

Das ist etwas, was ich nachvollziehen kann, da ich

meinen Ehemann nicht nur einmal, sondern zweimal getötet habe.

Peter nickt, um mir zu zeigen, dass er mich gehört hat, und steht auf, um den Tisch abzuräumen. Ich trinke weiter meinen Wein, während er die Teller in den Geschirrspüler stellt, und das warme Gefühl durch den Alkohol verstärkt sich, die Kerzen vor mir ziehen durch das hypnotisierende Flackern der Flammen meine Aufmerksamkeit auf sich.

»Lass uns ins Bett gehen«, meint er, und als ich aufsehe, bemerke ich, dass er sich gerade die Hände am Geschirrtuch abtrocknet. Ich muss eine Weile abwesend die Kerzen betrachtet haben. Entweder das – oder er kann wahnsinnig schnell aufräumen. Höchstwahrscheinlich war ich einfach abwesend, was bedeutet, dass ich betrunkener bin, als ich dachte.

»Bett?« Ich zwinge mich dazu, mich zu konzentrieren, als er zu mir kommt, mein Handgelenk ergreift und mich hochzieht. Obwohl ich dank des Weins ein wenig verschwommen sehe, erinnere ich mich an den Grund dafür, warum ich wütend gewesen bin, und als er mich zur Treppe führt, kehrt der Knoten in meinem Magen zurück, und mein Puls erhöht sich. »Ich möchte nicht mit dir schlafen.«

Er schaut mich kurz an, und seine Finger an meinem Handgelenk spannen sich an. »Ich will nicht schlafen.«

Meine Furcht verstärkt sich. »Ich will auch keinen Sex mit dir haben.«

»Nein?« Er bleibt vor der Treppe stehen und dreht

sich zu mir um, um mich anzuschauen. »Also, wenn ich jetzt in deine Jeans fassen würde, würde ich keinen durchnässten Slip fühlen? Und keine geschwollene und bereite Muschi, die nur darauf wartet, von meinem Schwanz ausgefüllt zu werden?«

Hitze steigt in meinem Nacken auf und breitet sich bis zum Haaransatz aus. Ich *bin* nass, von davor und durch die Art und Weise, wie er mich jetzt anschaut. Es sieht aus, als würde er mich verschlingen wollen, so als würden seine schmutzigen Worte ihn genauso sehr erregen wie mich. Mein vom Wein benebeltes Hirn ist auch keine Hilfe, und mir wird klar, dass ich einen Fehler gemacht habe, als ich versucht habe, meinen Kummer im Alkohol zu ertränken.

Es ist schon mit einem klaren Kopf schwer genug, ihm zu widerstehen, und in meinem jetzigen Zustand ist es beinahe unmöglich.

Aber ich muss es trotzdem versuchen. »Ich will nicht ...«

»Ptichka ...« Er hebt seine linke Hand und legt sie um mein Kinn. Sein Daumen streicht über meine Wange, während er mich anschaut und seine Augen wie geschmolzener Stahl aussehen. »Müssen wir noch einmal die alternativen Arrangements durchgehen?«

Ich starre ihn an, und in meinen Adern bilden sich Eiskristalle. Zum ersten Mal verstehe ich die volle Bedeutung seines Ultimatums. Er erwartet von mir nicht nur, dass ich mich nicht mehr gegen gemeinsame Mahlzeiten mit ihm wehre, sondern dass ich in allen

Punkten entgegenkommend bin, ihn in mein Bett lasse, so als führten wir eine wirkliche Beziehung.

So als hätte er nicht meinen Ehemann umgebracht und sei gewaltsam in mein Leben eingedrungen.

»Nein«, flüstere ich und schließe meine Augen, als er seinen Kopf nach unten beugt, um mit seinen Lippen über meine zu fahren … sanft und zärtlich. Seine Zärtlichkeit lässt mich trotz seiner entsetzlichen Drohung zerbrechen. Wenn ich gegen ihn ankämpfe, wird er mich entführen, mir auch meine restliche Freiheit nehmen.

Wenn ich mich wehre, werde ich alles verlieren, was mir etwas bedeutet, und wenn ich es nicht tue, werde ich mich selbst verlieren.

———

ICH STOLPERE, als Peter mich die Treppen hinaufführt, also hebt er mich in seine kräftigen Arme und trägt mich mühelos hinauf. Seine Stärke ist genauso angsteinflößend wie verführerisch. Ich weiß, wie es ist, sie am eigenen Leib zu spüren, aber etwas Primitives in mir fühlt sich davon angezogen, sehnt sich nach diesem Versprechen von Sicherheit.

Als wir im Schlafzimmer ankommen, stellt er mich hin und zieht mich aus, schält mich ruhig und ohne Eile aus meinem Pullover und meiner Jeans. Allein die dunkle Hitze in seinem silberfarbenen Blick verrät seinen Hunger, das Verlangen, dem er nachgeben wird, koste es, was es wolle.

Als ich nackt bin, zieht er sich ebenfalls aus, und ich erhasche einen Blick auf ein metallisches Glänzen in seinem Jackett, als er es über den Stuhl hängt. Eine Pistole? Ein Messer? Der Gedanke, dass er Waffen in mein Schlafzimmer bringt, sollte mich entsetzen, aber ich bin zu überwältigt, um zu reagieren, da meine Gefühle bereits zwischen Schock, Wut und Angst umherspringen. Und unterschwellig spüre ich eine eigenartige, unlogische Erleichterung.

Da ich keine Wahl mehr habe, kann ich nachgeben.

Das ist der einzige Weg.

Eine Träne läuft meine Wange hinunter, als er zu mir kommt, nackt und erregt mit seinem großen Körper mit seinen harten Kanten und gemeißelten Muskeln, seiner gewaltigen Schönheit und gefährlichen Männlichkeit. Monster sollten nicht so aussehen, sollten nicht genauso faszinierend wie tödlich sein.

Das ist viel zu verwirrend.

»Nicht weinen, Ptichka«, murmelt er, als er vor mir stehen bleibt. Seine Finger streicheln meine Wangen und wischen die Feuchtigkeit weg. »Ich werde dir nicht wehtun. Es ist wirklich nicht so schlimm, wie du denkst.«

Nicht so schlimm, wie ich denke? Ich will laut auflachen, aber stattdessen schüttele ich den Kopf, der von dem Wein und der Hitze seiner Nähe benebelt ist. Er hat recht: Ich will ihn. Ich sehne mich nach ihm, mein Körper brennt mit einem Verlangen, das so stark ist, dass ich es kaum unterdrücken kann. Und gleichzeitig hasse ich ihn.

Ich hasse ihn für das, was er tut – und das, was er mich fühlen lässt.

Seine Finger gleiten in mein Haar, bedecken meinen Schädel, und ich schließe meine Augen, als er mich erneut küsst, während seine andere Hand sich um meine Hüfte legt, um mich näher an sich zu ziehen. Seine Erektion drückt riesig und hart gegen meinen Bauch, aber sein Kuss ist sanft, seine Lippen locken die Empfindungen hervor, anstatt sie zu erzwingen.

Es fühlt sich einen Augenblick lang gut an, so unglaublich gut, dass ich vergesse, dass ich in dieser Sache keine Wahl habe. Meine Hände legen sich auf seine Seiten, spüren seine harte Muskelmasse, und meine Lippen öffnen sich, als sich die Hitze in mir ausbreitet. Er nutzt diese Chance, um in meinen Mund zu fahren, und seine Zunge bringt den schwindelerregenden Geschmack nach Wein und süßer Verführung mit sich. Das ist nicht unser erstes Mal, aber dieser Kuss ist eine Erkundungsreise, eine sinnliche Entdeckung und ein zärtliches Wunder.

Er küsst mich, als sei ich das kostbarste, begehrenswerteste Ding, dem er jemals begegnet ist.

Mein Kopf dreht sich durch diese nahezu unerträgliche Lust, und es ist reizvoll, mich völlig zu verlieren, der Illusion seiner Zuneigung hinzugeben. Die Art, wie er mich festhält, zeigt sein dringendes Bedürfnis, aber auch etwas Tiefergehendes, etwas, was in der verletzlichsten Ecke meines Herzens widerhallt.

Etwas, was den Graben der Einsamkeit, den die Ruinen meiner Ehe hinterlassen haben, füllt.

Ich weiß nicht, wie lange Peter mich so küsst, aber als er seinen Kopf anhebt, atmen wir beide abgehackt und die Hitze, die durch meinen Körper fließt, ist eine ausgewachsene Feuersbrunst.

Benebelt öffne ich meine Augen und schaue in seine, während er mich zum Bett trägt. In den grauen, metallischen Tiefen gibt es keine Kälte, keine brodelnde Dunkelheit, nichts außer der hungrigen Zärtlichkeit, und als er sich zwischen meine Beine begibt, mich mit seinem kräftigen Körper bedeckt, weiß ich, dass es leicht sein könnte.

Ich könnte aufhören, mich zu wehren, und seine Fantasie akzeptieren, diese düsterere Version eines Märchens leben.

»Sara …« Seine kräftige Hand legt sich um mein Gesicht, rahmt es mit unerträglicher Zärtlichkeit ein, und der Schmerz, der durch meine Brust fährt, ist genauso stark wie pervers. Er schaut mich an, als sei ich sein Ein und Alles, so als würde er mir alle Wünsche von den Augen ablesen wollen. Das ist genau das, was ich immer gewollt habe, immer gebraucht habe – aber nicht mit dem Mörder meines Ehemannes.

Ich kratze die zerbröckelten Reste meines gesunden Menschenverstandes zusammen und schließe die Augen, um der silbernen Verlockung seines hypnotisierenden Blickes zu entgehen. *Keine Wahl*, erinnere ich mich selbst, als sich seine Lippen für einen weiteren verzehrenden Kuss auf meine legen. *Keine Wahl*, wiederhole ich lautlos, als ich höre, wie eine Kondomverpackung aufgerissen wird, und seine behaarten

Beine an den zarten Innenseiten meiner Oberschenkel spüre, die er auseinanderdrückt, um mit seinem Schwanz mein Geschlecht zu berühren. *Keine Wahl*, schreie ich innerlich, als er in mich stößt, mich ausdehnt, mich ausfüllt ... mich mit brennend heißem Verlangen füllt.

Das ist falsch, das ist krank, aber es dauert keine ganze Minute, bis sein harter, antreibender Rhythmus mich mit einer Intensität kommen lässt, die mich aufschreien lässt und mir die Tränen in die Augen treibt. Mein Körper erzittert in dunkler Ekstase, krampft sich um seinen dicken, langen Schwanz, und ich schreie seinen Namen, kratze mit meinen Fingernägeln über seinen Rücken, während er mich weiter fickt, mich noch zweimal zum Höhepunkt bringt, bis er selbst kommt.

Danach liege ich entspannt auf ihm, unsere Beine sind verschlungen, und er streichelt langsam meinen Rücken. Da mein Kopf auf seiner Schulter liegt, höre ich das gleichmäßige Schlagen seines Herzens, und das Glühen der sexuellen Zufriedenheit weicht dem vertrauten Gefühl von Scham und Verzweiflung.

Ich hasse ihn und ich hasse mich selbst.

Ich hasse mich, weil etwas Perverses in mir froh über sein Ultimatum war.

Es hat sich gut angefühlt, keine Wahl zu haben.

»Du wirst nicht in einigen Wochen ausziehen«, murmelt er, ohne sein sanftes Streicheln zu unterbrechen. »Das Haus gehört nicht mehr dem Rechtsanwaltspaar – es gehört mir. Oder besser gesagt einer meiner Strohfirmen.«

Diese Nachricht sollte mich überraschen, aber das tut sie nicht. Ich muss das irgendwie erwartet haben. Meine Finger spannen sich an und zerknüllen die Ecke des Kissens. »Hast du sie bedroht? Sie umgebracht?«

Er lacht, und seine kräftige Brust bewegt sich unter mir. »Ich habe ihnen das Doppelte von dem gezahlt, was das Haus wert ist. Dasselbe gilt auch für deinen neuen Vermieter. Er ist gut für deinen Vertragsbruch kompensiert worden.«

Ich schließe die Augen, weil ich so erleichtert bin, dass ich weinen könnte. Ich weiß nicht, was ich getan hätte, wenn noch jemand meinetwegen gelitten hätte, wie ich dann noch mit mir hätte leben können.

Als ich sicher bin, dass meine Stimme nicht zittern wird, rücke ich ein Stück von ihm ab und blicke in seine jetzt dunkleren Augen. »Also, das ist es? Wir machen einfach so weiter?«

»Das machen wir … für jetzt zumindest.« Seine Augen leuchten dunkel. »Später werden wir weitersehen.«

Dann zieht er mich wieder an seine Schulter, legt seinen Arm um mich und hält mich dort, so als würde ich dort hingehören.

TEIL III

41

IN DEN NÄCHSTEN Tagen verfallen wir in eine eigenartige Häuslichkeit. Jeden Abend kocht Peter ein köstliches Abendessen für uns, und das Essen steht bereits auf dem Tisch, wenn ich hereinkomme. Wir essen zusammen, dann fickt er mich, oft zweimal oder noch häufiger, bevor wir einschlafen. Wenn ich morgens aufwache und er da ist, und das ist er häufig, macht er mir auch Frühstück.

Es ist so, als hätte ich mir einen Hausmann angeschafft, der allerdings in seiner Freizeit Morde im Black-Ops-Stil ausführt.

»Was machst du eigentlich den ganzen Tag?«, frage ich, als ich nach einem besonders anstrengenden Tag im Krankenhaus nach Hause komme und ein Gourmet-Essen aus Lammkoteletts und einem Russischen Salat mit Roter Beete vorfinde. »Du bleibst doch nicht nur hier und kochst, oder?«

»Nein, natürlich nicht.« Er wirft mir einen belustigten Blick zu. »Das, was wir tun, erfordert eine Menge logistische Planung, also arbeite ich mit meinen Männern daran und kümmere mich um die geschäftliche Seite.«

»Die geschäftliche Seite?«

»Kundenkontakte, Sicherung der Zahlungen, Investitionen und Verteilung von Geldern, Einkauf von Waffen und Zubehör, solche Dinge«, antwortet er, und ich höre fasziniert dabei zu, wie er mir einen Einblick in eine Welt gibt, in der irrsinnige Geldsummen die Hände wechseln und Mord eine Methode ist, um die Geschäfte zu erweitern.

»Wir arbeiten viel für Kartelle und andere mächtige Organisationen und Individuen«, erzählt er mir, als wir das Lamm essen. »Dieser Job in Mexiko war zum Beispiel ein Fall, in dem uns das Oberhaupt eines Kartells angeheuert hat, um seinen Rivalen zu beseitigen, damit er sich dessen Territorium sichern konnte. Andere unserer Kunden sind russische Oligarchen, verschiedenste Diktatoren, Mitglieder der nahöstlichen Königshäuser und einige wenige besser organisierte Mafiaorganisationen. Manchmal nehmen wir zwischen den Jobs auch kleinere Aufträge an und kümmern uns um lokale Gangster, aber dafür bekommen wir so gut wie kein Geld, also betrachten wir das als freiwillige Arbeit, durch die wir in Pausenzeiten in Übung bleiben.«

»Natürlich, freiwillige Arbeit.« Ich versuche gar nicht erst, meinen Sarkasmus zu verbergen. »So wie meine Arbeit in der Klinik.«

»Genau so«, stimmt mir Peter zu und grinst. Er weiß, dass er mich schockiert, und er tut es absichtlich. Es ist ein Spiel, das er manchmal spielt. Zuerst entsetzt er mich, und danach verführt er mich, bis ich mich nach seiner Berührung sehne, obwohl ich mich abgestoßen fühle – oder fühlen sollte.

Es gehört zu dem kranken Teil unserer Beziehung, dass fast nichts, was er sagt oder tut, längerfristige Auswirkungen auf mein Verlangen nach ihm hat. Meine Unfähigkeit, ihm zu widerstehen, ist wie ein blutendes Geschwür in meiner Brust, und ich kann es nicht heilen, egal, was ich tue. Jedes Mal, wenn ich das Essen esse, das er gekocht hat, jedes Mal, wenn ich in seinen Armen schlafe und durch seine Berührungen Lust verspüre, öffnet sich die Wunde erneut und hinterlässt mich krank vor Scham und verkrüppelt durch Selbsthass.

Ich lebe in einem häuslichen Glück mit dem Mörder meines Ehemannes, und es ist nicht einmal ansatzweise so furchtbar, wie es sein sollte.

Ein wenig liegt das daran, dass Peter mir nach unserem ersten Mal nicht mehr wehgetan hat. Zumindest nicht körperlich. Ich spüre die Gewalt in ihm, aber wenn er mich berührt, achtet er darauf, sich zu kontrollieren, die Dunkelheit davon abzuhalten, herauszuströmen. Es ist auch hilfreich, dass ich nicht offensichtlich gegen ihn ankämpfen kann. Dadurch, dass seine Drohung, mich zu entführen, wie ein Damoklesschwert über meinem Kopf hängt, habe ich keine andere Wahl, als mitzuspielen – das rede ich mir zumindest ein.

Das ist die einzige Möglichkeit, wie ich rechtfertigen kann, was gerade passiert, dass ich beginne, den Mann zu brauchen, den ich hasse.

Wenn er nur Sex von mir gewollt hätte, wäre es einfach gewesen, aber Peter scheint entschlossen zu sein, sich auch um mich zu kümmern. Ich bekomme romantische, selbstgekochte Abendessen, nächtliche Kuscheleinheiten, ich werde aufmerksam geduscht und manchmal sogar gekämmt. Wir gehen nicht aus – ich nehme an, dass er sich nicht in der Öffentlichkeit zeigen möchte – aber so wie er mich behandelt, könnte ich gut seine völlig verwöhnte Freundin sein.

»Warum tust du das so gerne?«, frage ich ihn, als er mir nach dem Duschen die Haare kämmt. »Ist das irgendein eigenartiger Tick von dir?«

Er wirft mir über den Spiegel einen belustigten Blick zu. »Vielleicht. Bei dir auf jeden Fall.«

»Nein, ernsthaft, was hast du davon? Du weißt, dass ich kein Kind bin, stimmt's?«

Peters Mund spannt sich an, und ich verstehe, dass ich unbeabsichtigt eine wunde Stelle getroffen habe. Wir sprechen nicht viel über seine Familie, aber sein Sohn war noch ein Kleinkind, als er getötet wurde. Könnte es sein, dass ich auf irgendeine kranke Art und

Weise ein Ersatz für seine ermordete Familie bin? Dass er sich auf mich fixiert hat, weil er sich um jemanden kümmern musste … irgendjemanden?

Könnte mein russischer Liebhaber so dringend Liebe brauchen, dass er sich mit einer perversen Version von ihr zufriedengeben würde?

Das ist ein verlockender Gedanke, besonders, da ich ab Ende der zweiten Woche feststelle, dass ich immer süchtiger nach dem Komfort und der Lust werde, die Peter mir bietet. Am Ende einer langen Schicht sehne ich mich körperlich nach den Nacken- und Fußmassagen, die er mir häufig gibt, und immer, wenn ich in die Garage fahre und die köstlichen Düfte aus der Küche rieche, muss ich aufpassen, dass mir nicht der Speichel aus dem Mund läuft.

Ich fange nicht nur an, mich an die Gegenwart meines Stalkers in meinem Leben zu gewöhnen, ich beginne sogar, sie zu genießen.

Oder zumindest teilweise. Ich bin immer noch weit davon entfernt, mich für die Bodyguards zu begeistern, die mir auf Schritt und Tritt folgen. Ich sehe sie fast nie, aber ich kann es spüren, wenn sie mich beobachten, und es beunruhigt und irritiert mich.

»Ich werde nicht weglaufen«, meine ich zu Peter, als wir eines Nachts im Bett liegen. »Du kannst deine Wachhunde zurückrufen.«

»Sie sind zu deinem Schutz da«, antwortet er, und ich weiß, dass er nicht die Absicht hat, in diesem Punkt Kompromisse einzugehen. Aus welchem Grund auch immer ist er davon überzeugt, dass ich mich in irgendeiner Gefahr befinde, etwas, vor dem gerade er mich beschützen muss.

»Wovor hast du Angst?«, frage ich, während ich die harten Wölbungen seiner Bauchmuskeln mit meinem Finger abfahre. »Denkst du, dass irgendein Irrer in mein Zuhause eindringen könnte? Mich vielleicht waterboarden und meinen Ehemann töten könnte?«

Ich blicke in sein Gesicht und sehe, dass er grinst, so als habe ich etwas Lustiges gesagt.

»Was?«, frage ich gereizt. »Denkst du, das ist ein Witz?«

Sein Gesichtsausdruck wird ernst. »Nein, Ptichka. Das denke ich überhaupt nicht. Und nur, damit du es weißt, es tut mir wirklich leid, dass ich dir damals wehgetan habe. Ich hätte einen anderen Weg finden sollen.«

»Okay. Einen anderen Weg, George umzubringen.«

Mir wird schlecht, und ich stehe auf, um ins Badezimmer zu flüchten, dem einzigen Ort, an dem mich mein Peiniger in Ruhe lässt. Manchmal vergesse ich, wie alles angefangen hat, da mein Gehirn praktischerweise gerne die entsetzlichen Anfänge unserer Beziehung überspringt.

Es ist so, als ob sich etwas in mir gern Peters Fantasie hingeben möchte, vorgeben möchte, alles sei genau so.

———

»Du hast mir nie erzählt, was zwischen dir und

George passiert ist«, meint Peter, als wir einen entspannten Sonntagsbrunch drei Wochen nach seiner Rückkehr haben. »Warum wart ihr nicht das perfekte Paar, für das euch alle gehalten haben? Du hast nicht gewusst, was er wirklich beruflich machte, also, was ist schiefgelaufen?«

Das Stück von dem pochierten Ei, an dem ich kaue, bleibt in meinem Hals stecken, und ich muss fast meinen ganzen Kaffee trinken, um es herunterzuspülen. »Warum denkst du, dass etwas schiefgelaufen ist?« Meine Stimme ist zu hoch, aber Peter hat mich völlig überrumpelt. Normalerweise vermeidet er, über meinen toten Ehemann zu sprechen – wahrscheinlich, um die Illusion einer normalen Beziehung zu verstärken.

»Weil du es mir gesagt hast«, antwortet er ruhig. »Während du unter dem Einfluss der Drogen standst, die ich dir verabreicht hatte.«

Ich starre ihn mit offenem Mund an, da ich es gar nicht glauben kann, dass er dieses Thema wieder angesprochen hat. Seit unserem Gespräch über die Bodyguards letzte Woche, und meinem darauffolgenden Weinen im Badezimmer, haben wir das Thema, was er mir angetan hat, vermieden, da keiner von uns in dieser offenen Wunde stochern wollte.

»Das …« Ich unterdrücke mein Entsetzen und sammele mich. »Das geht dich nichts an.«

»Hat er dich geschlagen?« Peter beugt sich nach vorn, und seine metallischen Augen verdunkeln sich. »Dir auf irgendeine Art und Weise wehgetan?«

»Was? Nein!«

»War er pädophil? Nekrophil?«

Ich hole tief Luft, um mich zu beruhigen. »Nein, natürlich nicht!«

»Hat er dich betrogen? Drogen genommen? Tiere geschändet?«

»Er hat angefangen zu trinken, okay?«, fauche ich gereizt. »Er hat angefangen zu trinken und nie wieder aufgehört.«

»Aha.« Peter lehnt sich zurück. »Also ein Alkoholiker. Interessant.«

»Ach ja?«, frage ich bitter. Ich nehme meinen Teller, gehe zum Mülleimer, um die Überreste meines Frühstücks wegzuwerfen, und stelle den Teller in den Geschirrspüler. »Dir gefällt es also, zu hören, dass der Mann, den ich geliebt habe und kannte, seit ich achtzehn war, der Mann, den ich *geheiratet* habe, sich ohne einen offensichtlichen Grund nach unserer Hochzeit verändert hat? Dass er innerhalb weniger Monate zu jemandem wurde, den ich kaum wiedererkannt habe?«

»Nein, Ptichka.« Er kommt hinter mich, und meine Atmung setzt aus, als er mich an sich zieht und mein Haar wegstreicht, um meinen Hals zu küssen. Sein Atem erwärmt meine Haut, als er sagt: »Es gefällt mir überhaupt nicht.«

»Ich habe es einfach nie verstanden.« Ich drehe mich in seinen Armen um, und meine alte Verletzung bricht wieder auf, als ich in Peters Augen schaue. »Alles lief so gut. Ich habe die Uni beendet, wir haben das Haus gekauft und geheiratet ... Er war wegen der

Arbeit viel auf Reisen, weshalb ihn meine Arbeitszeiten als Assistenzarzt nicht gestört haben, während ich kein Problem damit hatte, dass er so viel unterwegs war. Und dann …« Ich halte inne, da mir klar wird, dass ich mich Georges Mörder anvertraue.

»Und dann was?«, hakt er nach, und seine Finger legen sich um meine Hand. »Was ist dann passiert, Sara?«

Ich beiße mir auf die Unterlippe, aber die Versuchung, ihm alles zu sagen, ein für alle Mal die ganze Wahrheit loszuwerden, ist zu stark, um ihr nicht nachzugeben. Ich habe genug davon, Dinge vorzugeben, täglich die Maske der Perfektion zu tragen, die jeder zu sehen erwartet.

Ich ziehe meine Hand aus seiner und gehe zum Tisch, um mich hinzusetzen. Peter kommt zu mir, und nach einem Moment beginne ich zu reden.

»Alles hat sich einige Monate nach unserer Hochzeit verändert«, erzähle ich ihm ruhig. «Innerhalb weniger Wochen ist aus meinem warmherzigen, lebenslustigen Ehemann ein kalter, distanzierter Fremder geworden, jemand, der mich immer weggestoßen hat, egal, was ich getan habe. Er hat angefangen, diese eigenartigen Stimmungen zu haben, ist weniger für die Arbeit verreist und …«, ich atme tief durch, »hat angefangen zu trinken.«

Peter zieht seine Augenbrauen hoch. »Vorher hat er nie getrunken?«

»Nicht so. Er hat getrunken, wenn wir mit Freunden weggegangen sind, oder ein Glas Wein zum

Abendessen. Aber das war nichts Ungewöhnliches, nichts, was ich nicht selbst getan hätte. Aber das war anders. Wir reden hier über Trinken bis zur Bewusstlosigkeit, drei oder vier Nächte die Woche.«

»Das *ist* eine Menge. Hast du ihn jemals darauf angesprochen?«

Ein bitteres Lachen entweicht aus meinem Mund. »Ihn darauf angesprochen? Natürlich habe ich ihn darauf angesprochen. Die ersten Male, als es passierte, hat er mir erklärt, er habe Stress auf der Arbeit, danach war es ein Männerabend, dann musste er sich einfach nur entspannen und dann …« Ich beiße mir auf die Lippe. »Dann hat er angefangen, mich zu beschuldigen.«

»Dich?« Peters Stirn ist in Falten gelegt. »Wie konnte er dich beschuldigen?«

»Weil ich ihn damit nicht in Ruhe gelassen habe. Ich habe weitergebohrt, wollte, dass er eine Entziehungskur macht, zu den Anonymen Alkoholikern geht, mit jemandem spricht – irgendwem, der ihm helfen könnte. Ich habe ihm immer wieder dieselben Fragen gestellt und versucht zu verstehen, was passierte, warum er sich derart veränderte.« Mein Hals verengt sich, als ich mich daran erinnere, wie schmerzhaft das gewesen war. »Davor lief alles so gut, verstehst du? Meine Eltern, alle unsere Freunde, sie waren alle überglücklich über unsere Hochzeit, und wir hatten diese strahlende Zukunft vor uns. Es gab keinen Grund dafür, nichts, an das ich mich klammern konnte, um seine plötzliche Veränderung zu verstehen. Ich habe weiterhin nachgebohrt und ihn gedrängt, etwas zu ändern, und er hat weiterhin getrunken, immer mehr. Und dann habe ich …« Ich zwinge frische Luft durch meinen engen Hals. »Dann habe ich ihm gesagt, dass ich so nicht leben kann, dass er sich zwischen unserer Ehe und dem Trinken entscheiden muss.«

»Und er hat das Trinken gewählt.«

»Nein.« Ich schüttele meinen Kopf. »Am Anfang nicht. Wir gelangten in den klassischen Abhängigkeitskreislauf, in dem er mich bitten würde, zu bleiben, versprechen würde, sich zu bessern, und ich ihm glauben würde, bevor nach zwei Wochen wieder alles beim Alten war und die Dinge wieder so liefen wie zuvor. Und wenn ich seine Stimmungsschwankungen ansprach und ihn bat, zu einem Psychiater zu gehen, wurde er ausfallend und behauptete, dass *ich* der Grund für sein Trinken sei.«

Peters Stirnrunzeln vertieft sich. »Seine Stimmungsschwankungen?«

»Ich habe sie so genannt. Vielleicht waren es Depressionen oder eine andere psychische Erkrankung, aber da er sich geweigert hat, einen Psychiater aufzusuchen, haben wir nie eine Diagnose bekommen. Diese Stimmungsschwankungen haben kurz vor dem Trinken begonnen. Wir haben etwas zusammen gemacht, und plötzlich schien er völlig abwesend zu sein, so als sei er in eine andere Welt eingetaucht. Er war abgelenkt und eigenartig verängstigt, sogar nervös. So, als würde er Drogen nehmen, aber das hat er nicht. Zumindest sah es für mich nicht so aus. Er ist mit seinen Gedanken einfach irgendwo anders gewesen, und man konnte nicht mit ihm reden, wenn er sich in diesem Zustand befand. Es gab nichts, was man tun konnte, um ihn zu beruhigen oder ihn einfach wieder in das *Jetzt und Hier* zurückzuholen.

»Sara …« Peters Gesicht nimmt einen eigenartigen Ausdruck an. »Wann hat das alles begonnen, hast du gesagt?«

»Nur einige Monate, nachdem wir geheiratet haben«, antworte ich und runzele die Stirn. »Also etwa vor fünfeinhalb Jahren. Warum?« Und dann dämmert es mir. »Du meinst doch nicht, dass …«

»Dass die Veränderung deines Ehemanns etwas mit seiner Rolle in dem Massaker in Daryevo zu tun haben könnte? Warum nicht?« Peter beugt sich nach vorn und zieht seine Augen zusammen. »Denk doch mal darüber nach. Vor fünfeinhalb Jahren hat Cobakis Informationen weitergegeben, die dazu geführt haben, dass Dutzende unschuldiger Menschen, darunter Frauen und Kinder, abgeschlachtet wurden. Egal, ob das aus Ehrgeiz oder Gier oder schierer Dummheit geschah, er hat es einfach versaut, und zwar richtig. Du hast gesagt, dass er ein guter Mann war? Jemand mit einem Gewissen? Wie würde sich so ein Mann fühlen, wenn er der Grund dafür war, dass Unschuldige abgeschlachtet wurden? Wie hätte er mit dem ganzen Blut an seinen Händen leben können?«

Ich zucke zusammen, da die entsetzliche Wahrheit seiner Worte wie eine Kugel in mich einschlägt. Ich weiß nicht, wieso ich die Punkte nicht eher verbunden habe, aber jetzt, da Peter es ausgesprochen hat, ergibt es perfekten Sinn. Als ich das erste Mal von Georges Doppelleben erfahren habe, habe ich gedacht, dass vielleicht sein wahrer Job hinter seiner Veränderung stecken könnte, aber dann war ich so sehr mit Peters Eindringen in mein Leben beschäftigt gewesen – und damit, nicht über seine Enthüllungen zu grübeln –, dass ich den Gedanken nicht zu Ende gedacht habe.

Ich habe nicht in Betracht gezogen, dass die tragischen Ereignisse, die meinen Peiniger in mein Leben gebracht haben, dieselben sein könnten, die meine Ehe ruiniert haben … dass unsere Schicksale schon länger miteinander verbunden waren, als ich dachte.

Ich fühle mich, als würde mir gleich schlecht werden, also stehe ich mit zitternden Beinen auf. »Du hast recht.« Meine Stimme ist erstickt und rau. »Es müssen Schuldgefühle gewesen sein, die ihn zum Trinken gebracht haben. Die ganze Zeit habe ich mich gewundert, ob es etwas gewesen war, was ich gesagt hatte, ob ihn unsere Ehe irgendwie enttäuscht hatte, und dabei war es die ganze Zeit das.«

Peter nickt grimmig. »Außer wenn dein Mann während seiner Karriere mehrfach Massaker ausgelöst hat, ist das das Einzige, was Sinn ergibt.«

Ich atme abgehackt ein und drehe mich um, um zu dem Fenster zu gehen, das den Blick in den Garten hat. Die riesigen Eichen stehen wie Wächter da, aber ihre Zweige sind trotz der Hinweise auf den Frühling in der sich erwärmenden Luft noch kahl. Ich fühle mich gerade wie diese Eichen, nackt, in meiner ganzen Hässlichkeit bloßgestellt. Und gleichzeitig fühle ich mich leichter.

Wenigstens war es nicht meine Schuld, dass er getrunken hat.

»Der Unfall ist meinetwegen passiert«, sage ich ruhig, als Peter zu mir kommt und sich neben mich stellt. Er schaut mich nicht an, sein Profil ist hart und kompromisslos, und auch wenn ich weiß, dass er gerade seine eigenen Dämonen bekämpft, beruhigt mich seine Gegenwart auf einer fundamentalen Ebene.

Ich bin nicht allein, wenn ich ihn an meiner Seite habe.

»Wie?«, fragt er, ohne seinen Kopf zu drehen. »Im Bericht stand, dass er sich allein in dem Fahrzeug befunden hat.«

»Er hatte die Nacht davor getrunken. So viel getrunken, dass er sich im Laufe der Nacht mehrere Male übergeben musste.« Ich erschaudere, als ich mich an den Gestank nach Erbrochenem, nach Krankheit und an die ganzen Lügen und verlorenen Hoffnungen erinnere. Ich werde nur von einem seidenen Faden zusammengehalten, als ich fortfahre. »Am Morgen hatte ich genug. Ich hatte genug von seinen Entschuldigungen, von seinen endlosen Anschuldigungen und Versprechen, sich zu bessern. Mir wurde klar, dass George und ich überhaupt nichts Besonderes waren, wir waren einfach ein weiterer Alkoholiker und seine Ehefrau, die zu dumm war, es zu sehen. Das war keine schwere Zeit, die wir durchmachten. Unsere Ehe war einfach kaputt.«

Ich halte inne, da meine Stimme zu sehr zittert, um weiterzureden, als sich wieder eine große Hand um meine legt. Peters Gesichtsausdruck hat sich nicht verändert, sein Blick ist auf die Aussicht draußen gerichtet, aber die schweigende Geste der Unterstützung beruhigt mich, gibt mir den Mut, weiterzureden.

»Er hat noch geschlafen, als ich zur Arbeit gegangen bin, also habe ich mit ihm gesprochen, als ich zurückkam«, sage ich, so ruhig ich kann. »Ich habe ihm gesagt, dass er seine Sachen packen und gehen soll, und dass ich am nächsten Tag die Scheidung einreichen würde. Wir sind in einen riesigen Streit geraten und haben beide verletzende Dinge gesagt, und ich …« Ich schlucke den Knoten in meinem Hals herunter. »Ich habe ihn aus dem Haus geschmissen.«

Peter wirft mir einen leicht überraschten Blick zu. »Wie konntest du ihn rausschmeißen? Er war nicht der größte Mann, den ich jemals gesehen habe, aber er muss mindestens fünfundzwanzig Kilo mehr als du gewogen haben.«

Ich blinzele, da mich diese eigenartige Frage aus dem Konzept bringt. »Ich habe seine Autoschlüssel und seine Tasche in die Garage geschmissen und ihn ange-schrien, er solle verschwinden.«

»Ich verstehe.« Zu meinem Entsetzen formt sich ein leichtes Lächeln auf Peters Mundwinkeln. »Und du denkst, es sei deine Schuld, dass er gefahren ist und einen Unfall gebaut hat?«

»Es *ist* meine Schuld. Die Polizei hat gesagt, dass er doppelt so viel Alkohol wie erlaubt im Blut hatte. Er hatte getrunken, und ich habe ihn gezwungen, zu fahren. Ich habe ihn rausgeschmissen und ...«

Du hast seine *Schlüssel* rausgeworfen, nicht ihn«, sagt Peter, dessen Lächeln verschwindet, als seine Finger meine Hand fester umfassen. »Er war ein erwachsener Mann, der größer und stärker war als du. Hätte er im Haus bleiben wollen, hätte er das tun können. Außerdem, wusstest du überhaupt, dass er getrunken hatte, als du ihm gesagt hast, dass er verschwinden soll?«

Ich runzele die Stirn. »Nein, natürlich nicht. Ich war gerade erst von der Arbeit gekommen, und er sah nicht betrunken aus, aber ...«

»Kein Aber.« Peters Stimme ist genauso hart wie sein Blick. »Du hast das getan, was du tun musstest. Alkoholiker können auch mit viel Alkohol in ihrem Körper noch funktionstüchtig aussehen. Ich kann das beurteilen, ich habe viele von ihnen in Russland gesehen. Du warst nicht dafür verantwortlich, seinen Alkohol zu testen, bevor du ihn packen geschickt hast. Wenn er zu betrunken zum Autofahren war, hätte er sich nicht hinters Steuer setzen sollen. Er hätte ein Taxi rufen oder dich bitten können, ihn zu einem Hotel zu fahren. Zur Hölle, er hätte sogar erst in der Garage seinen Rausch ausschlafen und *danach* fahren können.«

»Ich ...« Jetzt bin ich diejenige, die aus dem Fenster starrt. »Das weiß ich.«

»Tust du das?« Peter lässt meine Hand los, ergreift mein Kinn und zwingt mich dazu, ihm in die Augen zu schauen. »Irgendwie bezweifle ich das, Ptichka. Hast du irgendjemandem erzählt, was wirklich passiert ist?«

Mein Magen zieht sich zusammen, und ein unangenehmer, starker Schmerz breitet sich in meinem Bauch aus. »Nicht genau. Ich meine, die Polizisten wussten, dass er getrunken hatte, aber …«

»Aber sie wussten nicht, dass er das immer tat, stimmt's?«, rät Peter und lässt seine Hand sinken. »Niemand außer dir wusste das.«

Ich schaue weg und spüre das vertraute Brennen vor Scham. Ich weiß, dass das der klassische Fehler der Ehefrauen ist, aber ich konnte es einfach nicht über mich bringen, unsere schmutzige Wäsche öffentlich zu waschen, zuzugeben, dass diese Ehe, die alle bewunderten, eigentlich innerlich verfault war. Zuerst war es eine Mischung aus Stolz und Verleugnung. Ich hätte eine clevere junge Ärztin mit einer strahlenden Zukunft sein sollen. Wie hatte ich einen solchen Fehler machen können? Gab es Warnsignale, die ich übersehen hatte? Und wenn nicht, wie konnte das mit dem wundervollen Mann geschehen, den ich geheiratet hatte, dem goldenen Jungen, der so vielversprechend war? Mit Sicherheit war es nur eine vorübergehende Situation, eine Regenwolke in einem sonst perfekten Leben. Und als ich endlich verstanden hatte, dass das Trinken nicht verschwinden würde, gab es einen anderen Grund zu schweigen.

»Mein Vater hatte etwa ein Jahr nach meiner Hochzeit einen Herzinfarkt«, sage ich und schaue auf die kahlen Zweige, die sich im Wind wiegen. »Einen schlimmen. Er ist fast gestorben. Nach einem dreifachen Bypass haben ihm die Ärzte geraten, sich so wenig Stress wie möglich auszusetzen.«

»Ah. Und zu erfahren, dass der Ehemann der geliebten Tochter sich in einen wütenden Alkoholiker verwandelt hat, wäre zu viel Stress gewesen.«

»Ja.« Ich hätte es dabei belassen können, Peter denken lassen können, dass ich einfach eine gute Tochter war, aber durch einen eigenartigen Impuls platze ich heraus: »Das war allerdings nicht der ganze Grund. Ich hatte Angst vor dem, was die Leute sagen würden, und den Urteilen, die sie fällen würden. George war gut darin, seine Sucht vor allen zu verstecken – rückblickend nehme ich an, dass seine Schauspielkünste einen Hinweis auf diese ganze Spionagesache gegeben haben sollten – und ich wurde auch ein Profi darin, heile Welt zu spielen. Unsere Jobs halfen uns ebenfalls dabei. Ich konnte immer ›Rufbereitschaft‹ haben, wenn wir eine Verabredung in letzter Minute absagen mussten, und George konnte mit einem dringenden Bericht beschäftigt sein, wenn er es nicht schaffte, rechtzeitig nüchtern zu werden.«

Peter sagt einige Augenblicke lang nichts, und ich frage mich, ob er mich für meine Feigheit verurteilt, dafür, dass ich keine Hilfe gesucht habe, bevor es zu spät war. Das ist die andere Sache, die mich beschäftigt: die Möglichkeit, dass ich etwas hätte tun können, wäre ich offener mit unseren Problemen umgegangen. Vielleicht hätte ich George in ein Entzugsprogramm stecken oder ihm psychologische Hilfe zukommen lassen können, und der tragische Unfall wäre verhindert worden.

Natürlich hätte der Mann, der neben mir steht, ihn sowieso getötet, also ist es auch egal.

Da ich mit diesem Gedanken gerade nicht umgehen kann, unterdrücke ich ihn genau in dem Moment, in dem Peter fragt: »Was war mit seiner Arbeit? Wie konnte er so weiterhin funktionieren? Außer natürlich … du hast gesagt, dass er keine Auslandsaufträge mehr angenommen hat?«

»Ja, genau.« Ich hole tief Luft, um meinen aufgebrachten Magen zu beruhigen, und konzentriere mich darauf, das hypnotische Schwingen der Äste zu beobachten. »Er ist nach unserer Hochzeit einige Male verreist, aber normalerweise untersuchte er lokale Geschichten – so wie die über die Mafia, die in Chicago die Polizei und Regierungsbeamte auf der Gehaltsliste stehen hatte.«

»Diejenige, von der sie dir erzählt haben, dass sie der Grund für seinen Personenschutz war.«

Ich nicke und bin nicht überrascht, dass er das weiß. Er hatte wahrscheinlich während meines Gesprächs mit Agent Ryson irgendeine Art Parabolmikrofon auf mich gerichtet. Nach dem, was ich in den letzten Wochen über meinen Stalker erfahren habe, ist das durchaus möglich.

Die Millionen, die er bei seinen Aufträgen verdient, verschaffen ihm Zugang zu jeder erdenklichen Ausstattung.

»Dann muss er damals aufgehört haben, für den

CIA zu arbeiten«, meint Peter, und als ich einen Blick auf ihn werfe, sehe ich, dass er ebenfalls die Äste betrachtet. »Entweder das – oder sie haben ihn gefeuert, weil er mit den Auswirkungen seines Fehlers nicht zurechtkam. Das ist das Einzige, was das Fehlen von Auslandsaufträgen erklären würde.«

»Stimmt.« Mein Kopf pocht quälend vor Anspannung, und mein Bauch krampft und zieht immer noch so, als würden meine Eingeweide immer weiter zusammengedreht werden. Mein unterer Rücken schmerzt ebenfalls, was mich darauf bringt, schnell etwas im Kopf auszurechnen.

Natürlich, ich bin kurz davor, meine Tage zu bekommen.

Wir stehen noch einige Minuten länger am Fenster und beobachten die Bäume draußen, bevor ich zum Medizinschrank gehe, zwei Ibuprofen herausnehme und sie mit einem Glas Wasser herunterspüle.

»Was ist los?«, fragt Peter, der mir mit besorgt gerunzelter Stirn gefolgt ist. »Geht es dir nicht gut?«

»Es ist nichts«, antworte ich, da ich nicht ins Detail gehen möchte. Dann wird mir klar, dass er es bald sowieso herausfinden wird, und füge hinzu: »Frauensachen, du weißt schon.«

»Ah.« Im Gegensatz zu den meisten Männern sieht er überhaupt nicht so aus, als sei ihm diese Information unangenehm. »Hast du normalerweise starke Schmerzen?«

»Leider ja.« Während ich spreche, spüre ich, dass die Krämpfe schlimmer werden, und ich danke den Göttern der Arbeitseinsatzplanung, dass ich heute keine Rufbereitschaft habe. Ich wollte heute Nachmittag in die Klinik gehen, aber ich überlege es mir anders und entscheide mich dafür, mich mit einem Heizkissen in meinem Bett zu verkriechen.

»Warum nimmst du nicht die Pille?«, fragt Peter und folgt mir, als ich nach oben gehe. »Ich habe sie dich nicht nehmen sehen, aber ich glaube, dass sie normalerweise bei Menstruationsschmerzen helfen.«

»Ach, du bist ein Experte für Frauenheilkunde?«

Peter lässt sich von meinem Sarkasmus nicht reizen. »Überhaupt nicht, aber ich habe für Tamila ein Rezept für die Pille besorgt, weil sie schlimme Krämpfe hatte. Ich nehme an, dass du einen Grund dafür hast, das nicht zu tun?«

Ich seufze und betrete das Schlafzimmer. »Den habe ich. Ich bin eine dieser seltenen Frauen, die keine hormonellen Verhütungsmittel vertragen. Ich bekomme selbst bei der niedrigsten Dosierung Migräne und Übelkeit. Ich bekomme sogar von Hormonspiralen Kopfschmerzen, also habe ich die Wahl, ob ich mich einige Tage pro Monat schlecht fühlen möchte oder die ganze Zeit.«

»Ich verstehe.« Peter lehnt sich gegen den Türrahmen, während ich beginne, mich auszuziehen. Ich kann die Hitze in seinen Augen sehen, als er mich dabei beobachtet, wie ich mich aus meiner Unterwäsche schäle, und ich hoffe, dass er nicht auf falsche Gedanken kommt und zu mir ins Bett kommen möchte. Er lässt sich selten eine Gelegenheit entgehen, mich zu ficken.

Ich ignoriere sein Starren, nehme das Heizkissen aus der Nachttischschublade, lege es unter meine Bettdecke und rolle mich in die Embryostellung, während ich warte, dass das Ibuprofen wirkt.

Ich höre leise Schritte, und danach bewegt sich das Bett neben mir.

Nein, Nein, Nein. Geh weg. Bloß keinen Sex. Ich kneife meine Augen zusammen und hoffe, dass mein Peiniger diesen Hinweis versteht, aber im nächsten Augenblick wird die Decke weggezogen, und eine raue männliche Hand streicht über meinen nackten Rücken.

»Kann ich dir etwas bringen?« Seine tiefe Stimme mit dem leichten Akzent ist leise und beruhigend. »Vielleicht Toast oder einen Tee?«

Überrascht rolle ich mich auf den Rücken, während ich das Heizkissen auf meinen Unterleib drücke. »Ähm, nein danke. Das geht schon vorbei.«

»Bist du sicher?« Er streicht die Haare aus meinem Gesicht. »Was hältst du von einer Bauchmassage?«

Ich blinzele. »Ähm …«

»Hier.« Er schiebt sanft die Wärmedecke von mir weg und legt seine warme Handfläche auf meinen Unterleib. »Versuchen wir es einmal damit.« Er bewegt seine Hand mit einem leichten Druck in einer kreisförmigen Bewegung, und nach einigen Minuten lassen das Ziehen und die Krämpfe nach, da die Hitze seiner Haut und die massierenden Bewegungen das Schlimmste der schmerzhaften Anspannung verjagen.

»Besser?«, fragt er leise, als ich meine Augen in glückseliger Erleichterung schließe, und ich nicke, während meine Gedanken abschweifen, als mich wohlige Müdigkeit überkommt.

»Das ist wirklich schön, danke«, murmele ich und schlafe ein, während er mich weiterhin beruhigend massiert.

42

*P*eter

ICH BETRACHTE Sara einige Minuten lang, während sie schläft, und stehe dann leise auf, um das Schlafzimmer zu verlassen. Ich könnte stundenlang an ihrer Seite sitzen und sie einfach nur anschauen, aber um zwölf habe ich ein Telefonat mit einem potentiellen Kunden und muss davor noch einige Dinge mit Anton besprechen.

Ich benötige einige Minuten, um die Küche aufzuräumen, und dann bin ich auch schon auf dem Weg. Ich verlasse das Haus durch die Hintertür und nehme die Abkürzung über den Garten des Nachbarn. Ilyas gepanzerter Geländewagen parkt zwei Straßen weiter, und während ich dorthin gehe, achte ich aufmerksam auf alles um mich herum: das entfernte Bellen eines kleinen Hundes, ein Eichhörnchen, das in Windeseile die Straße überquert, die Marke der Schuhe eines Joggers, der gerade um die Ecke verschwindet ... Diese Überachtsamkeit ist genauso ein Teil von mir wie meine Reflexe in Lichtgeschwindigkeit, und beide haben mir unzählige Male das Leben gerettet.

Ilya lässt den Wagen an, als ich mich nähere, und sobald ich einsteige, fährt er los, folgt der Straße in diesem Vorort genau 4,8 km/h zu schnell.

Er glaubt daran, dass man sich wie ein typischer Zivilist verhalten muss, um nicht aufzufallen, bis hin zu kleinen Verkehrsüberschreitungen.

»Irgendwelche Probleme?«, frage ich ihn auf Russisch, und er schüttelt seinen rasierten Kopf.

»Alles ruhig, so wie immer.«

Im Gegensatz zu seinem Bruder und Anton hört sich Ilya nicht enttäuscht an, als er das sagt. Ich denke, dass er unseren kleinen Aufenthalt in der Vorstadt genießt, auch wenn er es nie zugeben würde. Von den vier Personen, die den Kern unseres Teams bilden, sieht Ilya wegen seiner Totenkopftätowierungen und seinem starken Kiefer durch seinen jugendlichen Flirt mit den Steroiden am ehesten wie der typische Kriminelle aus. Sein Zwillingsbruder Yan könnte andererseits dank seiner penibel gründlich gebügelten Kleidung und dem konservativen Schnitt seines braunen Haars für einen Professor oder einen Banker gehalten werden. Was die Persönlichkeit betrifft, ist es allerdings Yan, der einen Lebensstil voller Adrenalin-hochs braucht, während Ilya sich lieber Strategien und der Arbeit im Hintergrund widmet.

Ich nehme an, dass Ilya, wenn er nicht seinem Bruder in die Armee gefolgt wäre, ein Programmierer oder Steuerberater geworden wäre.

»Gibt es etwas Neues von den Amerikanern?«, frage ich, als wir an einer Ampel halten. Da meine Männer ziemlich beschäftigt sind, benutze ich Ortsan-sässige als zusätzliche Sicherheitsmaßnahmen. Ihr Job ist es, Sara im Auge zu behalten, wenn sie nicht bei mir ist, und uns zu alarmieren, falls es in der Nachbarschaft ungewöhnliche Aktivitäten gibt.

»Nein. Dein Mädchen weicht kaum von ihrer Routine ab, aber ich bin mir sicher, dass du das weißt.«

Ich nicke und fahre mit den Augen die sauber geschnittenen Rasen in den Vorgärten ab, an denen wir auf dem Weg zu unserem geheimen Unterschlupf vorbeifahren. Irgendetwas stört mich, aber ich kann nicht genau sagen, was. Vielleicht ist es einfach zu still im Moment, ohne bevorstehende Jobs und kaum einem Fortschritt darin, den General aus North Caro-lina zu finden, der der Letzte auf meiner Liste ist. Dieser paranoide Ficker ist mit seiner ganzen Familie verschwunden und hat seine Spuren so gut verwischt, dass selbst die Hacker, die ich auf ihn angesetzt habe, Schwierigkeiten haben, ihn zu finden.

Wahrscheinlich werde ich irgendwann persönlich nach North Carolina gehen müssen, um zu sehen, was ich dort herausfinden kann.

»Sag ihnen, dass ich die nächsten Berichte selbst auswerten möchte«, meine ich zu Ilya, als wir in die Einfahrt zu unserer geheimen Unterkunft einbiegen. »Und sag ihnen, dass sie ihren Radius um zwanzig Straßen erhöhen sollen, nicht zehn. Sollte jemand in Saras Nachbarschaft oder in der Nähe ihres Krankenhauses nur niesen, will ich es wissen.«

»Verstanden«, erwidert Ilya, und ich springe aus dem Auto.

Vielleicht bin ich paranoid, aber ich werde es nicht zulassen, dass mir jemand das kaputtmacht, was ich mit Sara habe.

Ich brauche sie zu sehr, um das Risiko einzugehen, sie zu verlieren.

———

ALS ICH NACH HAUSE KOMME, liegt sie mit einem Heizkissen und einem Tablet auf dem Sofa, ihre schlanken Glieder sind anmutig an ihren Körper gezogen und ihre braunen Haare auf ihrem Kopf zu einem unordentlichen Knoten gebunden. Selbst in Jogginghose und einem riesigen Sweatshirt sieht mein Vögelchen immer noch so aus, als könne sie in einem Schwarzweißfilm mitspielen, da ihre zarten Gesichtszüge durch die losen, lockeren Haarsträhnen, die sich um ihr herzförmiges Gesicht legen, betont werden.

Ich kann kaum atmen, als sie aufschaut und mit ihren braunen Augen mein Gesicht betrachtet. Jedes Mal, wenn ich sie sehe, will ich sie, und mein

Verlangen nach ihr ist ein quälender Hunger in meiner Brust. In den letzten drei Wochen habe ich sie so oft gehabt, dass sich mein Verlangen nach ihr gelegt haben sollte, aber es ist nur stärker geworden, hat sich unerträglich intensiviert.

Ich will sie und ich will das – die ruhige Freude, ihr Leben zu teilen, zu wissen, dass ich sie mitten in der Nacht umarmen kann und sie am nächsten Morgen mir gegenüber am Küchentisch sitzen sehen kann. Ich möchte mich um sie kümmern, wenn sie krank ist, und mich in ihrem Lächeln sonnen, wenn es ihr gutgeht. Und manchmal, wenn meine Trauer aufsteigt, möchte ich ihr auch wehtun – ein Drang, den ich mit meiner ganzen Kraft unterdrücke.

Sie gehört mir, und ich werde sie beschützen.

Auch vor mir selbst.

»Wie fühlst du dich?«, frage ich und gehe zum Sofa. Ich hatte keine Gelegenheit, sie heute Morgen zu ficken, und ich bin schon allein von ihrem Anblick halb hart. Allerdings muss sich meine Lust mit der Rückbank zufriedengeben, da mein Bedürfnis, sicherzugehen, dass sie gesund ist und es ihr gutgeht, überwiegt.

Sara wird nicht von ihren Menstruationsbeschwerden sterben, aber ich möchte nicht, dass sie Schmerzen hat.

»Besser, danke«, antwortet sie und legt ihr Tablet neben sich. Es sieht so aus, als habe sie sich darauf Musikvideos angeschaut – etwas, was ich sie schon häufiger tun sehen habe, wenn sie sich entspannen wollte.

»Mach ruhig weiter«, sage ich und nicke Richtung Tablet. »Ich muss Abendessen machen, also hör meinetwegen nicht damit auf.«

Sie macht keine Anstalten, ihr Tablet wieder in die Hand zu nehmen, sondern legt ihren Kopf zur Seite und betrachtet mich, als ich zur Spüle gehe, um meine Hände zu waschen und die Zutaten für die einfache Mahlzeit herauszunehmen, die ich für heute Abend vorbereitet habe: die Hühnchenbrust, die ich letzte Nacht eingelegt habe, und frisches Gemüse für einen Salat.

»Weißt du eigentlich, dass du nie meine Frage beantwortet hast?«, meint sie nach einer Minute. »Wieso tust du das alles wirklich? Was ist dein Vorteil aus dieser ganzen Häuslichkeit? Hat ein Mann wie du nichts Besseres zu tun? Ich weiß nicht … zum Beispiel sich von einem Gebäude abzuseilen oder etwas in die Luft zu jagen?«

Ich seufze. Sie ist einmal wieder bei dem Thema. Meine ehrgeizige junge Ärztin kann nicht verstehen, dass ich das einfach gerne mache – für sie und für mich selbst. Ich kann die Zeit nicht zurückdrehen, um mehr Zeit mit Pasha und Tamila zu verbringen, kann meinem jüngeren Ich nicht den Rat geben, die Arbeit für die Dinge, die wirklich wichtig sind, zurückzuschrauben, weil alles in einem Augenblick verschwinden könnte. Ich kann mich nur auf meine Gegenwart konzentrieren, und meine Gegenwart ist Sara.

»Meine Frau hat mir beigebracht, einfache Gerichte

zu kochen«, erwidere ich, während ich die Hähnchenbrust in die Pfanne lege, bevor ich beginne, den Salat zu machen. »In ihrer Kultur kochten eigentlich immer die Frauen, aber sie war nicht sehr traditionell. Sie wollte sicherstellen, dass ich mich um unseren Sohn kümmern könnte, sollte ihr etwas zustoßen, und um ihr einen Gefallen zu tun, habe ich zugestimmt, einige Rezepte zu lernen – und dabei herausgefunden, dass ich gerne koche.« Ein vertrauter Schmerz zieht bei diesen Erinnerungen meine Brust zusammen, aber ich schiebe die Trauer beiseite und konzentriere mich auf die mitfühlende Neugier in den warmen, braunen Augen, die mich vom Sofa aus betrachten.

Manchmal bin ich mir sicher, dass Sara mich nicht hasst.

Zumindest nicht die ganze Zeit.

»Also hast du damit begonnen, für deine Frau zu kochen?«, fragt sie, als ich einige Augenblicke lang schweige, und ich nicke, während ich das geschnittene Gemüse vom Brett in die Schüssel gebe.

»Das habe ich, aber ich habe nur einige Grundlagen gelernt, bis sie gestorben ist«, sage ich, und auch wenn ich es nicht möchte, ist meine Stimme durch den unterdrückten Schmerz ganz rau und spröde. »Zwei Monate nach dem Massaker bin ich in Moskau an einer Kochschule vorbeigegangen und spontan eingetreten, um einen Kochkurs zu besuchen. Ich weiß nicht, warum ich das getan habe, aber als ich fertig war, und mein Borscht auf dem Herd köchelte, habe ich mich ein kleines bisschen besser gefühlt. Es war etwas, auf was ich mich konzentrieren konnte, etwas Greifbares und Reales.«

Etwas, was die kochende Wut in mir abkühlte und es mir ermöglichte, Strategien zu entwickeln und meine Rache wie ein Rezept zu planen, Schritt für Schritt und mit den Zutaten, die ich benötigen würde.

Diesen letzten Teil sage ich nicht laut, weil Saras Gesicht immer weicher wird. Ich nehme an, dass mein kleines Hobby mich in ihren Augen menschlicher macht. Ich mag das, also erzähle ich ihr nicht, dass ich in Moskau war, um meinen ehemaligen Vorgesetzten, Ivan Polonsky, dafür zu töten, dass er an der Vertuschung des Massakers beteiligt war – oder dass ich eine Stunde nach Ende des Kurses seine Kehle aufgeschlitzt habe.

Sein Blut hatte an jenem Tag sehr große Ähnlichkeit mit Borscht.

»Ich nehme an, dass man nie weiß, was man hat, bis man es verliert«, meint Sara nachdenklich, während sie das Heizkissen an sich drückt, und ihr wehmütiger Ton lässt meine Eifersucht aufflackern.

Ich hoffe, dass sie nicht an ihren Ehemann denkt, weil er meiner Meinung nach kein großer Verlust ist.

Dieser *sookin syn* hat bekommen, was er verdient hatte.

Als das Essen fertig ist, kommt Sara zu mir an den Tisch, und während des Essens rede ich von einigen der Städte, in denen ich Kochstunden genommen habe:

Istanbul, Johannesburg, Berlin, Paris, Genf … Nachdem ich ihr die verschiedenen Küchen beschrieben habe, erzähle ich einige Anekdoten über temperamentvolle Küchenchefs, und ein echtes Lächeln erhellt ihr Gesicht, während sie mir zuhört. Um ihr die Laune nicht zu verderben, lasse ich alle dunklen Teile aus – wie die Tatsache, dass Interpol mich in Paris aufgespürt hatte und ich meinen Weg aus dem Gebäude, in dem sich die Kochschule befand, freischießen musste, oder dass ich in Berlin vor der Kochstunde das Auto eines Opfers in die Luft gejagt habe – und wir beenden unsere Mahlzeit in einer harmonischen Atmosphäre, und Sara hilft mir beim Tischabräumen, bis ich sie wegschicke.

»Ruhe dich aus«, sage ich ihr. »Geh dich duschen und dann ins Bett. Ich komme gleich nach.«

Ihr Gesichtsausdruck wird vorsichtig. »Okay, aber ich habe begonnen zu bluten.«

»Na und? Meinst du, dass mich ein wenig Blut abschrecken kann?« Ich grinse, als ich ihren Gesichtsausdruck sehe. »Ich mache nur einen Scherz. Ich weiß, dass du dich nicht gut fühlst. Ich werde dich einfach nur im Arm halten, wie in der guten alten Zeit.«

»Aha, verstehe.« Sie antwortet mit einem Lächeln, das sich echt und warm auf ihrem Gesicht ausbreitet. »In diesem Fall sehe ich dich gleich oben.«

Sie eilt aus der Küche, und ich stehe einfach nur da, weil ich nicht atmen kann. Ich fühle mich, als hätte ich gerade ein Messer in den Bauch bekommen.

Scheiße, dieses Lächeln … Dieses Lächeln war alles, was ich brauche.

Zum ersten Mal verstehe ich, warum ich mich in ihrer Nähe so fühle.

Zum ersten Mal verstehe ich, wie sehr ich sie liebe.

# 43

S*ara*

Sonntagmorgen fühle ich mich besser und beschließe, meine Eltern zu besuchen. Ich habe sie seit Peters Rückkehr nur einmal gesehen, da ich zu sehr mit meinem Stalker beschäftigt war und Angst hatte, sie in Gefahr zu bringen. Allerdings bin ich immer mehr davon überzeugt, dass Peter ihnen nicht absichtlich wehtun würde. Er schätzt Familie zu sehr, um mir das anzutun.

Solange ich seinen Forderungen nachgebe, sollten meine Eltern sich in Sicherheit befinden.

Meine Mutter ist außer sich vor Freude, als ich sie anrufe, und wir planen, mittags Sushi essen zu gehen. Als ich Peter Bescheid gebe, nickt er abwesend und tippt etwas in sein Telefon.

»Was schreibst du?«, frage ich vorsichtig.

»Ich gebe nur meinen Männern Bescheid, dass ich heute doch vorbeikomme«, antwortet er und legt sein Telefon weg. »Warum? Wolltest du mich dabeihaben?« Seine grauen Augen leuchten, als er mich anblickt.

Ich lache. »Nein, ich denke, der Teil, in dem das FBI das Restaurant stürmt, um einen der meistgesuchten Verbrecher festzunehmen, könnte ein Appetitzügler sein.«

Peter lacht nicht, und ich verstehe, dass er es ernst gemeint hat.

»Du … du würdest dich mit mir in der Öffentlichkeit zeigen?«

»Warum nicht?« Er zieht seine Augenbraue kühl in die Höhe. »Ich habe mich ja auch bei Starbucks mit dir getroffen, oder etwa nicht?«

»Ja schon, aber das war, na ja, davor. Ich meine – ist auch egal.« Ich hole tief Luft. »Ich nehme also an, dass du keine Angst hast, in der Öffentlichkeit gesehen zu werden?«

»Ich würde nicht gerade vor dem örtlichen FBI-Gebäude hin und her spazieren, aber ich kann ab und an zu einem Mittag- oder Abendessen gehen, wenn ich den Ort vorher ansehen und sichergehen kann, dass es dort keine Überwachungskameras gibt.«

»Oh.« Ich kaue die Innenseite meiner Lippe, als ich meine Tasche nehme. »Vielleicht können wir ja nächste Woche mal abendessen gehen …«

»Aber nicht heute«, sagt er, und ich nicke, da ich

nicht weiß, was ich sonst tun soll. Ich werde auf keinen Fall Georges Mörder meinen Eltern vorstellen.

Es ist schlimm genug, dass ich ihm gerade angeboten habe, mit ihm Abendessen zu gehen.

»Alles klar. Wir sehen uns, wenn du zurückkommst«, sagt er, und ich gehe, bevor er noch etwas anderes vorschlagen kann – wie gemeinsame Tattoos oder eine Hochzeit am Strand.

Das ist völlig verrückt, und der verrückteste Teil ist, dass es beginnt, sich normal anzufühlen.

Ich gewöhne mich daran, Peter in meinem Leben zu haben.

———

BEIM MITTAGESSEN ERZÄHLE ich meinen Eltern, dass ich mich dazu entschieden habe, das Haus nicht zu verkaufen. Ich habe ihnen bereits vor zwei Wochen gesagt, dass das Angebot der Rechtsanwälte nicht hoch genug war, also sind sie nicht besonders überrascht von meiner Entscheidung. Eigentlich freuen sie sich sogar, da das Haus nur zwanzig Minuten von ihnen entfernt liegt, während es von meinem neuen Apartment mindestens fünfundvierzig Minuten gewesen wären.

»Es ist ein schönes Haus«, meint mein Vater, während er sich etwas Sojasauce eingießt. »Ich denke, das ganze Apartment-Ding war eine Überreaktion. Du bist jung, aber die Zeit vergeht schnell, und irgendwann wirst du vielleicht darüber nachdenken wollen, eine Familie zu gründen. Du weißt schon, ausgehen und einen Mann treffen …«

»Hör auf damit, Chuck«, ermahnt ihn meine Mutter. »Sara hat noch genug Zeit.« Sie dreht sich zu mir um und sagt mit sanfterer Stimme: »Lass dir so viel Zeit, wie du brauchst, mein Liebling. Lass dich von deinem Vater zu nichts drängen. Wir *sind* froh, dass du das Haus behältst, aber das bedeutet nicht, dass wir erwarten, in nächster Zeit Großeltern zu werden«

»Mama, bitte.« Es fällt mir schwer, nicht mit den Augen zu rollen, so als sei ich noch in der Highschool. Meine Eltern spielen guter Polizist, böser Polizist mit mir, wahrscheinlich, um mir den Gedanken »auszugehen und einen netten Mann zu treffen« in den Kopf zu setzen. »Wenn ich vorhaben sollte, Enkelkinder zu produzieren, werden du und Papa die Ersten sein, die davon erfahren, versprochen.«

Meine Mutter schenkt meinem Vater ein glückliches Lächeln. »Siehst du? Sie wird ausgehen, sobald sie bereit dazu ist.«

»Genau.« Ich beschäftige mich damit, meine Essstäbchen zu trennen. »Sobald ich bereit bin.« Was, so wie mein Leben gerade verläuft, niemals sein könnte. Oder zumindest nicht, bis Peter gelangweilt von mir ist – wonach es allerdings immer weniger aussieht. Wenn überhaupt, habe ich den Eindruck, dass er immer fixierter auf mich wird, dass seine grauen Augen mich mit einem besonderen Leuchten anschauen, das einen warmen Schauer über meinen Rücken jagt.

Bevor ich den Grund dafür analysieren kann, bringt der Kellner unser Sushiboot, und meine Eltern bewundern mit vielen *Ahs* und *Ohs* den kunstvoll angerichteten Fisch und verschonen mich mit weiteren ihrer nicht wirklich subtilen Überredungsversuche. Ich wünschte, ich könnte ihnen die Wahrheit sagen, aber es gibt keine Möglichkeit, ihnen von Peter zu erzählen, ohne ihnen wahnsinnige Angst zu machen.

Ich bin mir auch immer noch nicht sicher, wie ich überhaupt mit dieser ganzen Sache zurechtkomme.

———

AM ENDE der Woche ist meine Menstruation abgeklungen, und die darauffolgende Woche bin ich wieder mit vollem Einsatz dabei. Neben meinen normalen Schichten habe ich zwei Rufbereitschaften am Anfang der Woche und eine dreistündige Schicht in der Klinik. Ich arbeite so viel, dass ich kaum zu Hause bin, aber Peter beschwert sich nicht, auch wenn ich spüren kann, dass er mehr als unglücklich mit dieser Situation ist. Trotz meiner Periode hatten wir in den letzten Tagen Sex – er hat nicht über seine Unempfindlichkeit gelogen –, und jedes Mal war er ungewöhnlich hungrig, seine Berührungen hemmungslos und grenzwertig grob.

Es fühlt sich an, als habe er Angst, dass er mich verlieren könnte, so als höre er irgendeine Uhr ticken.

Freitag verbringe ich den Großteil des Tages in meinem Behandlungszimmer, aber gerade als ich nach

Hause gehen will, bekomme ich eine dringende Nachricht, dass bei einer meiner Patientinnen die Wehen eingesetzt haben. Ich unterdrücke ein müdes Seufzen und eile in die Umkleide, um mich für die Geburt fertigzumachen, als ich in Marsha renne, die gerade ihre Schicht beendet hat.

»Hallo«, sagt sie und schneidet eine mitfühlende Grimasse. »Fängst du gerade erst an?«

»Sieht so aus«, antworte ich und stopfe meine Kleidung in den Spind. »Geht ihr heute Abend wieder aus?«

»Nein. Andy schafft es nicht, und Tonya ist mit dem niedlichen Barmann beschäftigt. Erinnerst du dich an ihn?«

Ich binde mir meine Haare zu einem Pferdeschwanz zusammen. »Der aus dem Klub, in dem wir waren?« Als Marsha mir zunickt, frage ich: »Ja, warum? Sind sie zusammen?«

»Du hast es erraten.« Marsha grinst. »Aber ich sehe schon, dass du es eilig hast, also lasse ich dich in Ruhe. Ruf mich an, falls du dieses Wochenende etwas unternehmen möchtest. Andy macht morgen Abend ein Barbecue, und ich bin mir sicher, dass sie sich sehr freuen würde, wenn du kämst.«

»Danke. Ich melde mich, wenn ich es schaffe«, antworte ich und eile aus dem Umkleidezimmer. Ich weiß, dass ich sie nicht anrufen werde, und dieses Mal nicht, weil ich Angst um meine Freunde habe.

So gut sich Barbecue auch anhört, ich freue mich

wirklich auf eine ruhige Zeit am Wochenende zu Hause.

Mit Peter.

Dem Mann, den ich nicht hassen kann.

———

EINIGE STUNDEN später schleppe ich mich erschöpft zurück zum Umkleideraum. Die Gebärmutter meiner Patientin ist gerissen, und ich musste einen Notkaiserschnitt machen, um sie und das Baby zu retten. Zum Glück geht es beiden gut, aber ich habe von dem Hunger und meiner extremen Müdigkeit rasende Kopfschmerzen.

Ich kann es kaum erwarten, nach Hause zu kommen, das aufzuwärmen, was Peter gekocht hat, und wenn ich Glück habe, bekomme ich vielleicht sogar noch eine Massage zum Einschlafen.

»Dr. Cobakis?«

Die weibliche Stimme hört sich entfernt bekannt an, und ich wirbele mit rasendem Puls herum. Hinter mir steht Karen, die Agentin beziehungsweise Krankenschwester des FBI, die bei Agent Ryson war, als ich nach Peters Angriff aufgewacht bin. Wie das letzte Mal trägt sie einen Schwesternkittel, auch wenn ich weiß, dass sie nicht in diesem Krankenhaus arbeitet.

Sie muss versuchen, nicht aufzufallen.

»Karen?« Ich versuche, mich nicht nervös anzuhören. »Was tun Sie hier?«

Sie kommt auf mich zu und bleibt einen halben

Meter vor mir stehen. »Ich wollte mit Ihnen an einem Ort reden, an dem uns niemand sehen würde, und das hier schien eine günstige Gelegenheit zu sein.«

Ich schaue mich im Umkleideraum um. Sie hat recht: um diese Uhrzeit sind wir die beiden Einzigen hier. »Warum?« Ich wende meine Aufmerksamkeit wieder ihr zu. »Was ist los?«

»Vor einigen Monaten haben Sie sich an Agent Ryson gewandt«, sagt sie leise. »Sie haben gesagt, dass Sie sich beobachtet fühlten. Damals haben wir Ihre Beunruhigung abgetan, aber jetzt haben wir neue Informationen bekommen.«

Mein Hals verengt sich. »Was … was für neue Informationen?«

»Sie haben mit Peter Sokolov zu tun, dem Deserteur, der Sie in Ihrem Zuhause überfallen hat.«

»Ach?« Meine Stimme ist eine Oktave zu hoch.

»Er wurde in dieser Gegend gesehen, nur einige Straßen von diesem Krankenhaus entfernt. Eine versteckte Verkehrskamera hat sein Gesicht aufgenommen, und unser Gesichtserkennungsprogramm hat das Foto gemeldet.« Sie legt ihren Kopf schief. »Sie wissen nicht zufällig etwas darüber, Dr. Cobakis, oder?«

»Ich …« Mein Herzschlag dröhnt in meinen Ohren, und meine Gedanken drehen sich vor Panik rasend schnell im Kreis. Das ist sie, meine Chance, Hilfe zu bekommen, ohne dass Peter weiß, dass ich mit jemandem gesprochen habe. Das FBI weiß bereits, dass er hier ist, und es wird keine Ruhe geben, bis er nicht gefunden ist. Ich kann ihre Chancen auf Erfolg erhöhen, ihnen sagen, dass er höchstwahrscheinlich in meinem Haus ist, und wenn sie ihn und seine Männer fassen, wird es wirklich vorbei sein.

Ich würde mein eigenes Leben wiederhaben.

»Alles ist in Ordnung, Dr. Cobakis.« Karen legt sanft eine Hand auf meinen Arm. »Ich weiß, dass das alles ein sehr großer Stress für Sie ist, aber wir werden sicherstellen, dass Sie sich in Sicherheit befinden. Bitte denken Sie einfach an die letzten Wochen. Ist Ihnen vielleicht jemand gefolgt? Hatten Sie in letzter Zeit wieder das Gefühl, dass Sie beobachtet werden?«

Die ganze Zeit über, weil ich beobachtet *werde*. Das will ich ihr sagen, aber ich spreche diese Worte nicht aus. Stattdessen atme ich immer schneller, bis ich hyperventiliere. Peter wird sich nicht einfach ruhig festnehmen lassen, wenn die Agenten ihn holen kommen; er wird kämpfen, und Menschen werden ums Leben kommen. *Er* könnte getötet werden. Übelkeit steigt in meinem Hals auf, als ich mir seinen starken, von Kugeln zerlöcherten Körper vorstelle, seine durchdringenden, metallischen Augen leblos und vom Tod gezeichnet. Das sollte eine Vorstellung sein, über die ich mich freue, aber stattdessen macht sie mich krank, und mein Brustkorb zieht sich schmerzhaft zusammen, als ich mir vorstelle, wie mein Leben ohne ihn sein würde.

Wie frei – und wie allein – ich wieder sein würde.

»Ich … Nein.« Ich trete kopfschüttelnd einen Schritt zurück. Ich weiß, dass ich nicht klar denke, aber ich kann es einfach nicht sagen. Mein Mund kann die

Worte einfach nicht formen. »Ich habe nichts bemerkt.«

Karen runzelt ihre Stirn. »Nichts? Sind Sie sicher? Unseres Wissens nach sind Sie und Ihr verstorbener Mann seine einzige Verbindung zu dieser Gegend.«

»Ja, ich bin mir sicher.« Ich höre mich wie eine Fremde an, als ich diese Lügen ausspreche. Meine Kopfschmerzen werden immer stärker, bis sie zu einem Trommelschlag in meinem Kopf werden, und ich fühle mich, als müsste ich mich gleich übergeben. Meine Gedanken springen von einer Alternative zur nächsten, und mein Kopf fühlt sich an wie eine Ratte in einem Labyrinth. Ich weiß nicht einmal, warum ich lüge. Es ist vorbei. So oder so ist es vorbei – weil sie jetzt, da sie wissen, dass er sich in der Gegend aufhält, nach ihm suchen *werden*, egal, was ich sage. Und wenn sie es nicht schaffen, ihn zu töten oder festzunehmen, könnte er denken, dass ich ihn verraten habe, und seine Drohung wahrmachen, mich zu entführen, vielleicht sogar Menschen bestrafen, die mir nahestehen, um mir eine Lektion zu erteilen.

Ich *sollte* dem FBI helfen. Das wäre meine beste Chance, meine Freiheit wiederzuerlangen.

»In Ordnung«, sagt Karen, als ich nichts weiter sage. Wenn Ihnen noch etwas einfällt, hier ist meine Nummer.« Sie gibt mir eine Karte, während sie sagt: »Wir wollen ihn nicht warnen, falls er Sie aus irgendeinem Grund überwacht, also werden wir Sie nicht sofort in Schutzhaft nehmen. Stattdessen werden wir Sie diskret überwachen, und wenn wir etwas Ungewöhnliches bemerken – und ich meine schon die kleinste Abweichung –, werden wir schnell reagieren, um Ihre Sicherheit zu gewährleisten. In der Zwischenzeit tun Sie bitte die gleichen Sachen wie immer, und ich versichere Ihnen, dass der Mann, der Ihren Ehemann getötet hat, für das, was er getan hat, bezahlen wird.

»Okay. Das … das werde ich tun.« Da meine Selbstbeherrschung nur noch an einem seidenen Faden hängt, nehme ich meine Tasche aus dem offenen Schrank, schließe ihn und verlasse schnell den Raum.

Ich bin schon fast an meinem Auto, als mir auffällt, dass ich noch meine OP-Kleidung trage.

Dank Karens Überfall habe ich vergessen, mich umzuziehen.

———

HEAVY METAL DRÖHNT aus den Lautsprechern, als ich vom Parkplatz fahre und mich selbst für meine Dummheit verfluche. Trotz meiner Kopfschmerzen beruhigt mich die Musik, da die lauten Klänge geordneter sind als das verrückte Durcheinander in meinem Kopf. Ich kann gar nicht glauben, dass ich Karen nichts erzählt habe und sie auch nicht um die Hilfe des FBI gebeten habe, als ich die Gelegenheit dazu hatte. Jetzt weiß ich nicht, was ich tun soll, wie ich mich verhalten oder wohin ich gehen soll. Soll ich nach Hause gehen, obwohl das FBI mich überwacht? Und wenn ich es tue, werden sie bemerken, dass Peter da ist, oder werden seine Vorsichtsmaßnahmen, wie nicht in meiner Einfahrt zu parken, seine Anwesenheit verheimlichen? Vielleicht sollte ich lieber zu meinen Eltern oder in ein Hotel gehen – oder einfach irgendwo im Krankenhaus schlafen. Aber was ist mit Peters Männern, die mir überallhin folgen? Sie würden bemerken, dass etwas nicht stimmt, und Peter könnte mich suchen, und wer weiß, was dann passiert. Und überhaupt, wird das FBI zuerst meine Bodyguards entdecken oder werden diese zuerst die Agenten bemerken und Peter benachrichtigen? Wird er schon weg sein, wenn ich nach Hause komme, um den Behörden ein für alle Mal zu entgehen?

Wie schlimm habe ich es versaut?

Meine Hände am Lenkrad sind weiße Knöchel, und mein Kopf dreht sich von meiner Unterhaltung mit Karen, die ich immer wieder in Gedanken durchgehe. Mein Gott, ich hatte so viele Gelegenheiten, ihr die Wahrheit zu sagen, ihr die ganze Situation zu erklären und die Experten alles regeln zu lassen. Warum habe ich das nicht getan? Wie konnte ich nur so dumm sein? Nachdem mir aufgefallen war, dass ich mich nicht umgezogen hatte, bin ich zurückgegangen und habe mir gesagt, dass ich dieses Mal das Richtige tun würde, sollte Karen noch da sein – das war sie nicht.

Sie war bereits gegangen, und ich war erleichtert, weil ich tief in mir wusste, dass ich es nicht getan hätte.

Auch wenn Peters Drohung mich immer noch belastet, kann ich es nicht über mich bringen, die

Konfrontation auszulösen, die seinen Tod bedeuten könnte.

Während Metallica im Hintergrund dröhnt, fahre ich wie ferngesteuert und bin so sehr in Gedanken, dass ich nicht einmal bemerke, dass mein Unterbewusstsein bereits mein Ziel ausgewählt hat. Erst als ich in meine Straße einbiege, dämmert es mir, wohin ich fahre, aber da ist es bereits zu spät.

Ich bin zu Hause.

44

———

S*ara*

ICH ZITTERE, als ich aus der Garage ins Haus trete, mein Hals ist vor Angst wie zugeschnürt, und mein Herz schlägt synchron zu dem Pochen in meinem Kopf. Es ist schon weit nach Mitternacht, und alles ist dunkel, aber ich kann den leckeren Duft des Essens riechen, das Peter gekocht hat. Mein Magen knurrt, da mein Körper trotz des Adrenalins, das durch meine Adern schießt, auf Nahrung besteht. Ich muss gleich etwas essen, aber zuerst muss ich herausfinden, wo Peter ist und ob er weiß, was gerade passiert.

»Hast du Hunger?«

Die vertraute tiefe Stimme erschreckt mich so sehr, dass ich mit einem panischen Aufschrei wegspringe.

Ein Licht geht an und beleuchtet Peters Gestalt auf

dem Sofa im Wohnzimmer. Trotz der angenehmen Temperaturen trägt er seine Lederjacke, und sein kräftiger Körper liegt so entspannt da, dass er mich an ein dösendes Raubtier erinnert.

»Ähm, ja.« *Oh Gott, weiß er Bescheid?* Warum liegt er im Dunkeln? »Bei einer meiner Patientinnen haben die Wehen eingesetzt, und ich habe das Abendessen verpasst.«

»Hast du?« Peter stellt sich mit einer geschmeidigen Bewegung hin. »Das ist nicht gut. Komm, iss etwas, bevor du ohnmächtig wirst.«

Ich folge ihm auf zitterigen Beinen in die Küche. Die Tatsache, dass er hier ist und Essen für mich warm macht, muss bedeuten, dass seine Männer nicht bemerkt haben, dass mir das FBI folgt. Bedeutet das, dass das Gleiche auch umgekehrt gilt? Könnten die FBI-Agenten, die mich überwachen, ebenfalls diejenigen übersehen haben, von denen Peter mich überwachen lässt?

Meine Hände und Füße sind durch den Stress ganz eisig, und ich weiß, ich muss wie der aufgewärmte Tod aussehen, während ich meine Hände wasche und mich hinsetze. Ich hoffe, dass Peter meine Blässe auf meine Müdigkeit schiebt und nicht auf die Tatsache, dass das FBI jeden Moment mein Haus stürmen könnte.

Er stellt einen Teller herzhafte Gemüsesuppe und eine Scheibe knuspriges Sauerteigbrot vor mich, setzt sich danach mir gegenüber auf seinen normalen Platz und schaut mir mit ausdruckslosem Gesicht dabei zu, wie ich meinen Löffel in die Hand nehme und ihn in die Suppe eintauche. Meine Hände zittern leicht, eine Tatsache, die ihm nicht entgehen kann, die er aber hoffentlich auch meiner Erschöpfung zuschreibt. Wenn nicht, falls er etwas vermutet, könnten die Dinge schnell den Bach runtergehen. Er könnte mich schneller fesseln und in ein Versteck im Ausland schleifen, als meine Wachhunde des FBI Verstärkung rufen könnten.

Scheiße, warum gehe ich so ein Risiko ein? Warum habe ich Karen nicht einfach alles erzählt?

Doch auch wenn ich mich dafür in den Hintern trete, kenne ich die Antwort auf diese Frage. Sie sitzt vor mir und blickt mich so intensiv mit ihren grauen Augen an, dass mir gleichzeitig heiß und kalt wird. Ich sollte frei von meinem Peiniger sein wollen, sollte alles tun, was in meiner Macht steht, um ihn aus meinem Leben verschwinden zu lassen, aber ich kann nicht. Ich bin nicht verrückt genug, ihn zu warnen und das Risiko einzugehen, entführt zu werden, aber ich bringe es auch nicht übers Herz, den Moment zu beschleunigen, an dem die Gerechtigkeit ihn einholt und er entweder kämpfen oder fliehen muss.

Das wird sowieso geschehen, und alles, was ich tun muss, ist, zu überleben.

»Du arbeitest zu viel«, sagt Peter leise und legt seinen Kopf schief, während er mich anschaut. Ich atme zitternd aus.

Gott sei Dank. Er schiebt meine Nervosität auf meine Müdigkeit.

»Du solltest einen Gang runterschalten, Ptichka, die Dinge langsamer angehen«, fährt er fort, und ich nicke, wobei ich meinen Teller anschaue, um seinem eindringlichen Blick zu entgehen.

»Ja, ich nehme an, damit hast du recht.« Ich beiße vom Brot ab, nehme einen Löffel Suppe und konzentriere mich auf die köstlichen Aromen, um den Aufruhr in meinem Kopf zum Schweigen zu bringen. Ich bin nur teilweise erfolgreich, aber es reicht aus, um einen weiteren und dann noch einen Löffel zu essen.

Ich habe bereits mein Brot und fast die Hälfte meiner Suppe gegessen, als ich genug Mut zusammengenommen habe, um wieder aufzuschauen. »Warum hast du hier auf mich gewartet?«, frage ich, als ich mich daran erinnere, wie dunkel das Haus war, als ich zurückgekommen bin. »Ich dachte, du seist schon im Bett oder duschen oder so.«

»Weil ich dich in den letzten Tagen kaum gesehen und dich vermisst habe, Ptichka.« Seine Augen strahlen diese Weichheit aus, die ich diese ganze Woche gesehen habe.

Mein Magen zieht sich zusammen, und mein Hals wird eng. »Das … das hast du?« Das hat er mir noch nie gesagt. Auch wenn wir beide wissen, wie besessen er von mir ist, hat er nie irgendwelche echten Gefühle zugegeben.

»Ja. Hier, nimm noch ein wenig Brot.« Er schiebt eine weitere Scheibe zu mir herüber. »Du siehst immer noch viel zu blass aus.«

Ich nehme das Brot und beiße hinein, wobei ich

wieder nach unten blicke, um meinen Gesichtsausdruck zu verbergen. Mein Hals wird immer enger, und in meinen Augen brennen irrationale Tränen. Warum muss er ausgerechnet heute solche Dinge zu mir sagen?« Er soll furchtbar zu mir sein, nicht nett. Ich muss mich daran erinnern, dass er ein Monster ist, ein Mörder, der Dinge getan hat, die Ted Bundy erblassen lassen würden.

Er muss mich aus meiner Fantasie reißen, damit ich ihn nicht vermisse, wenn er weg ist.

Ich schaffe es, die Tränen zurückzuhalten, während ich den Rest der Suppe esse und Peter mich schweigend betrachtet. Die Art und Weise, wie er mich einfach ohne etwas zu tun anschauen kann, so als ob ihn mein Anblick völlig fasziniert, ist beunruhigend. Ich habe ihn schon häufiger dabei ertappt, einmal bin ich sogar nachts aufgewacht, als er mich derart angeschaut hat.

Es ist gleichzeitig beängstigend und schmeichelhaft, genauso wie sein endloser Hunger auf mich.

Als mein Teller leer ist, stehe ich auf, um ihn in den Geschirrspüler zu stellen, aber Peter nimmt ihn mir aus den Händen.

»Ich mache das«, sagt er sanft und küsst mich zärtlich auf die Stirn. »Geh hoch und mach dich fertig fürs Bett. Ich bin in einer Minute da.«

Ich nicke, blinzele, um erneut aufsteigende Tränen zurückzuhalten, und gehe ohne Widerspruch nach oben. Das macht er auch häufig: mich von jeglicher Hausarbeit befreien, wenn ich müde bin, egal, wie klein die Aufgabe ist. Er muss wissen, dass es mich nicht überanstrengen wird, einen Teller in den Geschirrspüler zu stellen, aber er behandelt mich wie einen Invaliden anstatt wie eine Ärztin, die nach vielen Stunden Arbeit erschöpft ist.

Er bemuttert mich, und ich liebe es, auch wenn ich das nicht sollte. Ich sollte alles, was er tut, hassen, weil nichts davon echt ist.

Das kann es nicht sein.

———

ICH BIN BEREITS GEDUSCHT, als Peter nach oben kommt, und er versperrt mir den Weg aus dem Badezimmer, indem er mich gegen den Waschtisch drückt, als ich gerade meine Zähne fertig geputzt habe. Ich habe das Handtuch um mich gewickelt, aber er nimmt es ab, lässt es auf den Boden fallen, und der Anblick von uns beiden im Spiegel – meine weiße und komplette Nacktheit, während er noch völlig in schwarz gekleidet ist – lässt mein Herz vor nervöser Erregung schneller schlagen.

Er ist heute Nacht besonders hungrig – und mehr als nur ein wenig gefährlich.

Er bestätigt meine Beobachtung, indem er eine große Hand um meinen Hals legt, und obwohl er nicht zudrückt, kann ich die Dunkelheit hinter der dünnen Schicht aus Selbstkontrolle und die implizite Drohung in seiner Geste spüren. Gleichzeitig legt sich seine andere Hand auf meine Brust, und die rauen Kanten seines Daumens reiben über meinen harten Nippel. Er blickt mir über den Spiegel in die Augen, und ich sehe einen eigenartigen Hunger in den silbernen Tiefen, Lust vermischt mit Besitzanspruch und diesem intensiven Etwas, von dem ich weiche Knie bekomme, während mir heiße und kalte Schauer über den Rücken laufen.

»Schau dich an«, haucht er in mein Ohr, und ich löse meinen Blick von seinen hypnotisierenden Augen, um mich auf den Anblick zu konzentrieren, den wir abgeben: er, so groß und tödlich gutaussehend, und ich klein und weiblich, fast zerbrechlich in seiner dunklen Umarmung. »Schau nur, wie schön du bist, wie süß und weich und rein. Deine zarte Haut, so dünn und empfindlich, so verletzlich …« Er streicht über meine Kehle, als ich schlucke, und mein Puls schlägt bei seinen Worten schneller.

»Weißt du, was ich mich manchmal frage?«, fährt er leise fort, und ich umfasse die Kante des Waschtischs, als seine harten Finger in meinen Nippel kneifen und ihn voller grausamer Absicht verdrehen. »Ich frage mich, ob ich eine Kette um diesen schönen Hals legen sollte, um dich an mich zu binden, und danach den Schlüssel wegwerfen sollte. Würdest du dann weinen, Ptichka? Wärst du wütend?« Er knabbert an meinem Ohrläppchen, seine weißen Zähne fahren über meine Haut und seine Hand bewegt sich von meiner Brust zu meinem Geschlecht. »Oder würdest du es heimlich mögen?«

Ich ziehe scharf Luft ein, zittere und bin so heiß,

dass ich jeden Moment in Flammen aufgehen könnte. Das Bild, das er malt, ist gleichzeitig beängstigend und erregend, genauso düster und erotisch wie unser Spiegelbild. Dadurch, dass er seine Arme um mich gelegt hat, kann ich das Leder seiner Jacke riechen, den metallischen Reißverschluss an meinem Rücken spüren, und ein Gefühl von Verletzlichkeit überkommt mich, als seine Finger meine nassen Falten auseinanderschieben, meine Klitoris berühren, scharfe Lust mich wie ein Peitschenschlag trifft und das Gefühl der Hilflosigkeit, des völligen Kontrollverlusts, verstärkt.

»Bitte.« Meine Stimme zittert. »Bitte, Peter …«

»Bitte was?« Seine Finger stoßen hinein und krümmen sich in mir, drücken gegen meinen G-Punkt, während seine Zähne wieder über meinen Hals fahren. »Bitte was, Ptichka? Bitte berühre mich? Bitte fick mich? Bitte geh weg?«

Ich presse meine Augen zusammen. »Bitte fick mich.« Mir ist schon nichts mehr peinlich, und ich kann es auch nicht mehr leugnen. Es fühlt sich an, als würde jede Zelle meines Körpers vor Verlangen pulsieren, aus dieser dunklen Begierde brennen, die er in mir erweckt hat. Vielleicht wäre ich unter anderen Umständen stark geblieben, hätte versucht, mich an etwas festzuhalten, um meine Würde nicht zu verlieren, aber ich bin zu erschöpft – und mir ist zu bewusst, dass es das gewesen sein könnte.

Heute Nacht könnte unser letztes Mal zusammen sein.

»Öffne deine Augen«, knurrt er, und ich gehorche

benebelt, während ich gegen diese berauschende Kraft der Lust ankämpfe.

Peters Blick ist dunkel und durchdringend im Spiegel, und sein Gesicht ist durch sein gewaltiges Verlangen verzogen. Und darunter spüre ich dieses beunruhigende *Etwas*, diese Weichheit, die ich nicht wirklich definieren kann.

»Sag es mir, Sara. Sag mir, wie ich dich ficken soll. Willst du es rau«, seine Finger stoßen hinterhältig erneut in mich, »oder sanft? Hart«, er reibt mit seinem Handballen über mein Geschlecht, »oder sanft?« Er verringert den Druck und beugt seinen Kopf nach unten, um mein Ohrläppchen zu lecken, bevor er rau in mein Ohr flüstert: »Willst du Blumen und süße Worte, Ptichka? Oder willst du lieber etwas Rohes und Echtes, auch wenn die Gesellschaft es für falsch hält … selbst wenn es nicht das ist, was du immer wolltest.

Ich atme keuchend und abgehackt durch meine Zähne, während sein Daumen meine Klitoris umkreist, und die Hitze unter meiner Haut macht es mir fast unmöglich, zu denken. Meine inneren Muskeln ziehen sich um diese rauen, eindringenden Finger zusammen, und ich verstehe nicht, was er fragt, was er von mir will. Ich brauche noch mehr dieser Lust an der Schmerzgrenze, und gleichzeitig muss ich von dieser sich immer weiter in mir aufbauenden Anspannung erlöst werden.

»Peter, bitte …« Mein Herz rast viel zu schnell. »Oh Gott, bitte …«

Sein Griff an meinem Hals wird fester, als seine

Finger sich in mir krümmen, um erneut gegen meinen G-Punkt zu drücken. »Sag es mir, und ich ficke dich,« Seine Zähne fahren über meinen Nacken, und ich erschaudere durch das Gefühl. »Ich werde dir genau das geben, was du möchtest, werde deine kleine, enge Muschi ausfüllen, bis du nach mehr bettelst. Sag mir, was du brauchst, und ich werde es dir geben, Sara. Ich werde dir alles und noch mehr geben.«

»Hart«, keuche ich, und meine Hände gleiten von der Kante des Waschtischs, um sich an den stählernen Säulen seiner jeansbedeckten Oberschenkel festzukrallen. Mein Geschlecht zieht sich um seine Finger zusammen, als ich meine Scham hart gegen seine Hand presse, da ich verzweifelt nach einem festeren Druck auf meine Klitoris suche. Ich weiß nicht, was ich gerade sage, aber ich weiß, was ich brauche. »Fick mich hart, Peter. Bitte …«

Sein Kiefer spannt sich an, und ich erhasche einen Blick auf die Dunkelheit in dem grauen Leuchten seiner Augen. Plötzlich lässt er mich los und wischt mit der Hand über den Waschtisch, um ihn von den Kosmetikartikeln zu befreien. Er dreht sich blitzschnell um, hebt mich hoch und setzt mich mit weit gespreizten Beinen auf den kalten Granit. Ich blinzele ihn an, aber er macht sich bereits den Reißverschluss seiner Jeans auf und zieht mich nach vorn, bis mein Po fast von der Kante rutscht.

»Peter – oh Gott.« Ich keuche, als er mich aufspießt und so dick und hart ist, dass es sich anfühlt, als verletze er mich innerlich. Er ist seit unserem ersten

Mal nicht mehr so hart gewesen, aber heute bin ich so nass, dass das gewaltvolle Eindringen mir keine Angst macht, sondern der drohende Schmerz meine Lust nur erhöht. Anstatt mich zusammenzukrampfen, bleibe ich nachgiebig und weich um seinen Schwanz, und als er in einen harten, festen Rhythmus fällt, und sich seine Finger in das weiche Fleisch meines Hinterns krallen, schlinge ich meine Beine um seine Hüften und meine Arme um seinen Hals, hänge an ihm, als sei er mein Anker im Sturm. Und das ist er vielleicht auch. Er fickt mich mit einer solchen Wut, dass ich mich wie ein Blatt in einem Sturm fühle, von seiner Gewalt überwältigt bin und von den Wellen seiner Lust hin und her geworfen werde. Das ist zu viel, zu intensiv, aber dieses Gefühl der Hilflosigkeit verstärkt meine wachsende Anspannung nur. Mit einem Schrei komme ich, ziehe mich um ihn zusammen, aber er hört nicht auf. Er macht weiter, bis ich erneut komme und dann noch einmal.

Erst als ich nach meinem dritten Orgasmus keuchend und benebelt gegen ihn sacke, lässt er seinen Orgasmus zu. Mit einem letzten, harten Stoß kommt er, und seine Scham reibt sich gegen meine, als er laut aufstöhnt. Ich spüre das Pulsieren seines Schwanzes in mir, als ich zitternd an ihm hänge, und mein Geschlecht zieht sich ein letztes Mal zusammen, ringt meinem übersensiblen Fleisch einen letzten Lustschauer ab.

Danach bin ich so fertig, dass ich kaum stehen kann, als er mich von dem Tisch hebt und mich

hinstellt. Unterschwellig bemerke ich, dass ich ungewöhnlich feucht zwischen meinen Beinen bin, sogar
eher klitschnass, aber erst als Peter zurücktritt und ich
merke, wie die Nässe an meinem Bein hinunterläuft,
verstehe ich, woher sie kommt.

»Oh Gott.« Mein Blick fällt auf seinen Schwanz,
der noch immer halb erregt ist und mit einer Mischung
aus unseren Flüssigkeiten glänzt. »Peter, wir …«

»Haben vergessen, ein Kondom zu benutzen? Ja.«

Er hört sich nicht besonders besorgt an. Stattdessen
sehe ich ihm entsetzt dabei zu, wie er sich wie selbst-
verständlich wäscht, seinen Schwanz wieder in seine
Jeans steckt und den Reißverschluss schließt. Danach
befeuchtet er einen Waschlappen und wischt sanft den
Samen von meinen Oberschenkeln.

»So, alles wieder verschwunden.« Er lässt den
Waschlappen ins Waschbecken fallen, und seine Augen
leuchten, als er sich zu mir herumdreht. »Mach dir
keine Sorgen. Du hast gerade deine Tage gehabt, also
sollten wir uns noch nicht in der Gefahrenzone befinden. Und ich bin sauber; ich benutze immer Kondome
und lasse mich regelmäßig testen. Ich nehme an, dass
das bei dir genauso ist?«

»Ja.« Ich starre zurück und bin von dem, was
passiert ist und wie er damit umgeht, schockiert. Theo-
retisch sollten wir auf der sicheren Seite sein, aber allein
die Tatsache, dass es passiert ist, mit *ihm* … Mein Kopf
beginnt erneut, schmerzhaft zu pochen, und meine
Erschöpfung kommt zehnmal so stark wie vorher

zurück. Wie hatte ich nur so nachlässig sein können? Bei George hatte ich immer daran gedacht, ihn daran zu erinnern, Kondome zu benutzen, und während der sogenannten fruchtbaren Tage hatten wir oft überhaupt keinen Sex, da wir nicht das bis zu 15 Prozent vorhandene Risiko eingehen wollten, trotz Kondoms schwanger zu werden, bis wir bereit wären, ein Baby zu bekommen. Mit dem Mörder meines Ehemannes war ich allerdings nicht annähernd so vorsichtig und hatte zu allen Zeiten meines Zyklus Sex. Und jetzt das …

Es ist, als wolle ein kranker Teil von mir mit ihm verbunden sein, diese unechte Beziehung in eine echte verwandeln.

»Es sollte also kein Problem geben«, meint Peter und kommt näher. »Obwohl …« Er macht eine Pause und betrachtet mich intensiv mit einem nachdenklichen Gesichtsausdruck.

»Obwohl was?«, frage ich, als er weiterhin schweigt. Mein Herz hämmert in einem dumpfen, schnellen Rhythmus. »Obwohl was?«

»Obwohl es mir nichts ausmachen würde.« Seine Worte sind leicht und ungezwungen, aber seine Stimme hört sich nicht so an, als würde er scherzen. »Nicht mit dir.«

»Du … was?« Meine Kopfschmerzen verstärken sich, und mein Schädel fühlt sich so an, als würde er jeden Moment explodieren. Er kann das, was er gerade sagt, unmöglich ernst meinen. »Warum würde es dir … Das ergibt keinen Sinn!«

»Tut es das nicht?« Seine Augen beginnen, amüsiert zu leuchten. »Warum nicht, Ptichka?«

»Weil … weil du *du* bist.« Meine Stimme ist vor Ungläubigkeit erstickt. »Du hast mir Drogen verabreicht und mich gefoltert, bevor du meinen Ehemann getötet und dich in mein Leben gedrängt hast. Ich weiß nicht, was du in dem hier siehst, aber wir sind nicht zusammen. Das ist keine Liebesgeschichte …«

»Nein?« Sein Gesichtsausdruck wird hart, und seine Belustigung verschwindet vollständig. »Was denkst du also, fühle ich für dich? Warum kann ich nicht eine einzige Stunde verbringen, ohne an dich zu denken, dich zu wollen … mich verdammt noch mal nach dir zu *sehnen*? Denkst du, dass ich aus Lust hierbleibe, immer länger, obwohl die ganze Welt hinter mir her ist und meine Männer vor Langeweile die Wände hochgehen?« Er tritt noch näher an mich heran, und ich atme schneller, als er seine Handflächen rechts und links neben mir am Waschtisch abstützt. Seine Augen funkeln erregt, als er sich nach vorn lehnt und seine Stimme immer rauer wird. »Denkst du, ich bin hier, anstatt den letzten *ublyudok* auf meiner Liste zu jagen, weil ich nicht genug von deiner engen, kleinen Muschi bekommen kann?«

Mein Gesicht brennt, als ich ihn anblicke, da seine vulgäre Wortwahl meine Verwirrung verstärkt. Ich weiß nicht, was ich sagen soll, wie ich das alles verarbeiten soll. Er hört sich wütend an, auch wenn sich das, was er sagt, fast anhört, als ob …

»Ja, ich sehe, du hast mich verstanden.« Auf seinem

Mund erscheint ein dunkles, ironisches Lächeln. »Für *dich* ist es vielleicht keine Liebesgeschichte, aber so beschissen das auch ist, für mich ist es genau das. Zuerst habe ich dich gehasst, aber irgendwann bist du das Einzige geworden, das mir etwas bedeutet, die einzige Person, die mir etwas bedeutet. Und ja, ich will sagen, dass ich dich liebe, egal, wie falsch das vielleicht ist. Ich liebe dich, auch wenn du *seine* gewesen bist … auch wenn du denkst, dass ich ein Monster bin. Ich liebe dich mehr als mein Leben, Sara, weil ich, wenn ich bei dir bin, mehr fühle als Qual und Wut – und ich mehr will als Tod und Rache.« Seine Brust dehnt sich aus, als er tief einatmet, und sein Gesichtsausdruck wird düster, als er leise hinzufügt: »Wenn ich bei dir bin, Ptichka, lebe ich.«

Mir fällt nicht auf, dass ich weine, bis sein Gesicht vor meinen Augen verschwimmt. Mein Brustkorb ist zu eng, und meine Atmung zu flach. Ich wusste, dass Peter von mir besessen ist, aber ich habe nicht gedacht, dass in seinem Kopf Besessenheit das Gleiche ist wie Liebe, dass er eine echte Zukunft mit mir möchte … eine, in der wir eine Familie sind.

Eine Zukunft, in der nicht gerade FBI-Agenten dabei sind, durch die Tür zu stürmen.

»Weine nicht, Ptichka.« Sein Daumen streicht über meine nasse Wange, und ich sehe wieder das ironische Lächeln auf seinen Lippen. »Das ändert nichts. Du kannst mich immer noch hassen. Nur weil ich dich liebe, bin ich nicht weniger ein Monster – und ich werde nicht aus deinem Leben verschwinden.«

Aber genau das wirst du. Ich will die Wahrheit herausschreien, aber ich kann nicht. Ich kann ihn nicht warnen, auch wenn mein Herz sich anfühlt, als würde es zerspringen. Ich liebe ihn nicht – das kann ich nicht –, aber es tut genauso weh, als täte ich es, so als wäre ihn zu verlieren das Schlimmste, was mir jemals passiert ist. Ein unterdrücktes Schluchzen entweicht meinem Mund, dann noch eins, und dann bin ich in seinen Armen, werde sicher gegen seine Brust gedrückt, während er mich aus dem Badezimmer trägt.

Als er bei meinem Bett ankommt, setzt er sich hin, hält mich auf seinem Schoß, und ich weine, vergrabe meinen Kopf an seinem Hals, während er langsam und beruhigend über meinen Rücken streicht. Er hat recht, seine Liebeserklärung sollte nichts ändern, aber aus irgendeinem Grund macht es die Sache schlimmer. Durch sie fühle ich mich, als würde ich etwas Echtes verlieren ... als würde ich ihn und *uns* betrügen.

Wie kann ein Monster mich nur so zärtlich halten? Wie kann ein Psychopath lieben?

Mein Schädel fühlt sich an, als würde er von innen aufgesägt werden, da mein Weinen die Kopfschmerzen verschlimmert, und ich drücke gegen Peters Brust, um mich aus seiner Umarmung zu befreien – nur um auf mein Bett zu fallen und zu wimmern, während ich gegen meine Schläfen drücke.

Er beugt sich über mich, und sein Gesichtsausdruck ist vor Sorge düster. »Was ist los, Ptichka?«, fragt er, während er meinen Arm streichelt, und ich kann gerade noch etwas über Kopfschmerzen murmeln, bevor ich meine Augen zukneife. Was ich fühle, ist eher eine Migräne, aber ich habe zu starke Schmerzen, um ihm das zu erklären.

Das Bett bewegt sich, als er aufsteht, und ich höre seine Schritte, als er aus dem Raum geht. Einige Minuten später kommt er mit Ibuprofen und einem Glas Wasser zurück. Ich zwinge mich dazu, meine geschwollenen Augenlider lange genug zu öffnen, um die Medizin nehmen zu können, und dann schließe ich sie erneut und warte darauf, dass aus dem Trommelschlag in meinem Kopf ein ertragbares Dröhnen wird.

Ich erwarte, dass er geht oder zu mir ins Bett kommt, oder was auch immer er jetzt vorhatte, aber stattdessen höre ich, wie die Badezimmertür geöffnet wird, und eine Minute später bedeckt ein kühles, nasses Handtuch meine Augen und meine Stirn und bringt eine angenehme Erleichterung mit sich.

Zum wiederholten Mal kümmert er sich um mich, unterstützt mich, wenn ich ihn am meisten brauche.

Die Tränen kommen zurück, laufen unter dem Handtuch heraus, während er die Decke fest um mich legt und sich auf die Bettkante setzt, um seine Hand unter meinen Hals gleiten zu lassen und die verspannten Muskeln in meinem Nacken zu massieren. Sie ist eine andere Art der Folter, seine zärtliche Fürsorge. Sie beruhigt meine Kopfschmerzen, aber facht den brennenden Schmerz in meiner Brust an. Ich habe mir selbst etwas vorgemacht, als ich das, was wir haben, eine kranke Fantasie genannt habe. Das hier mag vielleicht krank sein, aber es ist echt, und wenn er weg sein wird, *werde* ich ihn vermissen, genauso wie ich ihn vermisst habe, als er in Mexiko war. Was ich für ihn fühle, ist keine Liebe – Liebe kann nicht so düster sein, so unlogisch und verrückt –, aber es *ist* etwas.

Etwas anderes als Hass, etwas Tiefsitzendes und beunruhigend Süchtigmachendes.

Ein Hund bellt in einiger Entfernung, und ich höre, wie eine Tür zugeschlagen wird. Höchstwahrscheinlich sind es meine Nachbarn auf der anderen Straßenseite, aber trotzdem setzt mein Herz einen Schlag aus, und mein Magen zieht sich zusammen, als ich mir vorstelle, wie das Sondereinsatzkommando durch meine Tür bricht und Peter auf meiner Bettkante niederschießt. In meinem Kopf spielt es sich wie in einem Film ab: die schwarzgekleideten Gestalten stürmen herein, die Kugeln schlagen durch meine Bettwäsche, die Kissen, seinen Schädel …

Galle steigt in meinem Hals auf, mein Kopf explodiert erneut vor Qualen.

Oh Gott, ich kann das nicht tun.

Ich kann nicht schweigen, und es geschehen lassen.

»Peter …« Meine Stimme zittert, während ich meine Hände unter der Decke zusammenballe. Ich weiß, dass ich das auf Tausende verschiedene Arten bereuen werde, aber ich kann die Worte nicht davon abhalten, herauszusprudeln. »Sie haben dich gesehen. Sie suchen nach dir.«

Seine Hand auf meinem Nacken hält kurz inne, bevor sie mit der zärtlichen Massage fortfährt.

»Ich weiß, Ptichka«, sagt er leise, und ich spüre

seine Lippen auf meiner nassen Wange, während etwas Kaltes und Hartes in meinen Hals sticht. »Das weiß ich.«

Müdigkeit rauscht durch meine Adern, und mit einer eigenartigen Erleichterung wird mir klar, dass es das war.

Er wusste die ganze Zeit über das FBI Bescheid.

Er wusste es, und ich werde nie wieder frei sein.

45

Peter

»BEEIL DICH«, zischt Anton aus dem Beifahrerfenster, als ich mich mit Saras in eine Decke gewickelten Körper vor meiner Brust dem Geländewagen nähere. »Hast du meine Nachrichten nicht bekommen? Sie sind weniger als zehn Straßen entfernt.«

Ich umfasse mein menschliches Bündel fester. »Ich konnte nicht gehen, bevor ich nicht erfahren hatte, was ich wissen musste.«

»Was war das?«, fragt Yan, während er die Hintertür von innen öffnet. Er rutscht hinüber, und ich steige ein, wobei ich darauf achte, nirgendwo mit Saras Kopf anzuecken, als ich sie ins Auto schiebe.

Es ist schlimm genug, dass sie Kopfschmerzen hatte, als ich sie betäubt habe.

Ich ignoriere Yans Frage, setze Saras Körper zwischen uns und schließe die Tür, bevor ich Ilyas Blick im Rückspiegel erwidere. »Zum Flughafen. Schnell.«

»Bin schon dabei«, murmelt Ilya, während er das Gas durchtritt und wir nach vorn schießen, die leise Straße in dem Vorort entlangrasen.

»Was musstest du wissen?«, hakt Yan nach, während er einen Blick auf Saras Gesicht wirft – den einzigen Teil von ihr, der nicht in die Decke gewickelt ist. Mit ihren langen Wimpern, die wie Fächer auf ihren Wangen ausgebreitet sind, sieht sie aus wie eine schlafende Prinzessin von Disney, und ich mache meinem Mann keinen Vorwurf daraus, dass ich kurz Interesse auf seinem Gesicht aufflackern sehe.

Ich mache ihm keinen Vorwurf daraus, aber ich möchte ihn trotzdem dafür umbringen.

»Hat es etwas mit ihr zu tun?«, fragt er nichtsahnend, bevor er aufblickt, mein Gesicht sieht und erblasst.

»Ja.« Meine Stimme ist eiskalt. »Es hat etwas mit ihr zu tun.«

Er nickt und schaut dann weise weg, als ich meinen Arm um Saras Schultern lege und sie bequem gegen mich lehne. In einiger Entfernung höre ich Sirenen, die von dem Dröhnen von Hubschrauberblättern begleitet werden, aber trotz der sich nähernden Gefahr bin ich ruhig und zufrieden.

Nein, mehr als zufrieden – glücklich.

Sara hat mich gewarnt.

Sie hat sich für mich entschieden, obwohl sie keinen Grund dafür hatte. Vielleicht liebt sie mich jetzt noch nicht, aber sie hasst mich nicht, und während ich sie fest umarme, den süßen Duft ihrer Haare einatme, bin ich mir sicher, dass sie mich eines Tages lieben *wird* – dass sie eines Tages ganz mir gehören wird.

Sie hat mich gewarnt, sie hat sich dazu entschieden, mir zu gehören, und das wird sie jetzt auch für immer.

Ich liebe sie, und ich werde sie behalten.

Egal, was ich dafür tun muss.

Vielen Dank, dass Sie dieses Buch gelesen haben! Ich würde mich sehr über eine Bewertung des Buches freuen. Peters und Saras Geschichte geht in *Meine Besessenheit* weiter. Wenn Sie benachrichtigt werden möchten, wann das Buch erscheint, tragen Sie sich auf https://www.annazaires.com/book-series/deutsch/ für meinen Newsletter ein.

Wenn Ihnen *Mein Peiniger* gefallen hat, könnten die folgenden Bücher ebenfalls etwas für Sie sein.

- *Verschleppt: Die komplette Trilogie* – Die Geschichte von Julian und Nora, in der Peter als Nebenfigur auftaucht und seine Liste bekommt.
- *Ergreife Mich: Die komplette Trilogie* – Lucas' & Yulias Geschichte

- *Mia & Korum: Die komplette Krinar Chroniken Trilogie* – Ein dunkler Science-Fiction-Liebesroman
- *Die Gefangene des Krinar* – Ein abgeschlossener dunkler Science-Fiction-Liebesroman

Gemeinschaftsprojekte mit ihrem Ehemann, Dima Zales:

- *Mindmachines* – Techno-Thriller
- *Gedankendimensionen 0, 1 und 2* – Urban Fantasy
- *Die letzten Menschen: Die komplette Trilogie* – Dystopische/postapokaliptische Science-Fiction
- *Der Zaubercode* – High Fantasy

Wenn Sie über Neuerscheinungen benachrichtigt werden möchten, besuchen Sie bitte meine Homepage https://www.annazaires.com/book-series/deutsch/ und tragen Sie sich für meinen Newsletter ein.

Falls Sie Hörbücher bevorzugen klicken Sie bitte HIER, um zu dieser Serie und weiteren unserer Bücher zu gelangen.

Und jetzt blättern Sie bitte weiter, um einen kleinen Vorgeschmack auf *Twist Me - Verschleppt, Gefährliche Begegnungen* und einige meiner kommenden Werke zu erhalten.

AUSZUG AUS TWIST ME - VERSCHLEPPT

Anmerkungen der Autorin: Dieses Buch gehört zu
einer Reihe von Büchern, die auf Grund ihres sexuellen
Inhalts definitiv als Lektüre für Erwachsene gedacht
sind. Bewahren Sie deshalb dieses Buch am besten
außerhalb der Reichweite von Kindern im lesefähigen
Alter auf. Es unterscheidet sich außerdem von meinen
anderen Büchern, da die Hauptperson diese Geschichte
erzählt. Der Auszug und die Beschreibung sind noch
nicht editiert und deshalb können spätere Änderungen
nicht ausgeschlossen werden.

In dem Moment, als die Achtzehnjährige Nora Leston
die Aufmerksamkeit von Julian auf sich zieht, verändert sich ihr Leben komplett. Sie wird verschleppt und
auf eine einsame Insel im Pazifischen Ozean gebracht,
wo sie die Begierden ihres sadistischen Entführers

befriedigen muss — einem dunklen geheimnisvollen Mann, der genauso grausam wie gut aussehend ist ...

Hinweis: *Dieses Buch ist dunkle Erotik, kein Liebesroman. Es bietet: eine junge und unberührte Heldin, beunruhigende Szenen mit dubiosem Inhalt, Gefangenschaft, Machtspiele und sehr viel Sex, bei dem die Blümchen vor der Tür bleiben.*

Jetzt ist schon Abend. Mit jeder Minute, die vergeht, werde ich ängstlicher bei dem Gedanken daran, meinen Peiniger wiederzusehen.

Ich kann mich nicht länger auf den Roman konzentrieren, den ich gerade gelesen habe. Ich lege ihn weg und drehe Runden in dem Zimmer.

Ich habe die Sachen an, die Beth mir vorhin gegeben hat. Es ist keine Kleidung, die ich mir selber ausgesucht hätte, aber sie ist besser als ein Bademantel. Ein sexy Spitzenhöschen und einen dazu passenden BH als Unterwäsche. Ein hübsches blaues Sommerkleid zum vorne zuknöpfen. Alles passt mir verdächtig gut. Hat er mich schon eine ganze Weile verfolgt? Hat er alles über mich herausgefunden, einschließlich meiner Kleidergröße?

Mir wird schlecht bei dem Gedanken daran.

Ich versuche, nicht darüber nachzudenken, was noch alles passieren kann, aber das ist unmöglich. Ich weiß nicht warum ich mir so sicher bin, dass er heute Nacht zu mir kommen wird. Es ist natürlich möglich, dass er einen ganzen Harem voller Frauen hier auf dieser Insel festhält und jede nur einmal die Woche besucht, wie das die Sultane damals taten.

Und trotzdem weiß ich irgendwie, dass er bald hier sein würde. Die letzte Nacht hatte lediglich seinen Appetit angeregt. Ich weiß, dass er noch nicht mit mir fertig ist, noch lange nicht.

Endlich geht die Tür auf.

Er kommt herein, als würde ihm dies alles hier gehören. Was es natürlich auch tut.

Und wieder bin ich von seiner männlichen Schönheit beeindruckt. Mit so einem Gesicht hätte er ein Model oder ein Filmstar sein können. Wenn es auf dieser Welt Gerechtigkeit gäbe, wäre er klein oder hätte einen anderen Makel, der von seinem Gesicht ablenken würde.

Hat er aber nicht. Sein Körper ist groß und muskulös, mit perfekten Proportionen. Ich erinnere mich daran, wie es ist, ihn in mir zu haben und fühle ein unwillkommenes Aufflackern von Erregung.

Er trägt wieder Jeans und T-Shirt. Diesmal ein graues. Er scheint eine Vorliebe für schlichte Kleidung zu haben und das ist clever von ihm. So kommt sein Aussehen am besten zur Geltung.

Er lächelt mich an. Mit diesem Lächeln, dass ihn wie einen gefallenen Engel aussehen lässt — dunkel und verführerisch. »Hallo Nora.«

Ich weiß nicht, was ich ihm sagen soll, also platze ich mit dem ersten heraus, das mir in den Sinn kommt. »Wie lange wirst du mich hier fest halten?«

Er legt seinen Kopf leicht zur Seite. »Hier in diesem Raum? Oder auf der Insel?«

»Beides«

»Beth wird dir morgen die Umgebung zeigen und mit dir schwimmen gehen, falls du Lust dazu hast«, sagt er und kommt dabei immer näher. »Du wirst nicht mehr eingesperrt sein, außer du machst Dummheiten.«

»Wie zum Beispiel?« frage ich und mein Herz klopft, als er neben mir stehen bleibt und seine Hand hebt, um mein Haar zu berühren.

»Versuchen, dir oder Beth etwas anzutun.« Seine Stimme war sanft und sein Blick hypnotisierend als er zu mir hinunter sieht. Die Art und Weise, wie er mein Haar berührt, war sonderbar entspannend.

Ich zwinkere, um seinen Zauber zu brechen. »Und was ist mit der Insel? Wie lange wirst du mich hier festhalten?«

Seine Hand streichelt jetzt mein Gesicht und fährt an meiner Wange entlang. Ich erwische mich dabei, wie ich mich seiner Berührung hingebe, wie eine Katze, die gekrault wird, und versteife augenblicklich.

Seine Lippen verziehen sich zu einem wissenden Lächeln. Dieser Bastard weiß genau welche Wirkung er auf mich hat. »Eine lange Zeit, hoffe ich«, sagt er.

Aus irgendeinem Grund bin ich nicht überrascht. Er würde sich nicht die Umstände gemacht haben, mich bis hierherzubringen, wenn er mich nur einige Male ficken wollte. Ich habe Angst, aber bin nicht wirklich verwundert.

Ich nehme all meinen Mut zusammen und frage die

nächste logische Frage. »Warum hast du mich entführt?«

Das Lächeln verschwindet aus seinem Gesicht. Er antwortet nicht, sondern schaut mich nur mit einem undurchschaubaren melancholischen Blick an.

Ich fange an zu zittern. »Wirst du mich töten?«

»Nein, Nora, ich werde dich nicht töten.«

Seine Verneinung beruhigt mich, auch wenn er mich gerade anlügen könnte. Ich bin ein kleines bisschen ruhiger, aber es gibt da noch eine weitere Sache, die ich unbedingt wissen muss. »Wirst du mir wehtun?«

Einen Moment lang antwortet er wieder nicht. Etwas Dunkles flackert kurz in seinen Augen auf. »Wahrscheinlich«, sagt er ruhig.

Und dann beugt er sich hinunter und küsst mich, mit seinen warmen Lippen weich und zärtlich auf meine.

Eine Sekunde lang stehe ich stocksteif da, ohne irgendeine Reaktion. Ich glaube ihm. Ich weiß, dass er mir die Wahrheit sagt, wenn er behauptet, dass er mir wehtun wird. Er hat etwas an sich, das mir Angst Macht — das mir schon von Anfang an Angst gemacht hat.

Er ist überhaupt nicht wie die Jungs, mit denen ich Verabredungen hatte. Er ist zu allem fähig.

Und ich bin ihm völlig ausgeliefert.

Ich denke darüber nach, mich zu wehren. Das wäre das Normale, was man in meiner Situation machen würde. Das wäre mutig.

Und trotzdem mache ich es nicht.

Ich kann die dunklen Abgründe in ihm fühlen. Irgendetwas stimmt mit ihm nicht. Seine äußere Schönheit verbirgt etwas Grauenvolles im Inneren.

Ich möchte diese Dunkelheit nicht entfesseln. Ich weiß nicht, was passieren wird, wenn ich es tue.

Also stehe ich bewegungslos in seiner Umarmung und lasse mich von ihm küssen. Und als er mich aufhebt und zum Bett trägt, versuche ich überhaupt nicht, etwas dagegen zu machen.

Stattdessen schließe ich meine Augen und gebe mich den Empfindungen hin.

———

Wenn Sie wissen möchten, wann *Twist Me - Verschleppt* erscheinen wird, besuchen Sie bitte meine Webseite https://www.annazaires.com/book-series/deutsch/ und melden Sie sich für den Newsletter über meine Neuerscheinungen an.

AUSZUG AUS GEFANGENE DES KRINAR

Anmerkungen der Autorin: *Die Gefangene des Krinar* ist ein abgeschlossener Roman, der ungefähr fünf Jahre vor der Trilogie *Die Krinar Chroniken* spielt.

———

Emily Ross hatte in keinem Moment erwartet, ihren tödlichen Absturz im costa-ricanischen Dschungel zu überleben, und mit Sicherheit hatte sie nicht damit gerechnet, in einer eigenartig futuristischen Unterkunft aufzuwachen und von dem schönsten Mann gefangen gehalten zu werden, den sie jemals gesehen hatte. Einem Mann, der mehr als menschlich zu sein scheint …

Zaron befindet sich auf der Erde, um die krinarische

Invasion vorzubereiten – und die schreckliche Tragödie zu vergessen, die sein Leben zerstört hat. Als er den verletzten Körper des menschlichen Mädchens findet, ändert sich allerdings alles. Zum ersten Mal seit Jahren fühlt er mehr als nur Wut und Trauer, und Emily ist der Grund dafür. Sie gehen zu lassen, würde seine Vorhaben verraten, aber sie zu behalten, könnte ihn erneut zerstören.

––––––

Ich will nicht sterben. Ich will nicht sterben. Bitte, bitte, bitte, ich will nicht sterben.

Diese Worte wiederholten sich in ihrem Kopf, ein hoffnungsloses Gebet, das nie erhört werden würde. Ihre Finger rutschten weitere Zentimeter auf dem hölzernen Brett entlang, und ihre Nägel brachen ab, als sie versuchte, nicht den Halt zu verlieren.

Emily Ross krallte sich – im wahrsten Sinne des Wortes – an einer kaputten, alten Brücke fest. Hunderte Meter unter ihr rauschte das Wasser über die Felsen, da der Gebirgsbach durch die jüngsten Regenfälle angeschwollen war.

Diese Regenfälle waren zum Teil verantwortlich für ihre derzeitige Notlage. Wäre das Holz auf der Brücke trocken gewesen, wäre sie vielleicht nicht ausgerutscht und hätte sich auch nicht den Fuß dabei verdreht. Und sie wäre mit Sicherheit nicht auf das Brückengeländer gefallen, das unter ihrem Gewicht zerbrochen war.

Allein ihr verzweifeltes Zugreifen in der letzten Sekunde hatte verhindert, dass Emily nach unten in den Tod stürzte. Während des Fallens hatte ihre rechte Hand einen kleinen Vorsprung an der Seite der Brücke zu fassen bekommen, so dass sie jetzt einige hundert Meter über den harten Steinen in der Luft hing.

Ich will nicht sterben. Ich will nicht sterben. Bitte, bitte, bitte, ich will nicht sterben.

Das war nicht fair. Das hätte nicht passieren dürfen. Das waren ihre Ferien, ihre Zeit, wieder zu sich zu finden. Wie konnte sie jetzt sterben? Sie hatte noch nicht einmal begonnen zu leben.

Bilder der letzten zwei Jahre gingen Emily durch den Kopf, wie die PowerPoint-Präsentationen, mit deren Erstellung sie so viele Stunden verbracht hatte. Jedes Arbeiten bis spät in die Nacht, jedes Wochenende, das sie im Büro verbracht hatte – das alles war umsonst gewesen. Sie hatte ihren Job während der letzten Entlassungswelle verloren, und jetzt war sie kurz davor, ihr Leben zu verlieren.

Nein, nein!

Emily ruderte mit den Beinen und grub ihre Nägel tiefer in das Holz. Sie hob den anderen Arm in die Höhe und streckte ihn nach oben zur Brücke aus. Das würde nicht geschehen. Das würde sie nicht zulassen. Sie hatte zu hart gearbeitet, um sich von einem blöden Dschungel alles kaputtmachen zu lassen.

Blut lief an ihrem Arm hinunter, als sie sich an dem rauen Holz die Haut ihrer Finger abschürfte. Ihre einzige Hoffnung, doch noch zu überleben, war, zu versuchen, mit ihrer linken Hand die andere Seite der Brücke zu ergreifen, damit sie sich wieder hochziehen konnte. Es gab hier niemanden, der ihr helfen konnte, niemanden, der sie retten konnte, wenn sie sich nicht selbst rettete.

Die Möglichkeit, dass sie allein im Regenwald sterben könnte, war ihr nicht in den Sinn gekommen, als sie diese Reise angetreten hatte. Sie ging häufig wandern und zelten. Und trotz der Hölle, die ihr Leben in den letzten zwei Jahren gewesen war, war sie immer noch gut in Form, kräftig und durchtrainiert vom Laufen und den ganzen anderen Sportarten, die sie an der Highschool und an der Uni ausgeübt hatte. Costa Rica wurde durch seine niedrige Kriminalitätsrate und seine touristenfreundliche Bevölkerung als ein sicheres Reiseziel angesehen. Und ein billiges – ein wichtiger Aspekt bei ihrem schnell schwindenden Sparguthaben.

Sie hatte diese Reise schon vorher gebucht. Bevor die Börse erneut eingebrochen war, bevor eine neue Entlassungswelle kam, die Tausende von Menschen, die an der Wall Street arbeiteten, ihre Jobs gekostet hatte. Bevor Emily am Montag zur Arbeit gegangen war, übernächtigt von der ganzen Wochenendarbeit, nur um am gleichen Tag das Büro mit einem kleinen Karton zu verlassen, in dem sich alle ihre privaten Habseligkeiten befanden.

Bevor ihre Beziehung nach vier Jahren zerbrochen war.

Ihr erster Urlaub in zwei Jahren, und sie war kurz davor, zu sterben.

Nein, das darfst du nicht denken. Das wird nicht passieren.

Aber Emily wusste, dass sie sich selbst belog. Sie konnte spüren, wie ihre Finger weiter abrutschten und ihr rechter Arm und ihre Schulter von der Anstrengung brannten, das Gewicht ihres ganzen Körpers halten zu müssen. Ihre linke Hand war nur noch einige Zentimeter davon entfernt, die andere Seite der Brücke zu erreichen, aber diese Zentimeter hätten genauso gut Meter sein können. Ihr Halt war nicht stark genug, um sich mit nur einem Arm hochzuziehen.

Tu es, Emily! Denk nicht lange darüber nach, tu es einfach!

Sie nahm ihre ganze Kraft zusammen, schwang ihre Beine in die Luft und nutzte die Schwungkraft, um ihren Körper für den Bruchteil einer Sekunde etwas in die Höhe zu ziehen. Ihre linke Hand ergriff das hervorstehende Brett, hielt sich daran fest ... und das schwache Holzstück zerbrach. Die überraschte Emily schrie entsetzt auf.

Ihr letzter Gedanke, bevor ihr Körper auf dem Boden aufschlug, war, dass sie hoffentlich augenblicklich tot sein würde.

———

Der vollmundige und kräftige Geruch der Dschungel-vegetation umspielte Zarons Nase. Er atmete tief ein, damit die feuchte Luft seine Lunge füllen konnte. Dieses winzige Fleckchen Erde hier war so sauber, so unverschmutzt wie sein Heimatplanet.

Genau das brauchte er gerade. Er brauchte die frische Luft, die Isolation. In den letzten sechs Monaten hatte er versucht, vor seinen Gedanken wegzulaufen, nur den Augenblick zu leben, aber das war ihm nicht gelungen. Selbst Blut und Sex reichten ihm nicht mehr. Er konnte sich zwar während des Fickens ablenken, aber der Schmerz kam danach sofort zurück, genauso stark wie immer.

Schließlich war ihm das alles zu viel geworden: der Schmutz, die Menschenmengen, ihr Gestank. Sobald er nicht von einem Nebel der Ekstase umgeben war, wurden seine Sinne von der vielen Zeit, die er in menschlichen Städten verbrachte, überreizt. Hier, wo er Luft holen konnte, ohne Gift einzuatmen, wo er Leben anstatt Chemikalien riechen konnte, war es besser. In einigen Jahren würde alles anders sein, und er könnte vielleicht erneut versuchen, in einer menschlichen Stadt zu leben, aber jetzt noch nicht.

Nicht, bis sie sich nicht vollständig hier niedergelassen hatten.

Das war Zarons Aufgabe: die Niederlassung zu überwachen. Er hatte jahrzehntelang Nachforschungen über die Flora und Fauna der Erde durchgeführt, und als der Rat ihn um seine Hilfe bei der anstehenden

Kolonisation gebeten hatte, hatte er nicht gezögert. Alles war besser als zu Hause zu sein, wo die Erinnerungen an Laritas Gegenwart überall waren.

Hier gab es keine Erinnerungen. Trotz seiner Ähnlichkeiten mit Krina war dieser Planet fremd und exotisch. Sieben Milliarden Menschen auf der Erde – eine unglaubliche Anzahl –, und sie pflanzten sich mit einer schwindelerregenden Geschwindigkeit fort. Wegen ihrer kurzen Lebensspanne fehlte ihnen allerdings ein gewisses Langzeitdenken, und sie verbrauchten die Ressourcen ihres Planeten, ohne auch nur das kleinste bisschen an die Zukunft zu denken. Auf eine gewisse Weise erinnerten sie ihn an die Schistocerca gregaria – eine Spezies der Grashüpfer, die er vor einigen Jahren untersucht hatte.

Natürlich waren die Menschen intelligenter als Insekten. Einige Individuen wie Einstein ähnelten den Krinar in einigen ihrer Denkweisen sogar. Das überraschte Zaron nicht besonders; er hatte immer angenommen, dass das die Absicht des großen Experiments der Ältesten gewesen war.

Während er durch den costa-ricanischen Wald lief, dachte er über seine Aufgabe nach. Dieser Teil des Planeten war vielversprechend; er konnte sich leicht vorstellen, dass essbare Pflanzen von Krina hier gedeihen würden. Er hatte den Boden ausgiebigen Tests unterzogen, und jetzt hatte er einige Ideen, wie er ihn für die krinarische Flora noch verbessern könnte.

Der Wald um ihn herum war saftig und grün, roch nach blühenden Helikonien, und Zaron konnte das

Rauschen der Blätter und das Gezwitscher der einheimischen Vögel hören. In einiger Entfernung ertönte der Schrei eines Alouatta palliata, eines in Costa Rica heimischen Mantelbrüllaffen, und etwas anderes.

Zaron runzelte seine Stirn und hörte genauer hin, aber das Geräusch wiederholte sich nicht.

Neugierig eilte er in die Richtung, aus der es gekommen war, da seine Jagdinstinkte in Alarmbereitschaft versetzt worden waren. Eine Sekunde lang hatte das Geräusch ihn an den Schrei einer Frau erinnert.

Zaron, der mit Leichtigkeit die dichte Vegetation des Dschungels durchdrang, begann zu rennen, wobei er über einen kleinen Bach und einige Büsche sprang, die sich in seinem Weg befanden. Hier draußen, weit entfernt von menschlichen Augen, konnte er sich wie ein Krinar bewegen, ohne sich Sorgen machen zu müssen, dabei gesehen zu werden. Nach einigen wenigen Minuten nahm er einen durchdringenden, metallischen Geruch wahr, durch den sein Mund wässrig und sein Schwanz steif wurde.

Blut.

Menschliches Blut.

Als er sein Ziel erreichte, blieb Zaron stehen und starrte auf den Anblick vor ihm.

Vor ihm befand sich ein Bach, ein Gebirgsbach, der wegen der jüngsten Regenfälle angeschwollen war. Und auf den großen schwarzen Steinen in der Mitte, unter einer alten Holzbrücke, die über den Bach führte, befand sich ein Körper.

Der gebrochene und verdrehte Körper eines menschlichen Mädchens.

———

Die Gefangene des Krinar ist jetzt erhältlich. Falls Sie mehr darüber erfahren möchten, besuchen Sie bitte meine Homepage https://www.annazaires.com/book-series/deutsch/.

AUSZUG AUS GEFÄHRLICHE BEGEGNUNGEN

Anmerkungen der Autorin: *Gefährliche Begegnungen ist das erste Buch meiner Science-Fiction Romanserie, die Krinar Chroniken. Auch wenn es nicht so düster ist wie Twist Me, enthält es doch einige Elemente, die die Leser von dunkler Erotik mögen könnten.*

———

Eine düstere und anregende Liebesgeschichte, die die Fans erotischer und turbulenter Beziehungen begeistern wird ...

In der nahen Zukunft herrschen die Krinar auf der Erde. Sie sind eine sehr fortgeschrittene Rasse aus einer anderen Galaxie und immer noch ein Geheimnis für uns — außerdem sind wir ihnen völlig ausgeliefert.

Mia Stalis, schüchtern und unschuldig, ist eine

Studentin in New York, die ein sehr normales Leben führt. Wie die meisten Menschen, hat sie nie etwas mit den Eindringlingen zu tun gehabt — bis zu diesem schicksalhaften Tag im Park, der ihr ganzes Leben auf den Kopf stellt. Da sie Korums Aufmerksamkeit auf sich gezogen hat, muss sie jetzt mit einem mächtigen, gefährlich verführerischen Krinar fertig werden, der sie besitzen möchte und vor nichts Halt machen wird, bis er sein Ziel erreicht.

Wie weit würden Sie gehen, um ihre Freiheit wiederzuerlangen? Wie viel würden sie aufgeben, um anderen Menschen zu helfen? Welche Wahl würden Sie treffen, wenn sie beginnen, sich in ihren Feind zu verlieben?

———

Die Luft war frisch und rein, als Mia mit schnellen Schritten einen gewundenen Pfad im Central Park entlangging. Überall zeigte sich schon der Frühling, in winzigen Knospen auf den noch immer kahlen Bäumen und in der rasch wachsenden Anzahl an Kindermädchen, die sich draußen mit ihren wilden Schützlingen über den ersten warmen Tag freuten.

Es war eigenartig, wie sehr sich alles in den letzten paar Jahren verändert hatte und wie sehr es doch gleich geblieben war. Wäre Mia vor zehn Jahren gefragt worden, was sie denke, wie ihr Leben wohl nach der Invasion einer anderen Rasse aussehen würde, hätte sie sich das bestimmt nicht so vorgestellt.

Independence Day, Der Krieg der Welten — keiner dieser Filme näherte sich auch nur ansatzweise dem, was tatsächlich geschehen würde. Die Menschen trafen eine höher entwickelte Spezies, als diese zu Ihnen auf die Erde kam. Es war weder zum Kampf, noch zu irgendeinem Widerstand auf der Regierungsebene gekommen. *Sie* hatten es nicht erlaubt. Rückblickend wurde klar, wie dumm diese Filme gewesen waren. Nuklearwaffen, Satelliten, Kampfjets waren nicht mehr als kleine Steine und Stöcke für diese uralte Zivilisation, die schneller als mit Lichtgeschwindigkeit das Universum durchqueren konnte.

Als sie eine leere Bank nahe am See sah, ging Mia dankbar auf diese zu. Auf ihren Schultern machte sich die Last des Rucksacks bemerkbar, in dem sie ihren schweren zwölf Jahre alten Laptop und einige altmodische, noch auf Papier gedruckte Bücher hatte. Mit einundzwanzig fühlte sie sich manchmal alt, fehl am Platz in dieser schnellen neuen Welt der extraschlanken Tablets und den in die Armbanduhren integrierten Handys. Die Geschwindigkeit der technischen Entwicklungen war seit dem K-Day nicht langsamer geworden, wenn Überhaupt, waren jetzt viele neue Spielereien durch das beeinflusst, was die Krinar besaßen. Nicht dass die Krinar irgendetwas ihrer kostbaren Technologie Preis gegeben hätten. Ihrer Meinung nach sollte ihr kleines Experiment ohne größere Beeinflussungen fortgeführt werden.

Mia öffnete den Reißverschluss ihres Rucksacks und holte ihren alten Mac heraus. Das Gerät war schwer und langsam, aber es funktionierte, und als arme Studentin konnte sich Mia nichts Besseres leisten. Sie loggte sich ein, öffnete ein neues Word-Dokument und machte sich bereit, sich durch das Schreiben ihrer Hausarbeit in Soziologie zu quälen.

Zehn Minuten und genau Null Worte später gab sie auf. Wem wollte sie denn damit etwas vor machen? Hätte sie wirklich dieses verdammte Ding schreiben wollen, wäre sie doch niemals in den Central Park gekommen. So verlockend es auch war, sich fest vorzunehmen die frische Luft zu genießen und gleichzeitig etwas zu arbeiten, in Wirklichkeit hatte Mia das noch nie hinbekommen. Eine muffige alte Bibliothek war ein viel besserer Ort für solche Tätigkeiten, die derartig das Hirn zermartern.

Mia gab sich in Gedanken einen Tritt für die eigene Faulheit, seufzte und sah sich trotzdem erst mal um. Die Menschen in New York zu beobachten amüsierte sie immer wieder.

Das Bild, was sie vor sich sah, war ein Klassiker, mit dem Obdachlosen auf der Parkbank — zum Glück nicht auf der neben ihr, er sah nämlich so aus, als würde er schon sehr streng riechen — und den beiden Kindermädchen, die miteinander auf Spanisch redeten, während sie langsam ihre Kinderwagen vor sich her schoben. Ein Mädchen mit leuchtend pinkfarbenen Reeboks, die einen schönen Kontrast zu ihren blauen Leggins bildeten, joggte auf einem Weg weiter vorne. Mias Blick folgte neidisch der Joggerin, als diese um die Ecke bog. Ihr eigener hektischer Tagesablauf ließ ihr nur wenig Zeit zum Trainieren und sie bezweifelte, dass sie derzeitig auch nur einen Kilometer lang mit diesem Mädchen mithalten konnte.

Rechts konnte sie die Bogenbrücke sehen, die über den ganzen See reichte. Ein Mann lehnte am Brückengeländer und schaute über das Wasser. Sein Gesicht war von ihr weg gedreht, weshalb Mia nur einen Teil seines Profils sehen konnte. Trotzdem zog irgendetwas an ihm ihre Aufmerksamkeit auf sich.

Sie war sich nicht sicher, was es war. Er war zweifellos groß und schien unter seinem teuer aussehenden Trenchcoat auch einen gut gebauten Körper zu besitzen, aber das konnte es nicht sein. Große, gut aussehende Männer waren in dem von Modells überlaufenden New York nichts Besonderes. Nein, es war irgendetwas anderes. Vielleicht war es die Art und Weise, wie er da stand — völlig bewegungslos. Sein Haar war dunkel und glänzte in der hellen Nachmittagssonne, vorne gerade lang genug, um leicht im warmen Frühlingswind zu wehen.

Außerdem war er völlig alleine.

Das ist es, bemerkte Mia auf einmal. Die normalerweise sehr beliebte und malerische Brücke war völlig leer, mit Ausnahme des Mannes, der dort am Geländer stand. Heute schien aus irgendeinem Grund jeder einen weiten Bogen um sie zu machen. Tatsächlich saß niemand außer ihr und ihrem hocharomatischen, obdachlosen Nachbarn auf den sonst so beliebten Bänken in der ersten Reihe am See, sie waren alle leer.

Als ob es ihren Blick auf sich spüren würde, drehte

das Objekt ihrer Aufmerksamkeit langsam seinen Kopf und sah Mia direkt an. Bevor ihr Hirn sich dieser Tatsache bewusst werden konnte, fühlte sie, wie ihr Blut gefror und sie sich bewegungslos dem Feind ausgeliefert sah. Während sie ihn nur hilflos anstarren konnte, schien er sie sehr interessiert zu durchleuchten.

———

Atme, Mia, atme. Irgendwo in ihrem Hinterkopf wiederholte eine kleine rationale Stimme immer wieder diese Worte. Diesem seltsam objektiven Teil von ihr fiel auch sein symmetrisches Gesicht auf und die straffe goldfarbene Haut, die sich eng an hohe Wangenknochen und ein energisches Kinn schmiegte. Die Bilder und Videos die sie von den Krinar gesehen hatte, wurden ihnen kaum gerecht. Dieses Wesen, das weniger als 10 Meter von ihr entfernt stand, war einfach atemberaubend schön.

Während sie ihn weiterhin bewegungslos anstarrte, richtete er sich auf und ging auf sie zu. Er pirscht sich eher heran, kam ihr dummerweise in den Sinn, da jede seiner Bewegungen sie an eine junge Raubkatze erinnerte, die sich geschmeidig einer Gazelle annähert. Seine Augen ließen sie die ganze Zeit nicht aus dem Blick. Als er näherkam, konnte sie einzelne gelbe Sprenkel in seinen goldenen Augen erkennen und auch die vollen langen Wimpern sehen, die sie einrahmten.

Sie sah entsetzt und ungläubig, wie er sich weniger

als einen Meter von ihr entfernt auf die gleiche Bank setzte und eine ebenmäßige Reihe weißer Zähne entblößte, als er sie anlächelte. Keine Fangzähne, bemerkte sie mit einem Teil ihres Gehirns, der noch zu funktionieren schien. Nicht die leiseste Spur von ihnen. Das war eines der Gerüchte über sie, genauso wie ihr vermeintlicher Abscheu vor der Sonne.

»Wie heißt du?« Das Wesen schnurrte die Frage förmlich. Seine Stimme war leise und weich, völlig ohne Akzent. Seine Nasenlöcher bebten leicht, als er ihren Duft einatmete.

»Ähm« Mia schluckte nervös. »M-Mia.«

»Mia«, wiederholte er langsam, und es schien, als würde er sich ihren Namen auf der Zunge zergehen lassen. »Mia, und weiter?«

»Mia Stalis.« Ach du Scheiße, warum wollte er denn ihren Namen wissen? Warum war er hier und redete mit ihr? Und überhaupt, was machte er eigentlich im Central Park, fernab aller Siedlungen der Krinar? *Atme, Mia, atme.*

»Entspanne dich, Mia Stalis.« Sein Lächeln wurde breiter und es kam ein Grübchen in seiner linken Wange zum Vorschein. Ein Grübchen? Die Krinar hatten Grübchen? »Bist du bis jetzt noch nie auf einen von uns getroffen?«

»Nein, noch nie«, stieß Mia kurz hervor und dabei fiel ihr auf, dass sie ihren Atem die ganze Zeit anhielt. Sie war stolz darauf, dass ihre Stimme nicht so zitterig klang, wie sie sich anfühlte. Sollte sie fragen? Wollte sie es wirklich wissen?

Sie nahm all ihren Mut zusammen. »Was, äh —« nochmal Schlucken. »Was willst du von mir?«

»Jetzt gerade, mich mit dir unterhalten.« Mit diesen goldenen Augen, die sich an den Winkeln leicht zusammen zogen, sah er aus, als würde er gleich über sie lachen.

Seltsamerweise machte sie das so wütend, dass sie dadurch ihre Angst verdrängte. Wenn es etwas gab, das Mia mehr hasste als alles andere, dann war das, ausgelacht zu werden. Mit ihrem kleinen, dünnen Körper und ihrem allgemeinen Mangel an sozialer Kompetenz seit Teenagerzeiten — sie hatte das komplette Albtraumprogramm absolviert: Zahnspange, krauses Haar und Brille — waren schon mehr als einmal Witze auf Mias Kosten gemacht worden.

Sie schob angriffslustig ihr Kinn in die Höhe. »Also schön, und wie heißt du?«

»Korum.«

»Nur Korum?«

»Wir haben keine richtigen Nachnamen, zumindest nicht so wie ihr das habt. Mein voller Name ist sehr viel länger, aber du könntest ihn nicht aussprechen wenn ich ihn dir sagen würde.«

Okay, das war doch mal interessant. Sie erinnerte sich daran, mal so etwas in der *New York Times* gelesen zu haben. So weit, so gut. Ihre Beine hatten schon fast aufgehört zu zittern und ihre Atmung wurde auch wieder gleichmäßiger. Vielleicht, hatte sie ja doch noch eine klitzekleine Chance, aus dieser Nummer lebend herauszukommen. Diese Unterhaltung schien recht ungefährlich zu sein, auch wenn es sie etwas aus der Fassung brachte, dass er sie die ganze Zeit mit diesen gelblichen Augen anstarrte, ohne zu blinzeln. Sie beschloss, ihn reden zu lassen.

»Was machst du hier, Korum?«

»Das habe ich dir doch gerade gesagt. Ich unterhalte mich mit dir, Mia.« Seine Stimme hatte wieder den Hauch eines Lachens.

Frustriert stieß Mia ihren Atem aus. »Ich meine, was machst du hier im Central Park? Überhaupt in New York City?«

Er lächelte wieder und neigte seinen Kopf leicht zu einer Seite. »Vielleicht habe ich gehofft, hier ein hübsches Mädchen mit Locken zu treffen.«

Also, das reichte jetzt wirklich. Er spielte ganz klar mit ihr. Jetzt, da sie ihren Verstand wieder gebrauchen konnte, fiel ihr auf, dass sie sich mitten im Central Park befanden, in der Gegenwart einer Unmenge von Zeugen. Sie blickte sich verstohlen um, nur um sicherzugehen. Ja, obwohl die Menschen diese Bank und das darauf sitzende fremdartige Wesen offensichtlich mieden, gab es tatsächlich einige mutige Seelen, die aus sicherer Entfernung zu ihnen starrten. Ein Paar wagte es sogar, sie vorsichtig mit ihren in die Armbanduhren eingebauten Kameras zu filmen. Wenn der Krinar ihr irgendetwas antun sollte, wäre es umgehend auf YouTube zu sehen und das müsste er auch wissen. Natürlich könnte ihm das auch egal sein.

Da sie immer noch davon ausging, dass sie relativ sicher war — sie hatte noch nie von Videos gehört, die

Übergriffe der Krinar auf Studentinnen mitten im Central Park zeigten — griff sie nach ihrem Laptop und hob ihn an, um ihn zurück in ihren Rucksack zu packen.

»Lass mich dir damit helfen, Mia —«

Und bevor sie auch nur blinzeln konnte, merkte sie, wie er den schweren Laptop aus ihren plötzlich kraftlosen Fingern nahm und dabei leicht deren Knöchel streifte. Als er sie berührte, durchfuhr Mia ein Gefühl wie ein elektrischer Schock, der, als er abebbte, kribbelnde Nervenverbindungen hinterließ.

Er nahm ihren Rucksack und packte den Laptop mit einer weichen und geschmeidigen Bewegung weg. »So, fertig.«

Oh Gott, er hatte sie berührt. Vielleicht war ihre Theorie über die Sicherheit auf öffentlichen Plätzen doch falsch. Sie merkte, wie sich ihre Atmung wieder beschleunigte, und ihre Herzfrequenz befand sich wahrscheinlich auch schon im Sauerstoff unabhängigen Bereich.

»Ich muss jetzt los ... Tschüss!«

Wie sie es schaffte, diese Worte herauszuquetschen ohne zu hyperventilieren, würde sie wohl nie herausfinden. Sie griff sich den Riemen ihres Rucksacks, den er soeben losgelassen hatte und sprang auf ihre Füße. Dabei fiel ihr irgendwo im Hinterkopf auf, dass die Lähmung von vorhin verschwunden war.

»Tschüss Mia. Bis später.« Seine Stimme mit dem leicht spottenden Unterton war noch lange in der klaren Frühlingsluft zu hören, als sie losging und fast rannte, weil sie es so eilig hatte, von ihm wegzukommen.

———

Wenn Sie mehr darüber erfahren möchten, besuchen Sie bitte Annas Webseite https://www.annazaires.com/book-series/deutsch/.

AUSZUG AUS DIE GEDANKENLESER

Anmerkung des Autors: Wenn Sie etwas anderes ausprobieren möchten – ganz besonders wenn Sie Urban Fantasy und Science-Fiction mögen – sollten Sie einen Blick in *Die Gedankenleser* werfen, dem ersten Buch der Serie *Gedankendimensionen*, einem Gemeinschaftsprojekt mit meinem Mann Dima Zales. Ich muss Sie allerdings warnen, dass es in dem Buch kaum um Liebe oder Sex geht. Statt Sex gibt es Gedankenlesen. Das Buch ist jetzt bei den meisten Händlern erhältlich.

———

Alle denken ich sei ein Genie.

Alle liegen falsch.

Sicher, Ich habe Harvard im Alter von achtzehn Jahren

abgeschlossen und verdiene jetzt eine unglaubliche Menge Geld mit einem Hedge Fund. Der Grund dafür ist allerdings nicht, dass ich besonders clever bin oder wie verrückt arbeite.

Ich betrüge.

Ich besitze eine einzigartige Fähigkeit. Ich kann die Gegenwart verlassen und in meine eigene persönliche Version der Realität eintauchen – den Ort, den ich die Stille nenne – an dem ich meine Umgebung erkunden kann, während die restliche Welt innehält.

Eigentlich dachte ich immer, ich sei der Einzige, der das tun kann – bis ich sie getroffen habe.

Ich heiße Darren, und das ist die Geschichte, wie ich herausgefunden habe, dass ich ein Leser bin.

———

Manchmal denke ich, dass ich verrückt bin. In diesem Moment sitze ich an einem Kasinotisch und jeder um mich herum ist bewegungslos, so wie eingefroren. Ich nenne das die Stille, so als würde es das Ganze realer machen, wenn es einen Namen hätte – so als würde der Name die Tatsache ändern, dass alle Spieler um mich herum wie Statuen sind. Sie sitzen einfach nur da und ich gehe um sie herum, schaue mir die Karten an, die sie gerade erhalten haben. Hört sich das verrückt an?

Das Problem an der Theorie, ich sei verrückt ist, dass auch wenn ich die Welt 'entfriere', so wie ich es gerade getan habe, die Karten, welche die Spieler aufdecken, immer noch dieselben sind. Wäre ich verrückt, sollten die Karten dann nicht vermischt sein? Außer natürlich, ich bin schon so verrückt, dass ich mir auch die Karten auf dem Tisch einbilde.

Aber selbst dann gewinne ich. Sollte das auch Einbildung sein – sollte der Stapel Chips neben mir auf dem Tisch nur eingebildet sein – dann könnte ich auch gleich alles in Frage stellen. Vielleicht heiße ich auch gar nicht Darren.

Nein. So kann ich nicht denken. Wenn ich wirklich so verwirrt sein sollte, dann möchte ich gar nicht aus diesem Zustand herausgeholt werden – weil, wenn das passiert, werde ich höchstwahrscheinlich in einer psychiatrischen Anstalt aufwachen.

Außerdem liebe ich mein Leben, verrückt oder nicht.

Meine Psychiaterin denkt, die Stille sei eine Erfindung, um die inneren Vorgänge meines Genies zu beschreiben. Das hört sich für mich verrückt an. Es könnte auch sein, dass sie mich begehrt, aber das steht außer Frage. Sie befindet sich komplett außerhalb der Altersgruppe, mit der ich ausgehe. Ihre Erklärung würde sowieso nicht helfen, da sie nicht auf die Art und Weise zutrifft, mit der ich Dinge weiß, die selbst ein Genie nicht erahnen könnte – wie den genauen Wert des Blattes der anderen Spieler.

Ich sehe dem Croupier dabei zu, wie er eine neue Runde eröffnet. Außer mir befinden sich noch drei weitere Spieler am Tisch. Der Cowboy, die Großmutter und der Professionelle, wie ich sie in Gedanken nenne. Ich kann die jetzt fast spürbare Angst fühlen, die mit dem Hineingleiten einhergeht – das ist der Name, den ich dem Prozess gegeben habe: in die Stille hineingleiten. Meine Sorge, ich könne verrückt sein, hat das Hineingleiten schon immer vereinfacht. Angst scheint diesen Prozess zu begünstigen.

Ich gleite hinein, und alles ist still. Daher der Name für diesen Vorgang.

Selbst jetzt finde ich das noch unheimlich. In diesem Kasino ist es normalerweise sehr laut Betrunkene Menschen, die sich unterhalten. Spielautomaten, das Läuten bei Gewinnen, Musik – nur in einem Klub oder bei Konzerten ist es lauter. Und trotzdem, genau in diesem Moment könnte ich wahrscheinlich eine Stecknadel fallen hören. Es ist so, als sei ich gegenüber dem Chaos um mich herum taub geworden.

So viele eingefrorene Menschen um mich herum zu haben macht das Ganze nur noch eigenartiger. Hier ist eine Kellnerin, die mitten im Schritt mit ihrem Tablett auf dem Arm angehalten hat. Eine Frau, die gerade dabei ist, eine Münze in einen Spielautomaten zu schmeißen. An meinem eigenen Tisch ist die Hand des Croupiers erhoben und die letzte Karte, die er gezogen hat, hängt unnatürlich in der Luft. Ich gehe von der Seite des Tisches auf sie zu und nehme sie in die Hand. Es ist ein König, der für den Professionellen bestimmt ist. Als ich die Karte loslasse, fällt sie auf den Tisch anstatt weiter in der Luft zu schweben, wie sie es vorher getan hat. Ich weiß allerdings genau, dass sie sich wieder dort befinden wird, in genau der Position in der sie war, als ich sie genommen habe, sobald ich mich aus diesem Zustand zurückziehe.

Der Professionelle sieht genau so aus, wie ich mir immer Menschen vorgestellt habe, die mit Poker spielen ihr Geld verdienen: ungepflegt, Schatten unter den Augen und generell ein wenig eigenartig. Er hat sein Pokerface das ganze Spiel über perfekt im Griff gehabt – es hat nicht ein einziges Mal ein Muskel gezuckt. Sein Gesicht ist so unbeweglich, dass ich mich frage, ob ihm vielleicht Botox dabei hilft, eine so steinerne Miene aufrechtzuerhalten. Seine Hand befindet sich auf dem Tisch und bedeckt beschützend die Karten, die ihm gegeben wurden.

Ich bewege seine schlaffe Hand zur Seite. Das fühlt sich normal an. Also gewissermaßen. Seine Hand ist schweißnass und haarig, weshalb es unangenehm ist, sie zur Seite zu legen. Es ist anormal, das zu tun. Der normale Teil des Ganzen ist, dass seine Hand eher warm als kalt ist. Als ich noch ein Kind war, erwartete ich, dass sich die Menschen in der Stille kalt anfühlen würden, wie Statuen aus Stein.

Nachdem ich die Hand des Professionellen zur Seite gelegt habe, nehme ich seine Karten auf.

Zusammen mit dem König, der gerade in der Luft hängt, hat er ein hübsches hohes Blatt. Gut zu wissen.

Ich gehe zur Großmutter hinüber. Sie hält ihre Karten in der Hand. Dadurch dass sie sie wie einen Fächer ausgebreitet hat kann ich es vermeiden, ihre faltigen und fleckigen Hände zu berühren. Das ist eine Erleichterung, da ich in der letzten Zeit meine Probleme damit habe, in der Stille Menschen anzufassen – genauer gesagt Frauen. Falls ich es tun müsste, würde ich das Berühren von Großmutters Hand rational als harmlos ansehen – oder es zumindest nicht gruselig finden – aber es ist trotzdem besser es möglichst zu vermeiden.

Auf jeden Fall hat sie ein niedriges Blatt. Ich fühle mich schlecht für sie. Sie hat heute Nacht eine ganze Menge verloren. Ihre Chips gehen zur Neige. Vielleicht sind ihre Verluste, zumindest teilweise, der Tatsache zuzuschreiben, dass sie kein gutes Pokerface aufsetzen kann. Schon bevor ich einen Blick auf ihre Karten geworfen hatte wusste ich, dass sie nicht gut sein würden. Ich konnte sehen, dass sie nicht glücklich mit dem war, was sie in der Hand hielt, sobald sie ihre Karten bekam. Ich habe sie außerdem vor einigen Runden bei einem fröhlichen Aufblitzen ihrer Augen ertappt, als sie ein Dreierpaar hatte, welches gewann.

Pokern ist zu einem Großteil eine Übung, um Menschen besser lesen zu können – eine Fähigkeit, die ich gerne besser beherrschen würde. Auf meiner Arbeit wurde mir gesagt, ich sei großartig darin, Menschen zu lesen. Aber das bin ich nicht. Ich bin einfach nur gut darin die Stille zu verwenden um Ihnen das vorzumachen. Ich möchte aber trotzdem lernen, es wirklich zu können.

Was mich am Pokern eher weniger interessiert ist das Geld. Mir geht es finanziell gut genug, um nicht auf den Gewinn durch das Spielen angewiesen zu sein. Mir ist es egal, ob ich gewinne oder verliere, auch wenn das verfünffachen meines Geldes an dem Black Jack Tisch Spaß gemacht hatte. Dieser ganze Ausflug zum Spielen findet überhaupt nur deshalb statt, weil ich es mit einundzwanzig endlich darf. Ich war nie ein Freund von falschen Ausweisen und deshalb ist das wirklich ein Meilenstein für mich.

Ich verlasse die Großmutter und gehe hinüber zum Cowboy. Ich kann seinem Strohhut nicht widerstehen und setze ihn mir auf. Ich frage mich dabei, ob ich dadurch Läuse bekommen könnte. Da ich noch nie leblose Objekte aus der Stille zurückbringen konnte und auch anderweitig die Welt nicht nachhaltig beeinflusst habe, denke ich, dass ich auch keine lebenden Viecher mit mir zurücknehme. Ich lege den Hut zurück und schaue auf seine Karten. Er hat einige Asse – eine bessere Hand als der Professionelle. Der Cowboy könnte auch ein Professioneller sein. Soweit ich das beurteilen kann hat er ein gutes Pokerface. Es wird interessant werden, die beiden in der nächsten Runde zu beobachten.

Dann schlendere ich zum Kartenstapel und schaue mir die obersten Karten an, um sie mir einzuprägen. Ich überlasse nichts dem Zufall.

Als ich meine Aufgabe in der Stille abgeschlossen habe, gehe ich zurück zu mir. Ach ja, habe ich erwähnt, dass ich mich selbst dort sitzen sehen kann? Genauso eingefroren wie alle anderen? Das ist der verrückteste Teil. Es ist so, wie eine außerkörperliche Erfahrung.

Ich nähere mich meinem eingefrorenen Ich, und schaue es an. Normalerweise vermeide ich das, weil es so beunruhigend ist. Weder sich selbst unzählige Male im Spiegel zu sehen, oder sich Videos mit sich selbst auf YouTube anzuschauen, kann einen auf den Anblick des eigenen Körpers in 3D vorbereiten. Das ist nichts, was dafür gedacht ist, es zu erleben. Außer vielleicht, man ist ein eineiiger Zwilling.

Es ist kaum zu glauben, dass ich diese Person bin. Sie sieht eher wie ein ganz normaler Typ aus. Vielleicht nach ein wenig mehr. Ich finde diesen Typen sehr interessant. Normalerweise ist für mich das Aussehen anderer Männer nicht interessant, aber ich bin neugierig, wie mein eingefrorenes Ich aussieht. Oder um ganz ehrlich zu sein: Ich mag es, wie mein eingefrorenes Ich aussieht. Es sieht cool aus. Es sieht clever aus.

Ich denke Frauen könnten es als gut aussehend bezeichnen, auch wenn es nicht bescheiden von mir ist, das zu behaupten.

Ich bin nicht gut darin, die Attraktivität von Männern zu bewerten – das war ich noch nie – aber einige Dinge sind allgemeingültig. Ich kann erkennen, wenn ein Typ hässlich ist, und mein eingefrorenes Ich ist es nicht. Ich weiß auch, dass generell ein symmetrisches Gesicht als schön angesehen wird – und meine Statue hat so eines. Ein starkes Kinn ist auch nichts schlechtes. Das habe ich. Breite Schultern zu haben ist gut und groß zu sein wirklich hilfreich. Diese Punkte decke ich auch ab. Ich habe blaue Augen – was ein Pluspunkt zu sein scheint. Mädchen haben mir gesagt, dass sie meine Augen mögen, auch wenn sie an meinem gefrorenen Ich jetzt gerade ein wenig angsteinflößend wirken – glasig und glänzend. Sie sehen aus wie die Augen einer Wachsfigur. Leblos.

Als mir auffällt, dass ich mich zu lange bei diesem Thema aufhalte, schüttele ich meinen Kopf. Ich stelle mir vor, wie meine Psychiaterin diesen Moment analysieren würde. Wer würde diese Selbstbewunderung schon als Teil der psychischen Erkrankung sehen? Ich sehe sie vor mir, wie sie Worte wie 'Narzisstisch' notiert.

Genug. Ich muss Die Stille verlassen. Ich hebe meine Hand und berühre mein eingefrorenes Ich auf der Stirn. Sobald ich meinen derzeitigen Zustand verlasse kehren die Geräusche zurück.

Alles ist wieder normal.

Der König, auf den ich noch vor einem Moment schaute – der König, den ich auf dem Tisch liegen ließ – befindet sich wieder in der Luft und folgt der Bahn, die ihm vorherbestimmt war. Er landet neben der Hand des Professionellen. Die Großmutter betrachtet immer noch enttäuscht ihre gefächerten Karten und der Cowboy hat seinen Hut wieder auf, auch wenn ich ihn in der Stille abgenommen hatte. Es ist alles genau so wie in dem Augenblick bevor ich in die Stille hineinglitt.

Auf einer bestimmten Ebene hört mein Gehirn nie auf, über diese Unterschiede zwischen der Stille und außerhalb überrascht zu sein. Es ist fast vorprogrammiert die Realität in Frage zu stellen, wenn solche Dinge passieren. Als ich versuchte, meine Psychiaterin am Anfang der Therapie auszutricksen, las ich einmal ein ganzes Lehrbuch über Psychologie während unserer Sitzung. Ihr ist das natürlich nicht aufgefallen, da ich es in der Stille tat. Das Buch handelte davon, dass Babys, auch wenn sie erst zwei Monate alt sind, schon überrascht darüber sind, wenn sie etwas Ungewöhnliches sehen – wenn zum Beispiel eine Sache gegen die Regeln der Schwerkraft zu verstoßen scheint. Kein Wunder, dass mein Gehirn Schwierigkeiten damit hat, mit diesen Vorgängen zurechtzukommen. Bis ich zehn war, war alles normal, aber dann begannen die eigenartigen Dinge, um es vorsichtig auszudrücken.

Ich blicke hinab und stelle fest, drei Gleiche in der Hand zu halten. Das nächste Mal werde ich mir meine Karten anschauen, bevor ich hineingleite. Wenn ich so ein starkes Blatt habe, kann ich es auch darauf ankommen lassen und fair spielen.

Die Partie verläuft wie erwartet, weil ich ja die Karten sämtlicher Mitspieler kenne. Schließlich gibt die Großmutter auf. Sie hat offensichtlich genug Geld verloren.

In diesem Moment sehe ich sie zum ersten Mal.

Sie ist heiß. Mein Freund Bert von der Arbeit behauptet ich hätte einen bestimmten Frauentyp. Er hat ihn mir sogar beschrieben, nachdem er einige der Mädchen, mit denen ich ausgegangen war, gesehen hatte. Ich lehne dieses Konzept eines 'Frauentyps' generell ab. Ich mag es nicht, von mir selbst zu denken, ich sei oberflächlich oder berechenbar. Allerdings könnte das schon ein wenig auf mich zutreffen, da dieses Mädchen genau in das Beuteschema passt, welches Bert mir beschrieben hat. Und ich bin milde ausgedrückt extrem interessiert an ihr.

Große blaue Augen, deutlich erkennbare Wangenknochen, ein schmales Gesicht mit einem Hauch Exotik. Lange, extrem wohlgeformte Beine, die zu einer Tänzerin gehören könnten. Dunkles, gewelltes Haar, das, wie ich es mag, zu einem Pferdeschwanz gebunden ist. Kein Pony – sehr gut. Ich hasse Ponys und kann mir auch nicht erklären, wie manche Mädchen sich so etwas antun können. Auch wenn die Abwesenheit des Ponys in Berts Beschreibung meines Frauentyps nicht vorkam, gehört dieses Kriterium definitiv dazu.

Ich starre sie weiterhin an. Mit den hohen Absätzen und dem engen Rock wirkt sie an diesem Ort overdressed. Oder vielleicht bin ich mit meiner Jeans und dem T-Shirt auch einfach underdressed. Wie dem auch sei, es interessiert mich nicht. Ich muss versuchen, mit ihr ins Gespräch zu kommen.

Ich denke darüber nach, in die Stille einzutauchen und mich ihr anzunähern. Auf diese Weise könnte ich etwas unheimliches tun, wie sie aus nächster Nähe anstarren oder sogar ihre Taschen zu durchwühlen. Irgendetwas, das mir dabei hilft, mit ihr zu reden.

Ich entscheide mich dagegen.

Dieser Verstoß gegen mein gewöhnlich Verhalten, falls man das überhaupt so nennen kann, ist sehr eigenartig. Und da ich gerade von voreiligem Handeln spreche – ich stelle mir die folgende Handlungskette vor: Sie stimmt zu, sich mit mir zu verabreden, es wird ernst zwischen uns und, weil wir diese tiefe Verbindung haben, erzähle ich ihr von der Stille. Sie erfährt, dass ich etwas Unheimliches tue, bekommt Angst und verlässt mich. Es ist natürlich lächerlich, sich so etwas auszumalen, bevor wir überhaupt miteinander gesprochen haben. Möglicherweise hat sie einen IQ von unter 70 oder besitzt die Persönlichkeit eines Holzstücks. Es könnte zwanzig verschiedene Gründe dafür geben, weshalb ich mich nicht mit ihr treffen möchte. Und außerdem hängt das ja auch nicht von mir ab. Sie könnte mir genauso gut zu verstehen geben, sie in Ruhe zu lassen, sobald ich versuche mit ihr zu sprechen.

Die Arbeit mit sicheren Geldanlagen hat mich allerdings gelehrt, mich abzusichern. So verrückt diese Entscheidung, nicht in die Stille einzutauchen, auch ist, ich bleibe bei ihr. Ich weiß, dass es so höflicher ist. Aus dem gleichen Grund beschließe ich außerdem, in dieser Pokerrunde nicht zu schummeln.

Sobald die Karten ausgegeben sind, denke ich darüber nach, wie gut es sich anfühlt so ehrenvoll gehandelt zu haben – auch wenn das niemand weiß. Vielleicht sollte ich häufiger versuchen, die Privatsphäre meiner Mitmenschen zu achten. *Ja, richtig.* Ich muss auch realistisch bleiben. Ich wäre nicht dort, wo ich heutzutage bin, wenn ich diesem Rat gefolgt wäre. Ich würde sogar innerhalb weniger Tage meinen Job verlieren, sollte ich anfangen, die Privatsphäre anderer Menschen zu respektieren – und damit auch die ganzen Annehmlichkeiten, an die ich mich gewöhnt habe.

Ich mache es dem Professionellen nach und bedecke meine Karten sobald ich sie bekomme mit meiner Hand. Ich bin gerade dabei, einen Blick auf sie zu werfen, als etwas Ungewöhnliches passiert.

Die Welt um mich herum wird still, so, als würde ich gerade eintauchen ... aber diesmal habe ich nichts gemacht.

Einen Augenblick später sehe ich sie – das Mädchen, welches mir am Tisch gegenüber sitzt, das Mädchen, an das ich gerade gedacht habe. Sie steht neben mir und zieht ihre Hand von meiner weg. Oder genauer gesagt, der Hand meines eingefrorenen Ichs – ich stehe ja daneben und schaue sie an.

Allerdings sitzt sie auch noch mir gegenüber am Tisch, eine eingefrorene Statue wie alle anderen auch.

Mir kommt nicht einmal der Gedanke, das zweite Mädchen könne ihre Zwillingsschwester oder etwas Ähnliches sein. Ich weiß, dass sie es ist. Sie tut das Gleiche, was ich vor einigen Minuten getan habe. Sie geht in der Stille umher. Die Welt um uns herum ist einge-froren, aber wir sind es nicht.

Sie sieht schockiert aus, als ihr das Gleiche klar wird. Mit einer Hand greift sie über den Tisch und berührt ihre eigene Stirn.

Die Welt wird wieder normal.

Sie starrt mich schockiert mit ihren großen Augen und dem blassen Gesicht an. Ich kann sehen, wie ihre Hände zittern, während sie aufspringt. Ohne ein Wort zu sagen dreht sie sich um und geht weg.

Als sie anfängt zu rennen, zögere ich nicht. Ich stehe auf und folge ihr. Das ist nicht sehr clever. Sie würde sich wohl kaum mit einem unbekannten Typen verabreden, der hinter ihr her rennt. Aber über diesen Punkt bin ich schon hinaus. Sie ist die einzige Person die ich jemals getroffen habe, die das Gleiche kann wie ich. Sie ist der Beweis dafür, dass ich nicht verrückt bin. Sie könnte das besitzen, was ich mehr als alles andere möchte.

Sie könnte Antworten haben.

———

Wenn Sie mehr über unsere Fantasy- und Science-Fiction-Bücher erfahren möchten, besuchen Sie bitte Dima Zales' Seite www.dimazales.com/series/deutsch/ und tragen Sie sich für seinen Newsletter zu Neuerscheinungen ein.

Anna Zaires ist eine *USA Today* und Internationale Nr.1 Bestseller Autorin. Anna Zaires hat sich schon im zarten Alter von fünf Jahren in Bücher verliebt, in dem ihr ihre Großmutter das Lesen beibrachte. Kurz darauf schrieb sie auch schon ihre erste Geschichte. Seitdem lebt Anna neben der realen Welt auch ständig in einer Phantasiewelt, in der ihr nur ihre eigene Vorstellungskraft Grenzen setzen kann. Zurzeit lebt die verheiratete Autorin in Florida, zusammen mit ihrem Traummann, dem Sience-Fiction und Fantasy Romanautoren Dima Zales, der auch eng mit ihr zusammenarbeitet.

Bitte besuchen Sie https://www.annazaires.com/book-series/deutsch/ um mehr zu erfahren.